PRAISE FOR
A SEVENTH SENSE

"With the wit and social insight of Vonnegut and the satiric humor of Heller, Steve Jam claims a place on America's literary landscape. *A Seventh Sense* is bold and brave, silly and sensible, imaginative and brash, and something quite unlike any piece of writing in recent memory. The book is a journey through chaos to enlightenment, a wild ride in the company of characters as quirky as they are memorable, and is in the end the most rewarding of reads. Jam has created something special, something that fits in the best of libraries."

—**Greg Fields**, author of *Through the Waters and the Wild*, 2022 Winner of Independent Press Award for Literary Fiction

"Steve Jam's novel was a fantastic ride reminiscent of Terry Pratchett, an exploration of nonsense with humor and wit. A must-read!"

—**Tracy Salzgeber**, author of *The Girl in the Gun Club: My Time as One of the Few Good Men*

"Steve Jam's novel *A Seventh Sense* is imaginative and offbeat in the tradition of Thomas Pynchon and Tom Robbins. Amusing and often bewildering, it is filled with weird characters graced with appropriate names doing oddball things, but it balances the absurd with often touching human drama.

"One is also reminded of the unconventional, unexpectedly delivered humor of the Nobel Prize-winning children's author Astrid Lindgren, most famous for her Pippi Longstocking stories. But beware, this story is definitely not for children. Steve Jam's *A Seventh Sense* is fun to read and enhances one's capacity for reflection on life's complications."

—**Ray Carson Russell**, author of *Philurius College Blues*

A Seventh Sense

by Steve Jam

ISBN 978-1-64663-669-3

Published by

köehlerbooks™

3705 Shore Drive
Virginia Beach, VA 23455
800-435-4811
www.koehlerbooks.com

A SEVENTH SENSE

A NOVEL

STEVE JAM

VIRGINIA BEACH
CAPE CHARLES

The seventh sense
is the one we live with daily,
yet fail to acknowledge.
We seek to understand it,
yet it belies understanding.
What we must do is accept it for the reality
that it is,
and the influence it exerts . . .

The seventh sense
is the sense that doesn't make any sense:
nonsense!

~ O. M. Spuggett

PROLOGUE

The sign above the office building door read,

BUMPS & SPUGGETT
Radically Stupid Suggestions

Inside the office, beneath a large, brightly colored banner emblazoned with the company's motivational motto—

IT'S NOT WHAT YOU DO, BUT WHAT YOU DO WITH IT.

—and, beneath that, a smaller, hand-lettered sign that read,

From Stupidity
Springs Lucidity

a devoted, conscientious staff of individuals performed their daily duties and the vital functions necessary to keep the business moving, shaking, whirring, vibrating, chugging, horfing, and spewing. Why? Because Bumps & Spuggett was the leading purveyor of radically stupid suggestions in North Corners, Ohio, and everyone took his or her job very seriously.

Every morning at 2:30 a.m., the employees of Bumps & Spuggett would arrive at the office by helicopter, dropped onto the roof to slide down the rooftop air-conditioning duct to the room below. This somewhat unorthodox method of ingress had resulted from the radically stupid suggestion that daily wear and tear to the front door and entry stairway could be cut in half by only using them once a day instead of twice.

The employees would assemble in the conference room, high-fiving each other and singing a song that went like this:

> "If ever you're sleeping alone in your bed
> And wake up to find a hen's hatching your head,
> Be thankful she isn't a hippo instead!
> Zippity-bippity-boppity-boodle-dee-doo . . ."

The song would be repeated until all of them were fast asleep on the conference-room floor. They'd sleep soundly until noon (largely due to the fact that they were dog-tired from having to be at work at 2:30 a.m.), then wake up and proceed with pounding out their radically stupid suggestions for the day.

The oddly shaped two-story building that housed the Bumps & Spuggett firm occupied a corner lot at the intersection of two seldom-traveled streets in the far outskirts of North Corners. The demand for radically stupid suggestions (precisely nil) eliminated the necessity for any foot or vehicular traffic to the area. Consequently, the firm of Bumps & Spuggett: Radically Stupid Suggestions was a mystery, anomaly, and enigma to the good people of North Corners. Yet despite the rampant rumors and widespread curiosity, no one had summoned up the courage to investigate the peculiar goings-on of the company and its individuals. As the mystery grew, so grew the legend. There was much conjecture on the part of the townsfolk as to exactly what transpired inside the mysterious building, who the company's employees were and what they were like, and why they would earn their living by working for a mysterious firm that manufactured radically stupid suggestions as its chief products.

Perhaps the most controversial enigma—or more appropriately, the *two* most controversial enigmas—were the individuals whose names adorned the sign above the office building door. They were reputed to be old North Corners natives, but no one now living could remember much about them. Certain particulars regarding the two company founders were believed to be true, though it was reluctantly acknowledged they were based mostly upon hearsay and speculation:

Old Man Spuggett was 103 years old. He spent most of each day sitting in the overstuffed easy chair behind his massive oak desk, or practicing free throws, layups, and slam dunks utilizing the basketball hoop, net, and backboard he'd installed above the massive stone fireplace in his private office.

He spent the rest of his spare time inventing and testing small, nondestructive explosive devices that made extremely loud noises but weren't capable of damaging anything. They were, however, extremely effective at frightening the pants off his staff on a fairly regular basis.

As one of the world's few multiscillionaires, his estimated worth was somewhere in the neighborhood of borkteen scillion dollars. He kept his fortune secretly stashed in an old duffle bag as big as the Library of Congress and disguised to look like a mountain; it took up most of the state of Vermont. (Another rumor: it *was* the state of Vermont.) This offered a plausible explanation as to how the Bumps & Spuggett firm was able to sustain itself financially, since no one had ever seen a dime of profit from the production of radically stupid suggestions.

For his part, Old Man Bumps, the other cofounder, only had a dime to his name. That was the dime of profit no one had ever seen, since he'd embezzled it from the firm when the company was new and actually *did* business, albeit only a dime's worth.

However, Old Man Bumps was now deceased. He died in '57 when he accepted a dare from one of his employees and got his head stuck in the copying machine just before both he and the copier plunged over a 6,000-foot cliff into a raging volcano. He was much loved by all of his employees because he *didn't* invent or test nondestructive explosive devices. Plus, being as dead as a doorknob and consequently never around, it was much less stressful working for him.

That was the sum total of dubious information regarding Messrs. Bumps and Spuggett. Vague as it was, it only added fuel to the fire of curiosity that raged in the minds of the town's populace.

Rumors began to trickle out that a trip to the Bumps & Spuggett firm would be tantamount to visiting a loony bin: a veritable chortle-fest rife with zany antics and laden with goofballs galore (though nobody knew for sure). This further piqued the interest and the curiosity of honest and dishonest citizens alike, the clergy, local politicians, and anyone else who felt the need for a good laugh.

＊＊

Barley Doodlebody was a local entrepreneur, restaurateur, merchant, loan shark, racketeer, and extortionist who'd lived in North Corners all his life and been elected mayor three times.

Barley's past was not only shady but downright Stygian: no one was certain of where or *who* he'd come from. Even Barley had no real recollection of his early childhood. His mother was unidentified, his father an unsolved puzzle. His motto: live in the present; the past is past. He *was* certain that his early life had helped him to become what he was today—a wealthy, ambitious, blustering, belligerent, unscrupulous, violently humorless prick.

Another certainty in Barley's life was that he'd somehow inherited a dimwitted younger half brother, an easygoing, easily manipulated, surprisingly good-looking, devastatingly inarticulate nincompoop named Frog Puppleman. Frog's parentage was as uncertain as Barley's (even the idea that the city councilman had a mother and father was debated heatedly), but the relationship between Barley and Frog, though befuddling to local citizens, was nonetheless accepted by all. They treated Frog with grudging respect (so Barley wouldn't use them as packing material), only ridiculing or deriding him behind his back or when he wasn't there.

For his part, Barley treated Frog with a patronizing tolerance whenever he wasn't beating the crap out of him. The two half brothers had grown up as street orphans in North Corners, living hand to mouth, getting by on Frog's good looks and affable personality and Barley's unbridled ambition and enthusiastic willingness to use his adversaries as packing material.

After tiring of serving as North Corners' mayor for three boring but financially rewarding terms, Barley installed Frog on the North Corners City Council to be his puppet and surrogate "voice." A bit strange, since Frog's *own* voice and vocabulary consisted of one utilitarian phrase—"Yeah, buddy!"—which he repeated over and over under any circumstances, in all situations and in response to anything. Barley chose to interpret his half brother's inarticulation as the complete and unflinching agreement with and acceptance of anything he himself might suggest, demand, state, or question. Frog was the perfect yes-man; that's all Barley wanted to hear.

Being a shrewd, far-sighted, free-thinking, ever-cynical, head-busting entrepreneur, Barley was the first local townsperson to recognize the commercial potential of organized sightseeing tours to the Bumps & Spuggett firm. The intention: to provide tourists with a day of mirth, merriment, and entertainment by observing the wild and crazy antics of the company's employees.

The town was *starving* for entertainment and a pleasant diversion. The closest thing to amusement in the vicinity was the Jell-O Museum on Highway 55, where a visitor could view ancient gelatin molds from the past, preserved in glass cases. That was it. A guided tour to a certifiable nut palace would be the perfect antidote to the stagnation endured by the town's citizens—a surefire winner!

He envisioned a jaunt by bus, beginning at the local Mystic Knights of the Heavenly Daze Lodge Hall in the downtown portion of North Corners, the final destination being the Bumps & Spuggett reception room and office lobby, with a rollicking good time guaranteed for all.

Barley wanted to lend an additional air of prestige and respectability to the enterprise and foster the impression that he, as a North Corners businessman, had an acute sense of civic pride and a deep commitment to community involvement. He decided that before the group arrived at the Bumps & Spuggett office building, passengers would be treated to culturally stimulating historical narratives and tales about points of interest, people, and events along the route.

But then again, Barley conceded, most of the historical points of interest were about as enthralling as a fried rock. Perhaps a side trip to a local strip joint could be substituted as an alternative? Even better, several of his *own* business establishments could be included, enabling him to squeeze additional dollars out of his "captive" audiences. Of course, the ultimate destination would be well worth the wait, easily making up for any potential annoyance the tourists might feel for shelling out a few extra bucks.

Barley was convinced he had a bulletproof gold mine in this Bumps & Spuggett guided tours thing. It provided a unique community service and was, without a doubt, the most ingenious business idea he'd ever cooked up. It actually had a chance of succeeding! He immediately set the wheels in motion for his first tour to that mysterious and intriguing office building out on the edge of town.

But Doodlebody was no dummy. He realized that he'd need ample funds to implement his plan—preferably someone else's money. He set off to acquire the necessary funding by making the rounds of North Corners' various civic organizations and fraternal orders, including the aforementioned Mystic Knights of the Heavenly Daze Lodge, the Masonic Temple, Rotary Club, Kiwanis, Lions, Elks, Moose, Wombats, Jellyfish, Oddfellows, Extremely Oddfellows, Ridiculously Weird Guys, and Blithering Cretinous Twits, among others.

"C'mon, you fat, smelly bastards!" urged Barley, addressing a special session of the high council of the North Corners chapter of the Fraternal Order of Fat Smelly Bastards. "Are you short-sighted, mush-minded knuckleheads so collectively stupefied that you can't see the potential for big bucks here?"

Stinky Summerhorse, the highest ranking officer of the fraternal order, stammered like a terrified chicken with a speech impediment:

"B-b-b-b-but has anyone ever asked Old Man Bumps or Old Man Spuggett if they want a bunch of sweaty, gawking tourists hanging around in their reception room and lobby?"

"That's exactly why we don't tell the old farts we're coming! We *want* to freak 'em out and watch 'em go crazy!" Barley bared his teeth at Stinky Summerhorse and offered his most threatening grimace. "Are you *disagreeing* with me, Stinky? Questioning the integrity of my enterprise? Giving me unwanted, unsolicited lip from that barrel mouth of yours? I oughta kick your fat butt from here to hallelujah!"

He addressed the rest of the assembled lodge brothers and added, "I oughta kick every *one* of your fat butts!"

Barley did kick the fat butts of every member. The lodge immediately granted his request for start-up funding. He left the hall with his pockets stuffed full of cash, the deeds to several family farms, some mountain property in Venezuela, and three sets of car keys.

Brimming with self-satisfaction, Barley decided to use the same tactics on the political and bureaucratic end. He paid a visit to the members of the North Corners City Council with the intent of procuring the proper paperwork and securing required permits to make the operation of a guided tour business completely legal.

As if any of that really mattered to him.

An intense one-hour emergency session of the city council ensued, in which Barley outlined his plans—and subsequently performed an impromptu "redecoration" of the council chamber, utilizing the council members as the decorations. After one of the shortest deliberation periods in city council history, a city ordinance was unanimously passed that gave Barley Doodlebody the right to operate the tour company.

Any money he made from the enterprise would be tax-free. Forever. His laundry would be done without charge for two years. And everybody had to address him by the title of "*Mister* Doodlebody, Your Impressive Majesty, *sir!*"

***

So it began. Soon, the unknowing, unsuspecting fools at the tiny North Corners, Ohio, firm of Bumps & Spuggett: Radically Stupid Suggestions would have their lives changed forever by people and events that were only moments from taking the stage in this unfolding play of life . . .

PART I:

THE BEGINNING

1

As smoothly, efficiently, and effortlessly as Doodlebody Enterprises functioned and flourished, there was nonetheless one flaw that Barley couldn't put his finger on, one cog in the wheel that Barley couldn't swat, one fly in the ointment that stuck out like a sore thumb. That nagging problem came in the form of a formidable rival in Barley's world of illicit endeavors: a hulking, brooding, smooth-talking adversary named Brufyss Bathwater.

Brufyss had never been as successful or imaginative in his operations as Barley, but he was as much a nuisance to the good people of North Corners and as much a disrupting factor to Barley's business operations as anyone or anything could be.

Brufyss's origins were equally as puzzling as Barley and Frog's. He'd grown up in North Corners with them, shared similar childhood experiences, and they had been the best of friends. All three had been abandoned by their parents; Brufyss and Barley carved out meager existences by becoming streetwise, devious, and resourceful, much to the dismay of the townspeople who could never quite catch up to the crazy kids long enough to aid in their welfare (which basically translated into placing them in the North Corners Home for Neophyte Nuisances).

For a few boyhood years they attended public school, where Barley and Brufyss first developed, then perfected, their intimidation techniques, eventually eschewing school in favor of playing hooky and "working the streets." For the two fledgling flimflammers, plying their developing cons, connivance, and scams on the town's citizens was all the school and sport they needed. Studying math was not as challenging as running the numbers. Instead of participating on the tennis team, they opted to play the rackets. Baseball was not as exciting as using the bats as bludgeons.

Frog Puppleman didn't possess the antisocial disposition of the other two and continued with his education, which for him consisted mainly of being handsome, saying "Yeah, *buddy!*" and following everyone around like a good-natured puppy.

Despite their friendship, it became apparent early on that an element of competition existed between Barley and Brufyss in the various enterprises they undertook. Barley held the edge in imagination and intelligence. He would build a sidewalk stand out of wood to sell hot dogs, while Brufyss would build a sidewalk stand out of hot dogs to sell wood. Barley would shine shoes for ten cents on a downtown street corner, while Brufyss would shine the downtown street corner with his shoes and charge Barley ten cents, which Barley never paid. Barley began amassing a fortune, while Brufyss was continuously in need of new shoes.

However, the downtown street corners sparkled in the sun.

As the years rolled by and the lads grew from childhood to adolescence, their "businesses" transitioned into more sophisticated and devious operations. Brufyss grew into a strapping, bruising, intimidating, and ambitious thug, while Barley developed into a strapping, bruising, intimidating, ambitious, and *crafty* thug. He masterminded each deal or venture, and Brufyss increasingly found himself relegated to second-in-command—enforcer, strong-arm guy, or collection agent.

Frog Puppleman, being basically an idiot (albeit a good-looking one), would simply do what either Barley or Brufyss (or anyone, for that matter) told him to do, and that was that. Life was just a bit too fast paced, complex, and incomprehensible for Frog. Supplying him with a box of thumbtacks would pacify any potentially aggressive behavior and keep him busy for hours on end.

But Frog was a lovable soul, and the North Corners girls adored him. His qualities of being good looking, affable, and easily manipulated made him the perfect potential future husband—and as it turned out, perfectly suited for a political career.

The rootless young boys grew into rootless young men. So grew the rivalry, motivated primarily by Brufyss's envy of Barley's entrepreneurial and financial success and his own lack of it. Barley had become far more adept at extortion and intimidation, and this rankled the young second-in-command to the point of distraction. Barley was making more money on each successive venture, while Brufyss's share of the take was comparatively minor. *He* was the one doing the "dirty work" while Barley was "cleaning up." Resentment simmered under his thick skin, threatening to break out like acne on the teenager's face, finally coming to a head in a debacle that became infamously known around North Corners as "The Great Doodlebody-Bathwater Brouhaha of '67."

It happened in the spring of that year and was initially caused by, surprisingly enough, a woman! However, this was no ordinary woman. No Normal Norma, this one! Mrs. Kookerly was the most bitingly beautiful, slinkily sexy ingénue to ever butter the biscuit of any ambitious entrepreneur or self-styled sultan of seduction. Mrs. Kookerly was such a stunner that men and women alike would froth themselves dry and weep copious tears of unmitigated ecstasy at a mere glimpse of her curvaceous shadow on the wall as she breezed past like a zephyr with sensible shoes.

Mrs. Kookerly's given name was exactly that: "Mrs. Kookerly." She had received it from two somewhat neurotic parents who were wary of the stigma should their only daughter never marry and become an old maid. They remedied this potentially embarrassing potentiality by christening their newborn daughter with a ready-made marriage moniker.

Saddling an innocent baby with such a confusing name was a cruel (albeit unwitting) joke for the parents to play upon their only child, but Mrs. Kookerly's unusual name did make for some amusing situations as she grew up, especially in her early youth. Any adult with whom she came into contact was completely befuddled by having to refer to someone much younger than themselves in the same context as they would one of their adult peers.

However, it was not just Mrs. Kookerly who paid the cost of having such an unusual name. Her father, Mr. Kookerly, bore the brunt of most criticisms resulting from the parents' bizarre choice of a handle for their little girl.

Having a young daughter named Mrs. Kookerly put the Kookerly household into the position of having *two* females who answered to the name. The fact that Mr. Kookerly had two Mrs. Kookerlys living under his roof was appalling to those upright citizens who paid attention to this sort of thing, and they regarded Mr. Kookerly as a raving polygamist. What's more, it was known that the younger Mrs. Kookerly was Mr. Kookerly's own daughter. This qualified him as an incestuous, polygamous pedophile.

Of course, anyone familiar with Mr. Kookerly would have seen in an instant that he was an extremely lucky man to have convinced one female to marry him, much less two. Nonetheless, Mrs. Kookerly the Younger was fated to grow from infancy to adolescence enduring the mistaken stigma of being the wife and daughter of North Corners' resident raving, incestuous, pedophile polygamist.

Mrs. Kookerly's parents seemed unlikely candidates for having such a ferociously beautiful daughter, but in spite of their obvious shortcomings, when they put their genes together, a perfect fit resulted. As the years rolled by, it became apparent that Mrs. Kookerly the Younger was becoming a drop-dead knockout. She was not only extremely pleasing to look at but also intelligent and completely aware of the effect she had on the opposite sex. She came to realize that everyone in town now thought she was a hottie and didn't give a hoot about all that "incestuous polygamy" crap.

When it came time for the beautiful young girl with the perplexing name to enter high school, she enrolled in the town's premier secondary educational institution, P. P. Piggford and His Wife Janice High School.

P. P. and Janice Piggford had been among the first citizens in North Corners to recognize the necessity of a decent, proper, and equal education for all, and founded the town's first academy of higher learning to accomplish this. They elected to name the school La Escuela de los Idiotas (The School of the Idiots), although they had no idea what the name actually meant. Hearing their Hispanic housekeeper utter those words in her native language, they simply agreed that it exuded a profound air of multicultural class.

The housekeeper had been scoffing at the idea of a school being run by two illiterates; both P. P. and Janice Piggford were uneducated (and obviously possessed no comprehension of the Spanish language). The two aspiring educators had no inkling that the school's moniker was a major factor in dissuading anyone from attending it, and shortly thereafter the institution went bust.

Undaunted, P. P. and Janice opened a specialized day care center for the children of indigent walrus trainers. Due to a profound lack of walruses in Ohio, this enterprise tanked as well. Now in despair, the two made a double-suicide pact, flinging themselves from the highest precipice in the area and landing in a huge cement mixer at the foot of the cliff, where a construction site for a new high school was located, founded by a group of educators who actually knew what they were doing (i.e., how to read and write).

The construction workers who witnessed the messy landing of P. P. and Janice were too grossed out by the sight to fish the two out of the concrete stew. They left the Piggfords in the mixer, the contents of which was poured to make the flooring for the town's new school. Upon completion, the school was named in honor of P. P. Piggford and his wife, Janice, the first two citizens of North Corners to create the foundation for education in the community—literally.

During her tenure at P. P. Piggford and His Wife Janice High School, Mrs. Kookerly earned exceptional grades as a student and participated in the school's extracurricular activities as a cheerleader. The Piggford High School's mascots were the Cloud Fairies, bestowed upon them by the institution's first principal, Mugbelia Dugbuckles, an aging and very un-hip spinster whose idea of competitive sports was attempting to knit as many pairs of socks as possible before she died. However, as time passed, the pathetic won-lost records of the school's various sports teams verified that the name "Cloud Fairies" was far too generous a description of the athletic teams' prowess; they ultimately became famed around North Corners for being an unchallenged powerhouse in crying, whimpering, whining, and shrieking like howler monkeys.

Be that as it may, with the arrival of the Mrs. Kookerly-led cheerleading squad, the Cloud Fairies' fortunes improved immeasurably. The reason: the cheerleading squad originated a notorious routine in which they performed a high-spirited "victory dance" on the faces of opposing team members—whether or not P. P. Piggford and His Wife Janice High's team had been victorious. This was especially gratifying to the opposing team members if the girls forgot to wear underpants beneath their cheerleading skirts.

Mrs. Kookerly had been elected head cheerleader by her fellow cheerleaders, who were also her best friends: Daphne "Tasty" Dogdaughter, and two other similarly striking female students—Lucinda "Jiggly" Luckybeans and Flagella "Bubbles" Nuggmuck. Like her peppy compatriots, Mrs. Kookerly was also given an affectionate nickname by the PPPAHWJHS student body, but *her* nickname was not so much a humorously descriptive epithet as a more guttural, visceral, primal noise that emanated from deep within the souls of the students who viewed her flawless form as she bounced around, cheering maniacally. It was a growling, earthy "*OOOAAAWWWRRRUUUGGGHHH*," accompanied by heavy breathing, heart palpitations, excessive perspiration, and effusive salivary discharge.

Together, these ubiquitous cheerleaders cheered, jeered, danced, jumped, and joogled at every activity that took place at P. P. Piggford and His Wife, Janice High: football, baseball and basketball games, wood shop class, even the school nurse's application of bandages to minor cuts, scrapes, and gunshot wounds. They were full of pep and school spirit, and their fellow students (particularly the boys) were always inspired by the buoyant personalities and effervescence of Mrs. Kookerly, Tasty, Bubbles, and Jiggly.

Mrs. Kookerly was every man's dream and every man's nightmare. She was nobody's fool and the object of every man's desire, but she was girlfriend to only one man: Brufyss Bathwater.

Yes, Mrs. Kookerly had just about everything—except good taste in men. And therein lay the problem.

Mrs. Kookerly met Brufyss in her senior year during the fateful spring of '67. Their meeting was quite by chance: in addition to being a raving, perverted, pedophile polygamist, Mrs. Kookerly's father also had a penchant for placing ill-conceived wagers on thoroughbred pig races that his chosen porkers never seemed to win. Much of the Kookerly family fortune (such as it was) had been thus frittered away. Mrs. Kookerly's initial introduction to Brufyss occurred when she came home from school early one day and discovered him beating the snot out of her deadbeat father.

As it turned out, Barley and Brufyss also dabbled as bookies in off-track thoroughbred pig race wagering; Mr. Kookerly's delinquency in paying off his track losses had prompted a visit from the intimidating Mr. Bathwater in an effort to "solicit" the outstanding balance of the funds now owed.

Seeing her deadbeat father lying on the floor in a steaming pile and realizing that Brufyss was the merciless culprit who'd meted out the pounding that put him there, Mrs. Kookerly was unabashedly captivated, fascinated, and turned on. She sashayed sexily over to him, flashing her pretty eyes with seductive innocence and saying "Hello!" in her deepest, most alluring voice. She'd found the man of her dreams, the lump of her life!

Brufyss succumbed instantaneously. The big fool had been bitten and smitten by the charismatic kitten, but when she burst into an impromptu performance of her patented "victory dance" on his face, it sealed the deal. Brufyss was in love!

Mrs. Kookerly's heart was also prancing like a polo pony; she immediately asked him to be her date for the upcoming P. P. Piggford and His Wife Janice High School Senior Prom and Vegetarian Intimidation Fest. Brufyss accepted her invitation on the spot, his enchantment complete. Mrs. Kookerly was irresistible—and apparently easy to please.

There was just one problem: Barley Doodlebody had also fallen in love with Mrs. Kookerly, having watched her "victory dance" many times from afar with lust and longing. But Mrs. Kookerly's gaze had never once fastened upon Barley's. When it came to romantic interest, Mrs. Kookerly was romantically uninterested. Her eyes locked onto Brufyss and Brufyss alone, a point not lost on the object himself, especially in regard to his burgeoning rivalry with Barley. He rubbed it in like carnauba wax on the hood of a '57 Chevy.

Barley was wracked with resentment, eaten with envy, and jostled by jealousy. Why did Brufyss get the goddess and Barley end up rejected and dejected? Instead of feeling happiness for his boyhood buddy, Barley felt only spite—and the need to set things right.

One sunny day, not long before the P. P. Piggford and His Wife Janice High School Senior Prom and Vegetarian Intimidation Fest was to take place, Barley and Frog sat in the backroom office of the Doodlebody Enterprises building. The building had been an old, run-down, and dilapidated fish-glue factory that Barley took as collateral after the owner defaulted on a loan to remodel, refit, and restart the faltering business. The poor wretch had believed with all his heart that the fish-glue industry was on the upswing, and had taken out a 3,000 percent loan from Barley to make his dream a reality. The only reality was the 3,000 percent loan; as a result, Barley owned his first piece of real estate.

While Frog occupied himself with a box of thumbtacks, Barley sat behind his desk, ruminating over his ill luck at having failed to win the heart of Mrs. Kookerly.

"How could a big, ugly bone-brain like Brufyss Bathwater come up with a girl like that and *I'm* nothing but a piece of lonely lunchmeat?"

"Yeah, buddy!" Frog agreed as he tinkered with the thumbtacks.

"I have brains and a potful of money! All he has is everything *I've* given him! He'd still be tying turnips together at the leather laundry if it wasn't for me!"

"Yeah, buddy!"

"Can't she see that I'm the one who's going places and Brufyss is stuck in a rut? Doesn't she realize that being my girl will make her a princess? A queen? An empress?"

"*Yeeaaaahhh!*" screeched Frog, writhing in agony. He'd mistakenly pushed a thumbtack through his upper lip.

Exasperated at his half brother's unintelligent response, Barley planted a five-fingered smasheroo onto Frog's nose and utilized the rest of the thumbtacks to fasten him to the ceiling. He stormed purposefully out of his office to win the love of Mrs. Kookerly, having hatched a nefarious plan by which he'd get to her heart through the use of her best friend, Daphne Dogdaughter.

Daphne "Tasty" Dogdaughter, another good-looking, extremely popular, and nubile young example of North Corners female stock, had the mental capacity of a soup spoon. For Daphne, holding a conversation with a hand puppet was an exercise in intellectual futility; the hand puppet used too many big words. She, too, was lusted after and considered a great catch by the boys but was regarded as "accessory eye candy."

Tasty had risen to prominence by virtue of an imposing effort to gain peer acceptance and popularity in her early high school years. While attending the P. P. Piggford and His Wife Janice High's annual "Greasy Food Gorge-a-thon BoogieBall," she'd surreptitiously immersed herself in a vat of beef stew while stark naked, and offered herself up as a scrumptious tidbit. She was subsequently slurped completely clean by the entire student body, which resulted in the revelation of her heretofore hidden birthday-suit surprise. Because of her burgeoning beauty and dynamic desirability, she was the culinary success story of the event, and earned herself an enduring nickname.

Needless to say, Tasty Dogdaughter's now immortal "beef stew bacchanal" (as it came to be known) cemented her popularity and social standing among the school's attendees. The menu in the school cafeteria featured beef stew as a perennial offering, in hope that one day Tasty would repeat her hallowed Greasy Food Gorge-a-thon BoogieBall performance during lunch hour.

Daphne was a sweet, naive, true-hearted girl with a sincere desire to please her parents, teachers, friends, fellow students, pastor, dentist, green grocer, guys at the car wash, pedicurist, any cab driver who picked her up, most garage mechanics, some guy named Pea Head Jones, and the entire rhythm section and most of the trumpet players in the school band.

Barley Doodlebody would attempt to add his own name to that list. He intended to exploit the fact that Tasty was also a trusted and loyal friend to Mrs. Kookerly. He would deviously capture Mrs. Kookerly's affections by getting Tasty to fall for him; in so doing, Mrs. Kookerly would realize the error of her ways—that her feelings for Brufyss were actually intended for Barley. She'd become insanely jealous of Tasty, rue her bad decision, and want Barley for herself!

It was a simple plan with somewhat bizarre logic attached to it, but this was the same guy who'd come up with the idea of starting a treehouse-manufacturing company called Stick It Up Your Aspen.

Up until now, the only people who'd ever "fallen" for Barley had either been punched out or run over with an eighteen-wheeler. Love was an entirely new enterprise for him, an untried, untested, untrusted, unfamiliar animal in the Barley Doodlebody menagerie of masterful manipulations. Implementing this risky plan wasn't going to be as easy as Tasty Dogdaughter was.

The fact that Barley was no longer a student at P. P. Piggford and His Wife Janice High was no deterrent to Tasty's acceptance of his invitation to be his date at the upcoming Senior Prom and Vegetarian Intimidation Fest. She took an immediate liking to him when he approached her in the school hallway, dumped a wheelbarrow full of cash all over her shoes, and said, "All this could be yours if you go to that frickin' dance with me and don't give me any crap!"

A silver-tongued proposition if there ever was one.

Tasty had never met Barley before, but she immediately liked his style (or lack thereof). She rolled around in the pile of money on the floor and squealed like a pig in a mud bath.

So far, so good; the first part of Barley's plan had come off without a hitch.

Next on the agenda: a new car. His detailed plan for Mrs. Kookerly's seduction called for him to show up at the dance in a fancy new automobile with her own best friend on his arm. He'd visit Googalug's Auto-Man Empire and drive away with the finest, fastest, flauntable-est set of wheels he could find—a shiny, sinewy, stunning new Smegmatti 502, the coolest ride around. If *this* car didn't impress Mrs. Kookerly with Barley's success and good taste, nothing would. Furthermore, the owner and proprietor of Googalug's Auto-Man Empire, Harvey Googalug, owed Barley. He was far behind in his monthly payments of extortion dues.

When Harvey Googalug saw Barley show up on the dealership doorstep, he immediately wet himself and turned into a quivering, pathetic mass of liquid meat, letting the intimidating young hoodlum have the pick of the car lot. Gratis, of course. It was either that or submit to having his ears turned into mittens.

Barley chose a prized "Special Edition" Smegmatti 502 with a custom full-blown lymphatic nomenclature system, forty-millimeter lube locks, overbearing ignition bars, and deluxe animated suspension. It was gorgeous in every respect except its color. Because Barley was colorblind, his hue of choice was "hideously bilious, projectile-vomit greenish brown," the one shade on the lot that Harvey Googalug hadn't been able to move. Interestingly enough, it was the perfect color to complement Barley's character and disposition.

At the conclusion of the deal (which consisted of Barley hanging Harvey by the lapels beneath the car while he revved the engine viciously and threatened to turn the terrified dealership owner into a greasy puddle of pavement oil), Barley burned rubber and noisily sped away from Googalug's Auto-Man Empire with the hottest, coolest, hippest, most coveted car on wheels. Everyone in his slipstream sighed with admiration, turned green with envy, and gagged convulsively at the sight.

Harvey was so relieved that he hadn't been turned into greasy pavement oil that he wet himself again—with tears of joy.

The essential components of Barley's devious plan had been acquired. All that remained was to implement the plan, and the P. P. Piggford and His Wife Janice High School Senior Prom and Vegetarian Intimidation Fest was nigh . . .

2

Through the years, whether out of an acute sense of boredom, innate sense of malice, the effects of alcoholic overindulgence, or a combination of all, the Senior Prom and Vegetarian Intimidation Fest evolved into a rock 'n roll celebration of youth dressed in tuxedos and ball gowns, featuring a ceremonious free-for-all bashing of vegetarians just for the hell of it.

Along with dancing and overindulging on highly caloric, aberrant snack foods, the evening's wanton festivities included two greatly anticipated highlights: the joyous crowning of the queen of the senior prom, and the vegetarian intimidation fest, the latter event deemed the must-do of the dance's activities and the true reason anyone came to the party in the first place.

The vegetable ingestors targeted as subjects for the intimidation fest were referred to as "grain brains" by the town's carnivores. They could usually be found hanging around North Corners' only health food store, Chorfis Chumbu's Gross Natural Product, where they tossed back crabgrass smoothies like shots of tequila or sipped steaming cups of log-bark juice, grazed upon acorn snack balls like gluttonous squirrels stocking up for the winter, chatted sanctimoniously about the spiritual healing powers of kumquats, and debated heatedly as to whether ginkgo biloba was more effective as a brain supplement or laxative.

These poor souls would be the unwitting designees supplying the prom's evening entertainment. No personal animosity was aimed toward the individuals beyond the fact that they did not include greasy cheeseburgers and fat globules in their daily repasts. For this reason alone, the students hated them with every fiber of their being. It was the only aspect of these carnivores' lives that contained any fiber at all.

Chorfis Chumbu, the health food store's cynical proprietor, always participated as an enthusiastic albeit clandestine accomplice in aiding the ambushers of the "grain brains." The consummate hypocrite, Chorfis hated his store's patrons with a seething ferocity, believing them to be a bunch of chlorophyll-saturated lunatics, only catering to their insatiable herbivore appetites because he saw them as an easy source of sucker money. Normally he kept a stash of greasy cheeseburgers and fat globules hidden in his office for his own repasts, disdaining vegetables, fruits, and herbs with the same passion his customers displayed in consuming them.

The task of procuring and purloining the unfortunate vegetarians destined for the big dance's much-anticipated intimidation fest was relatively simple. The only necessity was a length of rope attached to a large fishnet—and the elements of surprise and deception. This "procurement" was easily accomplished when the subjects were involved in their weekly Gross Natural Product Bowling for Carrots tournament, an activity Chorfis had initially instigated because he got a charge out of watching his flesh-eschewing customers compete so fiercely for the common garden root.

He took perverse pleasure in watching the poor, misguided herbivores making idiots of themselves as they hurled bowling balls at pins down the sidewalk in front of his store for the ultimate prize: a large bundle of carrots. He especially enjoyed the occasional fistfight that broke out after he secretly drugged the free wheatgrass cocktails he offered competitors with heavy doses of valerian root and other questionable ingredients. Soon, he looked upon a sidewalk filled with semi-somnolent, lurching, drooling "grain brains," all stoned on herbal tea, trying to bash each other's faces until the effects of the sleep-inducing concoction rendered most of them unconscious and they collapsed in a heap.

It was also a kick to see where the bowling balls landed after being haphazardly hurled down the sidewalk by the drunken bowlers. Usually, they knocked down innocent passersby or severely damaged other businesses located along the same block where Gross Natural Product was located. The sidewalk would become a bloody battleground of competitive carnage, much to the delight of the sadistic health food purveyor.

It was during this frenzied free-for-all that the trap was sprung most easily. The groping, griping, grappling group, focused on the fracas raging around them, were easily netted by the carnivorous PPPAHWJHS students charged with supplying vegetarians for the evening. Before the group's addled minds had time to comprehend what had happened to them, they were whisked away to a truck parked around the corner, and bound tightly in a cluster in a fishnet, still trying to poke each other's eyes out, completely oblivious to their new plight.

Only when ensconced securely in the darkness of the truck trailer would it dawn on them that things weren't quite right. By then, the ruse was successfully perpetrated, their respective fates duly sealed, and the effects of the sleeping potion administered by Chorfis Chumbu fully realized. Soon, they were sound asleep on the floor of the trailer, looking like a pile of dead fish. Next stop: P. P. Piggford and His Wife Janice High School and a specially prepared holding pen under the gymnasium stage, stocked with bunches of raw carrots.

The premise of the vegetarian intimidation fest was simple enough: to viciously harass and ridicule these people. The method for conducting this harassment, however, was far more complex than its premise and infinitely more diabolical.

At the heralded commencement of the intimidation festivities, the purloined vegetarian participants would be mechanically hoisted, pen and all, to stage level through a retractable trapdoor at the stage's center. Emerging into the white-hot spotlight, the poor creatures, still entangled in the fishnet and vainly trying to shield their eyes from the burning glare of the spotlight, would now be in full, unobstructed view of the audience waiting like famished jackals for their chance to get the intimidation going.

At the start signal, the encaged captives were subjected to the "abuse and aggravation" portion of the proceedings—derisive, vicious, and vitriolic threats, taunts, and ridicule. This was a prelude for the action to come, but the prom attendees relished the opportunity to persecute someone other than themselves for a change. They threw themselves into the activity with enthusiasm.

Savage and injurious insults flew at the entrapped prisoners. They included such epithets as "You broccoli-faced celery sucker!"; "You're too stupid to tell toilet paper from a corncob!"; "Shove a cucumber up your nose and sit on an artichoke, you gazpacho-guzzling goofball!"; or "You're a bodacious, blithering, bean-brained batch of bubbling bog-slop!" (a perennial favorite)—words flung like poison-tipped arrows, the intensity of the venomous verbosity thoroughly bewildering the persecuted. They cowered in the corners of the holding pen to escape the brutal barrage, but the "grain brains" had nowhere to hide.

The students showed no mercy. The bright spotlight effectively masked the tormentors from view, and this anonymity bolstered the courage and ardor of the crowd; the degree of derision became so feverish that many of the more sensitive vegetarian victims wept copiously and wished they were dead—or munching on a chili dog.

After an appropriate amount of time had passed, determined by how innocuous the insults became as the students grew bored, each audience participant was issued a portion of uncooked animal flesh or internal organ: a raw lamb chop, a kidney, a flank steak, a pig's foot, or a cow's tongue.

That led to the next stage of the intimidation process: the "ministration of meat," during which the crowd pelted the vegetarians until the pen was filled with bloody animal parts. The panicked prisoners wallowed, slipped, and slid in the squooshy, bloody mess while contending with the fishnet, unable to escape the ever-deepening meat morass. The terror would drive those with weaker constitutions to the brink of madness.

However, the piece de resistance, the coup de grace, the final finale to end all finales, was the "bubbling bilious beef broth bath" and "gurgling gooey glop drop." This was guaranteed to push any stalwart vegetarian holdout completely over the edge and into the abyss of insanity.

The holding pen had no top covering; it better resembled a corral than a cage. The pen's floor was the trapdoor, under which a giant vat of the most repulsive liquid emulsion was wheeled. This horrific concoction, the "bubbling bilious beef broth bath," consisted of pureed and liquefied animal parts and entrails in a broth-like stew. It reeked to high heaven, forcing the vat movers beneath the stage to cover their heads and nostrils with gas masks lest they be overcome by the noxious fumes.

For the second element to the messy mixture, known as the "gurgling gooey glop drop," a second huge vat was suspended directly *over* the spot occupied by the unlucky captives. This vat was full of a less-noxious potpourri of stewed vegetables, fruits, roots, and berries, simmered slowly for days in gallons of sticky tree sap until it congealed into gooey, gloppy gravy.

As the "ministration of meat" reached its frenetic zenith, these final two surprise intimidations were perpetrated in succession. The stage trapdoor would be retracted quickly to one side, literally pulling the floor from under the vegetarians' feet. The poor victims would drop straight into the vat, along with the piles of bloody raw meat and animal parts accumulated in their pen. After their submersion, they'd surface, thrash wildly in the murky muck, gasp for air, and unleash hideous shrieks and tortured, tormented howls that would linger for weeks in the memories of all who attended.

Just when it seemed that this bizarre spectacle had run its brutal course, the "gurgling gooey glop" was unleashed with the force of an Olympic-sized swimming pool being dumped on their heads. The dilemma: either pig out on the vegetarian goodies floating in the mucky mire, or paddle around, frantically trying to escape the morass before drowning like sewage-encrusted rats.

As the reader might imagine, the revulsion, confusion, and chaos incited by this turn of events tended to liberate any residual sanity remaining within the skulls of the unfortunates. This ultimate act of physical and mental torture culminated in an earsplitting chorus of yowls and a heretofore unexplored dimension of blithering lunacy, much to the delight of the sadistic assemblage of students.

Once this savagery was complete, however, there was little point in inflicting further damage. The victims were good for nothing except playing with their boogers, drooling, and mumbling—something most of the students did themselves every day. Where was the fun in *that*?

After their removal from the vat, the now insane "grain brains," still wrapped in the fishnet, were placed on a forklift, carted outside the gymnasium, and freed to run into the hills or the next county, where they'd become someone else's problem.

Without a doubt, this fun-filled festival topped the list as the biggest diamond in the crown of P. P. Piggford and His Wife Janice High School's social season.

✳✳✳

A balmy, beautiful, moonlit spring evening greeted the students on the much-anticipated night of the '67 Senior Prom and Vegetarian Intimidation Fest. All were decked out in the finest apparel they'd ever worn, primed and ready for a slam-bang shindig.

The promgoers pulled up to the front of the school gymnasium, some in old, battered, rattling cars, others dropped off by old, battered, rattling parents in their old, battered, rattling cars. These clattering arrivals were followed by a mass procession of nattily attired students to the gym's front-entrance ticket window, concluding when each couple had purchased tickets to the dance and entered a gymnasium gaily festooned with handmade decorations.

The theme of the dance this year was "fake Hawaiian holiday." Streamers of crepe paper and strings of balloons adorned the walls. Crudely fashioned, hand-painted volcanoes and coconut palm trees fabricated from paper-mache sprouted throughout the gym. Along each wall was a row of tables laden with snacks or refreshments.

School teachers serving as chaperones were dressed in fake Hawaiian clothing: floral-print muumuus for the women, brightly flowered Aloha shirts for the men. All wore flower leis bearing an aromatic resemblance to stinkweed, graciously supplied by Chorfis Chumbu. Chorfis dropped off the leis at the gymnasium and sped away before anyone had the chance to thank him for his generosity or ask what type of flowers he'd used. However, in the weeks afterward, those teachers who'd worn them scratched and wept a lot and behaved like swarms of killer bees were sprinting laps inside their skulls.

The chaperone teachers stood along the walls, manning the snack tables and dispersing cute comments and liberal amounts of foods rich in saturated fats and partially hydrogenated cooking oil. They smiled like hyenas and acted as cool and affable as possible, hoping to avoid a physical attack upon themselves later in the evening by alcohol-saturated, disgruntled teenagers who might hold grudges. During regular school hours, these same teachers treated the students like fugitives from a Center for Disease Control hospital ward.

In one corner of the room, a professional photographer was taking photographic portraits of the teenage couples. He would sell the photos back to them at exorbitant prices, as either keepsakes or blackmail, whichever was applicable. The photographer's flash strobes were far too powerful for the space; each time his flashes exploded, the retinas of his subjects were scorched. The poor sufferers screeched in agony, clutched at their burning eyes, and staggered into the fake Hawaiian backdrop, which in turn crashed down upon their heads, knocking them silly. As each successive couple went through this routine (seemingly unaware that the couple preceding them had just had their eyeballs nuked and their heads crunched), they were quickly shepherded by a teacher chaperone to a room where they could revive. Once the backdrop had been reset, the whole procedure began again.

A small orchestral combo of musicians from the freshman class sat in chairs on the gymnasium stage, blowing, puffing, strumming, and thwomping various instruments in an attempt to recreate Hawaiian music. This transformed the culture's normally languid, lilting lyricism into a sound reminiscent of chickens and wildebeests being pureed in a blender. None of the attendees knew the difference or cared. They had never been to Hawaii.

As each student couple entered the gymnasium, the previous arrivals eyed them like vultures, ready to pounce and pronounce harsh judgment on their choice of coiffeur, dress, suit, or shoes. However, when the class vice president—the good-looking, totally-oblivious-yet-puzzlingly-popular Frog Puppleman—entered the room with his date—a young, socially prominent ingenue named Mimsy Borogove—the vicious criticism stopped instantly. All the students recognized Frog for what he was: a handsome, completely innocuous idiot who liked everyone, was affable as a puppy, and befriended any and all simply because he was too dense to discern friend from foe.

Though each of the judgmental promgoers secretly yearned to ravage the poor fool with insults, no one dared utter a disparaging word in his direction—at least, nothing above a discreet whisper. They were not only aware of Frog's mental deficiencies but also knew he was the good-natured brother of the infamously bad-natured Barley Doodlebody. No one was prepared to be used as packing material.

In lieu of taunting, tormenting, and tenderizing Frog and Mimsy, the crowd opted to greet them with smiles and compliments, only snickering behind their backs after they passed by. Frog responded to their salutations with his usual, "Yeah, *buddy!*" Mimsy smiled demurely and, when Frog wasn't looking, licked her lips and flicked her tongue lasciviously at each of the boys. She was not only a youthful debutant member of North Corners high society but also a shameless minx with a salacious reputation of which Frog was completely unaware. He probably wouldn't comprehend it anyway.

After Frog and Mimsy moved past the students in the hall, things returned to normal. The gang resumed their regimen of demoralizing the next unfortunate couple to run their gauntlet. Frog and Mimsy proceeded to the portrait photographer's corner to have their pictures taken, their eyeballs flambéed, and to be knocked senseless.

Suddenly, amid the raucous laughter and hurled insults, the main entrance doors of the gymnasium opened ceremoniously. A rush of astonished gasps arose, followed by a ripple of full-throated, earthy, guttural growling. The quasi-Hawaiian music ceased. The gym exploded into tomb-like silence, the air hanging like a curtain of smog, the mouths of all self-anointed critics dropping open in abject awe, amazement lathering their faces.

There she stood. The exquisite Mrs. Kookerly demurely clutched the arm of her nattily dressed beau nouveau, Brufyss Bathwater, making her entrance like Cleopatra entering ancient Rome. No sound was heard save for hundreds of male salivary glands unloading a gurgling gush of excitement, admiration, and froth. Soon the gym floor was awash with drool, and Mrs. Kookerly's nickname filled the hall:

"*OOOAAAWWWRRRUUUGGGHHH*!!"

She was a radiant vision in crinoline and crepe, a glowing apparition of teenage temptation and tantalizing tempestuousness, tastefully attired and tacitly triumphant, her adolescent glory the object of all the squishy, slushy slurping and sighing. Helen of Troy may have possessed "the face that launched a thousand ships," but Mrs. Kookerly's was "the face that brought forth the ocean upon which they all sailed."

The awe-inspiring two-person procession floated gracefully across the freshly waxed gym floor. The massed crowd of student admirers parted to let the magnificent Mrs. Kookerly and badass Brufyss pass, like the Red Sea once gave way to Moses and the Hebrews. Everyone who witnessed the handsome couple's grand entrance was dazzled by the sight.

As they moved through the crowd, Brufyss glared at the male students enraptured by the spell of Mrs. Kookerly's beauty. Each had seemingly forgotten the existence of his *own* dance partner. Brufyss's icy eyes pierced their reveries, causing them to cease their salivary surges and snap quickly back into their respective fear-filled realities.

It was disconcerting to everyone that one of the infamous "Doodlebody-Bathwater Boys" (as Barley and Brufyss had come to be known) was in their midst, much less the fact that this Doodlebody-Bathwater boy had won the heart and affection of the goddess of Piggford High! Though this was the first time Mrs. Kookerly and Brufyss had appeared together publicly, all could see that the thug had staked his claim, and that his "claim" was consensual. Mrs. Kookerly occasionally glanced up adoringly at her intimidating escort, obviously enamored, secretly hoping that Brufyss would pause to beat the crap out of some unsuspecting dance attendee for no reason whatsoever (although she'd requested him to leave most of his weaponry in the car—at least that which needed reloading). Just about everyone knew from prior experience that the high school dropout who now escorted their angelic idol was capable of immeasurable violence whenever his "territory" was infringed upon.

The royal couple made their way into the hushed throng. Only when Mrs. Kookerly looked across the gym and spied fellow cheerleaders Lucinda Luckybeans and Flagella Nuggmuck did the suspension of time and the holding of breath cease. Letting out a girlish squeal, she broke from Brufyss's side and skittered over to her friends—the official signal that life could return to a semblance of normalcy. General hubbub and conversation resumed, the hurling of venomous insults continued (though decidedly *away* from the area occupied by Mrs. Kookerly and Brufyss), the horrendous quasi-Hawaiian music recommenced, and the flashes from the photographer's camera exploded, as did the screams of agony from those students who'd just had their eyeballs quick-seared.

"Mrs. Kookerly, you look absolutely *gorgeous* tonight!" enthused Bubbles Nuggmuck as the head cheerleader joined her friends and their dates. "You're sure to be the prom queen!"

"You really look like a queen!" agreed Jiggly Luckybeans. "But who's the handsome guy you've brought with you? Is he a prince?"

Mrs. Kookerly gave Brufyss an adoring smile as the hoodlum walked up to join them.

"Oh no, Lucinda! This is Brufyss—he's my king! Isn't he a dreamboat?"

Brufyss blushed and returned her smile.

"Oh yeah! He's one dreamboat I'd love to take a cruise on!" giggled Jiggly.

Bubbles grinned slyly. "He can dock his boat in *my* slip any time he wants!"

"Shame on you guys!" Mrs. Kookerly laughed in mock rebuke, inwardly pleased that her friends approved of her new man.

Brufyss was in absolute heaven. This evening was turning out exactly as he'd hoped.

The conversation continued, Mrs. Kookerly, Jiggly, and Bubbles chittering and chattering giddily about how chic each other's dresses were, how darling each other's hairdos were, how cute each other's dates were, and how exciting the atmosphere of the whole scene was. However, they wondered aloud where Daphne Dogdaughter could be—and who she was bringing as her date.

As the girls immersed themselves in their musings and gossip and Lucinda and Flagella's prom dates withered under Brufyss's formidable gaze, he scanned the room like radar, looking for something—some*one*. Barley Doodlebody.

The two hadn't spoken for a few days, but Brufyss was certain Barley would finagle an invitation to the dance. He looked forward to flaunting the fabulous Mrs. Kookerly in Barley's face. This would be his moment of supreme triumph over the so-called "friend" who was always one step ahead, one head higher on the totem pole of life. At last he, Brufyss Bathwater, had something unattainable to Barley Doodlebody, something he knew Barley desired more than the money and business enterprises. Brufyss wanted very much to witness the envy in his rival's eyes when he paraded Mrs. Kookerly around for all to see and admire.

This would be Brufyss's moment to savor, and the anticipation was testing his patience . . .

3

Spatch Huntoon was the high school's star athlete. He was quarterback of the Piggford Cloud Fairies varsity football team, forward for the varsity basketball team, and a pitcher on the varsity baseball team. He'd been president of his class through all four years of his attendance and led the top boys' fraternal service club for egotistical athletes with rock-star good looks. Additionally, and up until Mrs. Kookerly met and became enamored with Brufyss Bathwater, Spatch Huntoon held the enviable position of being the young beauty's boyfriend.

As he sat in a darkened corner of the gymnasium, watching his old girlfriend with her new boyfriend, a seething, jealous rage gripped him. As the "big man on campus" at P. P. Piggford and His Wife Janice High School (BMOCAPPPAHWJHS), Spatch was accustomed to being the center of attention and the object of envy among the youth of North Corners. But he'd been rejected outright by the only girl worthy of his exalted status, on the biggest night of the year, in front of all his friends and teammates.

Melanie Bupwanger sat next to the pouting BMOCAPPPAHWJHS, her escort to potentially the most significant event of her high school experience. She tried everything to distract Spatch's attention from Mrs. Kookerly and back to herself. Being no "Tired Tanya" in her own right, Melanie possessed a curvaceous figure, a quick and intelligent mind, and a glib tongue, none of which curtailed Spatch's jealousy-fueled surveillance of his ex-girlfriend.

Melanie had been elected prom princess along with Mrs. Kookerly, Tasty Dogdaughter, Jiggly Luckybeans, and Bubbles Nuggmuck. Being the only non-cheerleading prom princess, Melanie was a decided underdog for winning the coveted crown; Mrs. Kookerly had that locked up. Nonetheless, it was a prestigious honor: she was the first non-cheerleading prom princess to be elected in the last thirty-seven years, which gave her the credentials to land an invitation to the dance from Spatch. Her sharp intellect and high grade-point average were conveniently overlooked. Who cared about *that* stuff? She didn't mind that she'd been an afterthought; she fully intended to make Spatch forget about Mrs. Kookerly by giving him the time of his life.

The evening started off well enough: Spatch picked Melanie up and commented that she "looked gorgeous, and would definitely be worth a 'righteous grope' later in the evening." Melanie was cool with that, having figured she'd be doing most of the groping. They consumed the prerequisite amount of liquor in the front seat of his car, made their way to the dance without incident, and received stares of envy and admiration from the promgoers when they entered the gym arm in arm. Melanie was especially cool with that. The evening progressed nicely.

Until now.

Melanie had tried every trick in the book to regain Spatch's attention, to no avail. Coquettishly batting her big eyes at him accomplished nothing. Running her hands seductively through his hair didn't raise an eyebrow. Waving her underwear in his face and wrapping her bra around his neck elicited no reaction whatsoever. She resigned herself to playing second fiddle to Mrs. Kookerly's first violin. The evening was headed straight into the dumper.

Melanie heaved a heavy sigh, slumped in her chair in a most-unladylike fashion, and twiddled a lock of her hair-sprayed hair in frustration and boredom. Next to her, Spatch continued to fume, drink from his flask, stare balefully at Brufyss and Mrs. Kookerly, fume, and drink some more. Melanie grew increasingly frustrated and Spatch increasingly intoxicated.

A flash of misguided motivation lit Spatch's swill-saturated brain like a match igniting a bottle rocket. Resolve caught up with and passed anger and resentment, the sum total resulting in a mutant form of alcohol-induced courage. Spatch had reached his limit. He rose unsteadily from his seat and, much to Melanie's amazement, swaggered and staggered across the gym floor to where Brufyss stood with Mrs. Kookerly.

The crowd's attention was drawn to Spatch's drunken-but-determined advance. A hush spread through the hall, just as it had when the royal couple made their grand entrance. A confrontation was inevitable, once and for all, for better or for worse, come hell or high water, to be or not to be. This evening just kept getting better and better!

Brufyss had always despised the good-looking high school star and derived extreme pleasure from the fact that he, a high school dropout, had deposed "the king" from the throne, the throne being Mrs. Kookerly. Brufyss gloated; this confrontation with Spatch Huntoon would be yet another triumph for him this evening, along with his showdown with Barley Doodlebody.

Whenever Barley showed up.

As the two romantic rivals drew nearer to their respective destinies, the crowd watched, enthralled. Heavy breathing echoed throughout the hall; it came from Mrs. Kookerly, extremely turned on by the idea of Spatch getting his block knocked off. She drew nearer to Brufyss and clung to his arm, her chest heaving with excitement, frothing with anticipation and arousal in her own delicate way.

Brufyss turned to face Spatch squarely, pulling himself up to his full, menacing height. A smug grin creased the corner of his mouth.

Spatch was undeterred. He continued his advance with resolve etched upon his face, staggering and lurching violently from side to side as the dulling effects of the alcohol took a deeper hold on his motor functions. Finally, he stood defiantly before Brufyss, the cheerleaders, and their dates.

"Jus' whaddya shink yer doin' wif my girl, Brufyssh?"

Brufyss eyed his drunken accoster, not sure whether to pity Spatch or pulverize him.

"Do you mean what am I doing with Mrs. Kookerly, Spatch? Is that what you're trying to say? I don't see your girl anywhere!"

"Misshush Kookerly's my girl! You *sole* her from me!"

"Stole her from you? To my recollection, Mrs. Kookerly was the one who invited *me* to this party, and unless I've missed something, I haven't done one thing to force her into it! How can someone be stolen who hasn't been stolen, Spatch?"

"Oh yeah? Wull, Misshush Kookerly's *my* girl! She's wish *me*!"

"If she's with you, then why is she *not* with you, Spatch?" Brufyss grabbed his adversary by the shirt collar. Spatch's head lolled back on his neck as if it were hinged. The others held their breaths. Mrs. Kookerly released her grip on Brufyss's arm and backed away, wet and wide eyed. The entire assembled throng of promgoers gasped in delighted horror. This wasn't going to be pretty!

"If she's with *me*, then she isn't your girl—is she, Spatch?"

"Whaddaya mean?!"

"It's really quite simple, Spatch! If you had the girl you say you have, she wouldn't be the girl I have now, would she?"

"But—"

"Then it would be me who didn't have the girl you have—but the girl I have now, who's the girl you *don't* have, leaves you without a girl and me with the girl who used to be yours but isn't now because she's *mine*! Got it?"

"Wha'??" Spatch's brain spun crazily, awash with alcohol, confused as a chimpanzee learning fractions. "You're flippin' cracked, man!"

"*Wrong answer*, Spatch!" Brufyss grew bored with tormenting his intellectually addled adversary. He held Spatch by the shirt collar and reared back with his other fist to plant a crushing haymaker between Spatch's bleary eyes . . .

Before he could deliver the face-flattening blow, the main doors to the gymnasium exploded inward and off their hinges with a thundering crash! A deafening roar filled the hall; the place shook like it was in the throes of an earthquake. Faux-Hawaiian wall decorations clattered to the floor, shattering into fragments. Bowls of snack food vibrated on the tabletops, ultimately spilling their contents onto the gym floor. The students dropped facedown like soldiers trying to escape incoming mortar fire, clutching their ears, screaming in terror.

When the dust settled and the smoke cleared, screams of terror turned to gasps of astonishment. A bright, shiny, hideously bilious, projectile-vomit greenish-brown Smegmatti 502 sat in the center of the gymnasium like a purring, chugging monster on round rubber paws.

Barley Doodlebody had made *his* grand entrance to the Senior Prom and Vegetarian Intimidation Fest.

Brufyss released his grip on Spatch Huntoon's throat. Spatch fell and smacked the back of his head on the floorboards—WHUMP!—cold-cocking him instantly, sparing him the ignominy of having his rock-star good looks pushed out the back of his skull. He lay immediately forgotten amid the chaos created by the uproarious appearance of Barley Doodlebody.

Everyone coughed and retched from the car's exhaust as Barley gave the students a moment to admire the class and power of the Smegmatti 502 idling on the gym floor, not yet aware he was asphyxiating them. Only after the gymnasium began filling up with exhaust smoke and carbon monoxide did Barley realize he and Tasty Dogdaughter (who sat next to him in the car's passenger seat, beginning to cough and retch) were starting to succumb to the noxious fumes along with everyone else. He turned off the car's ignition. The mammoth, blubbing engine shuddered into silence.

Stunned teacher chaperones regained their composure enough to throw open every door and window to let the smoke and fumes escape. The groggy students picked themselves up off the floor, focusing their blurry vision on the magnificent contraption that initiated the hubbub. Was this a scheduled portion of the evening's entertainment? An expansion of the school's parking lot? An attempt by the teachers to kill them en masse? Whatever it was, it was really cool—except for the car's color, which induced gag reflexes in many of those who'd ingested too much alcohol and snack food or inhaled the exhaust fumes too deeply.

Brufyss shook off his own drowsiness and lumbered over to the Smegmatti 502. As he approached, the passenger door sprang open, and Tasty Dogdaughter leaned her head and upper torso out, her face matching the hue of Barley's car. Her cheeks were puffed out like she had an inflated balloon in her mouth.

Across the room, Mrs. Kookerly and the other cheerleaders, just now emerging from their carbon monoxide–induced head rushes, spotted Tasty and squealed with as much joy as they could muster under the circumstances. They started to teeter over to the car to welcome her but were abruptly taken aback when Tasty spat up onto the floor.

Gubb Chizzlewilly, the school's custodian, screamed hysterically and ducked inside a corner broom closet, overcome with revulsion. Cleaning up after the vegetarian intimidation fest was one thing—students were assigned to that unfortunate task—but this unanticipated mess would be his to remedy. He hated cleaning up barf. His evening was destroyed!

Relatively unaffected by the mass nausea exploding around him, Brufyss moved to the driver's side of the car. Barley opened the door, pulled himself out, and stood up, straightening his clothing and surveying the effect his automotive prize was having on the crowd. He turned and came face-to-face with his astonished business associate and romantic rival.

"Doodlebody! What the hell are you doing?! Who the hell do you think you are?"

Seeing the shock on Brufyss's face, Barley replied with smug satisfaction: "Which question do you want me to answer first, Brufyss?

You know who I am, and what I'm doing is coming to the dance—just like you. You got a problem with that?"

"I've got a problem with trying to *breathe*, just like everybody else! What's the idea of driving this rattletrap into the middle of the room? Are you trying to kill everyone?"

"Just trying to show my girl here a little class." Barley gestured toward the other side of the car where Daphne Dogdaughter retched and vomited. He glanced over at Mrs. Kookerly to see if she'd been impressed by his dramatic arrival. He saw only her own efforts at not being sick; she hadn't noticed Barley yet.

"Why can't you just walk in through the front door like everybody else, Barley? Why do you always have to try to be such a big shot?"

"I'm not trying, Brufyss; it comes naturally! Now, if you don't mind, I'm gonna pay some attention to my girl here—I suggest you pay attention to *yours!*"

Barley turned his back on Brufyss and walked to the passenger side of the Smegmatti 502. He pulled and lifted the sagging, gagging Daphne out of the car and onto her feet, trying to avoid getting vomit onto his new custom suit.

Brufyss grimaced at Barley's rebuke, turned brusquely, and walked back to rejoin Mrs. Kookerly.

As the smoke and exhaust fumes dissipated, and the hulfing, horking, and hacking of the stricken students slackened, the dance reanimated. Faculty members cleaned up the snacks that had fallen on the floor while Gubb Chizzlewilly's wailing inside the locked broom closet continued. The crowd took no notice, thinking only that the band had resumed playing.

As comprehension gradually returned to their addled brains, the crowd became aware that the male half of the party's two newest arrivals was the infamous Barley Doodlebody. Brufyss Bathwater's appearance had been disconcerting enough, but the arrival of the town's *other* most feared hoodlum struck renewed fear and apprehension into the harried promgoers. Having a good time now was going to take a lot of work! With Brufyss and Barley at the dance, no one was safe, and everyone was fair game. Nothing left to do but go into denial and try not to think about this disturbing turn of events.

Returning to Mrs. Kookerly's side, Brufyss shot baleful stares at Barley. Barley had one-upped Brufyss again in his attempt to garner attention, acceptance, and admiration. Brufyss seethed with resentment, vowing that before the evening was over, he'd make his archrival rue this day.

Barley had an awkward time gathering Tasty Dogdaughter back into herself. Inordinately susceptible to the carbon monoxide gassing she'd received, Daphne was in a sorry state. She gasped for fresh air to relieve her nausea, brushed her vomit-soiled hair out of her face, and put forth her best effort to stand up straight at Barley's impatient insistence; but she'd not regained her composure enough to allay his dissatisfaction.

"C'mon, you!" he hissed. "Get your act together before you embarrass me and make even more of an idiot of yourself. Everyone is looking at us like we're drunken fools!"

Daphne was acutely aware of how unladylike and ridiculous she appeared. She gasped to stifle the tears. "I'm sorry, Barley! I don't feel good!"

"You're gonna feel even worse if you keep acting like an inebriated slob! Shape up and stop humiliating yourself in front of everybody!"

Daphne struggled mightily to compose herself so her *own* happy evening could begin.

✳ ✳ ✳

Mrs. Gooberwart, principal of P. P. Piggford and His Wife Janice High School, calmed herself enough to survey the situation from her perch high atop the gymnasium's basketball backboard.

When Barley's Smegmatti 502 made its explosive entrance, shock and surprise sent a massive surge of adrenaline through her body, inducing her to spring straight up into the air—BOINNNG!—in a leap that would have made any of the school's basketball stars gawk with astonishment and envy, had they not been lying prone on the floor with their arms protectively over their heads, frightened out of their wits, squealing like suckling pigs. Mrs. Gooberwart's spry leap ended with her clinging by her fingers to the top of the backboard, her legs dangling.

The principal peered down on the crowd, sensing a growing restlessness and anxiety among the dance attendees. She'd somehow have to extricate herself from this ridiculous predicament to head off potential chaos and regain control of the evening. It would be wise to proceed with the ceremony to crown the queen of the senior prom, lest the current instability escalate into full-blown wanton violence. There was already enough of that in the school's day-to-day activities.

She screamed for assistance over the hubbub. A small clique of promgoers heard her desperate entreaties, saw her hanging there, and laughed hysterically. Sensing her vulnerability, they hurled derision, taunting and ridiculing her mercilessly. They pelted her with various loose items lying in the vicinity: highly saturated fatty snack foods from the floor, wadded-up pieces of wastepaper, handbags, basketballs. Some students ran outside to pick up stones and rocks from the flower beds.

Mrs. Gooberwart lost her patience and her temper.

"ALL RIGHT, YOU FAT-FACED LITTLE BASTARDS! WHEN I GET DOWN FROM HERE I'M GOING TO KICK EACH AND EVERY ONE OF YOUR SCRAWNY LITTLE BUTTS FROM HERE TO HALLELUJAH, AND YOU'RE ALL GOING IN WITH THE VEGETARIANS!"

The crazed students immediately regained their senses. Mrs. Gooberwart could easily make good on her threat; it was common to pass by the principal's office and hear bloodcurdling screams and whomping noises issuing out from under the vault-like solid steel door—the pathetic cries of wrongdoers sent there for punishment. Only God and Mrs. Gooberwart knew what went on inside that room, but seldom were these victims seen again without sporting some obscene disfigurement.

This did nothing to alleviate Mrs. Gooberwart's present circumstances. Her tenuous grip on the backboard was slipping, and her arms felt ready to pop out of their sockets.

Suddenly, the students below her gasped. She looked down to see them recoiling in fear, eyes wide with apprehension. The sound of a voice drifted into her ears:

"Well, well! What have we here? It looks like Mrs. Gooberwart's gotten herself into a bit of a *pickle!*"

The voice belonged to Barley Doodlebody.

Mrs. Gooberwart had been through a session or two with Barley and Brufyss behind the office door. She remembered being impressed that both had survived and were still ambulatory.

Barley remembered the disciplinary sessions too; he'd learned many valuable lessons in "applied violence" from Mrs. Gooberwart, lessons he and Brufyss had put to good use in their post-high school business ventures. Barley viewed Principal Gooberwart as something of a mentor in his growth process.

Noticing her current position of vulnerability, Barley was intrigued. He could utilize her precarious situation to his advantage.

"I'd say you could use a little assistance, Mrs. Gooberwart, and I have a solution to your problem. But maybe we could solve your problem in a way that would be mutually beneficial."

"Hurry up and spit it out, Doodlebody! I'm losing my grip here!" shrieked Mrs. Gooberwart as her fingers slipped off the backboard a little more.

Barley turned to the students and addressed them in an ominous tone: "*Beat it*, you slime-slinging sludgeballs!"

The frightened students melted back into the crowd, not needing to be told twice. Barley focused on the dangling high school principal. In a low voice audible only to Mrs. Gooberwart, Barley elucidated his "mutually beneficial" proposal, assuring her that acceptance of it would resolve her dilemma.

"Whaddaya think, Mrs. Gooberwart? Do we have a deal?"

The principal didn't have long to think, nor did she have to think long. She knew the deal was her only option and, being the unprincipled principal that she was, saw herself making out pretty well in the long run.

"Yeah, we have a deal, Doodlebody!" Her grip slipped a little more. "Get me down from here!"

"Done."

He scanned the room until his eyes fell upon Vice Principal Muzzlemonkey standing outside the broom closet door, attempting to entice Gubb Chizzlewilly to fulfill his janitorial obligations. Barley recalled that Mr. Muzzlemonkey was an easily manipulated, spineless wimp— exactly who and what he needed at this moment.

"Muzzlemonkey! Hey, *Muzzlemonkey!*"

Mr. Muzzlemonkey spotted his boss clinging to the basketball backboard. He gasped in astonishment, abandoned his solicitation of Gubb Chizzlewilly, and ran to Mrs. Gooberwart, staring up her floral-print muumuu.

"Heavens, Mrs. Gooberwart! What happened to you? How did you get up there?"

"That doesn't matter anymore," she replied calmly. "What does matter is that I get down from here right now. We have to start the prom queen coronation ceremony before things get any more out of control!"

Barley spoke up. "Listen to me, Muzzlemonkey, and listen good. We need to find a ladder to get Mrs. Gooberwart down from there, and we need it now. Get it!"

Instant panic gripped Mr. Muzzlemonkey. He was just as aware of Barley's reputation as everyone else in the room.

"B-but, Mr. Doodlebody, the only ladder we have is in the broom closet! The custodian has locked himself in there and won't come out—no matter what I say to him!"

"Chizzlewilly's ass is *mine* when I get back down there," hissed Mrs. Gooberwart.

"She's losing her grip, Muzzlemonkey. You're gonna have to catch her."

"*Catch* her?! I can't catch her! My bad back—"

Barley flashed a prearranged signal to the dangling principal. She released her hold on the backboard, dropped straight down, and landed on the poor vice principal's head. The force and weight of her body drove him into the floor, cushioning her fall but knocking him cold.

Mrs. Gooberwart untangled herself from Mr. Muzzlemonkey, and Barley helped her to her feet. Trying to appear composed and unruffled, she smoothed out the wrinkles in her muumuu.

"All right, Doodlebody, you've fulfilled the first part of our agreement. It's time to fulfill the second part."

"Of course, Mrs. Gooberwart! It'll be my pleasure."

Barley reached into his suit coat pocket and produced an object which he nonchalantly pressed into the outstretched hand of the principal. She brought her hand up to the cleavage of her dress and quickly placed the object there, withdrew her hand, and used it to shake Barley's, thanking him for his assistance.

"Once again, it was my pleasure, Mrs. Gooberwart. Soon it'll be time to fulfill *your* part of our little agreement."

Mrs. Gooberwart nodded.

Barley walked back to his parked sports car, his mind racing with possibilities. This unforeseen and fortuitous turn of events could provide a most effective new direction for his master plan of turning Mrs. Kookerly's gaze from Brufyss to himself. Circumstances and fate had miraculously dealt Barley a high-stakes hand.

He'd need to play those cards skillfully.

*** ***

While the previous scene played out, Brufyss was across the gymnasium, attending to Mrs. Kookerly. He glanced over to see Mrs. Gooberwart dangling helplessly from the backboard by her fingers, and he chuckled. There was no love lost between himself and the irascible Mrs. Gooberwart. However, when he noticed Barley standing beneath her, engrossed in conversation, Brufyss became suspicious. What was Doodlebody up to? Why would Barley concern himself with a person who'd been their chief nemesis in high school?

His interest and suspicion piqued, Brufyss was ready to excuse himself from the group to investigate these mysterious proceedings when a spate of coughing from his glamorous new girlfriend caused him to divert his attention back to her. When she'd finally settled down and was feeling better, Brufyss remembered his initial intention.

Mrs. Gooberwart had already been rescued. She was heading toward the gym stage, leaving the crumpled Vice Principal Muzzlemonkey behind her on the floor and a rabble of nearby students whispering furtively among themselves. Barley was walking back to Daphne Dogdaughter by the ugly sports car.

Brufyss had missed whatever had just taken place! Well, Barley would probably tell him about the whole thing sometime later, after the dance or maybe tomorrow—if they were still speaking after tonight! Brufyss let his mind dwell on that for a few pleasurable seconds.

If he knew Barley, the bum was probably just kissing up to that old crow Gooberwart.

Brufyss turned his attention back to his beautiful date.

4

Mrs. Gooberwart made her way to the gymnasium stage and the microphone. She turned to the quasi-Hawaiian musical combo screeching and thwomping behind her. "All right, put a cork in it! We're gonna get the prom queen coronation started!"

The young musicians ceased, and the gym became quiet, except for the continuing din of chatter and hurled insults out in the crowd.

The principal surveyed the throng on the huge gymnasium floor. She gazed up into the roof rafters directly overhead and saw Retchard Pumpstuck, the school's student stage-lighting monitor, standing on the catwalk in semidarkness, diligently operating the spotlight and directing its brilliant beam upon her.

Retchard Pumpstuck was an academic-minded, socially inept student who considered himself intellectually superior to the other students and faculty members at P. P. Piggford and His Wife Janice High School—and probably was. A total geek in the purest sense of the word, Retchard sincerely believed that activities such as operating the gymnasium lighting system were more challenging, meaningful, and beneficial to mankind than attending school events designed to supply mere entertainment and a momentary diversion from the truly important things in life. Retchard overlooked the fact that no female within a thirty-three-county radius of North Corners would go out with him, finding him to be pompous, boring, repulsive, and smelly.

After graduating from high school, he'd go on to become a multibillionaire.

Mrs. Gooberwart spied the huge vat containing the "gurgling gooey glop" a few feet from the catwalk on which Retchard stood. The vat hung over the stage like a storm cloud, waiting to unleash its confusing mixture of treats and terror onto the evening's unsuspecting vegetarian victims like manna from heaven and a deluge from hell. Retchard's secondary job was to activate the drop at the appropriate time.

Next to the left-front corner of the stage, a large bin full of raw meat, animal parts, and internal organs sat in place for the "ministration of meat." The meat and animal parts had been kept in the school cafeteria's freezer, then were thawed out that morning. Bloody water dripped from the bottom of the bin, forming small, gory pools on the floor beneath it.

Mrs. Gooberwart satisfied herself that everything was ready for the night's festivities. She reached for the microphone, found the on/off switch at the microphone's base, and flipped it on. A banshee-like screech of high-volume feedback blared, causing everyone to scream and drop to the floor again. The horrified students prostrated themselves, clutched their ears, and howled like wolves caught in automobile shredders. The freshman musicians in the onstage band dropped their instruments and fell between their chairs, writhing and screaming, sounding slightly better than they had while playing.

Mrs. Gooberwart, her own ears ringing like church bells, quickly switched the microphone off and beckoned backstage to the student audio monitor.

Unabashedly enamored with audio-visual equipment, Fifi "Fungus" Farglebarker was another member of the socially outcast at P. P. Piggford High. Fifi dreamed of someday establishing a career in radio. Thus far, the closest she'd come to achieving her aspiration was getting her head stuck in a loudspeaker while setting up the sound system. The nickname "Fungus" derived from her enthusiastic willingness to supply the biology lab with microbe cultures from the lining of her lunchbox.

As an audio-visual geek, Fifi knew from prior experience that no one was going to ask her to be their date to the prom. She'd pleaded with Mrs. Gooberwart to be the designated audio monitor and work the sound system, with the additional task of operating the levers for the stage trapdoor and elevator. At this moment, Fungus was whimpering in pain, curled up on the stage floor beneath the audio equipment table.

Mrs. Gooberwart shook her head to clear the ringing in her ears. "*Farglebarker*! Get up and fix the damn microphone! I'm not paying you to lie around like a lump. *Fix* the damn thing!" she shouted.

Actually, Mrs. Gooberwart wasn't paying Fungus to do anything (the young student volunteered for the audio monitor job), but Fifi got the message—or what she could hear of it through the ringing inside her head. She crawled from under the table and faced a bank of electronic audio equipment that included the amplifier to the public address sound system. Fifi adjusted a couple of knobs, threw a couple of switches, turned the volume level down a notch, and stood away from the contraption, her hands covering her ears.

"Okay, Mrs. Gooberwart, try it again!"

Once more, the principal flicked the on/off switch on and hesitantly put her mouth close to the device.

"Testing, testing . . ."

An electronic reproduction of her voice came back at her from the many speakers set up around the hall—with no horrific feedback and a comfortable level of audibility. She breathed a sigh of relief and prepared to address the crowd.

"All right, you little heathens. Get off the floor and pay attention! I'm going to announce this year's winner of the queen of the senior prom balloting."

The students started shaking off the horrid effects of the audio assault. Finally something was going to happen tonight that might not frighten, hurt, or kill them!

At the beginning of the month, the students had cast secret ballots for their choice of a queen. The top five finishers, designated as the royal court of prom princesses, had been announced to the general student population earlier in the week. Now the students would pay homage to the one fortunate female who'd wear the queen's crown.

The promgoers turned their attention to Mrs. Gooberwart with renewed enthusiasm.

"When I read the names, I want each of the five nominated princesses and their escorts to come up onto the stage, form a line behind me, and shut up! I'll announce the winner of the voting, and remember: the results are final, so don't start whining and complaining if the person you voted for doesn't win. *Understand?!*"

The throng nodded.

The group comprised of Mrs. Kookerly and Brufyss Bathwater, Bubbles Nuggmuck, Jiggly Luckybeans, and both of their dates struggled to their feet, banged on their heads to drive the ringing sensation away, and smoothed out the wrinkles in their clothing.

At Mrs. Gooberwart's announcement, the girls primped in anticipation of their moment in front of the admiring student population. Both Bubbles and Jiggly self-effacingly assured Mrs. Kookerly that she had the queen's crown securely in the bag, and Brufyss swelled with anticipation of the moment when he'd put Barley Doodlebody in his place once and for all. The excited group waited with bated breath for Mrs. Gooberwart's invitation to come up to the stage.

Barley recovered from his own eardrum lambasting while assisting Daphne in her preparation for the coronation ceremony. Tasty gathered what composure she could muster. She felt as disheveled as she looked, but this glorious moment would never come again in her lifetime, and she was determined to put on her best face for the occasion.

She looked over at her fellow cheerleaders and managed a weak smile and a wave, which was returned by her friends. Mrs. Kookerly was the odds-on favorite to win, but Tasty would not be denied this opportunity to be recognized for her own beauty and popularity. Excitement and anticipation welled up inside her, fighting through the overall discomfort.

Over in the corner, Melanie Bupwanger performed her own ritual of preparation, adjusting her makeup and clothing for the big announcement. Spatch Huntoon was still lying in a state of semiconsciousness on the floor by Brufyss Bathwater. She finished her primping and wended through the crowd to the spot where Spatch lay drooling on the floor, doing his impression of a squished garden slug. Like Tasty Dogdaughter, Melanie was determined to savor this one brief moment in the student spotlight. If she had to drag Spatch onstage by the seat of his pants or the hair on his head, so be it!

Approaching Spatch's sprawled body and the gathered group of cheerleaders and their dates, Melanie cleared her throat and lowered her eyes, truly in awe of being in the presence of bona fide P. P. Piggford and His Wife Janice High School royalty.

"*Ahem*! Excuse me, please."

"Why, hello, Melanie!" greeted Mrs. Kookerly sweetly. The head cheerleader immediately recognized Melanie as a member of the high school's Future Genius Housewives of America Club and was in a benevolent mood, knowing full well that Melanie didn't stand a chance in hell of capturing the queen's crown. "Congratulations on being named a prom princess! It's so exciting, isn't it? Good luck!"

She was seconded by Flagella Nuggmuck and Lucinda Luckybeans. The girls' prom dates silently ogled Melanie, with the exception of Brufyss, who towered above Mrs. Kookerly like an overprotective Angel of Death.

"Thank you, Mrs. Kookerly!" Melanie was truly thrilled that the school's reigning popularity goddess had recognized her and remembered her name. "Good luck to all of you too! I-I hate to interrupt, but Spatch Huntoon is my date for the evening, and I have to get him on his feet before we go onstage."

The group had completely forgotten about Spatch! They looked down to the floor where the high school's once famous, now forlorn BMOCAPPPAHWJHS lay in a disheveled heap, his head lolling from side to side, saliva spilling from his mouth. Spatch was a sorry sight indeed, and the group took pity on Melanie.

"Brufyss, *please* help Spatch off the floor so Melanie can have an escort to the prom queen ceremony too!" cooed Mrs. Kookerly. In her present state of euphoric magnanimity, she'd forgotten that only a short time ago, she'd been frothing at the prospect of Brufyss knocking Spatch's teeth out.

"Yeah, sure—whatever." Brufyss grabbed Spatch by the shirt collar and yanked him roughly to his feet.

"Gently, Brufyss! Don't hurt him!"

"Don't worry about that, Mrs. Kookerly!" said Melanie dryly. "After the coronation ceremony, *I'm* going to kick Spatch's ass—royally! C'mon, you disgusting jerk!"

Spatch stood drunk and unsteady, trying to clear the giant fuzz ball out of his buzzing skull. Melanie applied a stinging slap to his face— WHAP!—which aided his return to awareness immensely. Spatch's besotted brain remembered being upset and angry about something or other. As his blurred vision refocused, he noticed Brufyss standing next to him; the memories rushed back. He was just about to bash Brufyss for stealing Mrs. Kookerly! Feelings of jealously and anger surged through him again.

Another searing slap across the face—WHAP!—rocked him back on his heels. Once more, Melanie had administered the blow. She was beginning to enjoy it.

"C'mon, Spatch, you drunken bastard! I've put up with your whiny, jealous crap all evening! Wake up and get it together before I knock you through the freakin' *wall*!"

WHAP! Another slap across the kisser. Spatch forgot his ill feelings toward Brufyss and threw his hands in front of his face to fend off the stinging blows that Melanie delivered with increasing ferocity.

"You are *not* going to ruin this night for me, Spatch Huntoon! All my *life* I've dreamed of being a prom princess instead of a four-eyed, egg-headed bookworm brainiac, and I'm not gonna let a spoiled, big-headed, jealous, drunken prick like *you* screw it up for me. You do, and I'll *kill* you!"

WHAP!

"*Do you understand me, Spatch*!?!"

The slaps achieved their desired effect. Spatch was sobering up. "Okay, okay! I get it! I'll be cool, Melanie, I swear I'll be cool! I'm all right now— just quit slapping me!"

Mrs. Kookerly and Brufyss, Jiggly, Bubbles, and their dates watched incredulously as Melanie smacked the snot out of Spatch. Who would've guessed she possessed such a volatile temper? Melanie Bupwanger's stock soared with all of them as they watched; this chick was all right!

Mrs. Gooberwart's amplified voice boomed throughout the cavernous hall:

"All right, everybody, simmer down! We're about to proceed with the introduction of last year's queen, this year's royal prom court, and the announcement of the new queen of the prom for '67. Farglebarker, play the coronation music!"

The audio monitor reached into a box full of phonograph records, placed the disc of prerecorded coronation music that was also used at the graduation ceremony onto the spinning turntable, and dropped the needle in the record's groove. The amplified scratches, crackles, and pops of the old recording's worn surface sounded for a few seconds, followed by the recorded music itself: a hillbilly banjo, fiddle, and guitar ensemble playing a spirited rendition of "Turkey in the Straw"—not exactly an appropriate selection for the coronation. Somehow, the boisterous hillbilly hoot had been placed in the wrong record sleeve.

Mrs. Gooberwart hurled a venomous backward glance at Fifi, who was ignorant of the musical mistake and didn't notice the withering stare. However, when the principal looked at the audience and saw the promgoers happily bobbing their heads and tapping their feet to the rollicking beat, she decided to leave well enough alone. What the hell! Queen of the prom or queen of the hillbilly mountain gals—it didn't really matter as long as *somebody* got crowned! She just wanted to get it over with.

"Before I proceed with the introduction of the '67 prom court princesses, I want to introduce the queen of last year's Senior Prom and Vegetarian Intimidation Fest, who'll pass her crown on to this year's queen.

Please extend a warm P. P. Piggford and His Wife Janice High School welcome to the queen of the '66 senior prom, *Miss Spiffany Tonguehoister*."

* * *

Spiffany Tonguehoister: last year's queen and the coed who'd occupied the coveted position of head cheerleader as Mrs. Kookerly's predecessor. Possessed of a beautiful face and figure, she had the personality and presence to charm flies off a rotting corpse and pep, vim, and vigor enough to power a sausage grinder nonstop for weeks. Her "vim" alone was a wonder to behold. Spiffany was the role model for the Kookerlys, Dogdaughters, Nuggmucks, and Luckybeans of the world.

The Spiffany Tonguehoister years had been especially good for the male students at Piggford High. A tomboy, she held the distinction of being able to rebuild the entire engine, transmission, and chassis of a Sherman tank while blindfolded, a talent that impressed the boys immensely. Knowing there wasn't a Sherman tank to be found within 7,000 miles of North Corners, they'd goad Spiffany into performing her blindfolded tank-rebuilding stunt. Spiffany would accept the challenge with determined enthusiasm. While she waited, blindfolded, for the mythical tank to be delivered, the boys would look up her dress.

Eventually, she'd lose patience with waiting for the tank, question its whereabouts, and be told it had been unexpectedly called to war. This explanation usually satisfied her. Though disappointed, she'd go about her business, leaving a bevy of teenage boys anything but disappointed.

Most recently, Spiffany's mechanical expertise had been utilized by Mrs. Gooberwart to update and increase the efficiency of the motors, gears, levers, and pulleys used to open and retract the gymnasium stage trapdoor and work the elevator for this year's vegetarian intimidation fest.

Spiffany was escorted by Bronson Facockta, another Piggford High alumnus and the person who held the title of BMOCAPPPAHWJHS prior to Spatch Huntoon's ascension. Bronson had been the guiding light and mentor to all male students who aspired to be egotistical, good-looking, shallow, and conceited. Spatch worshipped Bronson like the golden calf.

In the year since his graduation, Bronson had put together a successful string of business failures and was currently working at the local North Corners discount department store, Everything—And More!, in ladies underwear, which looked extremely funny on him to say the least.

Spiffany wore the prom queen's crown atop her fashionably coiffed head; miraculously, the crown hadn't fallen off when everyone dove for the floor. She'd utilized her mechanical prowess beforehand to weld the crown to a steel skull brace anchored securely to her earrings. She designed this device not only to fasten the crown securely to her head but also to make it virtually impossible to remove without a crowbar, iron tongs, and a steam-powered crane.

Like his faithful disciple Spatch Huntoon, Bronson had drunk himself into a state of catatonic inebriation. And similar to Melanie Bupwanger, Spiffany was loath to let Bronson's drunkenness deprive her of the opportunity to stand once again in the spotlight. She passionately wished to savor the last vestige of the glories of her youth, the conclusion of which would signify her official emergence into the world of adulthood.

Spiffany and Bronson made their way to the stage, awash in the brightness of Retchard Pumpstuck's spotlight, marching in step to the twanging strains of "Turkey in the Straw." The crowd obliged Mrs. Gooberwart's command for "a warm P. P. Piggford and His Wife Janice High School welcome" for the outgoing queen by applauding enthusiastically and screaming explicitly insulting comments like "ragged old has-been" and "washed-up loser." This significantly hastened the couple's progress through the crowd. When the two finally reached the stage and climbed the steps, Mrs. Gooberwart instructed Spiffany to pause, turn, wave at the crowd with queenly elegance, and accept the admiration and appreciation of "her loyal subjects." She told Bronson to shut up, do what Spiffany was doing, and try not to fall over.

The shouted threats and insults increased. Mrs. Gooberwart quelled the potential riot by casting a toothsome, threatening grimace at the assemblage. Restive order returned to the gymnasium.

"Okay, you two just stand back there behind me and shut up while I introduce the prom princesses. Your personal safety may depend upon your compliance with this."

Spiffany and Bronson stepped back a few feet from Mrs. Gooberwart, standing quietly side by side. Satisfied, Mrs. Gooberwart addressed the audience:

"When I read each prom princess's name, she and her escort will come up onto the stage and stand behind me. Farglebarker, turn off that damn music for a minute! Now, everyone give me your attention."

Fungus pulled the needle off the record, and all eyes fell on Mrs. Gooberwart in the center-stage spotlight. Hearts pumped. Palms perspired. Breathing ceased.

This was the big moment!

Mrs. Gooberwart produced an envelope from the folds of her floral-print muumuu, opened it ceremoniously, and extracted a piece of paper. Utter silence pervaded. Even Gubb Chizzlewilly, sequestered in his broom closet hideaway, sensed that something important was about to happen and ceased his weeping and wailing.

Mrs. Gooberwart read the first name: "Princess Melanie Bupwanger."

Melanie gave an excited gasp, grabbed Spatch by the shirt collar, and dragged him toward the stage. The audience parted and began applauding, while from somewhere within the crowd came occasional off-color references to various parts of Melanie's shapely anatomy and editorial comments regarding Spatch's recent fall from grace.

The couple reached the stage and took their places behind Mrs. Gooberwart, standing close to Bronson and Spiffany (who was now beginning to get a bit teary-eyed). Spatch recognized his former mentor and grunted a salutation. All Bronson could muster in response was a growling burp that reeked of alcohol and sour stomach acid. Spatch's smile quickly faded, and he stared blankly out at the crowd, his humiliation complete—again.

Melanie ignored her escort, beamed with delight, and smiled at Spiffany, genuinely thrilled to be in the presence of a P. P. Piggford student celebrity from yesteryear.

Mrs. Gooberwart turned to the couple and smiled at Melanie in acknowledgement of her accomplishment, then scowled severely at the comely coed's inebriated escort before turning her attention back to the crowd and her piece of paper.

"Princess Lucinda Luckybeans."

Jiggly let out a squeal of excitement, seizing her prom date by the arm and trekking through the crowd, receiving cheers from her cheerleading comrades and applause from the student population. As she made her way toward the stage with the harsh glare of Retchard Pumpstuck's spotlight bathing her in its eye-scorching brilliance, individuals within the masses began chanting rhythmically:

"Jigg-*lee*! Jigg-*lee*! Jigg-*lee*! Jigg-*lee*!"

Soon the entire audience joined in. By the time Jiggly Luckybeans arrived at the stage, the gymnasium was thundering with the roar of a thousand encouraging voices—though only two hundred students had come to the dance.

Lucinda Luckybeans earned the nickname "Jiggly" by performing an accomplishment as astonishing as Daphne Dogdaughter's "beef stew bacchanal." The occasion was yet another of the high school's gala events, the Jolly Jiggly Jelly Jamboree. Lucinda had accidentally fallen into a huge vat containing the main ingredient for the Titanic Toast-Tasting tournament: apricot jelly. The upshot was Lucinda's creative method of self-cleaning after she'd pulled herself out of the morass. Covered completely by the gooey, sticky mess, Lucinda began to wiggle, jiggle, and vibrate her body like a dog shaking the water from its fur. So intense were her high-speed gyrations that as she divested herself of the viscous coat, she dispensed with the majority of her clothing as well.

Because of this historic vibratory act, Lucinda Luckybeans would be known forever after as "Jiggly." Her popularity among the students increased tenfold, and subsequent Jolly Jiggly Jelly Jamborees were highly attended events if Jiggly Luckybeans (now the event's namesake) planned a personal appearance.

Lucinda and her escort climbed to the stage. Suddenly, she stopped in the spotlight, let go of her date's arm, and whirled to face the crowd. Knowing what her public desired from her, she launched into the super-velocity, full-body vibrating spasm that made her famous. Jiggly jiggled like a jackhammer, the rhinestones, buttons, beads, and bows popping off her ball gown's fabric and into the audience like kernels of popcorn from an uncovered popper.

Realizing that her gyrations were putting her in jeopardy of losing her entire ball gown, she ceased her spasms and smiled sweetly, waving at the crowd.

The open-mouthed audience was at first disappointed at Lucinda's cessation but quickly recovered and burst into another roar of appreciation. Always a crowd-pleaser, Lucinda Luckybeans was a worthy candidate for prom queen.

The "Jigg-*lee*! Jigg-*lee*!" chant echoed throughout the hall as Lucinda took her astounded escort by the hand, passed in front of Bronson and Spiffany (whose face revealed a tearful trickle), and moved to their place next to Melanie and Spatch.

Mrs. Gooberwart was just as mesmerized by Lucinda's spontaneous performance as the crowd, but she regained her composure after Jiggly and her date had taken their designated places on the stage. The crowd quieted down and the principal resumed her roll call of the royal prom court:

"Princess Flagella Nuggmuck."

Bubbles let out a girlish shriek. After a hug and encouragement from Mrs. Kookerly, she proceeded with her escort to join the other members of the royal prom court. As with the previous princesses, the crowd once more hooted, cheered, and clapped for Bubbles. However, there was no one in the crowd brave or foolish enough to start a "Buh-*bulls*! Buh-*bulls*!" chant, out of fear that Flagella, like Jiggly Luckybeans before her, might perform an impromptu rendition of the act that made *her* famous and earned her the nickname by which she was known.

Flagella Nuggmuck, the third member of the frolicking foursome of PPPAHWJHS cheerleaders, had received the nickname "Bubbles" in a somewhat different manner than her two compatriots. It happened at the school's annual Hot Dog Hog-a-Thon, wherein the event's patrons gorged themselves on hot dogs and sauerkraut lathered with mustard. Rampant overconsumption of the marinated-cabbage-covered delicacies resulted in an ensuing windstorm of gaseous discharge from the participants and crowd alike. The airborne methane by-product of their ingestions would waft over the countryside, paralyzing livestock and destroying crops in a two-county radius—yet the Hot Dog Hog-a-Thon was nonetheless an extremely well-attended fete.

Bubbles gained notoriety by losing her footing and plunging into a gigantic vat of yellow mustard. Since she'd already consumed a record-setting number of sauerkraut-accessorized wieners herself, she began producing voluminous amounts of her own methane by-product as she flailed helplessly inside the huge vat. Submerged as she was, her resulting discharge manifested in the form of gaseous bubbles, which rose to the surface of the liquid mustard like a saucepan of water boiling on a hot stove. As Flagella splashed in the roiling, bubbling mustard, the crowd watched in stunned, fascinated amazement—though by now their appetites were lost, and the contest dissipated into a non-event as far as further frankfurter feasting was concerned.

Flagella wasn't finished yet. Her next act would immortalize her in the hearts and minds of her fellow students. Because she'd ingested so many hot dogs, an unbelievable amount of gaseous methane was expanding inside her stomach. The pressure grew until it reached unmanageable proportions, finally culminating in an expulsion of gas the likes of which few had witnessed in a lifetime!

The explosion launched Flagella out of the mustard vat—KAWOOOSH!

She shot straight up like a bright-yellow missile, spraying mustard everywhere and all over everyone. Up, up, up she hurtled, perhaps a hundred feet in the air. Down, down, down she plummeted, plunging into the same mustard vat. A wave of mustard washed over the awe-stricken crowd, but Flagella was saved from injury. She bobbed groggily back to the surface, still producing enough methane to keep the brew bubbling for hours after she'd extricated herself, tooting all the while like a mustard-covered whoopee cushion.

The throng reverently bestowed a new nickname upon her: "Bubbles"—a name deemed to be more delicate and respectful than "Rocket Ass" or "Queen of Farts."

The prom crowd opted to acknowledge Bubbles with simple applause, cheering, and whistling in lieu of initiating a chant they might later regret.

It didn't really matter to Flagella how the crowd chose to bestow the accolades. She was overjoyed to be recognized and honored. She floated through the audience, euphorically clutching the arm of her date. They smiled at Mrs. Gooberwart, paid brief homage to Queen Spiffany (whose tears now streamed in rivulets down her face), and took their places next to Melanie, Spatch, and Lucinda and her date. The three princesses giggled and wished one another luck once again, while the escorts simply ignored each other. Bronson wobbled and drooled.

The list had narrowed to the last two elected prom princesses, Daphne and Mrs. Kookerly. Their escorts were the most-feared desperados ever to tread or deface the hallowed halls of Piggford High. The crowd's collective apprehension, mixed with intense curiosity, created a raw atmosphere of electric, anticipatory excitement.

Mrs. Gooberwart leaned forward and spoke into the microphone once again:

"Princess Daphne Dogdaughter."

Adrenaline surged through Tasty's body. All traces of discomfort instantly vanished. She straightened out her barf-stained dress, brushed a stray strand of sprayed hair from her face, and grabbed Barley by the arm. Despite her frazzled appearance, Daphne's adolescent beauty was incandescent.

"Okay, Barley, I'm ready—let's *go!*"

"Are you gonna be all right? Can you *walk?*" Barley was still wary of Daphne embarrassing him further. It was imperative to his master plan that she maintained and projected whatever dignity she still had.

"Yes, yes, I'm fine, Barley! I'm really okay, I promise; you'll see. We can go up now."

Barley placed Tasty's arm in his. "Let's go. Walk slowly—and don't fall down!"

They marched to the stage. The students stepped aside to let them pass, almost bowing to the floor in fearful deference to Barley. There was no cheering, no catcalls. An eerie silence accompanied the two as they walked, Daphne aglow with pride and happiness, looking radiant and expectant despite her tousled appearance. Barley walked erect, immaculately dressed, exuding an air of supreme confidence and superiority, his eyes roaming over the faces of individuals he passed, sizing them up, staring them down. No one challenged his gaze.

Barley cast another glance at the head cheerleader to see if Mrs. Kookerly's interest was beginning to divert from Brufyss to himself. He saw only her joy and excitement for Daphne. No sign yet he was capturing her attention.

That would happen soon enough.

Brufyss's eyes were focused on Barley. *Enjoy it while you can, Doodlebody . . .*

Soon the silence became too awkward for the crowd. One by one, students began clapping for the couple. Hoodlum escort or not, Tasty Dogdaughter was a venerated P. P. Piggford High School cheerleader and therefore worthy of respect and courtesy. Intellect the size of a kidney bean or not, she was a North Corners beauty, therefore worthy of recognition and appreciation. Wasn't Tasty Dogdaughter always in the forefront when the pep squad broke into their famous "victory dance"? Wasn't Tasty Dogdaughter always right there when lonely Piggford High male students needed cheering up, encouragement through tough times . . . or a quickie? Wasn't Tasty Dogdaughter the reason the school cafeteria served beef stew for lunch every day? The very *least* they could do was honor her for what she meant to the student population of Piggford High, and not let the foreboding presence of Barley Doodlebody intimidate them out of rewarding their loyal, lusty, ditzy pepster with the recognition she deserved.

A rolling wave of applause reverberated through the gymnasium as the crowd acknowledged Daphne Dogdaughter, '67 prom court princess, and the rousing chant "Tay-*stee*! Tay-*stee*! Tay-*stee*!" filled the room.

Daphne giggled and glowed. She clung to Barley with one arm, occasionally raising the other to wave at her appreciative peers and revel in the applause. Things had definitely taken a turn for the better. She looked forward to joining her good friends on the stage, to sharing her happiness with them, and to honoring her very best friend, Mrs. Kookerly, as the '67 queen of the senior prom. This had finally turned into a night the young coed would remember for the rest of her life.

She cast a euphoric gaze upward at Barley, her important and influential escort for this momentous occasion, and gave him an angelic smile of gratitude for helping to make this happen for her. He was close mouthed, jaw set firmly with determination, his steely gaze fixed on the approaching stage. He didn't return her smile but rather pulled her inexorably toward her destiny.

At one point during their march to the stage, the sound of one lone voice issued out above the noise, the applause, and the chanting:

"Yeah, *buddy!*"

Hearing Frog Puppleman's unmistakable signature salutation, Barley looked over the heads of the surrounding students and picked out his brother and Mimsy waving their arms like two desperate pedestrians without umbrellas hailing taxi cabs in an acid rainstorm. He winked at his weak-minded sibling as he passed by and continued onward.

"Yeah, *buddy*," murmured Barley softly to himself, a smirk curling his lip.

The couple climbed the stairs, where Mrs. Goberwart awaited with her grim, thin-lipped smile. They passed the straight single-file line of Queen Spiffany Tonguehoister (who was now sniffling, snuffling, and weeping softly), Bronson Facockta, and Daphne's fellow prom princesses with their dates. Daphne smiled at them as she and Barley took their places. The girls wished each other luck once again, while the other escorts, Spatch Huntoon included, drew back from Barley like hikers who'd stumbled on a coiled rattlesnake.

Barley threw each of the other escorts a curt, contemptuous glance and turned to face the audience. His eyes briefly met those of Mrs. Goberwart, who flinched almost imperceptibly and turned away to face the audience once more, nervously fidgeting with the piece of paper.

Barley perceived this, and the haughty smirk that creased one corner of his mouth spread to the other. So far, he and his master plan had reached this point without a hitch. He focused his gaze beyond the glare of the spotlight to the blackness where the crowd was calming down after paying tribute to his prom princess date.

There was only one more name on the royal roll call . . .

5

This was the most glorious moment in the P. P. Piggford and His Wife Janice High School senior class's four-year term: the moment when its most glorious member received her most glorious honor. The students waited breathlessly to see how it would all come down. Would she distribute kisses of gratitude to every male member of the audience who voted for her? Would she give them a night to remember by performing the victory dance on *all* of their faces? Would Brufyss Bathwater be so overcome with joy and goodwill that he'd become a nice guy forevermore and stop beating the crap out of them?

The answers would reveal themselves within the next few minutes. All eyes were focused on the spot at the rear fringe of the crowd where Mrs. Kookerly and Brufyss awaited the signal from Mrs. Gooberwart to march to the stage. The gym was quieter than the library had ever been.

This was the big moment of the big moment!

Mrs. Gooberwart's electronically amplified voice boomed over the PA system's speakers:

"Princess Mrs. Kookerly."

The crowd erupted with a full-throated roar of frenzied approval and applause. Cheers, whistles, and shouts of complimentary encouragement resounded throughout the gymnasium, devoid of lascivious catcalls and anatomical references. They hadn't forgotten who her escort was.

Mrs. Kookerly, her heart pounding like a bass drum bashed by a cave troll, took a deep breath and looked up at Brufyss, her eyes as wide as two pepperoni pizzas with extra cheese. The accolades, like the similes, poured down on them like monsoon rain on a tin roof.

Brufyss gazed at her proudly, admiringly, adoringly. Never in his life had he been so filled with happiness, fulfillment, and accomplishment. He was crazy about this girl who'd given him so much to live for and set his heart on fire. He was overjoyed at having the opportunity to share this glorious moment with her—his *own* supreme moment of triumph as well. An uncharacteristic smile of unadulterated happiness spread across his face.

"Brufyss, I'm so excited!" She took a deep breath, straightened out her dress, and looked into the mirror on her face-powder compact for a quick perusal of the state of her makeup. *Perfect.* Putting the compact back into her small evening handbag, she turned once more to Brufyss.

"Well, it's time to go!"

Brufyss nodded, and the two set off toward the stage to live out the most exciting moment of their lives, accompanied by the spotlight tracking their progress through the audience. The ovation rang mightily in their ears. Brufyss lapped up every bit of the attention with greedy enjoyment. He knew every eye was fixed upon his princess; every male in the audience wished they could be in his place. He also knew Barley Doodlebody was burning with jealous envy.

It couldn't have been more perfect.

As she approached the stage, Mrs. Kookerly reveled in the happiness and excitement in the faces of her three cheerleading princess comrades. It was so wonderful that they could share and treasure the lasting memory of this moment forever.

The happy couple reached the stage. Brufyss looked smugly at Barley with the intention of savoring the envy in his rival's eyes. To his dismay, Barley's gaze was riveted on Mrs. Kookerly—revealing no envy but rather a look of lustful longing. As far as Barley was concerned, Brufyss didn't exist.

Raw determination seized the underdog; he wasn't about to let this long-anticipated moment slip away! Taking Mrs. Kookerly firmly by the arm, Brufyss led her purposefully past Principal Gooberwart and back to the lineup of Queen Spiffany (now blubbering openly and uncontrollably) and semicomatose Bronson, and the prom princesses and escorts. Brufyss steered Mrs. Kookerly directly to Barley and Daphne and past them. He looked his rival squarely in the eye, smiling haughtily. Barley's gaze fastened immovably on Mrs. Kookerly, ignoring her escort completely.

Frustration brewed inside Brufyss like lava in a restless volcano. Each of the girls reached out to Mrs. Kookerly to grasp her hand, congratulate, and wish her well. Each of the escorts drew back from Brufyss as if he were a leper. Brufyss paid them no mind—he was fuming over Barley Doodlebody's lack of deference to him. *That will change soon enough!*

The couple reached the end of the lineup and took their places.

Spiffany and Bronson stood apart from the rest of the group. The reigning queen was now sobbing loudly, weeping copious tears of regret, remorse, and recrimination, completely aware that her moment in the sun was rapidly fading. She was gripped by the profound realization that once the royal crown of queendom passed from her life, her teenage star would wane as well. Where would she go? What would she do? Who would she be? What did life hold for a well-groomed, pretty-faced former cheerleader and prom queen with mechanical aptitudes? All she could do was entertain the seemingly futile hope that the wars would finally end and the tanks would come home, in desperate need of repairs.

She wept bitterly for herself and what lay ahead on the road of life: adulthood.

Bronson was thinking he could use a hot dog right about now.

The '67 royal prom court stood side by side, ignoring Spiffany Tonguehoister's increasingly noisy histrionics, their hearts full of youthful exuberance and expectation. The two hoodlums, Brufyss and Barley, now stared directly at each other from opposite ends of the line. Brufyss wore a look of defiance, while Barley had a look of . . . It was hard to tell *what* emotion motivated Barley's look, but his eyes had finally unpeeled themselves from Mrs. Kookerly to meet those of her escort head-on.

The princesses fidgeted nervously, awash in the glare of the spotlight and the scrutiny of the crowd. Mrs. Gooberwart, who'd been impassively waiting for the last couple to take their place in line, turned to face the crowd once again.

"Students of P. P. Piggford and His Wife Janice High School, here they are: your '67 senior prom royal court."

Enthusiastic applause for the honorees.

"I will now announce this year's queen of the prom, elected by all of you."

The applause ceased. The gym grew silent. This was it!

Mrs. Gooberwart paused nervously, took a deep breath, and looked down at the piece of paper in her quivering hand. She was about to make the announcement when a disturbance erupted in the crowd.

"Mrs. Gooberwart!! Hold on!! Please, wait! I'll be right there . . ."

Vice Principal Muzzlemonkey had regained consciousness and was making his way toward the stage. He'd been mysteriously relieved of his floral-print fake Hawaiian shirt, and the hair on his head and chest had been shaved off. The crowd parted to let the bizarre, bald-headed, pink-chested wrinkly old man get through.

It was Mr. Muzzlemonkey's designated job in the coronation ceremony to take the crown from last year's queen and pass it to the new recipient. He emerged from the crowd, disheveled and bedraggled, and scrambled up the steps to stand beside Mrs. Gooberwart, panting heavily and looking like he'd just taken an extended holiday inside the carburetor of a bulldozer.

Mrs. Gooberwart stared contemptuously at her wretched-yet-loyal vice principal. "See me in my office on Monday morning, Muzzlemonkey! For now, just stand there and shut up. I have one more announcement to make."

"Yes, ma'am." The dutiful vice principal was apprehensive of the punishment his boss might mete out on Monday morning but grateful to be an integral part of this auspicious occasion once again.

"The winner, and this year's queen of the senior prom, *is* . . ."

The crowd held its breath.

"*Mrs. . . . Daphne Dogdaughter*!!"

6

Barricaded behind the bank of audio equipment at the rear of the stage, Fifi Farglebarker waited tensely for Mrs. Gooberwart's announcement. The principal had instructed that the reading of the new queen's name would be Fifi's cue to restart the coronation music— or in this case, "Turkey in the Straw." She was poised over the turntable with her fingers gripping the stylus arm, ready to drop the needle into the record's groove once more.

At Mrs. Gooberwart's pronouncement of the word "Mrs.," Fifi dropped the needle, and the exuberant hillbilly music exploded over the PA system. The crowd, the foregone results preprogrammed in their minds, burst forth with a spirited roar and hearty applause, yelling their hearts out until the realization of what had *actually* been said began to sink in. Their cheering and wild applause slackened as puzzlement replaced pandemonium.

Mrs. Who? Mrs. Daphne Dogdaughter? Wasn't that supposed to be Mrs. *Kookerly*? But Mrs. Gooberwart said, "Mrs. Daphne Dogdaughter." Why did she call Tasty "Mrs."? Was Tasty married? When did Tasty get *married*? Was she married to that guy she was up there with? But that was Barley Doodlebody, not Barley Dogdaughter! Shouldn't it be Mrs. Daphne Doodlebody?? Or was that guy's name really Barley Dogdaughter and *not* Barley Doodlebody, and Tasty married a guy with the same last name as hers?

"Did *you* vote for Tasty??"

"*I* didn't—*I* voted for Mrs. Kookerly! I thought everyone voted for Mrs. Kookerly!"

"Why isn't Mrs. Kookerly the prom queen??"

Despite their inability to comprehend what happened, the crowd began to accept the fact that Daphne and not Mrs. Kookerly had just been announced as the new prom queen. No one could remember voting for Tasty, but she commanded enough esteem from her fellow students to earn a fresh round of applause for the prestigious honor they'd (evidently) bestowed upon her. She was a worthy queen-elect in her own right; the dubious election results weren't enough to dissuade the students from paying their tribute. The hall filled with clapping and cheering, rollicking banjo music, and cries of "Tay-*stee*! Tay-*stee*! Tay-*stee*!"

Mrs. Kookerly was the first of the princesses to react, realizing that her complete name hadn't been uttered and Daphne's had. Mrs. Gooberwart said, "Mrs." first—but it was definitely *Daphne* who'd been announced as the new queen!

Daphne shrank back from Mrs. Kookerly as if her best friend had suddenly contracted contagious terminal warts, her jaw dropping in surprise and incomprehension. Flagella Nuggmuck's hand flew to her mouth to stifle a cry of alarm, her eyes wide with incredulity.

Lucinda Luckybeans shrieked, "*What!?*" and began an involuntary high-rate body spasm. Melanie Bupwanger sucked in her breath and dropped her arms limply to her sides.

Mrs. Gooberwart turned to Spiffany Tonguehoister, who was trembling and weeping. "Give up the crown, Tonguehoister!" To the vice principal, she added, "Muzzlemonkey! Get the crown and give it to Miss Dogdaughter!"

She bolted out of the spotlight, down the stairs, and through the puzzled crowd, scurrying to the broom closet occupied by custodian Gubb Chizzlewilly. Producing a set of keys from inside the folds of her muumuu, the principal flicked through them, glancing up furtively to see if anyone was watching. No one seemed to notice. She located the master passkey, unlocked the door, slipped inside, and locked the door behind her.

The amplified strains of "Turkey in the Straw," the crowd's chanting of "Tay-*stee*! Tay-*stee*!" and general hubbub and excitement filled the gymnasium. Nonetheless, shrill screams of abject, excruciating agony and dull, sickening thuds coming from within the re-locked broom closet were audible over the din. Mrs. Gooberwart was making good on her vow to claim Gubb Chizzlewilly's ass as her own, relieving a few frustrations in the process—and she was now conveniently out of the picture . . .

***

The poor vice principal was now presented with a perplexing situation: prying the queen's crown away from a reluctant Spiffany Tonguehoister.

After Daphne had been announced as the new queen, the outgoing monarch let loose a bloodcurdling scream and bolted for the edge of the stage on the heels of the retreating principal. She flung her arms around her head to fend off anyone who might try to wrest the crown from her, barreling past Mr. Muzzlemonkey and violently bowling him over. She tripped over the vice principal's legs as he fell to the stage, and they both wound up entangled on the floor, thrashing like two mating alligators.

The resourceful Mr. Muzzlemonkey did what he felt was best: he screamed for help and passed out. His squealing plea snapped most of the male escorts on the stage out of their momentary paralysis. The dates of Lucinda Luckybeans and Flagella Nuggmuck, and even Bronson Facockta and Spatch Huntoon, leaped forward to assist the now unconscious vice principal and wrestle the crown away from Spiffany as the rest of the prom princesses watched in mute horror.

They dogpiled onto the two bodies, pushing Mr. Muzzlemonkey out of the way to get to Spiffany. Bubbles and Jiggly's dates grabbed Spiffany's arms and legs and pinned them to the floor to immobilize her while Bronson and Spatch grabbed hold of the crown and tried to wrench it off her head. The ingenious contraption Spiffany devised to anchor it to her scalp proved a formidable obstacle; try as they might, the two couldn't budge or manipulate the crown in any way. They twisted Spiffany's head back and forth to such a degree that her noggin seemed ready to pop off, but the crown remained in place.

The bright stage was rapidly becoming a scene of frenzied conflict. A writhing pile of bodies struggled for the queen's crown in an escalating battle, soundtracked by blaring hillbilly banjo music.

Suddenly, Spiffany received a fresh surge of adrenaline that seemed to endow her with superhuman strength. She threw off her attackers, stood defiantly, snarled, and fought with renewed vigor to retain the crown—which she now believed was hers by divine right.

The four prom escorts fought just as valiantly to take it from her. Bronson and Spatch had been given a new purpose in life, and their inebriated state helped numb them to the pain the deposed prom queen inflicted upon all who'd deny her freedom. They group-tackled Spiffany, wrestled her to the floor again, and resumed rolling and flailing across the stage.

Only Barley and Brufyss remained unmoved, making no effort to join in the fray. Barley watched Brufyss intently, observing Brufyss's reaction to these new developments. Brufyss stared back at Barley, bewilderment etched across his face. He looked at his trembling cheerleader princess, saw her dismay and confusion . . .

The realization hit him like a thunderbolt. He flashed his flaming eyes over to Barley, who smirked back at him. Brufyss finally got it—too late.

"Doodlebody! You're behind this! You paid off Mrs. Gooberwart to throw the contest. You fixed the results!"

Barley laughed. "Is *that* what you think, Brufyss? Don't you think Daphne's capable of winning the contest herself? Do you really think I'd stoop that low?"

Brufyss knew Barley could and would stoop that low; he felt rage like never before. "Everybody knows Mrs. Kookerly was going to win! Even Mrs. Gooberwart! She almost said, 'Mrs. Kookerly'! Everybody heard it, you creep! *Everybody!*"

"No, everybody heard her say 'Daphne Dogdaughter.' That's what you heard—and that, my sour-grapes friend, is that."

Spiffany Tonguehoister again broke free of the multitude of grasping hands and bodies, labored to her feet, and bolted across the stage between the two rivals, toppling all of the princesses, which resulted in yet another writhing dogpile. The participants in the first dogpile scrambled to their feet and rushed to the new dogpile, creating one huge mass that contained nearly everyone in the center of the stage. "Turkey in the Straw" blared through the auditorium, and the crowd below the stage stood transfixed by the drama in the spotlight.

Focused as he was on the leering countenance of Barley Doodlebody, Brufyss saw nothing of Spiffany's dogpile-to-dogpile transition, nor did he see that Mrs. Kookerly had been sucked into the newer, bigger dogpile squirming at his feet.

"I've had enough of you, Doodlebody! You're gonna pay for this—and this time it won't be in cash!" Brufyss vaulted over the writhing lump of humanity and launched himself at his rival like a juggernaut. A lifetime of friendship (such as it was), camaraderie (such as it was), business ventures (such as they were), and triumphs (such as *they* were) came to a swift, violent end as Brufyss cleared the pile and advanced on Barley. Barley stood his ground, steeling himself for the assault to come, a taunting sneer spread across his face.

"Bring it on, Bathwater! Let's see what you got—which is pretty much *nothing* without me!"

Brufyss snarled with rage, hurling a powerful right-handed roundhouse punch at his now former partner, every ounce of his weight and strength behind his swing. The blow missed as Barley ducked away, causing Brufyss to spin off balance and plunge forward into the left uppercut Barley threw in response. The counterpunch caught Brufyss squarely on the chin, snapping his head up and back. His knees buckled, his weight sagged, and his mind reeled between blackness and consciousness. He staggered, tumbling into the pile of bodies undulating behind him.

Barley's hand throbbed from the punch to Brufyss's chin. He stared wide eyed as his former friend and business associate disappeared into the fleshy pile. He then noticed that Daphne had been swallowed up along with Mrs. Kookerly and the rest of the prom princesses. Arms, legs, and hands gesticulated, groped, and grasped. Disheveled people with saucer-eyed, terrified expressions would pop up out of the mass, shout something unintelligible, and disappear into the human globule once more. Bits of clothing—dresses, shoes, shirts, and pants—flew all over the stage. Screams, shouts, grunts, groans, crying, and cursing issued out of the pile, and the crowd below the stage realized to their delight that this slapstick drama was now completely out of control. A growing atmosphere of anarchy was brewing among the students. "Turkey in the Straw" blared loudly.

As he stood away from the fracas, Barley frantically searched for Mrs. Kookerly among the other bodies, hoping to find her before she was torn to shreds—and to step into her good graces by being her gallant rescuer.

Spiffany squirmed free and scrambled to her feet. Her clothes were in tatters, a caged-animal expression of desperation smeared across her normally pleasant face—but miraculously, the queen's crown was still intact and anchored firmly atop her head. She glanced around wildly, saw Barley standing there, shrieked, and turned abruptly, hurdling over the human dogpile and running to the back portion of the stage occupied by Fifi Farglebarker's audio setup. She darted behind the table where Fungus stood witnessing the unfolding madness in terror.

"Out of my way, geekface!" The crazed, erstwhile prom queen knocked the audio monitor to the floor and barged to the gym wall behind the stage where the levers to operate the stage trapdoor and elevator were located. Spiffany was familiar with their functions, having recently upgraded them.

In an effort to put an obstacle between herself and her assailants, she grabbed the first lever and pulled down hard, setting wheels and gears in motion. The trapdoor in the middle of the stage floor slowly began to retract, revealing the pen full of trapped vegetarians for the intimidation fest. At the same time, the elevator platform upon which the vegetarians' cage sat began its ascension to stage level, bringing the ensnared herbivores up into the spotlight for the first time.

***

The audience became increasingly emboldened by the realization that the scenario playing out before them was not part of the coronation ceremony. The slow emergence of the captured vegetarians' cage increased their excitement. They launched into a chorus of shouts, taunts, and exhortations for further violence and mayhem.

More male students leaped onto the stage and joined the scrimmage in hopes of doing a bit of their own rolling and groping. Who knew what might be found at the bottom of that pile? Definitely some cheerleading prom princesses! That alone made the effort worthwhile.

Chaos broke out all over the gym. Students tore the fake Hawaiian decorations off the walls, hurled snack foods at the stage and each other, and threatened the terrified teacher chaperones with decapitation. Gubb Chizzlewilly's cries of pain, and the thumps and thuds of Mrs. Gooberwart's tortures, emanated from the locked broom closet. The battle for the queen's crown surged across the stage, the participants unaware that the crown's possessor was now absent from the proceedings.

In the gymnasium rafters, Retchard Pumpstuck looked down from his catwalk perch and surveyed the escalating pandemonium with keen interest. His lofty vantage afforded him a wide, unobstructed panorama of the entire gymnasium floor, and Retchard whipped his spotlight around the room—back and forth, over and across, to and fro—finding action wherever it appeared. The spotlight's brilliant circle of light zoomed from place to place like a will-o'-the-wisp, revealing a surreal landscape of burgeoning insanity everywhere its beam fell. A throaty, low-frequency roar of human voices along with the maddening strains of hillbilly music issued upward as the bedlam escalated.

Wound tightly in the fishing net and woozy from the debilitating effects of Chorfis Chumbu's corrupted wheatgrass concoction, the incarcerated vegetarians had been oblivious to their impending ordeal and anything taking place in the auditorium above them. They were abruptly roused from the pleasant serenity by glaring light as the trapdoor retracted, and by the jerky motion of the floor of their cage as it began its rise to the stage. The harsh light grew brighter. Twangy tones of hillbilly fiddle and banjo music filtered into their ears, growing ever louder. Befuddled by the narcotic, they believed they'd all somehow died and were ascending into hillbilly heaven. The next sight revealed they'd actually descended into hillbilly hell.

At stage level they were greeted by a wall-to-wall mural of insanity. The only portion of the gymnasium untouched by violence was the small space within their cage! In front of them, a mass of humanity rolled back and forth like waves crashing and receding on a sandless shoreline. Beyond the stage, shadowy figures darted everywhere, screaming incoherently, ransacking and hurling debris at everyone and everything.

The harsh light moved away, popping and panning around the interior of the hall, pinpointing and illuminating various and sundry acts of random violence and savagery, the blaring music providing a frenzied accompaniment. The vegetarians struggled within their bonds to maneuver into positions affording better views of the craziness it had become their lot to witness.

Within the pile, Brufyss regained consciousness. A shoe-clad foot pushed off from his cheek, a flapping elbow needled its way into his stomach, someone's buttocks squashed his head against the floor, a wad of greasy hair stuffed his mouth, and the heel of a woman's dress shoe poked into his nostril. Twisting, squirming bodies pushed, pulled, kicked, and rolled over him, while arms, legs, fingers, and feet poked, pinched, punched, and prodded. As his brain cleared, he began to recall the events that landed him in this predicament. Where was Mrs. Kookerly? Where was Barley Doodlebody? Where was "up" and where was "down"?

He looked down. *Where are my pants?*

A pair of hands grasped his coattails from somewhere behind him. He jerked around and rolled over, twisting his torso like a contortionist, reaching out toward the feminine hands. He wrapped his fingers around a bare forearm and pulled. The hand clutched at his coat lapel and pulled *him*. Finally, after much squirming, clutching, and clawing, the two were face-to-face at the bottom of the pile.

Brufyss stared into the terrified eyes of Mrs. Kookerly. Her once gorgeous blond coiffure now resembled a tumbleweed. Her once long and lovely prom dress looked like it had undergone alterations in a blender and emerged as a miniskirt. Somehow, her fashionable shoes were still intact and on her feet.

"Brufyss! It's you! I thought I recognized your shoes—but where are your pants? *Aaack*!" A disembodied clutching hand found its way into the middle of her face. Brufyss reached for the clutching hand, grabbed it, and sank his teeth into the flesh. A muffled scream emerged from somewhere nearby in the pile; the hand withdrew quickly.

"C'mon, we're getting out of here! Put your arms around my neck."

Just as she was about to do so, two powerful hands gripped her ankles. Before Brufyss could react, Mrs. Kookerly let out a frightened yelp and was pulled feet-first out of the pile.

***

Barley had circled the edge of the writhing mass like the referee of a group wrestling match, trying to recognize anything that suggested Mrs. Kookerly's presence therein. He spotted Daphne kicking to free herself from the grasp of another dogpile denizen attempting to relieve her of a portion of her prom dress. Barley paid them no mind. With Brufyss out of the way, his objective was to find Mrs. Kookerly. Daphne would have to fend for herself.

Suddenly he saw her. Mrs. Kookerly was lying next to a guy with shoes but no pants—*Oh no! Brufyss!* They'd somehow found each other and reunited amid the jumble. Once Brufyss got his paws around the teen beauty, Barley knew it would take a team of horses to pry her loose! And finding a team of horses at this late date was pretty much out of the question.

Locating Mrs. Kookerly's feet, Barley reached down with both hands and grabbed each of her ankles like a farmer wielding an old-fashioned plow. With great effort, he pulled, and she slid free of the pile.

"What are you doing? Let me go!"

"What am I doing? I'm rescuing you! You'll be crushed if you stay down there. I'm trying to *help* you!"

Mrs. Kookerly kicked her feet sharply to free her ankles from Barley's grasp and scrambled to her feet. "*Brufyss* was helping me!"

"Brufyss is still at the bottom of that pile—a lot of help he's gonna be!"

"Quit worrying about me and go help your own date! Daphne's still trapped in there. You should be helping her!"

Barley was at a loss; theoretically, she was right, but he really didn't care what happened to Daphne. Tasty had only been a means for getting to Mrs. Kookerly, and he had the blond beauty all to himself now—but he hadn't anticipated this ungrateful response. This wasn't how it was supposed to work.

"Leave me alone! I've got to find Brufyss. Go help Daphne!" She turned from Barley.

At that moment, Brufyss rose like a half-clad Samson throwing off his shackles. He forced his way to his feet with a Herculean explosion of strength and saw Mrs. Kookerly and Barley standing just a few feet away.

"Brufyss! I'm here!"

Brufyss heard her, but all he saw was Barley Doodlebody with *his* girl. Seized by raging fury, he attacked.

7

Brufyss hurled himself at Barley with the force of a brakeless freight train hurtling down a steep mountain. Barley staggered backward, crashing into the vegetarians' holding pen and falling to the floor with Brufyss on top of him. The holding pen, anchored only perfunctorily to the elevator platform, was jarred loose by the blow and skidded back a few feet, thereby misaligning it with the platform's edge. The vegetarians reacted with terrified screams; the skirmish they'd watched from the sanctity of their cage was suddenly right in their faces!

Brufyss and Barley rolled on the stage floor, each wildly trying to land a punch in the face of the other. Only one would be standing when this fight ended, and Mrs. Kookerly would be the prize. She hovered above the wrestling pair, watching the contest.

"Get him, Brufyss! Bash him!"

The two banged against the vegetarians' holding pen again, knocking it further askew. If the platform was retracted into the stage floor and the vegetarians fell into the pit, the cage bars would remain in their cockeyed position—but there'd also be a gap between the cage bars and the edge of the opening. The terrified vegetarians frantically slid away from the encroaching fracas, crawling and caterpillaring across the floor a few inches at a time, encumbered by the fishnet and the confining cage.

When the vegetarians' cage had ascended into the middle of the stage behind the mountain of struggling bodies, one group of drunken hooligans saw an opportunity too good to miss. They descended on the bin that contained the raw meat and animal parts to be utilized in the "ministration of meat." With a spirit of single-minded cooperation they'd never shared in school, the band of determined conspirators forcefully overturned the meat container, sending a torrent of bloody water across the gym floor. They hurled the container's contents at the captive vegetarians, at the dogpile on the stage, at the nattily dressed students in tuxedos and ball gowns, the garishly dressed teacher chaperones in fake Hawaiian costumes, and any and all in the vicinity.

Each person pummeled by the pungent pieces of raw flesh also found their clothing and hair soaked with blood and bloody water. They screamed and ran hysterically around the hall, colliding with each other and crashing into tables and chairs. Students slipped, slid, and tumbled into the massive mess spreading across the gym floor.

The dogpilers gradually became aware that along with shreds and articles of clothing, shoes, hands, feet, and legs that pummeled, poked, pinched, and pulled at them, there was now an occasional bloody spleen, pancreas, liver, lung, or lamb chop pelting them as well.

The vegetarians received their own salvos and panicked, howling and shrieking like tormented tornados, scraping and scratching like frenzied cats to get away from this new terror. Bombarded by blaring banjo music, they could do nothing but scurry, scramble, and scream in their futile attempts to evade the bloody blizzard. They were surely right in the middle of hillbilly hell.

***

Daphne was dumbfounded her name was announced. She was the new prom queen and in a quandary over how to process it. Should she protest the outcome and turn the crown over to Mrs. Kookerly as the rightful winner? Should she accept the crown as the new queen and feel good about herself in doing so? Deep down, she felt the former choice more appropriate. Before the secret election had taken place, it was no secret that everyone would be voting for Mrs. Kookerly. But right here, right now, Tasty's latent desire to possess the crown began to surface; the latter choice loomed large as the one she'd ultimately make. After all, Mrs. Gooberwart had declared "Mrs. Daphne Dogdaughter" the new queen, and *her* name was Daphne Dogdaughter—although the "Mrs." part had confused her a bit.

The argument was rendered moot when Spiffany bolted and took the crown with her. In a few minutes of wild activity, Daphne had gone from being "bewildered bystander" to "bottom of the pile." She should have been praised, lauded, and applauded as the new reigning prom queen for '67. Instead she was ravaged, savaged, divested, and molested by unseen groping hands. Her beautiful prom dress—the one Barley had so generously funded—had become a shameful, tattered shambles. Her heels had broken off her shoes, her shoes had been ripped off her feet, her hair was matted, mashed, and mauled, and her makeup would have looked ridiculous on a clown.

Her screams for help had been drowned out. Somebody—or some *bodies*—were taking liberties with parts of Daphne she normally only liberated voluntarily! If that wasn't vexing enough, she'd just been smacked with a bloody piece of cow's kidney and some other yucky stuff that she couldn't identify but which smelled *really* nasty.

Why was this happening? Where was Barley? When would all this stop? Who was grabbing her butt?

This is no way to treat a queen! Anger and resentment welled inside her. She'd waited her entire life to be recognized and honored as something more than a bimbo, a plaything, decoration for some idiot's arm. Now she was queen of the prom! She wasn't going to let a has-been like Spiffany Tonguehoister deprive her of her moment in the sun. The new '67 queen of the prom resolved the issue: she'd go after Spiffany and depose her once and for all. The crown would then—rightfully—be Daphne's.

There! That was settled! Now all she had to do was locate her underwear.

Spiffany shrank behind the bank of audio equipment, frightened but resolved to hold on to her crown at all costs. She had to make a break for it. She'd brought the vegetarians' cage up from the depths to put an obstacle between herself and her pursuers, to create a distraction and buy herself time to think. Now she needed to create another diversion—and a new opportunity presented itself. She glared down at Fifi Farglebarker, who cowered in terror behind the equipment table. "All right, Fungus, do as I say, and you won't get hurt! When I tell you to, pull that second lever there on the wall as hard as you can. *Understand?*"

Fungus jumped up and ran to the wall where the levers were located. She wrapped both of her hands around the second lever and paused, waiting for Spiffany's next command.

"On 'three'! One . . . two . . . *three!*"

Fifi pulled the lever, setting motors, wheels, and gears into motion. The retractable elevator platform answered the mechanical call. The floor of the cockeyed cage of vegetarians began to draw back into the stage, gradually revealing the hole in which the giant tank containing the "bubbling bilious beef broth bath" sat.

Inside the cage, the terrified vegetarians realized that profound changes were taking place. The floor moved—disappeared!—and an ever-widening hole appeared where the floor used to be. It really smelled down in that hole, and the hole crept toward them, coming to swallow them up. Their frantic attempts to move away from the encroaching maw—scrambling, crawling, sliding, wriggling, falling, and clamoring over each other, trying to dodge the barrage of bloody animal parts and divest themselves of the encumbering fishnet—were to no avail.

The holding pen floor disappeared completely. The vegetarians plummeted into the vat like a mound of screeching potatoes. They immediately relinquished any vestiges of grogginess from their ingestion of Chorfis Chumbu's narcotic cocktails, and any vestiges of sanity as well. Hard, cold reality returned with a malodorous vengeance.

Howls blared forth from the pit as the vegetarians were subjected to a total immersion in the most horrific emulsion ever concocted by man. These were the screams everyone in the audience had been anticipating all evening. The vegetarians' pitiful cries attracted the attention of students who'd wandered away from the stage to wreak havoc in other parts of the gym. Once these renegades realized the vegetarians were taking their beef broth bath, they ceased whatever violence or mischief they were perpetrating and ran back to the main source of the hysteria.

Within moments, the mob surrounded three sides of the stage, chucking raw meat at everyone within the semicircle—a "ministration of meat" the likes of which had never been witnessed in all the years preceding it.

High above, Retchard Pumpstuck was in hysterics, beside himself with mirth. He'd never seen anything like the frenzied farce taking place below him! As the raging madness escalated to a crescendo, Retchard glanced a foot or so to his right, his eyes falling on a knotted rope tied to the railing of the catwalk. From its secured end, the rope ran out over the stage and was threaded through a block-and-tackle device attached to a ceiling rafter. From there, it dropped straight down, directly over the spot where the vegetarians swam for their lives. At the end hung the enormous vat containing the "gurgling gooey glop," poised to rain its cargo upon the unsuspecting inhabitants of the pit.

Averting his gaze from the vat back to the surreal circus below, Retchard absentmindedly reached out with his right hand to stroke the knot of thick, coarse rope as if it were a prized and pampered pussycat . . .

***

For Spatch Huntoon, being at the bottom of a massive, squirming dogpile was not unfamiliar. As the quarterback, the bottom of a pile was where he spent most of his playing time. The team's offensive line was as adept at keeping out opposing defensive linemen as a jellyfish balancing a checkbook. Not only did Spatch feel at home, he was actually *enjoying* himself. The dogpiles to which he was accustomed were made up of heavily padded, sweaty male players. *This* dogpile had a goodly amount of more pleasantly padded female participants smelling more like department store perfume counters than post-game locker rooms.

During his topsy-turvy travels, Spatch groped and rolled with every one of the females in the group: his own date, Melanie Bupwanger (who managed to get off one more resounding slap before disappearing back into the morass), all of the other prom princesses with the exception of Lucinda Luckybeans (her intense vibration "force field" rendering her untouchable), and former queen Spiffany Tonguehoister. Somehow even Mrs. Kookerly had been assimilated into the dogpile with everyone else. He'd not only discovered her but had started to grab and pull her to him until someone snatched his hand away—and *bit it*! Then she was gone.

Spatch's contemplation was interrupted by a resounding WHAP! in the face. His immediate thought: Melanie had located him again. He strove to confront his face-slapping attacker and realized that what had slapped him was *not* a resentful Melanie Bupwanger but a resentful piece of bloody beef entrails! SPLAT! Another chunk of raw meat found its way into his face. SPLISH! Another one! What was going on?

Others in the pile squealed in protest and alarm. It was impossible to stand upright in the squishy collection of bloody, soggy meat parts accumulating around them. They slipped and slid, staggering upright only to see their feet fly out from under them, slamming them sloppily to the floor again and bringing down anyone nearby in the process.

As Spatch tried to amass enough traction to get up and away from the pile, he saw a ragged, scantily clad female, whose foot had just been in his face, attempting to pull herself up and stand—and succeeding! Growling and snarling like a blood-spattered tigress, she fought to rid herself of the clutching, grasping hands that tormented her.

Suddenly she was standing triumphantly upright! She'd done it! Spatch marveled at the girl's determination. As she took her first step to freedom, he grabbed the hem of her tattered dress and used her forward momentum to pull himself up and out of the fray as well.

The girl was Tasty Dogdaughter!

Daphne whirled around to face her hitchhiker. She slapped at his hand and hissed, "Let me go, Spatch, or I'll tear your head off!"

Spatch shrank back quickly. Daphne stepped away from the fringe of the dogpile and scanned the surrounding crowd like a desperate detective seeking the pickpocket who'd just stolen her badge. She noticed Brufyss and Barley locked in combat a few feet away, with Mrs. Kookerly standing above them, shouting encouragement to Brufyss.

Daphne felt a twinge of guilt toward her best friend, unjustly deprived of the queenly honor she now wanted for herself. This feeling was quickly dispelled; her outrage at Spiffany's coup d'etat far outweighed any feelings of guilt. Besides, Mrs. Kookerly always got whatever she wanted. Tonight it was Daphne's turn.

"Tonguehoister, I'm gonna kick your bony ass and get that crown!"

"Tasty, I'm looking for her too!" cried Spatch. "I'll help you get the crown!"

Daphne grunted distractedly, suddenly spotting Spiffany cringing behind the audio equipment. "There you are, you washed-up loser. *Gimme that crown!*"

She bolted through the rain of meaty missiles, around the cockeyed cage bars, and toward the rear of the stage. Spatch set off in pursuit of the pursuer, trailing behind like an afterthought. As he rounded the corner of the holding pen, he was almost bowled over by a hard-charging Mrs. Kookerly, who'd abandoned her spectatorship of the Doodlebody-Bathwater confrontation and now pursued Daphne herself. She cut in front of him, hot on Daphne's heels. Spatch did a double take and pursued the pursuer of the pursuer.

***

Hemmed in by a new mass of bloodthirsty humanity, Spiffany had no alternative but to use the elements of surprise and brute force to bull her way to freedom. She still possessed the crown, securely anchored to her head. She'd use it as a battering ram to smash through the human wall. If she moved fast enough, the crazed throng might not realize what was happening until she'd already broken through them.

She took a deep breath and set off, scooting around the audio equipment, past the dislodged cage bars above the smelly beef broth pit, sprinting toward the front of the stage like a halfback headed for the end zone.

Spiffany Tonguehoister, Daphne Dogdaughter, and Mrs. Kookerly— the outgoing prom queen, the incoming prom queen, and the one deprived of being either—met blindly in mid-sprint—BONK-KABONK!— colliding head-to-head-to-head, the force of the blows bouncing them away from each other. The crowd groaned and empathetically clutched their own skulls.

The three staggered like drunken cotillion dancers, knocked nearly senseless but still standing. Spatch, who'd been right on Mrs. Kookerly's heels, sidestepped her and Daphne and threw his arms around Spiffany in a tight bear hug so she wouldn't slip away again. Spiffany was in no condition to go anywhere, believing herself to be frolicking with magic singing woodchucks in Ice Cream Land. Daphne stood where she was and began jamming and riffing with the imaginary jazz-funk combo that floated in slow spirals above her, while Mrs. Kookerly was in the process of graduating from Harvard and receiving her bachelor's degree from an alien named Ludlow from the planet Gloxnar.

Spatch wrestled Spiffany to the stage floor with no resistance. Once again, he attempted to wrench the infernal crown off her head. Once again, the well-constructed anchoring mechanism wouldn't budge. The gathered crowd shouted their approval of Spatch's efforts, contributing a hearty helping of hurled raw animal parts in the bargain.

"Don't just stand there, you jerks! Somebody give me a hand!"

A few male spectators realized that Spatch had come up with a rather brilliant idea, and decided to give *both* hands, to grope and grapple with the now vulnerable Spiffany Tonguehoister. Without further prompting, they leaped en masse atop her and Spatch, forming yet another dogpile. The whole mess began anew.

The members of the original dogpile finally had some luck in freeing themselves from the scuffle and putting together enough traction to stand upright without slipping and falling. Most of the bloody slime was now smeared all over them instead of the floor. They looked more like survivors of a chainsaw massacre than senior prom attendees.

To their dismay, they realized they were trapped on the stage by the surrounding crowd.

8

Barley and Brufyss were locked in a violent struggle, each trying to find a weak spot that would allow a decisive blow to finish the fight once and for all.

Brufyss fought with enraged determination, his pent-up anger, deprivation, and envy channeled into every punch. As Barley warded off the relentless attack, he calculated how he might gain the upper hand. Brufyss was operating on blind instinct—he always did. Those instincts were usually flawed.

They were close to the pit where the vegetarians thrashed and screamed. Barley could smell the hideously foul beef broth bath just inches from his head, and they'd been banging into the cage bars as they fought. He knew the bars had been moved off their footings; the retracted cage floor exposed a hole that led directly into the pit. If he could somehow maneuver Brufyss into that hole, his troubles would be over.

Brufyss managed to straddle him and was about to punch him in the face.

A flash of inspiration. "Let me up! Mrs. Kookerly's in trouble!"

"What? Where?" Brufyss twisted his head and looked up to see what was happening.

In an instant, Barley grabbed Brufyss's coat lapels and drove his knee into Brufyss's crotch, lifting and flipping him forward. Brufyss hurtled over Barley's prone body and plunged head-first into the exposed hole in the stage, dropping into the frothing depths to join the screaming vegetarians.

He was gone!

Barley scrambled to his feet, gasping and panting, covered with wet, bloody slime, and searched the frantic mob for Mrs. Kookerly. He'd seen her dash around the side of the vegetarians' holding pen—*there*! She stood unsteadily at the side of the stage next to Daphne.

Barley's first thought was to get Mrs. Kookerly away from the chaos and violence, but a massive throng had collected on and around the stage and stood between them. Extracting her from this madness wasn't going to be easy.

The car!

The Smegmatti 502 was still sitting in the middle of the gym floor, unnoticed and ignored by the preoccupied crowd. He'd use the Smegmatti 502 to ride into the fray like a knight in shining armor on his valiant high-performance steed, whisking his damsel in distress to safety and vanquishing a few slobs along the way.

To get to his car, he'd have to run the gauntlet.

"*Out of my way*! I'm comin' through; anyone in front of me's gonna be *more* raw meat!"

Crazed as they were with the false bravado that lawless, unrestrained violence can inject into a wild mob, the students were not crazed enough to confront a rampaging Barley Doodlebody—especially after witnessing what he'd just done to Brufyss . . . his *friend*! As Barley advanced, flashing grimaces at each person he approached, they stood aside to let him pass unmolested and unchallenged. He reached the front of the stage and barged down the steps, brutally muscling and bullying his way through the masses until he broke out of the crowd and sprinted to his waiting sports car, nearly losing his footing on the slippery floor.

Barley jerked the driver door open and slid into the seat. His car keys dangled from the ignition slot. The car's mammoth engine exploded to life with a shudder and a magnificent roar, the volume magnified a hundred times by the cavernous gym's hollow acoustics; the new explosion of sound caused heads to turn and eyes to widen in astonishment. Barley pointed the nose of the car toward the crowd. He eased forward cautiously to keep from losing control and spinning out on the blood-and-water-soaked floor.

Those in the crowd who noticed what he was doing were perplexed. It wasn't until the car pulled up to the fringe of the crowd that the students realized the situation: if the vehicle's present route remained unchanged, they'd be directly in its path! Sure enough, the car continued moving to the stairway. The hemmed-in students began pushing and shoving each other to move up the stairs, crowding onto the front of the packed stage. This group of panicking promgoers forced the students already there to move closer to the gaping hole where the bubbling bilious beef broth bath loomed like a pungent chasm of doom.

Illuminated by the brilliant glare of Retchard Pumpstuck's spotlight, Barley stopped the Smegmatti 502. He saw the panic and uncertainty in the promgoers' eyes as they ran up the backs of the students in front of them to get away from the advancing car.

This was going to be fun!

Barley set the car's gearshift lever into the neutral position and pressed his right foot down hard on the accelerator. The car's monstrous engine revved loudly and viciously.

VRRROOOOOOOMMM!!

The crowd shrieked in terror and mobbed up the stairs. Barley revved the Smegmatti's engine again; the resulting crowd surge introduced the first of the wretched students nearest the beef broth bath to its odorous horror. All those who'd occupied center stage just moments ago tumbled into the pit, desperately and futilely reaching out to grab the cockeyed cage bars straddling the hole, only to knock them further awry. The sound of screams from the pit increased by multiple decibels.

The stairs momentarily clear of fleeing students, Barley shifted into first gear, punched the gas, and popped the clutch. The powerful sports car lurched forward violently. The two front tires left the floor, and their momentum brought them down atop the first step. VROOOMM-ga-bunk!

He stabbed the brakes, and the car stopped, the front wheels one step up. Another bevy of screams issued from the terrified crowd, followed by more upward scrambling, followed by more additions to the beef broth bath.

Enough is enough! Where was the fun in letting these poor idiots fall piecemeal into the bubbling morass? Barley gunned the engine once more, popped the clutch, and guided the powerful automobile all the way up the stairs—VROOOMM-ga-bunk! VROOOMM-ga-bunk! VVROOOMM-ga-bunk! VVROOOMM-ga-bunk!—like a spiffy off-road vehicle climbing a rocky hillside one boulder at a time. The Smegmatti 502 sent the remaining students fleeing across the stage, piling into each other to ultimately plunge into the pit. So many of the promgoers were joining Brufyss and the vegetarians that the pit started to fill up; the displaced liquid slopped onto the surface of the stage, splashing the students still massed there.

With one final punch of the accelerator, Barley urged the car up the top stair. It now sat completely on the stage in front of the pit, at rest and idling like a satiated predator. The remaining students pushed and shoved around the sides of the open hole in the floor, still unable to flee the stage because of the sadistic, howling, unmoving crowd surrounding it.

Leaving the Smegmatti 502 in neutral and idling, Barley threw open his door, sending several more students sprawling into the backs of the students ahead of them. He jumped out of the car—and there she was! Mrs. Kookerly was no longer wobbling on her feet, having regained her senses; she searched the faces in the crowd and called out for Brufyss. Daphne was standing a few feet from Mrs. Kookerly with her back to the pit. It appeared she was still recovering from the head-banging collision.

Barley muscled his way into the panicked crowd, throwing bodies aside as he moved through. He reached Mrs. Kookerly, grabbed both of her shoulders, and spun her around to face him. "C'mon, we're getting out of here!"

Mrs. Kookerly looked up into Barley's face. "Where's Brufyss? I'm not going anywhere without Brufyss. Where is he?"

"Brufyss is *gone*—I don't know where he is," Barley lied, "but I have to get you out of here before you get hurt!"

"Gone? Where did he go? Brufyss would never leave me here!"

"Yeah, well he *did*! Now let's get out of here!"

A ferocious spluttering roar came from the open pit. Barley looked over to see hulking, reeking, sludge-encrusted Brufyss Bathwater struggling to pull himself onto the stage. His face was contorted with unfathomable rage, his gaze immutably fastened upon Barley and Mrs. Kookerly standing above him.

"Brufyss!" cried Mrs. Kookerly. "Brufyss, I'm here!"

"Barley!" cried another feminine voice. "Barley, I'm here!"

It was Daphne. She'd regained her senses, seen the chaos raging, and realized that her prom date was standing nearby. "Barley, what's happening? Get me out of here!"

Barley's head spun. At the moment of realizing his ambition of obtaining Mrs. Kookerly, his own prom date beseeched his aid—and his enraged rival reemerged onto the scene with murder in his flaming eyes.

With one final push off the shoulders of a wallowing student in the pit, Brufyss painfully hoisted himself onto the stage, struggling to stand. Daphne moved past a student in the crowd who had blocked her from getting to Barley's side. Mrs. Kookerly set off to assist Brufyss.

Barley's left arm flashed out to block Mrs. Kookerly's advance. With his right arm, he savagely pushed Daphne away as she approached him. Daphne staggered backwards, windmilling her arms to catch her balance, and stumbled and crashed into Brufyss, knocking him off his feet once more. Both of them fell head over heels into the open pit, disappearing under the raging surface of the bubbling bilious beef broth bath.

Mrs. Kookerly watched this split-second drama unfold in front of her eyes with dumbfounded incredulity. What kind of madness was this? She was too stunned to move, to speak.

Barley could see that Mrs. Kookerly was totally incapacitated. He had to press ahead, to get her away from the mayhem and out of the gymnasium before anything else upset his plans. He grabbed Mrs. Kookerly around the waist and lifted her, swinging her body over his shoulder like a roll of carpet. She offered no resistance.

Putting one arm securely around her waist to hold her steady, he set off toward his waiting sportscar. Anyone who blocked his way received a vicious straight-arm to the head, which knocked them into the person behind them, causing a chain reaction of stumbling, falling bodies. He reached the idling sportscar, opened the passenger door, and placed Mrs. Kookerly's pliant body onto the seat. Her eyes were wide open, fixed in an unseeing stare, a catatonic stupor, oblivious to everything taking place around her.

Barley slammed the door and scurried around to the driver's side. He heard a commotion above his head and looked up in time to see a massive, cascading wall of brownish liquid hurtling down, seemingly in slow motion, about to rain a hideous deluge on everyone's heads.

* * *

Retchard Pumpstuck's rampant cynicism was shaken to its core by Barley's sacrifice of Daphne. This was just *too* outrageous, even for someone as devoid of human empathy as Retchard Pumpstuck! Tasty Dogdaughter had been one of the few students at Piggford High who hadn't ridiculed or tormented him in the past four years. He could no longer stand by as a detached observer while such unrestrained injustice took place under his very nose—not when he had the power to do something about it.

Retchard saw Barley open the car's passenger door and push Mrs. Kookerly onto the seat. He had to initiate the gurgling gooey glop drop before Barley could get away!

He forced the knotted rope loose from the railing. The weight of the vat full of viscous liquid ripped the rope out of his hands, the block-and-tackle whirred and squealed as it spun, and the huge vat tilted, tilted, and tipped, dumping its entire contents onto the stage below in one fell swoop.

Barley dove into the car headfirst, reaching back to slam the door as the brown liquid avalanche crashed down into the pit and onto the beef broth bathers. The gurgling gooey glop, now mixed with the bubbling bilious beef broth, welled over the edge of the pit and surged across the stage. The torrent knocked students off their feet and swept them away, carrying them into those surrounding the stage, who were also knocked down and inundated. The roaring, rampaging flood swallowed and consumed everything in its path. Everyone in the gym was caught in the deluge; the panicked crowd screamed in horror, vainly struggling against the raging current, trying to find the nearest exit, doused thoroughly and carried along like flotsam.

Secure within the tight confines of the Smegmatti 502's interior, Barley and Mrs. Kookerly escaped the crushing blow of the glop drop, but the car was engulfed in the ensuing surge that cascaded off the stage into the gymnasium hall. The car floated lazily on the surface, buoyed atop the crest of the wave by the dense viscosity of the liquid. Once the flood began to widen out, the level of liquid dropped sharply, and the car's wheels touched the floor once more. Amazingly, the engine was still running in neutral.

Soggy promgoers began slipping, sliding, and scrambling toward the exits in a mass exodus. The insanity that the vegetarian intimidation fest meant to bestow upon the evening's vegetarian captives had been democratically redistributed to everyone present.

Except Barley Doodlebody.

The double doors through which he'd earlier made his grand entrance were knocked off their hinges, and a portion of the flood's runoff streamed through the opening. Barley revved the Smegmatti's engine to blow out any vestiges of gooey glop and eased off the clutch, guiding the car slowly across the wet floor and out onto the street. The car plunked off the curb, and Barley stopped to look in his rearview mirror. No one was chasing him.

A clean getaway.

Mrs. Kookerly sat rigidly, gazing out the car's windshield, her beautiful face expressionless. Without turning to look at Barley she said in a near whisper, "Take me home. I want to go home now."

"But it's still early. Why don't we go somewhere and get to know each other a little more?"

"I want to go home now. Please take me there."

Barley figured it was best not to argue. There'd be plenty of time for them to get to know each other. He put the car in gear and headed across town.

The sound of shrieking police sirens filtered into his ears. Someone had called the cops. *Ha! Let them clean up the mess!* Barley turned the corner and left P. P. Piggford and His Wife Janice High School behind. An armada of North Corners police cars sped down the street from the opposite direction, passing Barley with sirens blaring and red lights flashing.

The two drove for a while in silence. After a few minutes, Mrs. Kookerly spoke in the same subdued tone as before: "Pull over right here. Stop the car."

Barley peered out the window. They were on a deserted, poorly lit street occupied by large industrial warehouses. No homes in this part of town.

"This isn't where you live! Why do you want to stop here?"

"Please, stop the car. I see something I want to clean up."

Barley acquiesced grudgingly, pulling to the curb under a streetlight in front of a shadowy, dilapidated building. He stopped the car and turned off the engine.

She opened her door and slid out, standing on the sidewalk. "Get out of the car and come here."

Barley shrugged, opened his door, and walked around the front of the car.

She peered at Barley intently. "Wipe your face."

Barley took his disheveled shirtsleeve and swiped at his face with the dirty cuff. "Okay?"

"It's still there."

Once more Barley dragged the shirtsleeve across his face. "Okay now?"

"No, it's still there. Wipe it again."

Barley scrubbed his face until it was almost raw. "*Now?*"

"No, it's still there."

"*What's* still there?"

"Your *face!*"

She stalked away without glancing back, turning a corner into an alleyway and disappearing from sight. The lonely clip-clop of her thick-heeled shoes echoed in the hollowness between the warehouses, slowly fading into silence.

Barley stood in shock on the empty sidewalk. He jarred himself out of his befuddlement and raced to the end of the alleyway, peering into the darkness. No sign of Mrs. Kookerly—not a trace. She was gone, vanishing like a ghost.

Like Barley's glorious dream . . .

9

So ended the Great Doodlebody-Bathwater Brouhaha of '67.

Immediately after the tragic episode, the P. P. Piggford and His Wife Janice High School gymnasium was razed, the entire site deemed uninhabitable after its saturation by the most horrendous deluge of aromatic effluent ever seen—or smelled. However, in a twist of irony never anticipated, the ground on which the gym sat became the most fertile patch of earth on earth.

The organic ingredients in the bubbling bilious beef broth bath and the gurgling gooey glop transformed the area into a veritable Garden of Eden. Trees, flowers, plants, and shrubbery flourished on the spot thereafter—but no physical structure ever occupied the site again.

The P. P. Piggford and His Wife Janice High School Senior Prom and Vegetarian Intimidation Fest was removed forever from the school's social calendar, much to the delight of the surviving North Corners vegetarian population. Nevertheless, for a number of years after the debacle took place and before the horrid memories finally receded into the shadows of the past, there was massive student absenteeism from school on the anniversary of the event. They'd sequester at home, beating their breasts, wailing, lamenting, and gorging themselves on snack foods to the point of nausea.

Rampant PTSD and myriad neuroses and psychological ailments plagued many for the rest of their lives: pathological fears of fruit, meat, vegetables, grains, vegetarians, non-vegetarians, snazzy sportscars, tuxedos, ball gowns, hillbilly music, and Hawaii among them.

As a result of their dogpiling experiences on that fateful night, Spatch Huntoon and Melanie Bupwanger underwent extensive psychological rehabilitation, eventually reemerging into North Corners society as professional wrestlers.

Spatch competed under the name "Spatch the Whiner." His career was marked by a propensity to shriek hideously, weep copiously, and wet himself whenever he was forced to the mat by an opponent. Interestingly enough, this involuntary tactic was so completely unnerving and disgusting to his opponents that they'd usually cover their ears and run screaming from the ring, thereby forfeiting the match and giving "Spatch the Whiner" the default victory—and ultimately a near-perfect record, losing only once in his entire professional career. He was thoroughly reviled and grossly repugnant to fans everywhere he competed. In the world of professional wrestling, this translates into immense popularity.

Subsequent to his triumphant retirement from the ring, Spatch joined his former idol and mentor Bronson Facockta at the local department store, Everything—And More!, taking over Bronson's sales position in ladies underwear—which looked extremely funny on him, to say the least.

Melanie Bupwanger's pro wrestling career was markedly different from Spatch's, primarily because she was never forced to resort to the pathetic methods Spatch used to achieve victory. As a matter of fact, the only defeat "Spatch the Whiner" ever suffered in his wrestling career came at the hands of Melanie Bupwanger.

Melanie's unfortunate experience on prom night turned her from an intelligent, good-looking, aspiring social climber and future genius housewife of America into "Mad Melanie the Malevolent Mangler," a vicious, raging, psychopathic purveyor of brutality known for face-slapping her opponents into states of quivering hysteria before physically destroying them. She was a huge crowd favorite, although the majority of her fans weren't quite sure what "malevolent" meant.

So many of her opponents were horribly maimed and disfigured that she was eventually arrested on charges of attempted murder, mayhem, inciting a riot, and being very difficult to get along with. She was tried, convicted, and given a life sentence in the North Corners High-Security Prison for Overly Aggressive Individuals. As is normally the case with life sentences, she was released from prison in a year and a half, going on to become a prison guard. No one ever attempted or even considered escaping from the prison, out of an extreme fear that Officer Melanie would catch them. A torturously slow, hideously painful death would be preferable.

Spiffany Tonguehoister retained the infamous crown she'd refused to relinquish that night, but even she was never able to remove it from her head. Her superior mechanical design for the cranial-anchoring device and the ingenuity with which she'd constructed it proved to be so formidable that she was fated to wear the immovable headgear for the rest of her life. This situation ensured that Spiffany no longer needed to concern herself with decisions on hairstyles; a gas-powered weed trimmer would usually do the trick.

After her own recovery from the horrible experience, she went on to open "Queen Spiffany's Sherman Tanke Repaire & Service Shoppe." She became a familiar yet comically tragic figure in North Corners, cruising up and down the streets in her specially modified high-performance custom Sherman tank, her crown-bedecked head poking out of the tank's top turret like a prairie dog peeking out of its hole, waving benignly at everyone she passed.

She referred to these cruising forays as her daily "vigilance patrols," having convinced herself that the security and welfare of "her subjects" mandated an effort of this sort. A conscientious and responsible monarch who coincidentally happened to be in possession of a specially modified, high-performance custom Sherman tank could do nothing less. Occasionally an errant artillery shell accidentally fired by "Queen Spiff" would destroy a downtown business or residence, though Her Majesty was seldom prosecuted for the mishap. One does not willfully piss off the owner of a specially modified, high-performance custom Sherman tank who sincerely believes herself to be queen of the realm.

Fortunately for those displaced by the accidental shelling, their demolished structures would be rebuilt by the remorseful Queen Spiff herself, who was actually a far more ingenious construction engineer and builder than a tank mechanic, and probably would have made a fortune as a building contractor had she not been too goofy to realize it.

Bronson Facockta was rendered mute by his own traumatic experience that night. Afterward, he retained employment briefly at Everything— And More! However, his newly acquired disability forced him to assume a position as a mannequin. Eventually becoming dissatisfied with this inglorious demotion, he disappeared from North Corners life, never to be heard from again—although this could probably be attributed to his having been rendered mute.

Immediately following the indelible events of the senior prom, an emotionally scarred Flagella "Bubbles" Nuggmuck suffered through a severe period of depression wherein she binged incessantly on hot dogs and sauerkraut, trying to recapture the essence of her "glory days." Unfortunately, she was completely successful in her efforts. She so totally "recaptured the essence" that her body inflated to seven times its normal size due to an overabundance of methane gas. During one of her more intense culinary binge sessions, she blew up.

Alas, Bubbles Nuggmuck was no more, but Bubbles's memory lingered in the form of a mammoth gas cloud so all-encompassing that it necessitated a widespread evacuation of populated areas within a fourteen-square-mile radius of the explosion.

In later years, the saga of Flagella Nuggmuck attained the status of folk legend among the citizens of North Corners: a wronged young girl whose monumental sorrows, unrealized dreams, and hollow triumphs transformed her into a vengeful angel who flew off like a rocket, detonating and disappearing into the sky in a cloud of toxic gas to live forevermore in the Land of Eternal Nuk-Nuk. To environmentalists she became a symbol, a cause célèbre, a convincing argument for the immediate and total eradication of air pollution and greenhouse gasses.

Another sad postscript: the term *nuggmuck* soon took its place in the lexicon of North Corners slang, the word's definition being "to willfully indulge in massive food overconsumption, resulting in self-detonation."

Lucinda "Jiggly" Luckybeans had been lucky on prom night. Her ability to generate a vibratory "force field," making it virtually impossible to lay a hand on her, kept her relatively unscathed throughout the ordeal—other than most of her clothing supersonically oscillating off her body. It had *not* prevented her from being nearly suffocated by the mass of bodies that swarmed all over her on the gymnasium stage. Consequently, she was forced to keep up her defensive vibrations continuously—something she'd never done before.

To her dismay, Lucinda discovered that her defense mechanism became *stuck* in the "jiggle" mode. No matter how hard she tried to stop gyrating, she was unable to do so. She jiggled and joogled, wiggled and waggled, quaked and quivered, shook and shivered nonstop!

Her inability to quell her body's ceaseless vibrations prohibited her from leading a normal life thereafter. There were few items in her wardrobe that would stay on her body without disintegrating or flying off. Most people could never look at her without seeing more than a blurry, indistinct image. Every store window, car windshield, glassware shop, or full-length mirror she passed would shatter from high-frequency pulsations.

The simple act of eating became an ordeal as well. In trying to chew her food, her teeth would vibrate at such an intense rate that she'd inevitably tear her tongue to ribbons, ultimately forcing her to restrict her food consumption to an all-liquid diet. Due to excessive weight loss, Lucinda soon resembled a gaunt, wire-thin piano tuning fork. Unable to find conventional employment, she was reduced to accepting a job at the downtown hardware store as a paint mixer.

Brufyss Bathwater—who'd miraculously managed to survive the ordeal—disappeared from public view, enduring a period of seclusion in order to regain and rejuvenate his dignity and solidify his resolve to obtain retribution for the injustices suffered at the hands of Barley Doodlebody. Brufyss emerged from this voluntary period still filled with unrequited anger, ever resentful and never forgiving. In the ensuing years, he'd go on to do whatever he could to disrupt, disparage, dismantle, or destroy any operation or enterprise that Barley could concoct or conceive.

Brufyss was on his own thereafter. On his own, but not alone.

Mrs. Kookerly, whose steadfast loyalty to Brufyss remained unflagging, eschewed the life of an upstanding citizen to team up with him, becoming the figurative right arm of his operations. With her lingering beauty, she became the perfect counterpart to Brufyss's bullying brawn. She never forgot nor forgave Barley for what he did to Brufyss, her best friend, Daphne, and herself on that terrible night.

Daphne Dogdaughter was also deeply affected by the experience. She joined Bruffyss and Mrs. Kookerly in their disruptive operations, intent upon exacting revenge on Barley for his flagrant deception and manipulation of her. While still retaining her good looks, the once sweet, trusting, and generous young girl became a vindictive woman, spoiled by her unconscionable abuse at Barley's hands.

Together, Brufyss, Mrs. Kookerly, and Daphne gained notoriety around North Corners as the Bathwater Boys 'n Girls Gang, a perpetual thorn in the side of Barley Doodlebody and all that he sought to accomplish.

Barley went on to retain, augment, and develop his many business enterprises (both legitimate and illegitimate); in doing so, he prospered. He later entered the world of North Corners politics, and by virtue of his deviousness, manipulative nature, and overbearing strength of character— or lack thereof—was elected mayor for three consecutive terms.

Despite his apparent triumphs and successes, Barley journeyed through the later years alone, never collaborating with an associate in any business venture, never sharing the fruits of his labor, never feeling the sense of pride, accomplishment, and fulfillment those triumphs and successes might have brought.

He wouldn't have it any other way.

PART II:

THE INAUGURAL BUMPS & SPUGGETT TOUR

10

The big day arrived at last!

This would be the historic, groundbreaking day the very first Bumps & Spuggett tour would depart from the Mystic Knights of the Heavenly Daze Hall in downtown North Corners, its ultimate destination the reception room and lobby of the Bumps & Spuggett office itself.

To the people gathered, the significance of the event was titanic and twofold: not only did the inaugural Bumps & Spuggett tour give the town a much-needed reason to celebrate, but now there would finally be a resolution and refutation—or a final *validation*—to the rampant rumors circulating about what went on inside the walls of that mysterious two-story office building out on the edge of town. Only someone with the perseverance, tenacity, and guts of a Barley Doodlebody could ever have pulled it off, and everyone was grateful to the brooding, fearsome entrepreneur for taking the initiative to answer, once and for all, the myriad questions that rankled in everyone's minds.

The courageous participants in this auspicious inaugural run would be a busload of the social elite of the North Corners community: local dignitaries, politicians, and a respected member of the clergy. They all preened in chairs upon the stage of the Mystic Knights of the Heavenly Daze Hall, looking down magnanimously on the curious and somewhat envious throng of townspeople who'd assembled to witness the sendoff.

First and foremost among the gathered VIPs was His Honor, Mayor Roymul Wubbleduster, the first magistrate of North Corners, sitting unobtrusively beside Barley Doodlebody, accompanied by his porky little daughter, Margaret, and his *very* obtrusive bodyguard and public relations advisor, Biff Spoozma.

Mayor Wubbleduster was a low-class politician with a fat belly and an abundant shock of greasy, jet-black-dyed hair that stood straight up like stalks of scorched wheat over the dome of his bowling-ball-shaped skull. His Honor possessed the reputation of being completely incorruptible—unless, of course, he was offered bribes or special favors. Barley had bought off Mayor Wubbleduster easily enough: a big fat cheeseburger with fries and a one-year subscription to a raunchy men's magazine had done the job, and had even started Barley thinking about running for mayor yet again.

Sincerely determined to win the hearts and minds of his constituents upon first being elected, Mayor Wubbleduster initiated what he believed would be his most significant accomplishment and contribution as first citizen: the creation and establishment of the North Corners Municipal Children's Playground.

Unfortunately, there were very few municipal children to be found in North Corners, the great majority of the little tykes being members of the private sector and therefore not permitted by law to play at the playground. The mayor was completely unaware of this ordinance, which was strictly enforced by armed guards stationed around the park. Their explicit orders? To shoot any privately owned juvenile who attempted to trespass onto the public property.

Yet another factor contributing to the park's unpopularity was its ill-advised location next door to the North Corners Cemetery, Mausoleum, and Crematorium, across the street from the North Corners Slaughterhouse, and down the block from the North Corners Asylum for Shrilly Shrieking Lunatics.

Much to the consternation of the mayor and community, even the few municipal children avoided the place like a toxic waste dump. The very thought of playing at or even of being in close proximity to the facility caused them to experience traumatic nightmares.

The unused playground fell into ruin. The armed guards turned to marauding the nearby neighborhoods, and the park's land was eventually leased to a group of itinerant farmers who sought to convert it to a truck farm. This enterprise was doomed to failure as well; try as they might, the farmers were unsuccessful at getting even one small truck to grow there.

As a consequence of this catastrophic community service debacle, Mayor Roymul Wubbleduster gave up any hope of improving life in the community and resigned himself to faithfully catering to every whim and demand of the ever-whimsical, always-demanding Barley Doodlebody, and avidly ogling his monthly copy of the raunchy men's magazine.

The good citizens of North Corners tolerated the mayor because his ridiculous appearance kept them in stitches and made them feel better about themselves—when they weren't completely ignoring him.

Biff Spoozma, the mayor's blindly obedient public relations advisor and personal bodyguard, stood quietly behind His Honor's chair, attempting to project an air of importance and administrative efficiency, but mostly just trying to stay awake. Absolutely motionless except for his beady eyes, which scanned the audience for impending threats to his boss or the need for an emergency public relations intervention, Biff was gradually losing his battle with the Sandman. Everyone in the assembled throng was preoccupied with ignoring rather than acknowledging Mayor Wubbleduster's existence, and Biff had no one and nothing on which to focus his diligent attention.

Biff finally conceded defeat to dreamland. A snorting snore issued forth from his nose, and he keeled straight over backward, landing with a thud on the stage. The impact of his fall and the conk he received on his head succeeded in waking him up again. He quickly scrambled to his feet to resume his stoic stance behind the mayor's chair, unnoticed by anyone except Barley Doodlebody, who gave him an exasperated, piercing stare, then turned his attention back to the proceedings.

His Honor's young daughter, Margaret Wubbleduster, was a stubby, porcine little creature who personified the supposition "If a pig could change into a human being, *this* is what it would look like."

Margaret was expert at creating saliva, manufacturing bucketfuls of it and unselfishly sharing it with everyone around her, whether they liked it or not. She would stalk her prey, pounce upon them when they least expected it, hold them down, and lather their entire body with her plentiful supply of the sticky stuff until they resembled a tearful, quivering glob of jelly. It was an idiosyncrasy peculiar to Margaret alone, and came to be known as "high-intensity voluminous expectorant distribution" (or HIVED). To be HIVED by Margaret Wubbleduster was an experience akin to being dipped in a vat of horsehair glue and left to decompose in a swamp.

A typical school-day activity for her fellow students and the faculty members at My Dear Watson Elementary was eluding the mayor's daughter at all costs. It was not an easy accomplishment; despite her stubby physique, little Margaret could move quickly.

As the offspring of the town's highest-ranking politician, Margaret had received special permission from her school's principal—granted willingly, even *gratefully*—to skip academics for the day and attend the inaugural Bumps & Spuggett tour event. A day without Margaret was like a day without crotch rot; everyone at the school was ecstatic to be rid of her for at least one brief twenty-four-hour period. It would also give the school's janitor time to mop up.

On the stage above the assembled crowd, little Margaret shyly hid behind her father's wide girth, shrewdly assessing potential targets to be HIVED among the many upturned, expectant, and unsuspecting faces in the audience.

Also on the stage was North Corners' beloved chief of police, Binky Bohoguss. Chief Bohoguss was yet another public servant comfortably ensconced in Barley Doodlebody's pocket—literally. The good chief was a perfectly proportioned seven inches tall, and could usually be found riding in the breast pocket of Barley's business suit, cushioned by a handkerchief under which he sometimes hid to avoid dealing with police-chiefly matters when confronted by them. He was in his usual spot: tucked safely into Barley's suit pocket, looking self-important and feeling quite full of himself. Due to his diminutive stature, that was not saying much.

Chief Bohoguss was venerated by the good citizens of North Corners because he was so darn *cute* in his tiny police chief uniform and hat. The children of the town thought he was some kind of magical toy doll that kicked and screamed hideously when his belly was squeezed, and the adult female population eyed him covetously, secretly visualizing how they could utilize a little guy like him for their own self-gratification. The men of the town loved to sit on him and fart whenever they caught him away from the protective shelter of Barley Doodlebody's suit pocket.

The chief's North Corners Police Force subordinate officers, extremely fond of the spirited little sprite yet unsure of how seriously they should take orders chirped from a seven-inch-tall pixie, simply viewed him as a figurehead—or, more precisely because of his small size, a "figurine." They were all aware that Binky had received no law-enforcement training prior to being appointed to his position by Barley Doodlebody (the town's mayor at that time) and consequently did whatever they pleased. Chief Binky was so darn cute and so darn *useless*.

However, unbeknownst to most of the good citizens of North Corners, Binky Bohoguss had a dark, secret past. Long before his career in law enforcement, he had spent time in the hoosegow as punishment for a criminal career in another part of the country. Known then as "Hoboken BoBo," Binky "Hoboken BoBo" Bohoguss had been a member of a notorious ring of burglars and bank robbers known as the "Notorious Burglar and Bank Robber Ring," renowned for their incredible burglaries of bank vaults that were deemed burglar-proof. The robberies had baffled even the most experienced detectives and criminologists, who simply could not imagine how these impenetrable money storehouses could have been violated.

The missing piece to that puzzle was Hoboken BoBo. He simply squeezed his tiny frame into the vault's air vent system, slid or shimmied into the vault, and unscrambled the combination lock of the vault door, enabling his cohorts to open it and gain access to the hoard of cash that lay within. This talent eventually earned the little burglar the additional nickname "Slinky Binky."

"Slinky Binky Hoboken BoBo" Bohoguss had been among the most successful seven-inch-tall bank robbers of all time, spending wads of money like a politician on a taxpayer-funded junket, living the high life, racing around in fast, expensive miniature sports cars, and wining and dining wild and wanton seven-inch-tall women.

That ended one fateful night when the Notorious Burglar and Bank Robber Ring attempted to break into the vault of a small bank somewhere in the eastern part of the country. The bank was *so* small that the vault was only six inches tall, smaller than little Binky himself. (As it turned out, this bank catered primarily to wealthy chipmunks.) Slinky Binky Hoboken BoBo got hopelessly stuck while trying to squeeze into the tiny air vent system. The rest of the gang, realizing that their "secret weapon" had become irretrievably incapacitated and that the heist was headed toward a big fat bust, panicked and took it on the lam, leaving behind poor little BoBo with his kicking, squirming legs sticking out of the vent duct.

He was in this unfortunate position when discovered by the bank's night janitor, who at first laughed hysterically, then tormented the ensnared burglar by tickling his tiny feet and toes unmercifully. Finally, he reported the botched crime to the police.

Slinky Binky Hoboken BoBo Bohoguss was arrested for his complicity in the cutest armed robbery ever attempted. His wrists were far too tiny for conventional handcuffs, so the cops just stuffed him in a shoebox like a pet salamander and sealed it with electrical tape, poking little air holes in the top so he could breathe.

During the sentencing portion of his courtroom trial, Binky was given a "shorter" sentence than most for his crimes because of his tiny stature and inherent cuteness: seven dog-years—the equivalent of one human year. He was sent off to the big house to serve his prison time. Once he actually arrived, however, it was immediately determined that the big house was far *too* big to incarcerate an inmate the size of little Slinky Binky Hoboken BoBo. The bars on even the smallest prison cells were too wide to keep him from easily walking between them, so the tiny prisoner was moved into a doghouse in the warden's backyard, specially modified for an inmate of Binky's stature with little bars on the doggie door to keep him from wandering off. That's how Slinky Binky Hoboken BoBo wound up "in the doghouse" for his criminal activities.

The warden's displaced pooch, resentful at having been evicted from his own doggie digs, would spitefully urinate between the bars across the doggie doorway on a daily basis, which not only humiliated the tiny prisoner constantly but also heightened his feelings of regret and repentance. He vowed that once he served his time and got out of "the big doghouse," he would go straight and mend his wayward ways.

Upon his release, Slinky Binky Hoboken BoBo made his way westward, turning up one day in North Corners. He sought a better life for himself, and an escape from the stigma of being an ex-convict—albeit the cutest little ex-convict you ever laid eyes on. Barley Doodlebody first laid eyes upon Binky that same day, when the desperate, destitute, and famished teeny-tiny ex-convict was rummaging through a trash bin behind one of Barley's dining establishments, looking for a discarded chili-cheese fry.

At the time, Barley was in the middle of his second of three lucrative terms as the mayor. He immediately saw the potential usefulness of a little guy like Binky Bohoguss. Barley needed a "puppet" in high places—Binky definitely fit the size requirement for the job, and desperate as he was for a new and better life, the tiny fellow was not above having his strings pulled.

Barley capitalized on Binky's potential usefulness by installing him as North Corners' useless chief of police, claiming to the puzzled populace that Chief Bohoguss could and would be a powerful deterrent to crime in their fair town. How could anyone even think of committing a crime against someone as universally loved and adored as Chief Binky? Who would want to be responsible for upsetting such a cute little munchkin? It would be insensitive and utterly unthinkable! Mayor Barley had a good point; as they gazed upon Binky's endearing, nearly microscopic countenance, the populace had to agree.

As a reward for the little guy's acceptance of the bogus North Corners chief of police position, Barley promised to keep Binky's lurid past forever buried, as long as the little elf-puppy minded his itsy-bitsy Ps and Qs. For his part, Chief Bohoguss would be forever beholden to Barley for giving him a second chance at making good with his own diminutive life.

And life had definitely taken a turn for the better. The little chief peeked out at the assembled crowd and waved to the town's women, who tittered girlishly, blew him kisses, and drooled lasciviously, imagining what they'd do if they could only get their horny mitts on the little bugger.

Sitting to Barley's left on the stage was another notable: City Councilman Frog Puppleman, Barley's dimwitted half brother. Frog had been conscripted by Barley (his "election" to the public office highly suspect; not one citizen could remember voting for him) to be the then-mayor's voice on the city council—yet another lucky beneficiary of Barley's ambition to manipulate and control the machinations of North Corners politics.

Frog faced the crowd, scratching himself and saying, "Yeah, *buddy!*" in response to whatever was said by anyone. Brother Barley, fed up with the mindless interruptions and exasperated at himself for forgetting to bring a box of thumbtacks for Frog to play with, reached over and smacked the city councilman soundly on the nose. Frog keeled over in his chair and sprawled face-first onto the floor, unconscious, arms and legs splayed obscenely like a dead contortionist. The crowd responded with polite applause, not quite sure if this was part of the ceremony but relishing the moment just the same.

Sitting to Frog's left was North Corners' favorite physician, Dr. Humaylius Pudbid, MD, an ancient, wizened member of the community. He resembled everyone's ideal grandfather: an unkempt shock of white hair atop his head, tiny rectangular spectacles perched on the end of his nose, a wrinkled white shirt with the sleeves rolled up to his elbows, and a twinkle in his eye.

Dr. Pudbid was the embodiment of that archetypical, Norman Rockwellian, old-fashioned country doctor straight out of America's past, even utilizing a black buggy pulled by a sway-backed horse named Frank Winslow to make house calls. The kindly physician and his one-horse rig made a familiar, reassuring sight around the small town's tree-lined neighborhoods.

It was Barley Doodlebody's opinion that the good doctor was completely nuts, since no one else had used a horse-and-buggy rig around

North Corners for seventy-five years. Indeed, most folks grouched that the doctor's buggy tied up automobile traffic wherever he went, and that accidentally stepping into a pile of his horse's poop on a town street was a big pain in the butt—theirs, not the horse's. However, old Dr. Pudbid was just so dad-gum-down-home-small-town lovable that the townsfolk tended to look the other way, disregarding the horse droppings on the streets (and usually stepping in them again).

His presence around North Corners was truly appreciated due to his undiminished medical skills, especially since he would accept any form of payment for his services, just as it had been in the old days. This included freshly baked bread, home-baked apple pies, a tray of warm chocolate chip cookies, a bag of oats for his horse, or maybe even a live chicken. The good doctor also famously distributed lollipops to his patients, no matter how young or old they might be.

Dr. Pudbid had delivered most of the babies born in North Corners over the years—not as the attending physician but rather from the hospital to the parents' homes in his horse-and-buggy rig. He did this to earn extra money, since loaves of freshly baked bread, home-baked apple pies, a tray of warm chocolate chip cookies, a bag of oats for his horse, or live chickens were seldom accepted as payment by his creditors.

Despite Barley's opinion of the tenuous state of Dr. Pudbid's sanity, the old physician was deemed important enough by the savvy entrepreneur to merit a coveted spot on the stage and a seat on the bus for the inaugural tour to the Bumps & Spuggett office. Barley felt that a medically knowledgeable person might be handy on the trip in case horrific traumas were inflicted upon the tourists by the B & S lunatics—which could result in lawsuits filed against him by the victims as well as bad publicity for the tour business. Plus, the doctor worked cheap. Barley had loads of home-baked apple pies and chocolate chip cookies stashed on the tour bus.

Kindly Dr. Pudbid sat on the stage in his appointed chair, a serene, grandfatherly smile on his face, enjoying himself immensely, winking at the children in the audience, totally oblivious to an unconscious Frog Puppleman lying motionless at his feet like a mackerel in a market stall.

Also present among the group was Mimsy Borogove, the richest and most prominent socialite in the somewhat-tepid North Corners social scene—the very same Mimsy Borogove who had been Frog Puppleman's date to the '67 senior prom debacle.

Mimsy had inherited most of her money from her wealthy grandfather, Gozznagle "Footch" Borogove, known affectionately as the "sewer entrepreneur." A canny old industrialist, Footch Borogove had amassed his sizeable fortune by wisely subscribing to and living by the adage "The only sure things in life are death, taxes, and sewage," and had founded the Western Sewage Factory, which held the distinction of manufacturing some of the best sewage in all of Ohio. The rest of Mimsy's money had come from turning tricks on Main Street, more an avocation than an economic necessity.

Her main claim to fame was her sponsorship of the annual North Corners Society Debutante Ball and Rummage Sale. Each year, the event was held at the socialite's stately mansion on North Corners' fashionable east side, just south of the Western Sewage Factory.

One interesting aspect regarding the debutante ball and rummage sale: hardly anyone ever showed up. Those who did were usually sickened by the stench from the Western Sewage Factory and went home nauseated without ever entering the place. Amazingly, only City Councilman Frog Puppleman had been the unfailing exception to this.

As Frog's reward, Mimsy let him have his way with her in any way he wished. This normally translated to her playing the part of a coffee table while Frog watched TV, became confused by the commercials, and eventually fell asleep. At this point, Mimsy would have her way with *him*.

Both Barley and Frog had known Mimsy since their youth. Because of her ongoing connection to Frog, Mimsy had become one of Barley's chief financial supporters in his efforts to establish the Bumps & Spugget guided tour business, so Barley grudgingly extended the invitation for her to participate. Privately, he viewed her as a ridiculous blue-haired strumpet.

Mimsy sat regally on the stage of the Mystic Knights of the Heavenly Daze Hall stage, belted and pantsed in the latest high fashion but for an old purple feather boa wrapped around her bony shoulders. A scraggly, toothless toy French poodle named Gaggy fidgeted nervously in her lap. She rattled her jewelry, played with her dyed-blue hairdo, and scanned the audience, flicking her tongue lasciviously at her past, present, and potential future customers. She paid particular attention to tiny Chief Binky Bohoguss, who had yet to fall victim to her lurid solicitations. Binky cowered fearfully behind the handkerchief in Barley's coat pocket, trying to avoid her hungry stares.

Sitting to Mimsy's left (and looking exceedingly uncomfortable about it) was the local clergy's representative to the group of town dignitaries, the Reverend Doctor Mafumbus Snortworthy. Reverend Snortworthy was pastor of Saint Cucamonga's Church of Fast Food for the Soul, the town's unwavering and unquestioned bastion of sobriety and propriety. The reverend, who looked like a sanctimonious sea elephant, smiled benignly down at the members of his flock who were in attendance—that is, when he was not squirming away from the sly grasps of Mimsy Borogove or Gaggy's constant attempts to sniff his crotch.

Years ago, before he became a saintly vicar, Mafumbus Snortworthy had been a fry cook at Hose Monster, a local North Corners eatery owned and operated by a young and ambitious (albeit somewhat crooked and unprincipled) entrepreneur: Barley Doodlebody. Mafumbus had worked in the kitchen slinging hash, hot cakes, ham 'n eggs, burgers, fries, dishes, silverware, kitchen appliances, waitresses, and anything else he could get his hands on. To say he was an angry young man in those days would be putting it mildly. Having a name like Mafumbus Snortworthy had given the young fry cook a chip on his shoulder the size of Mount Rushmore.

Barley instantly liked the pugnacious kid's style and promoted Mafumbus to bouncer, an unusual position for a greasy-spoon hamburger joint, but not so when one realizes that Mafumbus's job was to throw customers *into* the place. The food sucked, and no one would eat there of their own volition.

One fateful day, as Mafumbus stood at the restaurant's entrance, bouncing people in, along came one of North Corners' less-fortunate citizens, Gudge Mucklehugger, a derelict wanderer who prowled the back alleys of North Corners, rifling through trash cans in search of discarded French pastries and woodworking tools. As scruffy Gudge shuffled past Hose Monster's front door, Mafumbus the bouncer rudely picked him up by the coat lapel and seat of his tattered pants and heaved Gudge like a sack of potatoes into the depths of the dingy eatery. Gudge landed unceremoniously on a stool at the lunch counter and was immediately inundated with piles of greasy food by the head chef, a Frenchman named Jean-Clod LeGufee who had replaced Mafumbus after his promotion to bouncer, and who was overjoyed at finally having a customer to feed who was too hungry to be horrified.

Gudge hadn't eaten much more than a few pieces of patio furniture in the last four or five days. He gratefully tore into the steaming piles of free food like it was his last meal (as, indeed, it turned out to be), shoveling heaps of saturated fats and high-cholesterol delicacies into his mouth by the potful, much to Chef LeGufee's delight.

Mafumbus, gazing into the gloomy establishment at the unfolding feast, watched in growing horror as Gudge began to inflate like a gas-filled balloon, growing larger and more rotund with each massive bite of food. He finally reached and exceeded his full capacity and exploded like the legendary Flagella Nuggmuck, spraying the premises with partially hydrogenated trans-fatty vapor—a nauseating case of history repeating itself.

The grisly sight of Gudge Mucklehugger nuggmucking right before his eyes—a fate for which Mafumbus himself had ultimately been responsible—so horrified the young Snortworthy that he experienced an epiphany of life-altering proportions. The remorseful greasy-spoon bouncer resolved he would devote the rest of his life to saving souls rather than manhandling them, and set off on a quest to do just that.

Mafumbus embraced this spiritual rebirth with gusto, eventually receiving his doctor of theology degree from Fritz and Tuffy's School of Theological Ruminations and Automotive Detailing. Years of exemplary behavior in the community, compassionate attention to its less fortunate members, and fanatical devotion to his parishioners eventually led the Reverend Mafumbus Snortworthy to the altar of Saint Cucamonga's Church of Fast Food for the Soul, appointed head pastor by the church's council of elders.

Each Sunday, Reverend Snortworthy would stand regally in the pulpit of Saint Cucamonga's and entertain his parishioners with lengthy, tedious sermons. Homespun fables like "The Incontinent Fish and the Spastic Alligator" and parables such as "The Good Samaritan and the Discounted Gasoline Coupons" seldom taught or enlightened his audience to any great degree but did enable most of them to sleep through the services more deeply and soundly than they had all week. His flock was profoundly grateful, and church attendance was booming. The one-time angry young greasy-spoon diner bouncer was now looked upon with great respect by all of North Corners' townsfolk—except for the atheists, who thought the big, fat preacher was Satan incarnate.

Sitting next to the good reverend was Rapunzel Trashtrumpet, intrepid reporter for the local newspaper, *The North Corners Daily Poop*. Rapunzel was a scrawny, gangly string bean with a protruding beak-like nose and thick-framed eyeglasses, the lenses of which greatly magnified her eyeballs, giving her the appearance of a slightly crazed puffin sporting a beehive hairdo. She was famous for her outlandish clothing ensembles, one of which she wore today—an outfit so eclectically surreal and indescribable that the town's high-fashion mavens were offended to the point of deep slumber.

In her neophyte years as a young cub reporter, Rapunzel set out to make a name for herself in the journalistic world, and perhaps garner a coveted award in the process, by authoring a scathing series of exposés. She sought to unmask then-mayor Barley Doodlebody's covert efforts to manipulate North Corners politics and business through surreptitiously threatening to use any opponents of his policies and methods as packing material.

The young sleuthing scribe left no stone unturned in her relentless quest for the truth. Rapunzel's youthful zeal, idealism, and tenacity at revealing the shady mayor's connivance made her a continual annoyance. He was constantly forced to respond with "no comment" to her allegations of corruption, extortion, intimidation, and lack of personal character and integrity. Ultimately, however, the idealistic and energetic reporter was dissuaded from continuing her inflammatory series of articles by the formidable mayor himself, who surreptitiously threatened to use her as packing material.

That did the trick. Rapunzel Trashtrumpet, aspiring investigative journalist and journalism-award hopeful, contented herself thereafter with writing fluff pieces about nothing of import or significance (which was the main reason she was attending today's festivities), and using her column in the *Daily Poop* to spread uncorroborated gossip around town like cheap marmalade on stale toast.

She sat upon the stage, feverishly engrossed in scribbling notes on her ever-present pad of note paper, pausing occasionally to look up and peruse the crowd in search of the next character to assassinate.

Sitting next to Rapunzel was Lahloolah Snorgmark, a gigantic Scandinavian woman who worked as Barley Doodlebody's loyal assistant. Lahloolah wasn't her real name, of course, but rather a Scandinavian nickname which translated literally to mean "person whose choice of hairdo reveals a penchant for overcooked pasta." Her true name was unpronounceable by anyone on earth, including her parents.

Everyone knew her as "Noodles."

She was a proud descendant of Viking used-reindeer salesmen, and exuded an air of quiet self-assurance as she sat on the stage, clad in a huge pair of garage mechanic's overalls, bored and oblivious to everything going on.

Barley included Lahloolah in the proceedings with the intention of utilizing her to scare the crap out of anyone who might entertain the idea of causing trouble on this inaugural Bumps & Spuggett junket. Thus far, the plan was working; even her fellow VIPs quaked in fear whenever her vacuous gaze inadvertently fell upon them, except for Mimsy Borogove, who thought Noodles was a drag queen and viewed her as competition.

Eleven of the small town's most notable notables, all assembled before an ogling audience, were about to set off on a journey of diversion and discovery. *Anything* to relieve the incessant tedium and boredom of daily life in North Corners, Ohio.

Anything for a good laugh . . .

11

The dignitaries and the audience fidgeted and murmured, waiting for the ceremony to begin. Sensing the time had come to kick things off, Barley rose from his chair, approached the edge of the stage, and faced the audience, looking down upon them with a threatening grimace. Everyone ceased fidgeting. The room became as quiet as a catacomb.

Barley turned and whispered to Mayor Wubbleduster: "All right, get up here and say something to these idiots before I rip out your esophagus! And keep it short, you flatulent moron!"

The mayor blinked and nodded profusely, then rose from his chair and ambled to the podium. He leaned forward into the microphone and said, "Is this on?" receiving a jolt of electricity that barbequed his eyeballs. He collapsed onto the stage, smoking like a dormant volcano and babbling like a used-car salesman. The crowd applauded approvingly.

It was one of the mayor's better speeches.

Dr. Pudbid leaped out of his chair and bolted to where the mayor steamed like a kettle of bratwurst. Unfortunately, his eyeglasses sprang off the end of his nose, flying through the air and landing somewhere behind him. Without his glasses, the kindly old doctor was as blind as an indulgent mother with a delinquent son. (It was rumored that in an instance of misplaced spectacles, he'd once attempted to perform an emergency appendectomy on a refrigerator.) As he sprinted toward the incapacitated Mayor Wubbleduster, it became apparent that the old guy was making a beeline for the edge of the stage, about to plunge headlong into the audience.

"*Noodles*! Stop him!" Barley couldn't do without Dr. Pudbid on this trip. People were already dropping like flies, and the tour hadn't even started yet.

Noodles, who'd been sitting quietly in her seat, absentmindedly twirling a strand of Rapunzel Trashtrumpet's scraggly hair (much to the reporter's dismay), catapulted across the stage. Like a linebacker stopping a quarterback sneak at the goal line, Noodles brought the good doctor down hard, her momentum causing both of them to skid to a stop only inches from the lip of the stage.

Biff Spoozma was roused from yet another flirtation with forty winks by the loud sizzling ZAP of electricity that cooked his boss, and the loud THWUMP on the stage floorboards caused by Noodles thwarting the charge of Dr. Pudbid. The sleepy public relations advisor and personal bodyguard shook out of his stupor and darted past the sprawled bodies of Noodles and the doctor to where the stricken mayor lay. He grabbed a shock of the mayor's greasy dyed hair with one hand, the lapel of His Honor's suit coat with the other, and dragged the unfortunate first magistrate back to his appointed chair, hoisting him into the seat. Biff propped the pliant body into a sitting position and went back to his former post behind the chair, happy for some activity to keep him from dozing off again. It would probably be necessary to drag the mayor around like a sack of horse feed for the rest of the day, which would certainly aid his attempts to stay awake.

Noodles assisted the spluttering Dr. Pudbid to his feet, retrieved his glasses, re-perched them on the end of his nose, and guided him back to his seat. He slumped down and panted heavily. His white hair was now a mess, a crazed-yet-puzzled look contorted his wrinkled face, and Frog Puppleman and Mayor Wubbleduster, two unconscious would-be patients, reposed nearby, unattended.

Barley turned toward the back of the stage where Fifi Farglebarker, the audio technician, was cowering in terror. This was the same Fifi Farglebarker who'd been present as audio monitor on that fateful night of the last Piggford High Senior Prom and Vegetarian Intimidation Fest so many years before. After her own extended recovery period from the traumas inflicted upon her at that infamous event, the aspiring electronics "whiz kid" had gone on to a successful career as a professional amateur volunteer audio technician.

Much to Fifi's surprise, instead of a coarse rebuke for her technical failing, she received a broad smile and a thumbs-up! Barley was pleased that the ridiculous mayor was no longer a conscious presence in the prestigious entourage. He vowed to keep Fifi in mind the next time he needed to achieve similar results.

Fifi adjusted a few knobs and flicked a few switches on her audio console to correct the problem that had so electrified the mayor, then returned Barley's thumbs-up. Barley nodded and addressed the dignitaries:

"So, who's next here? Somebody'd better say something, and *now!*"

The VIPs looked at one another in dismay, reluctant to suffer a similar fate as His Honor the mayor. Biff Spoozma realized that as the only public relations advisor on the premises, it might behoove him to address the crowd on behalf of his indisposed boss. If there was ever a need for a quick PR intervention, it was now. However, as a nonconfrontational personality pathologically terrified of speaking before large groups despite his intimidating size, Biff decided instead to feign another sleep attack. Once again his eyes rolled back in his head, and with a snorting snore he keeled over backward, thudding onto the stage like a dead walrus. This time he stayed down, waiting for the storm to pass.

As a conscientious public relations advisor, Biff Spoozma made a better useless personal bodyguard.

Only Mimsy Borogove accepted the challenge, rising from her chair, placing Gaggy the poodle in Reverend Snortworthy's lap, and resolutely moving toward the microphone. She swished her feather boa as she sashayed across the stage, flashed a toothy smile at the audience, and ran her tongue suggestively over her heavily lipsticked lips.

Barley winced and covered his face with his hands. It was too late for Fifi Farglebarker to re-rig the microphone for another debilitating electric shock. Barley sat on the edge of his chair, anxious, ready to pounce upon her at the first sign of anything amiss.

Twirling her feather boa like a drunken stripper, Mimsy sidled up to the microphone. She grabbed the microphone stand, tilted it toward herself, and began to sing with a high-pitched, whiny voice that resulted in numerous blown-out eardrums and skull-splitting headaches. Just as Barley was about to spring from his chair and tackle the would-be chanteuse, little Margaret Wubbleduster emerged from the shadows and took care of the problem for him.

Before her father's accidental electrocution, Margaret had been sitting quietly next to the mayor. When Mimsy rose to take the mayor's place, Margaret's reaction was akin to that of an enraged bull having a red cape waved in its face by a taunting matador: *attack!* She'd found her next victim, and Mimsy was making it *too* easy.

With the agility of a tree-borne chimpanzee and the power of a pouncing panther, Margaret sprang from behind her inert father's body and traversed the short distance between herself and Mimsy in a flash. All pretense of shyness and anonymity vanished from her countenance, replaced by the animalistic tenacity of a predator who's found her prey and is ready to devour it. Before anyone in the assemblage could comprehend what was happening, Margaret fell upon the trashy socialite.

Caught in mid-warble and taken utterly by surprise, Mimsy was overwhelmed by her porky little assailant. Margaret wrestled Mimsy to the stage and maneuvered her onto her back, then pinned Mimsy's arms to her sides and against the floor while sitting astride her like a disoriented cowgirl riding an upside-down horse. Immobilized by Margaret's bulk, the struggling socialite screamed and wailed, to no avail. Margaret positioned her face directly over Mimsy's, leaving a foot of space between them, and the high-intensity voluminous expectoration began.

As the crowd's comprehension set in, muffled gasps, soon replaced by horrified screams and shouts, rolled through the audience in a wave of revulsion—although having to make a choice between *this* atrocity or Mimsy Borogove's renditions of Broadway's catchiest little numbers created a perplexing dilemma.

Margaret Wubbleduster's glorious center-stage moment came to an inglorious end when Barley Doodlebody finally came to his senses. He grabbed the HIVED-ing little demon by her pigtails (a decidedly unironic choice of hairstyle for someone who looked like Margaret), yanked her off Mimsy's prone body, and smacked a couple lengths of Fifi Farglebarker's gaffer's tape across the child's mouth to seal the sticky stream at its source. Noodles Snorgmark finished the job by wrapping more gaffer's tape around Margaret's wrists and taping them together as improvised handcuffs. Chief Bohoguss read the child her rights from his pocket perch in Barley's suit coat, sounding so darn cute with his squeaky little voice that everyone within earshot was smitten with renewed indulgent affection.

Noodles escorted a shaken Mimsy back to her seat and offered the stricken socialite a deerskin chamois she had tucked into her overalls so Mimsy could wipe off the residual spittle from the viscous HIVED-ing. The crowd began to quiet down, and Margaret became much more subdued in her comportment, much like an angry alligator that's been flipped onto its back and is having its belly rubbed.

Barley took stock of the situation as it now stood. Judging by the way this whole opening-ceremony thing had progressed so far, it was probably high time to get the show on the road, quite literally.

"All right, beet-heads," he whispered to the individuals on the stage, "we're gonna head to the bus and get out of here!"

Then, addressing the audience: "Okay, it's over. You can all go home—*now!*"

The audience and tour group rose from their seats in the Mystic Knights of the Heavenly Daze Hall, moving like a flock of half-asleep sheep toward the exits and the waiting tour bus. Chief Bohoguss made unnoticed attempts to direct the flow of traffic from Barley's coat pocket.

Once outside, the crowd fanned out into a semicircle on the sidewalk while the parade of local dignitaries made its way to the curb where the tour bus had been parked. Included in the group once more was City Councilman Frog Puppleman, who'd regained consciousness and was wobbling unsteadily along with his fellow tour group members, as well as the *un*conscious Mayor Roymul Wubbleduster, trundled and transported like a sack of seed via the brawny back of a wide-awake public relations advisor and personal bodyguard, Biff Spoozma.

Margaret Wubbleduster, now docile and securely bound with gaffer's tape, looked like a small waddling sausage on a leash as she shuffled along, accompanied by Barley's assistant, Lahloolah Snorgmark. Noodles watched the child protectively like a mama sow guarding her piglet, shepherding her charge through the crowd.

Barley gazed around at the spectators and well-wishers, silently cursing himself for not having charged an admission fee to get into the hall. He'd just have to make up that lost-cash deficit once the tour got underway.

"All right, everybody, listen up! Here's how it's gonna go: I want you all to line up in single file and get on that bus, find a seat, and sit your butts down. We've got a lot of stuff to see and do today, and I don't want anything or anybody to mess it up! If anyone in the group has a problem with the tour, do not hesitate to discuss your feelings with me. I will take care of you—and I will take care of you *quickly*! But I can guarantee you this: you're all gonna have a good time!"

This last statement was delivered more as a threat than a "guarantee."

At the conclusion of Barley's instructions, the tour group participants formed a single line, preparing to climb aboard the tour bus. It was at this moment that Spiffany Tonguehoister, or "Queen Spiff" as she'd become known around North Corners, came rumbling up the street in her Sherman tank on a routine "vigilance patrol."

Spying the huge crowd assembled on the sidewalk, the tour bus parked at the curb, and the gaily festooned exterior of the Mystic Knights of the Heavenly Daze Hall, the crown-bedecked queen correctly surmised that some type of gala event was taking place and brought her tank to a halt in front of the building. She was perturbed that as the town's reigning monarch, she had not been invited to attend this prestigious and auspicious occasion. However, determined not to appear petty or petulant in front of her assembled subjects, she decided to fire off a celebratory round from the tank's cannon in a spirit of goodwill.

Spiffany had learned her lesson from previous tragic episodes in which she'd discharged the big gun within the city limits and accidentally destroyed numerous dwellings and business structures. This time, she made sure to elevate the cannon, pointing its huge muzzle skyward so the fired shell's trajectory would take it up, away, and out of town to land harmlessly somewhere in the countryside.

BOOOOOOOOOM!

The big gun roared, spitting flame like a belching dragon; the ground trembled and rumbled with earthquake intensity and apocalyptic fury. The percussive shock wave blew out all the windows of the tour bus and most of the other buildings in the vicinity, shook walls, shattered flowerpots, and temporarily deafened everyone within three city blocks. Fortunately, Queen Spiff's precautionary measure had paid off: no physical structures were destroyed—not *totally*, anyway.

The terrified dignitaries and the crowd on the sidewalk reflexively hit the ground, screaming and shrieking hysterically, momentarily convinced they'd entered a time warp and were in the midst of World War II. Once the eardrum-bursting sound of the cannon faded, the dust settled, and they realized they weren't going to die on the street, the chaos and terror subsided. Everyone picked themselves up from wherever it was they'd hastily sprawled, smacked their heads repeatedly in an attempt to quell the ringing in their ears, brushed off their dusty clothes, picked shards of broken glass out of their hair and teeth, and endeavored mightily to rekindle the sparks of their previous merriment. Thankfully, there were no serious injuries other than a minor blow to the dignity of the dignitaries and a few scuffs and scrapes among the spectators—certainly not enough to complain to Barley about without running the greater risk of ending up as packing material.

Barley extricated himself from the nearby rosebush he'd leaped into after Queen Spiff's booming one-gun salute, plucking out the thorns imbedded in his flesh. He pulled a trembling Chief Binky from the pocket of his suit and held the little guy up to see if he'd been squished or impaled. Ascertaining that the tiny chief of police was only a bit shaken up, he shot Queen Spiff a look that would have melted a freezer full of icicles, but judiciously remained silent. Angry as Barley was, the delusional queen was still sitting up in her tank turret behind the big cannon, perplexed, dismayed, and disoriented—but still fully capable of aiming and firing that infernal gun.

The process of loading the now windowless tour bus recommenced. One by one, the tour participants filed aboard, brushed off the fragments of window glass littering the seats, and sat down. The crowd on the sidewalk resumed its cheering and waving, spirits rising once more, the anticipation again extreme.

"Okay, Chumbuckets," said Barley to bus driver Roland Chumbuckets. "Get this bus moving before that nutball in the tank has a chance to reload!"

The engine sputtered to life. With a choking cough of black smoke, the bus lurched forward, narrowly missing several old ladies who'd been standing on the curb, holding *Good Luck!* signs.

The inaugural run of the Bumps & Spuggett Office tour was underway.

12

The first portion of the day's activities would consist of a mini-tour of local points of interest in and around North Corners, the points of interest having been determined by Barley himself, based entirely upon the fact that he owned and operated all of them. The unsuspecting tourists were about to become his next paying customers.

At this moment his patrons were simply enjoying the ride through town, oohing and aahing at the sights beyond the shattered windows of the bus, completely disregarding the fact that this was their hometown and they'd seen these very same sights every day for years. Desperate as they were to be entertained, when driver Roland Chumbuckets became confused and wound up circling the same city block four times in succession, the happy tourists continued to soak up the scenery and enjoy the trip as if they were seeing it all for the first time—and it probably *was* the first time they'd seen that same city block four times in succession.

Stop number one on today's itinerary would be Granny Mambo's Liverland, an eatery normally shunned by the populace of North Corners because the cuisine served there was slightly less appetizing than truck polish. Barley had gained a total monopoly in the liver market in North Corners because most meat packers and butchers in the area couldn't get rid of the stuff and happily gave it to him free of charge if he would get it off their premises.

Barley had done so willingly, believing that in the hands of an imaginative and competent chef, liver dishes could rival anything served in five-star restaurants anywhere in the world. Sadly, Barley hadn't been able to locate or recruit any imaginative and competent chefs willing to exercise their culinary creativity by working exclusively with liver. He'd been forced to settle for the services of Granny Mambo, a toothless old woman from the hill country of an isolated, little-known island somewhere in the Caribbean.

Granny Mambo continuously clutched an old corncob pipe in her toothless gums, reeked of home-distilled rum, spoke with a thick accent that was almost unintelligible, and was reputed to have been a witch priestess on her home island, where she used the internal organs of various unfortunate creatures in her rituals and ceremonies. Because of this witchly skill, she was adept at concocting recipes featuring liver (or any other internal organs) that wouldn't kill the consumer—unless she wanted them to.

After what seemed an eternity of twists, wrong turns, dead ends, and near-fatal collisions with eighteen-wheelers going the wrong way down one-way streets, the tour bus finally reached this first destination. Granny Mambo herself was waiting on the sidewalk with open arms and a toothless grin on her withered face. Once the bus lurched to a stop, Barley stood and addressed the group:

"All right, now listen up! We're gonna get off the bus and go inside for something to eat. Anyone who doesn't spend at least fifty dollars on food will be taken out to the alley and executed. To ensure this does not happen, I will collect the fifty dollars from each of you as you get off the bus. The terms and conditions in the contract you all signed before the trip stipulate that you must do this; therefore, anyone who dishonors the contract is in violation of the agreement, and I have the legal right to correct the situation by blowing your head off."

There was some confusion as to whether execution was a legitimate form of legal recourse in the matter, but no one was prepared to find out by dishonoring the contract. Indeed, no one actually recalled seeing a contract prior to the trip; all they remembered was that the tour ticket itself had cost seven hundred dollars, extracted from them by Barley with the veiled promise that noncompliance might result in their accidentally being turned into packing material. Maybe they had just been too unnerved by Barley's presence to remember having signed a contract—it *could* have happened . . . maybe . . . so everyone nodded in acquiescence.

At any rate, having missed breakfast that morning, everyone was a little hungry, and Granny Mambo's Liverland was a dining establishment heretofore unknown to this particular group. Their collective spirit of adventure was high, their collective appetite was sufficiently whetted, Barley's ominous threat was enough to persuade them to give the place a try—and they had no other choice.

Each of the passengers filed off the bus, receiving scrutinizing stares from Barley as they remitted their fifty dollars to him. Granny greeted each of her new patrons with a welcoming hug and a hearty, "You got to come *een*side an' eat 'em up, whydonchanow!" and sprinkled some kind of juju water on their heads as they walked through the door. She paid particular attention to Gaggy, Mimsy Borogove's quivering toy poodle, licking her lips hungrily as Mimsy scooted past on her way inside.

Throughout the chaotic bus ride, Rapunzel Trashtrumpet had been scribbling on her pad of paper, noting significant and pertinent points to be used later when writing her report of the trip for *The Daily Poop*. As she stepped off of the bus, Barley accosted her and smiled.

"Enjoy yourself, Trashtrumpet! Your visit today is gonna put this place on the map. I'm *confident* of that."

Of course, the only thing Barley was truly confident of was that his whispered remark would make its point and Rapunzel would write a glowing review of the place—if she knew what was good for her (and it certainly wouldn't be the food).

Rapunzel goggled at Barley from behind her mammoth glasses, handed over her fifty bucks, and continued with trepidation toward the doorway and the welcoming Granny Mambo. *Well, if the food is as good as Granny Mambo is friendly, maybe the ordeal won't be so bad.*

Yes, and maybe having a tooth extracted with a backhoe wouldn't be so bad either . . .

As rotund Reverend Snortworthy stepped off the bus, paid his dues to Barley, and approached Granny Mambo, the old lady bristled.

"Ah, da vicah from da chuch comin' in heah! We don' wan' no *preachin'* in dis place, mon! You jes' eat, you heah? Look like you do plenny o' *dat*!"

Not sure what to make of Granny Mambo (or exactly what she'd said), the reverend marched past the wary priestess chef, into the building. He glanced back over his shoulder at her just as the old woman gave him a healthy spray of juju water, which soaked the top of his balding head and trickled down his face and neck and under his frock collar.

The preacher whirled around, wiping the trickling juju water from his face with his sleeve.

"Madam, I am *not* Catholic!"

"Dis ain' no Cat'lic wahtah!" Her fiery eyes bored through him. "You get yo'sef' *een*side, whydonchanow!"

The reverend defiantly flicked a water droplet from the end of his nose, mustered his dignity, and marched into the darkened recesses of the restaurant. He wasn't quite sure what had just transpired, but was quite certain he wouldn't be seeing Granny Mambo in his church this Sunday.

Biff Spoozma was next, laboriously trundling Mayor Wubbleduster over his shoulder. As he passed Granny Mambo, she cackled stridently.

"Ya don't nahmally see 'em like dat 'til dey comes *outa* da place!"

This comment was extremely unsettling to those prospective diners within earshot.

Bringing up the rear of the procession was Lahloolah Snorgmark with her two charges, Margaret Wubbleduster—bound, gagged, and on a leash—and tiny Chief Bohoguss, perched on Noodles's shoulder like a pirate's parrot.

Spotting the little chief, Granny remarked, "Eh, woncha look at da cute leetle dolly police-mon now! Don't have no plate, no silvahware dat tiny fo' da little guy, but he gonna make a tasty bite his'self you fix 'im up!"

Binky shrieked and scrambled higher up Noodles's shoulder, trying to hide within the spaghetti-like strands of her disheveled hair.

And regarding little trussed-up Margaret: "Now *deah's* a juicy one! Look like she's ready to cook, you bringin' da chile in heah all wrapped up like dat."

Little Margaret's eyes shot flame, but constricted as she was by her gaffer's tape bindings, Granny was unknowingly saved from a fate worse than death.

Noodles hastened to get both of her charges into the restaurant and away from Granny Mambo before Chief Binky could be devoured or little Margaret unleashed.

Once the tour group reassembled inside the restaurant and found seats at the tables, they had their first opportunity to examine the features of the establishment's rather unusual interior decor—a motif that could aptly be described as "island pagan minimalist." The atmosphere and ambiance gave one the impression of being outdoors in the dead of night: No windows or lamplight illuminated the room. Instead, the interior was lit by several flickering torches placed in holders on the walls. There were no decorative pictures, paintings, or artwork of any kind. A large bonfire blazed in one corner, the smoke rising through a hole in the ceiling. The floor was compacted earth.

Granny Mambo, her toothless, welcoming smile and the old, tobacco-stained corncob pipe now replaced by a somber scowl, entered the room, closed the front door behind her, and stood in the corner near the bonfire, perusing her new clientele, her countenance bathed eerily in the shifting glow of the flames. She clapped her hands loudly; a recording of Caribbean drum music began playing over the restaurant's sound system while a trio of zombie-like young men from the same Caribbean island as their chef boss shuffled into the room, carrying trays piled high with plates containing brownish-gray slabs of steaming liver and pitchers full of a mysterious greenish liquid—nothing else. No first-course salads, no side dishes, no garnishes.

The zombie waiters fanned out around the room and lethargically distributed the liver and the liquid to the diners, each table receiving one heaping tray of liver slabs and one pitcher of greenish liquid to be shared accordingly. The tourists had no choice but to eat the simple, unadorned fare given to them, like it or not. There'd be no ordering from menus today.

Granny Mambo began a low, throaty monotone chant, dancing slowly in a small circle in the corner in front of the fire, sprinkling her juju water everywhere, and generally behaving as if the group in the restaurant didn't exist. The tempo and volume of the drums intensified and increased gradually, and her dancing movements became more wildly animated; it appeared she was entering a trancelike state as she leaped and bounced to the pounding pulse.

Her voice changed as well, progressively rising in pitch from the low monotone to a mournful, wailing chant, escalating in volume along with the thudding accompaniment. The tourists stared at the flailing Granny Mambo, wide eyed and filled with foreboding, their former healthy appetites abandoning them completely.

Mimsy Borogove joined in with Granny's chanting chorus, raising both arms over her head, throwing back her blue-dyed hair, and shimmying like a drug-whacked hippie. Gaggy the poodle cowered in Mimsy's lap, quaking and quivering in a superb canine impression of Jiggly Luckybeans, his little poodle eyeballs bulging out of his head like two oversized lightbulbs. Gaggy added his own yowling whine to the chorus, as if responding to the shrieking siren of a fire truck.

Seated at a table near the bonfire, Frog Puppleman was thoroughly enjoying himself. He rocked back and forth in time to the beat of the drums, clapping his hands and shouting, "Yeah, *buddy!*" when the shrill vocalizations of Granny, Mimsy, or Gaggy produced an occasional shriek.

Frog's rocking motions became more pronounced as the two women and the dog's caterwauling increased in excitement, until he toppled over in his chair. In one fluid sequence of motions, he conked his head on the hard dirt floor and sprawled head-over-heels in a backward somersault, coming to rest in an unconscious heap dangerously near the crackling bonfire in the corner.

Since Frog had been audacious enough to inject his presence into her dancing space, Granny Mambo began a wild boogie-bop, circling his prone body and liberally soaking him with juju water, interspersing her wailing and chanting with gleeful cackles. Dr. Pudbid and Noodles rose to assist Frog, but a gesture from Barley stopped them in their tracks. He was quite content to sit back and see what Granny intended to do with his idiotic nuisance of a half brother. Noodles and Dr. Pudbid retreated to their seats, and Barley edged forward in his, breathlessly anticipating the horror to come.

The drums pounded furiously. Granny Mambo towered over Frog Puppleman. Her eyes rolled back in her head, and her body shook violently, as if she were experiencing an ecstasy-induced seizure. The zombie waiters also responded to the hypnotic rhythm and Granny Mambo's chanting dance, becoming more animated, ominous, threatening, and decidedly *less* zombie-like as they completed their distribution of the plates of liver to each table. Now, with frightening grimaces spread across their craggy, fire-lit faces, they turned their attention to Granny, the bonfire, and the unconscious Frog Puppleman. The raging bonfire's glow cast groping, grasping fingers of light and shadow across the ceiling, the restaurant's interior, and the faces of the terrified tourist diners.

Reverend Snortworthy watched the scenario unfold in disbelief. Never in his life had he seen anything like this! Never in his life had he witnessed such a surreal display of heathen ritual!

"*Desist*! Desist, I say, with this outrageous display of blatant heathenism and effrontery!"

Through the deafening noise, all anybody heard was "*Ooo!—Ay!—Eeee!—Oop!—Beep!—Doot!—Deet!*"

There was no response from Granny Mambo and her waiters, or from any of the tourist diners around him. Undaunted, the reverend gesticulated wildly toward Frog Puppleman and cried out again: "Away, pagan she-demon! Ye shall not lay a hand upon nor defile this unfortunate soul with your evil rantings, writhings, and corrupting spells!"

All anybody heard was "*Ayk!—Gook!—Onk!—Goink!—Baap!—Eek!—Ott!*"

Seeing that his warnings were having no effect, Reverend Snortworthy heaved a sigh of resignation and sat down. He'd given it his best shot.

The scene became more ominous with each passing minute. Barley had insisted they each consume fifty dollars' worth in food or be executed forthwith, and it was becoming apparent that Frog Puppleman was in prime position to become the next source for Granny Mambo's internal-organ pantry if they didn't consume quickly and get out of there.

The tour group wolfed down liver as if their lives depended upon it—as indeed they probably did—choking it or washing it down with the aid of the mysterious greenish liquid, which tasted like recycled sheep dip (but not as flavorful).

Barley felt a twinge of guilt. Ever since their childhood, Barley had willingly taken upon himself the continued maintenance of feeble-minded Frog's well-being; he realized that Frog's being ritually devoured in a cannibalistic orgy on the floor of his own dining establishment was a cruel fate that even a nincompoop like his half brother didn't deserve.

The impassioned chanting and wailing of Granny Mambo and her waiters and the hideous yowling and yelping of Mimsy Borogove and Gaggy the poodle reached a roaring crescendo. Panic and fear were spreading through the group—not exactly a public relations bonanza for a brand-new business venture—and there were far too many witnesses here should things start getting homicidal. Barley needed to call a halt to this before these Caribbean crazies pulled a stunt that would spoil everything, like eating Frog Puppleman or asking Mimsy Borogove to come up and do a solo.

Reaching into the interior pocket of his suit coat, Barley located a silver police whistle. He took a deep breath and blew it with all his might. TWEEEEEEEET! The shrill sound cut through the wailing and the rumbling drums like a hot knife through a big block of lard at room temperature.

The feasting tourists, who were in a closer proximity to Barley than the dancers, paused in their frenzied gorging to determine what this new sound might be. They looked up in terror, some with half-devoured slabs of liver hanging out of their mouths like long grayish tongues, others with their gullets so packed full of the stuff that they resembled foraging squirrels attempting to store basketballs in their cheeks.

The dancing in the front of the room continued unabated. Granny Mambo and her waiters were far too involved with the unconscious Frog Puppleman and the performance of their ritual to hear or notice what was going on behind them.

Barley clenched the police whistle in his teeth and blew it again. TWEEEEEEEET! This time the tourists were able to pinpoint Barley as its source. They stopped their frantic chewing and looked at him questioningly. He shouted over the loud pounding of the drums:

"Okay, that's enough of this! We're getting out of here now—everybody back on the bus!"

The tourists couldn't believe their ears! Had they heard correctly? They continued staring, unsure of what to do.

Barley realized he'd not yet made his point. He gave his police whistle another blast—TWEEEEEEEET! This time, even Granny Mambo heard the whistle, paused in mid-gyration, and turned to see what the commotion was about.

"I *said* we're leaving now, so everybody get out of here and get back on the bus! Now! *Go!*"

A rush of relief and deep gratitude welled up inside each of the tourists. Barley Doodlebody was a saint, and they were his children.

They spit out whatever unchewed liver remained in their mouths, gathered what personal items they'd brought with them, and leaped up from their chairs to bolt as one for the front door. Chairs, tables, and bodies went flying willy-nilly as the stampede of tourist dignitaries beat a hasty and decidedly undignified retreat to the street.

Rapunzel Trashtrumpet, seated nearest the exit, stood and lit for the door like a skinny, bespectacled zebra with a geriatric lion on its tail—the "lion" being Dr. Pudbid. Like Rapunzel, he flew out of his chair as soon as he comprehended Barley's command to leave, having personally consumed more liver at this sitting than he had in all the days of his long life combined.

Their separate paths merged at the front door of the restaurant. They smacked into one another like two sumo wrestlers, bounced back a couple of feet, simultaneously hurled themselves at the door a second time, and collided again, once more bouncing backward from the impact. This process was repeated yet a third time with the same result. At the fourth attempt, Dr. Pudbid, becoming suddenly chivalrous, stood back while Rapunzel hurled herself at the door with all her weight and might. Meeting no resistance this time, the reporter whizzed past Dr. Pudbid and barreled headlong through the front door into the sunlight, shrieking at the top of her lungs, staggering and flailing her arms to catch her balance. She shot across the sidewalk and slammed head-first into the side of the parked tour bus—CONK!—collapsing in a dazed heap at the curb.

Granny Mambo signaled for the recorded drum music to be turned off and screamed plaintively at Barley: "Mistah Doodlebody, sah! Wheah dey *goin'*?! Wheah all da people goin'?! We just gettin' to da *good* paht!"

"We're gettin' outa here! Before you and your lunatic bunch of weirdos kills anyone!"

Granny stared incredulously at Barley. "*Kills* anyone?? We not gonna *kill* anyone, sah! Dis is da *flaw show*! We jest givin' da people some enna-*tain*-ment while dey's *eatin'*!"

Barley stared incredulously back at Granny Mambo. *Floor show?* Did she just say that this whole creepy episode was her version of *entertainment?*

"Whatever it is, it's *over*! You people scared the crap out of everyone in this group with your mumbo-jumbo, and I'm getting them out of here before any more trouble starts!"

Catching himself, he thought for a few seconds. *There's potential here . . .*

"Save the floor show for the *next* group!" He smirked, giving his priestess chef a conspiratorial wink. Maybe between now and the visit of his next group of tourists he could figure out a way to turn this into a money-making proposition.

Unmollified, Granny Mambo stamped and stammered in futile protest. Her zombie waiters stared helplessly as Barley supervised the mass exit of his tour group from the restaurant.

Frog Puppleman regained consciousness on the floor by the bonfire. He was on his back, the searing heat of the bonfire so close that it singed his hair. He gazed up at the patterns of flame undulating on the ceiling, blinking to clear his vision and his head, and came to the conclusion that he was in hell.

As Frog deliberated his fate and how it had come to this, Barley reached down, grabbed him by the lapels of his coat, and jerked him roughly to his feet. Standing on two legs again, Frog blinked at Barley, grateful that his big brother had saved him from the cruel fires of Hades.

"Yeah, buddy!"

Barley brushed the dirt and ash from his brother's coat, straightened and tightened the knot of Frog's necktie, and marveled at how his half-wit sibling could endure two bouts of unconsciousness in less than an hour yet not be one iota stupider. He spotted a very queasy-looking Noodles Snorgmark coming toward him, escorting little Margaret Wubbleduster on her leash. He beckoned his assistant to him.

"Noodles, see to it that Councilman Frog gets back on the bus without hurting himself, okay?" He glanced around for any stragglers left in the room. "Where's Chief Bohoguss?"

Noodles suddenly realized that during all the commotion and frenzied feasting, she had somehow misplaced the tiny chief of police! Little Binky had been sitting on an overturned water glass at the table with Margaret and her when the hideous feast began—but where was the little guy now?

She looked back to the table that Margaret, Binky, and she had been sharing. The tiny chief was floundering frantically in an almost-empty pitcher of the mysterious green liquid. Since there were no drinking glasses in the restaurant tiny enough for him to use, the little guy had been forced to climb to the pitcher rim and lean down inside of it to get a drink. He'd leaned over too far, lost his balance, plunged in, and was unable to escape. He splashed, slipped, and sloshed around in the green beverage, vainly trying to put together enough traction to get a grip or foothold on the slippery pitcher and pull himself out before he drowned.

Noodles gasped and rushed to the table, pulling him out by one foot and lifting him over her head where he dangled dripping wet and upside down. The little chief appeared to be none the worse for wear despite being soaked through with the sticky green liquid—and not too happy about it.

Noodles grabbed a napkin and set wet little Binky gently down on the tabletop, wrapping him up like an itty-bitty Egyptian mummy until the only portion of the chief still visible was his little face. It was just *too* cute.

She picked him up in one hand, clutched Margaret Wubbleduster's leash with the other, and marched them back to where Barley stood with the dazed Frog Puppleman.

"I'll keep Chief Bohoguss with me, Noodles. You can hang on to Councilman Frog and the kid. Hurry up and get them out of here!"

His loyal assistant handed the mushy tidbit that was Binky Bohoguss over to Barley, grabbed Frog by the hand, tugged on Margaret's leash to get her attention, and headed for the front door.

Barley unwrapped Binky so the little guy's head, hands, and arms were free of the constricting napkin and tucked him back into his usual hiding place in the breast pocket of his suit coat. Despite the crackling bonfire nearby, Binky shivered from the cold of his soaked uniform, curling up like a fetus in the bottom of Barley's pocket to keep warm.

Biff Spoozma shuffled past, dutifully trundling Mayor Wubbleduster over his brawny shoulder. The mayor had been unaware of the liver gorgefest, but Big Biff had devoured enough of the stuff to choke a famished moose. His complexion was a deathly green, nearly matching the color of the strange beverage he had quaffed by the pitcher. Biff cast Barley an anguished look as he passed by, fighting to suppress the convulsive reflexes his gut was experiencing every few seconds.

Realizing the show was over, Mimsy hoisted Gaggy into her arms, slobbered a rush of disgusting baby talk over the pooch, and joined the rest of her fellow tourists as they exited the premises. As she passed the bonfire, she stopped and matter-of-factly asked the distraught Granny Mambo if she and her boys were available to entertain at the next debutante ball and rummage sale. Granny let out an anguished cry and beat her breast in misery. Mimsy took this response to be a yes. The society belle smiled benignly, licked her teeth and lips suggestively at the waiters, said "We'll be in touch!" and flashed Barley a satisfied smile before waltzing serenely out of the building.

Barley took one last reconnoiter around the room and saw that all of his tourists had made it out the door.

Except one.

Having turned his attention from the pagan ritual dancing to the food in front of him, Reverend Snortworthy was oblivious to the fact that everyone else had left the premises. He was thoroughly enjoying himself, sitting alone at the table, shoveling huge bites of grayish-brown liver into his mouth and smacking his lips with unmitigated pleasure, then wiping his face on the sleeve of his frock.

Barley watched, stupefied, as the voluminous cleric mowed through plate after plate of liver, using his fork to spear the unfinished portions of his now absent tablemates' meals, downing them as well! He guzzled the mysterious green liquid directly from the pitcher, burped, and dove back into the repast. The ravenous reverend had the capacity to consume well over fifty dollars' worth of this stuff!

"Okay, Reverend, finish up! We're leaving now!"

Reverend Snortworthy stared at Barley with a vacant expression on his face, took his fork, and snagged a slab of liver off another absent diner's plate. His reply was a mushy-mouthed, "*Mmmmmm*, this is really *good!*" This was not the same Mafumbus Snortworthy who only moments earlier had threatened to wreak divine retribution upon Granny Mambo and her crew. Apparently the corpulent cleric's appetite for saving souls had been outmatched by his appetite for Granny Mambo's liver.

"Let's go, Reverend! The bus is leaving, and you're gonna be on it!"

Massive Mafumbus continued to wolf down the liver as if his food-consumption switch were stuck in the "decimate" position. Barley's patience was at an end. He recalled the days when Reverend Snortworthy worked for him as a bouncer at Hose Monster and dropped all pretense of respect and decorum. He leaned down, his face inches from the reverend's.

"All right, you fat, slobbering, sanctimonious soot-bag! Either you get your flabby butt back on that bus right now, or I'm gonna let Granny Mambo shrink your head to the size of a pea!"

That did the trick! The reverend immediately dropped his fork and leaped to his feet like someone who'd just sat on a porcupine, screamed, and dashed toward the door.

As he passed Granny Mambo by the bonfire, Granny recognized that the vicar she'd confronted earlier had subsequently become her most ardent diner.

"You likin' da leevah—I saw dat! Long as you don't go doin' no preachin' in heah, you come back an' see Granny anytime, whydonchanow!" She gave the escaping reverend one last spritz of her juju water.

The reverend shrieked, "*Get thee behind me*," his mind beset with the image of what he'd look like with a pea head perched between his shoulders. He smashed through the front door like a wrecking ball and disappeared into the harsh sunlight.

Barley surveyed the scene. No one had been killed, injured, or turned into a marsupial—the tour would continue.

Turning once more to Granny Mambo (who had taken some solace from the fact that at least *one* of her customers had enjoyed his meal), Barley suggested that in future visits by his tour groups she explain to the tourists—*before the drumming and dancing started*—that all the ritual stuff was just an act, thereby sparing herself a repeat of the panicky picnic that had just transpired.

Granny had to agree. Maybe her reenactment of the "Kill and Eat All Enemies" ceremony *was* a bit much. She'd take Barley's advice. Besides, Barley was the boss; thanks to his patronage, she and her boys had no further need of performing *actual* pagan ceremonies to earn their livings.

Barley gave the island crazies a nod and checked his pocket to see if Chief Bohoguss was okay. The little imp was freezing his diminutive butt off in his damp clothes, his teensy teeth chattering so rapidly that even Barley thought Binky was the cutest thing he'd ever seen. He patted the chief of police on his tiny damp head, bid the restaurant's chef and staff a cursory "Good morning!" and walked out through the smashed front door to gather his group and resume the tour.

13

While the tourists were in Granny Mambo's Liverland, bus driver Roland Chumbuckets remained on his bus and swept up the shards of glass. Once finished with that chore, he sat drowsily in his driver's seat, legs crossed and elevated, heels resting on the dashboard, his hat pulled forward on his head so his eyes were covered. A feeling of peaceful tranquility settled upon him, spreading like a warm glow throughout his body. His eyelids drooped as slumber nestled into his brain . . .

Suddenly, the terrified gaggle of tourists gushed forth from the restaurant and into the open air and sunshine, gasping, moaning, and clutching at their abdomens. Roland hastily attempted to pull himself together.

Rapunzel Trashtrumpet was the first to emerge. She shot across the sidewalk, screaming bloody murder, arms windmilling, and rammed headfirst into the bus, caroming off the side like a cue ball. She staggered and collapsed to the sidewalk in a sitting position, a sickly greenish cast to her complexion. Clutching her throbbing head, gagging convulsively, and mumbling something that sounded vaguely like "Blup ulk hulf-hulf-hulf!" she looked up at Roland plaintively as he peered at her from the driver's seat, her stomach making incredibly loud growling-roaring-gurgling noises evocative of a drunken rhinoceros with its head caught in a punch press. Roland recoiled in horror.

Dr. Pudbid was right behind Rapunzel. He saw her take on the tour bus single-handedly with the top of her head (and lose) and hastened to assist her. Having ingested kilos of Granny Mambo's solo culinary creation himself, he suddenly stopped in his tracks, clutched at his liver-overloaded stomach, and sat alongside Rapunzel on the sidewalk, succumbing to the same overpowering illness. He wailed in gastrointestinal harmony with the reporter, both of them sounding like howling wolves auditioning for a dinner theater production of *Dueling Duodenums*.

The other tourists soon joined Rapunzel and the doctor for a spontaneous hootenanny of sidewalk-situated sickness. When Barley came out, he was confronted with multiple moaning, groaning, nearly nuggmucked victims of panic-induced liver overconsumption. Even little Chief Binky was waging battle with overwhelming nausea, his upper body hanging halfway out of Barley's suit pocket, his tiny face contorted with distress.

Barley felt perfectly fine. He hadn't eaten a bite, nor had he ventured anywhere near the mysterious green liquid in the pitchers, but he knew that lingering at Granny Mambo's Liverland would exacerbate an already uncomfortable situation. Wisdom dictated that he press forward without delay. "All right, everybody, listen up!"

Preoccupied with their own suffering, the tourists did not respond.

"Listen up, people, we're gonna leave now!" He reached into his pocket, produced the silver police whistle, gripped it between his teeth, and blew with everything he had. TWEEEEEEEET! The shriek grabbed their immediate attention and threatened to implode their already aching skulls.

Chief Bohoguss, desperate to take his mind off his agony, blew his own police whistle, a teeny-tiny one that produced a high-frequency sound inaudible to any human ear. Only Gaggy the poodle could hear it, driving the poor creature totally out of his mind. The terrified pooch scrambled out of Mimsy's grasp and bolted down the street like a fuzzy, sweater-clad rocket, yipping and yelping hideously, his high-pitched squeals fading as he ran into the distance, never to be seen again.

Mimsy became hysterical, weeping, whining, and warbling inconsolably (which, interestingly enough, didn't sound any worse than her vocal performance inside the restaurant). This set off a new bout of agonized moaning and groaning by the rest of the group, who now had to contend with Mimsy's pitiful lamentations along with their own physical discomfort.

Barley was beside himself. Just when he thought he'd finally gotten a handle on the situation, all hell had broken loose! He had to shut up that crazy blue-haired buzzard before she drove him and everybody else completely nuts. Receiving a sudden burst of inspiration, he reached into the breast pocket of his suit and extracted the soggy little chief of police, holding him in front of the distraught diva's nose. "Mimsy, if you'll settle down and shut up, I just might give you *this* to replace your stupid little dog!"

That did the trick. Mimsy ceased her lamentations, giving Chief

Bohoguss such a lustful leer that the little imp's blood froze in his veins.

"Good girl! Now, get back on that bus and settle down! You'll receive your reward *after* the tour is over."

Mimsy nodded, gave Binky one more soul-searing, lustful leer, and walked regally to the tour bus, proceeding obediently to her assigned seat. Gaggy the poodle was now a distant memory, replaced by the anticipation of acquiring Binky as her new "pet" and knitting him his own little sweater.

With the harrowing task of placating Mimsy Borogove accomplished, Barley stuffed the terrified Chief Bohoguss into his suit pocket. The little guy sighed with relief, but the idea of being awarded to Mimsy Borogove gnawed at him. *Mr. Doodlebody was only kidding . . . wasn't he?*

Barley was sure about one thing: he had to get this sickly group of tourists on their way to the next destination, to get their minds off their maladies as soon as possible, before Granny and her boys decided they weren't pleased with the floor show's bad reviews and retaliated by placing *real* curses on them—or worse, fixing them lunch.

"All right, quickly now! We've gotta get going before Granny Mambo comes out here and gives you all doggie bags to take with you! Everybody back on the bus!"

The tourists grabbed their bellies, put hands over their mouths, and waddled back to the bus, pushing and shoving up the stairs and past the incredulous Roland Chumbuckets (who was still mystified as to what horrors had transpired behind the restaurant's closed doors).

As they departed Granny Mambo's Liverland, the majority of the passengers no longer felt the need to withhold the inevitable. They leaned out of the blown-out windows, engaged in surprisingly well-coordinated ensemble vomiting, and ingloriously ridded themselves of their hastily consumed liver breakfasts in a manner unbefitting their exalted status in the community. The exception was Chief Bohoguss, who was cute as a button as he scrambled out of Barley's pocket, hung himself out of a window, and contributed his own tiny stream of vomit onto the side of the bus.

Barley quietly ruminated on the progress of this inaugural Bumps & Spuggett tour. He had to admit (though only to himself) that even *he* wasn't particularly enjoying the trip, and he was the one making all the money!

The ultimate destination of the tour, the Bumps & Spuggett firm, was guaranteed to provide enough laughter, ridiculous behavior, and stimulating diversionary entertainment to overcome the discomforts and inconveniences the group had endured. However, Barley knew the group's word-of-mouth descriptions and evaluations after their return from the outing would be instrumental in determining his enterprise's subsequent success or failure. Only a psychotic masochist would have enjoyed himself so far, and at this late date, finding a psychotic masochist—much less a whole busload of them—was out of the question.

What should he do about these bedraggled and abused witnesses to the failure of his surefire vision? The tales of horror they'd undoubtedly tell (especially that big-mouthed reporter, Rapunzel Trashtrumpet) would kill the best entrepreneurial idea he'd conceived in years.

But not if those tales were *never told*. Not if the inevitable horror stories could be suppressed and the storytellers themselves silenced. Yes! He must see to it that no adverse publicity or negativity, not a whisper of anything contrary to his desired results, filtered into the community to jeopardize the success of this operation. Barley had a means to prevent those misfortunes—although not a method he was used to employing. Nor did it please him to resort to this extreme and admittedly distasteful solution.

However, circumstances dictated he had no other choice. He began to formulate a plan he knew he'd have to implement soon and without hesitation, no matter how unpalatable it might be. Convinced that this was logical, sensible, and the only plausible solution to the problem, Barley sat back and tried to relax. The tour moved on.

✳ ✳ ✳

The bouncy, jerky, rolling motions of the vehicle as it traversed the city streets had acted as a catalyst to induce in each tourist the physical response necessary to purge whatever remained of Granny Mambo's insidious breakfast banquet (at the expense of the aesthetic presentation of their noble touring vehicle). Most of the group now contended with mere motion sickness as opposed to food poisoning.

Roland Chumbuckets kept to the city streets on his route to the tour's second venue. Then Barley leaned forward in his seat behind the driver and mumbled some instructions—a spontaneous amendment to the tour's itinerary.

Roland redirected the bus to the main highway on the outskirts of North Corners. Once beyond the city limits, he turned off the highway and up an inconspicuous dirt road, a serpentine, pothole-laden course that led to the summit of a high hill overlooking the town, known to the locals as Mount Getoodah. Roland brought the vehicle to a scenic lookout at the end of the roadway, on a cliff known as Getoodah Point. Most members of the group were familiar with this location, or had been in their youth, as the favored teenage make-out spot.

There were no hormonal adolescents present when the tour bus arrived, however. Nothing moved but a few skittering squirrels and leaves rustling in treetops.

The bus stopped in the cleared area where the view was most inspiring, but among the passengers grew a collective sense of unease and foreboding. They'd not been told about this side trip, and there were rumors that the buried remains of a few of Barley Doodlebody's former business associates—with whom he was no longer "doing business"—also reposed amid the underbrush in this very out-of-the-way location. The tour group whispered furtively, taking care not to be overheard by Noodles Snorgmark, Frog Puppleman, or Barley himself.

Now that he had their money, was Barley planning to "eliminate" them in the wilderness, where they'd join the unfortunate victims of his previous business ventures? He seemed tense on the bus ride. One had to admit, if Barley chose to add the tourists to the purported "victims list," circumstances were perfect for him to do so. They were far away and sequestered from anyone who might come to their defense.

The bus parked. Barley rose to his feet and faced the terrified group. "All right, everybody, we're going to be stopping here so you can enjoy the view and get some fresh air. Don't fall off the cliff, and breathe as much as you can while you're up here. I don't want any more of you barfing all over my bus!"

Barley walked down the steps and stood outside the parked vehicle. The passengers looked at one another, filled with trepidation. Barley was obviously attempting to lure them outside under the pretext of a sightseeing stop on the lonely hill. They shuddered at the way he'd said, "Breathe as much as you can while you're up here." Would those breaths be their last?

"Let's go, people! Get your butts outside—right *now*!"

Frog Puppleman jumped out of his seat with a joyous, "Yeah, *buddy*!" He scrambled up the center aisle, down the steps, and out the door. Once outside, he complied with his big brother's suggestion to breathe as much as he could, gulping huge amounts of the spring air, inhaling and exhaling with such rapidity that he began to hyperventilate and swoon from too much breathing and not enough oxygen. He passed out, falling forward—SPLAT!—onto his face.

Barley threw up his hands in exasperation. Walking over to his gasping sibling, he turned him over, pulled him up to a sitting position by the lapels of his disheveled suit coat, and applied a stinging WHAP! to the side of Frog's face. Frog didn't feel a thing. No matter; the slap was for Barley's enjoyment.

"Noodles, get down here and take care of the councilman, will ya? He's driving me nuts! And the rest of you—*do I have to come up there and throw you out the windows?*"

Noodles rose from her seat and shuffled up the aisle. The rest of the group apprehensively followed her lead; they had no choice but to get this over with, whatever "this" might be.

Reverend Snortworthy, certain that his time on earth was coming to an abrupt and violent end, moved hesitantly forward, head bowed, quietly murmuring last rites to himself. He took some consolation from the thought that his faithful parishioners at Saint Cucamonga's Church of Fast Food for the Soul would most assuredly give him a glorious martyr's funeral—but *he'd* be the one who was dead! So much for consolation.

Rapunzel Trashtrumpet furtively scribbled, *If I am dead, Doodlebody did it . . .* on a piece of her note paper—incriminating and damning evidence should a criminal investigation follow her mysterious disappearance. She surreptitiously stuffed the note into the crotch between her seat bottom and the backrest. Barley would not get away with this; her note would be the "smoking gun" that would ensnare him in his own sticky "web of deception," eventually collapsing the corrupt "house of cards" that made up his world. Having exhausted her repertoire of clichéd metaphors, she edged up the aisle, sniveling pathetically, resigned to a hideous and untimely death. At most, a flowery obituary in *The Daily Poop* was all she could hope for now.

Biff Spoozma had been roused from his nap by Barley's yelling. Unaware and unconcerned as to the reason for it, he stood and robotically hoisted the unconscious Mayor Wubbleduster over his shoulder, shuffling his bulky burden toward the door.

Dr. Pudbid stealthily palmed a scalpel from his medical bag to use as a "shiv" should self-defense become necessary. If he was going down, he'd take a piece of Barley Doodlebody with him, by cracky! His ancient mind then became preoccupied with figuring out what "by cracky" actually meant.

They staggered out of the bus to stand as a group in front of Barley, fearfully awaiting his fatal judgment—except for Mimsy Borogove, who was motivated: *this* might be the moment she received her Binky reward!

Noodles stooped to tend to Frog Puppleman while little Margaret stood over him, ruefully pondering the lost opportunity of HIVED-ing an incapacitated, powerless, and otherwise luckless victim of circumstance. Today, Frog Puppleman was one lucky luckless victim of circumstance.

Barley eyed the motley group. He gathered his resolve, cleared his throat, and fixed the group with a steely eyed, grimacing glare, peeved at these pathetic idiots for forcing him to do what he now must do.

Finally Barley spoke, his tone ominous: "This trip is not turning out the way I planned it, and you people are not helping things with your behavior—screaming and yelling and moaning and groaning, spewing all over my bus, sitting there looking like death warmed-over."

At the word *death*, the group gasped and cringed. Knees wobbled.

"Before you got on the bus this morning, I told you that if you had any problems with this tour, I'd take care of you. It appears you're *all* having problems with it. I'm gonna keep my word to take care of you—*all* of you!"

Rapunzel Trashtrumpet shrieked in terror and fainted into Dr. Pudbid's arms. Dr. Pudbid gasped in shock and dropped Rapunzel to the ground. Reverend Snortworthy wailed, rolled his eyes to the heavens, and began to babble in strange tongues. Meanwhile, Mimsy Borogove rejoiced; she was *finally* going to be taken care of!

Barley stared at them and sighed. "So we're gonna take a little break here, and each one of you squash-heads is gonna have a chance to recuperate, rejuvenate, and invigorate. You've got ten minutes, you whining bunch of brisket-bonking banana-butts! *Are ya happy now?!*"

Barley brusquely snatched Binky Bohoguss out of his pocket, handed him to Noodles, and stalked back to the bus. He climbed aboard the vehicle and plopped into his seat.

There. He'd done it—something he'd rarely done in his entire career, be it legitimate or illegitimate. He'd actually been *nice.* And *accommodating.* As a rule, Barley didn't like doing what he didn't like doing—but he did what he had to do, and now it was done.

Would it work?

The tourists stood frozen in ragged formation by the bus, slack jawed and stunned, looking like they'd just had their brains sucked out. A moment ago, they'd each been making peace with their Maker, certain they were about to be murdered where they stood. Now they were told to breathe the fresh air, take in the view, and spend the next ten minutes *enjoying* themselves. This whole thing was completely stupefying, but

Barley seemed to be sincere—he was back on the bus, fuming and pouting like a spoiled little child. Also, no weapons were being brandished at them. Maybe he was really on the level. Heaven knew they could use a little "recuperation, rejuvenation, and invigoration."

Cautiously, hesitantly, one tourist after another gathered enough courage to break away from the group and wander around the Getoodah Point lookout site, taking in the lovely scenery, listening to the pleasant quiet of the wilderness (in sharp contrast to the furiously pounding drums they'd left behind), breathing clean air, and letting the sunshine bathe their faces.

Frog Puppleman lay on his back where Barley had left him, receiving care from Noodles and Binky Bohoguss. Binky stood on Frog's chest, enthusiastically slapping the groggy city councilman's face with both hands but having no effect whatsoever. Being slapped by the little police chief was about as galvanizing as being farted on by a bird. Be that as it may, no one could deny that the little guy looked as cute as could be as he indulged himself with unrestrained abandon in attempting to face-slap Frog Puppleman back to life.

Mimsy Borogove stood next to Noodles, towering over Frog's prone form like a leering vulture, eyeing the little police chief. Frog was old news to Mimsy now. Binky was the way of the future in her erotic fantasies, but Noodles Snorgmark's formidable presence effectively thwarted any attempt the horny sewage heiress might make at claiming the "prize" Barley had promised her. Noodles eyed the salivating socialite warily, and Mimsy was held at bay.

Responding to the fresh air and Noodles's ministrations, Frog opened his eyes, blinked, and sat bolt upright, toppling Binky to the ground. Noodles snatched up the tiny imp and perched him on her shoulder before Mimsy had the chance to pounce. Mimsy hissed in frustration and stomped away.

"Yeah, budd—*whoooaaahhh!*" A wave of dizziness washed over Frog; he'd risen too fast and was on the verge of passing out again.

This time it was Noodles who gave the councilman a slap—SMACK! Frog shook his head and blinked, fully revived. Noodles helped him to his feet and escorted him, Margaret Wubbleduster, and little Binky to the lookout point to admire the view.

Rapunzel Trashtrumpet was also reviving, on the ground where Dr. Pudbid had dropped her. The realization that she wasn't dead dawned in her dazed consciousness—and she was lying there all by herself! Once it had been established that Barley wasn't going to assassinate them, the good doctor wandered off with the rest of the group to see the sights, leaving the passed-out reporter to her own devices.

Rapunzel took a couple deep breaths to clear her head and sat up, adjusting the huge goggle-lensed eyeglasses perched on her nose. She looked around; Barley was nowhere to be seen. The others were strolling around the lookout site. Struggling to her feet, she joined them, hoping to learn exactly what had happened to change what she'd initially perceived to be a tragic turn of events.

The group gazed out over the green, spring-washed valley below them. They marveled at the thin, crisscrossing street grid of distant North Corners, the miniature houses, scurrying automobiles, the shops and parks—even the P. P. Piggford and His Wife Janice High School campus that had been reclaimed by nature at the foot of the cliff. (Indeed, this was the very same precipice that the despondent P. P. and Janice Piggford had leaped from, fulfilling their double-suicide pact and ensuring their immortality as part of the future high school's flooring.)

The tourists took extreme delight in locating various town landmarks and their own homes, pointing them out to each other. This spontaneous stop was turning out to be an inspired tactic indeed, generating a much-needed improvement in the group's morale.

They were in a new venue and a sunnier environment. Most were fully conscious (with the exception of Mayor Wubbleduster—Biff Spoozma seated the zonked-out mayor against a tree near the lookout while Biff admired the view). Most importantly, Barley Doodlebody hadn't brought them up to this gorgeous spot to kill them. If those rumors of purported homicidal indiscretions and buried associates were true, the group had seen no evidence of it; indeed, they were discovering that this irascible, inscrutable, incorrigible entrepreneur was not as predictable as they'd believed. The morning was still young, the sun was still shining, the birds were still singing, and, because of Barley, they began to feel "recuperated, rejuvenated, and invigorated."

Barley sat dolefully behind Roland Chumbuckets and gazed through the shattered window, watching the invigorated tourists gawk and gad about like a giddy bunch of moronic . . . tourists! He'd performed the unthinkable, bowing to the unspoken will of these baboons, but only to get the group over its maladies and back on its feet. The ploy worked; the tour was saved. There was still much to see and do.

Time once again to get this show on the road.

"Okay, Chumbuckets, fire up this buggy, and let's get ready to move out. I've had about all the fresh air I can take!"

Roland turned the ignition key and the motor coughed, sputtered, and roared to life. The tourists heard the engine reigniting and let out a collective groan. Immersed as they were in the pastoral pleasures of this idyllic moment, they'd temporarily forgotten there was more tour yet to come.

Barley walked down the steps and stood outside the bus. He produced the police whistle from his trouser pocket and gave it a blow, waving the group over to him. The tourists trudged back to the bus like children about to take a trip to the woodshed for a whuppin'. Casting one last wistful look at the pristine landscape spread serenely below them, they sadly acknowledged that they'd have to descend into that faraway world once more. It looked so much nicer (and definitely smaller) from up here.

"All right, we're going to our next stop, so get back on the bus. Anybody still feeling sick?"

No one answered. The group members had overcome their nauseous feelings, but they were in no frame of mind to leave this beautiful place, much less continue with the tour—a tour as culturally stimulating as a spelling bee for kangaroos. Still, they'd each contributed seven hundred dollars (well, seven hundred fifty, now), so the dejected group took one last deep breath of the clear, clean air and boarded the idling bus.

"Okay, Chumbuckets, back to the *original* stop this time."

Roland put the transmission in gear, and the lumbering vehicle slowly headed back down the dirt road, stopping only once to return and pick up Mayor Wubbleduster, whom Biff Spoozma had left behind, hoping no one would notice.

Once more, they were off to the flatlands below. The bus rejoined the highway and headed back into North Corners, the tourists doing their utmost to enjoy the ride and erase the bad memories. Each was again willing to make the best of the experience; after all, things couldn't get any worse.

Or *could* they?

***

After reentering the town and negotiating a confusing series of streets, avenues, and alleyways, the bus pulled to the curb and halted in front of what was now stop number three. It too was an establishment secretly owned by Barley Doodlebody. Roland Chumbuckets turned off the vehicle's ignition, and the tourists gawked at the little shop through the shattered windows of the bus.

It looked conventional enough from the outside. Then again, so had Granny Mambo's Liverland.

They peered at the sign above the shop's door with apprehensive uncertainty:

POCKETS FULL O' PUCKY

Pucky? Did the word mean what they thought it meant?

Barley addressed the passengers, once again exhorting the group to spend at least fifty dollars in the shop or face the "legally terminal" consequences of death by execution. So much for the kinder and more considerate Barley Doodlebody.

Since the concept of death had re-factored itself into the equation as a potential byproduct of noncompliance, the beleaguered bunch dutifully complied, filing slowly off the bus, desperately hoping that Pockets Full o' Pucky was not another dining establishment.

14

Pockets Full o' Pucky catered to folks with a penchant for collecting curios, curiosities, items, and artifacts fashioned from dried cow chips—yet another market commodity in North Corners that Barley had cornered. Surprisingly, the quaint boutique was losing money hand over fist.

While approaching the front door, an acrid aroma slammed into the tourists' noses like the front four of a defensive line. The tourists now realized why Barley had been so insistent they get a healthy dose of fresh air at Getoodah Point. They took one last deep breath of relatively non-toxic oxygen and entered the ominously malodourous shop.

Once inside, the tourists were amazed to see how many things could be made from dried cow chips. They stared in wonder at shelves and counters lined and stacked from floor to ceiling with merchandise and memorabilia manufactured from the stuff cows themselves manufactured: household appliances, dinnerware, sporting goods, stationary and office supplies, toys, clothing, musical instruments, cosmetics—you name it. It was a mind-boggling display of American ingenuity, creativity, craftsmanship, and mental illness at its best, and the tourists wept with pride to see it—along with the knowledge that, very soon, they'd own a lot of this crap themselves.

Though Pockets Full o' Pucky was bankrolled by Barley Doodlebody, the enterprise was managed by a jovial, rotund woman named Arletta Fizzyfingers, who greeted the tourists warmly and enthusiastically invited them to explore, experience, and enjoy the many wonders displayed therein.

Arletta had been an insightful choice by Barley to oversee the store's operation: she'd spent the majority of her life on a dairy farm, and was therefore inured to the overpowering effect that massive amounts of accumulated cow chips had on a normal person's sense of smell. Her love for the products she sold was so fervent that her own home was furnished with many of the store's myriad dried-cow-chip products, a significant reason why most people avoided Arletta Fizzyfingers's home.

For those individuals not accustomed to the oppressive odor that permeated the shop, Arletta made the concession of lighting a number of scented candles and distributing them around the store to counteract the caustic stench as well as give the premises a more quaint and pleasant ambience. Unfortunately, her choice of scents only exacerbated the problem; it was hard to mask the powerful odor of dried cow chips with scents like "Sweaty Marine Barracks" or "Slaughterhouse Kill Floor." As the tourists wandered the aisles, they experienced the familiar rumblings of nausea that had followed them out of Granny Mambo's Liverland.

Biff Spoozma managed to leave Mayor Wubbleduster on the bus without Barley being aware of it. Continuously hoisting the first magistrate's enormous weight was wearing him down to an exhausted heap, and there was no point in hauling the senseless politician around the shop; his lack of consciousness would prevent him from appreciating its many wonders.

As soon as Biff disappeared inside the shop, Roland (who completely forgot about both Mayor Wubbleduster's presence on the bus *and* his very existence) decided he should take this opportunity to wash the exterior of his bus. The encrusted vehicle was contributing its own reek to the atmosphere, and Roland knew of a fire station located a few blocks away. Perhaps the firemen would lend him their hose to blast away the coating of dried vomit; it would only take a few minutes, and he could return to Pockets Full o' Pucky in plenty of time to pick up his shopping passengers. Roland fired up the vehicle and headed for the station.

Inside Pockets Full o' Pucky, Biff Spoozma encountered Frog Puppleman standing inside the front door, his face a case study in bewilderment. Where should he start? Where should he finish? What should he do in between? Biff's protective instincts were aroused by Frog's predicament; he decided to accompany the city councilman through the labyrinthine shop.

"Yeah, *buddy!*" shouted Frog, realizing that Big Biff would be his companion. The mayor's public relations advisor and personal bodyguard had historically been a special comrade to Frog whenever they ran into each other at city hall. Biff would help the councilman back to his feet and could always be relied upon to supply Frog with a box of thumbtacks to entertain himself during the confusing city council meetings.

Side by side, Biff and Frog wandered up and down the aisles in search of adventure—and a box of dried-cow-chip thumbtacks.

Margaret Wubbleduster, tethered to Noodles Snorgmark by the leash, her hands securely bound together with gaffer's tape and her mouth sealed shut, began to choke and gag from the pungent aroma in the store. Margaret's enormous nostrils were the only orifices on her face permitting any oxygen intake.

Grabbing a corner of the tape covering the little girl's mouth, Noodles yanked it off. Margaret squealed as the tape's adhesive pulled the tiny hairs around her mouth out of their follicles, but once the initial stab of pain had passed, she sucked in a deep breath of the tainted air, then snorted and blinked up at Noodles, a smile of gratitude on her pudgy face. A cascade of pent-up saliva issued forth from between her smiling lips and splooshed to the floor to form a viscous puddle.

Noodles gagged at the sight.

Barley had delivered Binky Bohoguss to Noodles once again so the little guy could be supervised while Barley was supervising everyone else. Binky sat astride Noodle's left shoulder like a cowboy straddling a huge, two-legged Scandinavian horse. The little guy clutched at his stomach, making almost imperceptible "hulfing" noises at the sight of Margaret's gratitude. Noodles deemed it expedient that they evacuate their present location before the sickening sight of Margaret's sticky drool puddle caused the tiny police chief to spit up all over the side of her head. Flicking Margaret's leash like the reins of a horse and carefully sidestepping the slimy bog on the aisle floor, Noodles and her charges set off in search of an open window.

Mimsy Borogove and Rapunzel Trashtrumpet had never seen a store like Pockets Full o' Pucky before. Their natural shopping instincts were firing on all cylinders. The lure of merchandise was sufficient for them to ignore the discomfort as they prowled the aisles, searching for the "perfect whatever."

As the trashy socialite and the nosy reporter meandered around the shop's stinky interior, Rapunzel examined the various items and scribbled notes on her pad of paper, while Mimsy shrieked with excitement each time she came upon what she thought was a great bargain. There were "great bargains" aplenty; the majority of the items in the shop were sales markdowns, for the simple reason that in the entire time Pockets Full o'

Pucky had been in business, a grand total of zero items had been purchased.

The two women were having a ball, in their element, and enjoying themselves more than they had all day. They also had the easiest time coming up with items to fulfill the fifty-dollar-expenditure quota, since they were purchasing just about everything they saw. Conveniently, the two were also in blissful denial of the fact that everything on which they spent their money was made from cow chips.

At one point, a fistfight broke out when they simultaneously laid hands on the same fake-diamond-encrusted cow-chip eyebrow-plucking attachment ensemble. Reverend Snortworthy, who was nearby examining cow-chip underwear shape retainers, hastened to where the two women were beating the stuffing out of each other and attempted to intercede in the name of peace and harmony. For his efforts, the reverend received vicious roundhouse haymakers to the jaw from both squabbling shoppers and staggered backward, crashing into a display of cow-chip applesauce re-constitutors, which tumbled down on him and left him sitting in a stupor on the floor.

Mimsy subsequently decided she didn't want the fake-diamond-encrusted cow-chip eyebrow-plucking attachment ensemble after all, and conceded it to Rapunzel, who immediately made the same decision. The two walked off arm in arm to continue their shopping.

Meanwhile, kindly Dr. Pudbid perused the merchandise, intrigued and inspired by the concept behind Pockets Full o' Pucky. Perhaps there might be a demand for products made from dried *horse* chips as well, something he had in plentiful supply through the courtesy of Frank Winslow, the horse that pulled his old buggy around town. Profits from the sale of Frank's horse chips might boost his own income enough for him to pay his bills.

He approached Arletta Fizzyfingers and presented her with his idea. She quickly rebuffed him, good-naturedly chiding him for his ignorance on the subject and condescendingly informing him that horses didn't manufacture "horse chips." Horses manufactured "road apples," and there was no market for them.

Having been thus corrected and educated, the doctor hung his head in defeat, slinking off to find a cow-chip gelatin mold.

Barley sat comfortably in a plush, dried-cow-chip-stuffed easy chair, keeping an eye on things. When the group members brought an item for purchase to Arletta Fizzyfingers's cash register, he smiled contentedly and jotted down the amount each person spent, keeping a close tally of where they stood in relation to the fifty-dollar total he'd assigned them.

As he pored over his calculations, a troubling aspect dawned on him: because items manufactured from cow chips were relatively inexpensive, the tourists had to purchase massive amounts to make their quotas. The immense bulk would consume considerable space on the tour bus—and would also smell like huge amounts of cow chips, only adding to the discomfort and inconvenience that had plagued the tour from its start.

Barley rationalized that the group had spent more than an acceptable length of time in purchasing cow-chip toaster ovens, tooth polishers, fingernail adjusters, hog pacifiers, sausage humidifiers, fish cuspidors, jackhammer cozies, ice cream extenders, rabbit stuffers, custom-fitted walrus beheaders, and other items about as useful as a parrot with lips. Whether each had met his fifty-dollar obligation or not, enough money had been spent to float Pockets Full o' Pucky until the next tour group showed up.

Once more, the police whistle shattered the silence, and Barley loudly addressed the scattered group, informing them they'd all satisfied their fiscal obligation and it was time to move on to the next tour venue.

Noodles quickly extracted Chief Bohoguss from the cow-chip vacuum cleaner he'd gotten sucked into, yanked on Margaret Wubbleduster's leash to wrest her away from the cow-chip aquarium she was filling with saliva, and headed to the cash register with her charges. Meanwhile, Mimsy Borogove had been trying on a fake-mink cow-chip stole, and opted to wear it out of the store, replacing her purple feather boa.

Rapunzel Trashtrumpet's arrival at the clothing section was delayed because she'd been debating buying the cow-chip briefcase she'd seen in the office and business supplies section. She eyed Mimsy's newest acquisition enviously—*darn!* All the reporter could do was gaze longingly at the stole, convinced that it would have made the perfect accouterment to her own wardrobe, and would have looked far better on her than that rich old bag. She'd have to settle for her second choice: a sexy little cow-chip nightie with cute little cow-chip ribbons and bows. Reverend Snortworthy and Dr. Pudbid witnessed Rapunzel making her alternate choice and fervently prayed she wouldn't emulate Mimsy by wearing *her* purchase out of the store as well.

The two satisfied lady shoppers made their way to the front counter to pick up the packages and parcels they'd purchased, each quite certain that she'd outdone the other in the quality and quantity of items.

Biff Spoozma and Frog Puppleman strolled the shop's treasure-laden interior, enthralled with the various items and artifacts. When they arrived at the children's toys section, they were both helplessly captivated by the two shiny, steel-reinforced cow-chip tricycles gleaming from the floor display.

The shining metallic paint jobs attracted Frog much as a moth gravitates to a blazing light bulb. His eyes sparkled with childlike glee. "Yeah, *buddy!*"

Biff was likewise hypnotized. He covetously caressed each tantalizing curve with hungry eyes, wishing he were a kid again.

Pulling one of the shiny tricycles out of the floor display and into the aisle, Frog sat astride the small contraption's imitation-leather dried-cow-chip-upholstered saddle seat like an elephant straddling a barstool. His legs were bent fully at the knees, his knees stuck straight out on either side of the tricycle like a couple of mirror-image figure fours, and his feet were planted firmly on the foot pedals. Grabbing the handlebars, Frog looked up at Biff with sublime euphoria manifesting in the ear-to-ear grin blanketing his boyish face. He made gruff, growling "*Vrooom! Vrooom!*" noises, coaxing and cajoling the big guy to jump on his own "trike" and join him for a spin around the shop.

Biff needed no further encouragement. He pulled the other tricycle out from the display and positioned it in the aisle next to Frog, squatting down to take his place on the tiny seat, looking even more ridiculous than the city councilman on his three-wheeler. Biff's physique was twice the size of Frog's. The little toy sagged and nearly buckled from his weight, but the steel-reinforced frame held up. The two sat in the aisle on their respective vehicles and taunted each other with competitive "*Vrooom! Vrooom!*" noises.

To the two tensed-up tricycle jockeys, Barley's police whistle signaled the start of the impending race. Frog threw down the gauntlet, Biff accepted the challenge, and Barley unknowingly sent them on their way!

They shot down the aisle, faces set in grim determination, side by side, neck and neck, legs pumping furiously, eyes riveted to the course. The narrow aisle was barely wide enough to accommodate the two racers, and their outspread knees smacked into each other as they maniacally pedaled down the row.

Reaching the end of the aisle in a dead heat, Frog jerked his tricycle into an abrupt right turn and sped around the corner. Biff, taken by surprise at Frog's lightning-fast maneuver, attempted to turn his trike in pursuit, but his momentum was too great and his reaction too slow to make the turn cleanly. He skidded left and smashed into a shelf display of cow-chip table lamps, falling sideways off of his bike. The display and its merchandise crashed down on top of him. Everyone in the shop stopped and turned toward the sound, but Biff and Frog's antics were below everyone's line of sight.

Frog looked over his shoulder in time to see Biff's untimely collision. He cackled gleefully, turning right down the next aisle. Biff pushed away the mess of tumbled table lamps and their entangling electrical cords, spied Frog speeding up the next aisle, jumped back on his trike, and set off in pursuit, leaving a heap of smashed table lamps in his slipstream.

Frog glanced back once again; his eyes momentarily diverted from the road ahead, he plowed into and between Dr. Pudbid and Reverend Snortworthy as the two were making their way to the cash register. The impact sent the two men hurtling off in opposite directions, violently crashing into stacks of merchandise on both sides of the aisle. Two more impromptu avalanches of dried-cow-chip products resulted, filling the aisle with dust and debris, nearly burying them where they sprawled. Frog continued on his way.

Frog's momentary delay enabled Biff to regain the ground his accident had cost him. He zipped past the two dazed crash victims sitting groggily in their respective debris piles and reached Frog's rear wheels, breathing down his neck.

Biff hung back as they pedaled toward the upcoming turn. He craftily strategized that by giving the councilman a little space, he could see which way Frog was going to turn, keep tight to his tail until the turn was made, and "slingshot" his tricycle past Frog's to take over the lead once they were back on the straightaway.

Sure enough, at the end of the aisle, Frog whipped his tricycle into a sharp left turn, then another quick left around the corner to head up the next row. Biff was ready to make his move—but just as he was about to do so, something happened that the two racers could never have anticipated: Frog suddenly encountered the slimy puddle of Margaret Wubbleduster's saliva. When the wheels of his tricycle hit the viscous pool, Frog spun crazily off course and slammed into a stack of cow-chip bed linens. Biff was unable to react in time to avoid Frog's misfortune. He skidded through the slime puddle and followed the leader, barreling into Frog and the merchandise, which collapsed over both of them.

This time, there was a new wrinkle: the double tricycle crash occurred at a spot where Arletta Fizzyfingers had placed one of the scented candles. Along with everything else in the cow-chip bed linen display that had just been annihilated, the lighted candle tumbled into the mess, its tiny flame igniting a chunk of the shattered debris.

Applying fire to a dried cow chip was like building a bonfire in a hayloft. The tiny flame caught hold of the dry material and instantly erupted into a blaze that jumped quickly to nearby stacks of cow-chip products, igniting them as well. In a flash, a wildfire flared in the middle of the dried-cow-chip boutique!

Biff realized what was happening and jumped to his feet, throwing and brushing the crushed and crumbled cow-chip remnants off of Frog and himself before the flames could set fire to them both. He pulled the stunned city councilman to his feet and hustled him down the aisle, away from the blaze now growing by leaps and bounds.

Reverend Snortworthy and Dr. Pudbid, both still reeling from the suddenness of Frog's assault and shock of the impact, attempted to extract themselves from under heaps of destroyed merchandise. Seeing the flames break out the next aisle over, the two panicked. "*FIRE! FIRE!*"

Their hysterical warning shouts drew the attention of the group at the front of the store. They too saw the wild flames spreading rapidly and picked up the "*FIRE! FIRE!*" chant.

Barley saw what they saw. "*Arletta*, what do we do?!"

Before Arletta could answer, the store's automatic emergency fire sprinkler system kicked in to action. Overhead sprinklers simultaneously cut loose with hissing sheets of water, thoroughly dousing the interior of the shop. Like a raging tropical monsoon, countless gallons of water showered down on everyone's heads, completely soaking the tourists, Barley, and Arletta, and every bit of dried-cow-chip merchandise on the premises. The furious downpour extinguished the fire in a matter of seconds. Once the system sensed the danger had been eliminated, it automatically shut itself down. The flood of water from the ceiling was terminated, but the once quaint and pleasant interior of the little shop had been transformed into a dripping, foaming quagmire of saturated and smelly cow-chip merchandise.

Everyone in the building was now soaked to the skin and miserable, their clothes dripping wet and steaming. What they saw next hurled them into paroxysms of revulsion and terror: every item, artifact, curio, curiosity—every *everything* in the store—began to dissolve and melt!

In mute horror, the waterlogged people witnessed what happens to dried cow chips when they get wet. The shop's entire inventory, including the products the tourists had just purchased, slowly lost shape, disintegrating into an oozing, dripping, drooping, melting mass of liquefied cow poop. People screamed in panic as the melted residue oozed and trickled down the aisles in ever-growing rivulets of sludge, creeping inexorably toward them like molten lava down the slopes of an erupting volcano.

Dr. Pudbid, Reverend Snortworthy, Frog Puppleman, and Biff Spoozma had each received a thick coating of dried-cow-chip dust, which now turned to a veneer of wet-cow-chip slime. Mimsy Borogove was also in a particularly bad way: the fake-mink cow-chip stole had gotten thoroughly soaked in the sprinkler downpour, melting into a horrific blob that completely covered her bony shoulders and gradually her entire body and her clothes. No one wanted to be anywhere near or have anything to do with her, especially when they got back on the bus. (Rapunzel Trashtrumpet was now secretly grateful she had *not* purchased the stole.)

The group huddled together by the front counter, dripping wet, shivering, and spluttering with dismay and discontent. Because of the deluge, they were all out another fifty bucks with nothing to show for it! Barley sensed that mutiny was now a distinct possibility. How was he going to rectify this? He was fast wearing down from dealing with problems, problems, and more problems!

He spied waterlogged Noodles Snorgmark standing nearby with similarly saturated Binky Bohoguss and Margaret Wubbleduster. "Noodles, we'd better get going! We've got to get to Bumps & Spuggett now before all these twerps get pissed off and I have to obliterate someone."

Turning to the group of soggy, miserable tourists, he told them to quiet their disgruntled mumbling and addressed them forcefully: "This has all been an unfortunate misfortune! No one—I repeat: *no one*—could have anticipated this happening! Before all of you start crying and wailing like a bunch of spoiled babies, we're gonna get out of here. Get yourselves outside and back on that bus, and forget this ever happened!"

The group shuffled toward the front door in a soggy, smelly, disheartened procession. The greasy rivulets of melted cow-chip residue squished noisily under their wet feet as they walked. Arletta Fizzyfingers stood forlornly behind the front counter. As she watched them leave, she became profoundly aware that it would be *her* primary responsibility to clean up all this crap.

Noodles positioned herself by the shop's doorway, barring anyone's exit until she could organize them into single file for boarding the bus. Once she'd finished, Barley stepped forward, grasped the door handle, pushed the door open, stopped abruptly, gasped, and stood staring with his eyes wide and his mouth agape.

The tour bus was gone . . .

15

Roland Chumbuckets guided the tour bus down the empty avenue, looking for the fire station and reveling in his brief time away from the tourists. His beloved bus had suffered gravely—but there was more to come. According to the tour itinerary, they were a long way from arriving at their final destination, so Roland wanted to utilize this opportunity to clean the bus exterior. The quickest way to blast the mess off would be with a high-powered fire hose.

Roland spied the small firefighting outpost just ahead. The place appeared deserted: the wide doors of the station's garage were pulled shut, and the office seemed lifeless as well. Roland hoped the station hadn't been closed down and abandoned.

He had a big job to do and not much time to do it, so he pulled the bus to the curb and parked, then approached the big, windowed garage doors and peered through the glass. The dimness within revealed a big red fire engine, a shiny red hook-and-ladder truck, and the fire company captain's red car, all three vehicles sitting side by side, parked nose outward to enable a quick exit. No firemen were visible, but evidently everyone was inside the station, probably in the office or the living quarters.

Roland gazed at the sparkling red fire engine. When he was a kid, he fantasized about driving one of those big crimson screamers, speeding through the streets of town, red lights flashing, siren shrieking, pedestrians scrambling, every type of motor vehicle obediently pulling to the side of the road in deference as he zipped past to save lives and property.

He walked from the garage to the station office door and tried the knob. The door was unlocked and swung open easily, but the small front office was quiet and unmanned. A fire and police scanner radio sat on a table in a corner, and he noticed a stairwell at the rear of the room that led to the second floor.

"Hello? Anybody here?"

No response. The radio crackled, and a dispatcher's static-filled voice called out some numbers and the order for a particular fire company to respond to a blaze somewhere in town. Roland held his breath and waited—but there were no signs of corresponding activity from the living quarters at the top of the stairs; the call was probably not for this particular station.

All was silent again in the small office. There were no more transmissions from the radio, no phones ringing, and no signs of life from above. Gathering his nerve, Roland proceeded to the rear stairwell, slowly and cautiously making his way up the single flight of creaking steps. Nearing the top, he heard what sounded like the snoring of a sty-full of slumbering pigs. Heavy breathing, hefty snorts, and nose burps issued forth in a cacophony of sleep-induced blather.

Arriving at a doorway atop the stairs, Roland peeked into the room. A number of cots were lined up in orderly rows as in a dormitory or military barracks, each occupied by a sleeping, slurping, and snoring fireman, like hibernating bears in the dead of winter, only much noisier.

Reluctant as he was to disturb the tranquility, he'd have to wake someone up to accomplish his task in minimal time. He tiptoed to the nearest cot, located next to a large hole in the floor where a polished brass pole allowed the firemen easy egress. A sleeping man in long underwear lay on the cot, adding his own grunting harmony to the dissonant chorus in the room. Roland gently tapped him on the shoulder.

The man did not wake up.

The bus driver tapped him on the shoulder once again, this time a little harder. "Excuse me, sir—hello? Sir? Hello?"

The man remained asleep. A more forceful approach was necessary. Roland leaned over and positioned his mouth next to the man's ear, grabbed the man by both shoulders, and shook him gently but firmly. "Yo! Sir! *Wake up!*"

The man on the cot woke abruptly, shook his head drowsily, blinked, and looked into Roland's face, mere inches from his own. The man's sleep-addled brain and body received a jolt of adrenaline, and he shrieked in terror, springing high into the air—*SPROOOIIIING!*—and plunging headfirst down through the hole in the floor, his arms wrapped around the brass pole. Roland gasped and ran to the gaping orifice, peering down into the chamber beneath him.

A pair of knee-high fireman's boots at the pole's base cushioned the terrified fireman's landing; unfortunately, he got his head wedged into one of them. He remained upside down, still hugging the brass pole with both arms, his inverted, long-underwear-clad legs and feet kicking wildly. Muffled cries of "*Help!*" issued from within the stifling boot.

As the rest of the firemen in the upstairs dormitory roused in response to the man's panicked cry, Roland slid down the brass pole. He landed on top of the inverted fireman, who crumpled under Roland's weight, released his grasp on the pole, and splayed onto his back with the boot still stuck over his head.

Roland scrambled off the fireman and grabbed the boot, straining and pulling to unwedge it from the man's noggin. One good yank, and the footgear popped off; the man gulped fresh air, massaging his chafed face and skull with both hands and eyeing Roland apprehensively.

"Who are you?! What do you *want?!*"

"Sir, I'm so sorry! I was only trying to wake you up. You were sleeping so soundly, and there was no one else around who could help me!"

"We always sleep when we're not putting out a fire; don't you know that? Why didn't you just set off the fire alarm if you wanted to wake us up? Do you have a fire that we need to put out?"

"No, sir, I only needed to speak to one person, and I didn't want to wake up the whole crew. I need some help with a problem!"

"A *problem?*" The fireman's demeanor softened as he recovered from the effects of his rude awakening. "Well, we're not used to solving problems around here normally, but we *are* here to help. We're always here to help! We're firemen!"

A ring of puzzled, concerned faces appeared above, peering through the hole in the dormitory floor: the rest of the fire company, now wide awake.

"Hey, Cap'n! You okay? You need any help?"

"See what I mean?" said the fire captain to Roland. "We're *always* here to help! We're firemen! I'm fire company cap'n Moolly Chubbychuffle, at your service and pleased to meetcha."

Roland introduced himself and shook hands with Captain Moolly Chubbychuffle.

The fire captain shouted back up: "I'm fine, men! Had a boot stuck on my head there for a minute, but it's off now. Just a minor mishap; no problem."

"Okay, glad to hear that! We're not used to solving *problems* around here normally!"

The fire captain nodded to Roland. "See what I mean?"

The concerned faces quickly disappeared, and the crew returned to their cots. Within seconds, the faint but vaguely disturbing sound of their snoring, snorfing, and blubbering drifted down through the hole.

"So, what's the problem? We're not used to solving problems around here normally, but we are here to help!"

"Well, sir, I'm a bus driver by trade, and today my bus is being used as transportation for a guided tour. It's been through a few rough moments, and I came here to see if I might borrow your fire hose to clean some rather nasty stuff off the sides!"

"Nasty stuff? You mean 'nasty' like *haz-mat* stuff, where we need to get dressed up in big rubber suits with oxygen masks?"

"Oh no, sir! Nothing like that! Just some dried vomit, that's all."

"Dried vomit? *Yeeesh!*" The captain grimaced and wagged his head in disgust. "Why, that's just plain gross! What kind of a guided tour are you conducting, son? Don't answer that; I don't think I really want to know!" He paused for a moment. "Well, of course you can use our hose—and some water too! We haven't got any fires to put out at the moment, and it sounds to me like you've got yourself a *problem!*"

"Thanks very much, Cap'n! I'm kinda short on time here, so if you can show me where the fire hose is, I'll get to work."

"Wouldn't hear of it! We're *always* here to help—we're firemen! Besides, you don't have the experience necessary to handle our fire hose."

With Roland's assistance, the captain stood and brushed himself off. He slipped on the pair of boots that had accessorized his fall and walked over to the wall next to the fire pole, where a number of firefighting outfits—coats, helmets, pairs of boots—were hanging on wall pegs or lined up on the floor. Still clad only in his long underwear, he added nothing but his helmet.

"Like my old daddy used to say," said Captain Chubbychuffle as he fastened the chin strap on his headgear, "'You can't saddle a gator unless he thinks he's a horse!'"

Roland was puzzled. How did that apply to *anything*?

The captain continued, "Since I'm up and awake now, I'll give you a hand with the hose and we'll get that bus cleaned up in a jiffy."

He pushed a large button on the wall next to the hanging clothes. The fire station's two garage doors swung open, letting fresh air and sunshine pour into the room. The highly polished surfaces of the fire truck, hook-and-ladder truck, and fire captain's car caught the rays of sunlight and shone magnificently. Roland admired the huge, lovingly tended fire engine, wishing he could swap his bus and the tour group for the chance to pilot that gleaming behemoth through the streets of North Corners to heroically fulfill its daily missions of mercy.

"We'll use the spare hose to wash the bus." The captain hoisted a neatly spooled fire hose from a corner along the rear wall of the garage. "Gotta leave the one that's on the truck right where it is; you never know when we'll get the next alarm, and we sure-as-shootin' wouldn't want to get the call and not have a hose ready! Like my old daddy used to say, 'You can take the hose out of the fire truck, but you can't trust a duck to flip a flapjack!'"

Roland was at a loss again, but the truth in what the captain's old daddy said was undeniable.

"Your old daddy was quite the philosopher!"

"He was a blithering idiot—but he *did* have a lot to say about things."

Carrying the rolled-up fire hose in his arms like a bundle of dirty laundry, Captain Chubbychuffle waddled out to the red fire hydrant at the curb in front of the building and plopped the coiled hose onto the concrete. "Okay, son, park your buggy in the driveway while I hook up this hose."

Roland jumped on the bus, fired up the motor (which sounded pathetically weak compared to how a fire engine sounded), and pulled into the driveway. The captain returned with a large silver wrench, which he used to attach the fire hose to an opening in the side of the hydrant. Once the hose was firmly connected, he placed the wrench around a bolt-like valve opener and waited until Roland had parked the messy bus.

"Okay, Cap'n, she's ready to go, but I should warn you: all the windows were broken this morning. We'll have to be careful to keep as much water from getting into the bus as we can."

"*All the windows?* What kind of a 'guided tour' are you conducting, son?" The captain shook his head and stooped to pick up the nozzle end of the fire hose. "Well, I'll be as careful as I can, but *some* water is gonna get in, no matter how careful we are. You okay with that?"

Roland had no choice. He nodded.

"All right then, I'm gonna take the hose over by the bus. You can help me by turning that wrench on the hydrant when I tell you to. Wait for my signal!"

"Got it!"

The captain walked over to one side of the scum-encrusted bus, uncoiling the serpentine fire hose as he went. He stepped back a few feet and stood poised, tensed, and ready to direct the spray of water.

"*Whooooo*-boy! How'd this thing ever get so bad, son?" The captain shook his head in disgust. "Don't answer that—I don't think I really want to know! Like my old daddy used to say, 'Never look for what you don't want to see!' Now, give that wrench a good hard push counterclockwise! *Let 'er rip!*"

Roland pushed hard on the big silver wrench. The sidewalk trembled; a surge of water erupted from the hydrant and rushed into the fire hose. As Captain Chubbychuffle braced himself, the powerful stream spewed from the hose's nozzle onto the side of the messy bus.

"Thar she blows!" The captain directed the surging stream of water around the exterior of the vehicle, power-washing the areas soiled by the sick tourists. The crust was easily blasted off, and the residue ran down the driveway and into the gutter.

Roland was pleased. The problem of the stinky, crusty tour bus was solved!

However, his joy was soon replaced by a sinking feeling: the heavy spray soaked the interior much more than he'd anticipated. Despite Captain Chubbychuffle's efforts, the fire hose poured huge amounts of water through the open windows.

Roland would have a new mess to deal with: waterlogged seats and standing pools of water on the floor! *Oh well, too late to stop now*, he thought. One side of the bus had already been hosed off, and the captain was moving to the other side to finish the job. The tourists would have to live with this newest inconvenience, and *he* would have to figure out a satisfactory explanation for Barley Doodlebody.

Captain Chubbychuffle, resplendent in his long underwear, boots, and fire helmet, continued his power-washing; the vehicle looked clean and revitalized. But neither Roland nor the captain was prepared for what happened next.

As the captain applied a final rinsing spray, a drenched, soppy man's head popped up and stared wild eyed out the glassless rear window. Streaks of jet-black hair dye ran in rivulets down his face as he spluttered, coughed, and spewed his own stream of water out the window, having swallowed big gulps of the stuff when it showered down upon his unconscious form on the rear seat. His Honor Mayor Roymul Wubbleduster had finally been aroused from his electric-shock-induced coma.

Roland gasped, remembering Biff Spoozma's admonition: "Guard the mayor with your life!" Now the mayor was nearly drowning like a bilge rat!

He gathered his wits and yanked the silver wrench clockwise, turning off the flow of water from the hydrant. Roland witnessed his entire life flashing before his eyes and foresaw his own horrible death at the hands of an enraged Barley Doodlebody—and when Barley was finished, it would be Biff Spoozma's turn!

Captain Chubbychuffle spotted the mayor in the back of the bus as the heavy stream of water from the fire hose receded to a trickle. "Well, I'll be doused! What the heck do we have here? We got us a *stowaway*, Roland! Say, fella, you been in there the whole time?"

Mayor Wubbleduster pulled himself into the window frame and hung his upper body out, gasping for air and wiping the hair dye out of his eyes.

"Where am I?! What's going on?! Who are you?! Why am I all *wet*?!"

"Hold on, hold *on*! One question at a time, big fella! I was about to ask you the same thing, 'cept for the 'Where am I?' and 'Why am I all wet?' parts! Like my old daddy used to say, 'Don't answer the obvious questions until they ain't been asked yet!'"

"He's Mayor Wubbleduster!" blurted Roland. "He was riding on my bus today, and I forgot he was in there!"

Captain Chubbychuffle stared at Roland in amazement. "You *forgot* that the *mayor of North Corners* was in the back of your bus? Good grief, Roland! How could you do that?"

"It's easy! Everybody does! Anyway, he was—um, ah—he was sleeping!"

"Well, he sure-as-shootin' isn't sleeping *now*!" The captain addressed the mayor: "Begging your pardon, Your Honor! I sure do apologize for hosing you down like that! I'm fire company captain Moolly Chubbychuffle, North Corners Fire Department, at your service and pleased to meetcha!"

Mayor Wubbleduster, now fully revived, didn't acknowledge the captain but stared as would someone in a hypnotic trance who'd just witnessed a profound vision. He began to speak in a soft, low melodious voice:

"'Twas perchance a dream of a pilgrimage as yet unfulfilled, but if dream it be, 'twas one of enchantment and terror, mingled with promise of peace and tranquility . . ."

Roland and Captain Chubbychuffle stared at each other. What was this?

"... for I dreamt I was visited by a bolt of lightning, smiting me where I stood before the throng; transported in a chariot of thunder hither and thither to a place wherein the pounding of earthly drums and the ill-and-evil moaning of the doomed and damned rose, flying above me as on the wind, and I was sore afraid.

"Yea, but therewith followed a warming of the soul which washed o'er me as I betook of the sun's benevolent radiance alighting on the greening roof at the top of the world, and lo! I saw down 'pon the firmament below, hours yet ere the gloaming of the day, a teeming of the sons of sons of fathers and mothers, spreading like a fair spring blanket o'er the land ..."

Okay, this is just plain creepy! thought Roland. Why the heck was this loon-ball talking like a waterlogged, low-end William Shakespeare?

Captain Chubbychuffle continued to gawk as Mayor Wubbleduster (or whoever he was at the moment) proceeded with his soliloquy:

"'Twas thus that I came unto these lands to feel the loosing of the flood and the trembling of the sky and the shaking of the earth. Verily the chariot that bore me hence sits beneath my feet, e'en as I to thee discourseth ..."

Roland deciphered the mayor's soliloquy: he was relating what had taken place thus far on the Bumps & Spuggett tour, as seen through the veiled mist of one who'd been electrocuted, transported five hundred years into the past, and spent the morning in a semicomatose state. The mayor believed the whole thing to be a dream from which he'd just awakened!

The mayor addressed Roland: "Forsooth! Methinks mine legions have wandered, for verily I see them not and knoweth not wherefore! Prithee, good son, what news of the fold?"

From what Roland could ascertain, Mayor Wubbleduster was asking where everybody was. "Um, well, they're not here right now, sir, but they're not far away, and we'll be rejoining them in just a minute."

"Then all's right and well! But leave us not tarry! There be yet many roads to tread and deeds to do—deeds fell and triumphant, of which songs of great praise shall one day be sung!"

This being said, the mayor slid back inside the bus and plopped down on the rear seat.

"Hey, Cap'n Chubbychuffle, are we finished here? I think the mayor is getting impatient!"

"I'd say so, Roland. I think we've cleaned up this old bus about as much as we can for now. Hope the water that got in won't be a problem for you—we're not used to solving *problems* around here normally!"

"Everything's just great, sir," lied Roland, convinced that nothing was just great. "Thanks so much for your help! I know you'll want to get back to sleep now."

"You got *that* right! You just can't get enough sleep in my business. Like my old daddy used to say, 'I'd rather be sleeping than dead, but too much of either prohibits progress—'"

The wisdom of Captain Chubbychuffle's old daddy was cut short by the strident clanging of the station's fire alarm bell. Within seconds, shouting and commotion erupted from the upstairs dormitory.

"*Fire! Fire!*" screamed Captain Chubbychuffle. "We have a fire alarm! Get that bus outa the driveway!"

He dropped the fire hose and rushed into the garage, where his men were sliding down the brass pole. Each man hastily donned canvas pants, full-length canvas coats, big rubber boots, and wide-brimmed fire helmets—except Captain Chubbychuffle. Still wearing his big boots and fire helmet, he was so preoccupied with preparing his troops that he hadn't realized he was clad only in long underwear.

Roland marveled at the controlled efficiency of the crew as they hurriedly made ready for the battle ahead. He yearned to join them but quickly shook off his daydream. His lot in life was to drive the tour bus, and he had to vacate the driveway so the firefighting vehicles could be on their way.

He ran to the bus, climbed the dripping stairs, and took his squishy seat, praying that the motor would fire up. Luck was with him: the engine coughed, grunted, sputtered, and roared to life, belching a cloud of black smoke from the rear exhaust pipe.

"Hang on, Mayor Wubbleduster! We're gonna be backing out of the driveway, and we're gonna be moving *fast*!"

"Huzzah! Huzzah!" cried the mayor jubilantly. "Off wi' ye, lad, and may thy noble chariot bear thee hence to victorious pursuits, and anon!"

Roland threw the vehicle's transmission into reverse and backed down the driveway. No sooner had he done so than the big red fire engine, hook-and-ladder truck, and the captain's car exploded out through the garage doors, fully manned, sirens screaming.

Captain Chubbychuffle waved to Roland as he sped past, his car's siren joining in a dissonant harmony with those of the two big trucks ahead of him. Roland returned the captain's wave and inwardly wished them all well, happy to have experienced a few moments with such brave and heroic individuals as the affable fire captain and his sleepy crew, and happy to have gotten his bus cleaned up in the process.

It occurred to Roland that the firemen were heading in the same direction he'd take to return to Pockets Full o' Pucky. If he followed along at a safe distance, maybe he'd catch a glimpse of some of the action. He gunned the motor and sped off in pursuit of the three wailing emergency vehicles.

As they shrieked, twisted, and turned down the streets of North Corners, Roland knew that in just a couple more blocks he'd have to break off and return to where he'd left the tour group. However, at this moment, he was enraptured by his participation in the rapidly moving convoy and the speeds they were generating. Not a cop was in sight, and his foot held the accelerator pedal to the floor.

"Whither goest thou?! Whither goest thou?! *Whoooooaaaaaw!*" screamed Mayor Wubbleduster from his seat in the rear. At each sharp turn or corner, he was jerked roughly from side to side and slid back and forth on the long, slippery, wet bench seat, trying in vain to keep his balance and remain upright through the wild ride.

"Almost there, Your Honor! Just a couple more blocks!"

Roland was apprehensive about how Barley and Biff Spoozma would handle the fact that the mayor was back in the ballgame again, sporting a vocabulary and dialect not uttered since the time of Queen Elizabeth I. He theorized that the jolt of high-watt electricity the mayor received back at the Mystic Knights of the Heavenly Daze Hall must have changed him somehow, and profoundly. Roland had heard of this phenomenon before: many comic-book superheroes could attribute the origin of their superpowers to the very same phenomenon.

But what about all that Shakespearian stuff? In the past, no one had been able to comprehend the mayor because he was an idiot. Now, no one could comprehend him without the aid of an Elizabethan English dictionary! Well, the repercussions and ramifications would be revealed very soon; they'd be back with the tour group momentarily.

Sure enough, just ahead of the fire trucks and the captain's car was the intersection at which he'd need to make a right turn to Pockets Full o' Pucky.

To Roland's surprise and delight, the brake lights of the emergency vehicles lit up as they reached the intersection. Each made a wide right turn, screaming around the corner, their blaring sirens clearing the road before them. This coincidence was almost too much. He could continue participating in their convoy a little bit longer . . .

Delight turned to dismay when the vehicles reached the street where Pockets Full o' Pucky was located and turned in that direction.

Oh no! Oh no! *The tour group's been trapped in a terrible fire, and I've been off gallivanting around the countryside!*

The firefighting vehicles screeched to a noisy stop in front of the store. As the tour bus approached from behind, Roland saw the tour group, Barley Doodlebody included, assembled on the sidewalk in front of the building. He scanned the throng; they were all there, and everyone seemed to be okay, or relatively so—but it appeared they'd spent a goodly portion of the last hour partying under Niagara Falls. And they looked like crap. (Little did Roland know how accurate this observation was.)

He parked his bus behind the fire company captain's car, turned off the ignition, and prepared for the nightmare.

16

As Barley and Noodles shepherded the drenched and disheveled tour group through the front door of Pockets Full o' Pucky and onto the sidewalk, Barley's rage mounted like steam building inside a bag of microwave popcorn. The interior of the shop was obliterated, the store's entire inventory completely lost, and everything saturated and congealed into a melted mass that comprised the largest cow pie on the face of the earth. Everyone had been thoroughly doused by the emergency sprinklers, and a few were also dripping with liquefied cow-chip residue. To top it off, the group had emerged from the inundated shop to find that the tour bus—their ticket out of this hell—had disappeared!

The tourists grumbled and groused among themselves, no longer reserved about their dissatisfaction with the way the tour was progressing. They were beyond being intimidated by Barley's threats now, far too miserable to be concerned about anything Barley might do to them. This latest catastrophe in a long string of catastrophes was the camel's back that finally broke the straw.

As the group wallowed in misery, approaching sirens could be heard, the volume growing louder. A huge red fire engine screeched around a corner up the street, followed by a hook-and-ladder truck and a smaller red automobile, all with sirens howling. Trailing the three vehicles was . . . the tour bus!

The fire trucks and car slowed and pulled to the curb in front of the shop, their sirens winding down. The tour bus pulled to the curb as well, stopping a safe distance behind them.

A fast-moving gaggle of grim-faced firemen exited the vehicles. Some unspooled the fire hose and hooked it up to a nearby hydrant. Others began pulling fire axes and other equipment from storage compartments.

Out of the red car jumped a number of firemen and their captain, who was clad in heavy boots, a big fire helmet, and long underwear. He rushed over to his rapidly deploying crew, gesticulating wildly and barking orders to the firemen, who responded without hesitation. Working as a seasoned, well-rehearsed team, the firemen were fully operational within seconds. Two men trained the fire hose upon the front of the building, one man stood by the fire hydrant with his silver wrench, tensely waiting for the order to turn on the water, and a group of three individuals with fire axes at the ready rushed past the stunned tourists, barging courageously through the front door and entering the ruined shop.

"Stand by to turn on the water, Floyd!" shouted the captain.

"Ready!" confirmed Floyd, poised to give the silver wrench a vicious crank.

The captain produced a bullhorn and shouted at the gathered tour group: "All you people clear the area! Move off to the side, out of the way! Any injuries here?"

The members of the group (who were standing a few feet from the captain and didn't require his use of the bullhorn) shook their heads to clear the ringing in their ears, which the captain took to be a negative response to his question.

The tourists followed the captain's orders, shuffling to one side of the storefront and gawking at the fire company as they performed their duties.

Perched on Noodles Snorgmark's shoulder, Chief Bohoguss began squirming and fussing at her, adamantly insisting that in his official capacity as chief of police, he should be working in concert with the captain to coordinate the fire and rescue operation. Noodles, aware that there *was* no fire and rescue operation, ignored the chief. The little guy fumed.

With the firemen fully deployed, the commotion ceased, and a tense moment of silence followed as the captain waited for the reemergence of the three-man team who'd just charged into the shop.

The front door burst open violently, swinging back on its hinges with such force that it smacked against the wall with a loud crash. The three-man team came out staggering, coughing, and retching, hustling a bewildered Arletta Fizzyfingers with them. She was covered from head to toe with a fireproof blanket, only her face visible. The men surrounded their rescued "victim" protectively, and Arletta struggled to pull the heavy blanket away from her face to keep from suffocating.

"Men, what's going on in there?!"

"Holy crap!" gasped one of the firemen as he inhaled deep gulps of fresh outdoor air. "It smells like a milking barn in there, Cap'n! *Whooooeeee! Yeeesh!*"

"*Whooooeeee!*" echoed the fireman's two teammates, pinching their noses and grimacing in disgust. "*Yeeesh!*"

"But no *fire?*"

"Nope, the automatic emergency fire sprinkler system put it out. We got here too late!"

"Darn those automatic emergency fire sprinkler systems anyhow!" growled the captain petulantly, slapping his thigh in exasperation. "We made this whole trip for nothing!"

While the captain and his men discussed the utter futility of responding to fire alarms when the fires had already been extinguished by automatic emergency fire sprinkler systems, Roland decided to take his medicine for leaving Pockets Full o' Pucky without permission. He got off the bus, took a deep breath, and slinked over to Barley, who stood with the tourists. Mayor Wubbleduster remained on the rear seat, sound asleep, exhausted after the wild ride through town.

Barley watched the reticent approach of his bus driver. "Where the hell have you been? We go inside the shop for *five minutes*, and you're off joyriding all over creation! I oughta crunch you up and roll you like a bowling ball!"

"I'm sorry, Mr. Doodlebody. I only wanted to clean the bus off while you were all occupied in the shop. I thought there'd be enough time to take care of it before you came back out. I never imagined the place would catch fire, and I certainly didn't mean to leave you high and dry!"

"Well, 'dry' is definitely *not* the term to describe us right now, Chumbuckets! We've got ourselves one big, fat mess going here, and I don't know what I'm gonna do!" Barley pointed at the tourists shivering behind him, some with wet clothes, others glazed with cow manure. "Cleaning up your bus won't make a bit of difference unless all these people get cleaned up, too! Any ideas?"

Yes. Roland looked at the pathetic tourists and the frustrated fire crew gathered on the sidewalk. He formulated a plan that might remedy the predicament and get himself back into Barley's good graces as well. "Mr. Doodlebody, that fire captain over there is a friend of mine. I was just at the same fire station these guys came from. That's where I got my bus cleaned up, and the captain let me use his fire hose!"

Barley eyed the fire captain dubiously. "You mean that buffoon with the bullhorn standing over there in his underwear? That guy's a friend of yours? He looks like a blithering idiot!"

"He's no idiot, sir! That's Captain Chubbychuffle, and he just gets a little, um, *absentminded* about certain details when he's extremely busy. Why don't we ask him if he'd let us use his fire hose to clean up all these mucky people here?"

Barley thought for a moment. *At this point, what have I got to lose?* "All right, Chumbuckets, you just might have something there. I'm all out of ideas. Set it up!"

Roland walked over to Captain Chubbychuffle. The captain was pleasantly surprised to see the bus driver again, and Roland explained the tour group's dilemma to him. Seeing the sorry condition they were in, particularly those covered with wet, odorous, melted cow-chip residue, which he could smell from where he stood, the captain volunteered his crew's assistance. They had nothing better to do at the moment anyway.

"As I told you before, Roland: we're always here to help. We're *firemen*! But *whooo-boy*! What have you folks been doing today? Don't answer that—I don't think I really want to know! Whatever it is, it always seems to end up in a big disgusting mess! Like my old daddy used to say . . ."

Roland cringed.

"'For every old mess to clean up, there's a new one to make.'"

He directed his crew to man the fire hose. They would perform their jobs after all—or a facsimile thereof. Still using the bullhorn, he addressed the tourists: "Okay, I want all those people who are in exceptionally soiled condition—you know who you are—to form a single line along the front of the shop and stand by!"

Dr. Pudbid, Reverend Snortworthy, Biff Spoozma, Mimsy Borogove, and even Frog Puppleman were painfully aware that they were the "exceptionally soiled" persons to whom the captain referred. They complied with his command, arranging themselves against the wall like criminals in a police lineup, while the fire crew faced the five exceptionally soiled tourists like a firing squad sizing up condemned prisoners. The five waited in trepidation, their knees trembling as it dawned on them what they were about to be subjected to.

"*Let 'er rip!*"

The fireman gave the wrench a mighty counterclockwise yank on the hydrant. The fire hose hissed, and a powerful stream of water exploded from the shiny brass nozzle, the torrent barreling into the tourists with the force of a battering ram. They were knocked off their feet, slammed to the ground, and smashed against the storefront like flotsam borne on the crest of a roaring tsunami wave. The poor souls screamed their heads off between desperate gasps for air.

Realizing that the water pressure was perhaps a bit excessive, Captain Chubbychuffle hurried over to the man holding the fire hose and looked down at the nozzle's spray-velocity setting. Sure enough, the nozzle was set at the "Riot Suppression" position.

"*Cut it!*"

The fireman shut off the flow of water.

Everyone stood in stunned silence. The only sound came from the residual effluent cascading into the gutter. The bashed and beaten tourists lay in a grotesque, contorted heap on the sidewalk, soaked, silent, and unmoving. The remainder of the group stared in horror at the still forms of their comrades. The fire company gawked in mute shock.

Captain Chubbychuffle broke the silence: "Oops!"

After a tense few moments, the tourists began moaning, groaning, and moving. Mercifully, the vicious hosing had done nothing more than beat the living snot out of them.

Captain Chubbychuffle and his men heaved a heavy sigh of relief. The captain gave the order to attend to the stricken and struck and walked to where Barley and Roland stood with the remaining tour group members. "Whew, that was a close one! Thought we had ourselves a buncha stiffs there for a minute!"

"All's well that ends well," replied Barley, not quite sure whether to be relieved or annoyed. "Thanks for helping us out, Cap'n. I'm Barley Doodlebody, the tour director for this junket. I guess you've already met Chumbuckets here."

"Yup, we cleaned up his bus over at the station right before we got the call to come here. Seems like we've been doin' more cleanin' up messes than puttin' out fires today—but I guess that's a good thing, eh? The name's fire company captain Moolly Chubbychuffle, at your service and pleased to meetcha!"

Barley and Captain Chubbychuffle shook hands. "Sorry about the false alarm, Captain!"

"Darn those automatic emergency fire sprinkler systems anyhow! They're puttin' us out of business! Like my old daddy used to say . . ."

Roland knew what was coming and quickly interceded:

"Uh, excuse me, Cap'n, but I have an urgent matter I need to speak with Mr. Doodlebody about. Would you pardon us for a moment, please?"

"Why, o' course, Roland! We're almost finished here anyway. We'll make sure everyone gets back on your bus, and you'll be on your way!"

"Thanks again, Cap'n! You and your men are lifesavers!"

"Always here to help, Roland! Like my old daddy used to say, 'You can turn tricks in a cathouse, but you can't get drunk in a crowbar.'"

His voice trailed off as Roland led Barley to the tour bus.

"All right, Chumbuckets, what's this all about?"

"Mr. Doodlebody, there's . . . something that, uh, I think you need to know right away."

"Well, spit it out! We've got to get this show back on the road before these idiots start getting crazy ideas about wanting their money back."

Roland gulped nervously. "Well, sir, it's about Mayor Wubbleduster: He's awake again, and he's—how shall I put it? He's *different* now!"

Barley laughed derisively. "That pinhead has always been different! So he's awake again. What's the big deal?!"

"Sir, when I say 'different,' I mean *really* different!"

"What are you talking about? How fricking different can he be?"

On cue, Mayor Wubbleduster poked his head out the rear window of the bus, his puffy face streaked with caked black hair dye and his wet, scraggly hair hanging in stringy strands down the sides of his face. Spying Barley standing by the bus, he let out an exuberant cry of salutation: "Verily, Master Doodlebody, mine heart doth rejoice, thine fair countenance again to espy! Sooth, have I endured tribulation, yet return triumphant! The wisdom of thine counsel would I take anon!"

Barley's jaw dropped.

"Let us parlay, good Doodlebody, ere the waning of the sun!"

Barley was flummoxed but not entirely witless. He had no intention of chitchatting with this incomprehensible, newly revived mayor—or whoever he was at the moment. "Shut up, you fat moron! If you want to talk to somebody, talk to Spoozma! I've got more important matters to attend to."

The mayor clucked his tongue indignantly at Barley's impertinence and exclaimed, "Fie! Fie 'pon ye!" and ducked his ragged head inside the bus.

Barley spotted the mayor's battered public relations advisor and personal bodyguard being escorted slowly to the bus by one of Captain

Chubbychuffle's firemen. "Spoozma! Get your butt over here! Your nutball boss is looking for you!"

Biff's eyes widened, and an anguished moan issued forth from deep down in his soul. The episode in Pocket's Full o' Pucky had enabled him to forget the mayor's existence. Being reminded sank the big man's spirit like an overloaded garbage scow. The firefighter led him to the bus door, gave him a sympathetic smile, and hastily departed.

Roland and Barley watched as he staggered like a beaten dog down the center aisle to the rear seats. They heard the mayor cry, "Hail, good Master Spoozma! Mine true and loyal minion!"—which brought forth yet another agonized moan from the big guy. Biff's only consolation, now that His Honor was awake, was that he would longer need to trundle him over his shoulder. Hopefully.

The other tourists arrived at the bus, their fireman escorts assisting them to the stairway and wishing them luck. As she parted ways with the handsome young man who'd been guiding her, Mimsy Borogove fixed him with a salacious leer and licked her lips, flicking her tongue at him obscenely. What she didn't realize was that a good deal of the blue dye in her hair had been washed off her head by the hard stream of water and now covered her face so that she resembled someone who'd spent the morning with her head dunked in an inkwell. Her fireman escort deposited her at the bus steps and scooted away with a queasy look.

Once all of the tourists were back on board and in their places, Barley and Roland took their seats. The bus was ready to leave Pockets Full o' Pucky and Arletta Fizzyfingers to their respective fates. Roland started the motor and eased the vehicle away from the curb. The fire company was busy stowing the fire hose and the other equipment back aboard the fire trucks. Roland spied Arletta Fizzyfingers engrossed in a vigorous debate with Captain Chubbychuffle, attempting to convince the captain that it was the duty and responsibility of his men to clean up the shop's interior.

From the look on his face, the captain wasn't buying into the idea. He did, however, pause in the midst of his heated discussion to wave goodbye to the departing group. The rest of the fire crew joined in, and Roland returned their send-off waves. He sat back in his driver's seat and sighed in weary relief. The Bumps & Spuggett tour was underway again—for better or for worse.

* * *

The bright sun had done a good job of drying off the exterior of Roland's freshly washed tour bus. The tourists were another matter entirely. They sat morosely in their seats, drenched, depleted, and depressed, oblivious to the fact that the interior of the bus was also soaked and dripping. For all they knew or cared, the automatic emergency fire sprinkler system had gone off inside the bus as well.

Barley felt fairly miserable himself. It was crisis time again on the Bumps & Spuggett tour, and he needed to distract the tourists. He would bite the bullet again and accommodate these people, although admittedly, it wasn't so difficult this time. He wanted to ease their suffering because he wanted to ease his own.

The tour bus hadn't traveled more than a couple blocks before Barley instructed Roland to pull over to the curb and stop. He stood at his seat and addressed the passengers. "Everybody, listen up!"

The tourists raised their heads and gazed at him lethargically.

"I'm not going to kid you: things are rough here. None of this was supposed to happen, and I'm just as uncomfortable as the rest of you. Whenever you start a new business, there are going to be a few kinks that need to be ironed out—problems you can't foresee, obstacles you have to overcome—and we've had our share of those today."

"Yeah, *buddy*!" agreed Frog wholeheartedly.

Barley scowled at his brother, paused, and took a deep breath.

"But the pioneers who settled this great land of ours had to endure hardship, and their hardship was a lot harder than our hardship. They never allowed hardship to hold them back, no matter how hard the hardship!

"You are modern-day pioneers: overcoming the hardship, facing down the unknown, enduring these things so that the people who follow in *your* footsteps will have an easier time and a better life. They will owe it all to you and your pioneer spirit! They will travel on the trails *you* blazed; they will build upon the ground *you* broke!"

Barley paused to get a feel for the tourists' reaction to his oration thus far. They seemed to be listening, their haggard faces turned up to gaze at him. Maybe a little confused, but curiosity flickered in their eyes.

He took another deep breath and went on. "You've answered the call today. You've proven that your own pioneer spirit is equal to the task before you. We've almost reached our goal! We're so close to achieving victory over adversity. We *will* prevail! I challenge you now to gather your strength and your courage, bring forth that pioneer spirit with renewed vigor and determination, and let's finish the task before us. The generations of our future demand it. The tour must go on!"

Barley stopped again, peering intently at the tourists, who looked at him with resolve blazing in their eyes. "So we stand at the crossroads; the moment of truth is staring us right in the face and asking us, are we ready to honor the sacrifice and the commitment of our forefathers, and carve our own names into the tablets of history? Or will we crumble and bow under the paltry pressures of inconvenience and adversity, admitting defeat and our own inadequacies as pioneers and trailblazers? I will *not* crumble or bow! I will keep on to the bitter end and a brighter day! *Are you with me?*!"

"*Yeah, buddy!*" screamed Frog.

Barley waited tensely for the others to respond. It only took a few seconds. They shook their heads positively, gathered their enthusiasm, and focused their determination. Barley was asking for their continued support and participation. He was *asking* them, not telling them. He *needed* them!

Shouts of "We're with you, Mr. Doodlebody!" and "Yeah! We can *do* this!" erupted from the seats.

"Hallelujah! Glory be!" cried Reverend Snortworthy.

Chief Binky shrieked excitedly and waved his arms over his head like a cheerleader action figure. The reinvigorated tourists smiled with indulgent affection.

In the rear, Mayor Wubbleduster exploded with a rousing, "Huzzah! Huzzah! Verily, thou speakest truth, noble Doodlebody!" causing the rest of the group to turn in their seats and gape at him. The mayor was back! But what kind of eloquently unintelligible gibberish was *that*?

Barley was pleased. All the members of the group, even the normally skeptical Rapunzel Trashtrumpet, seemed to be on board with the program. He'd given them the inspiration they needed, and just in time. But inspired or not, everyone was still sopping wet and uncomfortable. His dramatic speechifying had calmed the tourists for the moment; now he needed to get everybody dried out posthaste.

How?

Suddenly, the concept of "high-intensity" struck Barley like a boxer with an iron-lined glove. It had worked with cleaning the tour bus and the slime-covered tourists; maybe the key to resolving this new issue would be a high-intensity *drying* machine. And he knew where to find one.

"Chumbuckets, get this bus over to Charlie Nutbooger's Drive-Thru Car Wash and Used Bookstore on east Blapp Street! Nutbooger's an old lodge buddy of mine—he might be able to help us out!"

Roland was puzzled. "Mr. Doodlebody, the bus is already pretty clean now, and it's too big to fit inside that drive-thru car wash."

"We're not going there for the bus."

17

Before establishing his present business on East Blapp Street, Charlie Nutbooger had been the librarian at the North Corners Municipal Library. He was fired for embezzling books and running them to rural areas of third-world countries as contraband. Charlie's motives were altruistic: he sincerely believed he was enriching lives with good literature. But Charlie failed to take into account that most of the third-world countries receiving the contraband books could not read English. They used them as fuel for their cooking fires, burning them to heat their homes in the winter, or as toilet paper. Ignoble applications, perhaps, but not entirely impractical.

When Charlie's subterfuge was discovered, he was summarily canned, subsequently arrested, and his career as a well-meaning book smuggler ingloriously ended. However, then-first-term mayor Barley Doodlebody liked Charlie's surreptitious style and pardoned his fellow lodge brother from a jail sentence, thereby making Charlie Nutbooger yet another North Corners citizen beholden to him.

Charlie was grateful for the pardon but forswore a further life of crime, opening his drive-thru car wash on East Blapp Street. He made good on his marker to Barley by giving the crooked mayor free car washes for all eternity or until he sold his car, whichever came first. Additionally, he still had a large stash of embezzled library books left from his smuggling days, so he opened a used bookstore along with the car wash.

It was only a few bumpy blocks to East Blapp Street. Within minutes, the bus arrived at the car wash with its drenched passengers. Barley instructed Roland to pull into the driveway near the automated car wash's drive-thru exit, then turned to the tour group. "I'll only be gone a minute, so sit here and relax. When I come back, we're going to put everything right again!"

He got off the bus and walked to the office.

The tourists were too exhausted and waterlogged to complain or be concerned. Barley's pioneer-spirit rhetoric had given most of them a sense of purpose, and they were determined more than ever to complete their mission, for now it had *become* a mission. Their attention was diverted from the fact the tour was originally intended to be frivolous entertainment. Now it was a quest, a crusade, a war to be won—and by golly, they were going to win it!

If they didn't become martyrs first.

While the tourists waited on the bus, Barley outlined his idea to Charlie Nutbooger. Barley's plan would eliminate the high-pressure spray washing and waxing phase of the drive-thru and concentrate on the final portion, the huge hot-air dryers. By placing the tourists underneath these big drying machines, they could accomplish in a minute what would take the sun a couple of hours to complete.

"Well, Barley, I've never dried out any people like that before—mostly *cars*, y'know? I can't be sure if it'll work or not, but hey! I'm willin' to give it a shot if it might help! Still gonna have to charge you for a full wash, though."

As far as Charlie was concerned, the huge busload of tourists didn't fall under his "free car washes for all eternity or until Barley sold his car, whichever came first" obligation.

Barley considered this. "Tell you what, Charlie, I'll trade you: you dry out my people there, and I'll treat you and your wife to a fancy gourmet dinner at one of my best restaurants. Unique cuisine, attentive service, and a live floor show! Whaddaya say to that?"

A great idea, Charlie thought. As a cook, his wife was most proficient at preparing poached pickled pork with sautéed hay, day after day after day. *Anything* would be a nice change from that menu, and Barley promised the added bonus of live entertainment. The offer was too tempting to resist.

"Done!" They shook hands on the deal.

"Okay, I'm gonna go tell everybody what's going on. You get everything ready!" Barley smiled to himself. *Granny Mambo will be pleased . . .*

He climbed aboard the bus and faced his passengers. "I told you I was going to put everything right again, and that's exactly what's gonna happen now. Everyone come outside and follow me over to the drive-thru car wash. Look alive!"

Looking as alive as they were capable of looking given present circumstances, the passengers laboriously rose from their seats and filed outside.

Roland figured he'd mop up the vehicle's soggy interior while the bus was empty. Barley approved the idea and pointed Roland toward the car wash office where he had noticed many items that would aid in the bus interior's restoration, among them a stack of towels. Roland hastened to the office to obtain the towels.

Once the tourists had assembled, Barley led them to the exit of the car wash. Charlie Nutbooger positioned himself in front of a control panel located on a wall inside the tunnel. He ogled the tourists: never had he seen a more haggard, harried, hassled, disheveled, and disheartened-looking bunch of people, especially that woman with the blue hair and face! They *all* could use a good drying out—but why did they need a drive-thru car wash to accomplish this? A simple handheld hair dryer would probably achieve the same results. Eventually.

Charlie made some adjustments to the dryers' temperature controls to hopefully ensure the tourists' flesh wouldn't be melted off their bodies, and waited for Barley's signal.

"Okay, everybody, we're gonna stand under those big dryers you see in there," Barley said. "It'll only take a minute, and we'll be as dry as a bone, back in business, and on our way!"

Barley walked into the tunnel and stood beneath the dryers, beckoning the tourists to do likewise. Seeing that Barley wasn't forcing them to experience anything he wasn't prepared to experience himself, they gathered their courage and followed, bunching together under the formidable drying machines. Once everyone was huddled in place, Barley flashed a thumbs-up to Charlie Nutbooger, who returned the gesture and threw a switch.

A mechanical whirring sound filled the interior of the tunnel, increasing in volume until it became a roar. Continuous, high-intensity heated air erupted out of the dryer nozzles. The searing wind staggered and buffeted Barley and the tourists like leaves in a hurricane, whipping at their hair and clothing, instantly sucking all moisture out of their bodies.

Barley battled the heated blast, desperately trying to keep Binky Bohoguss from being blown out of his suit coat pocket and off to who-knows-where. "*YEEEEEEEEK! YEEEEEEEK!*" the little guy screamed at the top of his tiny lungs. The other tourists were slammed into each other by the relentless, overpowering currents. Mayor Wubbleduster shrieked,

"Succor! Succor! I beseech thee!" Reverend Snortworthy bawled and blubbered like a blathering baby.

Barley cried out to Charlie Nutbooger, his voice barely audible over the cacophony of the howling winds and the screaming tourists: "*Charlie*! That's enough! Turn it off! *Turn it off*!"

Charlie watched the windblown drama anxiously, fully aware that the group had had enough. These high-powered dryers were for cars, not people! He cut the electricity; the whining, whirring, roaring sound waned, and the withering winds decreased, leaving Barley and the rest of the group gasping for air and struggling to stand upright.

"Is everybody okay?" Charlie asked.

"Lemme outa here! Gimme some air! I can't breathe!" Biff Spoozma staggered away from the group and out through the exit of the tunnel, making his way into the fresh air and sunshine where he stood, bent at the waist, taking deep breaths.

Barley, quite shaken himself, took a moment to gather his wits and take stock of everybody's condition. To his relief, and despite being completely disheveled, discombobulated, and blown out, everyone was nonetheless unhurt—and *thoroughly* dry. The method may have been unorthodox, but the result was exactly what he'd hoped for.

"Yeah, Charlie, I think everybody's fine. We're a little shook-up, but we'll survive."

The others joined Biff on the driveway outside. Biff had finally managed to rein in his emotions and catch his breath, but as soon as Mayor Wubbleduster emerged from the car wash and cried, "Noble and steadfast servant! Be thee not dismayed, yet rejoice for thine redemption from the flood, filled with tribulation though it be!" Biff covered his ears with both hands, screamed, "I can't *take* this anymore!" and sprinted away from the group. He made a beeline to the used bookstore and disappeared inside, the door slamming behind him.

The rest of the bedraggled group stared gloomily at the door of the shop. It appeared that all of the stress and strain of the day's activities had finally caused Big Biff to snap like a twig. Who could blame him?

Barley verified that Binky Bohoguss was still in his coat pocket and walked over to Charlie Nutbooger. "I appreciate your help, Charlie. I guess we'll be on our way now. Still got lots to do today. I'll come back tomorrow with the voucher for your dinners."

"Glad I could help out, Barley, and thanks for the free dinners! The missus will be pleased for the chance to get out of the kitchen—and frankly, I'll be overjoyed to have her out of there myself!" He grimaced at the thought of Mrs. Nutbooger's patented poached pickled pork with sautéed hay. "*Yeeeesh*!"

"Don't mention it." Barley was certain that once Charlie and Mrs. Nutbooger experienced Granny Mambo's Liverland, he'd become persona non grata around the car wash and used bookstore forevermore. So be it. Sometimes, in order to cross a river you had to burn a bridge.

"All right, everybody back on the bus!"

The group, Barley included, now looked more haggard than they had all day. Their wind-blasted hair stood on end as if they'd spent a frightening day in fifty-yard-line seats at the Super Bowl of the undead. Their clothing had been rearranged so that they now resembled a band of scarecrows in hand-me-downs previously sucked through a jet engine. However, they were all dry again, and still convinced that their places in the pioneer history books were secure.

They climbed aboard the tour bus to find that Roland had dried the wet interior. The mayor and his little daughter returned to their seats. Margaret, to her consternation, discovered that the intensive session under the big dryers had completely dried out, drained away, and evaporated all the saliva in her body! The massive inner reservoir of bodily fluid that normally enabled her to produce voluminous quantities of spit was now as devoid of moisture as a swimming pool on the moon. She quietly took her place next to her father on the rear bench seat and gazed morosely out the shattered window, contemplating how she was going to overcome this disturbing new development and keep anyone else from finding out about it.

A good portion of Margaret's mystique could be attributed to the fearful anticipation she inflicted upon others; one never knew if and when they might be her next HIVED-ing victim, an advantage the little girl relished. If people discovered she'd been rendered saliva-deficient, her advantage would be lost, her power and mystique nullified. Also, there were a lot of HIVED-ing casualties who'd love to get their hands on her. This lack of liquidity could be a very bad thing.

No one else seemed to be suffering any ill effects from their ordeal under the dryers. Once everyone was seated and settled, Barley told Roland to get underway.

As the bus pulled away, the bookstore's door burst open, and Biff Spoozma sprinted out, clutching something under one arm, waving the other over his head and frantically shouting for the bus to stop. Roland pulled to the curb to let Biff climb aboard.

Barley scowled as the big man clambered up the steps. "Where the hell have *you* been?"

"I saw the used bookstore, and I went in and got this!" Biff held up the item he'd been carrying under his arm: an Elizabethan English dictionary.

"All right, you made it here in time! Get your butt back there and sit down!"

Biff proceeded to his seat next to Mayor Wubbleduster. Everyone was glad to have the big guy back with them again and nodded approvingly at his new purchase. It appeared that Biff had used his head, not lost it.

A few moments later, Mayor Wubbleduster's nearly incomprehensible babbling filtered from the back of the bus, accompanied by the sound of Elizabethan English dictionary pages turning feverishly.

Barley sat back and sighed. After everything the group had undergone today, and after all the grief and aggravation he'd endured trying to put things right, *everyone* could use a good laugh right about now. The time had come at last.

Once more he rose from his seat. "Okay, enough is enough! We've gone through hell today, and it's only noon. We're not gonna wait another minute. Get ready to see some of the craziest people you'll ever see, and to laugh like you've never laughed before! We're heading for Bumps & Spuggett!"

The passengers could hardly believe their ears. They were *finally* going to view what they'd endured so much to see: the inner sanctum and workings of the fabled Bumps & Spuggett firm. The tourists burst into joyous applause; this was the highlight of the trip, and it couldn't possibly be worse than what they'd been through already . . .

Could it?

18

The sign above the office building door read,

BUMPS & SPUGGETT
Radically Stupid Suggestions

"**O**kay, Chumbuckets, this is the place!" shouted Barley. Roland turned off the ignition, and the idling vehicle sputtered to a silent standstill.

Barley stood on the sidewalk, studying the legendary Bumps & Spuggett building, the object of his most recent venture in a long list of ventures. This was the first time he'd ever been here himself, but from what he'd heard of the place and its reputation for eccentricity, he was sure his tour business was on the threshold of becoming a very lucrative enterprise. Even the building's exterior exuded eccentricity. Once this group of haggard and harried tourists walked inside and witnessed the hilarity for themselves, the tragedies of the day would be forgotten.

Edging forward on their seats, the tourists craned their necks and gazed with curiosity at the storied building and its odd design.

The firm was located at the intersection of Clown Balls Avenue and Guggbutt Boulevard. Clown Balls Avenue ran in an east-west direction, and the front of the building faced the avenue, looking south. Guggbutt Boulevard, running north and south, bordered the building's west side. The rear or north side of the building looked out on a smaller thoroughfare named Gob Street, which ran parallel to Clown Balls Avenue, and the eastern side was bounded by a service alleyway accessible by either Clown Balls Avenue or Gob Street. The building sat on the northeast corner of the Clown Balls and Guggbutt intersection.

This was a neglected, deserted portion of North Corners that few people visited because they didn't *need* to: it wasn't close to anything. Other than an occasional deliveryman, most passersby who did venture into the area were either lost, drunk, on their way to somewhere else, or all of the above.

The exterior of the building looked like any other normal business establishment in North Corners except for its decidedly *ab*normal design: it was a two-story brick structure, with the second story appearing less spacious than the first in square footage but much taller in height. The upper floor was set back from the footprint of the first floor and rose high up like a windowless monolith. A strange, narrow outcropping protruded midway up the receded second-floor monolith and connected to the building's front.

Only two windows were visible on the front of the building, both at ground level. One of them—narrow, oblong, and vertical—was just to the right of the front door. The other, rectangular, stood a few yards to the right. Both were made of opaque glass, which precluded Barley from seeing anything when he attempted to peer inside. Both were covered and protected by vertical metal bars.

"All right, everybody, we're here. Get off the bus and prepare for the biggest thrill of your little lives!"

The tourists scrambled off the bus, assembled in a circle, and prepared for the biggest thrill of their little lives.

"Listen up! No one in this loony bin knows we're coming today. We're gonna sneak in, and they'll go absolutely bonkers when they see us—which is exactly what we want them to do. I'll go first, and you follow me, two by two. Noodles, get 'em organized!"

Noodles arranged the group into a column, the tourists lined up two abreast. Barley would lead the way, with Chief Bohoguss hitching a ride in his usual spot inside Barley's breast pocket.

Once the line had been formed, Barley addressed them: "All right, I don't want trouble from any of you from now on! Stay together in line, and nobody say a word. Spoozma, if the mayor makes a sound—one little *peep*—I'm gonna transplant his brain into *your* head right where we stand, get it? And Noodles, you keep the mayor's little snot-dispensing demon daughter under control or I'm going to hand her over to the Bumps & Spuggett loonies and let them do what they will to her. Remember: the element of surprise is what we're going for here. Everybody ready?"

In his excitement, Frog Puppleman shrieked, "*Yeah, buddy!*" and was immediately knocked cold by Barley, who had lost all patience with his nitwit half brother's mindless babbling. Frog fell unconscious yet again, and Noodles, now quite familiar with the routine, heaved a sigh and hoisted his inert form over her shoulder.

Barley approached the front door of the building and gave it a push—it opened! He eased his head inside to look around. He saw a long, narrow, dimly lit vestibule, the only source of light coming from the oblong opaque window by the front door. The illumination it cast was minimal and somewhat eerie but enough to render the interior features discernible. The vestibule was not a reception room or lobby, although it may have served that purpose at one time. There were no furnishings or decorations, only a dingy, dusty carpet on the floor.

At the western end of the narrow room, directly across from Barley, a set of closed double doors presumably opened into first-floor offices. To his right, at the eastern end of the vestibule, a darkened stairway led up to the second floor. Nothing else presented itself to view. The place smelled musty, and cobwebs hung from the walls and ceiling. Dust bunnies curled in the corners, but a track in the dusty carpet indicated that there had been foot traffic through the room. This track passed from the front entrance to the stairwell.

Pushing the door wider, Barley eased inside and motioned for Biff Spoozma to hold the door for him while the others waited. Barley crept across to the double doors. They were both locked. Perhaps the firm's activities were taking place upstairs, if anyone was here at all.

He crossed the length of the vestibule to the eastern end and the unlit stairway, which ascended a few steps before abruptly turning to the left and continuing upward. A light emanated from above, and he heard a low, barely perceptible drone coming from the direction of the upstairs light. Puzzled but intrigued, Barley signaled for Biff Spoozma and the rest of the group to be quiet and follow him into the vestibule.

As Biff held the door open, the tourists entered and crept past him into the darkened room, apprehensive, trying desperately not to make any noise. When they'd all entered and were standing again in their line behind Barley at the foot of the stairs, Biff closed the front door and retook his place next to wide-eyed Mayor Wubbleduster.

It was done. They were inside the offices of Bumps & Spuggett!

Barley placed his finger to his lips once again, reminding them to remain silent and wait until he told them to move. He looked up the stairwell, listening to the odd droning, and began to climb cautiously, one step at a time. He methodically tested each successive stair's strength; if it didn't creak, groan, or collapse under his weight, he transferred himself to the next and so on. Reaching the stair before the staircase made its abrupt left turn, he looked down at the waiting group and beckoned them to follow while emulating his caution and maintaining their silence.

The procession of tourists began their painstaking climb, literally following in Barley's footsteps. Reverend Snortworthy mumbled, "Yea, though I walk through the valley of the shadow of—"

"Shut your drooling yap, cabbage head!" Barley hissed through clenched teeth. "Or the only valley you'll be walking through is the one between the two split halves of your big, fat skull!"

The reverend ceased his mumbling and crossed himself several times, an odd thing to do since he wasn't Catholic.

Barley paused to listen for any reaction from atop the stairs that would indicate they'd been discovered. Agonizing seconds ticked by; no sound save for that mysterious droning noise could be heard from above. Satisfied that their presence was still undetected, Barley turned his attention to the next stair.

The odd, monotonous sound grew louder. Barley felt a touch of apprehension, but the thought of all the money he'd be making from this deal bolstered his courage and spurred him on. Farther back, Roland Chumbuckets was reminded of his recent experience at Captain Chubbychuffle's fire station. He'd also climbed a deserted staircase to an unseen second-floor room with a strange, mysterious sound. Roland had subsequently discovered a room full of sleeping firemen. What would this group discover?

They neared the top of the stairs, the light very bright now, and Barley determined that the odd hum was a human voice. The voice became more distinct with each step, and soon he heard it clearly: "Chili-baba chili-baba jijjy-booboo jijjy-booboo chili-baba chili-baba jijjy-booboo jijjy-booboo . . ."

Barley scratched his head in bewilderment. A person obviously made the sound, but he hadn't a clue as to what the words meant. Still, it wasn't enough to daunt him.

The tourists were encouraged by Barley's lack of hesitation and followed faithfully. If anything horrible happened at the top of the stairs, it would happen to Barley first, giving the rest of them time to turn tail and get out of there. This did much to ease their apprehensions.

Barley reached a step just below eye level with the second floor. Above him was the second-floor landing, and just beyond, the reception area and lobby of the fabled Bumps & Spuggett office. It was time to implement his surprise attack and burst in upon the firm's strange little world, demanding entertainment from them. If threats and intimidation were necessary to accomplish this, so be it. He'd come too far today and been through too much to back down now.

He took another deep breath of the stuffy air. The incessant "chili-baba chili-baba jijjy-booboo jijjy-booboo" was beginning to drive him crazy. If nothing else, he intended to silence whoever was making that infernal sound!

Barley stood ramrod straight, threw back his shoulders, and bounded up the remaining steps to the second floor.

PART III:

INSIDE THE OFFICES OF BUMPS & SPUGGETT

19

Lollie Babajuju was originally from the tiny village of Splat in the small country of Bubba-Bubba-Bubba. She awoke one fine morning to learn she was the receptionist at Bumps & Spuggett in North Corners, Ohio. How did she get there? She had no idea then, and still didn't. She just knew that answering the phone all day was a big, fat pain in the butt. She spoke no English. The saving grace was the fact that the phone never rang at all, which rendered Lollie and her job useless and therefore indispensable to the Bumps & Spuggett firm.

Lollie compensated for her lack of useful activity by spending the lion's share of each workday sitting at her desk, hands folded neatly in front of her, shoulders and back arrow straight, expression blank, staring straight ahead in a trancelike state and saying, "Chili-baba chili-baba jijjy-booboo jijjy-booboo chili-baba jijjy-booboo." This was a comforting routine from her girlhood in Bubba-Bubba-Bubba, a way of relaxing, calming her mind, and escaping the boredom of her daily existence. If she chanted long enough, she could achieve a euphoric high and disappear from the world for a while, which was the main reason she did it and where she was most of the time. It also offered a possible explanation as to why she awoke one fine morning to find that she was the receptionist at Bumps & Spuggett in North Corners, Ohio, without a clue as to how she got there.

She was completely enveloped in the trance when Barley came charging up the stairway and across the room to stand before her desk like a huge pork sausage with an attitude problem.

The rest of the group remained on the stairway, low enough to keep hidden from view, too low to see what was going on in the lighted room above them. They listened intently. So far, so good; no one screamed or cried out. The mysterious droning chant continued unabated. They waited breathlessly for something to happen.

Barley stood quietly in front of the big reception desk, but received no acknowledgment from the receptionist. He took the opportunity to inspect the room: it was a typical business lobby and reception area, somewhat muted in its decor, furnished with one upholstered armchair and two overstuffed sofas positioned perpendicular to each other in a corner across from the reception desk. In front of each sofa, a coffee table held no magazines, books, or reading material of any sort. On either end of the sofas were small end tables, upon which stood small shaded lamps. Overhead fluorescent bulbs lit the rest of the room—typical uninspiring but efficient office lighting.

The receptionist and her reception desk were positioned across from the stairway and to the right as one entered the room. Hanging on the wall behind her desk were two large oil paintings, portraits of two elderly, distinguished-looking gentlemen dressed formally in dark suits and neckties. Each wore stern, dignified, businesslike expressions that exuded wisdom and control as they gazed stoically down at Barley. Engraved brass plaques were attached to the bottom of each frame, one with the inscription *O. M. Bumps, Founding Partner—Now Dead*, and the other with the inscription *O. M. Spuggett, Other Founding Partner—Still Alive, Kind Of*.

Barley gazed up at them in wonder. So, these two clucks had started all the insanity. They certainly didn't look like weirdos. Evidently you couldn't tell how goofy a person was by looking at them (case in point: Frog Puppleman), but weirdos they must have been. Barley was going to use his more practical business acumen to make his fortune from their bumbling efforts to operate a business. *You nutty old buzzards are gonna make me rich!*

To the left of the portraits was an open double doorway, presumably the entrance to the company's business offices. Barley peeked through the doors into this inner sanctum. The majority of the space beyond the doors was taken up by a very large, open room. He spied a couple paper-strewn desks positioned near the entrance, unmanned. No signs of life. Aside from this receptionist's chanting, he heard no other sound.

It sure seemed quiet for a nuthouse.

Finished with his perusal of the rather unremarkable lobby and reception room, and somewhat disappointed at its lack of flair (and the fact that the walls weren't lined with rubber, as he believed they might be), Barley stared at the receptionist. She stared at something in the fourth dimension. The incessant "chili-baba jijjy-booboo chili-baba jijjy-booboo" drone issued forth from her mouth.

After several more minutes of this one-sided stare-down, Barley could take no more. "Say something intelligent, you blithering idiot!"

The crowd on the stairs jumped, startled at his frightening interruption of the soothing chant. They were actually beginning to enjoy it.

Lollie's chant merely continued. She was far beyond Barley's reach.

"*Helloooooo*! Is anybody in there? What is going *on* with you!?"

The response: ". . . chili-baba jijjy-booboo chili-baba jijjy-booboo . . ."

Barley scratched his head again, puzzled. No one had ever before ignored him so successfully and effectively, and he was yelling his head off—right in her face. Be that as it may, he surmised that the receptionist was harmless and it would be safe for the group to join him in the lobby. He walked back to the stairwell.

"It's okay, you can come up now. Keep quiet and let *me* do the talking!"

The tourists cautiously climbed the remainder of the stairs and entered the lobby and reception room, crowding behind Barley in front of the reception desk. They too stared at the chanting receptionist.

"Prithee, a word, Master Doodlebody," interrupted Mayor Wubbleduster, his voice just above a whisper, "but by which attitude must our comportment be upheld, lest we in our correspondence err with those whom we hope to engage?"

Barley flashed a beseeching look at Biff Spoozma, who consulted his Elizabethan English dictionary, flipping furiously through the pages. "I think the mayor's wondering how we're supposed to act when we meet these people, so we don't offend or insult anyone," he said.

Barley laughed derisively. "How are we supposed to *act*? Act any way you please! Who cares if we offend or insult anybody? We're not here today to *accommodate* anyone. We're here to be accommodated! We're here to be entertained by these nitwits. It's their job not to offend or insult *us*!

"You think you've had it rough today? Take it out on them! Things haven't worked out the way you wanted them to? Take it out on them! Look at this receptionist here! She's a loony! Why should you care how you act with someone like *this*?!"

Then to Mayor Wubbleduster, he added, "We're not here on a diplomatic mission, you moron! We're on a flippin' holiday! You especially,

Wubbleduster, could use a lesson in what it feels like to know you're better than someone."

The tourists scowled. Barley's cynical appraisal of the situation didn't jive with all that pioneer-spirit rhetoric he'd plied them with earlier. They wanted to forget about the hell they'd been through today, not put it onto someone else. Why should they want to ridicule and mistreat this chanting receptionist? True, her lack of attention was somewhat impertinent, but she didn't seem to realize they were *there*—she wasn't purposely ignoring them. Besides, that chant was nice. Knowing their host as well as they did now, Barley's cynical attitude was expected and in character but nevertheless unappreciated and unwelcomed.

The mayor started to protest, but Barley cut him off. "I don't want to hear it, you time-twisted, blithering dunce! Now shut your barrel and let's *move on*!"

Mayor Wubbleduster cringed from Barley's blistering rebuke, lowered his head, and slipped back in line behind Biff Spoozma.

Back in the group, little Margaret snorted, indignant at the way that big, loud, blustery man kept reviling her father. He'd been doing so most of the day, starting with this morning's assembly in the Mystic Knights of the Heavenly Daze Lodge Hall when he stood by apathetically as the mayor was electrocuted. He'd even called for *her* to be bound and gagged with gaffer's tape! After that, and ever since the mayor had recovered from his electric-shock trauma, the big nasty man had screamed at her father and told him to shut up repeatedly.

Margaret didn't care much about politics. The affairs of grown-ups in general were of little interest to her, but she knew her father's title of "mayor" was supposed to accord him respect. None of the other people had called her father names or told him to shut up, so why was this big, loud, nasty man doing so? He'd called the mayor a "moron," a "lunatic," and a "dunce"—but that moronic lunatic dunce was her *daddy*. The constant ridicule of her daddy was unconscionable! It was lucky for that big, loud, nasty man that those hot-air dryers at the car wash had dehydrated her so thoroughly. At least, for now . . .

Barley faced Lollie Babajuju once more. "*Lady*! Hey, lady! I'm talkin' to you!"

Oblivious.

"*What the hell are you jabbering about*?! *Are you totally and completely nuts*?! *Answer me*!"

"... chili-baba jijjy-booboo chili-baba jijjy-booboo ..."

Barley was furious, but the tourists relaxed into the soothing groove of the chant. Chief Bohoguss began mumbling the strange words in his tiny voice. He was particularly susceptible to the seductive rhythm (perhaps because of his diminutive size) and quickly fell under the spell. Soon he was blissfully chanting away, his doll-like countenance mimicking the euphoric expression on Lollie's face. "Chili-baba jijjy-booboo chili-baba jijjy-booboo ..." The little guy's voice wafted up from inside of Barley's coat pocket.

The group sighed with renewed adoration; how darn cute can you *get*?

Lollie Babajuju had unknowingly succeeded in frustrating Barley at a level to which he was ill accustomed. Nor was he used to this new brand of passive resistance. Normally, other dogs heeled when Barley Doodlebody barked. But the man's determination to get into the Bumps & Spuggett sanctum was undiminished. Once more, he faced down the chanting receptionist.

"How does anybody get any service around this dump?!"

"... chili-baba jijjy-booboo chili-baba jijjy-booboo ..."

"Am I gonna hafta bust your butt, you stuporous psycho?!?"

Same response from Lollie. She wouldn't have understood a word he said, anyway.

Barley had finally reached his limit. He was about to launch himself across Lollie's desk to level her with a haymaker when a little man appeared at the double doorway to the inner office, yawning widely and rubbing his sleep-filled eyes. He was Fandango Slamson, the Bumps & Spuggett CEO in charge of being the office manager, an odd-looking man with the personality and body of a potato, although potatoes were more interesting conversationalists. The commotion in the reception lobby awoke him from the daily Bumps & Spuggett conference-room nap that all the employees participated in due to their having to be at work by 2:30 in the morning.

Of all the Bumps & Spuggett employees, Fandango Slamson was the only one not required to produce radically stupid suggestions. He managed the Bumps & Spuggett office, which primarily involved running around like a crazed sprinter, screaming, *"Aaaaaahhh! Aaaaaahhh!"* at the top of his lungs, and pausing now and again to jump up and down in one place and pull his hair with both hands, all performed at the speed of ninety miles an hour. He would repeat this process all day long, day after day, time and time again. To all the other B & S employees, Fandango personified the epitome of conscientious office management practice: diligence, efficiency, consistency—and blinding speed.

He stood in the doorway, taking in the situation. His sleepy brain processed the information available: a huge bunch of absolutely horrific-looking people (if "people" was what they truly were; they strongly resembled creatures from the planet Gloxnar, and one was *blue*) were standing here in the lobby, staring at him like *he* was from the planet Gloxnar. In all his years at Bumps & Spuggett, Fandango Slamson had never seen a customer, much less a room filled with them. As he began to comprehend the situation, a surge of adrenaline shot through his potato-shaped body.

"*Aaaaaaaahh*!! *Aaaaaaahhh*!!"

He jumped up and down, pulled at his hair, and sprinted back through the double doors into the mysterious depths of the Bumps & Spuggett office.

Barley's reaction was instantaneous and without deliberation. "C'mon, *let's go*!!" He dashed around the reception desk and through the doorway in pursuit of the terrified CEO in charge of being office manager.

The members of the group looked upon Lollie with envy. She sat there chanting so effortlessly, so blissfully serene. They wished they could remain in the lobby with her, partaking in the euphoric peace and enlightenment that she—and now Chief Bohoguss as well—must be experiencing.

But the truth of the situation held firm: if they didn't get their butts into that office on the double, they'd have to deal with the unenlightened wrath of Barley Doodlebody, who'd given the order to follow him into the unknown recesses of the Bumps & Spuggett sanctum and would be expecting them to comply forthwith.

The frazzled throng of tourists roused themselves and crept toward the open double doors beyond Lollie's desk. They were committed; no turning back now.

Lollie remained behind, the "chili-baba jijjy-booboo" chant cocooning her in blissful ignorance.

20

The first to poke her head through the double doorway was Noodles Snorgmark, with the unconscious Frog Puppleman slung over her massive shoulder like a big dead fish and little Margaret Wubbleduster by her side.

Noodles peered into the chamber, searching for her employer and a place to stash her charges. What greeted her eyes was a large central office space with smaller offices situated around its perimeter. The room was rectangular, open, and spacious, filled with a maze of unattended desks and chairs haphazardly arranged. Positioned out and away from the wall in the far right corner was one stand-alone cubicle. (*Figure 1*)

On the wall to her left were two doorways. The first, located in the corner of the room nearest to her, was set behind closed double doors. Approximately fifteen feet farther down, closer to the opposite wall, was a second door—a single door, also closed. Stretching from the near corner to the far one above the two doors and just below the ceiling, a large banner with the words

IT'S NOT <u>WHAT</u> YOU DO, BUT WHAT YOU DO <u>WITH</u> IT.

was suspended, and beneath that hung a smaller, hand-lettered sign that read,

From Stupidity
Springs Lucidity

The opposite wall also featured two single closed doors, located only a few feet apart from each other toward the room's center. Along the far-right wall were two more single doors, one in each corner of the room. The door in the far corner, nearest the solo cubicle, was open, while the door in the near corner was closed.

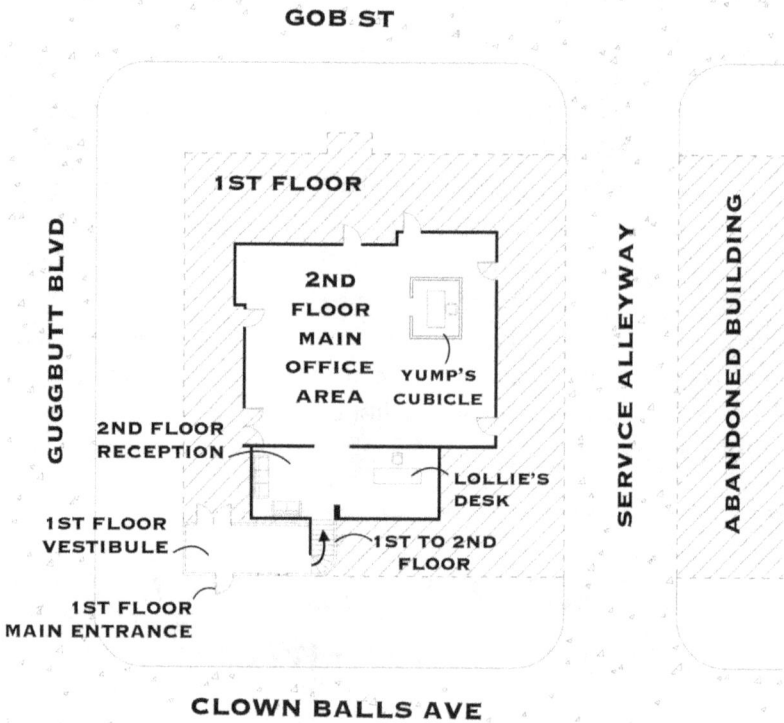

FIGURE 1 (2ND FLOOR)

The wall where Noodles stood in the double doorway was straight and windowless, its only aperture being this entryway from the reception lobby.

In the distant corner of the huge chamber, Noodles saw two blurred, speeding shapes: the sprinting forms of Fandango Slamson being pursued by Barley Doodlebody. In his attempt to elude Barley, Fandango's route took him around the room's perimeter from corner to corner to corner. His terrified screams echoed throughout the cavernous office.

"*Aaaaaahhh*!! *Aaaaaahhh*!!"

Noodles had to step back in the doorway to avoid colliding with Fandango and Barley as they sped past. Noodles clucked her tongue in amazement at the speed they were generating; she'd never seen Barley move so fast, although Fandango's speed was so much faster that he was actually lapping Barley, running two laps to Barley's one.

The huge frame of Noodles Snorgmark took up most of the double-door entryway. The tourists behind her could hear the agitated cries of the pursued and the pursuer as they ran their high-speed laps, and their curiosity was starting to get the better of them. They crowded behind Noodles, jockeying for positions that would enable them to see past her and observe.

Frog began to rouse on Noodles's shoulder, gradually coming back into awareness—at least, his version of it. He began to writhe and squirm fitfully. In order to keep him still (and because Barley was currently preoccupied elsewhere and wouldn't notice that someone was taking *his* prerogative), Noodles applied a quick uppercut to the councilman's jaw, cold-cocking him one more time. She wished Frog would help her out a little by staying unconscious; Mr. Puppleman was a lot more interesting, intelligent, and productive when he wasn't awake.

The unconscious city councilman weighed heavily upon her. She needed to rid herself of the uncomfortable burden to find out what Barley had in store for the group. Spotting a large desk and empty chair further into the room, Noodles waited until Fandango and Barley zipped past her on another lap, then waddled over to plop Frog into the chair.

Noodles had initiated the first foray into the big office. Biff Spoozma and Mayor Wubbleduster followed suit, tentatively working their way out from the edge of the room and into the interior maze of desks, sidestepping the two raving sprinters as they zipped past.

The mayor turned back to the remaining group members and whispered, "Come hither, but in softness tread!" Biff thumbed quickly through the Elizabethan English dictionary and in a whisper translated that the mayor was saying, "Follow us, but be quiet."

Across the room, the screaming Fandango Slamson deviated from his circuitous route around the room's perimeter and was doing laps around the solo cubicle, still pursued by Barley, both of them unmindful of the tour group entering the main office.

The tourists' attention was suddenly drawn to another sleepy figure standing and yawning in the right-hand doorway on the opposite side of the room, just to the left of the cubicle. This was Simpleton "Cheezy" Fabsmaggle, CEO in charge of smearing teriyaki sauce all over himself and rolling around on the floor.

Simpleton Fabsmaggle wasn't a simpleton. He'd received his name from parents who, intellectually speaking, were no threat to Albert Einstein—or Ding-Dong the Clown, for that matter. Ignorant of the fact that the definition of the word *simpleton* is "fool," his parents loved the name because it sounded dignified.

He'd been given the nickname "Cheezy" by his fellow Bumps & Spuggett coworkers, not because he loved cheese but rather because he hated oysters. Cheezy disdained being referred to as "CEO" because he mistakenly surmised the letters stood for "Cheezy eats oysters," which he most certainly did *not* do and took offense at the presumed implication.

Old Man Spuggett had promoted Cheezy to his present job of rubbing teriyaki sauce all over his body and rolling around on the floor after realizing that his young employee's creative juices were significantly stimulated by doing so. Cheezy's job required occupying one of the few private offices on the second floor because the performance of his duties required him to be naked. A naked Cheezy Fabsmaggle rolling around on the floor, covered in teriyaki sauce, was not a pretty sight and upset just about everyone.

Along with the rest of the Bumps & Spuggett staff, Simpleton Fabsmaggle had been asleep on the floor of the conference room and was awakened by the commotion in the reception lobby. Like Fandango, Cheezy was checking out the ruckus. While the office manager screamed as a matter of course, Fandango normally didn't start his maniacal shrieking until the rest of the employees were awake and at their desks, pounding out their radically stupid suggestions for the day. *This* seemed a bit out of the ordinary.

The tourists saw Cheezy's emergence from the conference room and stood rigidly silent, not wanting to draw attention to themselves until they were certain their reception would be a friendly one.

The fleeing Fandango Slamson suddenly veered off his circling course around the cubicle and came barreling down the north side of the room again, this time heading directly into Cheezy's path. Accustomed to traveling at high speeds through the office on a regular basis, Fandango neatly sidestepped the groggy CEO. Barley had never moved this fast in his life and was less adept at broken-field running than Fandango. He slammed into Cheezy like a runaway freight train, the impact launching the sleep-addled CEO airborne and headlong into the nearby office water cooler. The huge glass reservoir of water noisily exploded into a tinkling shower of shards. The water sloshed and splashed all over Cheezy, Barley, and the carpeted floor. Only a shattered heap remained as evidence of the cooler's existence.

Barley's momentum landed him atop the drenched CEO, sending both of them rolling through the debris until they stopped in a soggy, confused, semiconscious heap. Fandango sped off and continued running light-speed laps around the room, oblivious to the catastrophe behind him and the fact that he was no longer being pursued.

The force of the collision had violently ejected Chief Bohoguss from the breast pocket of Barley's suit. He hurtled in an arc over the gulf of the huge office like a rapidly spinning pinwheel, returning to earth to land miraculously in the soft cleft between Mimsy Borogove's breasts as she watched the escalating proceedings with the rest of the tour group.

Jolted out of his chant-induced reverie, Binky found himself submerged in the heaving bosom of the sex-crazed socialite, receiving a massive, suffocating dose of cleavage. The chief's little legs waggled fitfully between Mimsy's full breasts, and his tiny muffled screams of panic wafted up to the rest of the startled group.

It had all happened so quickly that Mimsy hadn't yet realized this was the scenario she'd been fantasizing about all day. She stood stunned, the bright whites of her widened eyes contrasting brilliantly with the dark blue of her face.

"Get him out of there!" Rapunzel Trashtrumpet cried, being the first to comprehend the extreme danger the little chief was in—and somewhat envious that Binky hadn't landed in *her* cleavage. If she'd had a cleavage.

Reverend Snortworthy answered Rapunzel's call and sprang to Binky's rescue, shoving his own hand down the front of Mimsy's blouse, groping frantically until he extracted the poor mini-cop and held him up triumphantly.

Mimsy had no idea why the reverend had just given her the righteous grope, but it was the most exciting thing that had happened to her all day. She expressed her appreciation by licking her lips at him suggestively and smiling, her white teeth standing out like a row of lanterns glowing in the dark.

The rest of the tourists sighed in relief as Reverend Snortworthy deposited Chief Bohoguss into the pocket of his clerical frock. The little fellow would be much safer there; the good pastor's cleavage was somewhat less formidable than Mimsy's.

The little chief peeked over the edge of the reverend's pocket, gasping for breath. His entire day had consisted of either being sucked into or shot out of something. Only when he'd chanted the Lollie Babajuju chant had he found any semblance of serenity, so he curled up at the bottom of Reverend Snortworthy's frock pocket and began chanting himself into another universe.

Being a seven-inch-tall pixie and cute as a button wasn't all it was cracked up to be.

* * *

Bimbo Spazzgate was Bumps & Spuggett's CEO in charge of water-cooler supervision (his job was to keep the water cooler from boiling over, which it never did, being full of cold water). Coincidentally, he emerged from the conference room at the moment when Barley and Cheezy Fabsmaggle collided and obliterated the water cooler. Although his awakening brain was at first puzzled by what he saw, a dim comprehension settled in as he realized that his small portion of the Bumps & Spuggett world was now wet, crunchy garbage on the office floor.

How can this be?

Bimbo let loose with an agonized wail that itself could have shattered glass. Deep within the confines of the conference room, snuggled in the midst of the other awakening Bumps & Spuggett employees, lay the inert form of Mux Muggsley, CEO in charge of believing he's a dog. When Bimbo Spazzgate's high-pitched whine reached the audio frequency that only Mux could hear, he sprang to his feet—it must be time for his afternoon walk!

Frothing with excitement, Mux bolted from the conference room into the main office, savagely bowling over any employee who strayed into the path of his exit. His frenzied progress carried him into the shrieking Bimbo Spazzgate with such force that their bodies lurched forward and cartwheeled over a desk, sprawling in a confused heap on the floor. Mux began yelping while Bimbo continued howling.

The tour group surveyed the unfolding mêlée in dumbfounded amazement. Pandemonium was breaking out around the office, spreading like ripples on a pond—and it was happening so quickly! As far as being loonies went, these guys were *good!*

Another Bumps & Spuggett staff member appeared at the conference-room doorway: Marshall Farkpucker, CEO in charge of anything and everything a deaf person can do. Marshall was hearing impaired but typically filled with magnificent radically stupid suggestions, his disability giving him a unique perspective the other aurally unchallenged employees didn't possess.

Marshall staggered out the door of the conference room with his head firmly wedged in a large wastepaper basket, where it had been deposited when Mux Muggsley made his mad dash out of the conference room, pushing Marshall roughly aside and sending him flying into the wall. Marshall had caromed off and stumbled headfirst in the waste receptacle, firmly wedging his noggin therein. Struggling to his feet and reeling blindly to the doorway, Marshall rebounded from side to side against the doorframe like a pinball. He fell through the doorway and received a cross-body block from the same office desk that had ambushed Mux and Bimbo, pitching headlong over the top. The wastebasket landed upright on the floor with Marshall's head as its contents, his body upside down, arms and legs protruding like the stalk and fronds of a flailing potted plant.

Directly behind Marshall was the CEO in charge of taking and administering quizzes, Bagmo Maltgoggles, who witnessed his coworker's unsuccessful confrontation with the office desk. Bagmo made a mental note to suggest that the rest of the staff wear wastebaskets on their heads for protection against dangerous doorjambs and office accidents. He sighed with self-satisfaction; he was going to be tough to beat today. Extremely competitive by nature, Bagmo was pleased to be so sharp, creative, and atop his game this early in the workday—definitely a step ahead of his coworkers—especially so soon after waking from the staff's morning nap, and *especially* especially since they'd received such an early and unanticipated wake-up call.

One by one, the rest of the sleepy Bumps & Spuggett employees made their way out into the main office. The odd procession hadn't yet noticed the tour group watching from across the room, their immediate attention focused on the coworkers raising a racket and avoiding Fandango Slamson as he zipped past them. However, the tourists were in a quandary as to what action to take once the staffers did notice them. Barley was still out of it after his collision (the B & S employees hadn't noticed him yet either) and wasn't in any condition to confront anyone.

They were on their own.

It all became moot speculation when Dork Snargmeyer emerged from the conference room and became the first member of the Bumps & Spuggett contingent to realize the presence of new and unfamiliar human life in the office.

Dork was a big Scandinavian from a portion of the country that was either unknown to most Scandinavians or wasn't spoken about because most Scandinavians were embarrassed to admit it was part of Scandinavia. He stood seven feet tall with the strength of a gorilla and the good-natured disposition of a child, and walked around the office saying, "Yah, shure, yabetcha!" most of the time. His greatest ambition in life was to lead a rousing Unnamed Part of Scandinavian celebration in which everyone would dance the *danzenfreekenboingadoinga*, an Unnamed Part of Scandinavia folk dance performed at parties, weddings, reunions of families or friends, and high-energy aerobics workouts.

Dork noticed the silent group of people standing across the room near the lobby entrance.

"Yah, shure, yabetcha!"

Busted! thought Roland Chumbuckets. *It was only a matter of time.*

"*Look!*" cried another staffer, noticing what Dork had seen. Narducci Palpatooti stood wide eyed and rooted to the spot, pointing and gesticulating wildly in the tour group's direction. "Look! Look! Look! Look!"

Staff member Yump Yup-Yup-Yup-Yup snapped rigidly to attention. Why was Narducci speaking like a chicken? Could it have something to do with those odd people on the other side of the office? Was that the language *they* spoke?

Yump Yup-Yup-Yup-Yup's national and ethnic heritage was entirely unknown to everyone at the firm, including Yump himself. Most people in the company theorized that, with a name like Yump Yup-Yup-Yup-Yup, he was probably from the planet Gloxnar and let it go at that.

His duties at Bumps & Spuggett consisted of watering the plants—an extremely difficult task since there wasn't one plant in the building. The resourceful Yump made up for this by hurling javelins into the wall. Old Man Spuggett realized that Yump's poor aim might result in other employees getting inadvertently skewered and, to alleviate this, sequestered him in a private cubicle where he could hurl to his heart's content. This was the stand-alone cubicle the tourists saw in the middle of the floor.

Yump Yup-Yup-Yup-Yup was now face-to-face with a large group of unfamiliar faces and a fellow employee speaking a foreign chicken language. His world—whether that be Earth or Gloxnar—was being turned upside down! Thankfully, gravity prevented him from falling off.

He suddenly received a flash of inspiration that almost blew out his eyeballs: perhaps the strange-sounding clucking language and the strange-looking people across the room had come from his own supposed home planet! After all, one of the members of the group staring back at him was blue. But that would mean that Narducci Palpatooti was *also* from Gloxnar. The place was positively crawling with Gloxnarians—and boy, were they ugly! They looked like they'd been doing aerobics inside a tornado (although the blue one was kind of intriguing).

Yump was overwhelmed by this new revelation. He was not alone here on planet Earth—there were others of his kind. It was even possible that this group of interplanetary travelers had come looking for *him*. He was now a major player in an historic occasion: the very first Earthly contact with really ugly, puffy, clucking aliens from the planet Gloxnar—besides himself, of course. And maybe Narducci Palpatooti, too. It was all so exciting! Yump felt humbled by his new role in this auspicious event. He knew what he must do.

Grabbing a pad of paper and pencil off a nearby desk, Yump scribbled feverishly, trying to transcribe and interpret what Narducci had said in the Gloxnarian clucking language. It was precisely then that Yump realized he had no idea how to speak Gloxnarian.

He noticed Marshall Farkpucker upside down with his head wedged in the wastebasket, feet and legs waving spastically in the air. The CEO in charge of nonexistent plant watering thought Marshall might be a new potted plant just introduced into the office—although he'd never seen such a specimen before, sheathed as it was in purple polyester slacks with florescent-pink socks and Cuban-heeled saddle shoes. Maybe it was from Gloxnar, too—a goodwill potted-plant offering.

Being the conscientious Bumps & Spuggett CEO in charge of plant watering that he was, and having an attention span that was not much longer than his name, Yump promptly forgot about the invading aliens and wandered off to look for his watering can.

Up to this point, the separate contingents had only been eyeing each other from opposite sides of the big room. The tour group stared at the Bumps & Spuggett employees with a mixture of amazement and apprehension. The employees stared at the tour group with a mixture of curiosity and incomprehension, but neither group had yet made an overture to the other.

That was about to change.

Frog Puppleman, who'd been sitting in the office chair where Noodles had deposited him, was just regaining consciousness from his most recent bout of sucker punches. Still wandering through that twilight world between awareness and dream, Frog stirred in the big chair and mindlessly cried out, "Yeah, buddy!"

Dork Snargmeyer's ears perked up. "Yah, shure, yabetcha!"

"Yeah, buddy!" returned Frog.

The tourists threw dagger stares at the reclining city councilman. Why wouldn't Frog just shut up? He was attracting attention.

"Yah, shure, yabetcha !"

"Yeah, buddy !"

"Yah, shure, *yabetcha* !"

"Yeah, *buddy* !"

The verbal ping-pong match continued for a few more minutes. The tourists and the staffers cringed in anxious anticipation of what the results might be.

At length, Dork could no longer contain his growing excitement and set off for the side of the room occupied by the tourists, all the while shouting, "*Yah, shure, yabetcha!*" and giggling like a plow horse high on nitrous oxide.

The terrified Doodlebody tour group sought shelter and safety from the advancing giant by huddling behind the monolithic Biff Spoozma and Noodles Snorgmark, who stood silently as he made his way toward them.

Noodles couldn't quite put her finger on it, but there was something about this huge, loping lummox that seemed oddly . . . familiar.

21

As the outsized encroacher drew closer, Biff and Noodles stood before the petrified group of tourists like a protective mountain range. Noodles held her body erect, her expression outwardly impassive, yet she pondered a gnawing question: *Why do I find this lummox so intriguing?* True, he was funny looking and currently making an idiot of himself, and he said, "Yah, shure, yabetcha!"—a phrase *she* used often enough—but there was something more that grabbed and held her attention.

Then it came to her: Dork's accent! It was the *way* he said, "Yah, shure, yabetcha!" Judging by his accent, he was from the same nameless part of Scandinavia as her. A homie!

"Yeah, buddy!" screamed Frog.

"Ya, shure, yabetcha!" answered Dork as he clumsily made his way toward the voice beckoning to him like the seductive lure of a siren.

Suddenly a new voice joined the chorus: "Ya, shure, *yuuuuuuuuuu*-betcha!"

It was Noodles Snorgmark, giving the traditional Unnamed Part of Scandinavia response to Dork's exhortation. She suddenly remembered this phrase from her early youth, before a confused Unnamed Part of Scandinavia postman, who had mistaken her for a huge, misshapen parcel of butter cookies, erroneously sent her to America. Hearing Dork's cries had jogged the dim memories of her girlhood.

"Ya, shure, *yuuuuuuuuuu*-betcha!"

Dork stopped dead in his tracks and stared at Noodles. "Ya, shure, yabetcha!" he offered cautiously.

"Ya, shure, *yuuuuuuuuuu*-betcha!" answered Noodles properly.

"Yeah, *buddy!*" screamed Frog. His entreaty was ignored by Dork, who was now entranced by the huge form of Noodles Snorgmark. She pulled herself up to her full height and spread her arms wide like the outstretched wings of an aggressive ostrich, a benign smile smeared across her face: the traditional greeting of the Unnamed Part of Scandinavia.

"Ya, shure, *yuuuuuuuuu-*betcha!"

Dork's joy exploded in a new rushing wave of excitement. Dork dearly loved his fellow Bumps & Spuggett employees and was dearly loved by them, but they were as much strangers to his Old Country customs as he'd been a stranger to theirs. Now, Noodles was formally extending him the salutation of his homeland. It had been so long since he'd seen and heard this traditional greeting—it was almost like being home again. At last! A friendly Unnamed Part of Scandinavian face! The big guy was ecstatic.

Dork returned the Unnamed Part of Scandinavian salutation to Noodles, who was feeling pretty good herself. It was rare to find a fellow countryman outside the Unnamed Part of Scandinavia—or *inside* the Unnamed Part of Scandinavia, for that matter. Noodles's sense of cultural isolation began to dissipate.

Dork shifted his gaze from Noodles to the bedraggled tourists. They were really scary looking with their rumpled clothes and shocking hair— and in Mimsy's case, her indigo-blue face and head. However, Dork was getting the impression that these scary-looking people were harmless, and this new friend he'd found had his undivided attention. He slowed his advance toward the group and stopped a few feet from Noodles, giving her a heartfelt Unnamed Part of Scandinavian smile.

The two stood facing each other, sizing one another up, hopeful optimism buoying their spirits. Noodles and Dork were undeniably from the same Nordic homeland and overjoyed at their mutual good fortune in finding each other in a mad metropolis like North Corners, Ohio. But now Dork had one more question to ask, to him the most important question of all. He paused in nervous reticence, gathering his courage. At last he spoke:

"*Danzenfreekenboingadoinga?*"

He held his breath.

Noodles's eyes widened in surprise and recognition. "Ya, shure, *yabetcha!*"

"Yeah, *buddy!*" screamed Frog hoarsely, effectively killing the poignancy of the mood, but Dork's euphoria knew no bounds. At long last he had an opportunity to perform his beloved friends-and-family reunion folk dance, and he'd found himself a willing partner.

Across the room, the Bumps & Spuggett employees watched raptly as the drama unfolded. Dork spoke a few foreign-sounding words to the big strange person he'd been talking with, raised his hand in a "Wait here for a moment!" gesture, and headed back toward his coworkers—specifically, a terrified employee named Ebenezer Snugnards. Grabbing the quaking fellow by the arm, Dork beckoned him to come along and motioned enthusiastically for the rest of the group to do the same.

Dork's singling out of Ebenezer Snugnards was purposeful: the big Viking was convinced that Ebenezer was a distant relative. In Dork's mind, the names "Snugnards" and "Snargmeyer" were just *too* similar to be coincidence. Ebenezer was terrified of Dork—and just about everything else on earth—so his confusion over what to do about his possible Unnamed Part of Scandinavian relative kept him in an almost constant state of anxiety.

Ebenezer Snugnards was highly educated, graduating with honors from North Corners' Institute of Profligate Ostentation with Benign Rapport Credenzas, an establishment of higher learning wherein he majored in "obscure if not totally meaningless verbal communication." He spoke a colloquial dialect of Complete Gibberish, and his conversation was incomprehensible to everyone. Ebenezer had done extremely well at school because the institute was run by a group of educators as unintelligible as Ebenezer. Only Complete Gibberish–speaking students were able to understand anything their professors said; consequently, class sizes at the institute were small, graduating classes even smaller. The school's alumni were an elite group of unintelligible intellectuals.

The other Bumps & Spuggett employees were in abject awe of Ebenezer's vast vocabulary and exquisite articulation, though no one could understand what he was talking about. He would extrapolate extravagantly with musings such as "The globulation thesis notwithstanding, matriculatory confabs wouldn't be the bone's bundle without the beetroot bubbly-booh!" and the staff would listen in wonderment. They accorded Ebenezer the utmost respect and went out of their way *not* to speak with him, which left him extremely lonely most of the time except for when he was by himself.

Shivering with fear in the vice-like clutches of Dork Snargmeyer, he found himself dragged by the arm across the room toward a group of hideous, puffy-haired people he'd never seen before. "Bean water! Bean water! Recalcitrant sublimation withheld and redundantly foregone!" he cried in dismay. He resigned himself to an untimely death.

For Dork's part, now that he finally had the chance to dance the *danzenfreekenboingadoinga*, he wanted to make sure Ebenezer wasn't left out of the fun. The Bumps & Spuggett employees followed like an obedient but curious flock of sheep.

As the throng drew nearer, the tourists realized that their initial feelings of foreboding might be unfounded. Noodles, on whom they relied for protection, seemed to be filled with excited anticipation. This was the first time they'd seen her smile today. The big guy with whom Noodles had been speaking seemed just as eager as she was—neither ominous nor angry in the least. On the contrary, he appeared to exude warmth and welcome. As for the rest of the approaching band of "lunatics," their expressions seemed less apprehensive as well—except for the guy who accompanied the "Ya, shure, *yabetcha!*" man.

At length, Dork, Ebenezer, and the other B & S employees stood before Noodles and the Doodlebody tourists. Members of the two groups stared at each other inquisitively. Dork looked at Noodles and flapped his arms like a gigantic flightless chicken as he performed several deep knee bends. "*Danzenfreekenboingadoinga!*"

"Yah, shure, yabetcha!" Noodles wiggled her buttocks in his direction with her arms folded behind her head. The tourists and employees were hypnotized by this Unnamed Part of Scandinavia ritual.

Dork and Noodles turned to their respective followers and organized them into a huge circle. Each person was led to a position in the ring and instructed to remain there. Tourists intermingled with employees. While everyone was puzzled by what was happening, they nevertheless smiled at their new neighbors in the circle, said "Hello," and politely introduced themselves.

Dork positioned Ebenezer in the circle next to Roland Chumbuckets. Roland politely said, "Pleased to meet you!" and Ebenezer, his apprehensions soothed by Roland's unthreatening manner, responded by smiling, bowing almost to the floor, and saying, "Thither hence, Tyrolian substitute! Ambiguity minus typewritten Renaissance biology absconds with a mixed porpienu, strung!"

This threw Roland for a loop. He nodded, shook Ebenezer's hand, and grinned feebly. Meanwhile, Mayor Wubbleduster reacted to Ebenezer's pronouncement with interest.

Now that any threat of danger or disaster had been alleviated, the group relaxed and directed their attention toward Dork and Noodles. Once everyone had been positioned in the circular lineup, the two took places in the center of the ring and faced out toward the group. They began to clap their hands rhythmically and in unison: *clap-clap* (pause), *clap-clap* (pause), *clap-clap* (pause), *clap-clap* (pause)—encouraging the others to join in.

Everyone followed Noodles and Dork's lead and picked up the beat. Once everybody understood the clapping idea, Dork and Noodles began a chant—"*Yoop*-dah! *Yoop*-dah! *Yoop*-dah! *Yoop*-dah!"—in time with the hand-clapping rhythm, again urging the group to do likewise.

Staffer Narducci Palpatooti was also a songwriter and the most musically talented member of the Bumps & Spuggett firm (Narducci had composed the "Zippity-Bippity-Boppity" song the employees sang each morning as they lay down for their naps). He grasped the idea, took over direction of the chorus line, and in short order had the circle organized into a cohesive, rhythmic chanting-and-clapping ensemble. *Clap-clap*-"*Yoop*-dah!" *Clap-clap*-"*Yoop*-dah!" *Clap-clap*-"*Yoop*-dah! *Yoop*-dah! *Yoop*-dah!"

As the group clapped and chanted, Dork and Noodles began to gyrate in the middle of the circle. Before long, they were pogoing up and down to the rhythm like painted ponies on a carousel, flinging their arms wildly over their heads and throwing one leg out to the side, then the other in an off-kilter high-kick: the *danzenfreekenboingadoinga* in all its glory.

The group in the outer circle gleefully watched the human pogo sticks bouncing around and up and down to their clapping, chanting accompaniment, and they began to pogo up and down with the clapping chant as well. Whatever this was, it was fun!

Clap-clap-"*Yoop*-dah!" *Clap-clap*-"*Yoop*-dah!" *Clap-clap*-"*Yoop*-dah! *Yoop*-dah! *Yoop*-dah!"

Noodles and Dork were in absolute heaven as they danced. Dork was thrilled that his long-time wish had been fulfilled and he'd made a new friend—in fact, a whole roomful of new friends. His fellow employees and the strangers seemed to be enjoying themselves immensely. Noodles was elated that she'd found a new friend and excited that everyone in the group was having such a good time after the ordeal they'd endured earlier in the morning. Things definitely took a turn for the better when they arrived at Bumps & Spuggett.

***

Also bouncing, clapping, and chanting was Bumps & Spuggett employee Faisal Herskowitz, the half-Arab, half-Israeli CEO in charge of both sides of an issue and argument and filthy-rag delivery. Faisal was a walking, talking, bouncing, shrieking dichotomy if ever there was one. His ethnic heritage consisted of an Israeli father and an Arabic mother, resulting in Faisal's vehement intolerance of himself—the Israeli half disagreeing with the Arab half and vice versa. This inner tussle kept him fighting and arguing with himself about practically everything.

The other employees were particularly fascinated by the occasional fistfight that would break out between himself when tensions ran high; watching Faisal throw punches at his own face and stomach and trying to sneak up and assassinate himself (he always seemed to show up too late to do the deed) offered a pleasant diversion during the workday.

After beating the crap out of himself until he could take no more, he'd reach the "peace negotiations" stage of the conflict, followed by a short period of bouncing joyously while singing and dancing around, waving his arms over his head, and shouting slogans. At this point, his coworkers knew that a temporary cease-fire was in effect. They'd return to their jobs until the next outbreak of discontent and violence. They usually wouldn't have long to wait.

Faisal came to America from the Middle East after failing miserably as a suicide bomber for a terrorist organization known as Cheezballah. This failure was primarily due to the fact that he didn't hold one iota of animosity toward anyone but himself. Even this was the result not of an antisocial personality but rather his genetic makeup. Despite his bravery, Faisal Herskowitz was an abject coward. The terrorists in Cheezballah were abject cowards as well, notorious for terrorizing chimpanzees and used car salesmen. They'd fired Faisal because he kept missing his targets and was somehow still alive.

After immigrating to the United States to escape his past, Faisal worked as a sheepherder and slept under a tree in a pasture outside of North Corners. He tended his flock, fought pitched battles with himself, and spent his free time trying to figure out why.

One day, the befuddled sheepherder confused Felicia Greenthing, a Bumps & Spuggett employee, for one of his flock who'd gone missing, pursuing Felicia up and down every street, avenue, and alley in town, whipping his crook about and screaming threats and curses at her, swearing that once he caught her, he'd turn her into a sweater.

The poor girl ran and shrieked all the way to the Bumps & Spuggett office, where she shinnied up the outside drainpipe to the roof, slid down the air-conditioning duct to the conference room (the normal method of entering the building), and ran into the main office to cower behind her desk, whimpering and quivering pathetically. This was Felicia's normal behavior around the B & S premises, so no one gave her a second glance.

Faisal shinnied up the drainpipe after her and slid down the air-conditioning duct, but being unfamiliar with this method of entry, he took a wrong turn and plopped down in Old Man Spuggett's private office. Startled, Old Man Spuggett accidentally set off one of his small, nondestructive explosive devices, which blew Faisal through the wall and onto the street. He landed, unhurt but dazed, in a large pile of filthy rags behind a delivery truck parked at the rear of the building.

This made Old Man Spuggett's day. Prior to this, the only thing his explosive devices had accomplished was pissing off a couple of ants wandering on his desktop.

Out in the street, the man who drove the delivery truck thought Faisal was part of the pile of filthy rags he was supposed to drop off at the B & S office (Bumps & Spuggett regularly received deliveries of filthy rags). He scooped him off the pavement and brought him through the second-floor delivery entrance. Trundling the disheveled sheepherder into the main office, the deliveryman dropped him in a heap on the desktop of the B & S employee whose job it was to receive, catalogue, and file the filthy-rag deliveries for future reference.

That employee was Felicia Greenthing.

Felicia let out a bloodcurdling howl that frightened everyone and brought Old Man Spuggett running out of his office to see what the trouble was. When the company founder saw that the heap of rags on Felicia's desk was the same heap of rags he'd just blown through the wall of his office, he was overjoyed. Faisal had played an instrumental role in the most successful detonation of a nondestructive explosive device in Old Man Spuggett's budding amateur explosives-manufacturing career. In gratitude, he hired the sheepherder on the spot.

Faisal launched into a spirited rendition of his bouncy dance of joy, which ignited a confrontation between himself during which he accused himself of exploiting the situation for personal gain, countering with the argument that he was jealous of his own success and good fortune. This was followed by a particularly brutal physical conflict wherein he nearly pummeled himself to death.

Old Man Spuggett and his staff watched in amazement as the dual-identity drama unfolded, although everyone was in a quandary as to which side to root for. However, what became apparent to the old man was that Faisal seemed to be a person who'd have a good grasp of both sides of an issue and an argument, a quality that could be valuable in manufacturing radically stupid suggestions.

Once Faisal had finished knocking himself silly, the old man offered him the position of CEO in charge of both sides of an issue and argument. This was the first time in his life that Faisal had ever been recognized for those qualities that comprised the basic makeup of his character. The now former sheepherder was unabashedly grateful.

All of this impressed the Bumps & Spuggett employees; their respect and admiration for their new colleague was boundless. The only employee who didn't share her coworkers' enthusiasm was Felicia Greenthing, who now lived in constant fear that Faisal would one day turn her into a sweater. To placate the typically hysterical Felicia, the old man promoted her to CEO in charge of finding the second-floor delivery entrance. Faisal took her place as CEO of filthy rag delivery.

Now, Faisal Herskowitz danced along with his fellow employees and the group of new arrivals. He was enthralled by the similarity of the *danzenfreekenboingadoinga* to his bouncy dance of joy. Mastering the steps of the boisterous folk dance was easy: the movements closely mimicked those necessary to avoid live rounds fired at the members of Cheezballah in the course of their regular training exercises. (Fortunately for Faisal, the Cheezballah marksmen were just as bad at their job as he was at suicide bombing.) Having so much prior experience with dodging bullets made Faisal a veritable *danzenfreekenboingadoinga* virtuoso.

✳ ✳ ✳

Barley Doodlebody emerged from the unconsciousness induced by cracking heads with Simpleton Fabsmaggle, an encounter he was destined to lose from the outset; Cheezy's skull had been the inspiration and model for military body armor.

Barley struggled to his feet and peered across the huge chamber. Through a blurry haze, he saw a group gathered in a circle. The people were chanting and clapping, and in the center of the circle, two giants were thrashing around, flinging their hands over their heads and bouncing up and down.

A clamorous cornucopia of questions boggled Barley's battered brain: *What are all those people and the two giants doing? Where am I? Why am I sopping wet? Why does my head hurt like I've just played a game of one-on-one with a herd of wild battering rams? Am I dead?*

Simpleton Fabsmaggle lay flat on his back at Barley's feet, soaking wet from the contents of the shattered water cooler and still semiconscious from the force of their collision. Gazing up at the ceiling, savoring the wetness that soaked his clothing, he imagined that he was in his working mode, covered in teriyaki sauce—but he was out in the big main room, and fully clothed to boot. Delighted as Cheezy was, he knew it was time to get busy. He rocked from side to side, warming up for the big surge of rolling around on the floor, his job at Bumps & Spuggett. Then the noise from the *danzenfreekenboingadoinga* folk dance filtered through the haze: *Clap-clap-"Yoop-*dah!" *Clap-clap-"Yoop-*dah!" *Clap-clap-"Yoop-*dah! *Yoop-*dah! *Yoop-*dah!"

Cheezy picked up the rhythm, rocking back and forth in time to the clapping and chanting, progressively enhancing and exaggerating his movements as he found the beat and slipped into the groove. He moved side to side and back and forth in an ever-widening path, sloshing in the slushy wetness. He didn't notice Barley Doodlebody standing over him, lost in his own moment.

It was inevitable the two would meet again.

Cheezy rolled into Barley's ankles. Barley tripped and staggered backward, conking his head—*Ka-BONK*—against a big oaken door. He collapsed and hit the watery deck, flopped onto his back, and lay across the door's threshold, stone-cold unconscious once more.

For his part, Cheezy Fabsmaggle was really getting into the spirit. Never before had he had so much fun while working. Never before had he enjoyed musical accompaniment while he worked. Never before had he been fully clothed while he worked! The *clap-clap-"Yoop-*dah!" groove really fired him up. He picked up the chant as well, parroting the "*Yoop-*dah! *Yoop-*dah!" portion of the medley as he sloshed through the water and debris without missing a beat, unaware that his wild rocking and rolling had just sent Barley Doodlebody boogaloo-ing back to Bonkville.

Yump Yup-Yup-Yup-Yup, who was watering the Marshall Farkpucker potted plant from Gloxnar, heard the commotion and was reminded of his previous concerns regarding extraterrestrial attack. He looked at the nearby revelers beneath the big banner and hand-lettered sign. Who were these strangers surrounding Dork Snargmeyer, screaming odd, threatening things at him and clapping like fiends? Who was that big Gloxnarian beside him? Could it be that big Dork was in mortal combat, valiantly fending off denizens of an evil alien empire whose aim was to take over the world, starting right here in the Bumps & Spuggett workplace? Did brave Dork Snargmeyer need aid? Assistance? Succor? Dancing lessons?

Yump had to choose sides in this rapidly escalating war of worlds. But which side? On the one hand, these were citizens from Gloxnar, his supposed birth planet—*his* people. If he chose to aid them, he'd be their "inside man." On the other hand, Yump had grown up here, been nurtured here, made friends here, and had a responsible position as an employee of an established company here. Earth and Earthlings made him feel welcomed, loved, and needed.

On the *other* other hand, he wasn't sure he was from Gloxnar at all. Maybe this whole argument and the ensuing dilemma was moot.

No matter which of those three hands was the right one (the left one didn't matter at this point), Yump realized he couldn't betray these good people of his "adopted" world. Earth was his home now; it would be Earth for which he'd fight!

Feeling a sense of urgency he'd never experienced before, except when he needed to visit the men's restroom, Yump grabbed his watering can and dashed off to his cubicle to find a javelin with which to ward off the attacking horde of Gloxnarians and save Dork Snargmeyer's life.

This plant-watering respite was welcomed by Marshall Farkpucker. *Not* a potted plant from Gloxnar, he was ensconced in the early stages of drowning upside down with his head stuck in a wastebasket.

Once the pain from their earlier violent collisions with the office desk and each other subsided, Mux Muggsley and Bimbo ceased their wailing and whining and listened to the ruckus. The chanting and clapping seemed like much more fun. The two saw no reason why they shouldn't join the revelry, and hurriedly got to their feet.

Bimbo recognized the purple polyester slacks, florescent-pink socks, and Cuban-heeled saddle shoes sprouting nearby but had no idea why Marshall was wasting his time doing an impression of a potted plant. He wasn't fooling anyone; Bimbo had recognized him right away. Perhaps

Marshall was hiding from all those strange-looking people across the room.

Whatever the case, when Bimbo saw faux cocker spaniel Mux Muggsley eying the Marshall Farkpucker potted plant (Mux had not yet been taken for his afternoon walk), Bimbo lifted Marshall by the legs to place him on a nearby desk, thereby saving him from another unsolicited watering. Marshall gave a swift, reflexive flail upon feeling himself being picked up, and Bimbo lost his grip, dropping Marshall back onto the floor. Marshall landed right side up, the wastebasket still firmly in place on his noggin, a trickle of water flowing from under it. Mux and Bimbo scrambled off to join the rollicking group on the other side of the room, and Marshall Farkpucker, CEO in charge of anything and everything a deaf person can do, never knew how close he came to being the substitute for a patch of grass on Mux Muggsley's afternoon walk.

On and on went the frenetic folk dance, Dork and Noodles throwing themselves wholeheartedly into their performance while the rest of the tourists and employees clapped, chanted, and bounced along. A genuine spirit of camaraderie fostered itself, and everyone participated with unbridled abandon. The tourists could put this morning's portion of the tour behind them.

Meanwhile, the Bumps & Spuggett employees reveled in the serendipitous change in their normal routine and the pleasant luxury of having guests to entertain. The positive atmosphere created by the group's uninhibited celebrating was contagious.

The energy and tempo were reaching a fevered pitch when, all at once and without warning, the group was rocked, rolled, and routed by the brutal impact of something hurtling into their midst from outside the circle.

CRASH! BOOM! BASH!

Struck and scattered like a stand of bowling pins, the *danzenfreekenboingadoinga* participants were launched into the air, spilling and sprawling wildly in all directions.

Yump Yup-Yup-Yup-Yup had arrived to save the day and, in the process, mankind itself . . .

22

Old Man Spuggett was sleeping blissfully within the comfy confines of his private office, his head and body wedged firmly up the chimney of his office fireplace. This was not his customary position, nor the place the old man usually occupied while taking his nap.

His presence in the chimney had resulted from an incident the night before. He'd been lying on the office floor in his bathrobe after an intense solo basketball slam-dunk session utilizing the hoop, net, and backboard installed above the fireplace. As he reclined on the floor, catching his breath, casually perusing the numbers in the company books (a relatively simple task since all of the numbers were zero), he rolled onto his side and inadvertently detonated one of his most recent nondestructive explosive devices that he'd absentmindedly stuffed into his bathrobe pocket. The small explosion, though harmless, nevertheless violently propelled the old gent headfirst into the fireplace.

In an instant, the ancient codger was snugly trapped up the chimney like a skinny 103-year-old Santa Claus, his hands still clutching the basketball but his arms wedged tightly at his sides and his legs dangling like two salamis in a delicatessen window.

Immobilized in this awkward position and unable to summon aid, yet feeling satisfied that his nondestructive explosive device had performed so well, the old man nodded off to sleep while humming contentedly, enjoying the echo the hollow chimney gave his tinny voice. Fortunately, prior to launching himself into the flue, the old man hadn't felt the need to light a fire in his fireplace.

Upon awakening, Old Man Spuggett began to squirm uncomfortably. This dislodged a bit of the soot from the sides, producing a cloud of ash that tickled the old guy's nose. Because his arms were pinned against his sides, he was unable to scratch the itch. The irritation increased in intensity until he snorted and burst forth with a powerful sneeze that sprayed up the chimney, propelling him downward into the fireplace below.

Still grasping the basketball, the old man rebounded off the hearth, setting off another nondestructive explosive device in his bathrobe pocket, which shot him out of the fireplace and back into the office like a rocket, rear end first. The oaken office door splintered like kindling as he "butted" through it and into the big main office just in time to barrel head-long (or "butt-long," as it turned out) into Fandango Slamson, who was performing one of his screaming, supersonic laps around the room. Fandango had remained completely oblivious to the other activities currently taking place in the office. He was moving so fast that everything around him was a blurred streak of color and was screaming too loudly to hear the raucous strains of the *danzenfreekenboingadoinga*.

The tremendous force of the impact with Old Man Spuggett hurled the office manager across the wide room like a cast-iron shot slung by a catapult. He hit the floor close to the folkdance participants and skidded like a stone skipping across a lake, through the double-door entrance to the main office, out the lobby, and past the reception desk, rolling like a potato-shaped bowling ball and bouncing all the way down the front stairs. He banked off the vestibule wall like a cue ball and spun through the front door of the building, rolling, rolling, rolling across the sidewalk. He rolled through the open door of the tour bus parked at the curb, bounced up the bus stairs, and finally came to rest (along with the metaphors) on his head, upside down and unconscious in the driver's seat.

Meanwhile, Old Man Spuggett landed in a heap of the splintered remnants of what had once been his beautiful office door. The basketball acted as a cushioning bumper, protecting him from being pulverized, but when he thudded onto the floor, the ball squirted out of his hands and shot across the room. It struck the far wall of the office and rebounded toward him, but its flight was intercepted by the panicked Yump Yup-Yup-Yup-Yup as he ran out of his cubicle, brandishing a javelin with which to threaten and, if need be, kill attacking Gloxnarians. The speeding basketball knocked Yump back into an office chair, the javelin flying up and out of his hands to stick fast in the ceiling.

The rolling chair spun across the office like a shrieking toy top with Yump holding on for dear life. It careened toward the group reveling in the joyous *danzenfreekenboingadoinga* and smashed into them full force, sending bodies flying everywhere before spilling Yump onto the floor as well. Bodies tumbled atop him, creating an enormous mass of human beings who, under the impression that this was part of the dance, continued chanting and clapping rhythmically. These Scandinavians knew how to shake it like no one they'd ever seen!

Yump was mortified. He'd tried in vain to come to the aid of Dork Snargmeyer in this life-and-death struggle against the aliens. Now he was trapped with Dork beneath a whole brigade of the monsters! They were all over and around him, trying to smother him. He soon realized that with all the clapping and "*Yoop*-dah! *Yoop*-dah!" stuff, none of them were taking any notice of him whatsoever—but they sure seemed to be having a good time. In fact, Yump had to admit that all of this seemed like a lot more fun than plant watering or throwing javelins at the wall of his cubicle. The chant was kind of catchy, too.

And that blue lady from Gloxnar was a cutie.

Within a few seconds, he too was clapping and chanting . These Gloxnarians weren't so bad after all! It might be cool being related, no matter how distantly, to such a hearty bunch of party animals.

Sitting amid the wreckage of his office door, Old Man Spuggett rubbed his aching 103-year-old buttocks as tweeting birds and stars spun around his head. He became aware that he was seated on something soft and squishy—the sprawled, unconscious Barley Doodlebody, although he had no idea who Barley was. Maybe when this cushion guy woke up, he'd offer him a job. You could never find enough good soft cushions around the office, and this fellow was really comfortable.

The old man's attention shifted to the big main room. The place was a bit messier than usual. Most interestingly, a wriggling, noisy mass of people was undulating on the floor under the big banner. What was that all about? A new work procedure? A replacement for Narducci Palpatooti's "Zippity-Bippity-Boppity" singalong and the morning office nap? A trendy physical exercise workout program? A radically stupid suggestion for ways of coming up with radically stupid suggestions? And who were those other people rolling around on the floor with his employees? And why hadn't he been invited to roll around *with* them?

Sheesh! You oversleep a few minutes and look what you miss!

Though still groggy, the old geezer's curiosity was now burning a hole through the fog. He wondered if he should inform Old Man Bumps about these new developments in the office's daily routine. As he regained more of his wits, he remembered that Old Man Bumps had been dead since '57, and decided to postpone telling him until he had a better idea of what was going on.

He dismounted from the cushion guy's stomach and set off to investigate.

23

"**S**higgydaygobah!"
Ebenezer Snugnards was having a wonderful time. He wasn't hurt in the fall, landing on something soft. By the sound of things, no one else had been hurt either; the group continued the *clap-clap*-"*Yoop*-dah!" routine around him without missing a clap, a "*Yoop*" or a "dah!" If this was part of the *danzenfreekenboingadoinga*, it *rocked*!

Usually anxious about one thing or another, Ebenezer was loosening up and emerging from his shell. The responsible individual was Dork Snargmeyer—the person he'd always been afraid of. It finally dawned on Ebenezer that Dork had wanted him to feel a sense of belonging, a sense of family. Dork succeeded in getting Ebenezer to let down his hair (pattern baldness notwithstanding), and he was having the time of his life because of it. As soon as he had the opportunity, he'd let big Dork know just how much his efforts were appreciated.

Then Ebenezer glanced down. Dork had cushioned his fall to the floor—yet one more instance in which he'd benefited from Dork's friendship. Dork was lying on top of someone else; it appeared to be the big woman with whom Dork had been dancing. Ebenezer leaned over to express his gratitude to his big Unknown Part of Scandinavian coworker-cum-landing cushion:

"Dork! O, Dork-Dork-Dork! Synonymous reticula somehow plasticized the matrix for prurient palpitation!"

Dork didn't respond, Ebenezer's landing having knocked the wind out of him. However, Mayor Wubbleduster heard Ebenezer and recognized the voice of the person who'd spoken to Roland Chumbuckets earlier. "I know whereof thou speakest, good sir, and behold! Thine noble-hearted wishes of goodwill go not unheeded by mine own ear! Verily, t'would please me to discourse with thee! Come ye hither—let us parlay, ere we be yet further indispos'd!"

Ebenezer's ears perked when he heard the mayor's entreaty. Someone was talking to him! Someone *understood* him! Was it another graduate of the North Corners Institute of Profligate Ostentation with Benign Rapport Credenzas? It was almost too much to hope for.

"Prenuptial incongruities aside, let the bong-bam banalities register raptoid redundancy! Zoom it or lose it!"

Mayor Wubbleduster was encouraged: "Hail fellow, and well met! Sit we together to share ken and tidings forthwith!"

Nearby, Biff Spoozma grabbed his Elizabethan English dictionary. Furiously thumbing through the pages, Biff pieced together a translation and realized that his boss was telling Ebenezer that he understood what he was saying. Biff had no idea what the Bumps & Spuggett employee was saying, but he recognized that a potential détente between the mayor and a credentialed representative of the Bumps & Spuggett firm could aid in establishing a good rapport with their hosts. This was great public relations. He had to get these two blatherers together.

Faisal Herskowitz was experiencing an uncharacteristic rush of happiness brought about by the impromptu merrymaking. His life before coming to work for Bumps & Spuggett had been fraught with failure, missed opportunities, and severe self-pummelings, so he had developed a somewhat morose personality and outlook. His heart was in the right place, and he was a hard-working, diligent, and conscientious CEO in charge of both sides of an issue and argument, but his first taste of success at Bumps & Spuggett came too late in life to change his basic disposition.

With the implementation of the *danzenfreekenboingadoinga*, he felt what it was like to laugh again. His "funny bone" had been tickled as it had never been before. He giggled and cackled as he clapped, chanted, and *boingadoinga*-ed, and continued doing so after the collision with the chair sent everyone flying. Faisal was beginning to realize that he couldn't *stop* laughing!

It was disconcerting, yet at the same time liberating.

Faisal had come down hard atop the sprawled body of Rapunzel Trashtrumpet, landing squarely on her back. She exhaled with a wheezing "*Oooof!*" while Faisal, whose laughter switch was stuck in the "guffaw" position, sat cheerily on her posterior and continued chanting and clapping, interspersed with roaring cackles of unmitigated glee.

Rapunzel was duly indignant, thinking Faisal's unbridled hysterics were obtained at the expense of her own misfortune. She spasmed to get him off her back. In so doing, she inadvertently smacked Felicia Greenthing in the mouth.

Felicia Greenthing, Bumps & Spuggett's CEO in charge of finding the second-floor delivery entrance, was a hardworking, excitable, somewhat-insecure, overly sensitive, good-hearted young company executive who was easy to confuse with an escaped sheep.

But Felicia Greenthing carried a deep, dark secret. She'd been born to parents who mistook her for an escaped sheep and shipped her off to a meatpacking house to be turned into lamb chops. While standing in line at the slaughterhouse, waiting to have her head bashed in, Felicia was befriended by a delusional female Bo Peep impersonator who spirited her out of the abattoir and took her home to be raised as part of the flock. During this formative period, Felicia developed many of the traits and characteristics that in later years would deceive then-sheepherder Faisal Herskowitz.

By the time Felicia grew to young adulthood, it had become apparent to her Bo-Peep benefactor that despite fervent hopes to the contrary, Felicia wasn't an escaped sheep after all. This was greatly discouraging to the young girl's adoptive guardian.

The disillusioned nursery-rhyme freak took Felicia for a one-way ride to North Corners, Ohio, dropped her on an out-of-the-way street corner, and sped away, leaving the poor girl to fend for herself. Felicia became hysterical and started screaming, crying, and howling like a one-woman tragedy. As luck would have it, the Bumps & Spuggett building stood on the very same out-of-the-way street corner. Felicia's ruckus drew the attention of Old Man Spuggett, who mistook her caterwauling for a pack of love-starved hyenas holding a cotillion dance in the street—or perhaps an entire flock of escaped sheep camping out on his doorstep.

Seeking to put an end to Felicia's histrionics, yet at the same time seeing special qualities in her that he felt might be useful in the radically stupid suggestion game, Old Man Spuggett offered her a job before she could start screaming again. She became the manager of the Filthy Rag Department at Bumps & Spuggett, eventually being promoted to CEO.

Felicia was working in this capacity when the aforementioned incident involving Faisal Herskowitz took place. Faisal took over Felicia's old job of being CEO in charge of filthy rags, and Felicia was promoted to CEO in charge of finding the second-floor delivery entrance, which she located within the first five minutes of her new position; it was situated directly across from her desk, but she opted to keep her discovery secret, fearing that her position in the company would be rendered obsolete if it became known that she'd actually accomplished her task.

She promised herself that she'd eventually petition Old Man Spuggett to change her title to "CEO in charge of *not* finding the second-floor delivery entrance," which would legitimize the job she was doing (or not doing). In the meantime, Felicia lived with her deep, dark secret and a deep-seated guilt that she was a fraud and a deceiver, taking advantage of Old Man Spuggett's patronage, generosity, compassion, and trust in her, all for her own selfish reasons. She spent hours each day whimpering, sniveling, and occasionally bawling her eyes out—when she wasn't hiding from Faisal Herskowitz or trying not to find the second-floor delivery entrance.

None of Felicia's fellow employees were aware of her deep, dark secret. They stuck cotton balls in their ears to avoid the noise of her ceaseless lamentations and went about their own business. The din became an everyday normality, and no one gave it a second thought, but cotton balls were always plentiful around the office.

After Yump's collision with the dancers, Felicia landed next to Rapunzel Trashtrumpet. Although the collision hadn't set the poor girl off, Rapunzel's inadvertent knuckle sandwich did. Felicia wailed and shrieked, not so much from the pain of Rapunzel's blow (delivered with all the force of an asthmatic mouse attempting to inflate a weather balloon) but rather because all she needed was an excuse to start.

She'd also landed in close proximity to the fiendishly laughing Faisal Herskowitz. He'd finally trapped Felicia with no escape! (Felicia overlooked the fact that, since joining Bumps & Spuggett, Faisal came upon many opportunities to "trap" her but never did so; the idea that her incessant screaming might have freaked him out as much as it did everybody else never crossed her mind.)

Initiated by Rapunzel Trashtrumpet's unintentional punch to the kisser and augmented by Faisal's cackling presence, Felicia's histrionics increased proportionately. The Bumps & Spuggett employees knew this was merely Felicia "going off" again, and that things weren't necessarily amiss.

The Doodlebody tour group was not aware that they were witnessing a typical day at the office. Hearing Felicia's agonized caterwauling, Dr.

Pudbid felt his aid was urgently needed. Some of his urgency might also have been attributable to the fact that Reverend Snortworthy was seated on the good doctor's head.

The kindly physician squirmed out from beneath the fat reverend's buttocks, pulled himself up , and tried to determine the source of the hideous wailing. He found Felicia lying on the floor next to Rapunzel Trashtrumpet, who was pinned beneath Faisal Herskowitz, who was lying next to Ebenezer Snugnards, who was sitting on top of Dork Snargmeyer, who was lying on top of Noodles Snorgmark.

Holding his ears so her screaming wouldn't blow out his eardrums, Dr. Pudbid asked what Felicia's problem was. He was immediately inundated with exclamations from the wriggling people on all sides, who thought he was talking to *them*. The tourists cried, "Help her! She's in trouble!" The Bumps & Spuggett employees cried, "Don't worry about her! She's fine!" The doctor didn't hear any of them through his hands.

He grabbed Felicia by the shoulders and strained to move her into a sitting position. She was screaming her head off but otherwise seemed healthy enough; there were no visible open wounds, no blood spurting, no bangs, bumps, or bruises he could ascertain. A more thorough examination was in order. "Young lady, where are you hurt? I can help you!"

Felicia stopped screaming and stared in disbelief. "*Hurt*?! I'm not hurt! What makes you think I'm hurt? I'm just fine! And stop poking me!"

The doctor was perplexed. "B-b-but-but—you're screaming!"

"Stop talking to my butt! There's absolutely nothing wrong with my butt, and it's not screaming! *I* am!"

"I just thought you might have sustained an injury and needed some help! I'm a doctor. My name is Humaylius Pudbid—"

"Well, Doctor, I'm just fine, and so is my butt!"

"Well, all right then. I'm sorry to have bothered you! I just thought—"

"Leave me alone! *Don't touch me*!"

The kindly doctor recoiled from Felicia as if she'd just turned into a giant potato bug. He apologized once more for disturbing her and slunk off dispiritedly, incredulous as to how bad his luck had been regarding patients in distress. Maybe he'd have better luck trying to assist Frog Puppleman; there was *always* something wrong with the city councilman.

Felicia resumed screaming her head off, happy as could be.

Until Dr. Pudbid turned his attention to semiconscious Frog Puppleman, the only other person who'd paid any mind to the city councilman was the executive secretary to Old Man Spuggett, Alpha Rae Sapoopa-LaBoobis. She'd first noticed Frog sitting in the big office chair during the "Yeah, buddy"–"Yah, shure yabetcha" exchange with Dork Snargmeyer. At that point, she had no way of knowing that Frog had suffered two knockout sucker punches delivered in rapid succession by Barley and Noodles. Once the dancing, clapping, and chanting commenced, the executive secretary threw herself wholeheartedly into carousing and forgot about Frog.

Alpha Rae Sapoopa-LaBoobis was a tall, thin, cantankerous old woman with purple hair done up in a bun. She was secretary to both Old Man Spuggett and Old Man Bumps, although she preferred working for Old Man Bumps because he was dead and had less for her to do.

Many years before, Alpha Rae had wandered into the office of the then-fledgling company in an amnesic stupor. She was hired immediately and spent the first few years helping to build the firm from a small, unproductive business into a larger unproductive business, as well as trying to figure out who she was and what she was doing there. Her duties consisted of taking dictation, which she never did. She refused to let anyone dictate to her.

When Yump joined the dancing group, Alpha Rae was upended along with the rest. Now she lay prone beneath Bagmo Maltgoggles and on top of Roland Chumbuckets. Roland and Bagmo made extreme efforts to untangle themselves from their pileup—Roland because the combined weight of Alpha Rae and Bagmo squashed the air out of him, and Bagmo because he wanted to get away from Alpha Rae as quickly as possible. Ms. Sapoopa-LaBoobis could be a holy terror when her anger was aroused.

Once the three separated from their entanglement and Alpha Rae sat up, she saw Dr. Pudbid abandoning his attempts to assist Felicia Greenthing. He moved to the chair in which Frog Puppleman slouched. Her prior curiosity toward the city councilman rekindled, she scrambled to her feet and followed the doctor.

* * *

Try as he might, Reverend Snortworthy hadn't found anything in this crazy *danzenfreekenboingadoinga* folk ritual to offend his sensibilities. There didn't seem to be any heathen practices being practiced, no one was acting inappropriately, no violence was being perpetrated, nor were there any indications that anyone was doing anything more than having a good time.

He felt utterly useless. His only option? To join the jocularity. He did so with a vengeance, bouncing to the beat like an enormous obese penguin with big rubber shoes and relieving all of his pent-up frustrations by boogying his brains out.

Nestled deep in the pocket of the reverend's clerical frock, little Binky Bohoguss remained cocooned within a warm shell of meditative tranquility, blissfully chanting, "Chili-baba jijjy-boo-boo." The little guy was completely unaware of the frolicking frivolity and would have felt no sense of deprivation if he'd known what he was missing. For someone seven inches tall, participating in an activity like the *danzenfreekenboingadoinga* would inevitably result in his being squashed like a bug.

When Yump's spinning chair collided with the rollicking group, Reverend Snortworthy's feet were knocked out from under him. He backflipped end over end like an Orca performing acrobatic tricks at a sea-life park. When he landed, Binky was ejected from the reverend's frock pocket in yet another graceful, soaring arc, culminating in an entanglement with the large banner hanging on the wall nearby. The little chief would have aroused the envy of NASA had the agency known how many successful launches he'd undertaken today.

Snapped out of his trance, he straddled the top edge of the banner like a teensy-weensy cowboy trying to ride the hitching post instead of the horse. To his dismay, the hanging banner was suspended ten feet above the floor. A ten-foot plunge for Binky Bohoguss was equivalent to a ten-story dive for a normal-sized person.

If there was one thing to enjoy on the banner, it was the splendid view. The office interior spread below him like a vast, hum-drum, economically furnished, fluorescently lit landscape. Spotting the undulating pileup on the floor, he screamed and shouted to attract their attention, to no avail. No one could hear his cries over their own strident vocalizations.

Binky realized that his rescue from this precarious perch was far from imminent, or even assured. He'd have to straddle the big banner until someone spotted him or realized he was missing. That might take a while. There was nothing to do but revert to what had worked successfully for him up to this point: escapism.

The little guy adjusted his seated position as best he could to ensure he wouldn't slip and plunge to his tiny death. He took a deep breath, did his utmost to calm his frayed nerves and quiet his fears, closed his eyes, and recommenced his "Chili-baba jijjy-boo-boo" chant. Within moments, he'd rejoined Lollie Babajuju in the peaceful, languidly swirling vortex of tranquility, and the potentially catastrophic consequences of his harrowing predicament were effectively consigned to blissful oblivion.

Below, Yump Yup-Yup-Yup-Yup had realized the Gloxnarian expeditionary force were a fun bunch of partiers. He set his eyes on one Gloxnarian in particular: the one with the blue face and blue hair. This alluring creature from his purported home planet fascinated him. No one else looked like her; perhaps she was a Gloxnarian princess or something— maybe even a queen! He had to introduce himself. He hoped she didn't only speak Gloxnarian; try as he might, Yump had yet to get a handle on that.

Locating his blue dream girl wouldn't be difficult. All he had to do was separate the various noise components permeating the room and listen for a random scream, shriek, or shout from within the pile that wasn't a "*Yoop*-dah!" or a Felicia Greenthing yowl. Mimsy would be groping those people as she rolled on the floor.

Mux Muggsley let out a high-pitched yelp from somewhere nearby. Sure enough, Mimsy was next to him, beckoning Mux with a lewd smile and a "Come hither!" expression spread across her indigo-tinted face. Mux wasn't showing much interest. He was trying desperately to put distance and other people's bodies between himself and the horny socialite when Yump scooted up beside her.

"Hi, I'm Yump. Do you cluck?"

Mimsy stared at Yump. That sounded like a proposition. *Now we're getting somewhere!* She liked his straightforward style and introduced herself, followed by suggestive flicking of her tongue over her lips and teeth. Yump believed this to be some sort of Gloxnarian gesture—perhaps a form of greeting. Not wanting to seem rude or impolite (in case she *was* a queen), he returned her flicks with his own. At least she wasn't clucking at him.

Mimsy was encouraged and gave Yump another dose of tongue action.

Yump now believed he was engaged in important negotiations with the blue queen of Gloxnar herself. He answered back, matching Mimsy flick for flick. The two of them lay side by side among the rest of the *danzenfreekenboingadoinga* participants, immersed in a world of their own, smiling broad, toothy smiles while flicking, darting, wiging, and wagging their tongues at each other like a couple of love-starved rattlesnakes.

Suddenly a new voice cried out above the hubbub: "*Gangway*! Everybody out of the pool!"

Everyone in the big pile on the floor sat up, trying to get their bearings.

They looked up to see a thin, white-haired old man clad in a bathrobe executing a perfect swan dive from atop a nearby desk. He arced into their midst and came down on them like a whacked-out teenager leaping into a mosh pit.

Old Man Spuggett was checking in for his share of the *danzenfreeken-boingadoinga* action.

24

Old Man Spuggett's 103-year-old body landed on top of the dogpile with all the weight of a feather pillow and plopped unceremoniously onto the floor. Unhurt, he sat up and surveyed the group scattered around him: some of these people were his employees and some weren't. None were doing the "*Yoop*-dah!" thing that brought him here in the first place. *Drat!*

The members of Barley's tour group recognized the old man in the bathrobe as one of the two gentlemen they'd seen in the large portraits hanging in the reception lobby—most likely the one who wasn't dead. He definitely resembled his portrait in the looks department. In real life, he dressed in a much less formal manner, having traded the dapper dark suit and necktie for a wrinkled, soot-covered bathrobe with battered old slippers on his feet. His thinning white hair was disheveled and scruffy looking. Having never met him before, the tourists' collective embarrassment and apprehension at meeting an actual company founder in this rather undignified manner intimidated them into awkward silence.

The Bumps & Spuggett staff realized their boss was now among them, and they weren't at their desks working as they should have been. Old Man Spuggett had never dealt with a full-throttle dance party during work hours, and the staff wasn't sure of his reaction. They were intimidated into their own stony silence, their faces bearing guilty expressions reminiscent of a man who's been discovered wearing women's lingerie in a biker bar.

"Well, why isn't anybody still doing what you were *doing*? Don't stop on my account! I wanna do it too!"

Everyone breathed a sigh of relief and looked at each other quizzically.

Who was going to take the reins and be the spokesperson? Who actually knew what was going on?

Old Man Spuggett studied the various members of the group. There were many faces he didn't recognize. Were they potential customers looking for radically stupid suggestions? Dancing instructors teaching his staff a new acrobatic routine that required violent physical contact?

"I see some faces here that are unknown to me. I'd like to meet you all and welcome you to the Bumps & Spuggett offices. To whom am I speaking, and to what do we owe the pleasure of your visit?"

The tourists looked at one another in panic. Barley Doodlebody still lay unconscious on the floor by the shattered water cooler—and they realized that they hadn't missed his presence at all. However, neither would he be of any help in the situation that faced them.

Mayor Wubbleduster took it upon himself to speak: "Hail, noble sire, and well met! We are but wayfarers amongst thee and these thy subjects; come we hitherto bearing no ill purpose nor malicious intent!"

The old man stared at the mayor. Biff dove into the pages of his dictionary. "Sir, the mayor is saying, 'Hi, nice to meetcha! We just came to see the place. We don't want any trouble.'"

Old Man Spuggett was puzzled. Where had he heard speech like that before? Then it struck him. "Sir, are you, perhaps, a friend or relative of Ebenezer's? Did he invite you here today?"

From his place on the floor, Ebenezer exclaimed, "Unctuous replenishment of an oligarchy's upper management lies deemed as unannounced! A froth betimes the munga-dunga-loofa-doofa-doo!"

"Was that a yes or a no, Ebenezer?"

Mayor Wubbleduster quickly answered, "Noble master, thine devoted minion sayeth verily, 'Nay, confesseth I to an ignorance of the man's intent, having ne'er his acquaintance receiv'd!'"

Biff Spoozma attacked the dictionary again. "The mayor is saying that the guy over there"—he pointed to Ebenezer—"says, 'No, I've never seen this guy before, and I don't know what he wants!'"

"The mayor, eh? That's Roymul Wubbleduster, the mayor of North Corners?"

"Yes, sir!"

"Well, this is quite an honor! The mayor of our town visiting with us today!" The old man bowed politely to the mayor. "Please forgive my total lack of comprehension of your speech, sir, but I've never been one who paid particular attention to politics. Had I known of your visit beforehand, we would've put out the red carpet for you—although we don't actually have a red carpet here at the office. Would you mind if we offer a somewhat faded, brownish-green carpet instead? We do have one of those—in fact, you're sitting on it right now! At any rate, you're most welcome here in our humble place of business."

"Sir, please don't be concerned about hospitality!" said Biff. "Our arrival today was unanticipated and unannounced, and the people we've already met have been exceedingly kind to us!"

"Well, I'm glad to hear that! And who are you, sir? And the rest of these folks?"

Biff realized it might not be wise to state that they were a curious group of tourists on hand to witness a bunch of purported lunatics behaving like lunatics. "Sir, I'm Biff Spoozma, the mayor's public relations advisor, and this is a group of distinguished North Corners dignitaries who've made the trip here today to observe the workings of your . . . your . . . *operation.*"

"Hmmm, 'dignitaries,' eh?" For being so dignified, these people looked thrashed! "We've got the mayor and North Corners dignitaries visiting us today? To observe our operation in action?"

"Yes, sir!"

"Oh my! And here we all are, running around like a bunch of drunken sport foofs! Well, at any rate, my name is Spuggett, and I'm the owner of this 'operation,' as you call it, although I must apologize for our seeming lack of professionalism. All this wild activity is not normal business procedure at Bumps & Spuggett, I assure you. We usually start our day with a good nap. And we usually sit at our desks when we work. Very rarely do we jump around and make noise—except for Faisal every once in a while, and maybe Felicia, and *definitely* Fandango, no doubt about that!"

He looked around—no Fandango. Now *that* was strange.

"But we never, *ever* carouse like a bunch of drunken sport foofs with visiting dignitaries—*never*! Not usually, anyway. Come to think of it, we've never had visiting dignitaries here before. As a matter of fact, we've never had customers here before. Did you come here in need of some radically stupid suggestions? If so, you've come to the right place.

"But what was it you were doing before I got here just now? It looked like a celebration, or a very terrible accident aftermath. And why did you stop when I got here? Even if it *was* a very terrible accident aftermath, it looked like fun!"

Ebenezer offered an explanation. "An aggrandizement with enamored tinsel erupted, espoused! Dork-Dork-Dork!" He pointed at Noodles.

Old Man Spuggett looked to Mayor Wubbleduster for the translation. "'Tis a humble custom of a rural peasantry, vigorously enacted by a duo of subjects of like ethnicity and heritage, one of whom be called 'Dork,' in concert with Noodles, a compatriot in our company who resideth here among us, yea, e'en as we now discourse!"

Now Old Man Spuggett turned to Biff. Following a brief but frenzied turning of pages, Biff responded: "The mayor says that the guy over there"—he pointed to Ebenezer—"says, 'We were doing a folk dance that Dork and Noodles"—he pointed to Noodles—"taught us, from the country they both come from!'"

"Aha! I thought it was a dance. It seemed far too organized and harmonious to have been a very terrible accident aftermath. Nice beat! What do you call this dance?"

"*Danzenfreekenboingadoinga!*" Dork and Noodles replied in unison. They blushed and smiled at each other timidly.

"Good name too—kinda catchy. But why did you stop?"

"I wasn't aware that we *had* stopped, sir!" Roland Chumbuckets said. "I thought we'd simply reconfigured from an upright to a prone position!"

"You can thank Yump for that!" interjected Narducci Palpatooti, the musically talented staff member, also an unabashed snitch. "Yump crashed into us with a chair and knocked everybody down. I don't think Dork intended there to be any rampaging office furniture in the dance. It was musically incongruous!"

"Well, let's ask Yump about that. Hey, Yump! Why'd you knock everybody down here?"

Yump did not reply, much too engrossed in his tongue gymnastics with Mimsy Borogove to answer Old Man Spuggett's inquiry. For all intents and purposes, he *was* on the planet Gloxnar.

"I don't think we're going to get much of an explanation out of Yump!" said the old man, grimacing in disgust. "Well, now that the dance has concluded, we can get to know each other a little better."

"Yeah, *buddy!*" came a cry from somewhere just beyond the pile.

"Who is that?"

"That would be City Councilman Frog Puppleman, sir," answered Biff. "He suffered a minor accident earlier today. He's still a bit groggy, but he's okay."

"My goodness! A city councilman! I must say, this is indeed a singular honor."

The company founder stood and peered over to where Frog reposed in the big office chair. Kindly Dr. Pudbid stood close by, but next to the good doctor was something the old man would never have expected to see: his executive secretary, Alpha Rae Sapoopa-LaBoobis, she of the rebelliously cantankerous nature and reluctance to perform the smallest of tasks, attending to the stricken councilman—even standing protectively over Frog, cradling his lumpy head in her hands and gently stroking his hair. Any attempt by Dr. Pudbid to intervene in her ministrations was met by threatening death stares.

Old Man Spuggett was amazed at Alpha Rae's sudden conversion to Angel of Mercy. He'd always suffered a devil of a time getting her to do anything constructive—or just about anything at all.

Dr. Pudbid nervously wrung his hands, once again with nothing to do, feeling impotent, useless.

"Our esteemed city councilman certainly seems to be out of sorts!" said Old Man Spuggett with concern. "Is he all right? Did one of my people do this to him? It wasn't Mux, was it? Sometimes Mux can be very aggressive. He thinks he's a dog, you know."

Mux Muggsley panted excitedly at the mention of his name.

"Not to worry, sir," answered Roland. "Councilman Puppleman's been like that pretty much all day—but Dr. Pudbid's looking after him. He's in good hands!"

Dr. Pudbid looked down at his empty, useless hands, fervently wishing that Roland would just shut up.

Old Man Spuggett gasped, wide eyed. "Did you say Dr. Pudbid? That wouldn't be Dr. *Humaylius* Pudbid, would it? My heavens, it *is*! Why Humaylius, you old hog-faced cattawarbler, I didn't recognize you without your horse! How long has it been, old friend? Fifty years?"

The good doctor grinned sheepishly. "More like sixty, I reckon."

"You two *know* each other?" asked Roland.

"Know each other? Young man, we were classmates at school together! Proud alumni of the North Corners Institute for Indigent Wannabes, class of aught-five!"

"That's one school in North Corners I've never heard of."

"Well, I don't suppose you would have, young fella—it went belly up years ago. Too many 'Wannabes,' and not enough 'Actually Ams.' They couldn't find anybody qualified to teach the classes. Humaylius and I graduated just in time, before anybody realized that fact. Had we waited another year, we would've been shipped off to Canada to fight in the Cannibal Wars! The two of us were inseparable in those days, weren't we, Humaylius? I used to call him Puddles, and . . . what was it you used to call me, Humaylius?"

"Spuggy."

"*Spuggy*! Indeed! That's what old Puddles used to call me: Spuggy. After graduation, Puddles went on to become a physician, as you know. The best country doctor in the country, I'll wager! I, along with my dead business partner—although he wasn't dead at the time—went on to become entrepreneurs and establish this company. Puddles, you old crank-dangling kleptomorphicide! How the heck are you? How goes the flow of the old heave-ho? And what are you doing *here*?"

The kindly old doctor shuffled his feet uncomfortably. "Well, Mr. Spugg—er, Spuggy—I'm doing fine, thank you. I guess the old heave-ho is still 'heaving' and 'ho-ing,' and I'm here to make sure no medical problems get out of hand. I intended to check on the city councilman's condition, but *this* woman"—he pointed to Alpha Rae—"seems to have taken it upon herself to look after him."

"You got a problem with that?" hissed Alpha Rae. "I'm gonna take care of this guy and he's gonna be *just fine*!"

Old Man Spuggett was incredulous. "My heavens, Alpha Rae! You've certainly staked your claim on the city councilman. What brought about this compassionate change of character? Up until now, you've shown no particular penchant for being a caregiver. I never knew you had it in you!"

"Frankly, I didn't either, Mr. Spuggett. I don't know what's come over me, but for some reason I've found myself wanting to help this gentleman, and I'm finding it more rewarding than not taking dictation—or not doing all the other things I don't do around here."

"Well, bravo for that, Ms. Sapoopa-LaBoobis! But despite your good intentions, I think it best that Dr. Humaylius should have the final say because of his formal training and expertise."

"As you wish, sir." Alpha Rae fixed Dr. Pudbid with a venomous stare, blood boiling in her eyes, her teeth bared in a threatening grimace. "Well, Doc? What's the '*final say*'?"

A showdown! Alpha Rae appeared to be the alpha dog. The room was quiet save for the muted giggling of Faisal Herskowitz and the sickening animal noises coming from Yump and Mimsy. Felicia Greenthing stopped sniveling. Everyone held their breath in anticipation of Dr. Pudbid's fateful decision.

The good doctor gulped and stuttered, "I-I-I don't s-see why Ms. S-S-Sapoopa-La-B-B-Boobis shouldn't be permitted to assist M-M-Mr. Puppleman if she chooses t-t-to do so! His condition is n-n-not serious."

The entire group exhaled in relief. Perhaps kindly Dr. Pudbid wouldn't get his kindly butt kicked after all.

"Very well, then. Carry on, Ms. Sapoopa-LaBoobis!" said Old Man Spuggett.

Alpha Rae smiled with grim satisfaction and returned to her jealous supervision of Frog Puppleman, who couldn't have cared less who supervised him.

The old man now addressed the good doctor warmly: "Humaylius, my old friend, since Ms. Sapoopa-LaBoobis will temporarily be assuming the care of the indisposed city councilman, perhaps we can reminisce and chew the fat a bit, eh? It's so good to see you again after all these years!"

Still visibly shaken by the harrowing challenge thrown at him by the executive secretary, Dr. Pudbid nodded and wiped his sweating brow.

"In the meantime, I suggest we all introduce ourselves. As I mentioned, my name is Spuggett, and I'm the owner of this place. I'd introduce you to my business partner, Mr. Bumps, but he's dead and doesn't show up for work much anymore. I suppose you could say he's my 'silent' partner."

At the company founder's behest, the Bumps & Spuggett staff members introduced themselves to the tourists, the tourists applauding politely after each had given his or her name and title. Once they finished, the tourists took their turn.

Old Man Spuggett cried out with delight when he spotted Margaret Wubbleduster in the group. "Hello, dear! What a lucky surprise to have you visiting with us today! We're going to have lots of fun, aren't we?" He gave her a grandfatherly hug and smiled.

Little Margaret had enjoyed herself immensely during the *danzenfreekenboingadoinga*, the first time she'd had fun all day. Free of the leash and the gaffer's tape bindings, she'd thrown her chubby little body into the activity with all the youthful energy she possessed, leaping and bounding like a playful piglet full of Mexican jumping beans.

Margaret had initially set her sights on Dork Snargmeyer as a solid HIVED-ing candidate, his tremendous size presenting an irresistible challenge to the squishy little hellion. Her current saliva deficiency had prevented her from acting, and since her inclusion in the *danzenfreekenboingadoinga* celebration, she'd determined Dork to be a *nice* man and a lot of fun. Dork was off the HIVED-ing hook. The big Viking had no inkling how lucky he was.

Now she was meeting Old Man Spuggett.

The tourists winced, prepared for some horrid response to his greeting. To everyone's amazement, Margaret snorted happily with a big smile creasing her porky little face. The tourists sighed with relief; it appeared the old man was off the hook as well.

Patting the girl gently on top of her head, the company founder turned his attention to Dork Snargmeyer, who sat on the floor next to Noodles. "It looks to me like you've made a new friend here today, Dork."

"Ya, shure, *yabetcha*!" replied the big Viking. "Vee gotten here Lahloolah!"

Noodles smiled at the old gentleman. "Ya, shure, *yuuuuuu-betcha*!"

"I'm pleased to make your acquaintance, Lahloolah!"

Old Man Spuggett bowed formally in his sooty bathrobe and slippers and then said to the entire group, "I'm very pleased to make *all* of your acquaintances! You've given us a most pleasant diversion from our everyday work routine, and apparently some rather amazing things have happened since you folks have been here: our Faisal Herskowitz, whose demeanor is normally anything but jovial, now seems to be fairly bursting with happiness . . ."

Faisal erupted with yet another explosion of laughter.

". . . and my dear executive secretary, Alpha Rae Sapoopa-LaBoobis, who heretofore has been reluctant to perform the smallest of tasks, has now thrown herself wholeheartedly into the diligent care of our city councilman."

Alpha Rae smiled at Old Man Spuggett, turned, and shot Dr. Pudbid a haughty smirk.

"So it is with great pleasure that I, along with my employees, look forward to showing you our 'operation.' In the meantime, I think this calls for *celebration*!"

The tourists looked at one another happily as the Bumps & Spuggett staff burst into approving applause.

The old man went on: "Unfortunately, due to the fact that we had no foreknowledge of your visit, we were caught unprepared and are unable to offer you proper refreshment."

A light went on in Bagmo Maltgoggles's head. "Mr. Spuggett! How about Gerald's cure for excess hair growth?"

The old man's face lit up like the sign above a Vegas Strip casino. "By Jove, Bagmo, you're *right*! Excellent suggestion!" He turned to staffer Gerald Foon-Package. "Gerald, we need you to whip up some of your special cure for excess hair growth right away! *Lots* of it!"

"*Will do*, sir!" cried Gerald, sensing the urgency in the old man's voice. He dashed over to a single door beneath the big banner, yanked it open, and sprinted up a flight of stairs to the building's attic, where he maintained his laboratory.

Gerald Foon-Package was one more CEO in a sea of CEOs at Bumps & Spuggett, a valued member of the staff and a person whose family history was a fascinating saga. His family had emigrated to North Corners from Merry Olde England early in the previous century, following the public disgrace of Gerald's great-great-great-grandfather, Trevor-Nigel Foon-Package. Trevor-Nigel had accidentally sneezed into Queen Victoria's face as she practiced her knighting technique. The queen was using Trevor-Nigel as a stunt-double knight, intending to bestow the honor on someone else in a ceremony to be held later that evening. She had astutely surmised that if something went wrong during the rehearsal, the stand-in stunt-double knight would take the lumps and not the actual subject. Her misgivings had validity: when Trevor-Nigel sneezed in her face, the queen jerked convulsively and cut off his ear. Thereafter, Trevor-Nigel gained infamy as "that one-eared bloke who blew his nose in Her Majesty's gob."

To escape the stigma of this humiliating ignominy, he high-tailed it out of the country to seek a better life for himself and his family, making the trip across "the pond" to America, where he settled near the newly established village of North Corners, Ohio. He built a miniscule, almost nonexistent farm and produced head-cheese-flavored ice cream, selling it to the Native Americans living nearby. This is a significant reason why Native Americans no longer live in North Corners.

As pioneer settlers of the area, the Foon-Package family members held the distinction of possessing "old money," although they actually had no money at all. Head-cheese-flavored ice cream wasn't a sought-after commodity.

Four generations of Foon-Packages and 150 years later, along came Gerald, modern-day scion of the famous blue-blooded Foon-Package clan.

Old Man Spuggett frothed at the chance to have a North Corners blue blood working under his roof, so he hired Gerald and put him to work under his roof, quite literally—up in the attic of the Bumps & Spuggett building. Gerald set up a laboratory to aid in his numerous scientific projects.

Science was Gerald's passion. He worked tirelessly to find a cure for excess hair growth, ultimately *not* discovering the cure for excess hair growth but creating instead a fantastic recipe for potatoes au gratin. For this, Old Man Spuggett promoted him to CEO and sent him back up to his attic to continue his relentless research—and perhaps inadvertently create another delicious side dish.

Old Man Spuggett addressed the assembled group once again: "Ladies and gentlemen, in lieu of the usual party fare, we can offer you the finest potatoes au gratin you've ever tasted in your lives, prepared by Bumps & Spuggett's own Gerald Foon-Package, scion of the venerated North Corners Foon-Package family!"

The B & S staffers burst into hearty cheering and applause. Some informed the tourists, "You're gonna *love* Gerald's cure for excess hair growth! It's the best potatoes au gratin in the whole world!" The tourists' excitement and anticipation increased accordingly, although a few of them cautiously asked, "He doesn't put any liver in them, does he?"

The old man studied the office water cooler, lying in shambles after its catastrophic run-in with Cheezy Fabsmaggle and Barley Doodlebody. "Since we're fresh out of champagne, I'm afraid the only beverage we can offer is water—but before that can happen we'll have to rehabilitate the water cooler. Mr. Spazzgate, may I entrust that task to you?"

Bimbo, the Bumps & Spuggett CEO in charge of water-cooler supervision, leaped from the floor to his feet, saluted Old Man Spuggett, and screamed, "Yes sir! Right away!" He hustled off to refurbish and replenish his disabled charge, overjoyed at the important assignment granted to him by the boss himself—despite the fact that this was already his everyday job.

The Doodlebody tour group was nearly overcome. Whatever else happened, this fortuitous meeting with these friendly people and this affable old man was the highlight of a very trying day.

"*Hallelujah*! Bless you, sir!" cried Reverend Snortworthy from his seat on the floor. "By your charitable deeds you have transformed a day of tribulation into one of joy and good fellowship!"

"*Shiggydaygobah*!" cried Ebenezer.

"Ebenezer doth rejoice!" translated Mayor Wubbleduster.

"The mayor says that Ebenezer says, 'Let's party!'" Biff said.

Rapunzel Trashtrumpet, who'd managed to get Faisal Herskowitz off her back, was also ecstatic. *At last! Something positive to write about in my article for* The Daily Poop!

"Yeah, *buddy!*" cried Frog Puppleman, who was emerging from his foggy stupor into full consciousness.

Alpha Rae gave Dr. Pudbid a triumphant smirk, unaware that Frog blithered, "Yeah, *buddy!*" whether he was conscious or not.

"All right then!" Old Man Spuggett was pleased with the enthusiastic responses. "But before we proceed, could somebody *please* separate the two people making those disgusting faces and animal sounds? We're going to be *eating* here soon!"

Yump and Mimsy were currently locked in a fevered embrace, tonguing themselves into a frenzy and producing bestial sounds. The two had miraculously found love amid the mayhem, but for those unfortunate enough to witness the "miracle," it was an emotionally scarring visual. The audio was fairly unsettling as well.

Noodles and Dork separated the two raunchy lovebirds and escorted them to opposite sides of the group. Yump and Mimsy continued to eyeball and tongue-flick from afar.

Old Man Spuggett continued. "Now that preparations are underway for our impromptu little wingding, let's have the members of the staff take a guest or two and show them what we do here each day at Bumps & Spuggett. I believe that's what they came here for in the first place!"

"Now you're talkin', sir!" said Bagmo Maltgoggles. "Okay, gang. Let's strut our stuff for these folks!"

The B & S staffers cheered; they'd never had the opportunity to display their individual talents and skills (such as they were) to anyone from outside the office. Today they were getting the chance to show off, and to party as well. Life was good!

"Let me remind you all," continued the old man, "that we have a special guest today: the Honorable Roymul Wubbleduster, distinguished mayor of North Corners!"

The employees responded with a collective, "*Oooooh!*"

"Perhaps, during the course of your demonstrating for our guests what it is that we do, you might come up with some suggestions to assist His Honor in the difficult task of running our beautiful municipality and overseeing our welfare."

Once again the staffers cheered. Mayor Wubbleduster swelled with pride, pleased that his office and duties as mayor were deemed important enough by Old Man Spuggett to charge his employees with assisting him. "Verily, mine heart doth sing and mine ears do rejoice in kind to hear pronouncement of such sweet sincerity! Wholly to thine counsel shall mine ears be lent!"

Biff went for the dictionary. "Mayor Wubbleduster says, 'I'll be very happy to listen to any ideas or suggestions you might have to offer!'"

"So be it! The mayor and all of our distinguished guests await the fruits of your labor! Suggest away, my loyal suggestionaires!"

With one more collective, full-throated cheer, each staff member scrambled to grab a tourist "buddy." The tour group members found themselves surrounded by friendly and enthusiastic company CEOs, eager to please and get to know their new friends.

"Shiggydaygobah!" cried Ebenezer.

Whatever he said needed no translation.

Shiggydaygobah, indeed.

25

As the excited B & S staffers scrambled to procure a Doodlebody tourist to entertain and enlighten in the ways of producing radically stupid suggestions, Dr. Pudbid remained forlornly near but more than an arm's reach away from Alpha Rae Sapoopa-LaBoobis and a recovered Frog Puppleman.

Old Man Spuggett approached the kindly doctor. "Humaylius, you reticulated old badger-bonker! Let's spend a little time together while we have the chance. We have sixty years of catching up to do. Come into my office. It's just over here."

The bathrobe-clad company founder led the physician to his private office, next door and to the left of the company conference room and easily identified by its now splintered oaken door. Coincidentally, the office was situated in close proximity to the smashed water cooler, the rocking-and-rolling Cheezy Fabsmaggle, wastebasket-headed Marshall Farkpucker, and unconscious Barley Doodlebody.

The doctor followed his old schoolmate to where Marshall sat motionless on the floor. The old man stopped and studied the seated figure. "Well, I can't be totally sure here, but judging by the look of this person's colorful wardrobe, it would appear that this is Marshall Farkpucker. I don't know why he's sitting here like this, but I would venture to say this fellow's fast asleep! Do I hear snoring beneath that wastebasket, Puddles?"

"Yes, by gosh, I think you do!" Dr. Pudbid was startled as Marshall cut loose with a snort that echoed loudly inside the metal receptacle.

Bimbo Spazzgate stumbled up to the two old gentlemen, having retrieved a replacement bottle of water for the water cooler. He stopped to rest and set the bottle on the floor.

"Mr. Spazzgate, is that Marshall Farkpucker sitting there?"

Bimbo scrutinized the seated bucket-head closely, recalling his very recent encounter with this very same wastebasket. "Yes, sir, that's Marshall. He's hiding. I think he's hiding because Mux tried to pee on him."

The old man scratched his head thoughtfully. "Huh! Well, I suppose one *would* want to hide from something like that, but why is he hiding with his head in a trash can? The rest of him is right out here in plain sight!"

"Well, I think Marshall's hiding with his head in a trash can because he can't get the rest of himself inside it."

"Hmmmm, you may be right. But please, Mr. Spazzgate, don't let us interrupt the doing of what you were doing!"

"Yes, sir!" Bimbo hoisted the heavy bottle onto his shoulder and waddled over to the stricken water cooler. "I hope you find Marshall, sir!"

"Thank you, Bimbo. I'm sure he's around here somewhere."

The two old friends walked over to find Cheezy Fabsmaggle preoccupied with his rampage on the floor. The old man stood just out of Cheezy's rolling range, watching his employee approvingly, then moved back a few steps and sat on Barley Doodlebody's stomach. "Have a seat here on Cushion Guy for a minute, Puddles. I want you to see what a diligent employee doing his job looks like. It's a joy to witness!"

Dr. Pudbid looked with uneasiness at Old Man Spuggett relaxing comfortably on Barley's midsection. Old Spuggy was skating on thin ice, and he had no idea.

"I think I'll just stand for a while. I've been doing a lot of sitting today, and I need to stretch my legs a bit." With one eye, the good doctor obligingly watched Cheezy Fabsmaggle "working." He kept the other eye on Barley, lest he wake up and turn Old Man Spuggett into a bona fide candidate for emergency medical care. The good doctor felt a twinge of guilt for not checking on Barley sooner. He'd witnessed the violent collision with Cheezy when the tour group first arrived but had become distracted by the subsequent goings-on. His negligence was now bothering him, but not overly so. Barley was still Barley, and it was nice having him out of the picture.

Old Man Spuggett marveled at Cheezy's uninhibited performance on the floor. "Y'know, Puddles, it does this old heart good to see the boundless energy of youth unleashed and focused with enthusiasm on worthy endeavors. Look at this guy go!"

The good doctor was puzzled. "What's he doing?"

"At this point, it's what he's *not* doing that I'm pleased with!" Old Man

Spuggett envisioned Cheezy's normally unclothed method of creating radically stupid suggestions. "For someone like Mr. Fabsmaggle here, producing radically stupid suggestions in the usual manner isn't really a possibility." He didn't elaborate. "By doing what he's doing now, his creativity is stimulated and his job is a lot more fun. See what I mean?"

Cheezy giggled and whooped happily as he wriggled on the wet floor.

"You mean he's actually working right now?" the doctor asked.

"Busy as a beaver! Simpleton loves his job. He comes up with radically stupid suggestions by the bucketful. Why, he's the only one of my employees with his own private office—although that's because he's normally undressed and covered in teriyaki sauce while he performs his job. Believe me, that's something you don't want to witness. Nor do I!"

"You mean, he's usually *naked* when he does this?"

"As a newborn babe."

"Why would you give someone a job assignment that requires him to be naked when he works?"

"Well, Puddles, you wouldn't ask someone to roll around on the floor covered in teriyaki sauce with their clothes on, would you?"

"Good point."

"But due to today's unusual circumstances and the fact that we have company at our company, I think it would be best if I give Simpleton some time off from his duties right now."

The old man stood and approached his engrossed employee. Dr. Pudbid sighed with profound relief; Barley hadn't awakened while Spuggy was utilizing him as a sofa.

"Simpleton? Simpleton. *Mr. Fabsmaggle!* Stop rolling for a minute, please!"

The CEO in charge of rolling around on the floor stopped his gyrations and looked questioningly up at his boss.

"Mr. Fabsmaggle, I'd appreciate it if you'd take a break from your duties. I need to speak with you briefly."

Cheezy obediently rose from his horizontal position and faced the old man. His clothing, still soggy from the water-cooler dousing he'd received, clung to his body like cellophane and dripped water onto the floor. "Yes sir, Mr. Spuggett. May I help you?"

"You most certainly can, Simpleton! Because of your diligence and preoccupation with performing your duties, I don't believe you noticed that we have guests with us here today at Bumps & Spuggett."

To his surprise, Cheezy saw the big office abuzz with a large group of new faces. "You mean all *those* people?"

"Yes, Simpleton, and because of today's rather out-of-the-ordinary circumstances, I'd like you to postpone your current work activities and accompany me and Dr. Pudbid here so we can get you into some dry clothes."

"Yes, sir!"

The company founder and Dr. Pudbid scooted past the prostrated form of Barley Doodlebody, but Cheezy gazed upon the cold-cocked entrepreneur in bemusement. The young staffer had no inkling that Barley was there because of the earlier collision with him; his memory of the incident had been conked right out of his head.

Old Man Spuggett's own curiosity was piqued again. "Puddles, by any chance would you happen to know who this cushion guy is? Did he come here with your group?"

"Yes he did, Spuggy. That would be Mr. Doodlebody. He's actually kind of, um, the director of our group."

Old Man Spuggett eyed Barley skeptically. "Director, you say, eh? Well, if you ask me, your Mr. Doodlebunny seems to be doing the majority of his directing from a prone position—sleeping on the job, as it were. But I do have to admit: he's pretty darned comfortable to sit on! Still, I don't suppose we should just leave him lying in the aisle like this."

"Perhaps we could move him into your office?"

"Good idea! We can lay him on top of my desk. I think it'll be big enough to accommodate him. C'mon, Simpleton, give the doctor and me a hand here!"

Together, Old Man Spuggett, Dr. Pudbid, and Cheezy Fabsmaggle hoisted Barley and muscled him into the old man's private office. Dr. Pudbid eyed the wreckage. "What happened here, Spuggy?"

The old man gazed upon the ruined portal and sighed. "Alas, I'm afraid I exited my office just a tad before the door was ready for me to do so. Such a pity—it was a beautiful door."

As they carried Barley's heavy body over to the big desk, Dr. Pudbid took the opportunity to peruse the interior. The spacious room occupied the entire northwest corner of the building's second floor, its four walls paneled with rich mahogany wood. In the northern wall, situated directly across from the smashed oaken door, stood the stately brick fireplace over which the company founder's basketball hoop and backboard were mounted. A few feet to the left of the fireplace was a large window, which the good doctor imagined looked out upon Gob Street.

To the right of the smashed doorway hung a large oil painting of a beautiful landscape. A green meadow ringed by lushly foliated trees occupied the foreground. The meadow was bisected by a pristine brook, and in the background, a majestic range of snowcapped mountain peaks looked down on the sylvan scene. On the floor beneath the painting stood a small table, bare except for a large, unlit table lamp. On each side of the table was a plush, comfortable easy chair.

Noticing Dr. Pudbid admiring the pastoral painting, Old Man Spuggett smiled. "Ah, Puddles, I see you appreciate the serene beauty and tranquility of that scene as much as I do. It's a very relaxing view, isn't it? I'll often gaze upon it in quiet moments, when all the world's problems seem a bit overwhelming. It helps me to realize that all the world's problems aren't necessarily *my* problems, and I shouldn't be worrying about all the world's problems but should instead be worrying about my own problems, which helps me to realize that my own problems might not really be problems at all and I'm just *imagining* them to be problems and worrying needlessly, although some of them actually *might* be problems, and I'm spending far too much time gazing at this lovely painting when I should be solving those problems which really *are* my problems—and then I find that my head is about to explode from thinking about all that stuff and I fall right to sleep! It's a very relaxing painting, indeed!"

Behind Old Man Spugget's desk was the office's other large window, overlooking Guggbutt Boulevard. Hanging on either side of the window were two small framed photographs, one a group portrait of Old Man Spuggett surrounded by his smiling staff, the other a photograph of the Bumps & Spugget building's exterior as seen from its front on Clown Balls Avenue, the exact view of the building the tour group encountered when they first arrived.

Paralleling this wall was Old Man Spuggett's massive oak desk and huge desk chair, and directly behind the chair and just beneath the window was a long, low credenza. Two bare, cushion-less armchairs faced the desk, ostensibly for business clients as they conferred with Old Man Spuggett. The wall upon which the broken doorway was situated sported another door a few feet to the right. This appeared to be a closet, though the door was closed. Hanging on the wall between the two doors was a framed printed poster with a motivational motto:

Seize the Day! Suck the Moment!

The image featured a wild-eyed college graduate dressed in cap and gown, with a toothy, grimacing, almost maniacal smile, clutching a rolled-up diploma like a bludgeon in one raised hand.

Both of the windows were framed by luxuriously heavy, matching red draperies that were pulled back, but the glass portion was covered by a closed Venetian blind. All of the light in the room emitted from overhead fluorescents.

The big desk was cluttered with papers, a desk lamp, and other items that would prevent the three from placing Barley on the desktop. The two armchairs also prohibited them from approaching the edge of the desk.

"It looks like I have a bit of a mess to clear away before we relieve ourselves of our burden," Old Man Spuggett said. "Let's put this guy back on the floor for the time being."

They laid Barley gently on the floor's thick carpet. Old Man Spuggett dragged the two armchairs to one side of the room while Dr. Pudbid and Cheezy began clearing the stacks of papers and other items from the massive desktop.

"Don't touch that, Puddles! *Put it down!*" screamed Old Man Spuggett as Dr. Pudbid fingered an odd-looking object he'd just grabbed from the desk. The doctor and Cheezy shrieked, and the doctor reflexively dropped the object onto the floor. In one fluid motion, Old Man Spuggett leaped headfirst over the massive desk, roughly pushed Dr. Pudbid to one side, and landed facedown on the floor, throwing his body over the dropped object.

The sound of a small, muffled explosion—*BOOF!*—followed by a puff of white smoke issued out from beneath the old man. Cheezy and Dr. Pudbid stood frozen, stunned. Suddenly realizing what happened, Dr. Pudbid screamed in horror:

"Spuggy! Spuggy, are you all right?! *Speak to me!*"

Old Man Spuggett did not answer but lay motionless on his stomach, a whisp of smoke curling out from under him. The doctor hurriedly stooped at the old man's side to administer whatever aid he could—if there was still time.

"You'd better step back, son!" he warned Cheezy, looking up at the frightened lad, who hovered over the two old men, his eyes like two round saucers. "And you'd better turn away if you have a weak stomach! This isn't going to be pretty."

"Well, *pretty* has never been a word used to describe me, Puddles, although I have been referred to as 'ruggedly handsome.' Of course, that was years ago when I was much younger and still had my gallbladder!"

Dr. Pudbid's head whipped around and his jaw dropped in dumbstruck amazement. There was Old Man Spuggett, lying casually on his side, staring up at the good doctor with a blithe grin on his wrinkled face. "Spuggy! I-I thought you just had your guts blown out!"

"My guts blown out? Don't be silly, Puddles. My explosive devices couldn't blow out a candle. I only wish they were powerful enough to blow my guts out! Even then, there wouldn't be much of a mess to clean up; as I mentioned, I don't have a gallbladder anymore."

The doctor was in a state of shock. "But . . . but when you threw yourself down on the floor like that and covered the explosion, I thought you were sacrificing yourself to save our lives! Like in a war movie or something!"

"Heck no, Puddles! I'm not that heroic! I figured the *noise* would startle you, so I was simply trying to muffle the volume a bit."

The doctor sat back on his heels and sighed with relief. Cheezy said, "*Whew!*" and wiped beads of perspiration from his forehead. Old Man Spuggett chuckled.

"Puddles, I have a penchant for dabbling in the creation and manufacture of explosives from time to time. It's actually a hobby, but the firepower that my amateur efforts generate is usually woefully inadequate for destroying anything more than my own foolish ambitions. You couldn't have known; I'm so sorry to have frightened you, old friend. Your concern for my welfare warms my heart! And you too, Mr. Fabsmaggle! Please forgive me."

"All is forgiven," sighed Dr. Pudbid. "I'm just glad you're all right!"

Old Man Spuggett pulled himself to his feet, the front of his sooty bathrobe still smoking from the harmless explosion. He glanced over at Barley on the floor in front of the desk. "We still have to take care of Mr. Diddlebooty here. I'll finish tidying up my explosive devices so we won't have a replay of that little drama. Puddles, why don't you and Simpleton lift Mr. Boodleditty onto the desktop."

Old Man Spuggett gathered the remainder of the nondestructive explosive devices and carefully placed them in the top drawer of the credenza under the window. The desk now cleared, they laid Barley onto its hard oak surface like a cadaver on a slab. The company founder placed a small throw pillow under Barley's head.

"Done! Now, Mr. Fabsmaggle, let me see what I have in the way of dry clothing for you to wear." He shuffled to the door beside the broken main door and opened it—a closet, just as the doctor had suspected. A garment rack stretched the width of the closet's upper interior, but the only hanging articles of clothing were bathrobes. A few pairs of battered bedroom slippers littered the closet floor, along with a couple of old basketballs.

"Oh dear, it looks like the only thing I have for you to wear is a robe and slippers, Simpleton! At least they'll be comfortable, and since you are approximately my size and height, they should fit you quite well."

Cheezy gratefully accepted the proffered bathrobe and bedroom slippers and slipped out of his wet clothes, tossing them onto one of the nearby armchairs, then put on the old man's donated duds, surveying himself with great satisfaction in the full-length mirror mounted inside the closet door.

Old Man Spuggett was pleased with the results. "Simpleton, if I didn't know better, I'd say you were *me*, seventy-five years ago—when I was ruggedly handsome and still had my gallbladder."

"Thank you, sir! What would you like me to do now?"

"Good question. What should we have you do? *Aha!* Gerald is working on a very important project. He's presently upstairs in his laboratory, manufacturing a large quantity of his special cure for excess hair growth to serve to our guests, and there isn't much time for him to complete it."

"Gerald's making his cure for excess hair growth? *Oooh*, yummy!"

"Yummy, indeed! But he has lots of work to do, and he could really use your assistance. Will you help Gerald for me?"

"I'd be *honored*, Mr. Spuggett!" He paused. "No oysters, right?"

"I can assure you that absolutely no oysters will be involved."

"Great! I'm on it, sir!"

"Give Mr. Foon-Package all the help you can. This task holds the greatest importance!"

Cheezy gave the old man a stiff salute and bolted through the broken doorway of the private office like a rack of barbecued pork ribs pursued by a pack of peckish predators. The two old men watched in awe as the young, enthusiastic, newly inspired CEO in charge of rolling around on the floor zipped upstairs to fulfill his mission in the attic laboratory. They followed him to the ruined doorway and stared into the depths of the huge main office.

The contented look of a proud, indulgent father spread across the old company man's face. "Look at them out there, Puddles! Each and every one of them is hardworking, conscientious, and loyal through and through! They work their hearts out every day. All they want is for me to be happy and satisfied with their efforts. Isn't that something? I'm an extremely fortunate man, Humaylius!"

"And extremely easy to please, I'd say."

The low voice came from behind them, dripping with derision. Old Man Spuggett and Dr. Pudbid whirled around to see Barley Doodlebody sitting upright on the edge of the big desk, fully awake, rubbing the back of his head with one hand. A cynical smirk warped the corners of his mouth.

"Extremely easy to please—or just plain stupid!"

26

Old Man Spuggett and Dr. Pudbid left the rest of the Bumps & Spuggett employees to compete for Doodlebody tour group members. Each was itching to demonstrate their radically stupid suggestion talents for the guests. The new faces were like a fresh blast of inspiration, helping to churn, shake, and stir their creative juices into a veritable frothing smoothie of radical stupidity.

However, due to the lack of a coordinated plan, the situation immediately descended into chaos and escalated into a brawl. Overzealous employees bickered heatedly with one another, the mood of cooperation and camaraderie rapidly deteriorating. Executive Secretary Rae Sapoopa-LaBoobis took it upon herself to stop the quarreling and divvy everyone into teams before anyone was murdered.

Alpha Rae normally avoided assuming responsibility when it came to administering the firm's affairs, unless it was to assume responsibility for absolutely nothing. In that case, she was as conscientious and responsible as could be. She'd been this way for as long as anybody could remember, but today something had come over her. The tall, skinny executive secretary was revealing aspects of her character heretofore concealed, even from herself. She'd not only voluntarily taken on the task of being Frog Puppleman's nurse and caregiver but now was also preparing to dictate policy as to who would be teamed with whom for the office show-and-tell.

This initiative was momentous, but its rarity had no effect upon the staff. They just needed someone to tell them what to do and didn't care who it was; it was either that or fight each other to the death.

"You people shut your yaps! I need to think about this for a minute."

There were many things to consider, and half of the faces looking to her for guidance were unfamiliar. She performed a quick head count, determining that there were nine staff members and nine guests available. Two members of the staff teamed with two guests seemed to be the solution.

Yump Yup-Yup-Yup-Yup and Mimsy Borogove weren't permitted to comingle for the sake of Margaret Wubbleduster's psychological well-being. The little girl was much too young to be subjected to the blatantly disgusting behavior those two were exhibiting. This problem could be avoided by having Dork Snargmeyer supervise Mimsy; his size and strength would enable him to control the blue-haired harlot relatively easily, and the big Viking would likely be impervious to any seductive overtures Mimsy might make toward him. Also teamed with Dork and Mimsy would be Frog Puppleman. Frog and Dork had hit it off rather well, their initial dialogue being the catalyst that brought the whole group together. Rounding out this first team would be Alpha Rae herself so she could keep a protective eye on the city councilman.

In determining the members of the next team of suggestionaires, Alpha Rae figured that since a big, intimidating guy like Dork would be guarding that disgusting woman with the blue face, a big, intimidating woman like that Lahloolah lady might be best for supervising Yump. Additionally, the executive secretary had spotted the flash of romantic interest between Dork and Lahloolah when they looked at each other. If the two Nordic compatriots decided to follow Yump and Mimsy's lead, separating them would avert the potential for another hideous display.

Alpha Rae placed Lahloolah Snorgmark and Yump Yup-Yup-Yup-Yup on the same team with Mux Muggsley and Margaret Wubbleduster. Being a child, Margaret had little interest in the workings of manufacturing radically stupid suggestions, but she probably *would* enjoy a good romp-and-fetch with the Bumps & Spuggett in-house canine wannabe. Having Yump on the same team with Mux would be a good move as well, since Yump usually took Mux for his afternoon walk. It was getting well past that time now.

The teaming of Ebenezer Snugnards with Mayor Wubbleduster was a natural: they were the only two able to understand each other. Biff Spoozma had his Elizabethan English dictionary for translating their incomprehensible conversation, so those three, along with Felicia Greenthing, would make up another team. Perhaps attempting to figure out what the mayor and Ebenezer were talking about, along with the tedious routine of waiting for Biff's translations, would distract Felicia from screaming her head off. It was worth a shot.

Alpha Rae felt confident that Bagmo Maltgoggles and Narducci Palpatooti would make compatible teammates with Rapunzel Trashtrumpet and Roland Chumbuckets. Being a reporter, Rapunzel was one of those "literary types," and Bagmo was probably the most "literary" of all the staff members, based on the fact that one of his most recent contributions to the firm's production had been the radically stupid suggestion of creating a magazine called *Mouth Garbage.*

Mouth Garbage was to be a gossip-oriented publication supplying its readership with stories, photographs, features, articles, and columns devoted to issues and events that attracted the public's interest but were merely rumor, speculation, conjecture, patently untrue, or, as in the case of the photos, so ambiguous as to be interpreted in any number of ways. The rag would employ the best irresponsible reporters in the business. Its slogan: *"Mouth Garbage Tells It Like It Is or Might Be—But Maybe Not."*

Old Man Spuggett had been absolutely thrilled at the radical stupidity behind Bagmo's suggestion but regretfully explained to his employee that actual publication of the magazine could not take place. Readers and TV viewers were inundated with plenty of that lowbrow, unsubstantiated rumor and gossipmongering on a regular basis—but nice try!

Alpha Rae recognized that when Bagmo truly applied himself, he could be quite productive. She decided that teaming him with Rapunzel Trashtrumpet would be appropriate. After all, Rapunzel herself had been under consideration to be one of *Mouth Garbage Magazine*'s irresponsible reporters.

Narducci was also a writer, albeit a writer of songs, like the ditty sung by all the employees to put themselves to sleep each morning in the conference room:

"*. . . If ever you're sleeping alone in your bed*
And wake up to find a hen's hatching your head,
Be thankful she isn't a hippo instead!
Zippity-bippity-boppity-boodle-dee-doo . . ."

A workday wasn't really a workday at Bumps & Spuggett without one or two impromptu songs belted out by the prolific in-house tunesmith. If nothing else came out of teaming Narducci with Rapunzel and Bagmo, at least he'd entertain them with a song or two, which would keep everyone occupied until the party got started.

She knew very little about Roland Chumbuckets. He'd spoken briefly to Old Man Spuggett a while ago and was wearing some kind of uniform—a military uniform? Postman? Policeman? It looked "official," but he hadn't been introduced earlier with the other "official" members of this group of guests. Who was this guy? Would he be a complement to the three "literaries"? She wasn't sure, but she'd give it a try anyway.

Finally, Faisal Herskowitz would take charge of the only two-man team, entertaining Reverend Snortworthy. Faisal was pretty much two people by himself, so Alpha Rae didn't feel like the good reverend was being shortchanged.

Her work was done. Now that all of the team rosters had been finalized and the participants assigned, Alpha Rae addressed the group. "To all our guests here today: once you get the hang of what's going on, please feel free to contribute any ideas or suggestions you might have to assist our staff members. Just don't expect to get paid for anything!"

With those words of encouragement, the group split into their respective teams and dispersed to their respective work stations to commence their respective radically-stupid-suggestion demonstrations.

＊

"Yeah, *buddy!*" exclaimed Frog as Mimsy, escorted by Dork, approached the desk where Alpha Rae and he were seated. Frog was happy to have his longtime companion on the same team. Mimsy was not of the same frame of mind; her head whirled over how she should handle the new turn of romantic events in her life. Frog Puppleman, her only real love interest of many years, was completely unaware that a new man had just swooped into her life on a spinning office chair and swept her off her feet (along with everyone else), carrying her heart away in the process. What could she say to dimwitted Frog Puppleman that would make him understand?

Frog and Mimsy had been introduced to each other at P. P. Piggford and His Wife Janice High School. Through the years, she'd clung to Frog like a wet T-shirt. Their relationship, such as it was, had endured from youth to adulthood.

But everything had changed! She'd found someone who accepted her for who and what she was, blue face and all! (Not that Frog hadn't . . .) She'd found someone who truly wanted to be with her! (But so had Frog . . .) She'd found someone who was just as *horny* as she was! (There! That was it! Frog was about as romantic as a bowlful of exploding dog food.)

There was no denying it: Mimsy Borogove had fallen in love with Yump Yup-Yup-Yup-Yup. She would have to sever her romantic ties with Frog Puppleman. It was the right and fair thing to do.

"*Yeah, buddy!*"

Mimsy stopped next to Frog's chair and stared down at him sadly.

"*No, buddy.*"

Frog cocked his head and stared up at her questioningly.

Meanwhile, staffers Ebenezer Snugnards and Felicia Greenthing, and their guest counterparts Roymul Wubbleduster and Biff Spoozma, removed themselves at Ebenezer's suggestion to the company conference room. Biff hoped to sneak in a quick snooze; after all, why did the mayor and this Ebenezer guy need him? If all the talking was done between the two of them, who else would need to listen?

However, Biff was not considering the additional presence of Felicia Greenthing, and Felicia absolutely demanded consideration.

"Why do we have to listen to these two blabbing on and on?" she complained to Biff. "I can't even understand what they're saying; can you?"

Somehow, all four of the team members had seated themselves on the same side of the conference table in one long row: Biff to Mayor Wubbleduster's left, with Ebenezer Snugnards to the mayor's right. Felicia sat on Biff's left at the end of the line, and the big man's hulking form partitioned her from the mayor and Ebenezer. It drove her crazy that she couldn't see past Biff's obstructive frame.

"I can't understand them, but if I could *look* at them while they're blabbing, it wouldn't be so bad—but I can't see them because I can't see past *you*! I wanna hear what they're saying! I wanna see what they're doing! It's not fair! I can't see what's going on!"

"Bean water! Felicia's feckless bran muffin just spent the entire day with an amusement Jezebel, sheathed, spindled, and spooped!"

Biff looked to the mayor for Ebenezer's translation. The first magistrate obliged:

"Sayeth Ebenezer, 'Yea, unbeknownst to thee and thy minion, tempest and tragedy shall explode forthwith should this youthful maiden her woes 'pon us unburden! Few will elude the roaring demise it portends!'"

Biff dove for the dictionary. Pages flew as his increasingly proficient research skills expedited a quick translation of the translation.

Ebenezer was trumpeting a warning to them in no uncertain terms that impending disaster and misery loomed large should Felicia commence caterwauling. Biff's mind raced to grasp a solution to the problem—and it came to him: "Miss Greenthing, perhaps if you took a seat across the table from us, your inability to see may be improved!"

He held his breath, waiting for her response.

"Okay." She rose from her chair and walked around the conference table, taking a seat directly opposite her three male counterparts.

"Crotchity-crotch-crotch! Restaurant legume wuggle-optious!" Ebenezer was duly impressed at the ease with which Biff dispatched the dilemma.

Before Mayor Wubbleduster could translate, Felicia interrupted again:

"What is he saying?! What is he *saying*?! I still can't understand him or the other guy! I don't know what they're saying!" She barely suppressed a sniveling wail that threatened to explode into a cappella cacophony.

Biff was at a loss. He couldn't understand these guys either—not without a round-robin translation by committee and his trusty Elizabethan English dictionary. "Miss Greenthing, we'll have to be patient and wait for the translations when they're finished talking. I'm afraid there's just no other way to do it!"

Another thought: "Or you and I could just go to sleep!"

Before long, Felicia and Biff were snoozing peacefully, their heads cradled in their folded arms on the conference tabletop. Mayor Wubbleduster and Ebenezer prattled on and on about anything that came into their minds, touching at least cursorily upon a plethora of fascinating and diverse topics.

Back out in the main room, Faisal Herskowitz and Reverend Snortworthy arrived at Faisal's desk in the center. Giggling like a schoolgirl, Faisal pulled up an extra chair and placed it on one side, directing Reverend Snortworthy to make himself comfortable. "I am saying first thing we should doing is to have ideas for suggestions to making," offered Faisal.

He burst into a paroxysm of belly laughs and guffaws that he was unable to quell until he shoved a fist into his mouth, nearly choking himself to death.

The reverend stared at him, slack-jawed.

Once Faisal managed to get a handle on his outburst, he continued in his broken English: "I am trying to say is we are putting ideas together before coming with suggestions . . ."

Pause.

"*No*! Is *not* what I am saying—*pig*!"

Reverend Snortworthy rocked back on his heels.

Faisal continued calmly. "If we are each writing idea on piece of paper without anyone sees it, then we are dropping pieces of paper into big hat and shuffle them. Then we are taking one paper piece *out* of hat, then we are *eating* paper piece from hat, then we are cutting up hat into many pieces, then we are eating hat—"

He stopped in midsentence, refutation and rebellion seething in his eyes.

"What in hell you are talking about?? You are silly clown with face of camel!

Faisal shrieked, slapped himself soundly several times, and grabbed the reins again. "How we are thinking when so much noise is making?! I am making suggestion first to being silence from scream!"

"Is good point well taken!" replied Faisal. "Argument and shouting no good. We take advice of Faisal in this: be sense-making and agreeing before fighting and screaming."

Pause.

"But man is terrorist nincompoop who can be not trusted!"

Faisal was upset with his repeated insults and casting of aspersions upon his own character. He angrily cried, "Go to da hell, Faisal! Go to da hell!" and bounced up and down vigorously in his chair. He exploded into another spate of side-splitting laughter, falling off the chair, tears of mirth squirting from his eyes like leaks from a garden hose. Realizing that his response to his diatribe was just another seizure of jolly hysteria, Faisal became incensed at being so cursorily dismissed by himself and shouted in an apoplectic rage, "So, *this* is how you are replying me, peasant?! You are to me outcast!"

The predictable pause . . .

"We are being too much judgment and unreason! We are criticizing innocent man's ancestors and believings! Perhaps is yourself, Faisal, who is being ashamed to yourself!"

He paused. He scratched his head and rubbed his chin thoughtfully. He pondered his words in silent rumination.

In a flash his hands lurched to his throat. He began strangling himself, rolling and writhing fitfully once again. He paused to grab his hair and bang his head on the carpeted floor a few times, and resumed his self-garroting, squealing, screaming, choking, chortling, grunting, gurgling, and guffawing, laughing his head off, ripping his head off.

The volume he generated with his dual-personality histrionics caused others to stop their own activities and stare in amazement at the two-man team—or was it the *three*-man team?

Reverend Snortworthy was utterly flummoxed. He'd never witnessed anything like this before—but he *had* heard of demonic possession. In the realm of his own experience, this smacked more of possession than anything else.

Once again, the spiritual sensibilities of the preacher kicked in. Fire blazed in his eyes, and the spirit of castigation moved and drove him. He leaped from his chair and towered over the "possessed" victim like an enraged, overweight avenging angel, exploding with a voice that boomed as thunder:

"ARREST THYSELF! ARISE AND BE GONE, DEMON OF EVIL CONNIVANCE AND SUBVERSION OF THE SOUL! I CAST THEE BACK INTO THE FOUL DEPTHS FROM WHENCE THOU'ST COME! BE GONE! RETURN NO MORE!"

That did the trick! Faisal ceased his hysterics and lay on the floor, stock-still and silent, looking up fearfully at the towering reverend, eyes wide, mouth agape. He had just been out-ranted and out-raved.

"Okie-dokie," he said matter-of-factly, jumping up off the floor and retaking his seat. The reverend remained standing, breathing heavily. "We are coming back at work!" giggled Faisal.

Across the room, Bagmo Maltgoggles led Narducci Palpatooti, Rapunzel Trashtrumpet, and Roland Chumbuckets to his desk close by Yump Yup-Yup-Yup-Yup-Yup's solo cubicle and only steps from the smashed door to Old Man Spuggett's private office. This desk had been extremely busy already, having waylaid Bimbo, Mux, and Marshall as they first emerged from the conference room after their nap. Just a few feet away, Bimbo was rehabilitating the office water cooler and fitting it with a new, full bottle.

Bagmo's team was greeted with the sight of wastebasket-helmeted Marshall Farkpucker, still seated and asleep on the floor. Bagmo recalled his earlier idea of making it mandatory for *all* employees to wear wastebaskets on their heads to prevent injuries. Considering this wastebasket-as-head-protector idea might be a good starting point for today's suggestion discussions, to get the ball rolling and the creative juices flowing. Bagmo voiced this opinion to his teammates:

"We have Marshall sitting right here before us as a living example of how this idea could be implemented!"

"Yeah, but he might be dead," interjected Narducci.

"Good point."

"Well, ask him a few questions and find out!" suggested Rapunzel Trashtrumpet absentmindedly as she scribbled on a pad of Bagmo's note paper. Always the reporter, she attempted to catch up on taking notes for what she now believed would be a feature piece for *The Daily Poop*.

"That's a good idea!" agreed Roland Chumbuckets. "Ask him some questions!"

Bagmo's eyes brightened. "You mean, like a *quiz*?"

Bagmo excelled at taking and administering quizzes. His competitive nature drove him to accept almost any question as a direct challenge to his intellect and quizmaster skills. "I'll take Marshall on in a quiz any day of the week!"

"Well, I think today is as good a day as any," said Narducci. "Go for it!"

"But if it's a quiz, Marshall's supposed to ask *me* questions too! If he's dead, he probably won't do that!"

"Good point."

"How 'bout if I ask him if he's *not* dead?"

"Might work."

"Hey, Marshall! Are you not dead?"

Although he *was* not dead, Marshall didn't answer. He was asleep, and he was also deaf. He also had a wastebasket stuck on his head.

Bagmo shrugged and looked at his teammates in frustration. "He won't say!"

"Or he can't hear what you're saying because he has a wastebasket on his head," offered Roland.

"Good point."

"Yeah, Bagmo," said Narducci. "How's he gonna hear you if he's got a wastebasket on his head? Especially since he's deaf! And possibly even *dead*!"

"Maybe we should see if we can get the wastebasket off Marshall's head," suggested Roland.

"How're we gonna do that?"

"Well, there are four of us here who don't have wastebaskets on our heads. Why don't we try pulling Marshall's wastebasket off his head *for* him?"

"Oh, I get it! And once it's off his head, he can tell us if he's dead or not!"

"Exactly! Narducci, grab ahold of the bottom edge of the wastebasket. Bagmo and I will hold on to Marshall's shoulders. When Mizz Trashtrumpet counts to three, pull *up* on the wastebasket, and we'll push *down* on Marshall. Hopefully, that will pop this thing off."

"Right-o!"

Bagmo and Roland took their places on each side of Marshall Farkpucker, their hands firmly pushing down on his shoulders while Narducci stood behind him and grabbed the edge of the inverted trash can with each hand. As they stood poised and ready, Narducci asked, "Shall we sing a song first, to help us get into the mood? That always works for me!"

"If that will help, Narducci, then by all means," sighed Roland.

"Okay! I will now sing a composition of my own composing, which I will sing for you now. I hope you'll enjoy it. It goes something like *this* . . .

"Hey there, Marshall! Be aware,
We know your noggin's stuck in there,
And we're about to free your head.
But are you still alive, or dead?
And how are we out here to know
If we can't hear you tell us so?
Don't give up! No need to fret!
We haven't set you free, as yet,
But trust me—when all's done and said,
We'll have that sucker off your head!"

"Thanks, that's all I have." Narducci concluded the song with a graceful flourish and a gracious bow. His other three teammates paused to give him a brief round of applause.

Roland was genuinely impressed. "Good song!"

"And based upon a true story, I might add," confided Narducci.

"All right, now that the mood's been properly enhanced, I suggest we return to liberating Marshall," said Roland. The three reassumed their positions. "Mizz Trashtrumpet, would you please count to three for us?"

"*One! Two!*—"

A split second before she shouted, "*Three!*" Reverend Snortworthy burst forth with his high-decibel tirade against the demon possessing Faisal Herskowitz. Roland and Bagmo instinctively jerked around to see what the commotion was, releasing the downward pressure on Marshall's shoulders. Narducci pulled up on the wastebasket; because there was now no counter-pressure, Marshall was lifted off the ground by his "headgear" and flung high up into the air, flipping end over end like a Chinese acrobat. As Narducci, Roland, Bagmo, and Rapunzel watched in horror, Marshall's high-arching trajectory took him directly over Bimbo Spazzgate and the water cooler.

"Bimbo! *Look out!*" screamed Bagmo.

Bimbo looked out. Unfortunately, he didn't look up. Marshall's descent deposited him directly on top of Bimbo and the water cooler— ʀASSPOOOSSHH! In seconds, the water cooler, Bimbo, and Marshall were separate ingredients in yet one more catastrophe casserole. Marshall lay spread-eagled atop Bimbo, the wastebasket still unstuck. The water cooler was upended again and the newly installed bottle of water smashed to smithereens, soaking both of its assassins and the carpet beneath them. Although Marshall was unhurt, he wasn't sure if he was awake or dreaming. Bimbo was crunched but coherent; he sat up and surveyed the ruin in dismay.

Roland scurried over, and the others edged up behind him. "Bimbo! Are you all right?"

"Don't ask *me*, ask the water cooler!" cried Bimbo, aghast at the destruction.

Bagmo did ask the water cooler, but received no response. "It won't say!"

"Of course it won't!" lamented Bimbo. "How could it? It's *wrecked*! Marshall wrecked it!"

"He didn't do it on purpose!" insisted Narducci.

Roland examined the wreckage. The water bottle had shattered and spilled onto the floor, but the rest of the water cooler remained intact and relatively undamaged. "I think we can salvage things here, Bimbo! You replaced the water bottle once before—would you have another replacement for this one?"

"Course! We got tons of 'em downstairs. That's where I got this one."

"Downstairs? When our group arrived here today, 'downstairs' was all locked-up."

"It is if you came through the *front* door—but you can get down there if you take the back stairs. We keep lots of stuff downstairs."

"Then let's go downstairs and get another water bottle!" Roland turned to Narducci, Bagmo, and Rapunzel. "While Bimbo and I are downstairs, why don't you continue getting that wastebasket off Marshall's head?"

"You found Marshall?" asked Bimbo. "He was hiding from Mux! Mr. Spuggett was looking for him. Where'd you find him?"

"Actually, Bimbo, *you* found him. That's why the water cooler's broken."

"Marshall thought he was so clever hiding inside that wastebasket," scoffed Bimbo. "*I* found him right away!"

"There you go! And that, Bimbo, is why you are you, and Marshall is Marshall."

"*Ha*! You got *that* right."

"So, let's you and me go downstairs and get another bottle of water. Bagmo, Narducci, and Mizz Trashtrumpet can take care of Marshall while we're gone."

Roland felt guilty for leaving his teammates to contend with Marshall Farkpucker—Bimbo could have easily retrieved the bottle by himself, having done so once already—but the lure of discovering the mysteries of the building's lower depths was irresistible to the inquisitive bus driver.

He set off with Bimbo for the downstairs storage room.

27

Yump Yup-Yup-Yup-Yup, Mux Muggsley, Noodles Snorgmark, and Margaret Wubbleduster tramped across the main office to Yump's cubicle. On the way, the possible Gloxnarian detoured to retrieve the javelin he'd accidentally flung into the high ceiling after being smacked by Old Man Spuggett's runaway basketball. The slender spear was stuck fast, but Yump successfully extracted it with Noodles's assistance.

Once it was down, Mux eagerly encouraged Yump to give the javelin a fling so he could chase and fetch it, but Yump refused. Old Man Spuggett had specifically forbidden him to hurl the javelin within the confines of the main office. The deprived puppy impersonator whimpered and slumped in disappointment, perking up when Margaret patted his head. The four teammates continued to Yump's cubicle, which was situated in the northeast corner of the main office, away from the perimeter walls, its doorless entrance opening into the big room's center. (*Figure 2*)

Noodles and Margaret noticed that its interior walls were perforated like Swiss cheese. The cause became evident when Yump screamed, "*Yeeeaaaah!*" and hurled the javelin at a wall on which a target had been suspended. Several more javelins stuck out of the other walls, and an entire quiver of the slender projectiles was propped in one corner. Apparently, Yump had been utilizing his cubicle primarily as an oversized pincushion. A watering can with a long, slender spout rested on an otherwise uncluttered desk. A comfortable swivel chair was pushed beneath the desk.

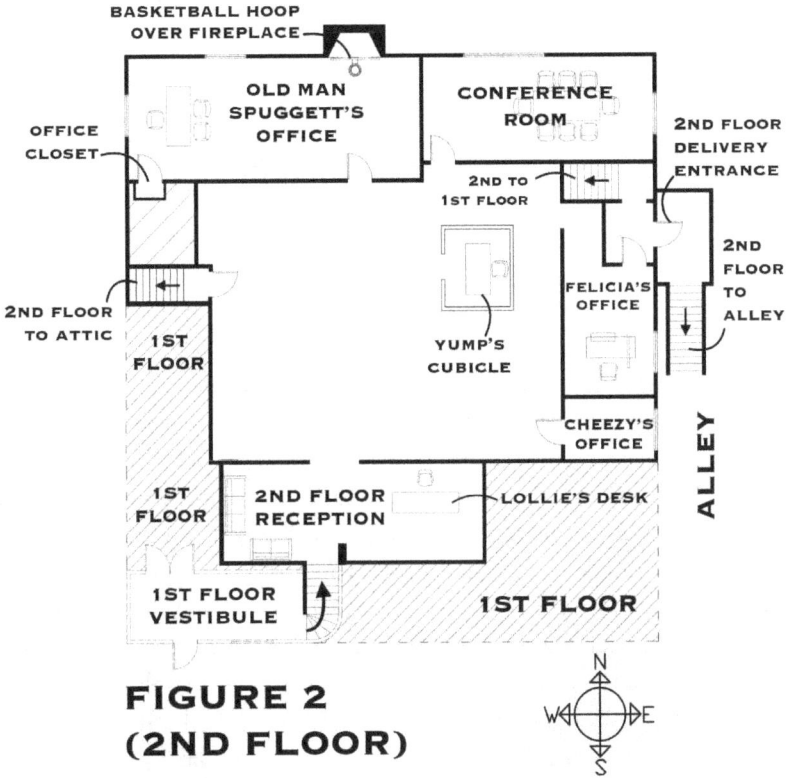

FIGURE 2
(2ND FLOOR)

Margaret spied the watering can on the desk and picked it up, tilting it just enough so a pencil-thin stream of water poured from the long spout and splashed onto the empty desktop. Since she'd had nothing to drink since the dryer episode at Charlie Nutbooger's automated car wash, Margaret wrapped her lips around the end of the narrow spout and swigged deeply until the can was drained. After the longest dry spell she'd ever endured, her depleted reservoir of HIVED-ing fluid was somewhat replenished.

Mux watched Margaret guzzle from the watering can; its liquid contents reminded him that he still hadn't taken his afternoon walk, and the realization struck him like a sucker punch to the bladder. He bounced like a bunny, whimpering frantically, trying to keep himself from exploding.

Thankfully, he was house-trained.

Before Mux Muggsley's personality transformation took place, he'd been a productive B & S employee, responsible for numerous outstanding radically stupid suggestions. Tragically, what he initially believed to be his greatest achievement would become his ultimate downfall.

He'd conceived the idea of establishing a psychiatric clinic for disoriented ducks. The clinic would be staffed by people who'd give psychiatric counseling to ducks with severe mental problems—neurosis, personality disorders, and delusional behavior such as imagining themselves to be cartoon characters.

After extensive research, however, serious problems presented themselves. Only actors who provided voices for cartoon characters would be able to speak duck language to the disoriented ducks. The dilemma: how was a person who *worked* as a cartoon character supposed to dissuade a duck from wanting to *be* a cartoon character? A definite conflict of interest!

Yet again, who could be sure the duck language spoken by the actors was authentic? Maybe it was just *people* duck language and not *duck* duck language! No one could actually understand duck duck language except the ducks themselves, and the ducks wouldn't advise anyone whether they understood what people were saying or not. Even if they did, they'd be speaking duck language, which no one would be able to understand.

Another issue: duck-speaking actors would most likely not possess the proper medical and psychiatric accreditation to be licensed duck psychiatrists. It would be illegal if they were to actually practice duck psychiatry. Where did one obtain credentials like that?

Additionally, it was determined that anyone working in the facility who was not a duck or a duck psychiatrist would probably go bonkers from hearing nothing but duck talk, day after day. They'd eventually need counseling themselves, which would prompt the necessity of creating a psychiatric clinic for people who work in psychiatric clinics for disoriented ducks. Who could say what future problems *that* would bring?

Mux bitterly abandoned the idea. A sensitive guy, he took this as a personal defeat and began a quiet, gradual retreat into a world of canine behavior. Nowadays, a scratch behind the ears or an occasional romp with a soft rubber ball kept him happy for most of the workday. He made one heck of a good watchdog, although fleas were sometimes a problem.

Mux's physical reaction to the watering can was becoming impossible to control. Yump, the person normally responsible for taking the office mascot for his daily afternoon walk, recognized the symptoms.

"I think we'd better help Mux before we do anything else here. We're all gonna be sorry if we don't. Ready for your walk, Mux?"

Mux yelped enthusiastically and sank his teeth into the edge of Yump's desktop.

"Okay, boy!" To Noodles and Margaret: "Would you mind if we took Mux for his afternoon walk before he pees on everything? We could get a little exercise ourselves while we're at it!"

"Ya, shure, yabetcha!" replied Noodles. Margaret snorted and nodded.

Suddenly, a scream exploded from outside the cubicle in the big main office, followed by a noisy crash and the shattering of glass.

"*Yipes*! What was that?!" shrieked Yump. Peering out of the cubicle, all four gazed in awe at the mess newly created by Bimbo and Marshall's unfortunate encounter with the water cooler.

Yump was impressed. "Wow! I wonder whose suggestion that was! That's gonna be a tough one to beat!"

Seeing the wet aftermath of the water-cooler catastrophe reinforced Mux's desire to divest himself of his own inner liquidity. He leaped in front of Yump and resumed jumping up and down, emphatically yipping, "*Yiy*! *Yiy*! *Yiy*! *Yiy*!" Extreme agony contorted his face.

"Okay, boy, we're going now! C'mon, guys, we'd better get a move on!"

Yump led Noodles, Margaret, and Mux around the corner and to the rear of his cubicle, over to the doorway in the northeast corner of the wall, where they were joined by Bimbo Spazzgate and Roland Chumbuckets. "What're you doing here?" asked Bimbo.

"I've gotta take Mux for his walk, and I'm bringing the rest of my team with me. What about you?"

"Gotta get a new water bottle. Marshall just wrecked the one I was installing."

"Where are we going?" asked Roland.

"This is Felicia's office. We have to go through here to get to the back stairs."

They were joined by a new arrival. Gerald Foon-Package had left Cheezy Fabsmaggle in his attic laboratory to make a trip to the first-floor storage room. The North Corners "blue blood" realized that his supply of enriched flour (an essential ingredient in his excess-hair-growth recipe) had run out and would need replenishment before Cheezy and he could continue their work. As was the case with so many of the office's other necessities, Gerald's stockpile of enriched flour was stored in the same first-floor storage room as Bimbo's replacement water bottles. He arrived at the door to Felicia Greenthing's office just as the others were preparing to enter.

The doorway opened into a short hallway that ran to the right a few feet, into the office itself. Felicia's desk sat along the opposite wall, facing them as they entered the room. Around the corner was another wall, in which another door was situated. When sitting behind her desk, Felicia would look directly at this door, which opened into a small, anteroom-sized vestibule. In the vestibule were two more doors: one straight ahead, which led to the first-floor stairway, the second located to the right.

The right-hand doorway was the fabled second-floor delivery entrance. It was Felicia Greenthing's job as CEO in charge of finding the delivery entrance to find it—or, as Felicia perceived, *not* to find it. The large, single door with a window in its upper half overlooked a second-floor porch landing from which a stairway descended into the alley on the building's east side.

The door was nearly adjacent to the first-floor stairway (which was regularly utilized). Since keeping the door's location a secret was imperative to Felicia's plans, she'd resorted to disguising it by posting a sign prominently on the door itself. The sign read,

---

This is definitely NOT a delivery entrance!

It is only a FAKE door, not a real one! Ha-ha.

The joke's on you.

If you try to use it, you will plunge to your

death and be killed!

Thus far, the ruse had been successful. Not one B & S employee had shown any interest in the door, or awareness of its existence. The one exception was the filthy-rag deliveryman, who used the door when bringing his daily filthy-rag deliveries to Faisal Herskowitz.

The party passed through Felicia's office, into the vestibule, and straight across to the door leading to a flight of steps down to the first floor. Bimbo switched on a light in the stairwell. The group proceeded down the stairs, which descended to a small landing, made a 180-degree turn, and descended again to the first floor.

"What's down here, Bimbo?" asked Roland.

"This is the first floor. The first floor would be down here."

"The storage room where we keep stuff is down here too," added Gerald, "and the restrooms. There's other stuff on this floor, too, but we can't get in there 'cause the doors are locked."

They reached ground level. Directly ahead of them was a set of large, windowless, metal double doors that presumably opened to the outside alleyway. Each of the doors was fitted with a horizontal metal push bar instead of a doorknob. Roland surmised that the double doorway constituted a first-floor delivery entrance. He gave the bars a push: both doors were locked.

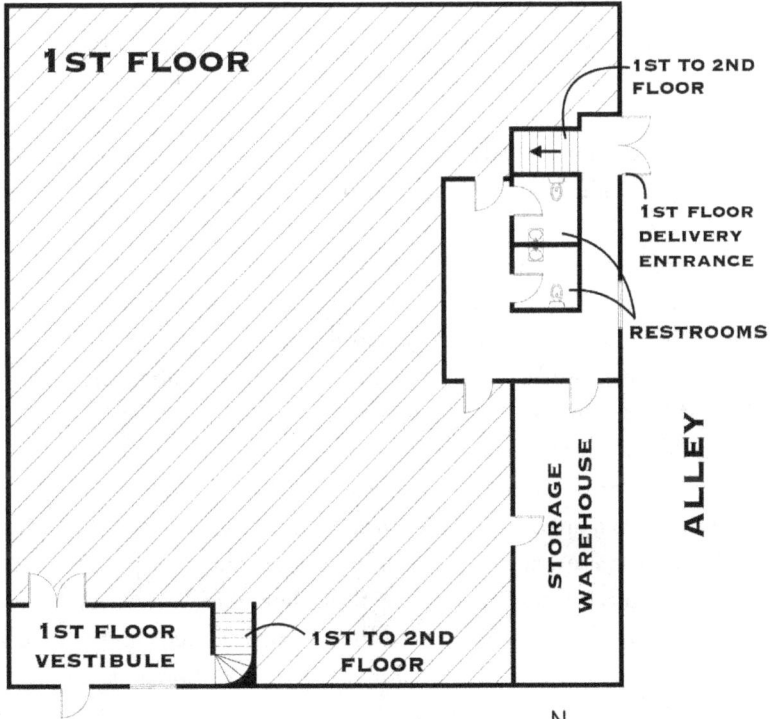

FIGURE 3 (1ST FLOOR)

They turned out of the stairwell and proceeded to the right down a long, cold, uncarpeted concrete hallway, their footsteps echoing noisily. Sun filtered through a large barred window on the left wall, which looked out onto the service alleyway, their sole source of light. The fluorescent indoor lights weren't on.

At the far end of the hallway, a single door faced them. The passage then made a turn around a corner to the right. (*Figure 3*)

Mux suddenly bolted past the rest of the group, sprinting down the remaining length of the hallway and disappearing around the corner.

"Hey, Yump, where's Mux running off to?" asked Roland. "Shouldn't someone be chasing him?"

"Nah. This is where we take Mux for his afternoon walk. The restrooms are just around the corner—that's where he's going."

"You don't take him outside for his afternoon walk?"

"Nah. If we took Mux outside, he'd probably run away! We just take him to the restroom. He only *thinks* he's a dog, you know. He's really a person."

A door slammed around the corner where the dog-man had disappeared.

"Whew!" sighed Yump. "I'm glad that's taken care of!" Mux was in, and all was well.

The group approached the wide metal door facing them at the end of the hallway. This door also had a horizontal push bar instead of a doorknob. "What have we here?" asked Roland.

"This is the door to the storage room," replied Bimbo, "and I gotta go in and get another water bottle."

"And I gotta get a bag of flour!" added Gerald.

Bimbo gave the bar a push, and the door opened. He reached inside the door and switched on the overhead lights, revealing the room's inner recesses.

The room was expansive in depth but not height; the top of Noodles's head was about two feet from touching the ceiling. Racks of shelves lined its perimeter, and aisles of shelving stood in the room's center, almost as tall as the ceiling and piled with all sorts of items, mainly janitorial products and office supplies. The continuity of the perimeter shelving was broken once, by another single door in the middle of the wall on the right side, which Roland determined to be the west wall. "Where does that door lead, Bimbo?" he asked, pointing to the portal, barely visible through the storage racks.

"Oh, that goes into the other part of the downstairs, but that door's always locked. The only door that's open is the one we just came through."

Roland was intrigued, wondering what secrets lay hidden behind that unnoticeable door.

Some supplies sat on floor palates: replacement drinking-water bottles for the upstairs water cooler, and stacks of professional-sized bags of flour, sugar, and various other products that Gerald used in his work.

Gerald made a beeline to a palate of flour bags, hoisted a bag off the pile, and positioned it on his shoulder. "Okay, I'm good. I got lotsa stairs to climb, so I'm outa here."

"I'll go with you!" said Roland. "I want to see what's on the rest of this floor."

"Not much to see, really," said Yump, "unless you like lookin' at closed doors that are mostly locked. You can use the restrooms, though; that's where Mux is right now."

"I'll be right back. Let's go, Gerald! Do you need some help with that flour bag?"

"Nah, thanks! I'm used to doing this, so I know what I'm doing. But if you're goin', let's go! I gotta get *goin'*."

Roland followed as Gerald lumbered toward the door.

Gerald headed up the concrete hallway to the staircase they'd just descended. Roland broke off and turned left, following this portion of the passageway; it ran for ten feet or so before making another abrupt turn to the right to become another hallway, running parallel with the back stairs hallway.

As he approached the turn, Roland saw another single door situated in the corner on the left wall. He gave the knob a try. It was locked. Roland hadn't seen this door from the storage room. Did it lead to another hallway that ran past the second mysterious door he saw in the storage room, and into the depths of the first floor's interior?

The locked door withheld the answer from him.

Roland turned to reconnoiter the passageway he'd just come upon. It had been painted a pastel yellow, now dingy and faded. As he peered down the corridor's cold, bare length, he saw two widely separated single doors in the right-hand wall, marked with signs that read *Men* and *Women*, obviously the restrooms. The left-hand wall was bare, with no doors or windows.

Past the restrooms, another single closed door faced him, a mirror image of the door in the corner behind him. That door was most likely another portal separating the restrooms and the storage room from the rest of the first floor; it would probably be locked, too.

Roland recalled that the tour group had seen another entrance to the first floor when they initially entered the downstairs vestibule. That entry had double doors, also locked, when Barley tried them. What was hidden in that locked-away portion of the building? Why was it abandoned?

As Roland ruminated, the door marked *Men* burst open, and Mux emerged, having completed his "afternoon walk." He was now more relaxed and cheerfully loped up to Roland's side, panting happily, his tongue lolling out of his mouth.

"All set now, Mux? Feeling better?"

"*Yeowp!*"

Roland followed Mux back to the storage room, where Bimbo had retrieved the replacement bottle of drinking water he'd sought. Lifting the large glass container onto his shoulder, he spotted Roland in the doorway. "Hey! You missed my tour! It was one of the best tours I've ever given!" Pause. "Actually, it was the *only* tour I've ever given."

Roland wasn't sure how disappointed he was to miss an exclusive guided tour of spare water bottles, sacks of flour, janitorial products, and office supplies.

"I was doing some exploring and I'm afraid the time just slipped away from me, Bimbo. Maybe the next time you're down here, I could join you for another tour!"

"No problem! There's nothing to see down here anyway but spare water bottles, sacks of flour, janitorial products, and office supplies. Well, since Mux has finished his afternoon walk and I got what I need here, I suppose we'd better get back upstairs—I gotta fix the water cooler before the party starts!"

Bimbo headed back to the stairway with Yump, Mux, Margaret, Noodles, and Roland. As they passed the window in the hallway that looked out to the service alley, Roland noticed a lone, unoccupied black sedan parked across the thoroughfare.

28

Old Man Spuggett and Dr. Pudbid stood in the broken doorway of the old man's private office and stared at Barley Doodlebody, who sat awake and upright on the edge of the big desk. He gingerly rubbed the areas on his head and neck where he'd received his sundry knock-out blows.

"So, this is how you welcome visitors to your place, huh?"

"Heavens no, Mr. Doodywinkle! Normally we're extremely hospitable here at Bumps & Spuggett! I'm terribly sorry about your misfortune, although I must admit I don't know what that misfortune is. We found you reposing on my floor like a dead fish, as senseless as a nonbinding legislative resolution, and moved you here into my office so no further misfortune might befall you. Do you need Dr. Pudbid's assistance? How are you feeling?"

"I feel like gorillas are thwomping a bunch of anvils inside my head! I oughta sue you 'til you bleed red ink!"

"Well, if that would make your head feel better, then by all means! But I might ask you in the meantime why you came to us unannounced and unexpected. I don't recall your having made a prior appointment with my secretary."

"If that was your secretary I saw out in the lobby when we first came in, then trying to make an appointment with her is like trying to fricassee a sedan with a cigarette lighter!"

The old man chuckled at Barley's exaggerated simile. "My goodness, that would definitely be daunting, wouldn't it? But I think you must be referring to Lollie. Lollie Babajuju."

"*Gesundheit!*" offered Dr. Pudbid.

"No, Puddles, 'Lollie Babajuju' is Lollie Babajuju's name! Mr.

Doubledribble, Lollie is actually a *receptionist*, so she's not the person you'd talk to regarding appointments. That person would be Alpha Rae Sapoopa-LaBoobis. She's my executive secretary—"

The old man caught himself. "Come to think of it, she wouldn't help you either. Yes, I guess I see your dilemma, Mr. Doodybumple!"

"That's Doodlebody!" corrected Barley.

"*What's* Doodlebody?"

"My name!"

"Oh! Sorry there, Mr. . . ." The old man looked confused. "Puddles, what did you tell me his name was?"

"Puddles?" Barley looked at Dr. Pudbid with a derisive smirk on his face. "Doc, am I hearing this guy call you *Puddles*?"

"Puddles is Humaylius's nickname. That's what I called him many years ago when we went to school together."

"And just what did you and the good doctor study when you went to that school? Idiocy?"

"It seems to me that there was a course of study offered in idiocy while we were attending the institute, but I don't think Puddles or I took the classes required to obtain a degree. However, I believe my business partner, the late Mr. Bumps, went through the entire program."

"Might've done you some good too!" snickered Barley. "Helped you to recognize lunacy when you saw it!"

Old Man Spuggett was receiving his first eye-opening glimpse of Barley Doodlebody's contentious, combative personality and general orneriness. This conscious version of Barley Doodlebody was far less entertaining and not nearly as comfortable as the unconscious one. Old Man Spuggett decided to have some fun with Barley and settle him down.

"Mr. Doobydipple, you seem to possess a certain biased attitude regarding our intellectual capabilities here at Bumps & Spuggett, be they my own, my employees', and it appears even the intellectual capabilities of Humaylius here. If this is so, then might I ask why it is you should choose to make a special, dedicated effort to transport yourself and your associates all the way out here specifically to see us? Your motivations are unclear and puzzling to me."

He raised one eyebrow and fixed Barley with a steady, inquiring stare.

Barley realized that any attempt to fool the old man would be futile; it was apparent that Old Man Spuggett was a crafty old bird and already wise to him, though the old geezer hadn't yet called his bluff. He couldn't afford to alienate the company founder if his ultimate aim was to establish Bumps & Spuggett office tours as an ongoing enterprise. What if it came down to striking some kind of partnership deal with this old croaker? It might be prudent for Barley to have Old Man Spuggett playing ball on *his* team. Diplomacy was in order.

Barley rose to the old man's unspoken challenge with as much tact and civility as he was able to muster. "Well, Mr. Spuggett, you're the talk of the town! You run a business that produces something . . . *unusual!* We came here today to learn how you do it, and why."

"You believe the business of producing radically stupid suggestions is unusual?"

"Well, yeah!"

"And why do you perceive this as being so? What led you to this belief?"

"With all due respect, Mr. Spuggett, the whole idea of producing radically stupid suggestions seems pretty stupid in itself!"

"Hmmm . . . 'stupid,' you say. Then I must ask you a question regarding your evaluation: is that good, or bad?"

"Whaddaya mean, good or bad? Stupid is just *stupid!*"

"Let me ask you another question, sir, if I may. How do you perceive stupidity?"

Barley thought for a moment. "Stupidity is everything I've seen since I've been here today: a receptionist you can't talk to because she's blithering some incomprehensible mumbo-jumbo and won't pay attention—"

"Yes, we've already established that you met Lollie Babajuju, our receptionist, and you say you couldn't talk to her or get her attention. Do you speak any Bubba-Bubba-Bubba dialects, Mr. Dumpledinky?"

"That's *Doodlebody!*"

"*What's* Doodlebody? A dialect you speak?"

"It's my name! Get it right, will ya?"

"Oh dear! My deepest apologies, Mr. Doodlebody. Doodlebody. *Doodlebody!*"

"It's *not* 'Doodlebody Doodlebody Doodlebody'! It's just Doodlebody! One time! Is that too hard for you to remember?"

Old Man Spuggett shook his head. "No, it's not too hard for me to remember your name, Mr. Doodlebody. It's just more fun forgetting it!"

"Yeah? Well, you'd better quit forgetting it. I haven't forgotten *your* name!"

"Wouldn't matter a jot if you did," laughed the old man. "From time to time, even *I* forget it! What's a name, anyway? Just something to call someone or something, but it's not who or what they really are! Mr. Doodlebody, you can call me anything you want to, or nothing at all, if you'd prefer—I won't mind either way. You can even call me Spuggy like Puddles does, if that would be more to your liking!

"But *you*, Mr. Doodlebody! You have such a musical-sounding name! *Doodlebody-Doodlebody-Doodlebody.* See what I mean? Music! What I wouldn't give to have a musical name like yours. We should get Narducci Palpatooti to compose a melody for your name, and we could all sing 'The Doodlebody-Doodlebody-Doodlebody Song.' Why, you'd be famous! At least, you would be around here."

Barley stared dumbly at Old Man Spuggett; he'd never experienced a conversation like this in his entire life. Not even with his brother, Frog.

"Now, let's get back on the subject here. We were discussing prerequisites and parameters useful when dealing with certain members of my staff. Regarding Lollie: she speaks no English, so you wouldn't have been able to communicate with her anyway, unless you speak the language of Bubba-Bubba-Bubba, Lollie's home country."

"She doesn't speak English? How can she receive guests? This isn't Bubba-Bubba-Bubba! We speak *English* here in North Corners!"

"Mr. Hoogledingy, up until your visit today, it didn't matter that Lollie spoke no English or didn't receive guests, because she didn't need to. We never *had* guests at Bumps & Spuggett! And you didn't call for an appointment ahead of time!"

"What's the use of making an appointment to visit a company that doesn't receive guests?"

"Our company didn't have guests before today, but since you're here, we've now *become* a company that has guests, so it stands to reason that we now need a receptionist. Well, it just so happens that we already *have* a receptionist: Lollie Babajuju. Bingo! Right there, Johnny on the Spot. Perfect timing, and an amazing stroke of luck!'

"But she doesn't speak English!"

"The way I see it, there's no need for you to speak with Lollie anyway. The person you need to speak with regarding an appointment is Alpha Rae Sapoopa-LaBoobis, and *her* English is just fine."

"But what happens once I do make an appointment? When I get upstairs to the reception room, I'm still faced with someone who won't let me in because she can't understand a word I'm saying!"

"Mr. Humperdinkle, if you have an appointment, you just walk right on in. You don't have to speak with Lollie at all. It won't matter one way or another to her; she'll probably be doing that chant thing she does, and she won't pay attention to you anyway. Because you're visiting with us here today, in future visits you will have already been here before. You'd already know your way around the place, so you'd just come on in. I don't see any problems with that. We're a pretty informal bunch here."

Barley's head was spinning. He shook off this perplexing bit and tried another one: "Okay, then how about this? What about the lunatic who runs circles around the office, screaming his head off like some maniac? I had to chase after him to talk to him, but I never caught up with the guy."

"Based on your description, that was our office manager, Fandango Slamson. He's the one who usually runs around and screams a lot, although I must admit I've seen neither hide nor hair of him today, which is very unlike Fandango. Perhaps you might know where he is?"

"No, while I was chasing him, I ended up smashing into someone else, and that's all I remember until I woke up on this desk."

"Hmmm, very strange, indeed!" The old man scratched his chin. "But please understand, Mr. Finkledooty: Mr. Slamson is an office manager. It's not his job to communicate with anyone but Bumps & Spuggett personnel. In not speaking with you, he was simply doing his job. Nor did he do anything inappropriate when he ran from you. He runs from everybody!"

"Well, then I won't take it personally," said Barley sarcastically. "So, let me get this straight: you have an office manager who won't talk and runs away from everyone, screaming like a little girl—and it's what he's *supposed* to do. If you ask me, that's pretty stupid!"

"Why should anyone be concerned if Fandango runs around and screams a lot? He keeps the staff awake, productive, and on their toes, and he does it diligently, consistently, and efficiently, which is what I want my office manager to do. He does it in his own way, to be sure, but who's to judge or criticize how success is achieved as long as it doesn't hurt anyone and it's legal?"

Barley's head was pounding, from both his headache and the old man's logic. Somehow, when the old man spoke, everything seemed to make sense—but what *kind* of sense was hard to determine. Still, he was feeling worn out by his own arguments. "Who *can* you talk to around here?" he asked.

"Well, for starters, you and I seem to be conversing rather easily. Seeing as how I'm the owner of this company, whatever you're getting from me you're getting from the horse's mouth!"

"The horse's mouth, eh?" sneered Barley. "The only thing I've ever gotten from a horse's mouth is a mouthful of stupidity. That's what one usually gets from a horse's mouth, and I haven't heard anything here to refute that yet!"

"Ah, I see we've come back around to the subject of stupidity," said the company founder. "A fascinating subject, indeed. Why, stupidity is the very foundation of our company! But I must ask you again: in *your* mind, how do you define stupidity?"

Barley thought for a moment. "I guess I define stupidity as 'ridiculous'— something that doesn't make sense."

"Precisely!" cried Old Man Spuggett. "So let me ask you this once more: do you think of stupidity as being a bad thing?"

"What are you asking me? Stupidity is something everybody can do without!"

"Ah, but we *cannot* do without stupidity, good sir! Without stupidity, there would be nothing to rise above."

"What are you talking about?"

"Mr. Doodlefinger, we here at Bumps & Spuggett see stupidity as indispensable because we view it as a starting point—a place to begin! Did you notice the sign that hangs on the wall out in the main office?"

Barley shook his head; he'd been so absorbed in chasing Fandango Slamson that he hadn't seen much of anything but the office manager's rear end.

"Well, that sign says, 'From Stupidity Springs Lucidity.' If you see stupidity as the very lowest level of perception, the bottom of the barrel, or the lowest rung on the ladder—and I think you do—then look at it this way: if stupidity's the bottom, then there's nowhere to go from there but up! We see stupidity as a foundation to build upon."

"What's 'up' from stupidity?"

"Clarity from confusion! Intelligence from ignorance! Sense from nonsense! Inspiration! Revelation! Illumination! *All* of those things can be gleaned from any statement, circumstance, or situation—no matter how 'stupid' they might seem initially—if that stupidity is viewed not as a place to end but as a place to *begin*!"

Barley's head whirled, but not his defiant attitude. "And all this from the horse's mouth, eh? So you're telling me that stupidity doesn't really exist except as a launching pad for brilliance? That a horse *isn't* just plain stupid?!"

Old Man Spuggett considered Barley's questions. "I see we've come back around to the subject of horses—what a splendid conversation! It's very cyclical; just like life itself! But let me clarify something here for you, Mr. Dunglebuggy: horses aren't stupid. Horses are horses."

"Okay, if horses aren't stupid, then how come they can't talk?"

"They *can*—and quite articulately! But they don't speak English; they speak Horse. They communicate with each other quite well. Since we're on the subject of horses again, let's get a few facts straight before we continue: like Lollie Babajuju, horses don't speak English—but they understand more of our language than we do theirs."

"How do you figure that?"

"If you say, 'Giddiyap!' to a horse, it knows you want it to run, and it runs, right?"

"Yeah, I guess so . . ."

"But if a horse whinnies or neighs at you, what do you do? You stand there scratching your head, but you don't do anything. Why? Because you didn't understand what it said—you don't speak Horse! Maybe it was telling you to move out of the way because a runaway freight train was about to mow you down. But because you didn't understand what it was *saying*, SPLAT!

"Horses don't speak English. Lollie Babajuju doesn't speak English. If Lollie were to speak to you in *her* language and you didn't understand her, would that mean she was stupid? Not necessarily. Would it mean *you* were stupid? Not necessarily!"

"C'mon, man, horses are stupid!" cried Barley, still clinging tenaciously to his last remaining argument.

"Indeed? When you give a horse something to eat, he eats it, right? When you smack a horse with a whip and tell him to run, he runs, right? When you harass, annoy, or anger a horse, he kicks you, right? What's stupid about that? To my way of thinking, when you do those things to a horse, the horse responds in a most intelligent fashion. I mean, after all, the horse could just *kill* you if it wanted to and be done with it!

"We need to establish something, Mr. Doofynoodle: stupidity is produced in massive quantities all the time. It's officially sanctioned and practiced on a regular basis by the entire human race. However, the way it's *perceived* is the key. Perception is everything!

"To a horse breeder, a thoroughbred racehorse is a ticket to fame and riches on the racetrack. To a farmer, a thoroughbred is a useless nag because it can't pull a plow. One man's brilliant political, scientific, or philosophical utterance might be another man's idea of the most ridiculous political, scientific, or philosophical utterance ever uttered! These attitudes are subjective: it all depends on how an individual perceives these things. The very nature of stupidity is subjective as well. One man's radically stupid suggestion might be another man's answer to a perplexing problem!

"Mr. Doodlefanny, throughout our conversation here, I've sensed that you want me to reveal some great secret to you—something more profound than the subject of horses—to justify what we're doing or why we're doing it. Well then, let me oblige you. I will now divulge the heretofore-forbidden great secret of Bumps & Spuggett to you:

"Within the walls of this building, my employees are free to be *themselves*, and free to exist on whatever level they choose to exist, unfettered and liberated from forces, prejudices, and individuals that neither understand them nor seek to understand them. Here they are understood, validated, appreciated, indulged, and involved. They mean everything to this organization, and this organization means everything to them. They contribute joyfully, their efforts are encouraged, applauded, and rewarded, their feelings of belonging are reinforced continuously, and all they're doing is being themselves! Their jobs are based on and determined by the skills, aptitudes, and perceptual levels each possesses as an individual, then custom designed especially for them. My employees are happy, fulfilled, looked after, and cared for."

"So, what's the big jolt you get from bankrolling all this?"

"By that I assume you mean why do I show them kindness, interest, good humor, direction, encouragement, and love? Because in return, I'm constantly surrounded by feelings of happiness and fulfillment, and receive my own feelings of accomplishment and a sense of belonging as well!

"Now, I suppose there's a certain amount of selfishness in me that I should desire this for myself, but I admit that I derive extreme enjoyment from seeing how these people blossom when given the chance. It also keeps me young: I got to be 103 by absorbing their energy and enthusiasm and attempting to perceive the world seventh-sensually, as they do."

"*Whoa*, wait a second there!" Barley's eyes narrowed. "Whaddaya mean, 'seventh-sensually'? What the heck is that? Some kind of spell? Some porno or cult thing?"

"No, Mr. Binglederry, it's not magic, it's not cultish, it's not sinister or naughty in any way. Nor is it anything that you yourself haven't experienced at one time or another. It's simply a particular sensory perception of the world. It's being able to sense the nonsense and the degree thereof in certain circumstances, focus upon and grasp that 'nonsense,' and make it the operative reality of that moment: make the *nonsense* the sense that makes sense, then deal with the circumstances on that level. When one does that, one is operating on what I call the seventh-sensory level, utilizing seventh-sensory perception.

" *This* sense comes not from the five basics of taste, touch, smell, sight, and hearing, nor do we operate with the mysterious *sixth* sense; that one's a bit too 'otherworldly' for us here. Instead, we function under and rely upon a *seventh* sense—the one that doesn't *make* any: nonsense!

"When one perceives the world from that perspective, things tend to make whatever sense the perceiver chooses to make of them. Things are as sensible or unsensible as they need or don't need to be, because the perceiver dictates how he will proceed in dealing with them. Try looking at things from *that* angle and our goings-on will make sense! At Bumps & Spuggett, we utilize the seventh sense to perceive the world. We find that in doing so, the world is made more understandable, or at least more manageable.

"Why do we produce radically stupid suggestions? Because from a seventh-sensory perspective, producing radically stupid suggestions makes as much sense as producing anything. Life is much more pleasant, fun, relaxing, and a heckuva lot less stressful when you're operating on that level!"

Barley was confused but intrigued. "Okay, assuming that's all true, and it's why you're in this business, how do you make any money?"

He had a genuine desire to know the answer to this. If he could make it pay, producing radically stupid suggestions seemed much easier than operating a liver-only specialty cuisine restaurant, running a diner where people blew up, managing a retail cow-pie boutique, or maintaining *any* of the businesses he'd ever conceived.

"How lucrative can the market for radically stupid suggestions be?" Barley asked. "How can you pay your employees' salaries? How could you possibly live the good life if you can't make all of it *pay*?"

"First of all, I'm already living the good life! I just elucidated for you the many reasons why I feel that way. Secondly, and perhaps most importantly . . ." Here he paused, chuckling to himself. "I'm a *scillionaire*, Mr. Noodlemonkey! I don't give a toot whether I make money or not!"

It became clear to Barley. Old Man Spuggett's world lay inside these walls: insulated, secure, happy, self-sustaining, harmless, and inconsequential. Outside these walls, the world existed as Barley knew it, with its frustrations, disappointments, failures, hollow triumphs, empty feelings of accomplishment and self-worth. *That* was the world most familiar to Barley.

Kindly Dr. Pudbid had been listening attentively to Old Man Spuggett's debate and discourse with Barley. So, *this* was what Ol' Spuggy had been up to in the sixty years subsequent to their graduation from the North Corners Institute for Indigent Wannabes: founding and developing a company that was a world within itself!

From what he'd seen, it was a very *nice* world, too. He liked everyone he'd met here—except perhaps the Sapoopa-LaBoobis woman, who stared at him with her cold, wild eyes. Still, he'd seen a genuine spirit of compassion and caring in her desire to look after Frog Puppleman. There was obviously more to this Mizz Sapoopa-LaBoobis woman than met the eye—indeed, more to *all* of Spuggy's employees! His college friend's last sixty years had been well spent in assembling such an amusing and amazing aggregation under his office building's roof.

At that moment, the enactment of the flying, acrobatic water-cooler destruction took place, as interpreted by Marshall Farkpucker and Bimbo Spazzgate. Old Man Spuggett and Dr. Pudbid whirled around to peer out the broken door. Barley slid off the edge of the old man's desk and joined the other two, staring over their shoulders at the chaos. He piped up triumphantly: "There you go! This is what I'm talking about. Insanity! What I'm seeing here is ridiculous!"

"It's a mess is what it is," answered Old Man Spuggett. "But accidents happen, whether stupid, insane, ridiculous, or otherwise. No one appears to be hurt, Puddles, so there's no need for a medical intervention."

Dr. Pudbid shrugged it off; what else was new?

"But now, Mr. Dirtybottle, you have an opportunity to evaluate how insane these affected employees really are! Let's see how they handle this tragedy, shall we? If your thesis is correct, it should prove to be amusing."

As Barley, Old Man Spuggett, and Dr. Pudbid observed, the small group discussing Marshall and Bimbo's predicaments came to the conclusion that one group would assist Marshall while Bimbo and Roland procured a replacement water bottle from the first-floor storage room.

Inside the private office, Old Man Spuggett turned to Barley. "Mr. Digglebooby, as I saw it, there were a couple of problems, and the group came up with the solutions. There didn't appear to be much in that little vignette that smacked of stupidity or insanity, did there?"

"Yeah, well, okay—so the people weren't running around like chickens without heads, but the fact that such a weird accident happened here in the first place is evidence enough that this joint is nuts. You don't see things like that happen anywhere else!"

Old Man Spuggett was growing weary of being on the defensive with this Doodlebody character. "Let me inform you of something, Mr. Boogynoodle! In our normal everyday activities here, we suffer very few accidents at all, 'weird' or otherwise. Nothing out of the ordinary, I can assure you. The spate of accidents we're currently experiencing did not commence until *your* group arrived on the scene unannounced, threw everything into disarray, and had us running around like a bunch of drunken sport foofs!

"By the same token, I must also acknowledge that since your group arrived here today, my staff has been treated to one of the most enjoyable experiences they've experienced in quite some time, and they've befriended those members of your group with whom they've interacted. As a matter of fact, even as we speak, my employees are preparing to throw all of you a party!

"If this is all insanity and stupidity, I don't see anything wrong or bad. I'm seeing it as *good*—and from the look of it, everyone else out there is, too!"

Gerald Foon-Package walked briskly past the broken door of the old man's private office on his way to the back stairway. "Going downstairs, Gerald?" asked the old man.

"Yes, sir! I just ran out of flour and I gotta resupply—but don't worry, Mr. Spuggett, the cure for excess hair growth should be ready soon."

"Very good, Gerald, glad to hear it. Carry on, by all means!"

Gerald proceeded to the doorway of Felicia's office and his rendezvous with the other groups congregating there.

"Busy as beavers!" exclaimed Old Man Spuggett with delight as he surveyed the scene. "Things are going rather well at the moment. Everyone seems to be getting along; everyone seems to have something to do."

Once more Old Man Spuggett turned to Barley. "You see, Mr.

Dinkydoodle? Everything is running smoothly, and everyone is involved. While you were sleeping on the job, your fellow guests established a rapport with my staff, and it's all leading up to one big, exciting wingding! How cool is *that?*"

"Well, I guess that's good, as long as you're not charging me for it!"

The old man was indignant. "How in good conscience could we possibly charge your group money for joining us as honored guests at a big party?"

A pang of guilt surged through Barley at the old man's question; that's exactly what he was doing with his *own* group.

"Why don't you join the rest of us at the party, Mr. Tinkledoodle? Consider this my personal invitation to you, right from the horse's mouth. You're our guest, just like all the other folks, and right now, it seems to me that you're one guy who could really *use* a good party. Enjoy yourself! At least, for as long as you're with us today."

Barley sighed heavily. His head pounded like the Army drum corps was holding auditions inside his skull. He was windblown, dried out, and weary from too much thinking, conniving, and accommodating. Whatever the old codger was prattling about, Barley needed a respite from this day-long beleaguered state of being.

He found the old man's philosophizing a bit tiresome, his continuous postulation a bit annoying, and that stuff about seventh-sensory perception somewhat bewildering, but it began to dawn upon him that the more he heard, the less contemptuous he was of this strange world and more envious—even covetous!—of their carefree existence. He didn't quite understand it all yet; what he did understand was that this world seemed rather inviting. Barley found himself less concerned with what *he* should be doing and more relaxed and interested in observing what was going on around him—to try to make sense out of all this.

One more question: "Mr. Spuggett, what does that sign on your office wall mean?" He pointed to the framed poster between the broken office door and coat closet, which read,

Seize the Day! Suck the Moment!

"Oh, *that*!" chuckled the old man. "That's another one of the many motivational and inspirational observations I live by. 'Seize the Day!' *Carpe diem*, in Latin. I'm sure you've heard that expression before; it's rather a cliché. Quite figurative, of course. One cannot actually put one's arms around a twenty-four-hour period of time and give it a hug, but it basically translates into making the very best and the most of every day.

"'Suck the Moment!' simply takes that *carpe diem* concept down one more notch to each minute of every day. Once again, a figurative image; one cannot actually draw life by wrapping one's lips around a few ticks of the clock and sucking, but one *can* draw life from every moment of every day by participating in each moment to the fullest and living those moments with gusto, deriving all one can from each second that passes by.

"Mr. Dinklefanny, my suggestion to you would be to forego worrying yourself with what we do here and how we do it. Grasp the precepts put forward on my office wall: seize the day and suck the moment, at least while you're here with us. We're gonna have a wingding! Seize it and suck it dry!"

Once more, Barley scanned the depths of the big main room. He ruminated on the old man's words while attempting to pinpoint and identify members of his tour group. It didn't prove difficult; the members of *his* group looked like they'd spent the last week spelunking inside a vacuum cleaner. And they were dispersed all over the premises, effectively out of his control. Interesting how the tourists carried on so well with these supposed "idiots." His group was not laughing at the staffers, nor making fun of them, nor frightened of them in the least! In fact, his tourists were treating the staffers as if they were the best of friends, and vice versa. How could that have happened? What had he missed while he was zonked out?

Rather than kill Barley's contemplative mood, the old man opted to keep quiet and let the incorrigible skeptic work it out for himself. Some time passed in silence while the three men observed the rest of the office buzzing with industrious activity. After a few minutes, Gerald Foon-Package returned, huffing and puffing with a large, heavy sack of enriched flour perched on his shoulder.

"Gerald is replenishing his flour supply so he can finish concocting the culinary fare for the upcoming party," said the old man. "I guarantee you're going to love the results of Gerald's work. He's quite an artist, really, although he thinks of himself more as a scientist. Either way, the findings of Gerald's research are invariably lip-smacking good!"

"He's an artist who thinks he's a scientist, and he invents food—but he's *not* a chef."

"Well, it's not quite like that," explained the old man, "because, you see, Gerald doesn't really *intend* to invent food when he does his research and experimentation. It just seems to come out that way! Truth be told, Gerald usually thinks his products are something entirely different from what they become. We don't set him straight because, when it comes right down to it, it doesn't really matter what you call his creations—and it doesn't really matter what Gerald thinks they are. They are what they are! You'll enjoy some yourself in a short while."

"Okay, well, that oughta be interesting," said Barley. Unprepared to argue the point, he adopted a go-with-the-flow attitude. *How bad could it be?* He needed a break.

Another ruckus and racket arose from the main office: a loud, frantic chorus of choking, coughing, and spluttering that sounded like it came from survivors of a whitewater rafting plunge through a washing machine's rinse cycle

Gerald Foon-Package and Simpleton Fabsmaggle emerged from the attic stairwell in a thick cloud of white dust and staggered out to the middle of the floor, desperately gasping for oxygen.

29

With a ponderous fifty-pound bag of enriched flour slung over his shoulder, Gerald huffed and puffed his way back from the first-floor storage room and through the main office, grim determination on his red face. He had to hurry; everyone was counting on him.

He'd left the door to the stairwell open in anticipation of his return. Without slowing, Gerald lunged through the open door and charged up the stairway as fast as his burden would allow, barreling headlong into the descending Simpleton Fabsmaggle. The impact of their collision sent both tumbling head over heels to the bottom of the stairs. The bag of flour ripped and spilled a healthy portion over Cheezy, covering his head, neck, and upper body, much like a piece of chicken before frying. Soon he was inhaling more dust than air. He coughed, hacked, and sneezed as he rose to his feet, trying to escape the small attic entryway for the fresh air in the big main room.

"My heavens!" cried Old Man Spuggett. "What could have happened to those two? And what's all that white dust?"

The old man and Dr. Pudbid scurried over to the two gasping employees. Barley, alone in the old man's private office, decided to sit this one out and observe the proceedings, having refrained from offering a smug "I *told* you so!" in response to the new crisis.

"Gentlemen! Are you all right? What happened?" the concerned company founder asked.

"Stand back, Spuggy," cried Dr. Pudbid as he ran up behind his old friend. "I'll see what's going on here!"

"We're fine! We're fine!" gasped Gerald. "We just inhaled a bunch of flour from that bag I was carrying. Now we're trying to get some fresh air. We don't need a doctor."

Dr. Pudbid sighed. Same old same old.

Old Man Spuggett inspected the damage—mainly confined to Cheezy, whose upper body looked like he'd spent the night snoozing upside down in a snowdrift. Gerald emerged from the catastrophe relatively unscathed, other than a few developing bumps and bruises. The majority of the flour was still contained within the damaged bag.

"Will you guys excuse me? I gotta get the rest of this flour back up to the lab!"

"Carry on, by all means, Gerald! Will you need Simpleton's help in the next few minutes? I think we'll have to re-outfit poor Mr. Fabsmaggle yet one more time. He's a mess!"

"No problem, sir!" Gerald headed to the attic stairway, carrying the remaining enriched flour as gingerly as he would volatile nitroglycerine. "Take all the time you need. There really isn't a lot for Cheezy to do at this point anyway."

He disappeared into the stairwell.

"We'll get you into some clean clothes again, Mr. Fabsmaggle," said Old Man Spuggett to Cheezy. "I hope you won't mind putting on another bathrobe."

Cheezy and Dr. Pudbid followed Old Man Spuggett to the wreckage of the broken water cooler. Nearby, Bagmo Maltgoggles, Narducci Palpatooti, and Rapunzel Trashtrumpet had momentarily ceased their debate over the ultimate fate of Marshall Farkpucker when the incident involving Gerald and Cheezy occurred.

"Yeesh! Cheezy's really a mess, Mr. Spuggett!" exclaimed Bagmo as they approached. "How's he gonna get clean again? Do you need some suggestions?"

"Well, Mr. Maltgoggles, what Simpleton really needs is a shower or bath, but since we don't have that type of facility and the only source of water in close proximity is there on the floor, that will have to do. Folks, please resume what you were doing. Simpleton, if you would step over here."

The company founder stooped down, grabbed a corner of the hem of his bathrobe, and dipped it in a puddle of water on the carpet to wipe Cheezy's face.

"There! Now we can see your face again, Simpleton, but I'm afraid there's far too much flour in your hair for me to wipe away with my bathrobe. Let's return to my office, shall we?"

Cheezy and the doctor followed the old man back to where Barley had been watching the unfolding drama. Cheezy noticed Barley. "Hey, that's the guy we just carried into your office, but he was asleep then!"

"Exactly right, Simpleton! This is Mr. Doodlebody, and now that he's awake, he'll be joining us at our party. Mr. Doodlebody, let me introduce you to Simpleton Fabsmaggle. He assisted Puddles and me in moving you into my office."

"Thanks for your help, I guess," said Barley as he shook Cheezy's hand.

"No problem! Glad to help out, Mr. Doodlebuggy."

"That's *Doodlebody*!"

"*What's* Doodlebody?"

"Never mind."

Old Man Spuggett opened his office closet and perused the remaining bathrobes. He grabbed one from the rack and held it up. "Will this do, Simpleton?"

"Oh, yeah! That's a *cool* one!" Cheezy doffed the flour-covered bathrobe, throwing it onto the same armchair his wet clothing currently occupied. Slipping into the new robe, he admired himself in the mirror on the back of the closet door. He was relatively clean again, and his face was flour-free. The only reminder of the previous disaster was his whitened hair.

"Spuggy, he looks like you now," chuckled Dr. Pudbid.

From a distance, Cheezy did resemble Old Man Spuggett—white hair, bathrobe, and slippers—in addition to being approximately the same height. Only upon closer scrutiny did the old man's wrinkles give him away. If one squinted a bit, they looked like ancient identical twins.

"My goodness, Puddles, you're right! He does look just like me, when I was much younger and ruggedly handsome. Why, Simpleton, you could be my great-great-grandson!"

Barley tried to stifle his own chuckle but gave up the effort and joined in heartily when Dr. Pudbid, Cheezy, and the old man burst into a chorus of guffaws.

Barley was laughing! He was actually *laughing*! This was the first good laugh he'd experienced in . . . How long had it been? He couldn't remember the last time he'd "broken up" at anything.

"Now I know who's going to inherit this business after I'm gone," sniggered the company founder. "I'm going to will it to *me*!"

Bagmo, Narducci, and Rapunzel appeared at the broken doorway and spied the two giggling "Mr. Spuggetts." Realizing that one was Cheezy, they joined in the laughter.

Rapunzel saw that Barley was awake and present; he'd been out of the picture for so long she'd completely forgotten about him. If there was anyone who could kill a happy mood just by being awake and present, it was Barley—but she noted that he was laughing along with everyone else. She never thought she'd see that.

✳ ✳ ✳

Executive Secretary Alpha Rae Sapoopa-LaBoobis sat at a desk in the big main office just below the

> # IT'S NOT <u>WHAT</u> YOU DO, BUT WHAT YOU DO <u>WITH</u> IT.

banner, studying Dork Snargmeyer and Frog Puppleman as they joyously relived highlights from their previous dialogue. Alpha Rae peered at the seated city councilman; she had no idea why this goofball should fascinate her so, but fascinated she was, and filled with feelings of protectiveness toward him as well.

What an interesting day for Alpha Rae. Feelings she hadn't experienced in quite some time, if ever, awakened within her. She'd been imbued with a new sense of responsibility that, up until now, had been quite foreign to her, but she *relished* the feeling.

Someone else piqued her interest as well: that blue-haired harpy who stood a few feet away, gazing wistfully across the wide expanse of the main office, absentmindedly twirling her poofy indigo locks—the woman who'd put on such a disturbing display of affection with Yump that the executive secretary had been forced to physically separate the two of them.

"Hey, *you*! Blue lady!"

Mimsy snapped out of her reverie and stared at Alpha Rae.

"Me?"

"Yeah, you! I don't see any other blue ladies around here."

"Well, your hair's purple, and that's almost blue."

"Even if it is, why would I be screaming at myself?"

"What do you want?"

"Who does your hair?"

Mimsy was taken aback; her hair was one subject she hadn't anticipated Alpha Rae to broach. Still, if the cranky old executive secretary wanted to talk girl talk, Mimsy was more than happy to oblige.

"I go to Fern Fuggle's Follicle Follies. Fern's been doing my hair for years!"

"Nice color," complimented Alpha Rae as she fingered a strand of her own purple coif, done up in a bun. "I like the style too."

"Oh, Fern didn't do the style! That was taken care of by those big hot-air dryers at Charlie Nutbooger's Automated Car Wash."

"So, you go to Fern Fuggle's Follicle Follies to get your color done, and Charlie Nutbooger's to get it styled—who does your face?"

"Oh, the face just kind of happened."

"Nice color."

"You like it?"

"I like the color. I think your *face* looks ridiculous."

So much for girl talk.

At that moment, the dual incidents of Reverend Snortworthy's strident castigation of Faisal Herskowitz and Marshall Farkpucker's destruction of Bimbo Spazzgate's water cooler shattered the industrious hum of the office, replacing it with a blanket of total, shocked silence.

Alpha Rae thought she detected, faint though it was, a continuous droning or buzzing close to where she sat. She listened intently. Yes, there was an almost imperceptible buzzing, right above her. She glanced up—and saw it! The tiny North Corners chief of police straddled the sagging banner on the wall above her, deep in the throes of a meditative trance, a serene smile spread across his cute little face. He seemed completely oblivious to the events around him.

Well, will you look at that: a teensy-weensy, itsy-bitsy little person in a cute little policeman's uniform. What the heck is he doing up there on that banner? One false move and he's gonna plunge to the floor. A fall like that could kill the little guy!

Alpha Rae rose from her chair as if entranced herself and stood under the big banner, staring up in awe at the chanting little Binky Bohoguss.

"Dork, get over here! I need your help!"

The big Viking halted his minimalist conversation with Frog Puppleman and hurried over. Frog's eyes followed his new friend, and he spotted Binky on his unstable perch and the potential danger the chief faced. "Yeah, buddy!" He leaped out of his chair and dashed to where the others stood.

Mimsy noticed Alpha Rae, Dork, and Frog gazing up at banner-bound Binky. *So that's where the little bugger's been!* She joined the other three, trying to appear nonchalant despite the fact that her heart pounded with excitement. She'd originally been fixated upon the little guy as the promised replacement for Gaggy the poodle, but her subsequent interaction with Yump had diverted her attention from her "promised reward." Since her new beau was presently occupied with other things, Mimsy re-entertained the thought of what a fun little plaything the tiny chief could be if she could just get her hands on him.

Alpha Rae pointed to Binky. "Dork, you've got to get that little person before he falls to the floor!"

"Ya, shure!" Dork plucked Binky from the big banner, gingerly holding the little guy in the palm of his massive paw. The tiny policeman remained unperturbed and unaware, his euphoric chanting uninterrupted.

"Well done! Bring him over to the desk, please—and don't break him!"

The big Viking deposited Binky gently onto the desktop and propped him into a sitting position. Mimsy determined it was time to make her move.

"Mr. Doodlebody said he was mine. I'm supposed to take care of him!"

"Well, if that's the case, you've done one heck of a great job so far! I suppose you put him up there in the first place? And just who is this 'Mr. Doodlebody' you're talking about?"

"Mr. Doodlebody is our group director, and he told me he wanted me to take care of him, so I'll take him now."

"You touch this little guy and I'll cut off your fingers!" If this blue-faced aberration couldn't be trusted with Yump, she sure couldn't be trusted with fragile little Binky. "He's staying right where he is. If this Mr. Doodlebody character has a problem with that, he can take it up with me!"

Mimsy decided to drop the issue. She doubted even Barley Doodlebody would make much headway against the iron will of this purple-haired lady. At least she still had Yump.

Under the watchful eye of Alpha Rae Sapoopa-LaBoobis, Dork, Frog, and Mimsy stood around the desk, softly poking, prodding, and petting the tiny police chief, who remained unmindful of the attention he was receiving.

***

Bimbo Spazzgate, Yump Yup-Yup-Yup-Yup, Mux Muggsley, Roland Chumbuckets, Noodles Snorgmark, and Margaret Wubbleduster ascended the back stairway with Bimbo leading the way, the big glass water bottle balanced on his shoulder. Roland was lost in thought. After exploring the small portion of the first floor accessible to him, he now pondered what mysteries lay beyond the locked doors he'd encountered.

"Hey, Bimbo, how come nobody's using the downstairs floor of this great big building? There seems to be more room down there."

"'Cause we don't need it. We're saving it for later."

"What's gonna happen later?"

"The second floor's gonna wear out."

"Wear out? What do you mean, 'wear out'?"

"Somebody made a radically stupid suggestion to keep the first floor locked up so we wouldn't use it and it would last longer."

"But the second floor is smaller! Why wouldn't you just use the first floor and keep the second floor closed up?"

"Because if the first floor wore out first, the second floor might collapse on top of it. Then you wouldn't have any floors!"

Roland contemplated the logic. *So this is an example of a radically stupid suggestion?*

"Who came up with that?"

"How should I know? I just work here!"

"I've got another question for you, Bimbo."

"Geez! My name is *Bimbo*, not Bagmo. Do I look like a quizmaster to you?"

"Just one more question, I promise!"

"Oh, okay—shoot."

"How can everyone in this company be a CEO?"

"Someone made the suggestion that making everyone a CEO would prevent anyone from feeling left out, or from receiving special treatment. So, since we all do our own jobs and nobody else tells us what to do because the only person who knows how to do his job is the person who does his job, we're *all* CEOs!"

"What about Mr. Spuggett? Is he a CEO too?"

They reached the top of the stairs. "Oh no, he's not a CEO," replied Bimbo. "Mr. Spuggett is Mr. Spuggett."

Proceeding to the main office, the group noticed Marshall Farkpucker still sitting on the floor where they'd last seen him, but Bagmo, Narducci, and Rapunzel were now clustered around the doorway to Old Man Spuggett's private office, looking into the room and laughing raucously. As the newly arrived group approached the private office, the cluster around the entrance broke apart, and Old Man Spuggett emerged from within, strutting like a peacock. His movements were comically exaggerated, and the group around the doorway laughed without restraint.

Roland, Bimbo, Yump, Noodles, Mux, and Margaret moved closer to learn why.

* * *

"Simpleton, you make a better me than *I* do!" laughed Old Man Spuggett. "Let's show the others—but don't tell them who you really are. We'll see if they can tell the difference between you and me."

"You want me to be you? Can I give people orders and tell them what to do?"

"By all means! It should be a real hoot!"

"But who are *you* going to be, Mr. Spuggett?"

"I'm not going to exist for the time being," replied the old man with a wink. "I think I'll just take a break from being me for a few minutes."

To all those in the room and standing at the doorway: "Everyone, play along! Let's see who figures out the masquerade first."

The young Old Man Spuggett moved out into the main office. Cheezy mimicked the old man's voice: "Out of my way! Everybody listen to me, 'cause I'm the *boss*!"

He strutted and swaggered into the big room just as Bimbo, Yump, Mux, Roland, Noodles, and Margaret drew near. Cheezy pointed and called out, "Bimbo, fix the water cooler! Yump, water the plants! Mux, don't pee on anything!" To Roland, Noodles, and Margaret he added, "I don't know who *you* are, so just start doing stuff. I'm the boss here! You have to do what I say!"

The newcomers stared in puzzlement at the old man. Why was he being so silly? And *bossy*? When Old Man Spuggett stealthily poked his head out the door and said, "*Shhhhh!*" with a wink, they realized it was a put-on.

Reverend Snortworthy and Faisal Herskowitz stared at the growing commotion. Alpha Rae Sapoopa-LaBoobis, Mimsy Borogove, Dork Snargmeyer, and Frog Puppleman interrupted their adulation of newly discovered Binky Bohoguss and peered toward the source of the noise. Everyone focused on "Mr. Spuggett" as he moved to the center of the room.

Cheezy sashayed up to an empty desk, climbed on top, and began dancing vigorously like a flapper from the Roaring Twenties, shouting, "I'm feelin' it in my feet! Wooooo-hooooo!"

Everyone stared, agog at the display. They'd never seen Old Man Spugget like this! It was one of the most uproariously funny demonstrations they'd ever seen by *anyone*—much less their own venerated boss.

The "old man" stopped dancing abruptly, executed a perfect back flip off the desktop to land feetfirst on the floor, and pointed around the room at every individual. "You there, get to work! Do what I say! What are you sitting around for? C'mon, you goldbricking goof-offs! Work! Work! Work!"

Old Man Spuggett looked over at Dr. Pudbid and Barley and giggled, "My goodness! I'm really quite a taskmaster, aren't I? Somebody oughta tell me to keep my big mouth shut!"

"But boy, can you dance!" gasped Barley between belly laughs.

Nearly everyone in the main office had caught the joke and abandoned any attempts at stifling laughter. They howled merrily as the faux Mr. Spuggett danced, pranced, and strutted around the room, spouting orders, acting sillier than the genuine article ever had. The entire room was in hysterics, the sound of their laughter filling the second floor.

30

Ebenezer Snugnards and Mayor Wubbleduster had heard the commotion from the conference room and ascertained that it wasn't the result of radically stupid suggestions.

"Inhospitable latchkeys constitute snowplowed rat confutation! The nonesuch exists plainly regardless, yet moribund in sequence!"

"Aye, noble compatriot, 'tis indeed a bellowing wind that blows, yet methinks with softness of purpose and no sense of peril impending!"

The two walked to the door, peering into the big room. It appeared that Old Man Spuggett was the culprit, cavorting about and acting extremely silly.

"Prithee, Ebenezer, but were I to infer that yon frolicsome incarnation of thy liege, Master Spuggett, seemeth somehow younger of appearance and disposition, wouldst thou not agree? Or do mine eyes deceive me?"

Ebenezer affirmed the mayor's supposition. "Nuptick buptick dooby-dooby-*doo*!"

At that moment, Cheezy Fabsmaggle's attention was drawn to the mayor and his Gibberish-speaking friend in the conference-room doorway. Gesticulating wildly in their direction, he cried out: "You there! Ebenezer and that mayor guy! Trying to hide out from me, eh? Well, you'd better get back to work!"

Ebenezer recognized the voice: Cheezy Fabsmaggle was the imposter! He informed the mayor, and both of them joined in with giggles and guffaws of their own.

Seeing that Big Biff Spoozma was sound asleep and missing all the fun, Mayor Wubbleduster shouted back into the conference room: "Spoozma! Good Spoozma, awaken from thine sweet repose to marvel at verily the finest jest thou may'st e'er live to see!"

Biff groggily raised his head, a thin stream of saliva drooling from the corner of his mouth. "Huh?"

"Come thee hence! Witnesseth the merriment, mine loyal servant! 'Tis a soothing tonic for any abundantly taxed soul!"

Biff roused himself and shook his head to clear the cobwebs. He thumbed through the pages of his Elizabethan English dictionary, translated what the mayor had said, rose from his chair, and joined the other two in the doorway.

Felicia Greenthing had also been awakened from her catnap by the mayor's urgent cry and followed Biff's lead. Still groggy from sleeping on the tabletop, struck with the disparity in age between the Old Man Spuggett she was familiar with and this newer, younger version, she jumped to a conclusion only she could jump to: "Oh my *heavens*! Mr. Spuggett is being sucked backwards in time!"

This realization set off a new round of hysterical screaming by the CEO in charge of finding the delivery entrance, her warbling shrieks sharply at odds with the hearty laughter from the rest. Their laughter ceased, and they stared at Felicia in bewilderment.

"Mr. Spuggett is being sucked backwards in time! He's getting *younger*! He's getting younger even as we *speak*! He's gonna be a *baby* pretty soon—until he completely disappears! Help him! Somebody help him!"

Felicia launched so far out of control that Old Man Spuggett knew he'd have to set her straight before everyone's ears blew up. He dashed out of his office. "Miss Greenthing, Miss Greenthing, please! There's no reason to panic. That's just Simpleton Fabsmaggle *pretending* to be me. See? Here I am, the real Mr. Spuggett, just as old as I can be. It's only a joke, Miss Greenthing! Don't you think he looks funny?"

Seeing the authentic Old Man Spuggett standing there, Felicia stopped screaming.

"That's *Cheezy*?"

"The very same! Pretty good resemblance, eh? He even had you fooled, Miss Greenthing! Indeed, it's Mr. Fabsmaggle doing his impression of me when I was much younger and ruggedly handsome!"

"Oh! Well, that's different!" Felicia burst into roaring laughter.

The rest of the group relaxed. The snickering and giggling started up again. Cheezy resumed his cavorting and capering, and Old Man Spuggett sighed with relief, walking back to his office where Barley and Dr. Pudbid were watching the shenanigans.

"*Whew*! I'm glad we were able to dodge that bullet. Felicia tends to be somewhat excitable—once she gets going, the only solution to the problem requires the insertion of cotton balls into the ears. Fortunately, that will not be necessary.

"But seeing as how you've arrived on the scene again, Mr. Bellynoodles, I think we need to incorporate you into the overall scheme of things. I believe the first order of business would be to introduce you to the rest of my staff. I assume the majority of *your* group already knows who you are."

"Oh yeah, you can bet they do!"

As he watched the fun taking place from Old Man Spuggett's private office, Barley was filled with a sense of wonder. He was amazed at how quickly his tourists had been accepted and welcomed by the staff, amazed at how the tourists had so quickly embraced their friendship, and amazed at how Old Man Spuggett had deftly handled the menace and malice with which Barley initially confronted him. The company founder had shown him only kindness, friendliness, patience, acceptance, and a tolerance for his cantankerous skepticism. With his inimitable brand of seventh-sensory logic, the old man had blunted the sharp edge of each and every argument Barley had proffered and skillfully deflected Barley's belligerence without a hint of anger. He'd succeeded in making Barley reconsider his previous attitudes and prejudices—even made him laugh! And he'd asked nothing from Barley except his participation.

Barley was genuinely unaccustomed to such treatment. Up until now, the only other person on earth who'd given him any sense of belonging was his half brother, whom he'd always considered to be nothing more than a cretinous idiot, and who was accepted readily by these people. Feeble-minded Frog was being *respected* by the Bumps & Spuggett staff!

Barley's feelings of anger, contempt, and connivance gradually dissipated, replaced by a relaxing sense of relief and even curiosity, born out of a desire not to exploit but rather to *absorb*—to learn more about these people and this fascinating world. The attitudes of superiority, skepticism, and cynicism he felt earlier in the day now seemed misguided, out of place, and unnecessary. Barley was actually starting to enjoy himself!

But he was an outsider: left out, alone, and lonely. Once the tourists saw he was back in the thick of things again, their mood would change from happiness to horror. For the first time in his life, he felt sorry to be the cause of such discomfort. For the first time, he wanted to be accepted and not dreaded. And for the first time, Barley Doodlebody felt the desire to be . . . liked!

He knew he'd need to earn the friendship of this group. Due to his lack of experience in that regard, he wasn't sure what to do.

"C'mon, Mr. Boogynoogle! We must introduce you to the rest. A gala wingding looms large in our futures!"

Barley took a deep breath. *Okay, I guess there's nothing to do but get this over with.* He prepared himself for the unwelcoming reception he'd have to face.

The old man put his skinny arm around Barley's shoulders and turned to Dr. Pudbid: "Puddles, let's go out there and share Mr. Dinglefinger with everyone, shall we?"

The good doctor feared that his old college chum's intention of assimilating Barley into the group would surely meet with disaster; Barley Doodlebody was not the type who assimilated easily into anything. Dr. Pudbid gritted his teeth, prepared for the worst, and tried to sound a positive note: "Okay, Spuggy! If nothing else, this oughta be interesting."

Together, the three walked through the broken doorway of the old man's office. The small group at the doorway parted to let them pass. Barley noticed that most of the members of his tour group were staring at him apprehensively, with the exception of Noodles. And little Margaret. She scowled at him menacingly.

They moved out into the center of the main room.

As soon as all of the suggestionaire teams and Cheezy Fabsmaggle saw the three emerge, a hush fell once more. The tourists were filled with dread. *Barley's back!* The Bumps & Spuggett staffers, most of whom had been unaware of Barley's presence until now, stared at him curiously.

"Yeah, *buddy*!" screamed Frog happily.

"Excuse me for interrupting your labors, everyone, but I want those of you on my staff to meet another one of our honored guests here today, a gentleman who, up until very recently, had been slumbering peacefully on our office floor but who is now ready to join us in our impending celebration. I've been told that *he* is actually the person responsible for bringing us all together here today, so it is to him that we owe our gratitude! Let me introduce . . ."

He turned to Barley.

"What did you say your name was again? Your *real* name?"

"Just call me Barley, please."

"Done! Ladies and gentlemen, let's give Mr. Barleyplease a warm

Bumps & Spuggett welcome, shall we?"

The staffers applauded, stamped their feet, and whistled enthusiastically.

"Would you like to make a speech, Mr. Barleyplease? I'm sure my staff would enjoy anything you'd have to say to them, as long as it doesn't involve too much math."

Normally, Barley felt no reticence in speaking to a large group, although normally he'd be the bossy bad guy, threatening them, extorting them, or telling them what they could or couldn't do. But he had no control or authority over anyone except his own tour group, and even more significant was the fact that Barley didn't *want* to be the bad guy! He'd just received a standing ovation from these people, and the old man had given him credit for bringing everybody together today. To them, Barley was the good guy.

"Speech! Speech!" cried the staff.

Barley was speechless.

"Um, thanks, everybody! It's nice to meet you all too." He smiled wanly.

His words were met with another hearty round of applause and whistles.

"Huzzah! Huzzah! Well spoken, Master Doodlebody!" cried Mayor Wubbleduster.

"Well spoken, indeed!" agreed Old Man Spuggett. "I bid you an official welcome to our humble business, Mr. Barleyplease! Mr. Spazzgate, how are we progressing with the refurbishment of the broken water cooler?"

"All finished, Mr. Spuggett! I just gotta clean up the mess from the other broken bottles and we're ready to go!"

"Excellent! The wingding draws ever closer!" Of Bagmo Maltgoggles he asked, "How are we doing with our efforts to free Marshall Farkpucker from his wastebasket?"

"Only a matter of time, sir. We *have* discovered that he isn't dead!"

"Good news!"

Gerald Foon-Package called down the stairwell from his attic laboratory: "Hey, Cheezy! The cure for excess hair growth is just about ready! I need you to go downstairs and get the plates 'n cups 'n stuff!"

"Okay, Gerald, I'm on my way!" shouted Cheezy.

"I'll go with you, to get some stuff to clean up this mess," said Bimbo. The two staffers excused themselves and headed to the back stairs. Felicia panicked: they were about to venture past the second-floor delivery entrance again!

"Just remember, you guys: that doorway you're gonna pass is absolutely *not* the second-floor delivery entrance."

"What doorway?"

Bimbo and Cheezy disappeared into her office.

Felicia sighed with relief. Her deep, dark secret would remain a secret—for the time being.

* * *

Alpha Rae had watched with amusement as Cheezy did his "bogus Mr. Spuggett" routine. It stimulated an odd recollection from within the dark recesses of her memory: long ago, when she first started working for the B & S firm, Old Man Spuggett had looked just about like Cheezy did. And when the *real* Mr. Spuggett had introduced Mr. Barleyplease to the rest of the group, another mysterious feeling welled inside of her, just as it had upon seeing Frog Puppleman: the feeling that for some reason she should take responsibility for him. For the purple-haired executive secretary, this day had seen many changes and a few surprises as well.

But right now, Alpha Rae had a surprise to share.

"Hey, Mr. Spuggett! Look what I found!" She held tiny Binky aloft like a mumbling action figure.

Before Old Man Spuggett had a chance to answer, Barley cried out, "Chief Bohoguss!" He rushed over to Alpha Rae's desk. "Please, let me have that little guy."

Alpha Rae held Binky behind her back. "And just who are *you*? Why should I just hand him over to *you*?"

"I'm Barley Doodlebody, and you're holding North Corners' chief of police Binky Bohoguss. Chief Bohoguss is in my charge today."

"You? You're in charge of him? Well, I found him hanging from that banner up there on the wall, just about to hurtle to his *death*. Some caretaker you are!"

"Madam, I was involuntarily indisposed until a short while ago, so I was unable to look after him. Let me assure you, I'm ready to resume custody of the little guy. I thank you for your temporary supervision of him. What's he saying?"

Old Man Spuggett recognized the symptoms. "I believe this tiny man—who's simply adorable, by the way—is reciting the same meditative chant that Lollie our receptionist is reciting. I can assure you, he's quite well and apparently quite content at the moment. I would even venture to say that everything is rainbows, green grass, and chocolate bunny rabbits where he is right now. This cute little fellow is the chief of police?"

"Correct."

"My goodness! We have the mayor, a city councilman, *and* the chief of police with us! I must say, our humble firm has been greatly honored. Mizz Sapoopa-LaBoobis, I would ask you to turn over custody of this impish crimefighter to Mr. Barleyplease, won't you?"

"Oh, okay—if you say so." Alpha Rae handed Binky to Barley, all the while studying Barley's face with ferocious intensity. It was unsettling, being scrutinized so closely. "What did you say your name was again?"

"Barley, ma'am. Barley Doodlebody."

"Hmmm, you don't say . . ."

She turned abruptly and walked away.

Barley held the little police chief in his hand and inspected him. Other than a wrinkled, rumpled uniform and looking like he'd been shot out the tailpipe of an automobile, the little guy was all there. His tiny eyes were closed as he mechanically chanted his "Chili-baba jijjy-booboo" mantra, a placid smile curling his lips. Barley carefully slipped him back into his usual place in the breast pocket of his suit coat. Little Binky remained unperturbed and undisturbed.

The tourists were relieved to have the little man back in the fold again. They'd momentarily forgotten about him in the frenzy of the *danzenfreekenboingadoinga*—but the Bumps & Spuggett personnel were spellbound by the teensy-weensy chief of police, having never seen anyone like him before. They rushed over to Barley, begging him to pull Binky out of his pocket so they could admire him again.

Barley obliged, and they all stood around in a big group, fawning over the tiny imp like he was a newly opened, genuinely appreciated Christmas present.

"What an absolutely delightful little man!" gushed Old Man Spuggett. "My goodness! Sometimes big things come in extremely small, if not downright microscopic packages."

Faisal Herskowitz was seized with another uncontrolled spasm of laughter. Then he paused and cried out indignantly: "Faisal! Laughing you should not be doing! This little person of smallness is to be important man for respecting from you."

Before he had the chance to pause and then rant from the opposing viewpoint, Reverend Snortworthy fixed him with an icy stare. "Truly, if you start screaming again, I will send you to Hell!"

Faisal trembled and turned several shades of green in rapid succession. "But I am not to screaming! I am to laughing! Laughing is coming out, but *I am not making!*"

Old Man Spuggett had dealt with Faisal's broken English for so long that he was confident he understood. "Faisal, are you telling us that you have no control over your laughter? You're not doing it on purpose?"

"Oh yes! Oh yes! Stopping to do I cannot!"

"Well, this is most unusual," marveled the old man. "Normally, it would take a miracle to get Faisal to crack a smile, much less cut loose with the cackles he's producing now. It does my heart good to see the old boy in such a jolly state. Tell me, Puddles, do you think he's okay?"

Dr. Pudbid, realizing that Old Man Spuggett was actually requesting his medical expertise, dashed over to Faisal and put one hand on the former shepherd's forehead, scrutinizing him carefully. Faisal tittered like a schoolgirl.

The good doctor finished his examination and sighed. "Other than laughing uncontrollably, he seems fine to me. His pulse and heart rate are normal, he's not running a temperature, his pupils are not dilating—I can't find anything wrong with him. He's just laughing, that's all!"

"Well, I suppose we should just leave him be," mused the company founder. "I'm no doctor, but I don't think anyone's ever died from too much laughter!" He watched with amusement as Faisal vainly attempted to flip his giggle switch off.

A new question popped into his mind: *Where is my CEO in charge of being office manager?* "Everyone seems to be present or accounted for with the exception of Mr. Slamson. This is highly unusual, and somewhat of a mind-boggler."

"Maybe Fandango got sucked backwards in time just like you almost did, Mr. Spuggett," offered Felicia. "Maybe he got sucked backwards so far that he just disappeared, or got un-born."

"*Oooh!* Then maybe I could have Fandango's desk," said a hopeful Bagmo.

"Fandango doesn't *have* a desk, Bagmo," said Narducci. "He just runs around and screams all the time. Besides, you already have a desk."

"Oh yeah, I wasn't thinking about that." Bagmo sat back down at his desk.

Felicia persisted. "So, what're we gonna do about Fandango if he has to be born again? Does he have to wait until he grows up before he can get his job back?"

"*Oooh*! Then maybe I could have Fandango's job!" said Bagmo hopefully.

"Don't be ridiculous!" countered Narducci once again. "Fandango can run way faster and scream way louder than you can!"

"Oh yeah, I wasn't thinking about that."

"How can you two be so heartless?" cried Felicia. "You're talking about Fandango like he isn't even here."

"But he *isn't* even here!"

"Oh yeah, I wasn't thinking about that." Felicia's upper lip curled and trembled into a grimace. She was about to blow again!

Old Man Spuggett realized it was time to dodge another bullet: "People, please! I'm sure Fandango has a perfectly plausible explanation for his absence. He hasn't really been gone that long. In the meantime, I think we should concentrate on getting that wastebasket off poor Marshall's head. He's not yet aware that we're having a party."

"That's because he's been trying to hide under that thing all day," declared Bagmo. "But Bimbo found him right away, and I know where he is too, so we might as well let him know the game is up."

"Good idea," said the old man. "But I think you're going to need some assistance with getting that clumsy headgear off his head!"

"I'll give you a hand with that," volunteered Barley. "My brother gets those things stuck on his head all the time."

"Yeah, *buddy*!"

Alpha Rae looked quizzically at Barley, then back to Frog, then back to Barley again, then back to Frog. "That Doodlebody guy over there is your *brother*?"

"Yeah, buddy!"

"I am *not* your buddy!" she stated huffily, continuing to direct her stare back and forth between the two brothers.

Barley had contributed nothing to the activities at Bumps & Spuggett thus far, while his tour group had been deeply involved. The need to belong possessed him. Helping remove the wastebasket from Marshall's head seemed to be the best tactic.

Barley called out to Biff Spoozma, who stood in the conference-room doorway with Felicia, Ebenezer, and Mayor Wubbleduster. "Hey, Biff! Come over here and give me a hand with this trash can, will ya?"

Big Biff, fairly certain now that a resumption of his catnap was no longer an option, joined Barley.

"Okay, Biff, you hold down his shoulders, and I'll yank the trash can off. On 'three.'"

Biff stood in front of Marshall, applying downward pressure on his shoulders. Barley walked behind the seated bucket-head and grasped the rim of the wastebasket with both hands.

"That's what *we* were gonna do," whispered Narducci to Bagmo. "But we sang a song first."

"I know, Narducci, but those guys are a lot bigger than we are, so they don't need to sing a song first!"

"Good point."

Barley prepared himself for the yank that would set Marshall free.

The crowd held its breath.

"Here we go! One . . . two . . . *three*!"

Biff pushed down on Marshall's shoulders, and Barley gave the wastebasket a vigorous pull. The receptacle popped off of Marshall's head, but along with it came Binky Bohoguss, expelled once again from Barley's suit coat pocket. Still chanting and oblivious to his newest plight, Binky soared high into the air and plummeted toward the floor.

Yump came to the little guy's rescue this time. The CEO in charge of watering the plants reacted instantly, hurtling over Bagmo's desk, making a spectacular one-handed diving catch of the tiny policeman inches from the floor.

The crowd gasped and erupted in wild cheering and applause, for both the success of Barley and Biff's liberation of Marshall and Yump's amazing acrobatic prowess in saving little Binky from splatting like a tomato on the office floor. Barley, Biff, and Yump were showered with accolades accorded conquering heroes.

Marshall sat on the floor and shook his head in shock. He massaged his head and shoulders and blinked rapidly as the first light he'd seen all day threatened to blind him. He noticed the new and unfamiliar faces in the crowd. Who were all these people? What momentous event had he missed that caused them to be here?

Chief Binky continued chanting, unaware of the frenetic goings-on.

"Well done! Well done!" cried Old Man Spuggett.

"Huzzah! Thine mettle prevaileth, O brave and powerful sires!" seconded Mayor Wubbleduster.

Mimsy leered at Yump and gave him a tongue-flashing demonstration that would have embarrassed the scales off a dead fish.

As the group surged around the three heroes, shaking their hands, slapping their backs, extolling them with "Attaboys!" aplenty, Narducci Palpatooti spoke up loudly over the joyful din: "This calls for a song of celebration. I've just composed one, and I'll sing it for you now."

The crowd squealed in joyful anticipation and settled down. When all was quiet, Narducci cleared his throat and began to sing:

"A figure sat there on the floor:
Two arms and legs, but not much more.
The figure's head, encased within
A trash receptacle of tin,
Was quite impossible to see!
The question was: Who could it be?

The person's form, though only partial,
Was determined to be Marshall!
Only Marshall F. would dare
To wear the clothes he loves to wear:
The purple slacks, the saddle shoes
And socks of many different hues,

But certainly it seemed most odd
That Marshall chose that tin facade
To hide behind! Or could it be
That Marshall was himself not free?
Was he imprisoned? No one knew,
And Marshall offered not a clue!

All those around him were perplexed:
What is the course we should take next?
But then, just like a bolt of light
Came Barley, saying, 'It's all right!
Big Biff and I will save the day
By freeing Marshall, come what may!'

No idle boast, as it turned out!
The men shared not one shred of doubt;
They yanked the trash can, pried it off,
And Marshall, glad his hat to doff,
Was back among us once again—
But who knew what would happen then?

The tiny chief in Barley's pocket,
Now a microscopic rocket,
Shot straight up and then, free-falling,
Hurtled toward a doom appalling!
What if he should hit the floor?
The tiny chief would be no more!

Yump, a lithe, fine-tuned machine, a
Leaping, soaring ballerina,
In-house spaceman, fancy dancer,
Saw the problem, knew the answer!
Leaped across the desk and caught
Chief Binky ere the farm he bought!

And so it went: our timely heroes,
Making positives from zeroes!
Barley, Biff, and Yump are three
As grand as gentlemen can be!
They saved the day and two lives, surely!
Now we party! It's still early!"

At the conclusion of Narducci's song, the group burst into another round of hearty applause. Narducci bowed, gesturing magnanimously toward Barley, Biff, and Yump as if to say, "No, please! *They* deserve all the credit, not I!"

"Very nice, and most appropriate, Narducci," said Old Man Spuggett.

"And based on a true story, I might add!" added Narducci.

Barley saw the admiration on everyone's faces. He felt the warmth of their smiles, shook their hands, accepted their compliments, and realized that he'd never been treated with this much respect in his entire life. Old Man Spuggett slapped him on the back with unabashed pleasure, and his tour group looked at him in a completely new light. This was a different Barley Doodlebody they were seeing, and they liked this new incarnation. *I guess there's something to be said for being a good guy!*

"Yeah, *buddy!*" screamed Frog as he fervently pumped his brother's hand.

"Ya, shure, *yabetcha!*" cried Dork.

Alpha Rae stared intently into Barley's face. "What did you say your name was again?"

"Doodlebody, ma'am. Barley Doodlebody."

"A name worthy of remembrance," said Old Man Spuggett. "But it probably won't be by *me!*" He burst into laughter and threw his arm around Barley's shoulder.

The milling crowd was settling from all the excitement when a hard, cold voice cut through the celebratory chatter like a scythe through stalks of wheat:

"I hate to put a damper on what appears to be a wonderful gathering here, but you people are currently in serious violation of the *law!*"

Heads turned in surprise toward the ominous-sounding voice. Silhouetted in the reception lobby's double doorway, his arm draped patronizingly around the shoulders of Fandango Slamson, was a smiling Brufyss Bathwater.

PART IV:

CRISIS, CHAOS, CATHARSIS

31

Brufyss Bathwater's voice cut through the chatter in the big office like a machete through marshmallows. He calmly surveyed the scene before him, towering over the terrified Fandango Slamson, whose narrow shoulders were draped in a confining embrace by the big man's arm.

Old Man Spuggett, his employees, and the majority of the tourists knew nothing about this formidable-looking man in the reception room doorway, but to Barley, Frog, Mimsy, and Rapunzel, Brufyss was a familiar figure. Rapunzel's recognition of Brufyss stemmed from an encounter with him a few years after that fateful senior prom in '67. After Barley had intimidated Rapunzel into abandoning her exposé pieces on his mayoral corruption with his go-to packing-material threat, Rapunzel set her sights on Brufyss Bathwater. In turn, Brufyss threatened to turn her into a pallet of cat food.

Realizing that further journalistic pursuit of Brufyss and Barley would only result in her being turned into some sort of inanimate object, whether cushioning for transported goods or a nosh for peckish pussycats, she redirected her ambitious investigative efforts into producing journalistic tripe.

Brufyss surveyed the room with his penetrating gaze, although a beguiling smile spread across his face and his demeanor exuded an exaggerated friendliness.

"Aaaaaah! Aaaaaah!" stated Fandango flatly, in a voice barely above a whisper, his eyes wide with fear. Brufyss held the Bumps & Spuggett office manager solidly in place by his side, and Fandango, unable to sprint to safety and too afraid to scream, trembled visibly.

"Well, what do we have here? Looks like a whole roomful of lawbreakers and trespassers! I see some very important people: Mayor Wubbleduster,

Councilman Puppleman, Reverend Snortworthy, Rapunzel Trashtrumpet, and so many others! Distinguished dignitaries I've always believed to be law-abiding citizens, and yet here you are, breaking the law blatantly and willfully. I must tell you: frankly, I'm shocked and not a little disappointed. However, I'm not the least bit surprised to see Mr. Doodlebody among you. 'Law-abiding' is not a term one would normally associate with him."

Barley stared at his old nemesis incredulously. "What are you talking about, Brufyss, and what do you want? How did you get in here, anyway?"

"Well, Barley, I 'got in here,' as you so coarsely put it, the same way I suspect you did. I walked in through the front door. But before I did, I rescued this little fellow here, who was upside down in the driver's seat of a ratty old bus parked at the front curb. He was just regaining consciousness when I found him."

"Aaaaaah! Aaaaaah!" stated Fandango, verifying Brufyss's statement.

"So *that's* where you've been, Mr. Slamson!" cried Old Man Spuggett, relieved to account for his office manager at last.

Brufyss ignored the old man's outburst. "Now, as to what I *want*, I want to see justice served! I want to see the law upheld, and I want to see those who would flagrantly flaunt their breaking of the law punished for doing so, as the law itself dictates!"

Barley snickered. "Since when did you become so law-abiding?"

"I believe it's never too late to turn one's life around and stand on the side of the right and the just!" retorted Brufyss. "Since my own rights have been so callously trodden upon by you, I've been forced to acknowledge that the paths of fairness and justice are roads I myself have avoided traveling to this point. Henceforth, I fully intend to do so!"

"Excuse me, sir," interrupted Old Man Spuggett, "but I'm the owner of this establishment, and I'm not aware of any laws that have been broken on these premises. Are you a member of one of the North Corners law enforcement agencies? If so, please be advised that we have the chief of police with us here today, and he's made no mention of any laws being broken or ordinances being violated."

"I shouldn't think the chief of police would have a problem with Barley and his group being here today unlawfully," snorted Brufyss, "since Mr. Doodlebody's dirty dealings and political manipulations have placed the chief securely in his own pocket!"

The Bumps & Spuggett staff gasped. They'd in fact seen Barley place little Binky into his suit coat pocket just a short while ago!

"Be that as it may, sir," continued Old Man Spuggett, "I'd appreciate enormously if you'd elucidate further upon your allegations for my own edification. We here at Bumps & Spuggett hold the laws that govern us in high esteem."

"I'm sure you do, sir. And may I assume that you are either Mr. Bumps or Mr. Spuggett?"

"You may! In fact, you may assume me to be the king of the Rangoon pirates if you so choose, though you'd be grossly in error. In a manner of speaking, I *am* either Mr. Bumps or Mr. Spuggett; that assumption would get you close to the reality of the situation, and if you *really* want to zoom in on the truth, I'm the latter. That is to say, I'm Mr. Spuggett—and I'm currently the sole proprietor of this business, at least until that time when my business partner, Mr. Bumps, returns from the dead."

"Let me assure you, Mr. Spuggett: it's not you, nor are any of your employees in violation. Mr. Doodlebody and the individuals who accompanied him here today are the culprits."

The old man was perplexed. "But, sir, Mr. Doodlefinger and his associates are here as my guests today!"

"That's Doodlebody!" corrected Brufyss.

"*What's* Doodlebody?"

Barley smirked to himself. He'd already traveled down this road.

"His name!" replied Brufyss.

"Whose name?"

"Why, Mr. Doodlebody's, of course!"

"You mean to say, Mr. Doodlebody's name is Mr. Doodlebody? Well, *there's* a shocker for you!"

"*No!* I mean—"

"No?? You mean Mr. Doodlebody's name is *not* Mr. Doodlebody? I'm getting a little mixed-up here . . ."

"No, no! What I mean to say is that Mr. Doodlebody's name is not what you *called* him just now."

"But I didn't call Mr. Doodlebody just now! I'm currently talking to you! What did you say your name was?"

Brufyss scratched his head; this conversation was getting confusing. "Uh, m-my name is Brufyss Bathwater."

"Well, Mr. Breathwater—"

"Bathwater!"

"Where?"

"Bathwater is my name!" answered Brufyss, now totally unnerved.

"And a good name it *is!*" stated the old man with finality. "Now, Mr. Buttwhomper, what is it that you want?"

"I want to see justice served!"

The old man seemed puzzled by Brufyss's statement. "So say we all, Mr. Beefwiener! As I mentioned previously, this firm is as law-abiding as they come, and we long for justice to be served as well. I don't know any law-abiding citizen who doesn't! However, I suggest you might be better off looking for a *courtroom*. Here at Bumps & Spuggett, we only serve radically stupid suggestions. Perhaps we might help you in that regard?"

"I could whip up something and have it ready for him right away, Mr. Spuggett," offered Bagmo.

"There you go. We're always here for you, Mr. Bedwetter: service is our business! Well, actually, producing radically stupid suggestions is our business, but we'll throw in the service at no extra charge. How about *that?*"

"I don't *need* any radically stupid suggestions! That's not what I came here for!"

"So, when you said you came here to see justice served, that's actually what you *meant?*"

"Yeah! That's actually what I meant!"

"Mr. Spuggett! Mr. Spuggett!" It was Narducci. "Pretty soon we're going to be *serving* Gerald's cure for excess hair growth—at the party, remember?"

"Good point, Narducci. Mr. Bandwagon, do you like potatoes au gratin?"

"What do potatoes au gratin have to do with anything? And why can't you get my name right? What's wrong with you people?"

Bagmo's eyes lit with excitement. "Oooh! It's a *quiz!* I love quizzes—but if you're gonna play the game, you can only ask one question at a time!"

"Are you nuts?" cried Brufyss incredulously.

Bagmo frantically waved his hand at Brufyss. "Oh! Oh! I think I know this one! But give me a hint first: does it have anything to do with polar bears or suitcases?"

"*What are you talking about?!*"

"Hey, no fair! You can't ask another question until we finish with the first one! And you're not supposed to scream!"

"*What?*"

"What kind of a question is '*What?*' It doesn't even have an ending to it! You can't just ask, 'What?' I mean, what '*what*'? Mr. Spuggett, will you please explain the rules to this guy?"

Barley had been content to listen to the amusing repartee taking place between Brufyss, Old Man Spuggett, and now Bagmo Maltgoggles, but he knew that Brufyss's motives for being there were far from noble or driven by a conscientious sense of civic duty.

"Pardon the interruption, Mr. Spuggett, but I believe this man's business here is with me." He looked Brufyss squarely in the eye. "All right, cut the crap! Just where are you going with all this?"

Rescued from the bizarre conversation with Old Man Spuggett and the other nutcase, Brufyss collected his wits and fixed Barley with a smile. "What I'm talking about, Barley, is that you're here illegally."

"What do you mean? I've got a business license and a permit, signed and sanctioned by the North Corners City Council, that says I have every right to be here. I've got the papers to prove it right here in my pocket." He reached into his suit coat and produced a sheaf of official-looking documents, which he held out for Brufyss. "Check it out for yourself."

"That I will!" Brufyss walked to Barley and Old Man Spuggett. His arm was still draped around the shoulders of Fandango Slamson, whom he guided along as he moved forward. He snatched the papers out of Barley's outstretched hand, and the rest of the room's occupants gathered around.

As Brufyss perused Barley's official papers, the smirk he'd been wearing grew into a full-fledged grin. At length, he finished his examination of the documents and looked up at Barley, a smug, triumphant smile spread across his face. "Well, these papers certainly appear to be authentic and valid."

"You're damn right they're authentic and valid!"

"Well, you're still in violation, and I'm going to have to ask you and your associates to leave this room immediately."

"What're you talking about? You just said the papers were in order!"

"It's all quite easily explained." Brufyss's manner was calm, his voice confident as he scanned Barley's documents again. "The permit and business license you possess have given you authority to operate '*a guided tour business which runs from the local Mystic Knights of the Heavenly Daze Hall in the downtown portion of North Corners, Ohio, to the reception room and lobby of the Bumps & Spuggett office.*' Does that sound about right to you?"

"Yeah, so what?"

"Well, as I look around these premises, in particular where we're standing now, I see that we're *not* standing in the reception room and lobby of the Bumps & Spuggett office. We're right out in the middle of the general working space, deep within the confines of the building. Having just passed through said 'reception room and lobby of the Bumps & Spuggett office' only a moment ago, I didn't see you. In fact, the room was completely empty except for a possibly demented woman who sat at the reception desk and blabbered incomprehensible nonsense which I gave up trying to understand."

"Lollie Babajuju!" cried Narducci.

"*Gesundheit!*" Brufyss continued. "Bottom line, you and your group are not where you're supposed to be, and are consequently in violation of your own permit and business license. In effect, you're *trespassing* on these premises and in violation of the law! How's that for an explanation?"

Barley was stunned and silent.

Brufyss gloated at the barrel over which he now had Barley. "All I can say is, thank you, Mr. Legal Loophole! My own permit and business license, which I'll graciously allow you to review should you so desire, gives me *unlimited access* to the entire Bumps & Spuggett building and its surrounding property. Of course, you're quite welcome to remove yourself and your associates to the reception room and lobby and view as much of these premises as you're able from that vantage point, as long as you don't overstep those legally defined boundaries. What's fair is fair, right?"

Brufyss took his own permit and business license and thrust them at Barley. In a daze, Barley glanced over the documents. They seemed to be just as valid and authoritative as Barley's, signed by the same city officials, bearing the same official seals. It was true! Brufyss had found a loophole in the legal language of Barley's permit and had managed to squeeze through it! By rights, he and his tour group would have to vacate the area they now occupied and move back out into the reception room and lobby, or leave the building entirely and go home.

"I-I-I don't know what to say!" stammered Barley as he turned to Old Man Spuggett with desperation in his eyes. "He's right, Mr. Spuggett! According to his papers, we have to go back outside."

The old man had been listening with keen interest as Brufyss enunciated the legalities and illegalities of the situation. He now spoke up somberly: "Mr. Brothmonger, may I see those papers, please? And, Mr. Doodlefeather, may I see your papers as well? I'd like to take a look at all this . . . *justice* for myself."

Brufyss jauntily handed Barley's paperwork to the old man. Barley, quite humiliated by this whole ordeal, handed Brufyss's paperwork over. Barley had come to know, like, and respect this wily old gentleman. The recollection of the actions he'd taken to brazenly and "legally" invade the old man's business and privacy with his uninvited presence was coming back not only to haunt him but to overwhelm him with feelings of guilt and remorse.

"I'm sorry, Mr. Spuggett, but when I originally took this action, I felt differently about things. I didn't know then what I do now! I was ignorant, selfish, and greedy. I ask you to forgive me—"

"Let's just see what we have here, shall we?" interrupted Old Man Spuggett without acknowledging Barley's contrition. His face impassive, he accepted the documents and sat on the edge of Alpha Rae's desk to examine them.

"Aaaaaah! Aaaaaah!" stated Fandango Slamson, trying to reestablish in everyone's mind that he was still here.

"Mr. Bilgewater, I would request that you please release my employee from your grasp immediately," said Old Man Spuggett as he examined the papers. "You have my implicit gratitude for rescuing Mr. Slamson from what I gather was an awkward predicament, but he appears to be sufficiently recovered now and no longer in need of a shepherd."

At the word *shepherd*, Faisal's ears perked up. He cut loose with a long-winded series of shrill cackles and belly laughs, startling Brufyss.

"What's up with that guy?! What's so funny?!"

"May we return to the matter at hand? Unhand Mr. Slamson, sir, if you please!"

"Oh, yes, of course!" Brufyss released his grip on Fandango's shoulders. The diminutive CEO in charge of being office manager zipped around the desk to cower under the protective wing of Alpha Rae Sapoopa-LaBoobis. Faisal continued to chortle.

Barley fixed Brufyss with a hard scowl. "What are you doing, Brufyss? What is it you're really after here?"

Brufyss shifted his gaze from the tittering Faisal Herskowitz to level his fiery eyes at Barley. All pretense of cordiality was now replaced by seething hatred.

"What am I *really* after, Barley? Let me clue you in: For years now, I've watched you terrorize and torment this town with your bullying, manipulation, and criminal callousness as you stifled and extorted anything and anyone who came between yourself and whatever it was you wanted from them. You deceive, demolish, and destroy the hopes, dreams, aspirations, and egos of all who oppose you, and the individuals who've suffered from your greed, cunning, and cruelty are too numerous to catalogue."

Barley cringed under Brufyss's withering verbal blows. Just moments ago, he'd been made the good guy by the group, but now his bad-guy past was being revealed to them all by someone who knew it firsthand.

"Years ago, I counted you as my friend, Barley. My *only* friend! It was you and me against the world! We may have been misguided in our aspirations; lost as we were then, we pursued a roundabout and wrongly directed course in achieving what we thought was our due, but I still counted you as my friend."

He let out a long, painful sigh. Barley knew what was coming now. Brufyss was still hurting, and he was about to inflict the pain of his own past on Barley.

"But with you, friendship wasn't enough. To *share* the success or the glory of what few triumphs we attained wasn't equitable. You needed more! You always had to be one step ahead or one rung higher on the ladder, and to get there you saw to it that I, your best friend, was kept down, in my place and beholden to you!

"I might've been able to live with that, Barley; I knew you were the more talented of the two of us, the more creative, the more ambitious— how could I not know it? You threw it in my face every day! But when Mrs. Kookerly came into my life—when it finally came time for you to acknowledge a success that I'd achieved on my own—could you be happy for me? Could you give me an ounce of credit, encouragement, or even congratulations for finding happiness? How did you handle *my* success?

"You tried to destroy me! You tried to take away the only accomplishment, the only satisfaction, the only love I'd ever achieved in my entire shabby life so you could have her for yourself. In order to accomplish that, you weren't averse to deceiving, manipulating, or hurting *anyone!*"

His venomous words dripped of a poisonous truth. Barley's mind spun, remembering his shameful actions, his shameful attitudes, the shameful person he'd been . . . and the shameful person he was now.

Brufyss continued, "I suppose I could cop out and say that the origins of the person I've become can be traced back to the abuse and degradation I suffered at your hands, but I have enough integrity left to take responsibility for my own actions and fate, and to acknowledge that I've made myself into a laughable loser who seeks nothing but revenge and retribution from you for your double-dealing! This is the level I've brought *myself* down to.

"For all these years I've followed you, seeking to disrupt or dismantle anything and everything you've undertaken. I've lurked in the background like a scavenger, observing your successes and failures, doing all I could to thwart, sabotage, and interfere, praying for the day that I might somehow turn the tables—to make you feel the pain of failure and disillusionment that you've given to me, to those I love, and to so many others!

"When I found out about your latest business venture, the guided tours to this establishment, I had to admit it was a darn clever idea, a surefire winner—and my long-awaited chance to finally turn those tables. I found a loophole in your paperwork, and I've gotten the jump on you! I've finally ended up on top! I've finally been able to make you feel that pain of defeat . . . But you know what, Barley? *It's not enough!*"

The B & S staffers listened to this newcomer vehemently slam the guy who'd just rescued Marshall Farkpucker from having to coordinate his wardrobe around trash-can headwear. Barley didn't seem as bad as Brufyss indicated. Narducci Palpatooti had even composed a song celebrating his heroics, which didn't jive at all with the horrible person this fellow was describing.

The tourists were well aware of the shortcomings Brufyss detailed; they'd witnessed a sizeable chunk of those shortcomings earlier in the day. And yet, Barley Doodlebody had changed before their eyes! Since awakening from his brief period of unconsciousness, he'd been helpful, sociable, and polite. They'd even seen *contrition* from their ill-tempered tour director, and they'd just witnessed him wither in shame beneath the brutal verbal thrashing meted out by Brufyss, offering nothing in his own defense. Maybe Barley was simply getting what he deserved, but Brufyss Bathwater was no angel, either. Which evil was the lesser?

While Brufyss unburdened himself of the pent-up anger and resentment stemming from his mistreatment at the hands of Barley, Old Man Spuggett impassively leafed and shuffled through the pages of business licenses and permits submitted to him by the two archrivals, his attention ostensibly focused on these documents that so neatly and adroitly enabled his autonomy and privacy to be invaded and violated.

At length, he determined that Brufyss was finally vented out; the malevolent monologue had ended. The old man gathered the papers together, tossed them haphazardly onto Alpha Rae's desk, and looked at the two antagonists, one of them steaming like a colander of broccoli, the other wilting like a wok-full of sautéed cabbage.

"It's like I said, isn't it?" Brufyss was triumphant. "All perfectly legal!"

The old man sighed and looked at Brufyss with weary, wizened eyes. "Frankly, I wouldn't have a clue. Didn't read a word."

"But you were just reading. I saw you!"

"I was actually listening, sir. Listening to what you had to say. Now *I* have something to say—that is, if *legally* I may be allowed to say it."

"By all means."

"First off, let me address the issue of your paperwork. It appears that with all the 'proper documentation' you've procured, enabling you to have unlimited access to my business—and that includes *both* of you"—he glanced over at Barley—"the only individual who's been left out of all this is me!

"Perhaps I've been enclosed within the walls of this building and out of touch with the outside world for so long that laws, statutes, and ordinances have passed me by. Perhaps some type of regulation has come into existence during my absence that allows individuals or groups such as yours to intrude upon privately owned establishments such as mine without having to go through the rigmarole of asking permission, receiving clearance, or just checking to see if it's okay.

"Indeed, by what you've shown me here, it appears that individuals or groups such as yours now have the so-called legal power to launch a parasite business without having to come to any sort of agreement with the host business! You may now waltz in here whenever you so desire and make money for yourself by exploiting my business, and there's no need or requirement for you to communicate with me, establish partnership with me, or compensate me for this incursion.

"If that's the case, then it appears that I, as the proprietor of the exploited business, am simply out of luck; I have no say and no choice in the matter whatsoever. I must tell you, gentlemen, that in my opinion, this new incarnation of free enterprise is quite surprising, extremely disappointing, and immensely unfair. Frankly, I'm shocked that our lawmakers would allow this to happen—that our esteemed mayor or our honorable city councilman, both with us today, would not view this as contrary to established free-enterprise principles!"

"Nay, nay, prithee, but *hold*, good sire!" Mayor Wubbleduster's cry of protest erupted from the crowd. "Verily, 'tis not as it seemeth! I beseech thee, hear me now! The deed done belieth convention and decorum! 'Twas a connivance of violence—aye, and treachery—by which the desired edicts were procured!"

Brufyss was incredulous. "What the hell is up with the mayor?"

Biff Spoozma attacked his Elizabethan English dictionary. "The mayor says, 'Mr. Doodlebody requested and received those documents through the use of *threats* and *violence* rather than the normal channels of conventional legislative and bureaucratic procedure. Those concessions were granted to him under duress!'"

Barley swallowed hard. Recollections of his violently intimidating visit to city hall flashed through his mind. Here was another guilty admission he would have to make to the old man to rectify the injustice he'd perpetrated. "Well, ah, um, actually, Mr. Spuggett, what the mayor means to say is that I acquired my license and permit in a somewhat *irregular* manner—"

"What the mayor means to say is that Doodlebody beat the crap out of everyone at city hall to get his permits," said Brufyss smugly.

"I see, and how did you go about acquiring *yours*, Mr. Birthbladder?"

"I proposed prior legal precedent! I simply told the city council that since Barley had already been granted his permit and license, a precedent had been set that would qualify me for the same permit and license. I amended it by adding the verbiage which allowed me total access to the premises, and no violence was perpetrated in the process. It's all perfectly legal."

"Very upstanding of you, sir," said Old Man Spuggett with just a hint of sarcasm. "But I have something more to say on this subject. I would inform you that nothing is 'perfectly legal'! The phrase is an oxymoron. The words *perfect* and *legal* used together are incongruous; there is no legality that is perfect. As any lawyer would tell you, everything is subject to interpretation, and interpretation itself is an imperfect tool."

"Call it what you will, then," interrupted Brufyss. "It's all just a bunch of words anyway! If you want to know the truth, Mr. Spuggett, I have no intention of starting a guided tour business to invade your company. My only objective in obtaining those documents and coming here today was to keep Barley Doodlebody from doing so—to finally win one battle in this war we've been waging for so many years."

The old man rubbed his chin thoughtfully, considering Brufyss's words. "'War,' you say, Mr. Bathwater? This is a *war* we're talking about here?"

"Yeah, *war!*"

The old man leveled his gaze at Brufyss and for the first time all day assumed a serious demeanor. "Mr. Bathwater, let me remind you: history has shown us irrefutably, and continues to show us to this day, that war— *any* war—is evidence of the greatness mankind has *not* achieved." He now included Barley in his gaze. "It is my opinion, gentlemen, that in your situation, to win a battle would not be a victory but merely a prolongation of the war. I believe that in your war there will be no victor."

"What do you mean?"

"War is a brutal confrontation in which self-interest is the motivation and destruction is the objective. War is only pain and devastation, gentlemen. Can't you see these tragic consequences in your own conflicts with each other? Given what you've so articulately expressed, can't you see that a lifetime of wasted life is all you have to show for this so-called 'war' you've been waging?

"If a state of war truly does exist between the two of you, be advised that there will be no resolution to those disputes on these premises. If emotional violence is what you choose to inflict upon each other, there will be no disruption of the harmony now present and existing within these walls. Be further advised that while you occupy space within these walls, you're under *my* jurisdiction, and a mandatory truce is now in effect between the two of you!

"Whatever you choose to do with each other after you leave these premises is of no concern to me, but for the duration of your visit to this office and the well-being of my 103-year-old skull, I'm compelled to exercise a legal loophole of my own:

"*Whereas* the submitted legal documents under consideration have *not* indicated that I am no longer the lawful proprietor of this business, which by inference would indicate that *I am* legally the lawful proprietor of this business . . .

"And *whereas* the submitted legal documents outline procedures concerning *trespassing* into said business but do *not* cover the admission within said business of guests invited freely by myself as the lawful proprietor of this business . . .

"*Be it resolved* that by my declaration, each and every individual presently occupying physical space within this business is, by executive order of myself, a freely invited guest upon these premises, thereby entitled to all privileges and benefits prescribed by myself as the lawful proprietor of this business.

"*You are hereby advised* that we're gonna have a party today, and you're *all* freely invited guests! If you and your legal documentation have a problem with that, I suggest you sue me. Then, perhaps, you'll get your opportunity to see justice served. In the meantime, while you're under my roof, you're gonna play by my rules! The rules? Relax! Party! Enjoy yourself!

"I rest my case."

While Old Man Spuggett presented his arguments, the Bumps & Spuggett staffers and tourists were mesmerized by the drama, trying to figure out what all the legal gobbledygook meant.

The only sentence they easily comprehended was the last uttered: the old man's proclamation of a gala party to which they were all invited, including the newcomer, Mr. Bathwater. At the conclusion of the company founder's proclamation, the tension broke. Employees and tourists alike burst into boisterous applause, cheering, whistling, stomping, whooping, and hollering, relieved that all the bickering and contentious accusations were over and a truce had been declared. Now maybe they'd heard the last of all this serious stuff.

Old Man Spuggett, worn out from the somber discoursing, sat to rest on the edge of Alpha Rae's desk with Dr. Pudbid by his side. The two old friends watched as the joyful revelers caroused.

Barley was reeling from the emotional roller coaster ride he'd just taken. He stood amid the pandemonium and marveled at the skill and precision with which Old Man Spuggett had defused and dismantled a potentially explosive situation yet again, employing his own inimitable brand of patience, kindness, tolerance, and logic—although he'd managed to get in a little butt-kicking along with it!

The company founder was a crafty old bird all right, but it always seemed that the end result of his extrapolations, illustrations, and demonstrations was positive, thought provoking, and conciliatory. He was indeed the master of his own world, and to Barley this world seemed to make more and more sense.

The old man had deflected Brufyss's determined onslaught, and in the process had made clear to Barley the evils and errors of his own ways. He was paying for those evils and errors now, but not because of Old Man Spuggett. Barley's own change of heart motivated him to clean up his act, make amends, and redeem himself.

Brufyss was right. Barley had dealt his best friend inexcusable and perhaps unforgivable injuries. As Brufyss detailed the cold and heartless methods Barley employed to wrong him back in those days, the "new" Barley had shriveled in humiliation and self-loathing. If he was truly going to change, he must first atone for the evils of his youth. He had to begin by making things right with Brufyss Bathwater—if that was at all possible.

**

Brufyss scratched his head in perplexity. In the blink of an eye, he'd gone from being in a position of authority and superiority to feeling like an ineffectual, bumbling fool! What just happened here? In one fell swoop, Old Man Spuggett deftly rolled that barrel Brufyss had Barley over out from under him and positioned it squarely under Brufyss. And he was now a "freely invited guest" to a big party!

Old Man Spuggett had him completely confused and at bay—for the moment. However, Brufyss had come too far, gone to too much trouble, waited too long, planned too thoroughly, and harbored too much malice and resentment toward Barley Doodlebody to be dissuaded from the task at hand.

He took a deep breath and collected his thoughts. Until he figured out the old man's game, got the "lay of the land" of the Bumps & Spuggett offices, and determined a new plan of attack, he'd keep cool and play along, waiting for the right opportunity to make his move.

No one was going to neutralize or defeat Brufyss Bathwater with the use of clever arguments, tricks of semantics, smoke, mirrors—or brute force! He'd reserve those options for himself, to be utilized when the time was right or the necessity arose.

In the meantime, he had another surprise for Barley . . .

32

When Mrs. Kookerly appeared in the double doorway to the reception room and lobby, Barley froze as if he'd turned to cast iron. She stood next to a disoriented Lollie Babajuju, one hand clutching Lollie's arm, surveying the celebratory scene while searching for Brufyss Bathwater.

Barley was thunderstruck by her appearance. Older and more mature since her halcyon days as the head cheerleader at P. P. Piggford and His Wife Janice High School, she still possessed the striking beauty that graced her youth. However, missing was the radiant smile that so prominently accentuated her magnificent features in those carefree high school days. Her look was focused and intense, her sumptuous lips pursed, her eyes flashing with a fire born of malice rather than youthfully innocent happiness.

Framed in the big double doorway, she was nonetheless a captivating vision to behold. The sight of her left Barley breathless. As Mrs. Kookerly's presence became known to the others, they stilled and riveted their attention upon her, staring in awe at the beautiful apparition.

Brufyss also noticed Mrs. Kookerly. His eyes immediately went to Barley, and a smile crossed his lips. Brufyss gloated at the spell she easily wove around Barley; just as with a magician's illusions, Barley was only seeing what she wanted him to see.

"Still got it going for my girlfriend after all these years, eh, Barley? Well, why don't you say hello? I'm sure she'd be delighted to see you again. Hey, Mrs. Kookerly! Over here!"

Mrs. Kookerly nodded knowingly and focused her attention on Barley, flashing a smile that struck him like a bolt of lightning.

She guided the bewildered Lollie as she entered, gliding regally across

the floor toward Brufyss and Barley. By this time, all of the tourists and B
& S staffers were aware of her presence and parted to let the women pass.

Long accustomed to the admiring stares of lesser humans, Mrs.
Kookerly acknowledged the crowd like visiting royalty, glancing from
side to side, bestowing glowing, condescending smiles upon everyone
she passed. Spying Frog Puppleman and Mimsy Borogove, she paused to
greet her old schoolmates.

"Hello, Frog—or should I call you Councilman Puppleman now?
What a pleasant surprise to see you here today. My, but you've certainly
come a long way since our days at Piggford High. A North Corners city
councilman! And just as handsome as you were then."

Frog grinned sheepishly. "Yeah, buddy!"

Mrs. Kookerly smiled at Frog's signature response. "It's so nice to see
you haven't changed a bit, Frog—still short, sweet, and to the point. I'm
sure North Corners is in good hands with an astute politician like you at
the helm."

She moved on to stand in front of Mimsy. "Do my eyes deceive me,
or is this not the lovely Mimsy Borogove? My heavens, Mimsy, what
happened to your face? Feeling a little *blue* today, are we? And your hair!
Did you get your head stuck in a blender, or is this the new look that high
society is touting nowadays?"

Mimsy blushed, the blood under her skin mixing with the blue tint of
her face to turn her a bright purple. "I-I suffered a small accident today."

"A small accident? It looks more like a catastrophe, Mimsy! Well,
whatever happened, this new look really suits you. I'd stick with it. You
always were a high-fashion beacon in the darkness—among other things."

She smiled her beguiling smile. "It's almost like a class of '67 reunion,
isn't it? Such a shame that our seeing each other again after all these years
couldn't be under more pleasant circumstances. Maybe later we can sneak
in a few minutes to talk about old times—if you're still here."

She gave her former classmates a wink and moved through the
silent crowd. Still clutching Lollie Babajuju's arm, she floated through
the throng, finally arriving to stand in front of Barley and Brufyss. Her
blistering gaze fixed upon the former as she softly addressed the latter:

"Hello, Brufyss, I almost didn't see or hear you in this noisy crowd.
Who do we have here? So nice to see you again, Barley! It's a shame you
can't stick around so we all might reminisce about the old days together."

Barley gulped nervously, knowing full well the degree of animosity the former teen queen held for him, despite her pleasant demeanor.

"I, er, um, I—ah, hello, M-Mrs. K-Koo-Koo—" stammered Barley.

"Mrs. Koo-Koo? Why, Barley, have you forgotten my name?"

"Oh, no! I-I—well, it's just that I, ah . . ."

"I see you haven't lost your flare for urbane conversation." She kept her gaze fastened on Barley but spoke to Brufyss. "Dear, have you informed Barley of his unfortunate mistake in coming to these offices today? It appears that his presence here has thrown the entire place into chaos! I'm sure Messrs. Bumps and Spuggett must be at their wits' end trying to cope with the havoc he's causing—"

"Actually, young lady, Mr. Bumps reached his wits' end long ago with an unfortunate 6,000-foot plunge into a raging volcano!"

Old Man Spuggett, like everyone else, had watched Mrs. Kookerly's dramatic entrance with a mixture of awe and curiosity. He rose from Alpha Rae's desk to greet her, gallantly shaking her hand and offering a chivalrous bow.

"However, as the current proprietor of these premises, I'd be most happy to welcome you into this seeming den of chaos. My name is Spuggett, and unlike my poor business partner, I am—to the best of my knowledge—still in possession of a modicum of wit, alive, kicking, and at your service, though not necessarily in that order!"

Mrs. Kookerly smiled indulgently at the old gentleman; she was aware of the Bumps & Spuggett firm's reputation for eccentricity, and Old Man Spuggett's quirky introduction confirmed the fact to her. "Thank you, Mr. Spuggett, it's a pleasure to meet you. My name is Mrs. Kookerly, and I must apologize for our unannounced visit here today. We're actually here to perform a service for you. As I'm sure Mr. Bathwater's already indicated, Mr. Doodlebody is here illegally, and we've come to see to it that he troubles you no more with his presence. I'm sure you understand."

"Oh, I do understand!" responded the old man cordially. "Prior to your glorious appearance on the scene, Mrs. Kookerly, these two gentlemen and myself underwent quite a thorough examination of the circumstances surrounding your and Mr. Doodlebody's reasons for being here today. I'm pleased to say that all those issues have been remedied and resolved in a most amicable fashion!"

Mrs. Kookerly scowled in confusion. "Then why is Mr. Doodlebody still *here*?"

Brufyss cleared his throat to get Mrs. Kookerly's attention, frowned, and subtly shook his head as if to say, "Don't press it right now!"

"In answer to your question, dear lady, I myself remedied and resolved the situation by exercising a legal loophole in *your* legal loophole, proclaiming all of you my freely invited guests here today! Therefore, everyone here—including yourself, now that you've arrived—is not only permitted but heartily welcome on these premises. Everyone! And you're just in time to help us celebrate the making of new friendships by joining us in a special party. Isn't it wonderful?"

"Uh, yeah, sure. Wonderful . . ." She turned to Brufyss and whispered through clenched teeth, "*Brufyss*, what's going *on*?"

Before Brufyss could answer, Old Man Spuggett spoke up again. "However, I do have one question for you: how did you manage to rouse my receptionist from her daily meditation, and why are you holding her arm so tightly?"

"Mr. Spuggett, that's actually two questions," said Bagmo. "You know the rules."

"Oops, sorry! You're right, Mr. Maltgoggles. Only one question at a time! In that case, if you please, Mrs. Kookerly, could you answer the *second* question first?"

Mrs. Kookerly's eyes widened. "Er—what was the question?"

"Which question?" asked the old man. "The first question, or the second one?"

"Which question did you want me to answer first?"

"I believe I'd like the second one answered first, and the first one answered second."

"Well, what was the second question again?"

"You mean the one I want you to answer first?"

"That's the one!"

Old Man Spuggett scratched his head thoughtfully. "Now that I think about it, answering the second question first would actually make the second question the *first* question, wouldn't it? Tell you what: to keep the order less confusing, we'll make the second question the new first question, which means you'd be answering the new first question first— then we'll move on to the new second question, which was the old first question. You can answer the new second question second, which is logical enough—that is, after you've answered the formerly second question first, since that will now be the new first question. I think this will keep things from getting too confusing, wouldn't you agree?"

"*Huh?*"

"Oh dear! Now I've gone and really confused things, haven't I? Tell you what, just answer me this: why do you feel it necessary to hang on to Miss Babajuju so tightly? She appears to be fully conscious and awake now—indeed, she appears to be rather uncomfortable with you clutching her that way."

"Babajuju?"

"*Gesundheit!*" offered Felicia.

At the mention of her name, Lollie snapped out of her bewildered state. "*Labaloolah um gaboola!*"

She looked down at Mrs. Kookerly's hand and roughly jerked her arm out of Mrs. Kookerly's grasp, clucking her tongue in reproach.

"Repository matricide unbeknownst!" said Ebenezer, looking from Lollie to Mrs. Kookerly and back again.

"'Tis well thou'st spoken, good friend," said Mayor Wubbleduster, "lest unannounced the misdeed in tragedy resulteth!"

Everyone in the room instinctively diverted their attention to Biff, who quickly thumbed through his dog-eared dictionary for the translation. "The mayor says that Ebenezer says that Lollie says to Mrs. Kookerly, 'Get your hands off me, or I'll rip every one of those pretty blond hairs out of your head one by one!'"

"Why, Ebenezer, I had no idea you could understand what Lollie is saying!" exclaimed Old Man Spuggett. "When did this development come about?"

"Blapfoggily macrobiotic buckets regurgitate seminal restitution!"

Mayor Wubbleduster: "Spake Ebenezer, 'Thus has e'er it been, but for mine own misspoken efforts comprehension hath no advocate!'"

Biff Spoozma: "The mayor says that Ebenezer says, 'I've *always* been able to understand what Lollie says, but no one understands *me* when I tell them!'"

Ebenezer turned to Mayor Wubbleduster and spoke to him in Complete Gibberish. The mayor translated what he'd said to Biff. Biff translated the mayor's translation:

"The mayor says that Ebenezer says, 'In my school days at the North Corners Institute of Profligate Ostentation with Benign Rapport Credenzas, I majored in obscure if not totally meaningless verbal communication—but I *minored* in understanding every language in the world. That's why I can interpret what Lollie is saying.'"

Mrs. Kookerly looked at Brufyss, absolute mystification blanketing her pretty face. "What's going *on* here, Brufyss?" she whispered.

"I haven't got a clue. I told you this place was bonkers!"

Narducci was elated. "Now that Lollie's here, she can come to our party, Mr. Spuggett!"

"Indeed, this is a rare but fortuitous development! It's not often that we're graced with the pleasure of Lollie's company, as she's generally out there at her desk, lost in a deep meditative trance—which leads me back to what is now the new *second* question I asked earlier, Mrs. Kookerly: how were you able to rouse her from her normally unresponsive state?"

Mrs. Kookerly swallowed uncomfortably at the question, reluctant to admit that she'd grabbed the catatonic receptionist by the shoulders and shaken her vigorously until she snapped out of her trance. "Oh, well, I— well, I simply used a bit of *insistent persuasion* to convince her that she'd be missing all the fun if she didn't wake up. I-I guess that did the trick!"

"Well, because of you, Mrs. Kookerly, we now have our full complement of staff members along with our other guests, and we can all communicate with each other—however indirectly. We humbly thank you for your assistance."

The crowd of employees shouted their concurrence and gave Mrs. Kookerly a hooting round of applause. Lollie stared, trying to comprehend the unfamiliar faces and what was going on.

"It-it was nothing, I'm sure," mumbled Mrs. Kookerly. She turned once again to face Brufyss and whispered, "Brufyss, please! Tell me what's going on here!"

"I'll fill you in later. Suffice it to say, our legal paperwork is useless. Just play along for the time being—and be careful of the old man. He's not as scatterbrained as he seems!"

"I think I've just seen him in action! He quieted me down pretty quick. Do you think he's wise to us?"

"I *know* he's wise to us. He's wise to all of us! We're under a mandatory truce at the moment."

"Speaking of the party," said Old Man Spuggett, "I'm beginning to wonder when we'll actually be ready to *start* the celebration."

He walked to the attic doorway and called up the flour-dusted stairwell: "Gerald? Gerald, are you up there?"

After a few seconds, Gerald Foon-Package called down. "Is that you, Mr. Spuggett? Yeah, I'm here!"

"Gerald, how much longer will it be before you're ready with the excess-hair-growth formula?"

"It's ready now, sir. I'm just waiting for Cheezy to get back up here so he can help me bring it downstairs. Is he down there with you?"

Old Man Spuggett scanned the crowd. "No, I don't think he's returned from the storage room yet."

"Jeez Loo-eez! What's taking him so long? All he had to do was get the plates and cups and stuff."

"Be patient, Gerald. I'm sure he'll be back up as soon as he can! Maybe he's just having trouble locating them!"

"Well, if he doesn't get up here pretty soon, this stuff is gonna start getting cold!"

"Gerald, I'm sure it will be absolutely delicious, no matter the temperature." The company founder turned to address the entire crowd. "You know how it is with temperamental artists who see themselves as scientists. Everything's gotta be just right."

Mrs. Kookerly used the exchange between Old Man Spuggett and Gerald as her opportunity to confront Barley. His insides tightened up like a sailor's knot as she faced him, looking into his eyes with the ferocity of a ravenous lioness about to devour her prey.

"So, here we are, Barley, face-to-face again after all these years. I hope you haven't forgotten us! Brufyss and I have thought about *you* almost every day—"

"I haven't forgotten you."

Barley's voice was barely a whisper. His meek response momentarily took Mrs. Kookerly aback, but her puzzlement was quickly replaced by raw hatred. "How does it feel to finally meet your match, Barley? How does it feel to know you've been a snake in the grass all your life and your own poisonous past has finally come back to bite you?"

She paused to let the venom of her words sink in.

"Not good."

Again, not the response she expected to hear from their archenemy. "Not good? *Not good?*! That's all you have to say? That's the best you can come up with?"

Barley stood like a repentant child taking his medicine for being a bad boy.

"What more can I say? I can't change the person I was. I'm trying to change the person I am today. There's no excuse for my past behavior—I know this, and I'm sorry for what I did to you both. *Sorry* is a word that doesn't adequately express the regret I feel. You're right. You're both right! Everything you've said is true."

"You're damn *right* it's true!"

"But I can never make it up to either of you, and that's painful to me. I deserve everything I get."

"You'll never get everything you *deserve!*" Barley's passivity shook her. She felt frustrated at his submissive acceptance of her vicious attack. He not only acknowledged every accusation she hurled at him but agreed with it as well. This was not the Barley Doodlebody she'd expected to encounter. This Barley Doodlebody was a *wimp!*

"All right, what's your game here? What are you trying to pull? You think you can erase forty-plus years of double-dealing by being apologetic?"

"Of course not! But how can I atone? I'm completely aware now of what I've been and what I've done—how I've wronged you and just about everybody else I've dealt with over the years. I know that doesn't mean much to you, but it's the truth."

Mrs. Kookerly and Brufyss stared in amazement at this person for whom they'd carried so much animosity, unsure of what to say next. Was Barley asking for *forgiveness*?

Brufyss piped up in rebuttal: "It's easy for you to be remorseful and apologetic now that you've been soundly whipped, Barley. I'll bet you wouldn't be talking like this if you'd beaten *us* again!"

"Brufyss, you did whip me, fair and square. Today, almost everything has conspired to put me in my place and smack me down—and you know what? I'm glad it's happened! I *needed* this to happen."

"What the hell are you talking about?"

"Coming here today has been both the craziest thing I've ever done and the most sensible. It's made me see the futility of the way I've been living my life, and it's helped to reveal the ridiculousness of just about everything I've ever accomplished."

Brufyss and Mrs. Kookerly stared at Barley with a mixture of skepticism and confusion. They took a measure of satisfaction in hearing his candid confessions of past injustices and iniquities and, now, the painful consequences they'd wreaked upon him. He did seem sincere enough—some of what he said was even thought-provoking to an extent—but they were also aware of Barley's notorious capacity for canny deception and manipulation. Was he trying to diffuse their anger by utilizing these tactics now? If so, more caution was in order. If not, and Barley's remorse was real, then to continue their merciless pounding in front of all these people would put the two of them in the position of being no better than he. They were faced with a perplexing dilemma—but how to proceed?

"So, you attribute this amazing 'epiphany' you've received to your visiting this place today?" Brufyss asked. "Are we to believe that your miserable life has been revealed to you simply by coming to this loony lair? Like this is some kind of a magical place or something? What do you take us for?"

"I'm not trying to take you for anything, Brufyss. I'm telling you that going through everything I've gone through today and coming to this place has helped to change me—or at least to show me that I need to change myself. Believe what you want to believe, but if you're going to stay here, see and judge for yourselves. Just don't involve the rest of these people in the problems you have with me."

"Sure, Barley, whatever you say. But don't worry: we have no interest whatsoever in the nutcases here. C'mon, Mrs. Kookerly, let's find out how 'magical' this place is. Maybe *we'll* get changed too!"

"Of course, dear—but since Barley's finally seen the error of his ways and become a repentant, sensitive, noble human being, don't you think the *other* person we brought with us would be an especially pleasant surprise for him?"

Brufyss smiled. "Honey, I believe you're right. I think seeing his old friend again would be just the thing to pick up Barley's spirits!"

Mrs. Kookerly brought two fingers to her lips and gave a loud whistle. The high-pitched signal brought the noisy chatter of the tourists and staffers to an abrupt halt. Almost immediately came a rattling sound from the double doors on the same wall as Gerald's attic entryway, the big hanging banner, and the hand-lettered sign. Everyone's attention was drawn to this previously ignored portal. (*Figure 4*)

The double doors wouldn't open. They were locked, and whoever was outside didn't have the key. The rattling sound increased in volume, accompanied by an increasingly violent shaking as the person on the other side struggled fitfully to get them open.

Felicia Greenthing shrieked. "Great Scott! A *monster's* trying to get in here!"

Mrs. Kookerly and Brufyss gawked at Felicia as she began to scream and yowl.

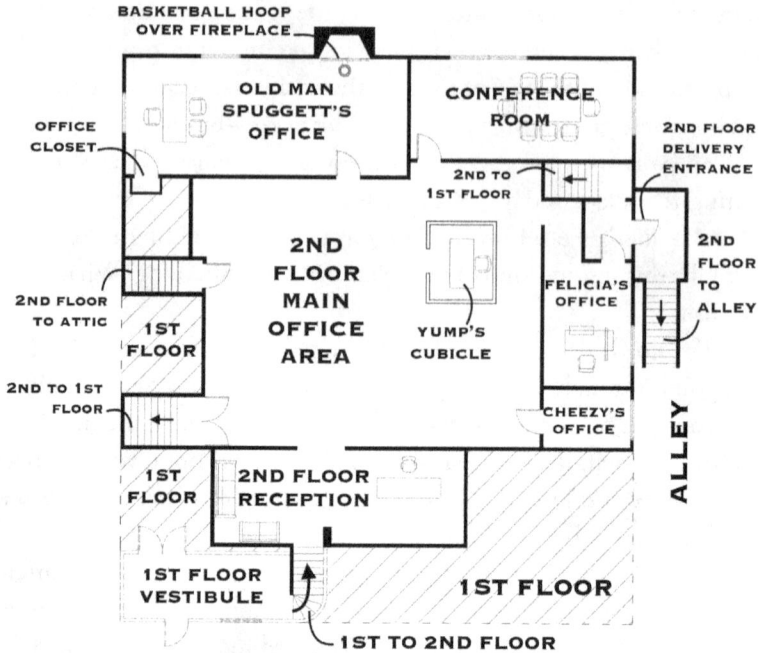

FIGURE 4
(2ND FLOOR)

"No, no! That's not a monster! I'll get it!" shouted Mrs. Kookerly, dashing over to the rattling doors.

Felicia stopped her wailing, watching nervously as Mrs. Kookerly whispered something through the crack between the doors. A muffled voice answered her. Mrs. Kookerly turned to Old Man Spuggett, who was now gawking at the rattling doors himself, having concluded his conversation with Gerald Foon-Package.

"Excuse me, Mr. Spuggett," she said, smiling sweetly at the old man, "but it appears that these doors are locked. Would you or any of your employees happen to have the key? There's another person outside."

"Of course, dear! I have the keys to all the doors right here in the pocket of my bathrobe, but I'm puzzled as to why this person is trying to get in through *those* doors! Behind them is a stairway that leads to a portion of the first floor not currently in use. It's supposed to be locked up."

Mrs. Kookerly blushed. "Is that so? Well, the person out there is notorious for getting lost and disoriented. I'm sure it's an honest mistake."

"No matter," said Old Man Spuggett as he fished for the key ring. "There's nothing down there anyway, just a maze of empty offices in which it would be easy to become lost and disoriented. No harm done."

Roland Chumbuckets sighed in disappointment at the company founder's revelation. The dark mysteries he'd imagined the first floor concealing were no longer quite so mysterious.

"Don't worry, Mr. Spuggett," said Bagmo as the old man fidgeted with his keys. "We'll be right behind you, to make sure there *isn't* a monster out there! C'mon, Narducci! C'mon, Dork! C'mon, Yump! C'mon, Reverend! C'mon, big guy who helps us understand what Ebenezer and the mayor and Lollie are saying! Give me a hand here!"

All responded to Bagmo's summons, standing protectively behind Old Man Spuggett as he unlocked the doors. "I'm sure these precautions won't really be necessary, gentlemen!"

"You're absolutely right, sir," agreed Mrs. Kookerly. "I know who that person is, and it's not a monster."

"You just can't be too sure!" cried Felicia in a voice one step shy of raving panic. "Who knows *what's* been living down there in that dank, dark hole all these years?"

Old Man Spuggett chuckled. "Miss Greenthing, although the first-floor offices have been unoccupied for a rather long period of time, it would be an exaggeration to think of them as a 'dank, dark hole'! A bit dusty perhaps—but we'll learn the truth soon enough, I suspect."

A sharp *click* was heard as the latch unlocked. The company founder clasped the two doorknobs, gave them a twist, and pulled the double doors open.

The person on the other side was rearing back to give the doors a solid shoulder-bashing. Forward momentum sent them whizzing through the suddenly opened entry, flying into the room like a juggernaut, barreling into Old Man Spuggett, and smashing and knocking down the assembled cluster behind him. The toppled group slowly untangled themselves, revealing the intruder, lying facedown on the floor.

Barley stared in horror at the disheveled figure, who attempted to regain a semblance of dignity as she regained her feet.

It was Daphne Dogdaughter.

33

D r. Pudbid shrieked as Old Man Spuggett and the rest flew backward from the force of Daphne's ramming. "Spuggy! Everybody! Are you all right?"

"I believe we're okay, Puddles, just a little shaken up. *Wow*! Who was that cannonball?"

"This young lady here!" The good doctor suddenly recognized her as one of the many North Corners babies Frank Winslow and he had delivered in the distant past. "Why, it's Daphne Dogdaughter! Daphne, dear, tell me where it hurts."

"I don't think it *does*," replied the uncrowned '67 senior prom queen shakily as she hoisted herself slowly off the floor. "I think I'm okay. Are you Dr. Pudbid?"

"Yes, I am!"

"It's been a long time, Doctor. How's your horse?"

"Oh, Frank's doing just fine, and thanks for asking. Now, are you sure you're not hurt?"

"Yep, I think I'm just fine." She recalled her favorite memory of visiting his office during her childhood. "But I'd still like a lollipop if you've got one."

"I'm sorry, dear, but I don't think I have any lollipops at the moment. Why don't you come by and see me at my office? I'll give you a whole handful of 'em."

"Do I have to be hurt or sick first?"

"Heavens no! The healthier, the better!"

Daphne's face lit up. She gave Dr. Pudbid her sweetest smile, enchanting every tourist and staffer in the room with the innocent expression of happiness on her pretty face. As with Mrs. Kookerly, the passage of time had deprived Daphne of very little of the captivating beauty that so enthralled her fellow students, who knew her then as "Tasty." Age left its mark upon her but had enhanced rather than diminished the allure of her features. She thanked the good doctor for his help and began to rearrange her disheveled clothing and recompose her discomposed composure. Both Mrs. Kookerly and Brufyss rushed to her side.

"Daphne, I'm so glad to see you're all right," said Mrs. Kookerly, checking for residual effects from her friend's nasty collision—and perhaps grounds for a lucrative lawsuit.

"Yes, I think I am. But somebody needs to get that door fixed. It's like a booby-trap!"

Barley stared at Daphne in dismay, vividly remembering how he'd taken cruel advantage of her kindness and childlike naïveté. Although she'd never been known for her intelligence, Daphne's kind, loving heart had been the stuff of legend, before Barley tore that heart heartlessly to shreds. He retreated behind the huge form of Reverend Snortworthy, hoping to postpone the inevitable reunion with his former date to the '67 senior prom. He anticipated it being yet another bad experience in a day filled with them. This might turn out to be the worst one of all.

"Good gracious!" cried Rapunzel Trashtrumpet. "It's the entire Bathwater Boys 'n Girls Gang!"

"The *who*?" asked Old Man Spuggett.

"The Bathwater Boys 'n Girls Gang," repeated Rapunzel, pointing at the three new arrivals.

"A misnomer if there ever was one," protested Brufyss. "Do we look like a gang to you? We're three old friends who've formed a business association."

"A 'monkey business' association!" snapped Rapunzel. "You three have been as much a thorn in the side of this community as Mr. Doodlebody!"

Barley wilted yet again, but Mrs. Kookerly quietly marched over to face Rapunzel.

"Who are *you* to make this accusation against the three of us? How dare you lump us into the same category as Barley Doodlebody! Brufyss, I believe this is your old friend Rapunzel Trashtrumpet, the misinformed gossip-monger for the local rag! When did you give up writing stupid fluff pieces full of unsubstantiated garbage to devote yourself to blatant and libelous defamation of peoples' characters, Miss Trashtrumpet?"

Mrs. Kookerly's intimidating gaze set the goggle-eyed reporter on her heels. Perhaps it was time to stop editorializing, shut up, and simply take notes. After all, fluff pieces did have their place.

Old Man Spuggett quietly observed these antagonistic exchanges and deemed it prudent to speak up again. "Good people, I suggest we place all this contentious behavior on hold for the time being so we might have a better chance of getting to know one another before the party begins—in keeping with the terms of the mandatory truce."

He turned to Daphne. "Young lady, I've heard you called Daphne. Is that your name?"

"Yes, sir!" Daphne smiled at the pleasant old man. "Daphne Dogdaughter."

"And may I ask, is that Miss, Ms., or Mrs. Dogdaughter?"

"Miss!"

"Well, Miss Dogdaughter, you are most welcome here today at Bumps & Spuggett, although I must request that in the future you enter our premises through the *second-floor* reception area, to avoid future accidents like the one we've all just experienced. How did you get in there, anyway?"

"I-I'm sorry, sir! I-I—" Daphne quickly averted her panicked eyes to Brufyss and Mrs. Kookerly.

"I think she must have . . . gotten lost," interjected Mrs. Kookerly.

"And disoriented," added Brufyss.

A look of relief crossed Daphne's face. "Yes! I got lost—and disoriented. But I certainly will be careful so that doesn't happen again, sir. From now on!"

"No need to call me 'sir,' Miss Dogdaughter," said the old man with a warm smile. "I'm used to being called Mr. Spuggett by my staff, but anyone who so chooses may call me Spuggy."

"Thank you, Mr.—er, Mr. Spuggy! But I heard someone mention Barley Doodlebody's name. Is he here?"

Before Old Man Spuggett could respond, Barley mustered the courage to speak up, determined to get this next assault on his character over with. He knew he couldn't escape it; he knew he deserved it.

"I'm here, Daphne." He stepped out from behind the shelter of Reverend Snortworthy. "I know you're here to see me."

Daphne's eyes widened, ignited in blazing contempt, and narrowed into a piercing stare, boring through Barley like a laser beam through a steel vault door. She said nothing, simply walked over to him, stopping a foot away. Total silence descended. Brufyss and Mrs. Kookerly exchanged surreptitious glances in anticipation of the vicious excoriation to come.

But something else happened. Daphne's upper lip began to quiver, and her eyes softened and grew moist. Her pretty face contorted into an expression of tortured anguish, and a stream of tears rolled down her cheeks. Instead of exploding with anger in Barley's face, Daphne Dogdaughter began to cry.

"Barley, how—how could you do that to me? Why did you have to hurt me so badly?" She spoke as if it happened only a few hours ago. "When you asked me to go to the dance with you, I was so happy! I felt so honored and pleased that such an important, famous man in North Corners noticed me and wanted to take *me* to the senior prom. You bought me a beautiful dress, you took me to the dance in a beautiful car. It was the most wonderful, exciting night of my life!"

She stifled the sobs and continued, "Brufyss said y-you bribed Mrs. Gooberwart to throw the prom queen election—so I-I would win over Mrs. Kookerly. Even though I knew Mrs. Kookerly was the *real* prom queen, I thought it was really sweet of you to do that for me! No one had ever done anything so nice for me before. It made me feel so good! I thought you wanted me to win because you . . . because you . . . *liked* me!"

Had Daphne used a broadsword to run him through, she couldn't have inflicted more pain on Barley than this heartrending story. He'd completely expected both Brufyss's and Mrs. Kookerly's hateful diatribes against him, but Daphne's aching confessional was almost too much to bear. Her pain, vulnerability, and inherently loving heart—the very qualities tearing Barley to pieces—all contributed to an involuntary dulling of her anger,.

She wasn't finished. "Then everything started to go wrong! Spiffany Tonguehoister wouldn't give up the crown, and instead of helping me to get it, you started to fight with Brufyss. When everybody was going crazy up on the stage and I was in trouble, you pushed Brufyss and me into that horrible pit—on purpose! You got away with Mrs. Kookerly and left me drowning in that horrible, *horrible* mess!

"Barley, if you didn't like me, why did you ask me to the dance? If you didn't like me, why did you try to make me *think* you did? Why did you do all those nice things to make me so happy, and then try to hurt me so badly? What did I do to you to make you *hate* me so much?"

She broke into anguished, wracking sobs, the terrible memories of that traumatic night rushing in and overwhelming her. The others in the room were overcome with emotion as well.

Brufyss and Mrs. Kookerly had heard Daphne's story countless times and had played significant parts when it happened. Nonetheless, they too were overcome as they watched the confrontation between their dear friend and their archenemy. Neither had anticipated it would turn out like this.

Daphne sobbed quietly. Barley stood stricken and helpless. Dr. Pudbid walked up and held out his hand, his own weathered cheeks wet with tears. "Here, Daphne, I found this tucked in my pocket. It isn't much—I didn't even know I had it."

Daphne stared at the doctor's outstretched palm, looked up into his eyes, and smiled. Taking the lollipop from his hand, she unwrapped the cellophane covering and put the candy into her mouth, savoring the sweet flavor. A childlike grin lit her pretty, tear-streaked face.

"Thank you, Dr. Pudbid! I *love* strawberry—it's my favorite!"

"Mine, too."

34

aphne Dogdaughter's wrenching recitation of the horrors Barley had inflicted upon her was the final stone block completing the bridge from Barley's past to the present, spanning the gap between his ruthlessness and his repentance. Prior transgressions roiled in a torrent under that bridge. Instead of draining away, they pooled into a reservoir in which he saw his misspent life reflected back.

He gathered his courage. "Daphne, I realize what a terrible person I've been, not only to you but to just about everyone I've ever known or come into contact with. You, Brufyss, and Mrs. Kookerly were my friends and I betrayed you. I did it for no good reason; it never benefited me in any way. You didn't deserve my cruelty and selfishness. You're completely justified in feeling hatred for me, but I must tell you this: I never hated you. I see now that the person I really hated was me. I know I can never take back what I did to you that night. All I can do is ask you to forgive me."

Daphne sniffed back her tears. Brufyss and Mrs. Kookerly had warned her that he would vilify and ridicule her mercilessly if she confronted him, but unless her ears were deceiving her, she'd just heard Barley ask for forgiveness. Forgiveness for destroying her life!

Her mind flooded with doubt, suspicion, anger, and bewilderment. Soon, her emotions became too much for her to understand or handle. This time she did explode, hammering on Barley's chest with her forearms and clenched fists.

"What are you trying to *do* to me?"

"Daphne, stop! *No!*" Barley grabbed her wrists to keep her from smashing his chest, leaving her squirming in a futile effort to escape his clutches. She ceased her exertion and looked into his eyes with resignation and defeat.

Brufyss sprang to her defense.

"Brufyss, no! Wait a minute!"

Barley released Daphne's wrists and pushed her away. Before she could attack him again, he reached into the breast pocket of his suit coat and extracted Binky Bohoguss, who was still chanting away in his deep meditative trance.

Brufyss stopped his advance in surprise. Barley held Binky aloft so Daphne could see him.

"Oh!" she cried. "It's a little tiny man in a policeman's uniform!"

"You almost *killed* him!" shrieked Felicia.

The rest of the congregation gasped in shock. With all the drama, they'd forgotten about little Binky again! Seeing the placid look on his face, and hearing the almost imperceptible "Chili-baba jijjy-booboo" chant issuing from his little mouth, everyone erupted with a simultaneous spontaneous "Awwww!"

Brufyss laughed derisively. "So *that's* the pocket you keep the chief of police in."

Lollie Babajuju stared at Binky in surprise. "*Bumba jaboola boomba-loo!*" she exclaimed, then asked in a puzzled voice, "*Kapoola bamba shabooh?*"

The crowd looked to Ebenezer.

"Lollie lays rectangulated in satiation, yet writhing—forthwith besmirched! Hullabaloo for two?"

Mayor Wubbleduster added, "Thus spake Ebenezer: Lollie in amazement lingers, the speaking of the cherub well within her ken, yet filled is she with puzzlement! How cometh the imp by the words uttered thus?"

After a hasty consultation with his dictionary, Biff translated: "The mayor says that Ebenezer says that Lollie says, 'Hey! That's *my* chant! Why is that cute little doll-man doing it too?'"

"I think the answer to that is obvious," said Old Man Spuggett. "I believe our little chief of police knows a good thing when he sees it, saw a good thing and knew it, and did something about it. He used Lollie's chant to escape from a world teeming with giant souls like ourselves who care little the tribulations of a tiny one like him. See how peaceful he is? Makes you envy the little guy, doesn't it? I think we all could do with a dose of serenity right about now."

"*I* sure could," sighed Bagmo.

The old man continued: "Now, I think everyone here would agree that our newly arrived guests have contributed to an atmosphere thick with tightening tension, rife with rampant resentment, alive with acidic acrimony, and coursing with caustic contention—and after listening to the numerous complaints of Mr. Bathwater, Mrs. Kookerly, and Miss Dogdaughter, it seems to me that they each have good reasons for feeling that way.

"The past deeds and misdeeds of our Mr. Doodlebody here have apparently been outrageous and outlandish, vindictive and venomous, selfish and solicitous, blatant and brutal. Perhaps one could even throw 'unreasonable,' 'intolerable,' 'unconscionable,' and 'inexcusable' into the mix as well!"

Brufyss and Mrs. Kookerly nodded in agreement. Barley sank deeper into the carpet. Daphne scratched her head, mystified at all the big words.

"However, due to the mandatory truce now in effect and the fact that one heck of a wingding looms in the near future, I hereby proclaim that all differences and disparagements be temporarily relegated to the proverbial back burner. I propose additionally that at the conclusion of the wingding, we all gather together as a group in a spirit of camaraderie and cooperation, and my impartial staff and I will be happy to mediate and provide insights in a productive colloquy wherein all grievances shall be aired, discussed, and debated, and equitable accommodations and recommendations to all contentions will be achieved and appropriately administered. Whaddaya say to *that*?"

Daphne said nothing; she still hadn't figured out the first part of the old man's speech.

Barley smiled; he couldn't wait to see what kind of "insights" Old Man Spuggett and his "impartial staff" might come up with.

Brufyss and Mrs. Kookerly looked at each other, their faces mirroring skepticism.

"Suppose we choose not to follow your recommendations?" Brufyss asked.

"Regrettably, you'd be asked to leave these premises and resolve your differences at some other time, in some other place. That would be unfortunate for all of us. I suggest you put them aside for a time—long enough, at least, to savor our hospitality and enjoy yourselves at our party."

Brufyss and Mrs. Kookerly looked at each other once again, this time in resignation. It appeared that, however feigned, cooperation was the best tactic.

Daphne heard a word she did understand. "A party? We're going to have a *party*?"

"One heck of a wingding, Miss Dogdaughter! You, Mrs. Kookerly, and Mr. Winkboffer are all invited to join us!"

Daphne turned to Brufyss and Mrs. Kookerly. "Did you hear that? We're invited to a party!"

A thought flashed through her mind: "But what about—?"

"Daphne, *shhh*!" hissed Mrs. Kookerly through clenched teeth. "Keep quiet about that!"

"Oops, sorry!" Daphne shot a guilty glance at Old Man Spuggett to see if he'd overheard what she said. Apparently, he hadn't.

"He's inviting the Bathwater Boys 'n Girls Gang to the party," mumbled Rapunzel under her breath, "*and* Barley Doodlebody! This oughta be some wingding."

"Hey, Mr. Spuggett! When are we gonna *have* our party?!" shouted Bagmo over the excited buzz of the crowd.

"Well, Mr. Maltgoggles, the cure for excess hair growth hasn't arrived yet, but I see no reason why we can't start right now!"

"Yeah, *buddy*!" bellowed Frog.

The somber mood changed to exuberant celebration once again. The staff and tourists launched into a renewed frenzy of dancing, singing, whooping, and hollering.

"Looks like you're off the hook for the time being, Doodlebody," whispered Brufyss as he and Barley watched the excited throng.

Barley ignored the veiled threat and joined Old Man Spuggett, who was watching the celebration with Dr. Pudbid. "Sir, might I ask a favor of you?"

"Why, certainly, Mr. Doobydipple! What might that be?"

"Do you think we might find a safe place to stash Chief Bohoguss while all this partying is going on? I'm afraid he's going to get stomped or squished!"

"My heavens, you're right! We need to hide the little fellow someplace where all this frivolity won't kill him. I haven't seen this many fancy dancers in one room since the last session of Congress. We should put him in my office—that would be out of harm's way."

The old man took Binky from Barley and cradled the tiny chief of police in his own hand, then gazed at Barley with concern. "Mr. Fondlebody, how are you feeling? Your character, ego, and past appeared to have undergone some rather brutal assaults by our new guests."

Barley smiled wanly. "Well, sir, I guess you could say I'm going through a few growing pains at the moment."

The old man returned Barley's smile with a twinkle in his eye. "Yes, Mr. Funkydoodle, I can imagine that 'growing pains,' as you call them, are hurting a bit right now, but please remember—without growing pains, one isn't growing!" To Dr. Pudbid: "Puddles, you pragmaticated old spongethumper! Why don't you accompany me to my office? We'll deposit the little law enforcer in a safe place and get out of this noise ourselves."

The old friends took leave of Barley and headed across the room to Old Man Spuggett's private office, transporting Binky Bohoguss to what they believed would be a secure, party-proof place of refuge.

The wingding was finally underway. Bumps & Spuggett employees mingled with their freely invited guests, releasing tensions that had built with the consecutive confrontations between Barley, Brufyss, Mrs. Kookerly, and Daphne. Narducci Palpatooti realized that despite all the unbridled celebrating, a major ingredient was missing: music! He decided to compose another song, and in moments was surrounded by a gaggle of receptive tourists and staffers.

"The following is an original composition of my own, which I composed myself just now and humbly present to you," he said. "Please remain silent whilst I singst."

His audience settled down, and Narducci cleared his throat, coughed a few times, let go with a big sneeze, recomposed himself, and began to sing:

"To those of you newcomers who
Are puzzled by our habits
And wish to see the reason we
Behave like frenzied rabbits,
Then gather close! Receive a dose!
The medicine we're taking
Is bound to do the same for you!
It's merriment we're making!
Ahay! Ahoy! We're whompin' at the wingding!

We haven't room for gloom or doom,
For pragmatists or purists!
We strive to be a family
Of employees and tourists!
There's Kookerly and Brufyss, he,
There's Barley and there's Daphne!

We're best of pals, us guys and gals,
And . . ."

Narducci paused, scratching his head. "What rhymes with 'Daphne'?"
Many additional heads were scratched.

"Half knee?"

"Calf tree?"

"Laugh spree?"

"Staff key?"

"Frab-jahola glaff-schnee!" offered Ebenezer.

The rest of the group looked at him questioningly. "What the heck
does 'frab-jahola glaff-schnee' mean?" asked Alpha Rae.

"I have no idea," replied Narducci, "but I like it! It's *in*!"

Narducci resumed his performance, picking up where he left off:

". . . There's Kookerly and Brufyss, he,
There's Barley and there's Daphne!
We're best of pals, us guys and gals,
And frab-jahola glaff-schnee!
Ahay! Ahoy! We're whompin' at the wingding!

We'll tolerate no anger, hate,
Recalcitrance or whining!
Closed-mindedness is, more or less,
Constricting and confining!
The gang's all here, we're full of cheer,
The mood is copacetic,
So if you doubt, then please, BUG OUT!
You'll blow the whole aesthetic!
Ahay! Ahoy! We're whompin' at the wingding!
We're stompin' at the wingding!
Whomp with us at the wingding!"

Narducci concluded his song with a sweeping bow. His audience
rewarded him with a rousing round of applause and cheering. "Narducci,
that's gotta be the best song you've *ever* written!" exclaimed Bagmo.

"Shiggydaygobah!" confirmed Ebenezer.

"Thanks! And it's based on a true story, I might add," added Narducci.

The group dispersed to resume their revelries, now fueled with a new song to sing, warbling, "Ahay, ahoy, we're whompin' at the wingding" as they *danzenfreekenboingadoinga*-ed around the big main office.

Bagmo bounced over to Daphne, who stood with Brufyss and Mrs. Kookerly in the center of the room.

"Hey, Daphne! Wanna dance? C'mon, it's really *fun!*"

Daphne turned to Brufyss and Mrs. Kookerly. "Can I? Can I?"

Brufyss looked at Mrs. Kookerly, who returned his look with a "Why not?" expression. She knew Daphne's encounter with Barley had left her emotionally drained and saw no reason why her old friend shouldn't enjoy herself a bit.

"Sure, go ahead, Daphne!" shouted Brufyss over the noise. "Just keep an eye out and be ready in case we need you."

"Will do." She turned back to Bagmo. "Okay, let's go!"

"C'mon, then! Show me what you got, pretty mama!"

Bagmo and Daphne eased into the frenzied fray and were soon lost amid the sea of bobbing heads.

✳ ✳ ✳

Gerald Foon-Package sat in his attic laboratory, impatiently drumming his fingers on a tabletop and listening enviously to the rowdy celebrations below him. Where was Cheezy Fabsmaggle? It had been *ages* since Cheezy went down to the storage room for plates, cups, and utensils to aid in the consumption of the cure for excess hair growth, but he still hadn't returned. The huge covered pot simmered and bubbled, slowly cooling down. Unless the partygoers wanted to devour his lovingly concocted cuisine with their bare hands like cavemen, it was imperative that Cheezy supply them with a civilized means of devouring it. *Where is he? He should have been back a long time ago!*

Gerald rose from his chair, stalked to the head of the stairs, and shouted down the stairwell:

"*Hey!* Is anybody down there??"

Anybody *was* down there. So many anybodies were down there making so much noise that no one heard him shouting. Gerald's frustration was reaching the boiling point, hotter than the potful of cure for excess hair growth would be before too long.

"*Hey, Mr. Spuggett, Alpha Rae, anybody!* Can anybody hear me??"

No answer. The party raged on uninterrupted. Gerald raged on unheard.

＊

Bagmo led Daphne into the crowd of dancers, dodging flailing legs and bouncing bodies in their attempt to find an open patch of floor upon which to commence their own flailing and bouncing.

After a quick tutorial for Daphne, the two launched into a spirited rendition of the dance, accidentally smacking into nearby dancers and having a wonderful time.

"Hi, I'm Bagmo!"

"Hi, I'm Daphne!"

"Come here often?"

"Actually, I've never been here before."

"Oh, right! That's probably why I've never *seen* you here before! So, what brings you to Bumps & Spuggett this fine day?"

"I came here with Brufyss and Mrs. Kookerly so we could confront Barley Doodlebody!"

"Seems kinda like you don't like him very much! He seems okay to me; he helped rescue Marshall Farkpucker from a fate worse than death a little while ago."

"Well, he almost killed me a few years back!"

"Really? Wow! It's a good thing he didn't kill you, otherwise you'd be *dead* now! And you wouldn't be here at our party. See? Everything all works out in the end!"

"Yeah, I guess . . ."

Someone tapped on Daphne's shoulder. It was Frog Puppleman, standing awkwardly, smiling his crooked-yet-appealing smile, his face flushed with embarrassment.

"Frog! What a pleasant surprise!" Although he was Barley Doodlebody's brother, Frog had done nothing in the past to incur Daphne's wrath or rancor. "It's been years, hasn't it?"

"Yeah, *buddy!*"

"It looks like Councilman Puppleman wants to cut in on our dance, Daphne! Do you wanna dance with him for a while?"

"Is that true, Frog? Would you like to dance with me?"

"Yeah, buddy!"

Bagmo waved to them and made his way to the side of the room to catch his breath. Daphne and Frog waved back and were soon swallowed up in the frolicking maelstrom.

***

Brufyss and Mrs. Kookerly drifted near the newly opened double doors at the first-floor stairway. As Mrs. Kookerly watched the rambunctious celebration, Brufyss's attention was drawn to the big banner stretched across the top of the wall nearest them.

"What do you suppose 'It's not <u>what</u> you do, but what you do <u>with</u> it' means?"

Mrs. Kookerly looked up at the sign. "I haven't the slightest idea. It doesn't make any sense—like everything else around here."

"But if it doesn't make sense, then why is this banner so huge? Obviously it's there to be read; it must mean something important enough to warrant a huge banner, up high enough for everybody to see. I think I understand what 'From Stupidity Springs Lucidity' means, but 'It's not <u>what</u> you do, but what you do <u>with</u> it' has me completely bamboozled!"

"Don't sweat it, Brufyss. Why should you be concerned about a banner in a nuthouse?"

"But that's just the point! Do you have to be a crazy person to understand what it means? If not, then how come I don't understand it? It's beginning to drive *me* crazy!"

"If it's bothering you, why don't you ask someone?"

"Maybe I will! But I'll feel like an idiot if a nutcase knows something I can't figure out."

"Ask that guy over there." She pointed to Bagmo, who was leaning against the wall under the banner.

The couple approached the office quizmaster.

"Excuse me, son, but my name is Brufyss, and I'd like to ask you a question, if I might."

"Yeah, I know who you are—and you too." Bagmo pointed to Mrs. Kookerly. "Narducci just mentioned your names in a song he wrote a few minutes ago. You're the ones who don't like Mr. Doodlebody, right?"

Brufyss and Mrs. Kookerly exchanged glances.

"Uh, yeah, right! Mind if I ask you a question or two?"

"Is this a quiz? Sure, man, I love quizzes! But you gotta follow the rules. Only one question at a time. Otherwise, it just gets too confusing."

"I can well imagine. One question at a time, I promise."

"Okay then, I'm ready—*shoot!*"

"First of all, what's your name?"

"Ooh, I know this one! My name is Bagmo Maltgoggles!"

"One for one!" said Brufyss, giving Mrs. Kookerly a wink and Bagmo the benefit of the doubt that he'd know his own name.

"Okay, gimme another one!"

"All right, Bagmo, question number two: what does that banner hanging above us mean?"

Bagmo peered up at the huge motivational sign over their heads and read the words. "What does it mean?" he repeated contemplatively. His face lit up as the answer came to him: "I know, I know! It means *what it says*!"

"But what it says is, 'It's not <u>what</u> you do, but what you do <u>with</u> it'!"

"Um, is that a question?"

"No, that's what the sign says!"

Bagmo considered this for a moment, then smiled wryly. "Oh, I get it. This is a *trick* question! Okay, the answer is yes."

"Yes what?"

"Yes *what*? You can't ask, 'Yes what?' It doesn't mean anything!"

"Neither does that sign, Bagmo. I'm trying to figure out what the sign means when it says, 'It's not <u>what</u> you do, but what you do <u>with</u> it'!"

"I think what's important is what it doesn't mean."

"Okay, then what doesn't it mean?"

"Well, it doesn't mean just about everything in the world. That covers a lot of stuff!"

Brufyss wasn't getting it, but he stubbornly refused to let this deter him. "One more question: why is that sign there?"

"Mr. Spuggett put it there to give everybody something to think about while we're working."

"And have you thought about it?"

"Sure. Everybody has!"

"Well, what do you make of it?"

"I don't make anything of it—it's hanging up too high. But if I *could* make something of it, I'd make a tent."

"Look, Bagmo, here's what I'm getting at. When I read that sign, I'm not able to understand what it's talking about because it doesn't make any sense to me. I was hoping you might give me an idea because you've thought about it more than I have."

"So, what's your question?"

"Okay, let's take it one step at a time. Firstly, 'It's not <u>what</u> you do . . .'—what does that part of the phrase mean?"

Bagmo thought for a moment. "It means, 'Whatever it is you're doing, that's not *it*!'"

"*What's* not 'it'??"

"Whatever it is you're doing."

"But I'm not doing anything!"

"Right!" cried Bagmo triumphantly. "See? That wasn't so hard, was it?"

Brufyss didn't see but decided to press on anyway. "Okay, Bagmo, let's try the second half of the phrase: 'but what you do <u>with</u> it'—what does that part of the phrase mean?"

"It doesn't mean anything all by itself."

"Then what do you have to put *with* it to make it mean something?"

"Whatever it is you're *not doing*, of course! Hey, what do I get for answering all these dumb questions, anyway?"

Brufyss ignored Bagmo's question, intent upon having his own answered. "So, let me get this straight. What the banner means is 'Whatever it is you're not doing, then <u>that's</u> what you have to <u>do</u> something with!' Is that right?"

"More or less," replied Bagmo, now bored with this whole conversation.

Brufyss slapped his hand to his forehead in frustration. "Come on, Bagmo! Level with me. What do you know that I don't know?"

"Hey! That's not a fair question! In order for me to answer that, you'd have to tell me everything you know so I'd know everything you know. Then I'd have to compare that with everything I know and tell you all the stuff you don't know that I do know. I don't have that kinda time, dude! There's a party goin' on here, if you haven't noticed. Hey, Mrs. Kookerly, wanna dance? It's really fun!"

Bagmo grabbed Mrs. Kookerly by the hand and led her in a beeline for the center of the room, abruptly terminating the "dumb quiz."

✳✳✳

After handing Binky Bohoguss off to Old Man Spuggett, Barley stood by the wall outside of the old man's office, watching the merry antics of his tour group and the B & S employees. His attention was drawn to Brufyss and Mrs. Kookerly standing beneath the big banner on the western wall, Brufyss locked in discussion with Bagmo Maltgoggles. Barley wondered what the subject of this *tête-à-tête* could possibly be.

After a long discussion, Bagmo grabbed Mrs. Kookerly by the hand and hustled her into the revelers in the middle of the room, leaving Brufyss alone. Barley saw an opportunity to approach his former friend and try to clear the bad air between them. He set off for the spot where Brufyss stood lost in thought. He turned left at the corner and walked past the doorway to the attic stairs, suffering a minor collision with Gerald Foon-Package, who was heading downstairs in search of Cheezy Fabsmaggle.

"Oh! Sorry, there!" Barley grabbed Gerald to prevent him from toppling over. "Are you okay?"

"Yeah, no problem!" Gerald brushed himself off. "No harm done; could've happened to anybody. It's already happened to me once today."

"It's Gerald, right?"

"Well, *I'm* Gerald, if that's what you mean. You're that Doodlebody guy, right?"

"Right!"

"You haven't seen Cheezy Fabsmaggle, have you? He's supposed to help me bring the cure for excess hair growth down to the party. I've been up in my lab screaming for him to come back upstairs, but nobody can hear me over all this noise!"

"I haven't seen him since he went downstairs a while ago. Can I give you a hand with it?"

"Nah, thanks, that's Cheezy's job, and you're the guest of honor. I've gotta find him and get his butt back up here; he's probably just goofin' off, but I'm afraid the cure for excess hair growth is gonna get cold if we don't get it down here."

"From what I've been told, your cure for excess hair growth is worth waiting for. I hear you're quite the chef."

"I'm a scientist, actually, but thanks for the compliment. Food's been a tradition in my family goin' way back, and I've had lots of practice eatin' the stuff. Well, I gotta go—nice talkin' to ya, Mr. Doodlebody. See ya at the party!"

"If I see Cheezy, I'll tell him you're looking for him."

"Thanks!" Gerald headed for the back stairway.

As Barley took another step toward Brufyss, he was waylaid again. Alpha Rae put her hand out to stop him. She stared intently into his face, scrutinizing it closely, her own face wrinkled with a puzzled scowl. "So, you're Barley Doodlebody, right?"

"Yes, that's correct, ma'am," answered Barley politely, not wanting to ruffle the feathers of this famous grouch.

"And that Frog Puppleman character is your brother, right?"

"Yes, my half brother."

"Which half?"

"Oh, I dunno—the better half, probably."

"And who's that Brufyss Bathwater fellow over there? What's he doing here?"

"Brufyss? Well, he's an old friend of mine—at least he used to be. We had a falling-out a few years back, and he's been holding a grudge against me for a long time now."

"Hmmm, has he?" Her gaze was still steadfastly riveted on Barley's face. "*That's* not good."

Barley was uncomfortable with Alpha Rae's penetrating stare. She never took her eyes off his face, yet she seemed distracted somehow. "Uh, no, that's *not* good. I'm just on my way over to talk to him now, to try to straighten things out."

"Hmmm, you are, are you? Yes, that's good—you should do that."

"I certainly will, Alpha Rae. Will you excuse me, please?"

"Of course, go right ahead—and don't call me 'Alpha Rae'!"

Barley paused and looked at her questioningly. "I'm sorry, ma'am, what should I call you?"

"I . . . I don't know yet." She turned and wandered into the midst of the dancing throng.

Unnerved, Barley tried to push away the unsettling thoughts and concentrate on the task at hand: speaking man-to-man with Brufyss. Brufyss was still staring at the big banner as Barley approached him.

"Brufyss, can we talk?" Barley extended his hand.

Brufyss lowered his gaze from the banner and saw Barley's extended hand. He did not take it. "Talk about what, Doodlebody? What do you want?"

"Just to talk. I noticed you and Bagmo having a discussion a moment ago. Did he enlighten you on whatever subject you were talking about?"

"*Enlighten* me?" scoffed Brufyss. "How could a complete whacko enlighten me?"

"I wouldn't be too sure he's a whacko. You might be surprised—"

"Are you as loony as he is? Nothing that guy told me made any sense!"

"What kind of sense were you expecting him to make?"

"What are you talking about? No sense is *no sense*!"

"In one sense these people make *a lot* of sense, Brufyss."

"Doodlebody, you're starting to give me the creeps! You sound like that Bagmo guy I was just talking to. You've been hanging around with these idiots too long!"

"Not long enough, Brufyss. These people are not idiots. What did Bagmo tell you?"

Brufyss laughed derisively. "We were talking about that banner. I asked him to explain what the sign means. First, he told me the sign means what it says! Brilliant! When I asked him to be more specific, he told me it said, 'Whatever it is you're *not doing*, then *that's* what you have to *do* something with!' Can you understand that?"

"I can understand why *you* don't understand it. Let me ask you this: was what he told you wrong? Think about it carefully. Was it incorrect in any way?"

Brufyss thought hard for a moment. "Well, it was a little weird—but I suppose it wasn't exactly *wrong* . . ."

"Uh-huh, and if you think about it a little more, was *anything* he told you actually wrong or incorrect? No matter how weird it sounded to you?"

Brufyss thought hard again. "Well, no. I guess." He gave Barley a piercing stare. "What are you trying to say?"

"What I'm trying to say is that you're mistaking an alternative perspective for stupidity. What Bagmo told you made complete sense—to Bagmo. You're seeing things from a different perspective than he does. Bagmo makes his own kind of sense."

"Are you trying to mess up my head as a way of getting back at me for beating you today?"

"No, Brufyss. Earlier today I got caught in the same mix-up as you did with all this convoluted logic and alternative perspectives, and I was just as confused as you are now. Old Man Spuggett clued me in to what it was all about. If you want to understand it, then while you're here, you have to change the way *you* perceive things to the way *they* perceive things, and everything will make a lot more sense. That's what I'm trying to do."

Barley's words made Brufyss's conversation with Bagmo seem less obtuse, but Brufyss's understanding was still not clear. Plus, he was suspicious of Barley's motives. "What are you trying to pull, Doodlebody? It's too late to make amends for what you've done to me. The past is gone."

"I'd like to think that it's never too late to talk things out. What is the alternative?"

"The alternative would be for me to put your lights out."

"Would that make you feel better?"

"I don't know—but it might be worth a shot just to see!"

"Brufyss, I don't want to fight with you. I don't want any more bad blood between us. If I did, don't you think I would have taken some kind of action against you when you first arrived?"

"Are you telling me you're mellowing with age? What brought about this miraculous change of heart?"

"My realizing that you and I make better friends than we do enemies."

"Pity you didn't realize that forty years ago! It would have saved both of us a lot of grief."

"Yeah, it's a pity, Brufyss, but I realize it now, and now is better than never."

"I think 'never' is a little closer to reality for me."

"What would remaining enemies accomplish? Didn't you hear what Old Man Spuggett said? How all we have to show for our years as adversaries is a lifetime of wasted life? Well, I'm sick and tired of wasting my life! You were a great friend to me—I could always count on you. You were a better man than I was, Brufyss, because our friendship was the only thing that mattered to you, and I was too young, stupid, greedy, and self-centered to see, or to feel that way myself. Because of that, I played you for a sucker.

"But you not only succeeded in holding on to everything I tried to steal from you then, but you've continued to hold on through all these years, while I've succeeded in holding on to nothing!"

Brufyss stared at Barley. "Why are you telling me all this? What do you really want from me?"

"What I really want is for us to be friends again!"

"And what if I don't believe you?"

"Then I guess I'll have to prove it to you somehow. I want to make things right in my life—as right as I can, anyway. In my mind, the best way to start is to patch up our differences."

"And you think everything is gonna be just like nothing ever happened?"

"Of course not! But we've both got to start moving forward—"

BANG!!

The celebration screeched to a halt, and heads snapped around to pinpoint the source of the thunderous explosion. It was like no report ever made by any of Old Man Spuggett's nondestructive explosive devices, and it didn't come from within the old man's private office.

The silence was shattered by Narducci Palpatooti. "*Look! Look! Look! Look!*"

He pointed frantically at the doorway to Felicia Greenthing's office: there stood a large, craggy-faced, evil-looking man, surrounded by Simpleton Fabsmaggle, Bimbo Spazzgate, and Gerald Foon-Package, their arms pinned behind them and securely bound with electrical tape. All three were wide eyed and trembling with fear.

The evil-looking man was not smiling. He held a shiny, steel-gray handgun that he'd just fired into the ceiling, a wisp of acrid white smoke curling from the end of its snub-nosed barrel like a slowly writhing serpent.

35

"**B**illy! What the hell are you doing? Have you lost your mind?"

Barley stared quizzically at Brufyss. "Brufyss, do you know this guy? Is he with you?"

Brufyss kept his eyes riveted on the thug in Felicia's doorway. "That's Billy Jelly, and yes, he's with me—but this wasn't supposed to happen! Billy, I told you *no guns!*"

The evil-looking man's name set Barley back on his heels: Billy Jelly—or as he was tagged throughout the criminal underworld, "Smelly Billy" Jelly. Barley had heard of Smelly Billy, and the recollection sent a shiver through his body. Billy was one tough, vicious criminal—an out-of-towner, a freelancer who sold his sinister services to the highest bidder. If the venture was promising and potentially lucrative, he donated his time in return for a cut of the spoils.

He stood in the doorway of Felicia Greenthing's office, a gun in his hand and three terrified captives cowering in front of him.

"What's the problem, Bathwater? I'm just tryin' to attract some attention. It's too damn noisy in here!"

"Okay, you got our attention. Now put that gun away!"

"What are you doing upstairs, Billy?" cried Mrs. Kookerly from within the frightened crowd. "We told you to stay downstairs until we gave you the word."

"And miss all the fun up here? This seems to be where all the action is! There's nothin' downstairs but a bunch of empty rooms. Besides, it looks to me like you weren't gonna give me the word, anyway. Don't you think I like a good party, too?" Billy Jelly prodded Bimbo in the back with the barrel of his gun. "C'mon, boys, let's join the party. Why should these chumps have all the fun?"

The three captives awkwardly shuffled out through the doorway and into the main office, shepherded by the gun-wielding hoodlum.

"Billy, put that gun away! I told you there wasn't going to be any trouble!"

"Oh, there ain't gonna be no trouble, Bathwater. Not while I got this gun!"

"Billy, we only came here today to get Barley Doodlebody out of here," said Mrs. Kookerly. "These other people mean nothing to us. Let them go!"

"They don't mean nothin' to you, maybe, but to me they represent an excitin' new career opportunity."

"You're working for me here!"

"*Was* workin' for you, Bathwater," Smelly Billy replied with a sinister chuckle. "I've recently since seen fit to dissolve our partnership, seein' as how our individual objectives in comin' here today are now at cross-purposes."

"What do you mean?"

"I mean I'm through foolin' around with you and your two empty-headed women friends. What the hell do *I* care about this Doodlebody guy you're all so heated up about? What *I'm* heated up about is the fact that the owner of this dump is worth a few scillion bucks. As long as we're here, I feel compelled to score myself a hefty portion of 'em!"

"Don't be a fool, Jelly. You think Old Man Spuggett is gonna fork over a scillion dollars to a thug like you?"

"I dunno, Bathwater, why don't we ask him? He's right here."

Smelly Billy gave Cheezy Fabsmaggle a sharp poke in the center of his back with the barrel of the gun. "*Ow!* Hey, cut it out! I already told you, mister. I'm not Mr. Spuggett!"

"*Brufyss!*" whispered Barley. "That's not the old man. He's just a kid! It's one of the old man's employees dressed up to look like him!"

"This is a whole roomful of earning potential, Bathwater. I heard the mayor, a city councilman, and the chief of police was gonna be here today, too. We have a lot of collateral to negotiate with, and I don't think our old friend here"—he gestured at Cheezy—"would like to see anything bad happen to all these important people. We're standin' in a gold mine."

"No, no! This isn't a gold mine," corrected Narducci. "We manufacture radically stupid suggestions here!"

"Yeah, the gold mines are in a whole different part of the country," added Bagmo. "You're in the wrong place, mister."

"Shut up, creeps! I ain't in the wrong place!"

"Well, there goes the wingding—again," groused Bagmo.

Anger built inside Reverend Snortworthy as he watched the unfolding drama. "Your criminal intentions, sir, reveal you to be possessed of great evil. I entreat you now to cease this intrusion and intimidation. Fall to your knees and seek forgiveness for your sins and your transgressions. *Redeem thyself ere the yawning abyss swallows thee in vengeful retribution!* *So sayeth—*"

BANG!!

"That's what *I sayeth!*" mocked Billy, having fired another shot into the ceiling. The reverend shrieked and dropped to the floor.

So much for the righteous rebuke.

Most of the crowd hit the floor along with Reverend Snortworthy. Felicia curled into a fetal position and howled like an air raid siren. Faisal Herskowitz doubled over on the carpet, exploding with raucous belly laughter. However, Billy's shot ignited one employee in a way he never could have anticipated. Unable to suppress his gripping fear, Fandango Slamson sprang to his feet and took off, running madly around the big rectangular room, screaming, "*AAAAAAHH! AAAAAAHH!*"

Too stunned to react, Billy gawked in amazement at Fandango racing around the room at a speed he never imagined a human being capable of, and at the two employees on the floor reacting to his intimidation most peculiarly.

"Barley, this was not part of my plans at all," whispered Brufyss. "I told Jelly to wait downstairs and guard the door—that's it! He's doing all of this on his own now. I never wanted anyone to get hurt!"

"I can see that, Brufyss!" They scooted quickly to one side to avoid Fandango whooshing past them. "Your mistake was letting a thug like Smelly Billy Jelly work for you in the first place."

"But he came to *me*, Barley! He was in town and found out we were coming here today. He said he'd heard this place was crazy and wanted to see it for himself, for a good laugh! I thought I might be able to use the extra help, but I'll bet he intended to pull this off the whole time."

"That doesn't matter now. We've got to make sure he doesn't hurt or kill anyone—and we've got to keep him away from Old Man Spuggett."

"Where's the old man now?"

"He's with Dr. Pudbid and Chief Bohoguss in his office, probably scared out of his wits!"

BANG!!

Smelly Billy attempted to bring down Fandango with his next shot. The pitch of Felicia's air raid siren jumped an octave, and Faisal whooped with unbridled hilarity. Billy's shot slammed harmlessly into the north wall of the big main office; Fandango's amazing speed presented a mere blur to everyone. But Barley and Brufyss saw that the unscrupulous gangster was prepared to perpetrate not only mayhem but murder as well.

BANG!!

Billy fired off one more attempt to stop Fandango's supersonic lapping of the big room. Once again the shot missed, Felicia screeched, and Faisal cackled, but this time it was Mux Muggsley who could no longer contain his fear. Mux leaped to his feet, made a beeline for the side of the room, and began running the same course around its perimeter as Fandango, but in the opposite direction. Fandango screamed "*Aaaaaahh! Aaaaaahh!*" and Mux yelped, "*Yiy! Yiy! Yiy! Yiy!*" Felicia shrieked like a teenaged she-demon, and Faisal harrumphed like a hyena, creating a huge racket.

Despite the noise nearby, Fandango and Mux seized Billy's undivided attention as they headed for the southwest corner. Although they were approaching from opposite directions, their speeds would bring them to just about the same place at the same time. Billy calculated that Mux and Fandango would meet at the corner between the two doorways. He'd wait until they crossed paths and try to bring them both down with the same bullet—then he'd take care of those noisy weirdos on the floor.

The two speedsters were almost at the corner. Billy took aim at the spot and squeezed the trigger . . .

Barley realized Billy's intentions. "Mux, Fandango! *Look out!*"

BANG!!

To Billy's dismay, Fandango executed a high-speed turn to the right, disappearing down the stairway. His "Aaaahh! Aaaaah!" echoed in the hollow stairwell, fading into the downstairs distance.

Fandango was gone!

Mux reached the double doorway to Lollie's reception room and made a quick left turn, zipping through the waiting room and down the stairway there. His "Yiy! Yiy! Yiy! Yiy!" echoed in the hollow stairwell and faded downstairs. He, too, was gone.

The bullet slammed harmlessly into the corner, and Billy cursed in frustration as he watched the two escape to the first floor.

Felicia's screaming went hypersonic; nobody could hear her anymore. Had Gaggy the poodle still been there, he would have blown up. Faisal hee-hawed, hyperventilated, and passed out.

Mrs. Kookerly stood up in the middle of the prostrate crowd. "*Billy!* Stop this insanity, *now!*"

Billy turned the gun to her. "Shut up, lady! If you ain't with me, I got no problem puttin' you down. Get your hands up where I can see 'em!"

Mrs. Kookerly immediately complied, realizing that a further attempt at bravado would be a useless endeavor, and possibly a fatal one.

Brufyss panicked. "Barley, I gotta do something! I gotta do something *now!*"

"Go! Keep him distracted. I'm gonna see what I can do."

Brufyss stood and raised his hands over his head. "Leave her alone and deal with me, Billy. She's no threat."

"And neither are you, Bathwater." The thug trained his weapon on Brufyss. "No threat and no use to me! I got business to take care of here, and you're wastin' my time."

"So, you think you're gonna get a load of money out of Old Man Spuggett?" Brufyss laughed. "I've got news for you, Jelly. You've got the wrong man there! Take a good look at him. Does that guy look like he's a hundred years old to you?"

"A hundred and *three*," corrected Bagmo from his place on the floor.

Billy grabbed Cheezy by the collar of his bathrobe and roughly jerked him around so that he faced the gangster. "I got a *picture* of the old coot, and the picture shows him with white hair, wearin' a bathrobe. If this ain't him, then who is it?"

"My name is Simpleton! I've been tryin' to tell you that for the last hour. Mr. Spuggett gave me these clothes to wear because my own clothes got wet. My hair's white 'cause I got *flour* in it!"

"He's telling the truth, mister," confirmed Gerald. "I was there when it happened."

"Shut up, you!" Billy smacked Gerald on the back of his head with an open palm. "I don't give a damn *what* happened to him."

Suddenly, another loud voice boomed throughout the big room: "Stay thy treacherous hand, foul brigand! 'Tis I with whom thou must confer!"

Billy snapped to attention at the sound of this new, commanding voice, and he searched for its source. In the center of the room, moving slowly to stand next to Brufyss and Mrs. Kookerly, was the rumpled figure of His Honor, Mayor Roymul Wubbleduster.

With Smelly Billy Jelly's attention focused on Brufyss, Mrs. Kookerly, and now Mayor Wubbleduster, Barley crawled on his belly like a soldier under fire, making his way to Old Man Spuggett's private office from his spot under the big banner. He was boggled by the bravery—and perhaps the foolishness—the three were showing with their unarmed challenges to Billy's threats, but their time was running out. The company founder, Dr. Pudbid, and Chief Bohoguss had undoubtedly heard the gunshots out in the main office, and were most likely cowering behind the big desk or hiding in the closet. It would be only moments before Smelly Billy came looking for the old man. Time was running out for Old Man Spuggett, too.

Barley calculated the crook had fired off five rounds since his surprise emergence from the first floor. If his handgun held six, there was one left. If Billy fired ineffectually one more time, maybe the group could wrestle the weapon from him before he reloaded. Outnumbered, his possession of the gun was the only factor keeping him from being overpowered.

Was Billy aware of the number of shots he'd fired? If not, it would be important to keep him distracted so he didn't have the presence of mind to do the calculations himself.

But what if Barley was mistaken with his own calculations?

Whatever the case, he had to get to Old Man Spuggett's office to place himself between the company founder and the threatening crook. So far, he'd remained undetected. Mrs. Kookerly, Brufyss, and Mayor Wubbleduster were engrossed in debate with Billy and effectively screening Barley from the hoodlum's line of sight. He wended through the tourists and employees, gesturing for them to remain silent so they wouldn't give his presence away.

The broken door loomed closer . . .

***

Billy stared in amazement at the defiant, disheveled Mayor Wubbleduster, whose face was streaked with black hair dye from his fire-hose dousing, his hair blown out like a puffy dust mop.

"Who the hell are you?" Billy leveled the gun at the first magistrate's corpulent midsection. "And what the hell did you just say to me?"

Before the mayor could reply, Biff pulled himself off the floor and moved to the mayor's side. "He's Mayor Wubbleduster, mister, and he's with me!"

"Who the hell are *you* then?"

"I'm Biff Spoozma, the mayor's public relations advisor. You wanna speak to the mayor, you gotta go through me."

"Oh, so you're a big shot too, huh? Well, you certainly got the size for it! Welcome to our little gatherin', Mr. Big Shot. Now, both of you jerks put your hands up over your heads." The mayor and Biff complied with Billy's command, staring down their captor with defiant eyes.

The gangster scanned the rest of the crowd on the floor. Barley ceased his crawling and lay still. "It looks like I got just about everybody I need except for that city councilman and the chief of police. I don't see no cops here, so where's the councilman? You here, Councilman? We almost got ourselves a quorum!"

"Yeah, *buddy*!" shouted Frog, standing and placing himself between Daphne and the gun-toting criminal.

Daphne stared up at Frog with terror in her eyes. "Frog, what are you doing? Don't you realize you could get killed?!"

"Yeah, buddy!" Frog smiled wanly, gazing down at Daphne. He then raised his hands over his head and worked his way through the crowd to stand next to Biff, the mayor, Brufyss, and Mrs. Kookerly.

Barley realized to his horror that his dim-witted brother had voluntarily placed himself in harm's way.

"Oh, good! I got just about everyone, and it was much easier than I thought it would be."

"Vile knave! Holdest thee thine false and spiteful tongue and *be gone*! Thine evil purpose be feckless, as it be in kind egregious!"

"What're you blitherin' about, you fat creep? Speak English, or I'll blow your brains out!" Billy aimed his pistol at the mayor's head.

"He *is* speaking English!" Biff moved subtly to stand in front of the mayor. "He just told you to shut up and get out of here!" He'd made the translation without referring to his Elizabethan English dictionary.

"Oh, that's what he said, is it?" Billy leveled the gun at Biff. "Okay, Mr. Big Shot. Let's see what language your idiot mayor uses when I blow *your* head off!"

Billy cocked the hammer of his pistol and pointed the barrel directly into Biff's face. He slowly squeezed the trigger . . .

✴ ✴ ✴

Across the room, Barley scrambled on his belly, sluicing through the mushy carpet, past the remnants of Bimbo's shattered water cooler, finally reaching the doorway to the old man's private office. He slithered inside, stood up, and flattened himself against the wall, his eyes scanning the room. The old man, Dr. Pudbid, and Binky Bohoguss were nowhere in sight.

Sidestepping past the *Seize the Day! Suck the Moment!* poster on the wall, he peeked inside the open closet; it was empty, except for the old man's remaining bathrobes hanging limply on their hangers. He glared at the floor behind the massive desk, expecting to see the three crouched there. The space was occupied only by the old man's plush desk chair. He checked behind the curtains framing the two windows, then the interior of the big fireplace.

Nothing.

Now panicked and out of time, Barley realized that the trio had vanished into thin air.

Out in the main room, Brufyss knew that this nightmare was playing out because of his own bad judgment. "Jelly! If you're going to shoot someone, it had better be me, 'cause I'm going to kill you if you *don't*!"

Billy slowly pulled the pistol from Biff and trained it on Brufyss. His evil smile drilled a hole through Brufyss nearly as lethal as the bullet he was about to fire. "My, ain't we the gentleman! No problem—I'm sick of you shootin' off your big mouth!"

Mrs. Kookerly realized that Brufyss was about to die. "Billy, *please*! *NO!*" She leaped in front of Brufyss just as the thunderous report of the gunshot rang out—

BANG!!

Like a flash of lightning before the thunderclap, both Mrs. Kookerly and Brufyss were slammed by a flying body. They hit the floor hard from the jarring impact of the human projectile, who landed on top of them— and who'd taken the bullet in their stead.

Barley Doodlebody, his left shoulder bleeding from where the bullet had torn into it, rolled painfully off the two and lay on his back, breathing heavily and staring up at Brufyss. Brufyss scrambled to his knees and leaned over him.

"Brufyss, he's out of bullets!" gasped Barley hoarsely. "*Get him!*"

He let out a long sigh, closed his eyes, and lapsed into unconsciousness.

36

Only moments had passed since the main office of the Bumps & Spuggett building's second floor was the noisy scene of joyful celebration. The big room was now as quiet as a stone, everyone frozen in shock.

Barley Doodlebody had just been shot.

Brufyss knelt above Barley's prone form, trying to comprehend what had happened. Mrs. Kookerly lay on her back, staring blankly at the ceiling.

Frog Puppleman was the first to react. Seeing his brother lying stricken on the floor near his feet, he looked from Barley to Billy, and connected Barley's wound to Billy's firing of the gun. Anger oozed from him. "*Yeeeaaaah, buddy!*"

Frog lurched toward Billy, bowling over Cheezy, Bimbo, and Gerald as he charged past with the ferocity of a tornado. Billy pointed the gun at his enraged attacker and pulled the trigger.

Click.

No shot rang out. Barley had been right: the gun's firing chamber was empty. Frog was on Billy in an instant. Brufyss regained his senses enough to comprehend that Billy was now without firepower and Frog Puppleman was taking on the would-be murderer by himself.

"Get him! He's out of bullets!"

Biff and the mayor snapped out of their respective dazes and moved on the gangster.

"*YABETCHA!*" Dork struggled to his feet and rushed to the burgeoning scuffle to lend a ham-sized hand.

Reverend Snortworthy flashed back to his youth. In his bouncer days, he was no stranger to a good roughhouse. Having just witnessed his former employer take a bullet for an old friend, the good reverend jumped up with a rebel yell and vaulted over the sprawled people on the floor to "do unto others" with a vengeance.

Smelly Billy realized that just about every outsized individual in the room was joining the battle against him, his gun was out of bullets, and he was seconds from being overwhelmed. He lashed out viciously with the steel weapon and scored a crunching blow to the side of Frog's head.

Frog spun around drunkenly from the force of the blow, his head throbbing and his eyes seeing only brilliant, stabbing flashes of light as unconsciousness beckoned him yet again. He fell backward into Biff. Both hit the floor heavily.

"*Frog!*" Daphne surged toward the exploding fracas.

The others in the assault party were momentarily taken aback, which presented Billy with a split-second opportunity for escape. He swung out wildly with his gun-wielding hand, hitting no one but causing his assailants to hesitate for an instant. Staggering away, he turned to his rear and dashed toward Felicia Greenthing's office and the only means of escape of which he was aware in this unfamiliar building: the back stairway to the first floor.

"He's getting away!" cried Brufyss as Billy disappeared through Felicia's doorway. Biff scrambled to his feet and joined Brufyss, Dork, Mayor Wubbleduster, and Reverend Snortworthy in pursuit, smacking into each other as they tried to squeeze through the doorway simultaneously.

The delay caused by their confusion gave Billy time to charge through the doorway of the second-floor delivery entrance vestibule, slam the door behind him, and push the door's lock button. He took a deep, gasping breath and darted for the back stairs.

He knew where he had to go.

His pursuers clambered into Felicia's office and around the corner to the vestibule door. Brufyss grabbed and twisted the doorknob.

"It's locked! You two!" He pointed to Dork and Biff, the largest members of the posse. "Break the door down!"

"Ya, shure, yabet—"

BOOOM!

The door quivered under the blow but did not open.

"Again!"

BOOOM!

The wooden doorjamb cracked. The door still held.

"One more time!"

BOOOM! CRACK! CRASH!

The door slammed back on its hinges. One by one, the five big men burst through and scurried down the stairs. Smelly Billy had gained a sizeable lead on them. Undeterred, the five descended to the Bumps & Spuggett building's first floor.

✳✳✳

The group in the main office was finally shaken out of inaction. Mrs. Kookerly and Daphne knelt by Barley and Frog while Ebenezer, Narducci, and Bagmo ran to assist Gerald, Cheezy, and Bimbo out of their electrical tape bindings. The former hostages got up, brushed themselves off, and verified that no one else had been hurt.

"We've got to get Barley to a hospital!" cried Mrs. Kookerly, placing both of her hands over Barley's wound and applying pressure to stem the bleeding.

Daphne gingerly felt the huge welt on the city councilman's head. A trickle of blood ran down the side of his face. "Frog needs a doctor, too!"

"Dr. Pudbid! Where's Dr. Pudbid?!" shouted Rapunzel.

Faisal Herskowitz, now revived, pointed frantically at the old man's broken door. "I am seeing him and Mr. Spuggett to going inside of private office before now!"

Bagmo dashed to the doorway and scanned the room. "Nobody's in here!"

"What are we gonna do?" shrieked Felicia. "Oh my heavens, what are we gonna do?"

A voice boomed, the sound ricocheting off the walls like rolling thunder.

"All right! Everybody calm down!"

Standing majestically in the room's center, arms akimbo, hands resting on her hips and a stern scowl on her face, was purple-haired Alpha Rae Sapoopa-LaBoobis. "As Mr. Spuggett's executive secretary, along with the fact that Mr. Spuggett has apparently taken a powder for the moment, I'm taking over this operation."

"Oh, thank heaven," cried Felicia, still teetering on the brink of hysteria. "Alpha Rae is going to save us all!"

"Felicia, *shut up*, or I'm gonna knit you into a sensible outerwear ensemble!"

"Yes'm."

"Listen up! I want all the men to help Mr. Doodlebody and Councilman Puppleman. Carry them out to the reception room and lay them on the two sofas! Hurry! *Go*! The rest of us will prepare the reception room to receive the injured parties. *Everybody* will stay on the lookout for that crook!"

They hurried into Lollie's reception room. Under the benevolent gaze of the company founders' portraits, they grabbed throw pillows from the chairs and piled them onto the sofas.

Out in the main office, the men hoisted the unconscious Barley and Frog; Daphne and Mrs. Kookerly assisted them. The latter had removed her jacket and was using it to apply pressure to Barley's shoulder wound. Daphne continued stroking Frog's hair, using the sleeve of her blouse to dab the trickle of blood on his face.

The two brothers were carefully laid on the sofas. Lollie pulled her chair out from behind the reception desk, offered it to the executive secretary, and Alpha Rae sat down, eyeing the two wounded brothers possessively; it was apparent she was taking on the job of supervising the two injured men, although both Daphne and Mrs. Kookerly continued their ministrations. After handing the charge of Margaret over to Narducci, Noodles took up a sentry position atop the stairway, occasionally casting a concerned glance at her stricken boss.

Narducci took Margaret to one corner and sat on the floor with her, quietly entertaining the frightened little girl with soothing songs and melodies. The rest of the employees and tourists stood in small groups, feeling helpless.

"We've got to find something to wrap Barley's shoulder and Frog's head," said Mrs. Kookerly. "If we don't, they could bleed to death."

"Right you are," agreed Alpha Rae, "and we need to get them water."

"That's what I was doing when that guy surprised us," said Bimbo ruefully. "I was getting a water bottle to bring upstairs for the water cooler. I had to leave it down there when he tied us up!"

"Then we're gonna have to go back and get it. And we've got to find a large quantity of fabric that we can make bandages from."

She thought for a moment. Her eyes brightened behind her big eyeglasses.

"There are curtains in Mr. Spuggett's office. Cheezy, Bagmo, get over there, tear down those curtains, and bring them back here. Bimbo, go get that water bottle!"

"I don't wanna go back down there by myself, Alpha Rae," protested Bimbo. "If that guy's still got a gun, he might kill me!"

Alpha Rae considered this. "There are some very competent—and very *big*—members of our group chasing after that thug, Bimbo. You'll be safe, but both of these men right here are liable to die if we don't get them some water."

"I'll go downstairs with Bimbo," offered Gerald. "If there are two of us, it'll be safer!"

"All right—you two get down there and bring that water bottle back."

"I'll go with Bimbo and Gerald." It was Yump. "If there are three of us, it'll be safer than two of us!"

"All right—you three get down there and bring that water bottle back."

Roland Chumbuckets finally saw a way of contributing. "Mizz Sapoopa-LaBoobis, I want to help! I was downstairs earlier today, and now I know my way around, too."

"And," added Yump, "if there are *four* of us, it'll be safer than three of us!"

"All right, enough! You *four*—and nobody else!—get down there and bring that water bottle back upstairs as fast as you can. But if there's any trouble, get out of there and run! Mr. Doodlebody and Mr. Puppleman tried to be heroes, and look where it got them. Now go!"

Yump, Gerald, Bimbo, and Roland set off across the big room.

"*Wait!*" cried Mrs. Kookerly, jumping from Barley's couch and stopping in the double doorway. "You've got to be extra careful. There's someone else besides Billy down there!"

Alpha Rae scowled at Mrs. Kookerly. "You mean you brought *more* people with you?"

"Yes, one more. He came along with Billy. It wasn't Brufyss's or my idea."

"Oh, that's just great! You got any more surprises you wanna tell us about?"

"No! That is, no, there are no more surprises. I've told you everything."

"She's telling the truth; I can vouch for that," verified Daphne.

"All right then," yelled the executive secretary to the four out in the main room, "you heard what the lady said: be on the lookout for someone *else* down there!"

Yump cried, "Hold on a second!" and dashed into his cubicle. He emerged holding one of the javelins he used for target practice. "Anybody messes with us now and they'll end up as shish-kebab! Okay, Mizz Sapoopa-LaBoobis, we're ready to go."

"Look after yourselves, and each other as well." Alpha Rae turned her attention to the two unconscious brothers lying on the couches. "And I'm going to be looking after you."

Cheezy and Bagmo stood in the broken doorway of Old Man Spuggett's private office and peered into the room. "Wow! Those curtains are really big," said Cheezy, sizing up the heavy red draperies that framed the two windows. "It's gonna take a lot of work to get 'em down. C'mon, Bagmo, you take one window and I'll take the other."

Cheezy ran to the window behind Old Man Spuggett's desk while Bagmo took the window next to the big fireplace. For Cheezy, the job would be relatively easy: he could stand on top of the low credenza beneath his window, thereby giving himself an easier reach to the curtain rod overhead.

Bagmo didn't have a cabinet or a stepladder to stand on. He decided to avail himself of one of the old man's desk chairs. Pulling it over to the window, he stepped onto the seat and reached up to unfasten the drapes. The chair's added height still didn't give him the elevation he needed. Standing on his tiptoes, Bagmo strained to get a hand or even a finger on the elusive curtain rod. Despite his best efforts, he simply wasn't tall enough. He knew Cheezy would fare no better; Cheezy was shorter than he was!

Bagmo stared in frustration at the curtain rod above him.

"Here, Mr. Maltgoggles, maybe I can help you with that. I think my reach is a bit longer than yours."

Bagmo looked down at Old Man Spuggett, who stood next to the chair, peering up at him. At the old man's side was Dr. Pudbid.

"Thanks, Mr. Spuggett! I guess I'm just not tall—*hey*! You're Mr. Spuggett. You're *here*!"

"That I am, Mr. Maltgoggles. Dr. Pudbid and I have actually been here all along, though not necessarily in this room."

Cheezy turned from his curtain and saw the two old gentlemen. "Mr. Spuggett! Dr. Pudbid! We thought you disappeared. We were searching all over for you!"

"Not *quite* all over, Simpleton. But why are you dismantling the curtains in my office?"

"Oh, right!" Bagmo remembered their urgent mission. "Someone shot Mr. Doodlebody and hit Councilman Puppleman on the head! Alpha Rae sent us here to get your curtains to use for bandages."

"Spuggy, I've got to help them," Dr. Pudbid announced.

Old Man Spuggett ushered Bagmo off the chair and jumped on himself. "I just knew something terrible was going to happen when I heard the gun! How badly are they hurt?"

"Well, they're still alive, but unconscious."

"Where's the man with the gun now?"

"He ran down the back stairs to get away. The *big* guys ran after him."

"So he's downstairs! Come on, boys, let's finish tearing down these drapes. Puddles, you'd best attend to Mr. Doodlebody and the councilman. Where are they, Bagmo?"

"Over in Lollie's room. Alpha Rae's in charge."

"Bless her soul. Puddles, be on your way!"

Dr. Pudbid dashed out through the broken door of Old Man Spuggett's private office. *Finally! Somebody needs me!* But the reason he was now so desperately needed troubled him greatly—and he'd left his black medical bag on the floor of Roland's tour bus.

* * *

Brufyss, Dork, Reverend Snortworthy, Mayor Wubbleduster, and Biff thundered down the back stairway to the first floor. Now that Billy was unarmed, the pursuers felt sure they could overpower him.

If they could catch him. "Does anybody know where we're going?" puffed Brufyss as they neared the bottom of the stairs.

"Ya, *shure*!"

"We'll follow you!"

The group reached the first floor, and Brufyss tried the double doors of the first-floor delivery entrance. They were locked, just as he'd discovered when he first arrived and tried opening them from the outside. He suddenly raised his hand for silence.

"Listen!"

A door slammed in the distance. The sound was so faint that it was only possible to pinpoint the general direction from which it came. "He's down here! Dork, lead the way!"

The big Viking bolted down the hallway, followed by the rest of the group. The passage was brightly lit, as daylight still poured through the window. Reaching the end of the corridor, they faced the storage room's metal doorway and the continuation of the hallway to the right. (*Figure 3*) Dork led them in this direction, making the sharp right turn which abruptly turned into another right turn with another closed doorway in the left corner.

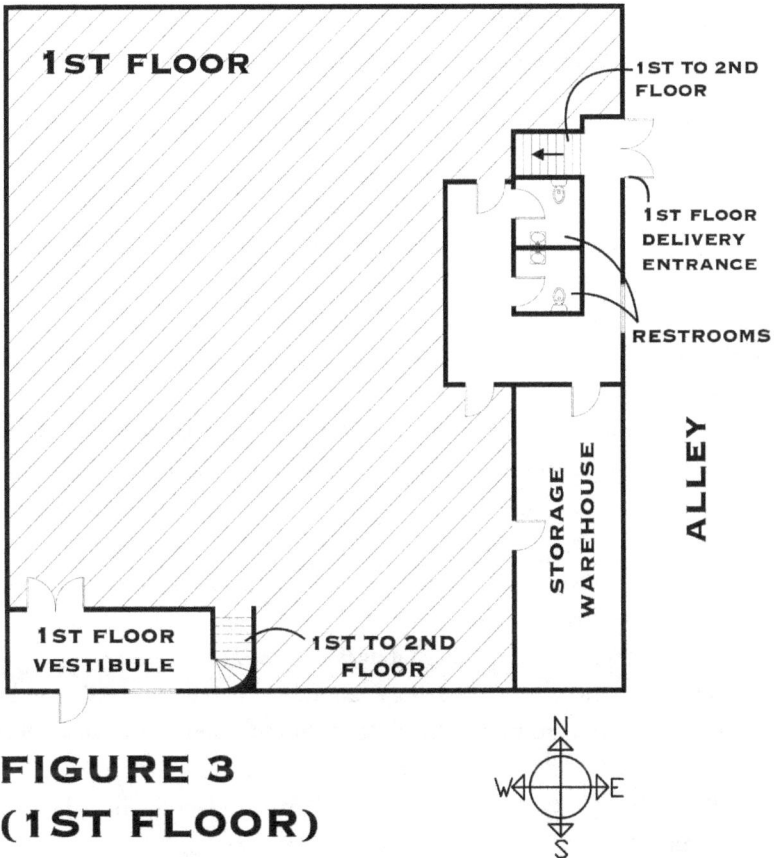

FIGURE 3
(1ST FLOOR)

Dork tried the door. Locked.

They ran down the length of the restroom corridor, hurling open the restroom doors. Both rooms were empty. Another closed door faced them at the end of this corridor. It too was locked.

"Dork, is there anywhere else he could have gone?"

"Ya, shure!"

He darted back down the hall to the storage room. The door swung open easily, and the group poured into the room one by one.

"Everybody, spread out! If he's in here, we'll find him!"

They all split up, searching the aisles of racks and shelves. At one point Reverend Snortworthy was tripped by a large water bottle abandoned in the center of an aisle, but the group found nothing to indicate Smelly Billy's presence in the room.

The four congregated in the center of the room, out of breath and exhausted. "That guy has . . . just up and . . . disappeared on us!" lamented Biff between gasps for air.

"No, he hasn't," objected Brufyss. "He's got to be in this building somewhere!"

"'Tis not a thing of certainty!" countered Mayor Wubbleduster. "The villain hath, mayhaps, a path to the outside procured—and thence to freedom!"

"The mayor says, 'He may have left the building and gotten away,'" translated Biff, again without the use of his dictionary. He was getting good at this!

"I don't think he's going anywhere until he gets what he wants out of Old Man Spuggett," argued Brufyss. "I know Billy; he's greedy. This is his chance to make the biggest score of his life, and don't forget: he reloads that gun, and all bets are off again!"

Suddenly, from over by the western wall of the room, Dork cried out, "Ya, shure, yabetcha!"

The others scrambled to see what he was seeing. He stood next to a gap in the shelving along the wall, staring at another closed door. Could this be the door they heard slamming in the distance from the foot of the back stairs?

Brufyss swallowed hard, his stomach knotted in apprehension. "Okay, boys, I'm going to try this door. You with me?" All nodded. "Here we go—be sure to whisper from now on."

He grasped the doorknob and gave it a gentle turn. A metallic *click* disengaged the latch. The door was unlocked!

Brufyss eased the door open gently and poked his head through into a semi-darkened hallway. The corridor ran to his right for twenty feet or so, terminating in a closed door. To his left, the corridor ran for another twenty feet and made an abrupt right turn. Unlike the bare concrete floors leading to the storage room and restrooms, the floor of this hallway was covered with a dark, dusty carpet.

Biff strained to peek over Brufyss's shoulder. "What can you see out there?" he whispered.

"Just an empty hallway. It looks clear."

He eased the door open and stepped into the hallway. A little light streamed from around the corner to the left. The overhead fluorescents weren't on; perhaps sunlight was glancing through a window somewhere. Slowly, quietly, Brufyss tiptoed down the left portion of the hall toward the source of the light. His compatriots emerged one at a time from the storage room and followed.

They neared the end of the hall, about to make the right-hand turn that would take them into parts unknown.

"Okay, boys, here we go . . ."

They rounded the corner and slammed to a dead stop. Billy Jelly stood in the center of the corridor, his gun leveled at them. He calmly surveyed his pursuers with a sneering, triumphant smile, although his face now sported a series of nasty welts from his scuffle with Frog Puppleman. Nonetheless, his attitude was haughty as he addressed the stunned group.

"Hello again, you stupid bunch of creeps! Lookin' for me, eh? Well, ya *found* me!"

"My son, you've already shot one person, injured another, and you're greatly outnumbered," said Reverend Snortworthy. "You're digging yourself into a hole you'll never be able to climb out of."

"Diggin' my own grave—is that what you're sayin', preacher man? Well then, I might as well dig it deep enough for *all* of us to fit in, and the first one o' you twerps to make a false move is gonna be the first one in the hole! You was havin' a little party when I came upstairs; I hope you're still in the mood, 'cause now you're gonna join me in a little party I'm havin' down here. Let's go!"

They had no choice but to comply. They had no idea if he'd reloaded the gun. He might be bluffing, but if not, Billy could kill them with his eyes closed at this range.

The thug motioned the five pursuers to proceed down the hallway in the same direction they'd been traveling, further into the depths of the first floor.

37

Cheezy Fabsmaggle stood on the credenza behind Old Man Spuggett's desk and unfastened the window curtain. "That guy with the gun thought I was *you*, Mr. Spuggett!"

"Yes, Simpleton," replied the old man as he assisted Bagmo with the other curtain. "That wasn't a joke that stayed funny very long, was it?"

"No, sir! But he wants to get money from you, Mr. Spuggett—a lot of money!"

"Hmmm, we'll see . . ."

"Mr. Spuggett, where did you and Dr. Pudbid go when we were all looking for you?" asked Bagmo. "We couldn't find you anywhere, but no one saw you go anywhere either! How did you just disappear like that?"

"Many are the mysteries an old man like me accrues and carries in the course of a long lifetime," he said cryptically. Then he smiled. "Can you boys be trusted to keep a secret?"

"Oh yeah!" cried Bagmo excitedly. "I *love* secrets—even more than quizzes!"

"Me too!" enthused Cheezy.

"Well, I'll share my secret with you; I may have to reveal it to just about everyone fairly soon."

"Can we be first?" asked Cheezy.

"You can be first because you're the closest! Are we finished taking down the curtains?"

"I am!" Cheezy held up the bulky drapery triumphantly.

"I think we are too, sir!" said Bagmo, surveying the curtain he and Old Man Spuggett had taken from its window.

"Come with me, but we must be quick. As soon as you see what I'm going to show you, we'll run these curtains to Ms. Sapoopa-LaBoobis."

He moved to the half-opened doorway of his office closet. "Simpleton, you may remember this closet from a while ago, when we put together your current wardrobe ensemble. But this closet is more than just a closet." He beckoned his two employees to look inside. "See anything?"

"Uh-uh! Just some bathrobes, a couple pairs of bedroom slippers, and a basketball," replied Bagmo. "Are we supposed to see anything more than that?"

"Not yet. But how about *now*?" The old man stepped into the closet and pulled the hanging bathrobes to one side. He pushed firmly on the closet's rear wall. The wall swung open and inward like a door, revealing a narrow staircase winding downward. (***Figure 5***)

"*Holy cow!*" cried Cheezy. "You've got a secret door in your office closet!"

"That I do, Mr. Fabsmaggle. I'd always dreamed of having a secret door—a secret door to a secret room, where I could hide and no one would be able to find me."

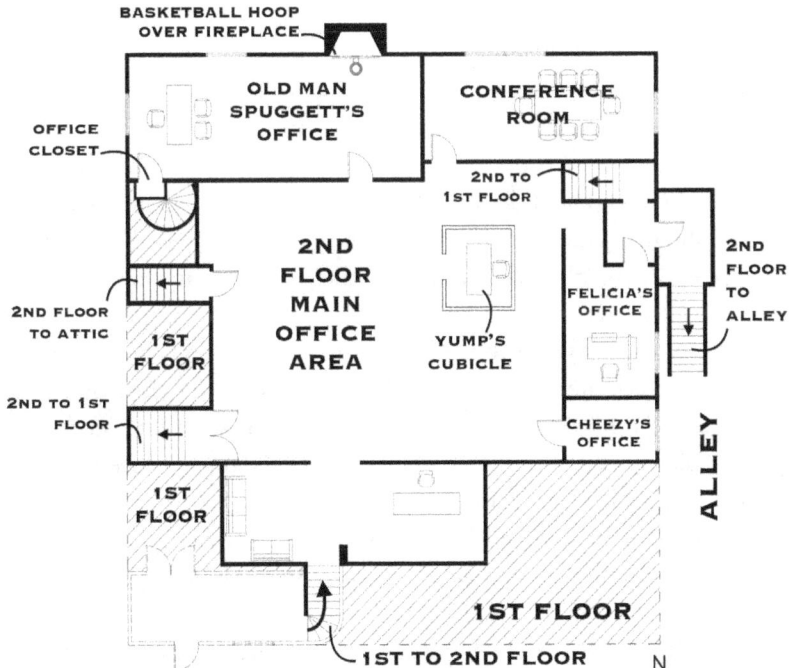

**FIGURE 5
(2ND FLOOR)**

Bagmo marveled at the hidden doorway. "I think *everyone* wants one of those," he said.

"Well, years ago, when we built this building, I vowed that just for the fun of it I'd make my dream come true—and here it is! But it doesn't actually lead to a secret room."

"Where does it go?

"To a couple of rooms directly below us: what used to be Mr. Bumps's office, and the old Bumps & Spuggett library. The doorways down there are hidden too, behind great-big bookshelves."

"Ooh, could we try it out?" asked Bagmo. "I've never been in a secret passageway before, and I've never been anywhere downstairs except the restroom and the storage room."

"Not just yet, Mr. Maltgoggles. I'm sure you'll have your chance in due time, but we have more important things to accomplish first."

"And nobody else knows about this?"

"Just Dr. Pudbid, Chief Bohoguss, and the two of you. Mr. Bumps used to know about it; his office was on the first floor, and we'd use the secret passage to go back and forth to visit each other without the employees being aware of it." He gave the boys a conspiratorial wink. "Nobody ever suspected that Mr. Bumps and I were goofing off during business hours—it was wonderful! But Mr. Bumps has been gone a long time now, and I haven't used the passageway in years."

The old man pulled the secret door closed. "This is where the doctor, Chief Bohoguss, and I disappeared to when that man with the gun came into the main office. I didn't want the little policeman to get hurt, so we got him out of here and took him down there. Boys, we must keep the existence of this passageway to ourselves for the moment. Besides, we've wasted too much time talking here. We've got to get these curtains over to Alpha Rae, and I have some very important information for everybody."

A look of deep concern was etched into his ancient face. His two employees stared at him questioningly.

"When Dr. Pudbid and I were downstairs, I peeked out the library door to look around. There's a rear entrance to the building close by the library, and I saw a fellow—a *different* fellow from the one with the gun—putting a padlock and chain on the door. If he's done the same for the other entryways, then I believe we've been locked inside the building, and all the windows on that floor are barred. None of us will be able to get out."

✳ ✳ ✳

Bimbo, Gerald, Yump, and Roland cautiously descended the back stairway to the building's first floor. Yump led the way, brandishing his javelin.

"Let's keep our eyes and ears open down here, fellas!" warned Roland.

Gerald: "Will do!"

Bimbo: "Righto!"

Yump: "Got it!"

"Keep a lookout for that Billy Jelly guy, and the other person Alpha Rae told us about too!"

"Will do!"

"Righto!"

"Let 'em come!" sneered Yump, fingering his javelin. "I'll turn 'em into fondue!"

"And watch out for *our* guys!"

"Should I kill them too?"

"No, Yump, we want to help them if we can!"

"Got it!"

Gerald: "Will do!"

Bimbo: "What's fondue?"

As they passed the window in the hallway, Roland noted a golden cast to the sunlight streaming in; it was late afternoon.

"Hey, Bimbo, what exactly happened when that bad guy showed up?" asked Yump as they trudged along. "Did he surprise you guys? Did he hurt you?"

"Well, yes and no. Yes, he did surprise us, and no, he didn't hurt us—at least not until he wrapped us up with that electrical tape. We almost got ourselves electrocuted, man!"

"Bimbo, you can't get electrocuted from electrical tape," corrected Gerald. "Electrical tape is supposed to keep you from getting electrocuted."

"Oh yeah, Mister Smarty-Pants Scientist? Then how come I couldn't feel my arms?"

"'Cause he wrapped the electrical tape around us so tightly that it was cutting off the circulation."

"Well, it sure *felt* like I was being electrocuted!"

"But didn't you see Billy coming?" asked Roland. "Why didn't you run?"

"He snuck up on us!" The group reached the door to the storage room. "He didn't come through this door; he came through the other one—the one that's always locked. We weren't paying any attention to that door, and besides, we didn't think anyone else was down here."

As they entered the storage room, Bimbo pointed toward the door in the room's western wall, the locked one Roland had noticed on their earlier visit.

"That one, eh?" mused Roland. "Unless Jelly Boy had a key, that would mean it unlocks from the other side."

"When that guy captured us I had to leave the water bottle in the middle of the aisle," said Bimbo. "I'll just go get that one again."

"I'll go get cups for the water," added Gerald, "and the plates and silverware, just in case we can start up the wingding again."

Yump planted himself by the storage room entrance, clutching his javelin tightly with both hands. "I'll stand guard. Any bad guys try to get by me, I'll make Swiss cheese out of 'em!"

"Yump, if anyone was going to threaten us, I don't think they'd come through that door," said Roland. "I think they'd probably come through the door over there." He pointed to the door in the west wall.

"Yeah, you're probably right. I should guard that door—is that what you're saying?"

"Yup!"

"That's *Yump*!" Yump walked down the aisles until he reached the west door. "Hey, this door's wide open!"

They scrutinized the dim hallway beyond. "Wow! I'll bet that's where that Jelly Belly guy ran when he escaped down here," said Yump.

"And I'll bet that's where our guys chased him," added Roland.

"In fact, I'll bet they've probably caught the guy by now."

Roland's curiosity began to get the better of him again; he'd been itching to explore the first floor's hidden depths since his first trip, and now he finally saw his chance. "Y'know, Yump, none of our guys has any weapons, but we've got your javelin. Maybe we should give them a hand bringing that guy back upstairs! Whaddaya say?"

"I don't see why not!"

Roland shouted across the room: "Hey, Bimbo, Gerald! Do you guys need any help? If not, Yump and I are gonna go help catch the bad guy!"

"Nah, I'm ready to head back upstairs!" shouted Bimbo. "I got the water—for the *third time* today!"

"I got everything I need," shouted Gerald. "I'll go with Bimbo."

"Okay, then we're gonna take off! Be careful, and we'll see you back upstairs."

"Righto!"

"Okay, Yump, let's go get ourselves a bad guy!"

Yump smiled and nodded. The two would-be bad-guy apprehenders took their first steps into the dark hallway, having completely forgotten that *two* bad guys lurked somewhere ahead . . .

✳ ✳ ✳

As Alpha Rae kept a quiet vigil, her head spun with a kaleidoscope of fragmented thoughts, memories, and distorted images—disconnected, yet seemingly related. They drew her, combining to move her forward and somehow pull her backward. She just wasn't able to put her finger on what it all meant or where it was heading.

She shared the room with the remaining Bumps & Spuggett employees and tourists who were not currently occupied with running errands or pursuing enemies, as well as Mrs. Kookerly and Daphne. Everyone in the room stared forlornly at the injured brothers, contemplating how the joyful celebrations of just a short while ago had degenerated into the serious situation that faced them now.

Dr. Pudbid dashed into the room. "Where are they?!"

"Simmer down, sawbones," growled Alpha Rae. "They're right here— not gallivanting all over who-knows-where like *you*! Where the hell have you been?"

"Mr. Spuggett and I were attending to other important matters, and were unaware of what occurred. We've only just heard."

"Then get busy! These guys aren't getting any better with you standing around!"

The doctor was incredulous. "I actually have your *approval* to examine them?"

"Do I look like a doctor to you?"

He checked each patient and made a quick diagnosis of the extent and seriousness of their wounds. "You've done well to get them in here and make them comfortable as quickly as you did. From what I can see, neither has injuries that are life-threatening, but we've got to get some water in here for them right away."

"Bimbo went downstairs to get some water a few minutes ago," offered Narducci.

"Good! We need to rehydrate them and clean their wounds. Mr. Spuggett and two of your fellow employees are bringing something to make bandages; that'll do the trick until we can get them out of here for some proper medical treatment."

Old Man Spuggett, Cheezy, and Bagmo entered the room with the curtains. "But as you know, that won't be possible for a while yet, Puddles." Old Man Spuggett addressed the assembled group. "Ladies and gentlemen, I don't want to alarm you, but I must inform you: it appears we've been padlocked into the building by those two crooks downstairs."

He saw the dismay on everyone's faces.

"I'm sure we'll come through this with flying colors in the end, but for now, let's just stay together and try to remain calm. Here, see what you can do with these."

The dismantled draperies were handed over to Mimsy and Rapunzel.

"Start tearing those curtains into strips!" ordered Alpha Rae. Everyone joined to prepare the fabric in an effort to help and also take their minds off their new dire predicament.

Mrs. Kookerly wore a look of confusion. "You saw Sauce Fingerbanana? How did you do that? He didn't come upstairs with Billy!"

"So, those are the names of our two adversaries, eh? Yes, we did see this 'Sauce' Fingerbanana you're talking about, Mrs. Kookerly. As to *how* we did it, I'm sure you'll learn that in a short time."

"Me and Bagmo already know," boasted Cheezy.

"Cheezy, *shut up*, will ya?" cried Bagmo.

"Well, Mr. Spuggett brought it up first."

"Hey! We've got the water out here!"

"Ebenezer! Get out there and give Bimbo a hand," barked Alpha Rae. "Don't break the bottle again. Faisal, Narducci! Get the water cooler!"

Ebenezer relieved Bimbo of the heavy water bottle while Faisal and Narducci placed the water-cooler cabinet upright in the center of the floor. The four lifted the heavy bottle and turned it upside down, placing it securely on top of the cabinet.

"Cups, Gerald! *Cups!*"

Gerald gave two of the packaged paper cups to Lollie, who filled each cup with the precious liquid. The executive secretary motioned for Lollie to give the cups to Mrs. Kookerly and Daphne. "See if you can get the boys to drink a little of that water. *You!*" She pointed to Rapunzel. "Take a couple strips of this curtain and soak them to use as wet towels. Give them to Dr. Pudbid!"

"Where's Yump?" asked Mimsy of Gerald and Bimbo. "He went

downstairs with you two, didn't he? Why didn't he come back with you?"

"Yump and Roland stayed down there to look for the bad guy," answered Bimbo.

"But that guy had a gun! They could be killed!"

"It's okay," Gerald reassured her. "Yump has his javelin with him."

"I don't believe a javelin is a match for a gun," said Old Man Spuggett. "Oh dear, I wish those boys hadn't done such a foolish thing!"

Mrs. Kookerly and Daphne were having some success getting Barley and Frog to drink the water. The two injured men seemed to be reviving. Frog began to moan softly, while Barley moved his head slowly from side to side.

At Frog's pained vocalizations and Barley's first tentative movement, Alpha Rae's head began spinning anew. She was dragged down into a thick fog, swept around and around with unseen voices and sounds beckoning to her, taunting her, entreating her, rebuking her, beseeching her, in a swirling maelstrom of rushing, gushing, tumbling, reemerging remembrance.

***

Roland and Yump stood in the hallway just outside the second doorway to the storage room. "Listen!" hissed Roland. "Do you hear anything?"

They strained their ears for any sound that might indicate someone nearby was pursuing them. "Nope," whispered Yump, "I think we're cool."

"I want to check something before we start. Stay where you are for just a second more, okay?"

Roland moved down the dim hallway to the right, toward the door that terminated the corridor in that direction. He reached it and saw that the door locked from the side on which he was now standing. He grasped the doorknob with one hand and gave it a clockwise turn; the knob offered no resistance, unlocking with a *click* as he twisted it.

Roland pushed the door open wide enough to poke his head through, and stared the length of the restroom corridor. Just as he'd suspected in his earlier exploration, this door acted as a partition, closing off the restroom hallway from the interior office complex. The closed door at the opposite end probably led to the other portion of the office complex—a back door to the restroom hallway.

He returned to Yump's position, leaving the partition door half open. "Okay, Yump, I found out what I wanted to know. Let's go!"

They tiptoed down the hallway in the opposite direction, unknowingly following in the footsteps of Brufyss, Biff, Dork, Mayor Wubbleduster, Reverend Snortworthy—and Billy Jelly. Roland determined they were moving toward the front of the building. Reaching the end of the hallway, they stopped and poked their heads around the corner. Another long, straight, and empty corridor led away in an east-to-west direction, following the portion of the building that fronted Clown Balls Avenue. This was the side the tour group had entered when they first arrived. Roland's bus would be parked outside at the curb.

Ahead of them in the left wall was a single open portal. A shaft of natural light streamed through the door from a window looking out onto the street and fell across the floor in front of them, illuminating another single doorway directly across the hall. They eased past the first two doors. Both rooms were vacant offices. The office looking onto the street featured an opaque window that appeared to be barred, and the room across the hall was dark and windowless.

They moved further down the corridor, past a second door located a few feet beyond the first on the right-hand side. This room was also vacant and windowless; Roland surmised that the absence of windows in these two right-side offices meant they were located in the center of the first floor's interior. In this office, the wall opposite the doorway contained another closed door. *There must be another room or hallway beyond it*, Roland thought.

They approached the end of the corridor. It terminated straight ahead with a large, barred, opaque window—Guggbutt Boulevard had to be outside—and the corridor made another sharp turn to the right. (*Figure 6*)

In the left corner was a set of closed double doors, most likely the locked doors the tour group had seen in the downstairs vestibule when they first entered the building. They reached the end of this southern hallway and stopped at the corner.

"Hear anything?" whispered Roland as they prepared to follow this new passageway.

"Hey, I think I do!"

They froze and listened. The drone of human voices was barely audible in the next corridor. It seemed to emanate from a doorway on the left side of the hall, in a room just beyond a wide staircase that led up to the second floor—probably the same staircase Daphne used when she made her entrance.

"They're in that room on the left!"

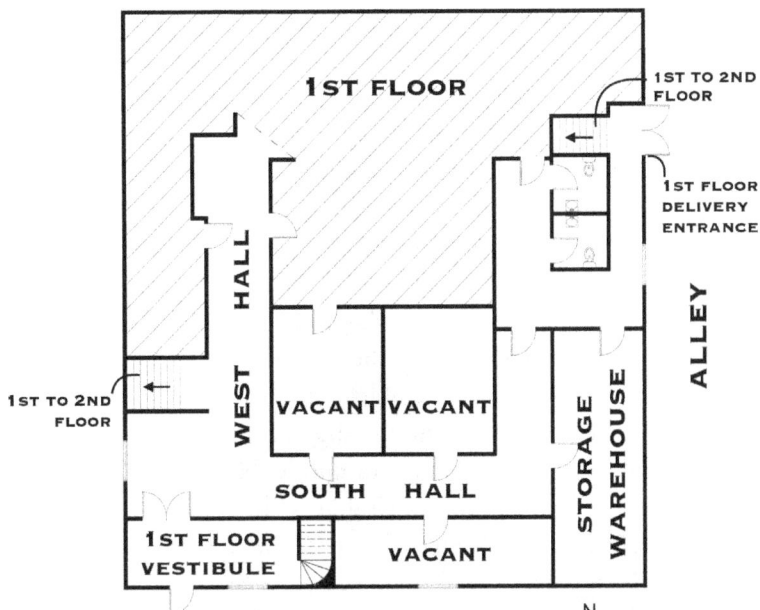

FIGURE 6 (1ST FLOOR)

Yump brought his javelin into a defensive position, and they inched toward the room, passing the staircase on their left. Another office door stood directly across the hall from the one they were approaching. As they crept nearer, they picked out two distinct voices:

"We've got everyone locked inside the building with us now, right?"

"Um, well, not everybody! When you shot your gun off, one guy came running down the front stairs, barking like a dog. He was able to get out through the front door. I hadn't gotten to that door to lock it yet."

"Are you tellin' me that he got away, Sauce? That he got *outside*?"

"Yeah, Billy. I didn't have enough time to lock all the doors before he came runnin' down here! But that door's all locked up now—and I did get the other guy."

"The little screamin' guy?"

"Yeah, that guy! He came flyin' down those stairs and crashed right into me! He was staggerin' around and I nabbed him. He's all tied up now in the other room."

"You're done, Billy!" came a third voice from inside the room; it sounded like that Brufyss fellow. "Somebody got away after all, and he'll be coming back with the cops."

Billy laughed. "Yeah, somebody got away, and he barks like a dog! The only thing that nut's gonna come back with is a slobbery stick."

"Look, Billy," said the Brufyss-sounding voice, "you're not going to get away with this. Give it up!"

"And miss my chance to score a scillion bucks? Are you crazy?"

"Huh? A scillion bucks?" It was the "Sauce" voice. "What's this, Billy?"

Billy ignored the question. "The only thing I'd regret, Bathwater, would be not takin' the shot when I had the chance. I know the old man's locked in here with us, so takin' the shot'll be shootin' fish in a barrel. In the meantime, I got you guys as insurance that nobody tries anything stupid. One false move, and Sauce is gonna blow you to pieces."

Roland pulled Yump down the hall until they came to the second-floor stairway and ducked into its alcove. "Yump, we've got to warn everybody! That Billy Jelly guy is going to be looking for Mr. Spuggett, and there's no telling what he'll do when he finds him. We've gotta do something now. Go warn everybody about what Billy's planning to do."

"What're you gonna do?"

"I think I've figured out my way around down here. I'll act as a decoy to distract Billy and give you enough time to get upstairs. Use this stairway— the double doors at the top are open now. I'll take off in the other direction and lure him deeper into the offices on this floor. Let me have your javelin."

Yump handed the needle-like projectile to Roland. "What're you gonna do with that? Spear him?"

"I'm not sure yet, but I'll figure something out! Okay, ready? Go!"

Yump scrambled up the stairs, and Roland darted back into the hallway, up to the half-opened doorway of the room occupied by Billy Jelly, Sauce Fingerbanana, and the prisoners. He poked his head inside, shouted "*Hey*! Jelly Boy!" and continued sprinting up the hallway toward the rear of the building.

Startled by Roland's shout, Billy ran to the door and looked up and down the corridor for the source of the impudent voice, spotting Roland's silhouette at the north end where the passage made another turn to the right. Roland concealed the javelin behind his back, stuck his tongue out at the hoodlum, gave him "the razzberries," and bolted off through the back portion of the building.

"Sauce, keep your eye on these guys! *Shoot anyone that moves!*"

Gun in hand, Billy took off in pursuit of Roland. Unnoticed, Yump bounded up the stairs to the main office and rushed into the reception room.

***

Barley and Frog had regained consciousness. Barley was groggy, his chest bare, a piece of red fabric wrapped tightly under his left armpit and around his left shoulder. Frog wore a piece of the red fabric wrapped around the top of his head and under his jaw so that one side of his face was covered. Everyone stared at Yump in surprise as he burst into the room.

"Where have you been, Yump?" cried Mimsy, running to him and throwing her arms around his neck. "I've been worried sick about you!"

She was immediately set upon by Noodles, who pried her off, separated the two, and reassumed her position at the top of the stairs, disaster mercifully averted.

"I was downstairs with Roland," gasped Yump, trying to catch his breath. "We found out where Jelly Belly was hiding, but he captured the big guys and Fandango and he's holding 'em prisoner. He's gonna be comin' up here to look for *you*, Mr. Spuggett!"

Mrs. Kookerly's eyes widened. "They captured Brufyss? They're holding him prisoner?"

"Yup, and all the other big guys too: Dork, the mayor, the reverend, Biff, and Fandango—but he's not a big guy, of course."

"Yump, which room are they being held in?" asked Old Man Spuggett.

"I think the room on the first floor that's between there"—he pointed to the stairway he'd just ascended—"and there!" He pointed to the stairway that led to Gerald's attic.

"Hmmm, that would be Mr. Bumps's old office," said the company founder. "Is that where Mr. Slamson is, too?"

"The other bad guy said Fandango was in another room, but I'm not sure which one."

Barley spoke up weakly from his seat on the couch. "Where's Roland?"

"He's still down there, being a decoy to distract Jelly Belly from coming up here."

Old Man Spuggett was horrified. "Good heavens! He's taking on two armed and dangerous hoodlums by himself?"

"Yeah! He said he knows his way around down there and for me to come up here and warn you about Jelly Belly!"

Barley looked up at Old Man Spuggett. "Sir, we don't have any time to waste. We've got to get out of here!"

"I appreciate your enthusiasm, Mr. Doubleduty, but aren't you and Mr. Puppleman still too weak to move?"

"I think I can make it. I'm pretty much awake now—a little woozy, but I'll be okay. How about you, Frog?"

"Yeah, buddy!" slurred the city councilman.

"Mr. Doodlebody, I think you're getting ahead of yourself here!" objected Dr. Pudbid. "You two are in no condition to be moving around right now!"

"Doc, we can't just stay here like sitting ducks while Billy runs rampant. I can hold it together long enough for us to get out of here— how about you, Frog?"

"Yeah, buddy!" slurred the city councilman.

"We've got to get out of this building, Mr. Spuggett!"

"I'm afraid that's impossible at the moment, Mr. Boobledoody. You've been unconscious up until now, so you aren't aware. We've been locked inside this building by those thugs. We're *all* prisoners!"

Barley thought for a moment. "In that case, if they've locked us *in*, we've got to lock them *out*. Is there a room on this floor big enough to hold all of us? One we can lock from the inside?"

"Yes, we can use the conference room! It's big enough for everybody, and we can barricade the door with the big table. Another thing: now that people are occupying the downstairs portion of the building, the lack of sufficient light down there is most likely aiding the bad guys more than the good guys. Switching on the first-floor lights will help equalize the situation."

"Can you do that from up here?"

"There's a box on this floor with circuit breakers for the whole building. I'll take care of that."

Alpha Rae jumped in. "I'll take care of getting us all out of here, Mr. Spuggett! We'll meet you in the conference room!"

The old man nodded and crossed the main office. He felt some relief now that a plan of action was forming. He ruminated on the next important items on the agenda: how to resist, combat, and overcome the threat from the intruders. Friends and enemies were dispersed all over the building, on two floors. There was no way to communicate with everyone, and no way of knowing where everyone was. He rounded the corner in Felicia's office and walked into the vestibule, stopping in front of an electrical circuit box opposite the second-floor delivery entrance door. Scanning the columns of switches, he threw the switch that would illuminate the murky depths of the ground-floor office complex for the first time in many years.

38

Roland Chumbuckets dashed down the rear hallway of the first floor, Smelly Billy Jelly in pursuit. When Roland poked his head into the prisoners' room to taunt Billy, he noted its layout and where the prisoners were sitting on the floor—and he'd gotten a look at Sauce Fingerbanana. As he ran to the rear of the building, he'd spotted a hallway that led to a rear exit, probably opening onto Gob Street. The door was padlocked. (*Figure 7*)

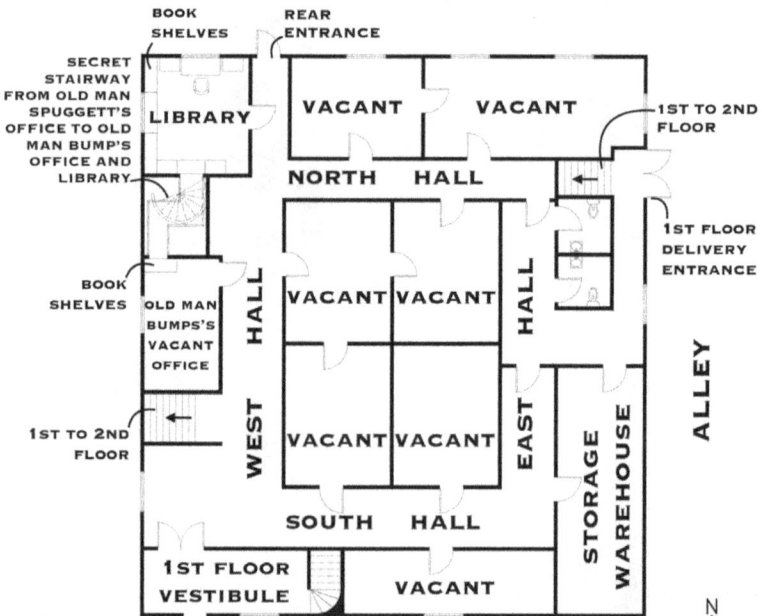

FIGURE 7
(1ST FLOOR)

Roland reasoned that the last door on the right of the hallway he was running through now would open into the restroom hallway. That would create an uninterrupted corridor running the length of the building's east side: the restroom hallway, past the storage room, all the way to the front of the building.

This meant that the first-floor office complex was linked by four main corridors forming a square circumnavigating the ground floor. By keeping to the four main hallways, he could lead Smelly Billy on a squared circuit of laps, keeping the thug occupied until Yump could warn the people upstairs of the impending danger.

He arrived at the terminus of the northern corridor and reached for the door in the right corner. If he was unable to open this door, Billy would have him boxed in and trapped, and be on him before he could reverse his direction and escape. He grasped the doorknob—the door opened into the restroom hallway!

Roland blasted through the door, into the bright restroom corridor, and down the concrete-floored passage. Up ahead loomed the door he'd purposely left half open. He reached it just as the pursuing thug entered the restroom hallway.

Roland dashed through the partition doorway, back to the point where Yump and he had first begun their downstairs exploration. He shouted, "Come get me, *chump*!" and bolted down the remainder of the eastern corridor, leading the thug back into the office complex. He turned right and ran along the front southern corridor.

Suddenly, the hallway was bathed in brightness as the overhead lights came on. Roland could clearly see where he was going—

BANG!!

So could Billy. His shot slammed into the wall by the opaque window. *Oops! Forgot about that gun!*

Roland turned the corner to the western corridor, beginning his second lap around the first floor's interior. He decided to gamble on the small offices in the building's center. If the office directly across from the prisoners' room connected to the one in the south hallway he'd just passed, he could double back on Billy and confuse him even more.

He reached the half-opened door to the prisoners' room. *Can't go in there—that Sauce guy has a gun too!* He ducked into the office directly across the hall. In the wall to his right was a connecting door, but this room also had a second connecting door ahead of him. He ran to the door on the right, opened it, and zipped through the next room and out to the southern hallway just as Billy rounded the corner and sped up the western corridor. By doubling back through the two small offices, Roland had placed himself *behind* his pursuer. If he was to open all the connecting doors to the inner offices and use their passages in conjunction with the four main corridors, he could create a labyrinth on the first floor.

Keeping track of the doors and corridors was confusing, but Roland counted on it being even more so for Billy. Roland was planning ahead as he ran. Billy ran mindlessly, bent only on apprehending Roland—or killing him.

Roland emerged from the small office and looked around the corner in time to see Billy passing the room where the prisoners were held. "Hey, doofus! I'm right here!"

Billy stopped in his tracks and spied Roland back at the corner he'd just turned.

BANG!!

The bullet whizzed past Roland's head and slammed into one of the double doors behind him.

"Ya missed, jelly head!" He took off down the hall toward the storage room. Billy reversed direction and pursued.

The bus driver turned left and headed up the eastern corridor, past the storage room, through the partition door, past the restrooms, through the doorway, and left into the rear northern corridor. He traveled the squared course in a counterclockwise direction. All of the small center offices were now on his left.

There was another door in the left wall. Did the room behind it adjoin the office he'd seen with *two* connecting doors? He jigged to the left, entered this room, and there was a door to his right. He opened the door, again entering the office across the hall from the prisoners' room.

Three of the four small central offices were connected by interior doors. The fourth office, in the southeast corner of the group, was a room unto itself. It could only be entered from the southern corridor—a dead end. If he could somehow maneuver Billy into that room, he'd have him trapped! *I gotta remember that!*

The only other rooms on this floor whose interiors he hadn't seen yet were situated around the building's perimeter and probably not interconnected. He wouldn't try to hide in any of those rooms—more dead ends—but maybe they could eventually be utilized to trap his pursuer as well. He didn't have the time to find out.

But Roland was now sure of where he was going. A new plan of action revealed itself to him; in order for it to work, Billy had to run at top speed. Roland looked back through the connecting door and saw Billy emerging from the restroom hallway into the northern corridor, heading west.

Roland crossed the small office and zipped through the room's other connecting door on the left, emerging into the southern corridor again. He positioned himself at the intersection of the southern and western corridors and waited for Billy to appear at the western corridor's opposite end. When he did, Roland shouted up the hallway:

"Hey, fat butt!"

Once again Billy raised his gun.

BANG!!

The bullet crashed into the double doors as Roland scooted down the south corridor. Billy gave chase, arriving at the end of the hall just as Roland entered the restroom corridor.

BANG!!

Missed again! Billy's inability to shoot or catch him had to be elevating the thug's frustration considerably; his thoughtless expenditure of bullets gradually leveled the playing field as well. Roland calculated that four shots had been fired. As Barley's experience had revealed, the weapon could fire six. Two more bullets remained, but with luck, his new plan would eliminate the opportunity for Billy to fire them.

I hope this works! I'm getting tired!

Roland shot past the storage room and reached the partition door. Instead of continuing up the hallway past the restrooms, he darted through the door, moved to the right, and flattened himself against the wall, clutching the javelin and breathing heavily.

Billy reached the end of the south corridor and headed up the eastern corridor, running hard toward the open doorway where Roland was concealed. Roland had to time it perfectly to take Billy by surprise.

Billy pounded closer.

Three more steps . . .

Just as Billy was about to burst through the doorway, Roland rammed the tip of the javelin into the wooden doorjamb across from him at ankle level. It stuck fast. He held on tightly to the other end of the spear with both hands.

Billy never saw the trap stretched across the doorway. As he barged through, one ankle and shin came in contact with the firmly wedged javelin. His forward momentum sent him flying headfirst through the air. He landed on the concrete floor of the restroom hallway, smacking his head on its bare surface—CRACK!!

Roland darted over and tried to pry the handgun from the crook's fingers. Although Billy was reeling from the blow to his head, he was conscious. He grappled with the bus driver, desperately trying to keep the only thing that gave him power. They thrashed and rolled as Roland grasped and grabbed at the handgun.

Billy wasn't giving up the prize.

BANG!!

The pressure Roland put on Billy's gun hand forced the crook to squeeze off another shot, which slammed into the wall nearby. Only one bullet remained in the gun.

Even in his discombobulated state, Billy was much stronger than the bus driver. Roland's attempts to get the gun from him were going nowhere. His only option was to incapacitate the thug. Roland released Billy's gun hand and grabbed his hair, banging Billy's head onto the concrete floor with as much force as he could muster. KONK!!

That did the trick! Billy ceased his struggling, and his body went limp. Roland collapsed beside him, breathing heavily, and extracted the gun from the unconscious hoodlum's hand. Sauce Fingerbanana was still in possession of another gun, but *this* gun was now the property of Bumps & Spuggett. As long as the remaining bullet wasn't fired, they'd be on nearly equal footing with the bad guys.

However, Roland was faced with a new quandary: Should he confront Sauce Fingerbanana gun-to-gun and try to free the imprisoned big guys, or should he return to the second floor and present his compatriots with this newly acquired firepower? And what should he do with the now incapacitated Billy Jelly?

*** *** ***

When Old Man Spuggett switched on the first-floor lights, the mass exodus from the second-floor reception room to the conference room commenced. The large, roomy chamber with its huge conference table and sturdy door would offer ample protection for them all.

Marshall Farkpucker, Narducci Palpatooti, and Mrs. Kookerly accompanied Barley, who moved stiffly but was able to negotiate the distance. Faisal Herskowitz, Gerald Foon-Package, and Daphne Dogdaughter escorted Frog, who was also walking under his own power, although his head pounded from the pistol-whipping Smelly Billy Jelly gave him.

Mrs. Kookerly gazed at Barley with a thoughtful expression. "You know, Barley," she said, smiling at her boyfriend's old nemesis for the first time, "that was a pretty amazing thing you did, saving Brufyss and me from being shot."

"Mrs. Kookerly, I just want to make things right between us and move forward."

"Well, I believe you now—and I'm sure Brufyss does, too. You could've let Billy finish us off right then and there."

"But that's just the point: I *couldn't* have! I want you as friends—*alive* friends, not dead ones."

"What do you think we should do now?" asked the former head cheerleader as they approached the door to the conference room.

"We've got to get Brufyss and the others out of trouble. We can't move *anywhere* until we accomplish that."

They heard a muffled report of a gunshot from the floor below. "Billy's reloaded his gun!" exclaimed Barley. "He might be shooting at Roland— or he might've already shot him."

"Or Brufyss," cried Mrs. Kookerly.

"Or *all* of the big guys, and everybody!" added Yump.

The company founder rejoined the group, having completed his errand. "It sounded to me like that shot came from somewhere toward the front of the building. If Yump's description of where Mr. Bathwater and the others are being held is correct, they wouldn't be where the shot was fired."

"Then he's probably shooting at Roland!" said Barley. "We've got to do something *now*, Mr. Spuggett! Roland doesn't stand a chance against that bum if he's got a loaded gun again."

"I agree. Let's get everybody situated inside the conference room. I think I've come up with a plan."

As the migrating group hurried into the conference room, Old Man Spuggett stood by the door with Barley and Mrs. Kookerly and outlined his strategy:

"It's going to take more than one of us to subdue those criminals, and we're handicapped by our lack of knowledge as to everyone's location. However, we do know how this building is set up—at least, I do—and I believe we can use that knowledge to compensate for what we still don't know. I have an idea that will enable us to gather the information we need, and I don't believe anyone will be hurt in the process."

The sound of another muffled gunshot came from the first floor. "We've got to move now. Puddles, please continue your medical ministrations to our two injured compatriots. Alpha Rae, please continue your supervision of our group. Bagmo, Simpleton, you boys come with me! We're going on a reconnaissance mission. I must ask that the rest of you stay here, and be sure to lock this door after we leave. We'll be back as soon as we can. Let's go, boys!"

"Wait! I'm going with you!" cried Mrs. Kookerly, leaving Barley's side and rushing to join the old man.

"Mrs. Kookerly, it's going to be very dangerous down there with two armed gunmen!" protested Barley.

"Listen, Barley, Brufyss is down there at the mercy of those two, and I'm not going to sit up here while his life's being threatened. Besides, I know Billy and Sauce. They came here with us today. I can deal with them."

"But Billy already tried to kill you once. He'd have no qualms about blowing your head off if he got the chance again!"

"Barley, if Billy kills Brufyss, how could I live with myself knowing I did nothing to prevent it?" She turned to Old Man Spuggett. "I'm going with you, sir. I will not be a hindrance."

The old man smiled at the fiery woman. "I truly believe those two hoodlums won't stand a chance against this young lady if she gets her hands on them, Mr. Doodyfellow. Come along, Mrs. Kookerly. We'll all keep a close eye on each other. No one will be harmed, but we must hurry!"

He motioned for his three coconspirators to follow him. They eased out of the room and around the corner, slipping quietly through the broken door into his private sanctum. Another gunshot rang out below, again toward the front of the building.

"All right, team, we've got to work fast now, but we've also got to be as quiet as we can."

Another gunshot, but on the opposite side of the building.

"Whatever's happening down there, the participants are on the move and moving away from where we're going."

"Are we gonna use the secret door, Mr. Spuggett?" asked Bagmo.

Mrs. Kookerly's eyebrows raised. "Did you say 'secret door,' Bagmo?"

"Yes, he did, Mrs. Kookerly. There's a hidden passageway in this room. Bagmo and Simpleton learned of its existence only a short while ago. We're going to use it to pass down to the first floor; however, we'll be heading into the hornets' nest, so it's imperative that you follow me and do as I say."

The company founder skirted around behind his desk. He opened a drawer in the low credenza beneath the window and extracted something, placing it into the pocket of his bathrobe.

The sound of another gunshot reached them, originating from somewhere on the east side of the building, possibly the restroom hallway.

"Whoever's firing that gun is about as far away from where we are as they'll ever be. This is our best chance. Follow me, and be as quiet as mice!"

The old man moved to the office closet and revealed the staircase within.

Mrs. Kookerly's jaw dropped.

"Cool, huh?" said Cheezy.

"Here we go!" whispered Old Man Spuggett. "Follow me in single file. It's dark in here, and the stairway is very narrow. Watch your step."

The old man began a cautious descent of the spiral stairs, commencing what the four hoped would be the successful rescue of their imprisoned friends, somewhere below and ahead of them on the Bumps & Spuggett building's first floor.

*＊＊

Roland decided he'd take Billy's gun upstairs to the rest of the group. Now that the crook had been incapacitated, the strength in numbers of the combined tourist-and-staff contingent, along with the newly acquired firearm, would have a much better chance of success in subduing Sauce Fingerbanana.

Any effort to transport the unconscious Billy Jelly back upstairs without assistance would be a time-consuming, if not futile endeavor. The hoodlum's bulk and dead weight was nearly impossible to trundle down the first-floor corridors and up the flight of stairs he'd have to negotiate to reach the second-floor reception room where he'd last seen his friends.

It would probably be wiser to leave Billy where he was for the time being and take the handgun up to his compatriots. While he was there, he could grab a few more capable hands to come back down and assist him in retrieving Billy before the thug regained consciousness.

Roland grasped the silver-gray handgun carefully and proceeded to the rear stairway. He now possessed valuable knowledge of the first floor's layout that would aid his companions immeasurably. He bounded up the stairs, sped through Felicia Greenthing's office, crossed the wide expanse of the main office, and entered the reception room.

The room was deserted.

He ran back into the main office.

"Hello! It's me, Roland Chumbuckets! Is anybody here? Where did everybody go?"

Silence.

After a few seconds, the door to the conference room opened a sliver.

"What do you *want*?" It was Alpha Rae Sapoopa-LaBoobis.

"Alpha Rae! It's me, Roland! I was downstairs with Yump, Bimbo, and Gerald just now, remember?"

Alpha Rae poked her purple-haired head partway out the door to get a look at the disembodied voice hailing her. She spotted Roland holding the gun in his hand.

"What the hell are you doing with a gun, Roland Chumbuckets? You didn't have one when you went downstairs!"

"I wrestled it away from that Billy Jelly guy! It's *our* gun now. But we've got to hurry. Will you let me in?" Roland heard a voice from inside the room—it sounded like Barley's—urging her to open the door.

"All right, get your keester in here!" Alpha Rae opened the door wide enough for him to slip inside.

Roland received the excited greetings of his friends, all of them relieved to see him safe. As he surveyed the conference room, he breathed his own sigh of relief at having survived the ordeal. This was the chamber in which the employees had been slumbering when the Doodlebody tour group first arrived. The rectangular room was partially filled with the large, heavy conference table now barricading the door. The plush chairs normally surrounding the table had been moved to the sides and were currently occupied by various staff members, tourists, Barley, and Frog. The north and east walls contained large windows that looked out onto Gob Street and the service alleyway. Both were adorned with open venetian blinds, revealing the sun sinking low on the horizon.

Close to the ceiling on the west wall was a large, gaping, round hole—the opening to the air-conditioning duct the employees utilized to slide down from the roof after being deposited there by helicopter each morning. An ornamental grating that covered the big hole had been removed so the employees could slip through the opening.

The idea of using the duct as an escape route to the roof had been entertained, but when Noodles boosted Marshall Farkpucker up to the opening, he repeatedly slid back out and plunked onto the floor. The steep incline, forces of gravity, and slipperiness of the conduit made it a snap to slide down. Sliding *up* was out of the question.

The group had already determined that none of the windows in any of the second-story offices could be used as avenues of escape. They were positioned too high above the ground for anyone to jump from without injury, and nothing on the exterior of the building could be used as a means to climb down.

Barley beckoned to Roland from his seat along the wall: "Chumbuckets, what were you doing down there? We heard the sound of the gunshots; we thought you were a dead man—and now you're standing in front of us with a gun in your hand!"

Roland rapidly recounted his harrowing chase and subsequent battle with Billy Jelly, informing Barley that Billy was still lying unconscious in the restroom corridor. "If we hurry, we might be able to capture him before he wakes up again. This gun still has one bullet left in it. I'm not sure if Jelly Belly knows that, but I doubt he'll try to find out with its barrel pointed at him."

"That was good thinking, Roland. It took a lot of guts to do what you did." Barley scanned the room's occupants. "Roland, Narducci, Ebenezer, and Yump—you guys come with me! We're going to bring that bum back up here, and it's going to take strong arms to do it."

"Hold on, Mr. Doodlebody!" cried Alpha Rae. "You're in no shape to go tramping all over the building with your shoulder bandaged up like that. You just got shot, for cryin' out loud!"

"I have to agree with Alpha Rae on this," added Dr. Pudbid.

"You're damn right you do! Mr. Doodlebody, you're much too weak to lift a big guy like that thug and carry him up a flight of stairs, even if you do have help."

"I'll be all right. I'm feeling okay now. I'll just hold the gun while the others do the heavy lifting. And Mr. Spuggett might need some help down there; we don't know where his group is or what they're doing right now."

"Mr. Spuggett's downstairs?" asked Roland, alarmed. "Mr. Doodlebody, we can't waste any more time! It's been a while since I knocked that Jelly guy out, and I'm not sure how 'out' he was when I left him. I overheard him say he wanted to find Mr. Spuggett, and now Mr. Spuggett could be walking right into his arms!"

"That settles it." Barley moved unsteadily to the conference-room door. "We're going downstairs—*now*! We'll bring him right back up here, so the rest of you stay in this room with the door locked until you hear me yell."

"I'm going with you!" Dr. Pudbid was adamant. "I'm not taking the chance of having you pass out cold in the midst of bloodthirsty hoodlums."

Narducci was indignant. "Come on, Doctor, we're not bloodthirsty hoodlums! Sure, we might argue sometimes, but—"

"He was talking about the hoodlums *downstairs*, Narducci," corrected Barley with a smile. "Doc, stay here! Take care of Frog."

"I'll make sure Frog has everything he needs," said Daphne. "He'll be okay with me here."

"And me too!" Alpha Rae gave Daphne her possessive scowl.

Barley was fighting a losing battle. "Okay, okay, you win! You're in, Doc! Now let's go! Chumbuckets, let me have that gun."

Roland turned the gun over to Barley. The group of six proceeded down to the restroom corridor. At the foot of the back stairway, Roland signaled for them to pause and spoke in a barely audible whisper: "We've got to be quiet! Jelly Belly should be just down this hallway, around the corner. If he's awake and hears us, he might try an ambush."

Reaching the end of the hallway, Roland peeked around the corner, toward the spot where he'd left Billy.

Billy was gone.

39

Old Man Spuggett led Mrs. Kookerly, Cheezy, and Bagmo down the steep, curving secret staircase. Light from the old man's private office vaguely illuminated the claustrophobic passageway. He'd left the secret door in the closet open for this purpose. (*Figure 7*)

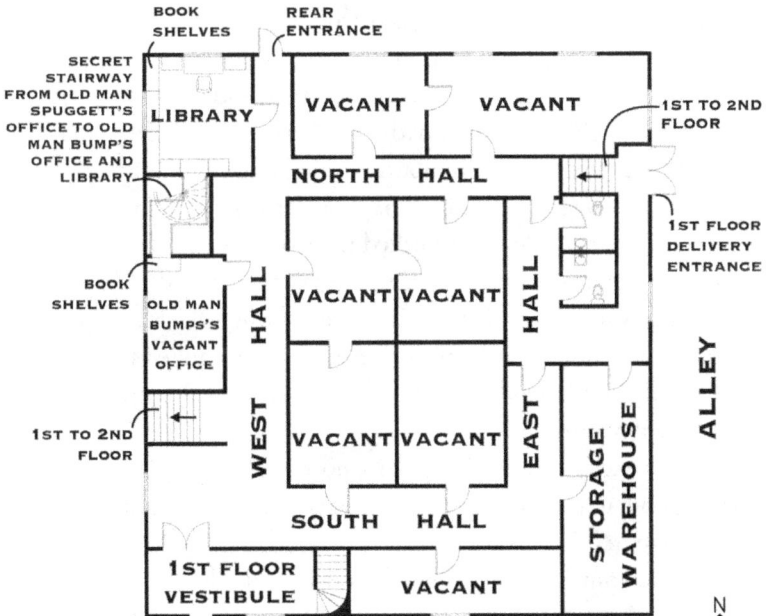

**FIGURE 7
(1ST FLOOR)**

His followers had been briefed as to what they'd find when they reached the bottom of the stairs: a narrow passage that led to two separate doors, both disguised to look like bookshelves. A door at the foot of this stairway opened into the library. A little farther down the passage, the second door opened into what had once been Old Man Bumps's private office, where Billy Jelly and Sauce Fingerbanana were imprisoning their friends. They'd exit into the library.

The old man paused at the bottom of the staircase, signaled for the others to remain silent, and pressed his ear to the secret library door to listen for movement within the room. Hearing nothing, he opened the door enough to poke his head through.

Overhead fluorescents shone on the library's dusty interior. The room was unfurnished, except for a small reading desk and chair. In the wall above the desk was an opaque window, closed and barred. Each of the room's four walls was lined with tall bookshelves (the secret door also functioned as one), extending in height from the floor almost to the ceiling with a gap of three feet between the tops and the ceiling itself. Since the library was not being used, the shelves were empty.

Only one other object occupied this room. On the floor by the reading desk, Fandango Slamson sat like a sad-eyed little baked potato, his knees bent to his chest, his legs tied together, and his hands and arms securely bound behind his back with electrical tape. An additional piece of tape was plastered across his mouth.

Old Man Spuggett turned to his followers, pointed into the room beyond the door, and silently mouthed the word *Fan-dang-o*. He pushed the bookshelf door open a little wider and whispered, "*Mr. Slamson!*"

Fandango's head jerked up in surprise. Spying Old Man Spuggett's white-haired noggin, the little spitfire's eyes lit up in wonder. From behind the slab of electrical tape that covered his mouth came his muffled cry of "Mmmmmm! Mmmmmm!"

"Mrs. Kookerly, Mr. Maltgoggles, and Mr. Fabsmaggle are with me too; we're going to get you out of here, but you must be absolutely quiet."

Fandango nodded.

"Here we come!" The old man pushed on the bookshelf door and stepped into the dusty room. The other three followed. Mrs. Kookerly marveled at this little fellow who'd outrun Billy Jelly's bullets.

They loosened and removed the electrical tape binding the diminutive office manager's legs, hands, and arms, and yanked the piece of tape off his face. While Mrs. Kookerly and the employees worked on Fandango, Old Man Spuggett walked a few steps over and peered at a spot above one of the large bookshelves, just below the ceiling. He noticed a small air-conditioning vent that once fed cool air into the room; the grating that normally covered the opening had been removed. He stared at the exposed vent for a moment and returned to assist the others.

Once freed, Fandango scrambled to his feet, massaged his face and limbs to restore the circulation, and gave each of his rescuers a grateful hug. He scooted over to the bookshelf-camouflaged door and peeked inside with obvious fascination, turning back to smile at his friends.

Convinced that their presence hadn't yet been suspected or detected by the hoodlums, and knowing that the interior of the library was relatively soundproof, the company founder addressed his compatriots in a hushed whisper:

"My friends, now that we've freed Mr. Slamson, we need to determine how to get our other friends. According to Yump, they're being held in the room next to this one—a room accessed from the same secret passageway we just used. However, we also heard gunshots being fired, presumably at Mr. Chumbuckets. We must determine whether he's been injured, captured, or in some way needs our help. The first thing I want to do is ascertain where our two adversaries are. I haven't heard any gunshots lately. Have you?"

His team members shook their heads.

"Then we might assume from the silence that the gunfire is concluded, in one way or another. I'm going to peek outside the room and see what I can see."

He walked to the library's entrance and gave the doorknob a twist. Evidently, the hoodlums hadn't felt the need to padlock the door after they'd hog-tied Fandango. He poked his head outside. The corridor ran fifteen feet to his left, terminating in a rear entrance, which he knew had been padlocked.

The rear-entrance corridor ran a few feet to his right and intersected with the north and west hallways. All quiet. Not a soul in sight.

He cautiously took a step outside and tiptoed to where the corridors intersected, peering down the length of one hallway, then the other. Both corridors were empty. The partially opened door to Old Man Bumps's office was a few feet down the western corridor. He heard no voices coming from the room.

Motioning for the rest of his party to follow him, the old man crept along the north corridor, heading for the eastern side of the building, the last area where a gunshot was heard. The others followed and noticed two closed doors on the left side of the passage, bordering the building's northern perimeter. There were also two open doorways on the right side—one in the middle of the corridor, the other in the corner at the end of the hall.

Suddenly, through that very door and around the corner to the right, *movement*! Someone shuffled toward them.

Old Man Spuggett motioned for everyone to duck inside the center office. The old man poked his head out far enough to see Smelly Billy Jelly careen through the doorway. As the villain turned into the northern corridor toward the hidden group, he drunkenly caromed from side to side, banging against one corridor wall and then the other like a pinball. He lurched down the hallway toward them, stumbling and moaning, clutching his head with both hands.

As he drew closer, Old Man Spuggett saw a nasty bump on his forehead.

The old man stepped into the corridor. Billy stopped and stared, swaying like a reed in the wind. "May I help you?" asked the old man in a whisper.

Billy didn't answer but stood unsteadily, blinking in a futile attempt to focus and determine who was talking to him.

"You seem to be lost, sir! Might I direct you somewhere?"

Billy continued to stare vacantly.

The old man motioned for the rest of his group to join him. As Cheezy came abreast, Billy's glassy eyes moved back and forth from the old man to Cheezy. His face contorted into a combined look of astonishment and dim recognition; he'd seen this old man before, but there was only *one* of him then!

"Billy's been knocked silly," whispered Mrs. Kookerly. "He thinks he's seeing *two* of you!"

"Huh? Wha'?" mumbled Billy.

The old man chuckled. "It appears that Mr. Jelly's confusion has blessed us with a temporary advantage. At present he seems incapacitated—"

"His head's gonna come off!" whispered Bagmo, alarmed.

"No, no, Mr. Maltgoggles! He's been *incapacitated*, not *decapitated*! He's just been conked a little coo-coo somehow. Merely a temporary condition, I'm sure."

"Whew! Glad to hear *that*! For a minute there, I thought that if we touched him, his noggin would fall off his shoulders and roll down the hallway like a bowling ball!"

The old man smiled. "Not at all, Bagmo. He appears to be grappling with unconsciousness at the moment, but eventually he'll be all right— just a headache and a bump on the forehead. But while we have him at a disadvantage, I suggest we take advantage of our advantage!

"Bagmo, would you and Simpleton have a look around the corner? See if you can spot Mr. Chumbuckets in the hallway. Mrs. Kookerly, Fandango and I will take care of Mr. Jellyball while you're doing so. And please, be careful, won't you? Don't venture anywhere near Mr. Bumps's old office."

Cheezy and Bagmo skirted around the woozy criminal and crept toward the restroom corridor to hunt for Roland.

"Let's get Mr. Jellybean into a room where we can interrogate him when he wakes up."

The old man addressed the befuddled Smelly Billy. "Please allow us to escort you to a quiet place of comfort, Mr. Bellyjilly. You can sit down, relax, and rest your head. That's a rather nasty bump you've got there."

"Huh? Wha'? *Ohhhhh* . . ." Billy clutched his aching head with both hands.

They guided the thug into a room off the northern hallway. Once the conference room for the first floor, it was a spacious chamber with three barred windows: two of them looking out onto Gob Street, the third facing the service alleyway. In the west wall was a closed door that connected to the next room.

The old man's reasons for choosing this particular chamber were threefold: Firstly, it was close at hand. Secondly, several stacks of unused office chairs stood in one corner of the room, something they could use to seat Billy. Thirdly, the room was situated well away from Old Man Bumps's former office in the west hallway. If Billy made any loud noises during their interrogation, the distance between the two rooms might be enough to preclude being heard by Sauce Fingerbanana.

The old man pulled one of the stacked chairs into the middle of the room. Fandango and Mrs. Kookerly assisted Billy in sitting down. "Here you are, Mr. Jellybelly, a nice, comfortable chair upon which to rest your weary body. Do sit down, won't you? I have a few questions I'd like to ask . . ."

As soon as Billy sat down, the inside of his bruised, aching head began spinning, his head slumped forward on his chest, and he lapsed into deep unconsciousness without uttering a single coherent word.

Outside the room, Cheezy and Bagmo reached the end of the north hallway and cautiously poked their heads around the corner to the restroom corridor. They looked down the eastern corridor, past the restrooms on their left and all the way to the front portion of the building, but saw no sign of Roland. What they *did* see gave them cause for great puzzlement: stuck into the partition door's jamb at ankle level and extending across the width of the doorway was one of Yump's javelins!

"If someone didn't see that thing, they could trip over it and crack their head open," whispered Cheezy.

"Cheezy, now that you mention it, I think that's exactly what happened to that Billy Jelly guy! He was acting like someone who just got his head conked big-time, wasn't he? And his forehead was bleeding, too. Maybe he tripped over that thing!"

The two boys heard whispers past the restrooms and around the corner to the left.

"Cheezy, there's someone *else* down here!"

"Well, it's probably not that Billy Jelly guy, 'cause we just saw him with Mr. Spuggett."

"Good point! Maybe it's that other guy Mrs. Kookerly was talking about!"

They ducked behind the doorway, peeking cautiously around the corner. Someone's head bobbed around the corner at the other end of the restroom corridor, looking up the hall in their direction.

"It's Roland!"

"Hey, Roland! It's *us*!" called Cheezy in a hoarse whisper. He and Bagmo stepped into the doorway.

Roland saw the two standing at the entrance to the north corridor and whispered to someone behind him. Narducci, Ebenezer, Yump, Barley, and Dr. Pudbid streamed into the restroom corridor and scurried up the passage. Roland detoured to the partition doorway, extracted Yump's javelin from the doorjamb, and joined his companions.

"It's good to see you boys!" said Barley to Cheezy and Bagmo. "I'm glad you're okay!"

"Shiggydaygobah!" added Ebenezer.

"We came down here to find Jelly Belly," whispered Roland. "I knocked him out a little while ago, but when we got down here to bring him upstairs, the dude was gone!"

"We found him," said Bagmo. "He was walking down the hall, all goofy! He's with Mr. Spuggett and Mrs. Kookerly right now. We found Fandango, too."

"Is Fandango okay?" asked Dr. Pudbid.

"He's just great, Doc! It's ol' Jelly Head who ain't doin' so hot at the moment."

Roland was puzzled.

"How did you guys get down here? You couldn't have used the back stairs; I would've seen you! Did you use the front stairs?"

"Nope," replied Cheezy. "We used the *secret* stairs!"

"Cheezy, *shut up* again, will ya?" whispered Bagmo in disgust.

"Oops, sorry again. I keep forgetting!"

"Look, guys," Bagmo explained to the rest of the group, "it's nothin' personal, but we're not supposed to tell anyone about the secret stairway in back of Mr. Spuggett's office closet until Mr. Spuggett says it's okay."

"That's not important right now, Bagmo," said Barley, trying to keep the group focused. "You mentioned that Mr. Spuggett, Mrs. Kookerly, and Fandango were taking Billy somewhere to ask him questions. Where?"

"C'mon, we'll take you to them," whispered Bagmo, "but you gotta be really quiet. The big guys are still being held prisoner, and Jelly Boy's buddy doesn't know we're down here yet."

"Smelly Billy Jelly, captured?" marveled Barley. "Fantastic job!"

"Shiggydaygobah!" reiterated Ebenezer.

Cheezy and Bagmo led the group into the north corridor and made their way noiselessly along the hall to the room where Billy Jelly was being held. Roland, once again filled with curiosity, this time about the newly revealed secret passageway, held his tongue but filed the memory for future reference.

***

Old Man Spuggett scrutinized the unconscious Billy Jelly, pondering what he, Mrs. Kookerly, and Fandango could do to keep the hoodlum under control once he woke up. It was a very precarious situation. If Billy tried to make a break for it once he regained consciousness, the old man was doubtful the three of them would be much of a match for his brute strength. But Simpleton and Bagmo were still on the first floor; if they rejoined the group in time, would their combined strength be enough to keep Billy subdued?

"It looks like Mr. Jellyfish won't be contributing much until he snaps out of his current funk," Old Man Spuggett said. "In the meantime, I suggest we make preparations for that moment when he finally does. Fandango, Mrs. Kookerly, please pin his arms around the back of the chair. That will have to do until we can find something to tie his hands behind his back."

Bagmo poked his head through the door. "Aha! So *this* is where you guys went!"

The three captors sighed with profound relief that there were extra hands to be lent.

"Come in, boys!" exclaimed the old man. "You've arrived just in the nick of time—whatever *that* is."

"We've brought reinforcements with us too," said Bagmo. "C'mon in, guys!"

Cheezy and Bagmo slipped into the room and beckoned to their followers. In moments, Barley, Ebenezer, Yump, Narducci, and Dr. Pudbid were inside the office, staring curiously at the unconscious crook. The old man was pleased to see Roland among them.

"Mr. Chumbuckets, my heart is filled with joy to see you unharmed. You had us all worried that you were in quite a fix. You're lucky Mr. Jellyball never got his hands on you!"

"I prefer to think that Mr. Jellyball was *unlucky* he never got his hands on me."

The old man smiled. "Considering his present condition, I'm sure Mr. Jellyball would agree with your assessment—if he was able to! Well done, Mr. Chumbuckets. We owe you a debt of gratitude."

He turned to Dr. Pudbid. "Puddles, you bunkdinkulated old fork-pusher, your presence among us is fortuitous as well. Could you please take a look at our Mr. Bellybubbles here? He received a rather evil-looking bump on the head, courtesy of Mr. Chumbuckets; it's rendered him a bit dead to the world right now."

"I'll check him out, Spuggy." The doctor pulled the gangster's chin off his chest, held his head back, and pried his eyes open to determine the extent of Billy's concussion. "Without a more thorough examination, I'd guess this poor devil will survive."

"Well, that's a relief!"

"We have more good news, Mr. Spuggett," said Barley, producing Billy's handgun from his pocket and holding it up. Old Man Spuggett gasped in surprise.

"My goodness, Mr. Dumblehoney! How did you get *that*?"

"Ol' Chumbuckets not only managed to turn the tables on Smelly Billy but came up with this in the process. Thanks to Roland, we're in a whole new ballgame—there's still one bullet left."

"And now that we've got Billy where we want him, we can start making plans to free Brufyss and the others," said Mrs. Kookerly.

"Most definitely," agreed the old man. "Our outsized comrades have languished in captivity long enough! But we must be wary of the hooligan guarding them. I'm told he has a weapon similar to this one."

"Yeah, but now that *we've* got a gun, we can meet force with force if need be!"

"*No*, Mr. Doubledooby! There'll be no more use of guns in this building. Look at yourself: a bullet tore into your shoulder, your arm's in a sling—because of a gun! Councilman Pupplemeister, Mr. Bathweather, Mrs. Kookerly, Mux Muggsley, Fandango, *and* Mr. Chumbuckets are extremely fortunate they weren't killed. No, there'll be no further use of any weaponry in this building as long as I have anything to say about it."

"How about this javelin?" asked Roland, holding up Yump's shiny spear. He pointed at Billy. "It helped me to capture him."

"But I can see by this hoodlum's injuries that you didn't use it to skewer him, did you, Roland?"

"No, sir, I used it to trip him."

"There you go! We can defeat our enemies just as Roland did—by using ingenuity."

"Your point is well taken," said Barley as Roland propped the javelin against a wall. "If that's the way you want it, that's the way it'll be. No weapons. With that in mind, I think the first thing we need to do is lure Sauce Fingerbanana away from Brufyss and his crew. Draw his attention from them."

"Excellent suggestion. Can you envision a way of doing it?"

"We need to create confusion. From what you and your employees have taught me today, and from what we know about these two thugs, I believe we can overload them with a healthy dose of seventh-sensory persuasion. For anyone not familiar with that level of perception, confusion would be the natural result."

"We can use the layout of this floor to assist us with that," added Roland. "I got to know the floor plan pretty well when Belly Boy was chasing me around down here. It's a maze for anyone who's not familiar with it."

"Indeed, it is," agreed the company founder. "I used to get lost down here myself back in the old days, and that was without anybody chasing me around!"

Barley locked into his plan. "So, if we tempt Sauce Fingerbanana out of the room where Brufyss and the boys are, we can confuse him enough to get that other gun away from him. We begin by causing a commotion in the hallways and having Bagmo engage Sauce in conversation to lure him into the maze. At that point, the rest of us will keep him occupied until our guys can be spirited out of the room."

"Why do you mention Mr. Maltgoggles specifically?"

"Mr. Spuggett, can you think of anyone with a better grasp of seventh-sensory perception, logic, and reasoning?"

"*Aha*! I see your point!"

"Is that a good thing?" asked Bagmo suspiciously.

"Bagmo, if anybody can talk some 'sense' into Sauce Fingerbanana, it's you," said Barley reassuringly.

"But what if he kills me?"

"Sauce Fingerbanana couldn't kill the *lights*, Bagmo!" interjected Mrs. Kookerly. "He's not very smart, and about as mean as a tubful of tapioca—not a cold-blooded maniac like Billy. Without Billy there to tell him what to do, Sauce will be lost. He doesn't do *anything* unless Billy orders it, and he'll probably start crying like a baby if you get him confused enough."

"Besides, Dr. Pudbid is down here in case he kills you," added Cheezy. "And I'll go with you to help out."

"You must remember, Mr. Maltgoggles, all you're trying to do is lure Mr. Fingerbanana out of the room. The rest of us will take over from there, and you'll be doing our captured comrades a great service."

Bagmo pondered the situation. "Okay, I'll do it!"

"Excellent!" The old man's face filled with admiration for his brave employee. "Keep in mind, we'll all be nearby to assist you should anything go awry. But I'd never put you in this position if I didn't think you could pull it off."

The old man turned to Barley. "Bravo, Mr. Donkeydoodle! You're thinking like a true suggestionaire! I believe your plan has a great chance of succeeding; as a matter of fact, I think *I* might even have a little something to contribute that will expedite the success of this operation without compromising the restrictions I've placed on our methodology."

Reaching into the pocket of his bathrobe, the old man extracted a handful of mysterious-looking objects. Barley and his tourists stared at them quizzically, but the members of his own staff recoiled in alarm. Their boss was holding a slew of nondestructive explosive devices!

"These little buggers couldn't maim a moth or annoy an amoeba," said the old man proudly as he admired the harmless handiwork of his explosives research, "but they make one heck of a lot of *noise*! They should create quite a ruckus and shake up our Mr. Fingerbanana a bit."

His employees nodded in enthusiastic agreement.

The plan was in place. The players were ready to play. It was time to let the seventh sense make sense of everything.

✳ ✳ ✳

In the second-floor conference room, the remaining staff members and tourists sat in quiet trepidation. No one had any idea what was happening with their friends on the first floor. All they knew was that circumstances were dire enough to require sequestration in their present accommodations.

Marshall Farkpucker absorbed the day's activities with keen interest. He was unable to hear anything because of his deafness, but he didn't *need* to hear to know things weren't copacetic. This day hadn't been typical by any stretch of the imagination. It had started with a metal trash receptacle becoming wedged on his head. Things regressed from joyful dancing to people getting shot or shot at, fighting, carrying injured casualties, shuffling like refugees from place to place, office to office—all ultimately leading them to where they were now: cowering in the B & S conference room, unable to leave the building through the exits or air-conditioning duct.

Marshall swung his legs back and forth as he sat on the conference-room tabletop next to the goggle-eyed newspaper lady, who scribbled furiously, filling page after page of writing paper she'd procured from Bagmo's desk. He became aware that Lollie the receptionist was surreptitiously attempting to attract his attention. She sat across the room from him, fixing him with an intense stare and subtly waving her hand, hoping to catch his eye.

Lollie and Marshall enjoyed a unique relationship: neither ever truly knew what anyone was saying to them, but through the years, the two

402 A SEVENTH SENSE

had developed an effective means of communicating with each other by utilizing hand signals and pantomime gestures.

He glanced around at the others; no one was paying attention, and no one else had spotted Lollie's stealthy attention-attracting gesticulations. Marshall realized that Lollie's gestures were meant for him alone. He furtively waved back at the receptionist.

Lollie proceeded to send him covert signals and signs, stating her intention of escaping the stifling confines of the conference room to learn what was going on downstairs. She wanted Marshall to accompany her.

Being cooped up with so many dour-faced people, Marshall felt fairly claustrophobic himself. He signaled to Lollie that he'd gladly accompany her—but how would they get past Alpha Rae?

"Leave that to me!" signed Lollie. She motioned for him to follow her to the conference-room doorway, where the executive secretary was acting as sentry.

Alpha Rae eyed them as they approached. "What do *you* want?"

She remembered that neither of these employees would understand what she said.

"Mumba-lala baloola!" said Lollie matter-of-factly, giving Alpha Rae her best "I mean business!" look. Marshall stood next to Lollie, smiling like a clueless moron.

"You *know* I can't understand you, Lollie!"

"Chalala-*ponk*!" Lollie indicated to Alpha Rae that she wanted to leave the room with Marshall.

"Oh, you wanna get *out* of here? Well, I can't blame you for that, but I'm sorry, dear. No one's leaving this room until it's safe to do so."

Lollie gathered from Alpha Rae's comportment that her request had been denied. She was prepared for this.

"Balla-baloolah! Balla-baloolah! Jabumba-jabumba-jabumb!" Lollie pointed insistently at the door, her voice rising in volume, her face betraying irritation.

"I said *no*, Lollie!"

Lollie would have none of "No." "Doopah-laboop! Doopah-*laboop*!" she cried angrily.

Everyone watched this confrontation between the executive secretary and receptionist. It was fast becoming a battle of wills between the two women.

"Sit your butts back down!" Alpha Rae's anger was building.

However, Alpha Rae was woefully unaware of the fact that in the "fearsomeness" department, she'd met her match in Lollie Babajuju. A bludgeoning blast of Babajuju belligerence could lay waste to continents full of the most ardently angry!

Lollie jumped up and down in place like a kangaroo with limited leaping space, screaming, "Gahlahlah-baloogoo! Gahlahlah-baloogoo!" over and over at the top of her lungs, flailing her arms wildly, a manic, seething homicidal ferocity blazing from her eyes like rocket engines a-firing. Even Marshall, who couldn't hear a word, stared in fascination at the infuriated receptionist. Lollie's performance was awe inspiring!

Felicia shrieked and howled. Faisal belly laughed. Everyone else in the room cowered in fear. No one had ever seen the normally sedate, heretofore placid, seemingly catatonic, usually meditating receptionist in this agitated state before.

Alpha Rae was completely overwhelmed by Lollie's powerful demonstration of raving petulance. "All right! All right, Lollie! By all means—*go*! If that's what you want to do, then *do* it. Just don't come cryin' to me if you get killed!"

Lollie could tell by the terrorized expression on the executive secretary's face that her hissy fit had done its job. She and Marshall had been given official clearance to leave the room. She relinquished her demanding demeanor, gave Alpha Rae a demure smile, and with an emphatic jerk of her head indicated to Marshall that they were now free to go. The Bumps & Spuggett receptionist and the CEO in charge of anything and everything a deaf person can do eased out into the main office, pulling the door closed behind them.

Alpha Rae turned to the remaining group and sighed. "*Sheesh*! I liked her better when she was just doing that chanting thing!"

The others nodded their agreement, happy that Lollie was on *their* side.

Out in the main office, Lollie signed to Marshall to follow her to Yump's cubicle. She stepped inside and grabbed one of Yump's spare javelins.

On rare occasions when she wasn't chanting "Chili-baba jijjy boo-boo" in the reception room, Lollie participated in javelin hurling with Yump. Having gained a formidable proficiency in spear throwing in her homeland (although it was only for sport; for hunting she used a .357 Magnum), Lollie kept her javelin "chops" up by utilizing the target hanging on Yump's cubicle wall.

Spotting the huge banner,

IT'S NOT <u>WHAT</u> YOU DO, BUT WHAT YOU DO <u>WITH IT</u>.

---

she raised the javelin to her shoulder, took precise aim, ran a few steps forward, and with a cry of "*Oooooff!*" flung the spear across the huge expanse. It hit the banner—T H W A N G!—imbedding itself perfectly within the *O* in the word *DO*. Lollie smiled at Marshall with satisfaction. Marshall smiled back with admiration.

She ran back into Yump's cubicle and grabbed another javelin from the quiver. Sufficiently armed, the two adventurous employees made an about-face and headed for the reception room and lobby. Lollie's objective was to use the front stairway to descend, explore the first floor, and determine what was transpiring in its mysterious depths.

40

Metaphorically speaking, Wiley "Sauce" Fingerbanana wasn't the brightest candle on the cake. His level of perception was on par with that of a ball-peen hammer, and his first name did not match the person who wore it. If there was anyone who was not wily, it was Wiley.

One curious fact about Sauce Fingerbanana was his disposition in relation to Billy Jelly's. Sauce was the very antithesis of Billy. Where Smelly Billy Jelly was evil, selfish, heartless, violent, cutthroat, cruel, and conniving, Sauce Fingerbanana was eager to please, easy to deal with or to ignore completely. Billy found it less of a hassle working with Sauce than with other, more ambitious henchmen because Sauce did whatever Billy said, without question. If he *did* have a question, it was usually something like "Did I put my pants on backwards?" or "Could you help me pull this fork out of my leg?" Billy gave him the nickname "Sauce" to describe the interior of his brain.

An incongruous quirk to Wiley Fingerbanana's character was his penchant for performing what he referred to as "scientific experiments." He had no scientific training whatsoever but endeavored to ascertain reasons for unreasonable things and solutions to unsolvable problems, discovering nothing and usually causing immense property damage and great bodily injury to himself, much to Billy's delight.

This was the person who now stood nervously with a gun in his hand in a furniture-barren room, his assigned task being to guard Brufyss Bathwater, Dork Snargmeyer, Biff Spoozma, Mayor Roymul Wubbleduster, and Reverend Mafumbus Snortworthy—five of the biggest men he had ever seen in his life—and see to it that they remained quiet and stayed where they were.

Sauce stood against the western wall of Old Man Bumps's former office, beneath a large opaque window directly across from the office door, a position which gave him a clear view of anyone who might try to enter the room. His handgun was trained on the prisoners clustered on the floor in the middle of the room, their hands and feet bound together with the ubiquitous electrical tape. The captive big guys gazed morosely up at Sauce, who gazed morosely down at them.

Of all the prisoners in Sauce's charge, only Brufyss was acquainted with the weak-minded thug. Both Billy Jelly and Sauce Fingerbanana had come to the Bumps & Spuggett building as hired henchmen of the Bathwater Boys 'n Girls Gang. With Billy now out of the room, Brufyss raced to capitalize on the thug's limited intellect.

"So, Sauce, why are you holding a gun on me here?"

"Because Billy told me to. It's nothin' personal."

"But you and Billy came here with *me* today! You wouldn't be here if I wasn't, right?"

"Right."

"You came here with me today because I'm the boss of this job. Aren't you supposed to be working for me? I'm paying you, right?"

"Well, yeah, I guess . . ."

"Then as your boss, I'm telling you to put that gun away!"

"But Billy told me to watch you."

"So, what are you saying, Sauce? That Billy's the boss and not me?"

"Billy's my *partner*!"

"So you're gonna do whatever Billy tells you to do?"

"Well, yeah! Billy takes care of me."

"Takes care of you, eh?" Brufyss laughed. "Well, Sauce, I'd say he's not taking very good care of you right now!"

"Whaddaya mean?"

"Did Billy tell you that he went upstairs because they're having a big party? Did he invite you to come up there with him? Billy's having a great time, Sauce! Lots of girls! He didn't tell you that, did he?"

"A party? With girls?"

"That's right. And what does Billy have you doing while he's upstairs partying? Padlocking doors, guarding prisoners, staying put and out of sight—doing all the dirty work while he plays and parties with the girls. If we weren't down here with you right now, you'd be all alone, wouldn't you?"

Sauce thought for a few seconds. "Yeah, I did hear a lot of noise and singing, and the ceiling was rattling and shaking—"

"It's a great party! I'll bet that's where Billy is right now."

Sauce began to fume. Brufyss's words were making an impact.

"Wanna know the *real* reason why he's up there and you're down here? I'll tell you why: because he's embarrassed to be seen with you. He doesn't want anyone to know that you and he are partners 'cause he thinks you're an idiot! Even more importantly, he doesn't want to split all the money he's gonna get from old Man Spuggett."

"Money?"

"Tons of it! Scillions of dollars! But he wants it all for himself. He didn't tell you about that, did he?"

"Well, no . . . But now that you mention it, I did hear him say something to you about it."

"Billy knows the old man has tons of money, and he wants it for himself. He has no intention of sharing it."

"Why are you telling me this?"

"Because Billy's trying to cut *all* of us out of our share! He's trying to give us the shaft, and I don't wanna see him get away with it! Do you?"

The weak-minded hoodlum was buying wholly into Brufyss's argument. "No! That dirty bum! You're telling me he's gonna walk outa here with scillions of dollars, and he's got me down in this hole, babysitting you guys?"

"Bingo!"

Suddenly, from somewhere out in the depths of the first floor came a loud **POP!—POP!—POP!—POP!** like the reports of multiple gunshots, followed by many agitated, shouting voices—and then dead silence.

Sauce's eyes widened and he cringed, pointing his gun toward the door. "What was that? I heard yelling! I heard shots!"

Everyone craned their necks, trying to see into the hallway through the half-opened door. They'd heard Billy shooting at Roland a while ago, but that noise had stopped. It had been some time since they'd heard anything else—and Billy hadn't returned yet.

Only a few seconds passed before a partially obscured figure appeared at the office entrance. A single hand and arm reached out slowly. The hand hesitated slightly—and knocked on the door.

"Excuse me! Hello! Knock knock! Is anybody in there?"

The prisoners recognized the voice instantly.

Sauce pointed the gun at the partially opened doorway. "Who is it?! Whaddaya want?!"

Bagmo Maltgoggles poked his head through the narrow opening and smiled. The big guys stared at him incredulously. "Hi there! Sorry to disturb, but you're Sauce Fingerbanana, right?"

"Yeah—who wants to know?" He leveled the gun at Bagmo.

"My name is Bagmo Maltgoggles, and I just really wanted to meet you, Mr. Sauce! You're pretty famous around here."

"I-I am??" Sauce was completely taken aback; the last thing he expected to encounter was a friendly visitor, but it amazed him that anyone else on earth was aware of his existence, let alone calling him "famous."

"Yeah, you are," said Bagmo. "*Everybody* around here knows about you, and lots of people want to meet you. Pleased to make your acquaintance, Mr. Fingersauce!"

"That's Fingerbanana!"

"What's Fingerbanana?"

"My name."

"Oh! Sorry about that! I get confused with names all the time. Yesterday, I called Felicia Greenthing 'Willard Bilbo'—and that's not even Felicia's name! Willard Bilbo! Jeez Loo-eez, where the heck did I come up with that one?"

Bagmo burst into laughter, shaking his head in amusement at his own absentmindedness. "But Mr. Spuggett always gets people's names mixed up too, so I guess I shouldn't feel too bad, 'cause he's the boss!"

Dumbfounded, Sauce stared at Bagmo with his mouth hanging open.

"Anyway," continued Bagmo, "all of that's neither here nor there. But then again, what *is*, right?"

He burst out laughing again, pleased with his own joke. Once he'd regained control, he went on. "So, Mr. Fingerbanana, I just wanted to meet you for myself, and I must say, now that I have, I'm glad I did."

Sauce realized the friendly visitor was passing the conversation over to him. "Yeah, um, thanks. Pleased to meet you too."

"Oh, by the way," added Bagmo, "I also wanted to let you know that your friend—Mr. Jelly, is it?—he's in a bit of a fix. Really a mess, actually."

Sauce stared at Bagmo, dismay contorting his face. "Billy? A mess? What happened?"

"Whoa! One question at a time, please! I sense a quiz comin' on here, but if we're gonna start one, we've gotta do it right!"

POP! POP!

More gunshots from somewhere down a distant hallway . . .

"Where's Billy? Where's Billy?!" shrieked Sauce.

Bagmo paused and nonchalantly rubbed his chin. "Okay, you asked two questions just then, but since it was the same question twice, I'll cut you some slack. Now, you asked me, 'Where's Billy?' My answer: Out *there*." He made a sweeping motion with his hand, indicating the rest of the first floor.

Bagmo's casual attitude toward this obvious emergency was working Sauce into a state of panic. "Billy's in trouble! I gotta go find him! He needs me, but I gotta watch these guys. What am I gonna do?"

"Okay, now you've got the idea! You said a lot of stuff there—tricky maneuver!—but you're not fooling me. You only asked one question, and I think I know the answer: help him!"

"But who's gonna watch these guys?" Sauce pointed to the prisoners.

"Aha! I know this one, too. *I'll* watch them!"

"*You'll* watch them? But what if they escape?"

"Two questions again!" snapped Bagmo. He shook his head in exasperation. "Doesn't anybody but me care about following the rules around here? I should be getting extra points for this!"

"Okay, okay. Never mind."

"*Never mind*?? If everybody had an attitude like that, people would be cheating on quizzes all the time! Then where would we be?"

"I dunno, man." Sauce was thoroughly discombobulated. "Look, Mr. Bagmo, it's just that Billy told me to stay here and watch these guys, and he told me to shoot anyone that moves. That's what I've been doing!"

Bagmo pondered the panicked henchman's words for a moment, glanced at the prisoners on the floor, then back at Sauce. "You say you're supposed to shoot anyone that moves?"

"Yeah!"

"Have you been doing that?"

"Yeah! Well, no—not really. I haven't shot anybody."

"Why haven't you shot yourself?"

"*What*?" Bagmo's question rocked Sauce back on his heels. "Why haven't I shot myself? What're you talking about, man?"

"Think about it! What did Mr. Jelly tell you to do before he left this room?"

Sauce wracked his brain, trying to recall Billy's last order to him. "He-he said, 'Keep your eye on these guys! Shoot anyone that moves!'"

"Okay. Let me ask you this: do you always do everything Mr. Jelly says?"

"Yeah."

"*Everything*??"

"Well, yeah!"

Bagmo pondered Sauce's words for a few seconds more. "'Shoot anyone that moves!'—that would be everybody in this room, right?"

"Well, yeah, I guess . . ."

"Mr. Fingerbanana, if Mr. Jelly meant for you to shoot anyone in this room that moves, you'd have to include yourself. Me and these other guys have been very still. We can't move 'cause you're holding a gun on us."

Brufyss recalled his own discourse with Bagmo about the big banner in the main office and his subsequent conversation with Barley. His old rival had attempted to explain the workings of Bagmo's mind to him; absurd though it was, it was beginning to make sense! He jumped into the dialogue:

"Y'know, you've been moving around a lot, Sauce! Billy must have figured you would. That's why he told you to shoot anyone that moves; he knows you'll shoot yourself 'cause we're not moving and you *are*—and you always do everything he says."

Sauce was utterly baffled. "Billy wants me to kill myself? Why?"

"I already told you! That's Billy's surefire way to avoid sharing Old Man Spuggett's scillions."

"Scillions? Whoa." Bagmo shook his head in disbelief. "That Jelly guy is one selfish dude."

Sauce frantically evaluated the dilemma now confronting him. "I don't know what to do! If Billy's trying to get me to kill myself so he can keep all that money, then I shouldn't be trying to help him."

"Good point!" agreed Bagmo.

"But if he's *not* trying to cheat me and he's really in trouble, then I *should* be trying to help him."

"Good point! Looks like you've got yourself one heck of a problem—I wouldn't want to be in your shoes. Then again, I don't even like being in mine. Marshall Farkpucker's got some cool ones though; they're Cuban-heeled saddle shoes, and—"

POP!—POP!—POP!—POP!

More gunshots!

"What am I gonna do?!" wailed Sauce.

"Man, the questions never stop with you, do they?" groused Bagmo. He paused and rubbed his chin thoughtfully. "Look, you're gonna hafta give me a couple o' minutes with this one, dude! It's a real toughie . . ."

✳ ✳ ✳

Lollie Babajuju and Marshall Farkpucker crossed the main office and entered the second-floor reception room in time to hear what sounded like four gunshots—*POP!*—*POP!*—*POP!*—*POP!* A cacophony of excited voices wafted up the front stairwell. Lollie looked at Marshall in dismay, and Marshall gazed questioningly back at her, having not heard a sound.

Lollie stopped at her reception desk, where the only telephone on the premises was located. She picked up the receiver—dead silence. The line had been cut. No matter; even if she could have used the phone to call for help, who'd understand her?

She peered down the front stairwell and saw nothing. The first floor was strangely silent again. She began her descent, Marshall following. The disturbing commotion indicated that some kind of trouble was afoot, but she felt relatively secure with the javelin in her hand.

Down they went, drawing closer to the first-floor reception room, negotiating the curve near the bottom of the stairs. At the corner of the stairway, she peered around the partitioning wall, listening for any sound or movement.

The silence was abruptly broken by another two gunshot sounds—*POP!*—*POP!*—and more agitated voices, coming from beyond the double doors at the far end of the room. She knew nothing about what might be behind them; as with most of the other Bumps & Spuggett employees, the first floor was unfamiliar territory to both Lollie and Marshall.

Overhead fluorescents lit the room, but no sunlight streamed through the small window facing Clown Balls Avenue. Darkness had descended upon North Corners.

They crossed the empty anteroom to the building's front entrance and saw that the door had been chained and padlocked. Turning to the double doorway, she tried both doors; they were locked as well.

Lollie was fed up with locked doors. Motioning for Marshall to stand aside, she rammed the needle-sharp tip of the javelin into the door lock's keyhole with enough force to shatter the locking mechanism. She signaled for Marshall to open the doors and brandished the javelin. Marshall grasped both doorknobs, turned them, and encountered no resistance; Lollie's javelin thrust had successfully "picked" the lock. He pushed inward on the doors. Lollie cringed, her javelin poised at the ready. The two doors swung open easily.

Old Man Spuggett, Roland Chumbuckets, and Ebenezer Snugnards stood only a few feet away in the intersection of two hallways, staring back at them in surprise. Further up the hallway, at an open doorway on the left side of the corridor, Bagmo Maltgoggles was apparently conversing with someone inside the room.

The old man raised a finger to his lips. Lollie nodded. She and Marshall stepped through the doors and into the hallway, and Lollie quietly closed the double doors.

Old Man Spuggett held out the palm of his hand to reveal several small objects. With pantomime gestures, he informed the newcomers that they were explosively charged, and he was going to detonate them on the floor. Immediately thereafter, they'd run down the corridor to the right. Lollie and Marshall nodded in acknowledgment.

The company founder separated four of the nondestructive explosive devices from the handful he held, gently placing the extras into the pocket of his bathrobe. One by one, he hurled each device onto the floor in rapid succession; the resulting *POP!—POP!—POP!—POP!* filled the empty corridor with noise. Lollie realized she was witnessing the source of the "gunshots."

Immediately following the explosions, Old Man Spuggett, Roland and Ebenezer screamed and shouted. Lollie shrieked, "Sha-lah-lah *boom*-tee-yay! Sha-lah-lah *boom*-tee-yay!" After a few seconds of rowdy noisemaking, the old man signaled for the group to dash down the front hallway to the eastern corridor. They reached the corner, turned north, and headed toward the restrooms.

At the intersection of the hallway to the back stairs, Old Man Spuggett raised his hand to stop the procession. "Our group has gotten too large for us to move quickly and effectively around the building. I propose we move back to headquarters and deposit Lollie and Marshall with the others there. They can assist with keeping an eye on our prisoner."

"Headquarters" was the first-floor conference room. It had become their first-floor base of operations and the room where Billy Jelly sat unconscious, surrounded by other members of the downstairs contingent.

Old Man Spuggett rapped softly on the door; Narducci let them in. Lollie and Marshall stared in surprise at the captured hoodlum.

Now that Old Man Spuggett, Lollie, Marshall, Roland, and Ebenezer had joined the party, the room was feeling claustrophobic. "There are too many of us in here now," Barley whispered. "If Sauce Fingerbanana was to find us, we'd be right in the palm of his hand with his buddy Billy sitting here in our midst! We also need to get back out there to support Bagmo—he's on his own right now."

"What do you propose, Mr. Dooglefoogy?"

"Let's send out two groups of decoys this time. Mr. Spuggett, you take Fandango and Narducci. Chumbuckets, you take Mrs. Kookerly and Yump. We'll need people in this room to guard Billy, so I'll stay here with Ebenezer, Lollie, Marshall, and the doc.

"Mr. Spuggett, keep using those 'firecrackers' of yours to make noise and work your way around the floor. Roland, Mrs. Kookerly, and Yump should concentrate on getting into positions far away from Mr. Spuggett's group and raising a ton of ruckus—there'll be commotion coming from all over this floor. Sauce might panic and give up if he thinks he's surrounded!"

They separated into the two smaller groups Barley had designated and moved back into the north corridor. Old Man Spuggett whispered to Roland that he'd take Fandango and Narducci back to the southwestern portion of the building, where they'd encountered Lollie and Marshall.

"We'll go this way," whispered Roland; he'd take Mrs. Kookerly and Yump down this hallway to the right, in the direction of the library. "We'll have both ends of the western corridor bottled up and blocked off. Sauce won't know which way to run!"

Barley was left in the room with kindly Dr. Pudbid, Lollie, Ebenezer, and Marshall. He was formulating a specific plan for this bunch.

✳✳

"Okay, I think I have an answer to your question," said Bagmo to a very agitated Sauce Fingerbanana. "But before I give it to you, I'll make you a deal. You have to agree that I won the quiz."

"Okay, okay! You won the quiz! Just tell me what I'm supposed to do."

"Ha! Victory is *mine!*" cried Bagmo triumphantly. He looked around for someone to high-five, but the big guys had their hands tied behind their backs, and Sauce was on the other side of the room.

"All right, here's what you gotta do: You go out there and find Mr.

Jelly. If he's in trouble, you help him—that is, if he's not trying to cheat you. But if he's not in trouble and he *is* trying to cheat you, then you help whoever's out there."

"If Billy's trying to cheat me, then I ain't gonna capture him. I'm just gonna shoot him!"

"Uh-uh! No way, dude! Mr. Spuggett said no weapons."

"*What?*" Sauce was overloaded.

Bagmo felt compassion for Sauce's predicament. "Look, Mr. Saucebanana, it's all pretty simple, really. You need to find out what's going on, but you won't really know until you check it out for yourself."

"But who's gonna watch these guys while I'm gone? Billy will kill me if I let 'em get away!"

"How 'bout if I watch 'em for you?"

Sauce considered this for a moment and made a decision. "Okay, great! Thanks, man." There was relief in his voice. "You're really helping me out of a jam here. Just shoot 'em if they try to get away."

"And what am I gonna shoot 'em with—my good looks? Besides, I already told you, Mr. Spuggett said no weapons!"

Sauce looked down at the gun in his hand. He contemplated handing it over to Bagmo, then realized he hardly knew this guy, other than the fact he was an ardent quizmaster who rigidly insisted on playing by the rules. But he *was* very helpful.

"Look, you just stay here in this room, keep watch on these guys, and I'll keep the gun. I might need it to help Billy—that is, if I *decide* to help Billy! But if I see you or any of these guys try to leave this room, I'm gonna come back here and blow you away. Understand?"

"Yes!" answered Bagmo with finality. "Okay, that's it: end of quiz! But I gotta tell you, Mr. Sauce, if you go out there and use that gun, you'll be breaking the rules. You know what Mr. Spuggett said!"

"Is Mr. Spuggett the guy who keeps making up all these rules?"

"Sorry, too late! The quiz is over. Ya just gotta draw the line somewhere!"

Sauce said nothing more but grabbed a padlock and a short length of chain from the windowsill behind him. He dashed around the seated big guys and over to the office doorway, just as another round of **POP!**—**POP!**—**POP!**—**POP!** reverberated from somewhere on the first floor.

Sauce shrieked in panic. "Someone out there is breaking the rules! Why can't I?"

"Good point!" conceded Bagmo, relieved that the quiz was over.

Sauce really had him with that one—unless he spilled the beans about the "gunshots."

Sauce muscled his way past Bagmo, turned, and pushed the quizmaster from the hallway into the room. "Stay here!"

He slammed the door. To the dismay of the prisoners, they heard him applying the chain and padlock. They were still trapped, and now Bagmo was trapped with them.

The frightened henchman ran down the corridor, shouting, "Billy! I'm coming! Where are you?" His voice trailed into the distance.

Brufyss stared at Bagmo from his seat on the floor, profound admiration in his eyes. "Bagmo, that was amazing—especially the part about him having to shoot himself. That bit was so over the top it was *brilliant*! You freaked Sauce totally out of his wits."

"I was only telling him the truth!"

Brufyss blinked in surprise, then comprehension dawned; he now clearly understood what Barley said about Bagmo's level of perception. The way Bagmo had perceived the situation, everything he told Sauce was truthful and logical. Sauce really *would* have been required to shoot himself.

"Be that as it may, I'm afraid you're trapped in here with us now. Good try, though."

Bagmo smiled mischievously. "Not to worry, Mr. Brufyss! We're not trapped. We're all getting out of here, right now."

Brufyss was nonplussed. They were all padlocked in this stuffy, dusty room. What level of perception did one need to believe they could get out of this?

Bagmo walked over to the empty bookshelf, said, "Okay, Cheezy!" and stood back as the bookshelf swung open to reveal a hidden passageway. There in the secret doorway stood Simpleton Fabsmaggle, smiling widely.

"Hi, guys! Check out the secret passage! Isn't it *cool*?"

The big guys gawked. "Huzzah!" cried Mayor Wubbleduster. "Forsooth, good Masters Bagmo and Fabsmaggle, thou hast 'pon us a reprieve to all our trials and travails most eloquently bestow'd, aye, and in a fashion most timely!"

"Huh?"

Big Biff translated. "The mayor says, 'Good work, guys! You saved our butts!'"

"Abundant thanks," added Reverend Snortworthy, "for delivering us from evil!"

"Ya, shure, yabetcha!" chimed Dork, a beaming grin smeared across his big Nordic face.

"No problem, guys," said Bagmo. "But we gotta get outa here now, before that Sauce guy comes back."

The boys proceeded to remove the captives' electrical tape bindings, help them to their feet, and lead them through the secret bookshelf door, into the passage, to freedom.

* * *

Roland, Mrs. Kookerly, and Yump peered down the western corridor where Old Man Spuggett, Fandango, and Narducci had positioned themselves and watched the old man detonate four noisy nondestructive devices on the floor.

POP!—POP!—POP!—POP! The explosions wobbled the walls and shook the ceiling. The screams, yells, whoops, and hollers generated by both groups sent Sauce Fingerbanana blasting past Bagmo and into the hallway.

After padlocking the door, Sauce whirled and sped down the hall toward Old Man Spugget's group. "Billy! I'm coming! Where are you?"

"Quick! This way!" cried the company founder. The panicked thug took off in pursuit.

They bolted down the south hallway, led by Fandango Slamson, his cry of "*Aaaaaaahhh! Aaaaaaahhh!*" echoing through the hollow corridor.

Roland's team ran up the north hallway, parallel with the old man's group, stopping in front of the center office on their right. (*Figure 8*) Within seconds, Fandango and the others came roaring up the restroom corridor toward them. When Fandango made the turn into the north corridor, Roland directed the speedy office manager into the center office. Fandango zipped into the room, Mrs. Kookerly and Yump followed him, and Roland guided Old Man Spuggett and Narducci quickly into the headquarters room. He closed the door just as Sauce careened around the corner. The bus driver yelled, "Sauce! In here!" and bolted into the center office, following in the wake of Fandango, Mrs. Kookerly, and Yump.

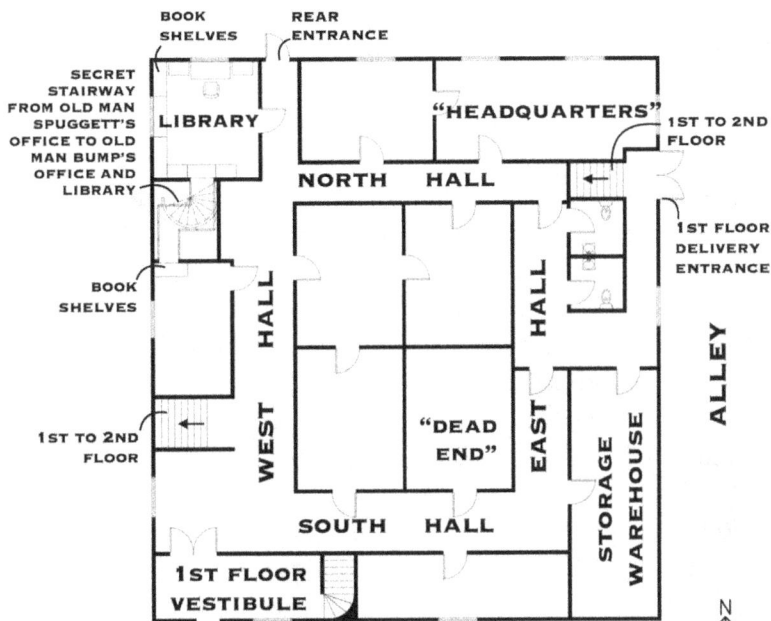

**FIGURE 8
(1ST FLOOR)**

Mrs. Kookerly and Yump ran through the center office and through the connecting door. Once inside the next room, the two split up, Mrs. Kookerly zipping through the office's main door into the western corridor. Yump followed Fandango's trail to the southern corridor. Mrs. Kookerly faced the door to Old Man Bumps's office; she knew Brufyss and the others were being held captive there, but with the padlock on the door, there was nothing she could do to help them. She looked back into the office just as Roland burst through the connecting door with Sauce Fingerbanana on his heels. Roland spotted her standing in the corridor and yelled, "Go right!"

She took off in the direction of the library just as the library door opened. Cheezy Fabsmaggle emerged from the room, leading the newly freed captives.

"Brufyss! This way!"

Seeing her beautiful visage, Brufyss reacted with surprise and relief, but her sense of urgency dictated that they move with all possible speed.

She sped up the north corridor to the headquarters room, flung open the door, and gestured frantically for the group to get inside.

She shut the door behind them just as Fandango made the turn into the north corridor and *whooshed* past the room, narrowly avoiding a head-on collision with the escaped prisoners. At last, the big guys were free and reunited with the group, and Mrs. Kookerly rushed into Brufyss's arms.

Barley watched the extreme happiness of the reunited couple with a trace of envy, but his envy was no longer inspired by jealousy. He conceded that Brufyss's and Mrs. Kookerly's love for each other was genuine. They were meant to be together. Barley realized that his feelings now were motivated by a distinct longing for a person he could share *his* life with. He'd been on his own much too long. Pangs of emptiness and loneliness surfaced within him. But he'd never again begrudge Brufyss Bathwater and Mrs. Kookerly their happiness. Now he just wanted his friends back.

Roland led Sauce on a wild romp through the first-floor office labyrinth. In Sauce's abject panic, all he could process was that the people he was chasing seemed to be trying to help him. They kept shouting at him, telling him where to go. The guy in front of him seemed to know exactly where to head next.

Roland knew that this wild goose chase had to end, and soon. He was getting tired. He could tell from Sauce's heavy breathing that his pursuer was approaching the same state of exhaustion. Where should he lead him? How could they finally catch him?

The bus driver burst into the southern corridor near the front entrance. He looked to his left—Yump was rounding the corner of the southern hallway, heading toward the restrooms.

A flashbulb went off inside Roland's head. He remembered that the office Yump had just passed was the only one of the four center offices with no connecting door. If he lured Sauce into this "dead end" room, the crook would be trapped. They'd have him!

Roland darted to the office and pulled the door open just as Sauce emerged into the south corridor and paused to catch his breath. "Sauce! He's in *here!*"

Sauce jerked his head to the left and saw Roland standing just a few feet away.

Billy's in there! He took a step toward the bus driver. Before he could take a second, he was blindsided by Fandango Slamson—*KABONK!*—

who'd hurtled around the corner after sprinting down the western corridor.

The collision of the office manager and panicked hoodlum was just a glancing blow. Fandango jigged a step and continued down the hall past Roland, but the blow spun Sauce like a top. His momentum carried him into the double doors of the front entrance. He banged against them. They remained stubbornly shut but bounced him off like a trampoline. Sauce staggered back into the corridor, completely disoriented.

Roland watched helplessly as the thug lurched up the western corridor, saw the stairs on his left, and scrambled up, still clutching his gun. "I'm on my way, Billy! I'm on my way!"

He disappeared up the stairwell.

Roland was now in a panic himself. Sauce was taking his gun upstairs, and everyone who could catch him was down here!

He closed the door to the dead-end room and dashed back to headquarters to deliver the bad news: Sauce Fingerbanana was loose on the second floor.

✳ ✳ ✳

Within the headquarters, the big guys were reunited with their compatriots. They exchanged a hearty round of handshakes and back-slapping. Brufyss turned to Barley, who stood next to Billy's chair, and looked down on the unconscious criminal. "I see you were able to nab this bum before he killed somebody."

"Yeah, my bus driver kayoed him. We've still gotta bag Sauce Fingerbanana."

Brufyss laughed. "Man, you should have seen Bagmo bamboozle that guy. It was a one-in-a-million moment. He totally lost it—tore out of that room like his butt was on fire!"

The group chuckled at Brufyss's vivid descriptive. "You said *butt*!" giggled Narducci.

Old Man Spuggett beamed proudly at Bagmo and Cheezy. "You boys both lived up to my expectations with flying colors. Bagmo, I assume you related the facts to Mr. Fingerballerina as you saw them?"

"Tried to, Mr. Spuggett, but mostly I just beat the pants off him in the quiz we played."

"That he did!" agreed Brufyss.

"No one stands a chance against Bagmo when it comes to quizzes," confirmed Cheezy.

Bagmo frowned. "Getting people to follow the rules is the toughest part."

"*Amen!*" seconded Reverend Snortworthy.

"Barley, you took a bullet for Mrs. Kookerly and me," Brufyss said. "I want to thank you; there's no way we can ever repay that."

Barley looked at Brufyss with a scowl on his face and snarled, "Don't flatter yourself, Bathwater. My motive was purely selfish."

Brufyss was taken aback. "Selfish?"

"Yeah, you heard what I said—*selfish!*" His face softened into a smile. "I want you to be my friends. I didn't want to lose you!"

Brufyss smiled and extended his right hand. Barley grasped it with his own. They shook hands warmly for the first time in over forty years, bringing to an end four decades of animosity.

The headquarters door burst open, and Yump stumbled into the room. The group stared at him in surprise, and Narducci quickly shut the door behind him.

"Yump, what's going on out there?"

"That Sauce guy has a gun and he's chasing Roland and Fandango! We gotta help 'em!"

Barley realized that with the exception of Roland and Fandango, the entire downstairs contingent was in this room again. Those two had been inadvertently abandoned and were now alone in attempting to mislead Sauce Fingerbanana around the first floor.

"Yump's right! We've gotta get back out there and give those two guys a hand!"

The words were barely out of his mouth before the door burst open again and Roland staggered in, gasping for breath. "Mr. Spuggett! Mr. Doodlebody! Something's happened . . . that we've gotta stop . . . right away!" He sank to his knees, nearly overcome with exhaustion.

An excited chorus of "Roland! What is it?" erupted from the room's occupants.

"Sauce got away. He's . . . headed upstairs . . . with his gun!"

"Good gracious alive!" cried Old Man Spuggett, aghast. "Those people up there are unarmed. We've left them unprotected!"

"Listen up!" shouted Barley over the resulting din of dismay. "We've gotta move fast here! Chumbuckets, which way did he go?"

"Up the front stairway . . . that comes out . . . into the big room."

"That's the stairway Daphne used! We're going to have to break up into teams again. We'll cover every access route to the second floor and work our way upstairs; he won't be able to come back down without running into us.

"Chumbuckets, you take Yump, Bagmo, and Cheezy and head up that same stairway. Reverend, you take Narducci and Dork and cover the back stairs. Mr. Spuggett, Brufyss, Mrs. Kookerly, Doc Pudbid, and I will take the stairway leading up to Lollie's reception room—"

"What about us?" interrupted Biff, pointing at Mayor Wubbleduster, Ebenezer, Lollie, and Marshall. "What're *we* supposed to do?"

"Biff, you guys stay with Billy. Someone's gotta be here when this bum wakes up."

Barley addressed the entire group. "When Billy and Sauce padlocked us into the building, they were locking themselves in as well. As long as things were going their way, that wasn't a problem, but they didn't count on things going south. Now they're trapped in here just like we are. We have to convince Sauce that he no longer wants to be here—to make him wish he was anywhere else in the world but in this building. Maybe *this* will help us accomplish that!"

Barley reached into his pocket and produced the same silver police whistle he'd used so effectively in grabbing his tour group's attention earlier in the day. He held up the shiny noisemaker for everyone to see; the tourists remembered it well. "I think it's time to put this to work for us. I don't think Sauce or Billy would be happy to hear anything that might sound like a *cop*!"

"This will be our time to shine," cried Old Man Spuggett. "Remember: seize the day and suck the moment!"

The teams moved to their assigned second-floor stairways. Barley gave one final instruction to the remaining group: "We're all counting on you guys to keep Billy quiet and under control when he wakes up. Don't let him out of that chair!"

He smiled and spoke pointedly to the mayor's public relations advisor and personal bodyguard: "Biff, no matter what, don't *you* say one word!"

Biff looked questioningly at Barley for a second, then back at his own group. A light suddenly dawned in his eyes, and he grinned widely.

Barley winked and left the headquarters room, pulling the door shut.

41

A subdued, somber air hovered in the second-floor conference room. In the aftermath of Lollie Babajuju's confrontation with Alpha Rae and her subsequent departure with Marshall Farkpucker, the remaining tourists and staffers settled into contemplative conversation, pondering their situation and that of their absent compatriots.

Out of the blue and for no apparent reason, Faisal Herskowitz burst into a raging fit of uncontrolled, riotous laughter. He rolled around on the floor, giggling, guffawing, and snorting wildly, clutching his midsection, tears of mirth cascading down his cheeks. His unbridled hysterics had a contagious effect on the psyches of the room's other occupants, inducing gradual chuckles throughout the group. One by one, they began to titter, chortle, and snigger. As more people caught the bug, the giggles morphed into guffaws. In a short time, everyone was swept up in side-splitting laughter.

Their revelry was brought to an abrupt halt by the *POP!—POP!—POP!—POP!* of Old Man Spuggett's nondestructive explosive devices being detonated around the first floor. Silence replaced laughter, their apprehension reignited. Since they were not briefed on the downstairs contingent's diversionary strategy, they had no idea that the old man's concoctions were responsible for the noise, believing instead that the muffled explosions were gunshots being fired by the crooks. The somber mood returned and more time crept by in quiet disquiet—until they could take no more.

Each individual resolved that he could no longer sit and bide time in this stifling room while friends and coworkers were being assailed, assaulted, and assassinated. It was time to get involved, whatever the consequences. As one, they all rose and approached Alpha Rae.

Noodles spoke first. Barley, her boss, and Dork, her new love interest, were both facing unknown dangers downstairs. "Veeer gettin' *outen* heeer, bygosh, yabetcha!"

It was not a request.

The rest of the group clustered around the executive secretary. "Yeah, Alpha Rae. We all wanna help!" exclaimed Bimbo.

"And that means all of us," added Gerald. "Even *me*!"

Mimsy: "And *me*!"

Rapunzel: "And *me*!"

"And I am to including also myself! *Whaaaa-hah-hah-haaaaaaaah!*" Faisal exploded into more unprovoked laughter, prompting a new round of giggles.

"And me too!" chuckled Daphne, trying to recompose her demeanor from gleeful to grave.

"Yeah, buddy!" chimed Frog, whose demeanor, like his conversation, never seemed to change from one mood to the next.

"But what if we all get *killed*?" wailed Felicia.

"My argument exactly!" cried Alpha Rae, jumping onto Felicia's bandwagon. "It's my responsibility to see that no one is hurt, dies, or gets killed! I can't in good conscience let all of you go out into the unknown unarmed and unprepared. There are murderers, thugs, and thieves lurking out there, people!"

"But our friends are out there too," argued Gerald.

"Look, Ms. Sapoopa-LaBoobis—if we get killed, we promise not to blame you. I'll give you a full report," Bimbo said.

The group's fervent loyalty made Alpha Rae realize that no matter what argument she presented or how much authority she attempted to exercise, she'd be outnumbered and overruled by them all. Deep down, she was in total agreement with them; the situation couldn't be allowed to continue.

"Okay—you win! When you're right, you're right. Why should we stay cooped up in this stuffy room? Let's go out there and kick some butt!"

Everyone cheered, and Faisal burst into more hysterical cackling, which stimulated a fresh spate of the same from his compatriots. When Alpha Rae pushed the conference-room door open and allowed the laughter-convulsed throng to stream into the main office, her inner apprehension at sending these people into harm's way was overruled by her conviction that this nightmarish episode must be brought to an end once and for all.

＊＊

Wiley Fingerbanana was feeling decidedly *un*-wily as he clambered up the front stairway to the second floor. He was frightened, confused, lost, desperate, and heading into unfamiliar territory. Thus far, his travels within the Bumps & Spuggett building had been limited to the first floor, but his fear of getting caught and captured outweighed his fear of the unknown. He'd take his chances—and he had his gun. Maybe he'd only have to use it to intimidate people into staying away from him.

He emerged through the double doors into the commodious main office. After his long sequestration in the stuffy confines of the first floor, the vast chamber seemed like the interior of a domed football stadium.

A small procession of people, all laughing like hyenas, streamed out of a doorway to his left, far across the room. He stopped at the head of the stairway as they flooded in; it appeared they hadn't noticed his presence. Their mass mirth was puzzling: what could possibly be so funny when everything in *his* world was so intensely serious?

To Sauce's chagrin, Billy Jelly wasn't among them. If Billy wasn't downstairs and wasn't with this group, where was he?

He spotted a familiar face—Daphne Dogdaughter. She entered the room, wheezing with laughter and escorting a guy with a red piece of cloth wrapped around his head. Sauce's first reaction was one of relief, until it struck him that she was in the company of their presumed enemies. Was she friend or foe, ally or enemy? Should he call out to her or run away?

These questions were rendered moot when Daphne spied Sauce. "*Wiley*! Wiley, there you are. Come over here!"

He'd always appreciated that Daphne eschewed using the nickname "Sauce" when addressing him. Now that he thought about it, Daphne had always been sweet and considerate, never talking down to him like Billy did; his first instinct was to trust his kindhearted compatriot. But when Daphne cried out to him, it also attracted the attention of the gleeful group of strangers. They ceased their laughter and stared at him.

Daphne saw the terror in Sauce's eyes and on his face. She walked into the center of the big room with Frog and called out like the owner of a frightened dog trying to coax her panicked pooch out from under the refrigerator: "Wiley, there's no reason to be afraid. These people are very nice. They won't hurt you!"

"Yeah, buddy!" agreed Frog.

Sauce froze in place. He heard Daphne's sincerity but also saw the rest of the people transfixed with as much apprehension as himself, all of them staring at the gun he clutched in his hand.

Then something unexpected happened. A young man walked across the room, passed in front of Daphne and Frog, and stopped a few yards from where Sauce was standing. "Hello, my name is Bimbo Spazzgate. It's my duty as an employee of this company to ask you the following question: are you going to kill us?"

Sauce was stunned. "*Kill* you? Why are you asking me if I'm gonna kill you?"

"Well, you're carrying a gun, and we already had a previous incident today when another guy with a gun tried to kill a whole bunch of us. Do you have the same intention? Please understand, if you do kill us, I have to make a full report to our executive secretary."

Sauce was aghast at the inference that he might be intending to commit mass murder. "You gotta be kiddin', man! I'm not gonna kill anyone; I'm just tryin' to find Billy!"

"Billy? Billy was the guy who tried to kill us!" Gerald said. "He captured me an' Cheezy an' Bimbo when we were downstairs, an' he *shot* Mr. Doodlebody! He was shooting at *everybody*!"

Gerald stood next to Bimbo. Soon, the entire upstairs contingent gravitated to join Bimbo and Gerald as they dialogued with the gun-toting stranger.

"Billy tried to kill you? He shot Mr., er, Somebody?"

"Not 'Mr. *Some*-body'!" corrected Bimbo. "Mr. *Doodle*-body! That Billy guy shot him right in the arm, but he was tryin' to *kill* Brufyss and Mrs. Kookerly and Fandango and Mux! Now, if you please, will you answer my question so I can prepare my report for Alpha Rae?"

"What question?"

"Are you gonna *kill us*?"

Sauce saw the apprehensive group waiting for his answer. His anxiety blossomed into full-blown panic. "Daphne, I don't wanna kill anyone. I *never* wanted to kill anyone! People are chasing me—*shooting* at me! I thought we were just coming here to kick some guy out of this place that you and Mr. Brufyss and Mrs. Kookerly didn't like! When you all went upstairs, Billy started acting real funny. He made me put locks on all the doors. He made me take this gun! He made me guard some big guys I never saw before, and he told me to shoot anybody that moved—*including me!*

"Mr. Brufyss told me that Billy was gonna rob scillions of dollars from some guy named Mr. Spuggett—he's the one who makes all the rules around here. But Billy never told me that! All he told me was to guard those guys and shoot 'em if I had to. But I *didn't* shoot anybody! I haven't shot this gun at all!"

"You weren't the one shooting just now?" asked Daphne. "We heard lots of shots!"

"I wasn't doing it, Daphne, I swear. Somebody was shooting at *me!*"

Sauce trembled like a leaf, broke down, and sobbed like a penitent waif. "Daphne, I don't wanna shoot anyone, I don't wanna kill anyone, I don't wanna rob anyone or hurt 'em, I don't wanna hold anybody prisoner, and I don't want anyone to hate me or be afraid of me. I don't wanna even *be* here! All I wanna do is go home and do my experiments!"

Bimbo: "So—is that a *no?*"

Sauce's pitiful protestations struck a chord of pathos in his audience. They were filled with compassion for this poor, lost, and lonely confessor. However, one individual in the contingent was struck by something more. Like a moth drawn irresistibly to a candle, Gerald Foon-Package gravitated toward the trembling fugitive. "Experiments? Would you be referring to *scientific* experiments? Are you a scientist, sir?"

Sauce stared nervously at the strange man who was staring so intently at him. "Well, um—I'd *like* to be a scientist, but I just do experiments. It's kind of a hobby. I don't think I've actually discovered anything yet—"

"But you're saying you'd *like* to be a scientist?"

"Well, yeah! Billy says I'm too stupid to be a scientist, but I wanna discover somethin' nobody's ever discovered before—instead of bein' a two-bit crook."

"Maybe you could discover how to put your two bits together," offered Bimbo.

"The only thing I've discovered so far is that I'm too stupid to be a scientist."

"Balderdash!" pronounced Gerald magnanimously. "Why, look at me! I'm a scientist. *Anyone* can look scientific. Even you!"

"You mean I could really *be* a scientist?" Sauce hardly dared to believe.

"You bet you could! That is, unless you're stupid enough to think you're too stupid to be a scientist!"

"But . . . but how? How can I be a scientist when I've never been to science school?"

"By working with me as my assistant! A person like yourself, who performs scientific experiments for the true love of science, even though you're too stupid to be a scientist—that's the kind of person I want working with *me*!

"I recently had another assistant, but he was a real klutz: falling down the stairs, spilling important ingredients all over the floor, all over me, all over himself—although to be fair, his true area of expertise is working with teriyaki sauce. But I see true potential in you, sir! True potential and scientific passion, which is most important! I believe that both of us, working together in tandem, could do great deeds, achieve great achievements, and create great creations.

"But first, we'll have to do something about that gun you're carrying. No true scientists carry guns—unless they happen to be gun scientists, of course, but I am not a gun scientist, I don't carry a gun, and I do not want a gun in my laboratory! It's hard enough for me to keep from blowing myself up with my experiments without having to worry about blowing my head off with a gun."

"Look, I don't even want this gun." Sauce held the gun out like it was a dead skunk. The group shrank back from the steel-gray weapon like it was a *live* skunk. "Billy's the one who made me carry it. Here, you can have it! *Anybody* can have it; I don't care! I just wanna be a scientist!"

Daphne scurried up to him and reached out. "Here, Wiley, I'll take that for you."

She eased the gun out of Sauce's trembling grasp and stepped back.

"There!" cried Sauce triumphantly. "Daphne's got the gun. Does that mean I can be a scientist now?"

Gerald's eyes lit up. "I don't see why not. Wait a second! I've got an idea."

He paused for a moment, lost in thought. The gathered group held their breaths expectantly. What brilliant inspiration had just hit their scientist-in-residence? At length Gerald broke his silent rumination and spoke with urgency.

"Mr. Fingerbanana, are there bullets in that gun?"

"Well, yeah, I told you—I didn't shoot 'em!"

"Is there gunpowder in those bullets?" Gerald's voice rose with excitement.

"I would imagine so," answered Daphne.

"*Great*! Give 'em to me!"

Daphne popped open the gun's revolving cylindrical chamber; it was indeed loaded with six potentially lethal projectiles. She emptied the bullets into her hand and placed them into Gerald's outstretched palm.

"What are you thinking, Gerald?" asked Alpha Rae suspiciously. "What do you need bullets for?"

"Yeah!" agreed Bimbo. "If you're gonna shoot someone, you need a gun. You can't shoot anyone by *throwing* a bullet at them!"

"It's not the bullets I need; it's the gunpowder. I think I can use it in my next experiment!"

"Really? You're gonna do an experiment?" Sauce was ecstatic. "Could I watch?"

"Watch? Mr. Fingerbanana, you can start your scientific apprenticeship right now by assisting me."

"And just who do you think is gonna *pay* him, Gerald?" Alpha Rae asked. "We haven't asked Mr. Spuggett about this yet!"

"Oh, I don't need to be paid, ma'am. I'm honored to be able to help. Maybe I could just have some food occasionally—"

"See? He's making demands already!"

"Alpha Rae, if he's working for Gerald, he'll have all the cure for excess hair growth he can eat," reasoned Bimbo.

"There you have it!" Gerald was excited and impatient to begin his work. "Mr. Fingerbanana will be my new assistant if he so desires. Do we have an agreement, sir?"

Before Sauce had the chance to reply, the shrill, piercing shriek of a police whistle cut through the air like a scythe through celery—TWEEEEEEEET!—and more **POP! POP! POP! POP!** explosions could be heard coming up the stairwell.

Shouting voices, great noise and commotion, and the clomping of heavy feet issued from all the stairwells, including the one from which Sauce had just emerged. They were coming up the stairs behind him.

"*Cops*! Cops are in the building! It's over! I'm busted!"

He sank to his knees in defeat and supplication.

The noise grew louder and closer as their perpetrators ascended the stairs to the second floor. Then, something new: a chant! "Seize the day! Suck the moment! Seize the day! Suck the moment!" The police whistle shrieked once more and another round of **POP! POP! POP! POP!** exploded from the front stairwell.

Sauce screamed in terror. "They're comin' to get me! I didn't hurt anyone! Billy made me do it! I don't wanna go to jail!"

"Quick! Come with me!" Gerald grabbed Sauce by the arm, pulled him to his feet, and steered him toward the door to the attic stairway. "I'm gonna get you out of trouble. No one's gonna come up to my lab."

"Please just get me out of here!"

"Seize the day! Suck the moment! Seize the day! Suck the moment!"

Gerald Foon-Package, intrepid inventor and aspiring mentor, led his new protégé up to the impregnable, inviolable sanctuary of his attic laboratory.

Or so he thought.

***

Below them, the tourist and guest members of the upstairs contingent were unaware of the reasons for this raucous cacophony; they panicked and scattered. Apprehensive at the prospect of facing the police, Daphne pulled Frog back into the conference room, blue-faced Mimsy cowered in a corner of Yump's cubicle, and Rapunzel took refuge in Cheezy's corner office, clutching her stack of writing paper like a security blanket.

Although the B & S employees were initially as confused and frightened as the tourists, it dawned on them that there was something familiar about that chant, which lessened their sense of dread.

In the midst of the pandemonium, Noodles grabbed little Margaret by the hand and looked for a place to hide. Just behind her was the broken doorway to Old Man Spuggett's private office. Noodles led Margaret into the old man's sanctum and perused the interior. The only place that might accommodate both of them was the closet. The open door beckoned.

She noticed the framed poster hanging on the wall next to the closet and realized the chanting throng was incanting those exact words! She was puzzled, but her instinct to protect little Margaret took precedence over her inquisitiveness. As the chaos and noise in the main office rose to a crescendo, Noodles and Margaret discovered that the closet's rear wall was a false one. Noodles's curiosity was piqued again; she had to explore this hidden opening. Perhaps it would give them added security from the mayhem in the main room.

Little Margaret was also thrilled by this new revelation and just as eager as her guardian to explore what lay beyond the mysterious secret door. She clasped Noodles's huge hand tightly, and the two of them entered, discovering a narrow, steeply inclined stairway that wound downward into darkness. With nothing but ambient light to illuminate their path, the two proceeded down the narrow spiraled stairs, negotiating each step with extreme care.

**

The veil of unconsciousness enveloping Billy Jelly was beginning to lift. The hoodlum slowly roused himself, his head ablaze with searing pain from the blow he'd received, his mind awash in a swirling, disorienting maelstrom of jumbled images and voices. He was in a chair but felt his arms pinned behind him. He squirmed in an attempt to free himself and realized that as he did so, even more constricting pressure was being applied to his limbs, holding him in place.

He lifted his chin, opened his eyes, and blinked several times. A blurry shape presented itself, inches from his face. He blinked again, trying to bring the shape into clearer focus; the inscrutable image was a person. The awakening thug was gazing straight into the face of Ebenezer Snugnards, who smiled.

"Rim-ta-tim-ta-tippity tay!"

Billy wasn't sure he'd heard correctly. Maybe he was having an auditory hallucination.

"Huh?"

"Resolutely raffish! Modernistically moderated! Resoundingly regurgitated!"

"Wha'?"

A female voice came from somewhere behind Ebenezer. "Malala bumbaloolah!"

Billy shifted in his seat, trying to see past Ebenezer. His movement instigated a fresh application of pressure on his constricted arms.

Yet another voice: "Methinks yon scoundrel the light of revival doth see!"

Billy didn't understand a word, but his vision was returning. He began to see who and what surrounded him. He surreptitiously cast his eyes from side to side. He was in a sitting in the center of an empty room. Straight ahead was a wall with a closed door, with another closed portal situated in the wall to his right. Obscuring these exits were the people speaking to him in strange tongues.

He saw the man standing in front of him more clearly. Behind him stood the woman he thought he heard a moment ago. She was brandishing what appeared to be a spear! Standing next to her was a large man with scraggly, dyed-black hair who looked vaguely familiar. Billy believed this guy had also spoken a moment ago, albeit unintelligibly.

Who was holding his arms? Billy cocked his head to the left. Out of the corner of his eye, he saw a very large man behind him who also looked vaguely familiar but who'd been silent. On his right side stood another strange-looking guy, dressed in such odd, colorful clothing that he looked like a circus clown without makeup. The clown said nothing as well.

"Where am I? Who are you?"

"But soft! The knave awakens, his eye in fevered quest a-wand'ring, his realm to ascertain . . ."

"What?"

"Justification apparent, forthwith resumed."

"Huh?"

"Papalappa-loopah-doopah-doop!"

The two men behind him remained silent.

"What are you people *saying*? Am I still knocked out? Where am I?"

He began to squirm in the chair. Biff and Marshall increased the pressure on his arms.

"*Ow*! Hey, lay off, will ya?"

Lollie raised the javelin over her head, bared her teeth, and grimaced fiercely. "Chubba-bumbily boola-babaloo!"

Ebenezer added support to Lollie's theatrical display. "Lollie, Lollie! Lock-tight lipperator loopy-tootle-too!"

"Chop-chop bobba-lop, shoo-shapoopy-doo!" cried the receptionist.

"Umber trenchant rubber mensche-a booty bungie-bumpers!" exclaimed Ebenezer.

Billy's eyes widened with terror. Whatever these raving maniacs were saying to each other, it didn't sound good, especially coming from that lady with the spear.

He looked imploringly at Mayor Wubbleduster. "What are they saying? What do they want? Is she gonna kill me?"

"Nay, miscreant, thy fears be naught and needless! Forsooth, the twain nor a word in anger spake; 'tis a play, a show, a mere contrivance, thine own fears to inspire!"

"What are you talking about?" Billy was convinced he'd awakened in another dimension. Was this a dream? A nightmare? What was reality? What *wasn't* reality? "Somebody tell me what's going on here!"

Lollie began shaking her javelin. "Ga-nuck! Ga-nooka! Ga-bimba-booka!"

Ebenezer shook his head. "Hat box momma, chuffa-choo, chuffa-choo!"

"'Tis but a spell thou hast 'pon thyself bestow'd!" explained Mayor Wubbleduster.

In frustration, Billy turned his head to Marshall Farkpucker: "*You*! You ain't said nothin' yet! Can you understand what these nuts are talkin' about?"

Marshall looked down upon Billy, a serene smile spread across his face. He said nothing.

Billy turned to Biff. "How about you, big fella? Can *you* say somethin' intelligent?"

Biff mimicked Marshall's placid grin, remaining silent.

Billy had another unsettling thought: "Am I dead?"

Biff, the mayor, and Ebenezer snickered at Billy's supposition. Lollie and Marshall joined in the frivolity; soon, everyone except Billy was giggling and laughing.

"Stop laughing and answer me! Am I dead, or not?"

Lollie walked up to Billy, bent down, and placed her face inches away from his. She said, "Habbalah-habbalah-habbalah babbalah-*booo*!" then shook her javelin and cackled like a chicken.

Ebenezer burst into laughter and began to chant, "Oh-mah, oh-mah yuppa-duppa-ding-dong!" while bouncing up and down and spinning around like a jack-in-the-box ballerina. Billy stared at him with eyes so wide that they were liable to pop out of their sockets.

"Nay, brigand! Death hath not its clammy hand 'pon thy brow yet lain! 'Tis thine own mind, aye, and thine own intemp'rate disposition with which thou must contend! We jest, but thou hast not the humor to digest it!"

Mayor Wubbleduster was informing Billy that the group was messing with his head. The bewildered gangster's messed-up head perceived something else: that he'd most likely been abducted by aliens from the planet Gloxnar who were about to devour him as a snack, or perform some type of perverse medical experiment with the javelin. He'd heard about that kind of stuff; he wasn't about to let it happen to him.

The rebellious aspect of his antisocial personality reasserted itself: "I dunno who you are or what you want, but you ain't gettin' away with it without a *fight*!"

The thug squirmed and struggled violently, thrashing from side to side, rocking the chair back and forth, fighting through the pain in his two pinned arms and the throbbing of his battered head to break free of the restraints. Biff and Marshall grappled with the panicked gangster, attempting to keep him pinned to the chair. The joke had run its course— the situation was now turning serious.

Lollie, the mayor, and Ebenezer dashed to assist Biff and Marshall. In seconds, the once tranquil headquarters room transformed into jumbled turmoil. Billy growled and snarled like a cornered tiger, oblivious to his own pain and discomfort. He had nothing to lose; these alien freaks were going to pay a stiff price if they wanted a piece of him.

Suddenly and without warning, Fandango Slamson burst through the door in the midst of the mayhem, screaming, "*Aaaaaahh! Aaaaaahh!*" He'd been performing his high-speed laps on the first floor until he realized he was all alone, having seen neither friend nor foe in his last few circuits. He'd come back to headquarters to find out what was going on and why he'd been forgotten.

Fandango's untimely interruption of the mêlée surprised the group and stopped them cold. Billy seized the initiative, violently wrenching himself out of their clutches and bolting out of the chair. The main door was blocked by his enemies. He scrambled for the door in the wall to his right.

"He's making a break for it!" cried Biff.

Billy reached the side door, pulled it open, and darted into the room beyond. Slamming the door and locking it, he was free from the clutches of the evil Gloxnarians—for the moment. He couldn't stay holed up; he was certain the aliens would send out a search party to bring him back. He had to find a way out.

"Okay, the game's over!" cried Biff. "We can't let that guy back upstairs again; the other guy with a gun went up there! Your Honor, we'll take Fandango and follow Billy through this door. Ebenezer, Lollie! Take Marshall and head out the main door!"

"Chibbily-chibbily bupkis!" Ebenezer motioned for Lollie and Marshall to join him.

Biff, the mayor, and Fandango sprang to the side door. They would have to break it down.

Billy felt the door behind him quiver and vibrate from the blows. He had to move fast. There was another partially opened door in the wall to his left. He ran to it, poked his head through, and saw a wide hallway just outside the door, deserted and vaguely familiar.

The door behind him burst open and crashed back against the wall. Biff, Fandango, and the mayor poured through and spotted him about to enter the north corridor. Billy stepped into the passageway and violently slammed the door in the faces of his pursuers.

He paused for a split second and looked down the western corridor. It was empty. Turning toward the north corridor, he realized that his choice of an escape route had already been made for him. Lollie, Marshall, and Ebenezer emerged through a doorway a few feet to his left and spotted him.

He bolted down the western corridor, chased by the three staffers, who were joined by Biff, Fandango, and Mayor Wubbleduster as they burst into the hallway. Everyone scrambled after the fleeing gangster, screaming and shouting like a wild mob.

As he ran down the western corridor toward the front of the building, Billy realized why this place was familiar. The memories rushed back into his throbbing brain: earlier in the day, Sauce Fingerbanana and he had come here with Brufyss Bathwater. He was in an office building on Earth, in North Corners, Ohio! His pursuers were *not* cannibalistic aliens from the planet Gloxnar, just very weird human beings. Nonetheless, these bizarre characters had him outnumbered and were intent upon catching him again, probably to put him back in that room and drive him nuts with their crazy jabbering. Or worse!

Passing by Old Man Bumps's office, Billy recalled that he and Sauce had been holding prisoners in that room. Seeing the padlock on the door, he surmised that Sauce was no longer inside—he'd have to be *outside* the room to padlock the door. Were the prisoners still inside? If so, where was Sauce? Was he still holding the prisoners, or were the prisoners holding him? It suddenly dawned on Billy that two of the loonies now chasing him were among the group he'd captured earlier. That idiot Sauce must have let them escape!

He no longer had his gun; his pursuers were probably in possession of it. Why hadn't they used it against him when they had the chance? *Goody-two-shoes suckers! You're gonna regret that!*

Billy arrived at the intersection of the western and southern corridors and saw the closed double doors to the first-floor reception room. He remembered that Sauce had locked them earlier but was unaware that Lollie's vicious javelin thrust had rendered the locks useless. He headed east along the front of the building, the route he'd taken earlier in the day when he first went upstairs.

There was a room up ahead where he'd captured those two idiots and the Old Man Spuggett lookalike—a room cluttered with lots of racks and aisles of shelves. Maybe he could give his pursuers the slip by ducking in there.

He reached the end of the hallway and turned left. The door to that storage room was still open. Hearing the pursuing mob, Billy dashed up the corridor and slipped inside the room, pulling the door shut behind him. The posse turned the corner in time to catch a fleeting glimpse of the closing door. They poured into the chamber, scattering among the aisles in search of their fleeing quarry.

Billy crouched low and worked his way purposefully across the cluttered room, up and down the aisles, through the maze of shelving, over to the doorway opening into the back stairway corridor. He had to find Sauce Fingerbanana; Sauce might still have a gun. Maybe Sauce was upstairs.

His head start enabled him to traverse the storage room while his trackers were still engrossed with trying to pinpoint his location. Billy knew where he wanted to go, and they didn't. He reached the door to the rear hallway, threw it open, scooted outside, and darted toward the back stairs before his pursuers knew he was gone.

Suddenly the shrill shriek of a police whistle shattered the air and *POP! POP! POP! POP!* echoed through the halls.

Gunshots! Cops!

The racket and excited chatter spread throughout the building—but it also came from just a few feet above him, on these very stairs! He'd almost blundered into them. His way was blocked, he was trapped inside this loony bin, and the upper floor was crawling with cops.

More sounds of gunfire—*POP! POP! POP! POP!*—came from the other side of the building. The police whistle screamed its biting scream, and the shouting and yelling transitioned into a chant: "Seize the day! Suck the moment! Seize the day! Suck the moment!"

Billy's head pounded with pain, his heart filled with fear, and his mind raced. Heading upstairs was out of the question now, but before he could hope to escape or hide himself in the network of rooms on this floor, he needed to double back and pass that storage room again. The crazy mob was still floundering around in there and hadn't pursued him into the hallway yet. Maybe he could slip past them without being seen.

He ran back down the bare-floored corridor and passed the storage room. In his haste to escape, he'd left the door open, and as he shot a glance into the room, someone saw him!

He heard the cry of alarm. Darting around the corner to his right, Billy sprinted up the restroom corridor and shot through the doorway to the north hallway, unknowingly coming full circle since his desperate escape from the headquarters room.

He had no idea where he was at the moment, but he had to find a place to hide until he could think of something better.

42

Barley, Old Man Spuggett, Brufyss, Mrs. Kookerly, and Dr. Pudbid waited at the foot of the first-floor reception room stairway while Roland, Yump, Bagmo, and Cheezy stood at the foot of the stairway accessing the second floor from the first-floor offices. Meanwhile, Reverend Snortworthy, Narducci, and Dork waited at the foot of the back stairs.

"Okay, everybody," whispered Barley to his teammates. "Once we get moving up the stairs, take 'em slowly, one step at a time. And make plenty of noise. Even Sauce won't be stupid enough to try to shoot it out with the whole police force!"

Mrs. Kookerly agreed. "He'll just throw in the towel and give up. He isn't the fighter Billy is."

"Be that as it may, he's still got the gun," whispered Brufyss. "Until we get it away from him, we can't be sure of anything."

Suddenly they heard a clamor from the first-floor offices closest to the reception room where they stood. The voices were muffled by the closed double doors. Biff Spoozma's group was pursuing Billy Jelly down the southern corridor, on their way to the storage room.

"What could that be?" asked Mrs. Kookerly, puzzled. "I thought all of our groups were in position already!"

"Better check it out, Brufyss," said Barley, "in case there's been a foul-up and somebody's not sure where they're supposed to be."

Brufyss ran across the reception room to the double doors, opened them cautiously, and peered up the western corridor, then down the southern corridor. By this time, the pursued and his pursuers had traversed the southern corridor and disappeared into the storage room around the corner. Brufyss saw only empty hallways.

He returned to the foot of the stairway. "Nothing there! Must have been hearing things. Maybe it was just Fandango, screaming."

Barley nodded. "I think the other teams have had enough time to get into position. Let's *go*!"

He clenched the police whistle between his teeth and blew—TWEEEEEEEET! The piercing sound sliced through the still air of the first floor, sending the assault teams on their way. Old Man Spuggett tossed his remaining nondestructive explosive devices down the stairs behind him, the resulting *POP! POP! POP! POP!* reports rumbling up the stairwell. Everyone shouted and shrieked, and raised voices could be heard from the other teams as well.

Barley ruminated on the day's events: the stairs were the same the tour group had ascended upon their arrival, seemingly ages ago. So much had happened since then—so many unanticipated events, shocking surprises, and mind-boggling metamorphoses.

Inspired by it all, Barley recalled the framed poster on Old Man Spuggett's office wall and its uplifting message. It sounded right, it felt appropriate, and he chanted its words softly but rhythmically as he took each step: "Seize the day! Suck the moment! Seize the day! Suck the moment!"

Old Man Spuggett smiled and picked up the chant himself. "Seize the day! Suck the moment!" Their voices gradually rose as they repeated each phrase. Brufyss, Mrs. Kookerly, and Dr. Pudbid joined in. The volume increased, and the other assault teams picked up the chant from their respective locations. The voices roared, the police whistle shrieked, and the explosions plunged the entire Bumps & Spuggett building into a sublime, controlled chaos.

As the step-by-step procession continued, Barley felt his blood pressure rising, and the gunshot wound in his left shoulder throbbed with pain. His breath came in shorter and shorter gasps, he was getting dizzy, and his vision clouded. He'd pushed himself too hard and too far; his injury was pushing back. The pain in his shoulder began to overwhelm him. He stumbled and slipped, nearly falling.

Brufyss was one step lower and behind Barley. The misstep nearly caused the two of them to collide. "Barley, what's going on? Are you okay?"

"I'm . . . not sure," gasped Barley, halting his climb, trying to steady himself by leaning against the wall. "I-I think the gunshot . . . is getting . . . to me!"

"Mr. Doodlebody! Stay right where you are and don't move," cried Dr. Pudbid. "Mr. Bathwater, please give me a hand!"

Brufyss draped Barley's uninjured right arm over his own shoulder, ensuring that Barley wouldn't pitch headlong down the stairs.

"Keep . . . the noise . . . up! Don't stop . . . on account . . . of me!"

Though gravely concerned with Barley's condition, Old Man Spuggett and Mrs. Kookerly complied with his wishes, recommencing their shouting and stair stomping.

"Here, Brufyss. Take . . . this!" Barley handed the police whistle to his old friend. "Keep up . . . the racket. We're almost there." His eyes rolled back in his head, his chin slumped to his chest, and he passed out.

"We've got to keep moving!" urged Old Man Spuggett. "We can't leave Mr. Dinkleflinky here! Someone might come stampeding down these stairs like a harried herd of kangaroos."

"Right, Spuggy! C'mon, Mr. Bathwater, let's get Mr. Doodlebody to the reception room. There's a sofa up there we can lay him on. We've already been through this once today."

Brufyss and Dr. Pudbid maneuvered Barley up the remaining steps and into Lollie's reception room. Mrs. Kookerly prepared one of the sofas. Once Barley had been positioned comfortably, Brufyss ran to the reception room's double doorway. He scanned the main office and saw that the other two assault teams had entered the room and were now scouring it for Sauce Fingerbanana.

Some gathered and calmed the tourists, coaxing them out of hiding with assurances that all was well. Daphne emerged from the conference room, guiding an unsteady Frog Puppleman. All the excitement and scrambling had aggravated his head wound, and the city councilman looked pale and wobbly.

As order and calm were restored, the tourists gravitated to the center of the room to join the staffers, curious to learn what had happened.

Brufyss spotted Roland Chumbuckets. "Roland! What's going on? Where's Sauce?"

Roland joined him. "I'm baffled. I don't see him anywhere, and we've searched all over."

"But that's impossible! There's no way he could've given us the slip. We had all the stairways blocked."

Old Man Spuggett poked his white-haired noggin into the room. "Has our rescue strategy been successful, Mr. Boatweather? Have we captured the fugitive?"

"Not yet, apparently," answered Brufyss. "We don't know where he is—but he couldn't have gotten away."

"You mean, he's not up here? Where could he be? Did any of our people up here see him?"

"I'm not sure, Mr. Spuggett," answered Roland. "We haven't talked to anyone yet, other than to calm them down."

Old Man Spuggett spotted Alpha Rae standing with Daphne and Frog. "Ms. Sapoopa-LaBoobis!"

Alpha Rae scurried across the big room. Daphne and Frog followed a short distance behind, the councilman shuffling unsteadily. "Mr. Spuggett, I'm so glad to see you're safe! It's been chaos up here! Was that you making all that noise?"

"Yes, me and a lot of our friends."

"I figured as much when we heard that 'Seize the day, suck the moment' thing, but I'm afraid our guests were a little freaked out. It sounded like the entire North Corners Police Force was conducting a running gun battle up our stairs!"

"That was the impression we intended to create, to convince Mr. Fingersandwich that further violence would be useless and escape impossible. But I'm puzzled: he's nowhere to be found. Have you seen him?"

"That Sauce guy? Oh yeah, we've seen him. He's up in the attic with Gerald, helping him with some kind of experiment or something. I told Gerald we'd have to run it by you first, but he's already hired the guy!"

"*Hired*? But he had a gun! Did he threaten you? Hurt anyone?"

"With all due respect, sir," interjected Bimbo, "are you kiddin'? That guy couldn't hurt an open wound!"

Felicia laughed. "When he thought he was gonna go to jail, he melted into a quivering, blithering blob, like an overheated piece of cheese." She overlooked the fact that *she* melted into a quivering, blithering blob like an overheated piece of cheese on a regular basis and for no apparent reason.

"And he gave Daphne his gun," added Bimbo.

"Yeah, buddy!" Frog gazed at Daphne and smiled.

Daphne blushed and held the gun aloft for the old man to see. "Gerald took all the bullets. He said he needed the gunpowder to complete his experiment, and Wiley went with him to help out."

Brufyss shook his head in awe. "Help out? You mean, Gerald's got Sauce Fingerbanana helping him out with some kind of experiment? Man oh man! This has got to be the most amazing place I've ever been!"

"It appears that while the rest of us have been running around this building like a bunch of drunken sport foofs, the supposed threat of Mr. Fingerbaloney has been neutralized by our own Gerald Foon-Package."

"Yup!" agreed Bimbo. "Gerald's gonna help him become a scientist!" Brufyss shook his head again, amazed.

"But lest we become too complacent here," continued the old man, "let me remind you that we still have a very dangerous criminal being held downstairs, and a seriously injured Mr. Bodydoodle lying on a couch in Lollie's reception room. I suggest we make haste to take care of our patient and reinforce the downstairs group."

"You caught Billy? Oh, that's wonderful!" exclaimed Daphne.

"Yes, yes, that's all well and good," interrupted Alpha Rae, "but what is Mr. Doodlebody's condition?"

"There's no need to worry, Ms. Sapoopa-LaBoobis! Even as we speak, Dr. Pudbid is tending to Mr. Doodlebuggy's every need, ably assisted by Mrs. Kookerly. He'll be just fine!"

Alpha Rae was horrified. "You're letting that Pudbid quack look after Mr. Doodlebody? Well, I have something to say about that!" The executive secretary dashed into Lollie's reception room. Dr. Pudbid and Mrs. Kookerly sat at opposite ends of a sofa, watching over the recovering tour group director, he by Barley's head, she at Barley's feet.

"Get away from that man, Pudbid, before you kill him and I kill *you*!"

"But, Ms. Sapoopa-LaBoobis, I've stabilized his condition, and everything's under control. There's nothing to worry about!"

"Fine, then send me a bill. *I'm* taking over now!"

"I can assure you, Ms. Sapoopa-LaBoobis," stammered Dr. Pudbid as he retreated slowly, "Mr. Doodlebody's absolutely fine. He's just a little exhausted!"

"*A little exhausted?* That's like saying he's 'kind of dead'!" She paused a moment to calm herself. "But none of that matters anymore. He's mine now."

The purple-haired executive secretary settled onto the sofa by Barley's head and stroked his hair soothingly, a faraway look in her eyes . . .

✶ ✶ ✶

Noodles and Margaret stood at the foot of the secret passage stairway, preparing to enter the library. Noodles poked her head through the bookshelf door to reconnoiter, saw no one, and determined it was safe. With little Margaret tightly grasping her hand, she moved into the deserted chamber.

The main door was open, and somewhere off in the distance, agitated voices could be heard as Biff, the mayor, Ebenezer, Lollie, Marshall, and Fandango pursued Billy Jelly through the storage room.

Noodles was wary but unwilling to retrace her steps to the pandemonium above. She decided to conduct her own reconnaissance, but first she had to deposit the little girl out of danger's way.

There was no obvious hiding place in the barren library. Perhaps it would be safer to place the little girl back in the secret passageway and close the door. She thought better: if someone descended the spiral staircase with bad intentions, they'd literally stumble upon Margaret hiding there.

She examined the empty bookshelves. Something caught her eye: a three-foot space between the top of the bookshelves and the ceiling. If she lifted Margaret and placed her atop the tall bookshelves, there'd be enough room for the little girl to lie flat and out of sight, away from the shelf's edge. As long as Margaret stayed quiet and didn't move, she'd remain unseen.

Noodles voiced her intentions. Margaret nodded and snorted excitedly; it would be *fun* to hide way up there! Noodles lifted Margaret to the top of the bookshelf closest to the secret door. Margaret scrambled out of Noodles's grasp and onto the wide, flat, dusty surface just below the ceiling. Noodles instructed her to flatten out. As she suspected, the little girl was satisfactorily hidden. She'd leave the secret door open in the event it became necessary to use the hidden passage as an escape route back to the second floor.

Noodles walked to the library door and peered into the hallway, spotting the padlocked rear entrance. To her right, two corridors intersected only a few feet from where she stood. Sounds of commotion could still be heard around the corner to her left.

She had no idea where Dork Snargmeyer had disappeared to, but the last time she'd seen him, he was heading down here. If Dork was still on the first floor, Noodles intended to find him. She had no way of knowing that her new boyfriend had just ascended to the second floor and the commotion he'd helped produce drove her down here in the first place.

She tiptoed to the intersection of the two main thoroughfares, peeked around the corner, and scanned the north corridor in the direction of the far-off noises. She saw nothing but an empty hallway. She stepped into the western corridor and crept toward the front of the building. Arriving at the junction of the southern and western hallways, she heard the distant sounds of the downstairs commotion grow suddenly louder and closer.

She looked back up the corridor toward the library in time to see a man materialize at the intersection of the two hallways.

The gangster who'd shot Mr. Doodlebody!

Breathing heavily, the man stopped and looked over his shoulder, then sprang down the western corridor in Noodles's direction, spied her huge silhouette looming like a monolith at the other end of the passageway, and skidded to a halt. His pursuers burst into the northern corridor. Noodles blocked one route of his escape, and the screaming pursuers blocked the other.

However, the hallway leading to the rear entrance was behind him. Billy did an about-face and sprinted up the short hallway. Noodles scurried along the western corridor and cried out in horror as the fleeing gangster saw the open library door and darted inside. The door slammed loudly, and the dead bolt clicked. The desperate, homicidal hooligan was locked in the library with little Margaret Wubbleduster!

∗

Billy twisted the lock only seconds before the door received a torrent of blows. The lunatics pursuing him were stymied. His quick thinking had bought him a few precious ticks with which to plan his next move. He pressed his back against the quivering door and surveyed the room. It looked like a place where books had once been kept.

What he saw next set his heart palpitating. There was a *door* in the midst of the bookshelves! One of the shelves stuck out of the wall at a cockeyed angle, and a void, like a room or some kind of passageway, was behind the aperture. He couldn't believe his good fortune; here was a way out of what seemed like a dead end!

He hurried over to the bookshelf and peered into the dark space beyond the disguised opening. There appeared to be a concealed passageway with a steep, narrow spiral staircase leading upward—exactly what he needed at this desperate moment!

He grabbed the edge of the bulky bookshelf, pulled it open, and was about to take his first step into the secret passage when something with the consistency of a heavy sack of potatoes dropped on him, knocking him roughly to the floor. The force of the blow and the ponderous weight now crushing him caused him to brutally smack the rear of his already traumatized head—*CONK!*

The last thing Billy remembered before another wave of unconsciousness swept over him was the feeling of being held down, immobilized, and the agonizing sensation of being sucked in, swallowed up, and slowly sinking, sinking, sinking ever deeper into a bottomless vat of viscous horsehair glue.

✱ ✱ ✱

Biff, the mayor, Ebenezer, Lollie, Marshall, and Fandango had been running helter-skelter through the cluttered storage room when Lollie spotted the gangster darting past the storage room door. She shouted an alarm; in an instant, the entire crew scrambled to resume the chase.

As they emerged into the restroom corridor, Biff motioned for them to stop and listen. In the distance, they heard the heavy tromp of running feet. Billy was heading past the headquarters room, toward the opposite side of the building.

The group turned the corner in time to spot their quarry stopped at the far end of the hallway, trying to catch his breath. Billy spotted them and bolted down the western thoroughfare, stopped dead in his tracks, and reversed his direction, darting back to the building's rear entrance. The group dashed the length of the north corridor in pursuit.

As they reached the intersection of the north and west corridors, they were met by Noodles gesturing frantically at a door in the rear hallway. They turned in time to see the door slam shut—Billy had ducked into the library!

Noodles explained that the secret door had been left open and little Margaret was now imprisoned in the room with the gangster. The mayor let loose with an anguished cry—"Woe is me! Mine own progeny to dire peril hath been subjected!"—and led a determined charge to the library door.

Biff, Noodles, and the mayor joined forces to bust the locked door off its hinges. They reared back and hurtled forward with pile-driver force; it would only take a few to smash the door to smithereens and burst into the room—but what would they find?

Once again, the three reared back and hurtled forward. The door burst open with a splintering crash, and they poured into the library, fully prepared to do battle and save an innocent child.

The hideous sight that met their eyes stopped them cold. Little Margaret smiled widely, perched astride the unconscious Billy Jelly, who was almost unrecognizable due to an ultra-spectacular "HIVED"-ing, the likes of which had never before been witnessed by the eyes of mortal men.

Since the whole ordeal began, the porcine little hellion had been forced to endure fear, frustration, and mortification. She'd been gaffers-taped into submission, paraded about on a leash like a disobedient doggie, soaked like a sponge, and dried out like a slab of jerky. She'd been disregarded, disrespected, profaned, reviled, ignored, and overlooked. She'd watched helplessly as her father had been ridiculed, humiliated, abused, and threatened, and she'd witnessed the nasty Billy man hurting and harassing *everyone*. Her inexhaustible reservoir of expectorant had been sucked dry by the massive hot-air dryers at Charlie Nutbooger's automated car wash, rendering her only means of defense and self-expression useless—until the contents of Yump's watering can replenished her depleted fluids and her confidence.

The little girl's pent-up emotions had reached the boiling point as she lay atop the dusty bookshelf. Then the nasty man who'd caused so much trouble suddenly appeared right beneath her . . .

She had him all to herself.

Margaret waited patiently until the unsuspecting thug moved close enough, and dropped on him like a vengeful ton of bricks.

When her rescuers arrived, Billy was laid out on his back, still as a stone, slimed and slathered, lubed and lathered into a pulsating, voluminous mass of liquid expectorant. The child had single-handedly— or single-*mouthedly*—accomplished what none of the grown-ups had. She'd defeated Smelly Billy Jelly in a most singular fashion!

"Daughter beloved! Thou hast . . . a palace of pride . . . 'pon the foundation of . . . mine heart constructed!" cried Mayor Wubbleduster proudly between gurgling gags and gasps.

"Your . . . father says, 'You've . . . made me . . . very proud, Margaret!'" translated Big Biff, struggling mightily to fend off his own wave of nausea.

Little Margaret blushed and snorted appreciatively. Once the group managed to becalm their twisting stomachs, she was showered with effusive praise. However, no one ventured to touch the wretched victim of her high-intensity voluminous-expectorant-distribution masterpiece.

Billy Jelly's reign of terror had come to an end, thanks to the little girl with the constitution of liquid.

✳ ✳ ✳

Now that the second-floor invasion had come to a peaceful conclusion and the pandemonium subsided, the staff and guests set about concluding the "operation." Dork Snargmeyer, concerned for the safety of Noodles and Margaret, had been dispatched to the first floor by way of the secret passageway in Old Man Spuggett's office, accompanied by Roland,

Brufyss, and the old man himself. The four would also check on the status of Billy Jelly and Biff Spoozma's downstairs contingent. If all was well, they'd transport the prisoner upstairs where the rest of the staffers and guests could keep an eye on him.

Sauce Fingerbanana was sequestered in the attic laboratory, working with Gerald on a scientific experiment. As a precaution, Cheezy and Narducci were stationed by the attic stairwell to act as sentries, although no one really believed Wiley Fingerbanana would jeopardize his newly attained status as a member of the Bumps & Spuggett scientific community by perpetrating any mischief.

The group in the second-floor reception room and lobby occupied themselves by conversing quietly, theorizing about the eventual outcome of the day's events, determining the course of action to break out of the padlocked building, and watching the poignant interaction between Alpha Rae Sapoopa-LaBoobis, the recovering Barley Doodlebody, and City Councilman Frog Puppleman. Frog was experiencing a resurgence of pain from his head wound and had reclined on the other sofa, attempting to quell the throbbing. His eyes were closed; he was falling asleep.

Daphne sat on the couch next to Frog, and Alpha Rae sat in Lollie's chair between the two sofas, watching over the injured brothers. Dr. Pudbid monitored their condition safely out of Alpha Rae's reach.

The ill-tempered executive secretary was once again beset and besieged by a whirlwind of conflicting, confusing, confounding, nearly overwhelming mental images and emotions. She'd been so since the midday arrival of the Doodlebody tour group. Suddenly, from somewhere deep within the seething tornado that scoured her subconscious mind, came the sound of *music*—a melody with words that resounded persistently within her, working through the fog into her waking brain and out through her throat. Softly, sweetly, soulfully, Alpha Rae began to sing . . .

> *"Hush, little darlings! Dark of night*
> *Soon makes way for morning bright.*
> *Until the sun lights up the day,*
> *Momma will sing your cares away!*
> *Momma will sing and dry your tears,*
> *Momma will sing and calm your fears!*
> *Sun will rise and morning beckon.*
> *Momma will still be here, I reckon . . ."*

As Alpha Rae softly hummed the lullaby's melody, the people in the room stared at her in wonder. The Bumps & Spuggett employees had never witnessed this tender side of the normally irascible executive secretary. Mrs. Kookerly and Daphne were touched by the scene as well. Her lullaby had a soothing, almost magical effect on everyone, easing the current concerns in their minds, quieting the myriad misgivings now dwelling in their hearts.

As the rest of the group looked on with adoration, Alpha Rae sang to the injured men. Then—amazingly!—the two men, emerging from the throes of pain and near unconsciousness, responded by *singing along*. Two mismatched, middle-aged half brothers, removed temporarily from the reality and gravity of the world, were singing a hazily remembered childhood lullaby with Alpha Rae Sapoopa-LaBoobis!

Frog paused in his singing. He opened his eyes and blinked several times, then turned his head slowly to gaze up at Alpha Rae with a childlike look of wonderment.

"Momma?"

43

The process of remembering began for Alpha Rae earlier in the day: rumblings of maternal recognition had stirred within her when she noticed Frog sitting unconscious in the office chair. Later, her brief meeting with Barley during the wingding celebration further jarred her subconscious, and as her mystified mind meandered ever deeper into this bewildering journey through the unknown, she was unknowingly finding her way home.

There was also an evolving change in her personality. She was willing to assume leadership responsibilities she'd diligently avoided until today. The feeling came upon her in a rush, and she'd felt no reticence in taking charge when the group needed her, but the reasons for her change in attitude weren't readily apparent. Questions remained in her mind.

The traumatic experience of witnessing Barley and Frog, the objects of her conundrum, lying in distress for the second time on the reception room couches had been the final, cataclysmic event that triggered the buried lullaby. The singing in turn triggered remembrance in her two apparent offspring.

There was no way that the trio's familiarity with the song could simply be labeled coincidence. The lullaby was Alpha Rae's creation, composed spontaneously one night many long-lost years ago while attempting to quiet her two crying young sons. Alpha Rae, Barley, and Frog were the only three people on the planet who could have known the gentle words and soothing melody.

The two brothers were awake now; they stared at Alpha Rae and she stared back.

"I-I-I can't believe it!" stammered Barley. "Are you really our mother?

Where were you all those years? Why did you abandon Frog and me?"

"Mr. Doodlebody, one question at a time, *please*!" pleaded Alpha Rae.

"Yeah, those are the rules!" confirmed Bagmo.

"Besides, you know as much as I do right now. This whole thing is freaking me out!"

"Yeah, *buddy*!" agreed Frog, fairly freaked out himself.

"Well, what can you remember?"

"I . . . I remember wandering into this building." She attempted to slow down the whirlwind of disjointed images in her mind and isolate one that would illuminate her elusive past for her. "It was many years ago, and I couldn't remember my name, where I came from—nothing! I can't remember anything before I was here."

"Can you remember how you got the name Alpha Rae? Is Alpha Rae your real name? And if Frog's name is Puppleman and my name is Doodlebody, how come your surname is Sapoopa-LaBoobis?"

Bagmo scowled at Barley's multiple queries but remained silent.

Alpha Rae thought hard. Suddenly, a flash of inspiration: "I think it was Gerald—and Ebenezer!" She seemed to fall into a trance as days gone by played through her mind like a grainy motion picture. She began to narrate:

"It was in this very room! I came up the stairs, and Mr. Spuggett was here speaking with Gerald about some kind of experiment he was doing, and Gerald was talking about alpha rays and gamma rays. Mr. Spuggett saw me and said hello and asked me what my name was—but I couldn't remember! So I told him it was Alpha Ray; it was the first thing that popped into my head. Gerald screamed, '*Alpha rays*! Of course! Not gamma rays! Thank you so much, ma'am!' and ran out of the room. Mr. Spuggett was so impressed that I'd solved Gerald's problem without even knowing what the problem *was* that he hired me right there on the spot!

"And then Ebenezer walked in and saw me, pointed at me, and shouted, 'Sapoopa-laboobis! Sapoopa-laboobis!' It seemed that he knew who I was, like he was calling me by name."

Had Alpha Rae known Ebenezer was actually saying, "Look at that woman! She's got purple hair!" she might have reconsidered her choice of surnames.

"And so I told Mr. Spuggett my name was Alpha Rae Sapoopa-LaBoobis, and that's what I've been calling myself ever since."

"Wow! That's a cool story, Alpha Rae, or whatever your name is," marveled Bagmo.

"But it still doesn't explain why you abandoned Frog and me, or when!" said Barley. "What happened that would cause you to do such a thing?"

Alpha Rae shot back, "Look, Mr. Doodlebody, there's a lot of stuff that hasn't clicked in yet—a flood of old memories and lost moments. It's overwhelming!"

"Focus on one thing! What happened the moment you abandoned Frog and me? Do you think you can remember that? It would be very important to both of us!"

Alpha Rae closed her eyes and concentrated. "Well, when you mention the word *abandon*, I get a distinct feeling that the word is somehow . . . wrong."

"Wrong? How so?"

"I don't think it was voluntary. The memories are very disjointed—"

"Go back to *before* that happened. Maybe you can remember events that led up to you separating from us."

Alpha Rae shut her eyes and tilted her head back, as if to let those memories pour into her brain. "The last things I remember are hazy before everything goes blank. I was not myself somehow."

"You mean you were being affected by something? Something else?"

"Yeah, like something was clouding my brain!"

"Were you drunk?"

"Not a freakin' *chance,* buster!" She opened her eyes and gave Barley a scalding stare. "Alpha Rae Sapoopa-LaBoobis—or *whoever* I am—doesn't drink! No matter what happened to me during my blank time, *that* would not have changed! I have two kids to take care of! I would never—"

She stopped short and gasped.

"Kids! Yes! *You* guys!" She paused and looked at Barley and Frog, shaking her head in amazement. She closed her eyes again, and the stream began to flow smoothly and uninterrupted: "I was single, raising you two. You were very young at the time. My husband—what the heck was his name? Oh yeah, *Boogzy!* Boogzy Puppleman, a two-timing jackass! He ran off with a door-to-door cosmetics salesgirl and left me with the nine hundred dollars' worth of lipstick, eyeliner, and hand cream she suckered him into buying—and the bill as well. I don't even use that stuff! Boogzy Puppleman! Boy, there's a name that brings back memories! Unfortunately, most of them aren't good.

"Boogzy was a good-looking, smooth-talking, stylishly dressed, goldbricking, conniving deadbeat," she said. "A real con artist. He sure had me lapping out of his dish! All he had to do was flash his boyish grin and I was a goner. I'd do anything he'd say! If he wanted me to stomp amoebas 'til the cows came home, I'd do it for him!"

"Why wouldn't you just wait until the cows came home and let *them* stomp the amoebas?" asked Bagmo.

"It's a figure of speech, Maltgoggles!" snapped the executive secretary. "I'm making a point: Boozy Puppleman was a con man who wrapped me around his finger and took advantage of me.

"He came upon me a year or two after my first husband vanished. I was doing all right financially; my first husband had provided for me with a humongous life insurance policy. Boogzy found out I was a wealthy widow with a young son and zoomed in on me like a Hollywood close-up. He started schmoozing me, wining me, dining me, fawning all over me . . . and I fell for him. We got married, and Frog came along a year or so later."

"Yeah, *buddy!*" cried Frog, pleased that his name finally made it into the conversation.

Alpha Rae frowned at Frog and took another deep breath. "I thought I had the perfect little family: a handsome, engaging, popular husband and two beautiful young boys—but I soon found that our perfect little family fortune was fast disappearing! That punk was siphoning money out of our bank account like a vacuum cleaner.

"Boogzy found out I'd found him out, he split with the door-to-door cosmetics lady, and that was that. Thanks to Boogzy Puppleman, I went from being a wealthy widow with a young son to a *poor* widow with *two* young sons! I had to get a job. I found one at a health food store here in North Corners, working for a terrible man. Oh yes, a bona fide crook if there ever was one! What was his name? It was something like Chumbis, or Choobis—"

"Ohmigosh! *Chorfis Chumbu!*" cried Mrs. Kookerly. "Barley, your mother worked for Chorfis Chumbu at the Gross Natural Product Health Food Store!"

"That's the guy, all right!" confirmed Alpha Rae. "Chorfis Chumbu—a first-class creep! That bum would always use me as the guinea pig when he tested his terrible herbal concoctions. He'd give me all these exotic potions and extracts and serums and brews and teas and toddies, and watch to see how they'd affect me. That's how my hair got like this!" She fingered her purple locks and gestured at Mimsy. "You think this is a dye job like Ink Head over there?"

Mimsy blushed the same hue as Alpha Rae's hair.

"He told me all his ingredients were natural, herbal, and restorative, so I shouldn't be afraid, no matter how they affected me—the effects would only be temporary. One day he made me test a drink he wanted to give to his customers during one of his weekly bowling tournaments on the sidewalk in front of the store."

Barley, Mrs. Kookerly, and Daphne looked at each other with raised eyebrows. "Um, that wouldn't be the Bowling for Carrots tournament, would it?" asked Mrs. Kookerly.

"Why yes, I believe that's the one! How would you know about that?"

"My high school used to . . . participate in those tournaments once a year."

She had a sinking feeling as to where this was heading.

"That's right! I remember! The last clear memory I have before everything goes blank is Mr. Chumbu telling me there was going to be a big high school dance that night, and all his Bowling for Carrots contestants were going to be guests."

"The Senior Prom and Vegetarian Intimidation Fest!" sighed Barley, Mrs. Kookerly, and Daphne in unison, looking at each other with dread.

"Piggford High School was still putting on that dance when Barley, Frog, Mimsy, Daphne, Brufyss, and I were that age," said Mrs. Kookerly. "We all attended it—once."

Recalling the heartless heartbreaker he'd been that night, Barley was filled with shame yet again, but his building apprehension about the possible ending to Alpha Rae's story was a greater concern at the moment.

"So, Chorfis Chumbu made you the guinea pig when he tested his poisonous potion . . ."

"Yes, and here's where the fog starts clogging up my memory. After I drank it, I began feeling woozy, dizzy, disoriented, and confused. Everything was spinning and became a blur." She shivered as she recalled the scene. "All of my visions get very disjointed and surreal from this point. I have quick flashes of different images in my mind: Mr. Chumbu up in my face, laughing at my reaction to the drink he gave me; being wound up in . . . it was a net or something, and I couldn't escape; squashed up against a bunch of other people, being taken somewhere in the back of a truck, in a cage in the dark. I see a very bright light overhead. I feel myself rising up to meet the light."

Barley, Mrs. Kookerly, and Daphne cast horrified glances at each other. They knew the ending to the story.

"I remember hearing awful words—and screaming, lots of screaming! I remember being slapped and hit with terrible, smelly, slimy things! I remember blood: blood all over me, all over the other people in the net— all over the place!"

Tears were in her eyes now, and Barley could take no more. "Alpha Rae, there's no need to torment yourself with this. You're getting upset—"

"I'm on a roll now!" she snapped. "It's nasty stuff, but it's only a *memory*. And I'm remembering things I haven't thought about in years."

She paused, closed her eyes again, took a deep, calming breath, and continued: "I was getting crazier and crazier with all the stuff that was happening, and all the stuff that was happening got crazier and crazier! Suddenly we fell into a pit of something—something repulsive, unspeakably vile! I almost fainted from the smell, but I had to stay on my feet. A deluge of something dumped on my head, nearly knocking me out and drowning me. That's where the memories stop. I can't remember anything after that. It just goes black."

"I know what happened next," said Barley, staring sadly up at the ceiling. "You went stark-raving mad and ran off into the hills. When your head finally cleared, you wandered out of the wilderness and came back into North Corners—on *this* side of town. Since the only inhabited building around here was this one, you came in to make human contact, and you met Mr. Spuggett. The perceptive old bird immediately saw that you were lost, alone, and confused; he took you in right then and there, and you became a part of this little world. It was the best thing that could have happened to you."

Barley turned on the couch to face Alpha Rae. "You didn't abandon us; I understand that now. You were made to *forget* us!"

The attendees of the '67 Senior Prom and Vegetarian Intimidation Fest fell silent and reflected on how in their callous youth they'd laughed and felt no remorse for the agonies inflicted on the captive vegetarians during those unspeakable annual rituals. Brufyss and Daphne had experienced those agonies firsthand. Too many people's lives had been irreparably damaged. It wasn't such a hoot anymore.

"At least no one will have to endure that agony again," said Barley. "The '67 dance was the last one they ever had—thanks to me, and what I made it into."

"Barley, that's in the past," said Daphne. "I forgive you, and I'm putting it behind me. I think we all have to do that now."

Mrs. Kookerly smiled at her best friend and addressed Barley: "We're moving forward, remember? Today you found your mother—and what an amazing person she is!"

"Yeah, *buddy*!" seconded Frog.

Alpha Rae sat back in her chair and sighed deeply, overjoyed at rediscovering her two lost boys and her past, finally able to make sense of all that didn't a few hours earlier.

"I've got one more question for you, Alpha Rae," said Barley. "How come I'm named Doodlebody? Boogzy Puppleman was your *second* husband, right?"

"That's right, dear. I married him a couple of years after your father, Fervis Doodlebody, was lost in a freak accident at our summer cottage on Lake Chuckanuggett—"

"Wow! We had a summer cottage on Lake Chuckanuggett? Where's Lake Chuckanuggett?"

"There *is* no Lake Chuckanuggett! Will you let me finish my story, please?"

"Sorry! You were saying that we had a summer cottage on Lake Chuckanuggett, which doesn't exist . . ."

"Yes, your father did quite well for us back then. He designed custom alpaca-wool lawn mower mittens, and they were quite the rage. Anyway, there'd been some gold mining around Lake Chuckanuggett years ago, and eventually they went bust. Thar just warn't no gold in them thar hills!"

"Thar never is," sighed Bagmo.

"They closed the mine down, saying the vein of gold was tapped out, but there was another reason: in the course of their digging, the miners accidentally stumbled into a huge subterranean cavern that contained an abyss. Turns out the abyss led to the center of the earth!"

"I remember when they found that cavern," said Dr. Pudbid. "Yes, it was years ago—all over the front pages of *The Daily Poop*! The mining company sealed off the mine and skedaddled out of North Corners. A few years later, the lake started spilling into the cavern, and in a short time there was no more Lake Chuckanuggett!"

"Correct!" said Alpha Rae. "And the cavern was situated directly below our cottage. We didn't even know it. One summer, the three of us were at the lake. I took a day to do a little shopping and brought Barley with me. Fervis stayed behind to work on some of his custom lawn mower mitten designs. While we were gone, a huge sinkhole formed beneath the cottage.

In a short time, the hole grew to mammoth proportions and swallowed the cottage in one gulp! And just like that, ol' Fervis was on a one-way-ticket ride to the center of the earth. Never saw him again—I suspect no one else did either. It goes without saying that the custom-designed alpaca-wool lawn mower mitten market was never the same."

Dr. Pudbid picked up the story. "The lake started spilling into the hole, and before long, the whole thing was gone. Nothing left but a big ol' bottomless pit. The authorities didn't know what to do. What *do* you do with a bottomless pit that leads to the center of the earth? Well, they used it for a garbage dump! Filled the whole thing up in a couple of years and built a big-box discount department store on the site."

Barley sighed. "That sure explains a lot. I could never really believe our mother would desert us for no reason. And now Frog and I know who our fathers were! My father was a respectable, responsible, creative businessman—a *family* man! That makes me feel good, but what a tragedy that he should meet his end like that."

"Yeah, but the dude got sucked down to the center of the *earth*!" marveled Bagmo. "That's a pretty prestigious place to get sucked down to!"

Barley smiled. "Finding out about Frog's dad has been a revelation, too. Even though the guy was a creep, look how Frog turned out in spite of it. Wouldn't hurt a soul, wouldn't deceive an oyster, and wouldn't think a harmful thought about anyone."

"Yeah, *buddy*!"

"No matter how things started out, the end result has been worthwhile: our family tree is intact again! And it's a good thing Chorfis Chumbu is no longer around, or he'd be getting a visit from me. Whatever happened to that guy?"

"I heard he was making chili dogs and fell into a sausage grinder," answered Mrs. Kookerly. "They buried him under a compost heap somewhere."

"There's an irony for you," chuckled Barley. "Destined to spend all eternity buried under the things he hated most in life: vegetables!"

"*Rotting* vegetables!" laughed Mrs. Kookerly.

"Eventually becoming fertilizer himself," added Rapunzel, "to help *other* vegetables grow big and strong!"

"Looks like I won't be eating any chili dogs in the near future," said Bagmo.

Everyone in the room familiar with the infamous health-food store proprietor shared a giggle in memory of Chorfis Chumbu, which triggered a cackling response from Faisal Herskowitz. Soon, the whole room convulsed with laughter.

"Alpha Rae, I think you've made an incredible breakthrough here today," said Barley once the hilarity had subsided, "and I'm sure the rest of the answers will come back to you in time. By the way, you don't have to call me Mr. Doodlebody if you're my own mother."

"Well then, Barley, you just call me Mom. You don't have to call me Alpha Rae if you're my own son!"

"Especially since that's not really her name," stated Bagmo.

"Yeah, *buddy*!" added Frog.

"Don't *ever* call me buddy!"

"Yeah—*Momma*!"

Everyone in Lollie's reception room was convinced they'd witnessed a miracle. What were the odds of something like this happening? Did they even *give* odds on something like this happening? The familial ties of Alpha Rae, Barley, and Frog had been reestablished beyond a shadow of a doubt. It was something to celebrate; however, the staff and guests were still trapped inside the building.

"Right now I'm as amazed as anybody is," said Barley, "but we'll have plenty of time to solve these puzzles and get more answers once we get out of here."

"Gettin' something to *eat* might be nice too," added Bimbo.

Bimbo was right. Everyone had been preoccupied with the events of the day and Alpha Rae's discovery, but now it was nighttime, and the gnawing realization of hunger dawned upon them. Had all gone according to the original plan, the cure for excess hair growth that Gerald intended to serve during the wingding would have alleviated that. The course of events prevented the anticipated feast from taking place. A roomful of empty stomachs began to sound a dissonant chorus of growls.

"Until Gerald and Sauce finish their experiment, a big ol' cheeseburger will have to do the job," reasoned Bagmo. "Anybody here got a big ol' cheeseburger?"

"That'll have to wait for a bit, Bagmo," said Barley. "We have Sauce Fingerbanana and Billy Jelly under control now, but we're gonna have to use the strength of our numbers to break down the doors and get out of this building."

"Maybe Mr. Spuggett can use his explosives to blow 'em up and knock 'em down!" offered Yump.

"Yeah, and scare the crap out of 'em," added Bagmo.

"That's a thought, guys," said Barley. "But I don't think Mr. Spuggett's explosives have enough power to do anything more than rattle the doors a little—"

BOOOOOOOM!!
CRAAASH!!

"Think again, Mr. Doodlebody!" cried Bagmo as he dove to the floor.

The sound, concussion, and shock of a *huge* explosion rocked the entire second floor, shaking the group in the reception room like rag dolls. Alpha Rae, Daphne, and Dr. Pudbid threw themselves protectively over Barley and Frog.

Out in the main office, one of the building's outer walls and part of the ceiling collapsed. The walls and floors of the entire structure wobbled, swayed, and shuddered, the overhead lights flickered and flashed, and plaster and dust rained down from the ceiling. Windows throughout the building shattered. The lamps on the end tables in Lollie's reception room and the two hanging portraits of the company founders crashed to the floor.

"*I repent! I repent!*" screamed wild-eyed Reverend Snortworthy as the floor trembled. "Behold, 'tis fire and brimstone from the very bowels of hell!"

"I don't like the sound of *that!*" shouted Bagmo.

Everyone hit the deck, covering their heads to shield themselves, quaking in terror as the building disintegrated around them. This was not the detonation of one of Old Man Spuggett's nondestructive explosive devices.

This was the end of the world!

44

Old Man Spuggett, Brufyss, Roland, and Dork entered the library through the disguised door to behold Smelly Billy Jelly, or what *appeared* to be Smelly Billy Jelly, lying unconscious on the dusty carpeted floor.

Margaret had arisen from her perch atop Billy's squelchy midsection and was standing over him, wiping her hands and surveying her work with grim satisfaction. Everyone else was struck dumb by the horrific-yet-somehow-pathetic sight of the hapless hoodlum.

"Yooooookta-fooookta!" blurted Dork, seeing Billy for the first time.

"Ya, shure, yuuuuuuuuuuuuu-betcha!" seconded Noodles.

"Goodness! What happened here?" asked Old Man Spuggett in shock and amazement—and a fair degree of queasiness.

"Billy got away from us . . . and Margaret got him," answered Biff, agog at the child's handiwork.

"Heavens, Margaret! *You* did this to Mr. Jellyball?"

Margaret beamed, nodded in the affirmative, and snorted as if to say, "Who else?"

"Thank you, my dear; you've saved us all from a very bad man." He reached down, stroked the little girl's head with a grandfatherly hand, and smiled. "I *knew* we'd be lucky to have you with us today, Margaret!"

The little child's beaming smile went nuclear.

"In turn, dear friends, we bring you joyous news: our mission to subdue Mr. Fingerbonanza was successful—he's been conscripted to be Gerald Foon-Package's assistant. We'll transport Mr. Bellyboy upstairs, and it's all over."

Brufyss was doing his best to suppress a gag reflex. "How are we gonna get Billy upstairs in this condition? *Yeesh!*"

"Perhaps we should just leave him where he is until the authorities arrive."

"How about putting him in the room where *we* were held prisoner?"

"Mr. Bumps's former office?"

"Yeah! Sauce padlocked it from the outside before he ran upstairs, and Billy doesn't know about the secret door in that room. We could drag him in there and leave someone to guard him until the police get here."

Margaret raised her hand to volunteer for the job . . .

BOOOOOOOM!!
CRAAASH!!

The building was rocked by the terrible sound and violent shaking of the mammoth explosion on the second floor!

"What was that?" shrieked Biff as the overhead lights flashed and flickered wildly.

"I'd know that sound anywhere!" exclaimed Old Man Spuggett. "I've never been able to reproduce it myself, but I can tell you: something big has blown up!"

"Mrs. Kookerly's up there!" cried Brufyss. "*Everybody's* up there! Biff, Dork, Noodles—drag Billy into the next room and meet us upstairs!"

The three hauled the slimy gangster into Old Man Bumps's office and left him on the floor, shut the bookshelf door, and beat a hasty retreat to join the rest of the group scrambling up the spiral staircase.

The crew sprawled in Lollie's reception room held their breaths and waited tensely for any follow-up to the massive explosion, or for the roof to cave in. All was still; only the sounds of plaster chunks falling from the ceiling in the main room and the buzzing and sputtering of the remaining overhead lights could be heard. Vaporous dust wafted into the reception room, clouding the air, making breathing difficult—but the worst seemed to be over, and no one had been injured.

"I am thinking my ears are to be falling off!" exclaimed Faisal, shaking his head to clear the ringing. He then cut loose with a fresh round of laughter, which provoked the usual contradictory response from himself: "Faisal! Always you are making the jokes and laugh when funny is not!"

The predictable pause . . .

"But to laughing is good, when we are wanting to crying instead!"

"What happened out there?" asked Bagmo from his hiding place under Lollie's reception desk. "It sounded like a chunk of the building fell in!"

"I think you're right!" said Barley. "We're gonna have to get out of here before the *rest* of the building comes down."

Mrs. Kookerly stood up in the middle of the room and brushed herself off. "Brufyss and the others were downstairs—they might be hurt or trapped! We can't leave them down there!"

From somewhere out in the main room, a weak voice called out: "Hello! What happened? Can anybody hear us?"

"Cheezy and Narducci!" cried Yump. "They were on guard duty out there. We gotta help 'em!"

Alpha Rae and Dr. Pudbid assisted Barley, Daphne helped Frog, the rest of the tourists and employees dragged themselves up from the floor, and Mrs. Kookerly moved to the wide doorway. She stared out into the ruined chamber in shock and disbelief.

"Ohmigosh! The room's been devastated! There's a big hole in the ceiling!"

The room had been blasted into shambles, choked with the dust of crushed plaster and smashed bricks from the building's inner and outer walls. The only intact items were the big banner and the smaller, hand-lettered sign hanging on the western wall.

Cheezy and Narducci sprawled on the floor by the attic doorway. They'd been far enough from the blast to escape serious injury, but flying debris and the explosion's concussive shock wave hurled them violently against the wall, knocking the wind out of them and conking them silly. They were reviving now, banged up and disoriented.

Mrs. Kookerly entered the demolished room, stepping over chunks of plaster and piles of debris, skirting around office desks and chairs knocked over and askew from the blast. "I think they're okay, just shaken up. I'm going to help them."

She looked over her shoulder to see a large hole blasted through the front of the building between Lollie's reception room and Cheezy's southeast-corner office. The entire southern wall of Cheezy's domain was gone. A sinister, flickering, red-and-orange glow appeared through the gap, and the cool air of the springtime evening wafted through the jagged opening, mingling with the lingering dust from the explosion.

"There's a huge hole in the wall, and it looks like there's a fire outside! We've gotta get out of this building *now*!"

One by one, the rest of the group entered the huge chamber. Everyone stared, aghast at the wrenching sight.

Rapunzel gathered up the papers on which she'd been scribbling most of the day, writing her *Daily Poop* article. The stack had become quite bulky.

"Rapunzel, how are you going to carry all that?" asked Mimsy of her Pockets Full o' Pucky shopping buddy. "Do you need help?"

"It looks heavy," said Yump. "Let us give you a hand."

"I appreciate the offer, but I wanna keep every scrap of this work under my own thumb. If we got separated during all the confusion, pages might be lost. Nothing's gonna keep me from getting this story out; I've just gotta figure out how I'm gonna carry it all!"

Yump had a flash of inspiration. "You could carry it on top of your head like they do in Bubba-Bubba-Bubba. Lollie can help you with that!"

"That's a wonderful idea, Yump," agreed Mimsy, "but Lollie's downstairs. Let's see if *we* can figure it out."

While Rapunzel organized her papers, Mimsy tore a strip of fabric from the remnants of one of Old Man Spuggett's red office curtains piled in a corner of the room. She eyed the fabric swatch disdainfully. "This is a horrid shade of red! I'm afraid it's going to clash with your outfit, Rapunzel. It's really not saying the right thing about you, fashion-wise!"

"Mimsy, I just wanna get these papers out of here. I'll adapt myself in any way I have to in order to accomplish that, fashion-wise or otherwise!"

The socialite was disappointed at the reporter's callous disregard for style and fashion sense at this critical juncture but didn't press the issue. She helped Yump lift the paper stack and place it atop Rapunzel's head. While Yump supported the paper and Rapunzel steadied herself, Mimsy draped the strip of fabric over the top of the stack and down both sides of the reporter's face, tying the two ends together under her chin. Rapunzel reached up and stabilized the paper-stack bonnet, seeking the balance point that would make it easier to carry the weight. She took a tentative step. The stack wavered, but she braced it with her hands to keep it in place.

"Y'know, if I can just keep my head from falling over, this might work!"

Supported on each arm by Mimsy and Yump, Rapunzel made her way into the main office, sporting her new headwear, weaving unsteadily like a drunken dental patient with a toothache on *top* of her head.

Meanwhile, Mrs. Kookerly reached Cheezy and Narducci and knelt beside them.

"It felt like a freight train smashed through the wall!" said Narducci. "What happened?"

"There was some kind of explosion, but it seems to be over now. Are you boys okay?"

"Oh, sure. Nothing a couple of weeks in Tahiti won't cure!"

"My *office*!" shrieked Cheezy, seeing his shattered workspace. "If I try to work in there now, I'll roll right into the street!"

Supported by Alpha Rae and Dr. Pudbid, Barley emerged from the reception room and witnessed the destruction. "You're right, Mrs. Kookerly, it isn't safe in here anymore. The ceiling is looking pretty shaky, too!"

Soft moaning came from a pile of rubble next to the ruins of Yump's cubicle, beneath the huge hole in the ceiling. "Somebody's over there," cried Mimsy. "It looks like *two* people!"

Two dust-covered figures struggled to free themselves from the debris. The coating of plaster dust and a mysterious gooey substance made their features unrecognizable. The employees and tourists scrambled across the wreckage to where the two sat on the floor, groggy and confused but conscious.

As the group approached, one of them addressed his rescuers. "I don't know what happened, but I swear—*we didn't do it!*"

It was Gerald Foon-Package and Wiley Fingerbanana. The two scientists had been hard at work in the attic laboratory when the monstrous blast caused a portion of the ceiling to cave in, bringing them down through the hole, along with Gerald's lab equipment and the large vat of cure for excess hair growth. Other than suffering a few bumps and bruises, they were relatively unharmed. The same could not be said for the vat of cure for excess hair growth, which spilled, splashed, and splooshed all over Gerald, Wiley, and the rubble-strewn floor.

"Well, it looks like it's gonna hafta be cheeseburgers after all!" said Bagmo sadly.

Bimbo was relieved but amazed. "Holy cow! You guys fell through the *roof*!"

Gerald coughed and cleared his throat of the choking plaster dust. "No, Bimbo, we fell down through the ceiling. If we fell through the roof, we'd be falling up, defying the law of gravity, and most likely hurtling off into space."

"Wow! Then that was a *close* one!" gasped Bimbo, marveling at their good fortune in not having fallen up.

"You might have landed on Jupiter or something," said Yump. His face brightened. "But I think I have family up there you could've stayed with."

"Indeed, it is fortuitous that you're both still here on Earth, unharmed and intact," Old Man Spuggett interjected. He had appeared with Brufyss in the broken doorway of his private office, surveying the scene of destruction. Behind them, the rest of the downstairs contingent craned their necks to see the mess. Ebenezer was on his hands and knees, peering between the legs of Brufyss and the old man.

"Bean water! Unanticipated redundancy mellifluously impregnated! Kapow! Kaput!"

"Verily, good friend, 'tis an observance well spoken," said Mayor Wubbleduster.

Mrs. Kookerly rushed over to Brufyss with joyous relief. "I'm so happy to see you're all safe and okay!"

"Yes, *we* are—but it appears our poor building has received a devastating and perhaps fatal blow," said the company founder. "We'd best make haste to evacuate these premises."

The ceiling began to creak, crack, and groan ominously as if to confirm his evaluation. The few working overhead lights flickered and buzzed.

Barley stood in the center of the room, staring at the threatening ceiling. "You've got that right, sir! Where's Billy? What happened to him?"

"Margaret Wubbleduster took care of Billy for us," replied Brufyss. "He's downstairs in Mr. Bumps's old office, out cold and totally incapacitated—"

"You mean his *head* came off again?" cried Bagmo.

"No, no, Mr. Maltgoggles! Remember? *Incapacitated*, not *decapitated*!"

"Whew, glad to hear that! Would've been the second time today."

"I don't think the first floor has experienced the same degree of damage that this floor has," continued Brufyss. "Billy should be okay where he is until we can get back to him."

The downstairs contingent emerged from the old man's private office and picked their way across the room, joining the rest of the employees and guests. All kept wary eyes on the weakened ceiling. Their numbers were large once again, and their predicament tenuous; no time could be wasted.

Lollie saw Rapunzel balancing the stack of writing paper on her head and smiled approvingly; in her home country, this was a standard and practical method of transporting goods. With a few appropriate gestures, she demonstrated how best to keep the load balanced and walk at the same time.

Rapunzel smiled at the receptionist. "Thanks, Lollie! You're helping to bring our story to the rest of the world."

"Wumba-lala laboola!" Lollie had no idea what Rapunzel said but was certain she'd never seen anyone look so ridiculous.

Once everyone had assembled in the big room, a head count was taken to ensure all were present. An escape plan had to be formulated quickly. "We don't have an idea of the full extent of the damage to the building," said Brufyss, "but every way out of here is chained and padlocked."

Mrs. Kookerly pointed through the jagged hole in the southern wall. The flickering red-and-orange glow lit the black of the night sky. "There might be a fire to contend with once we get outside!"

"We're just gonna have to batter our way out of here," concluded Barley. "There are enough of us to do it."

A voice came from the fringe of the assembled group. "Wait! That won't be necessary!"

It was Felicia Greenthing.

The feelings of guilt, selfishness and irresponsibility for not contributing her obvious solution had been building inside Felicia for quite some time. The CEO in charge of finding the second-floor delivery entrance had kept its existence and location secret, fearing that once she'd actually accomplished her assignment, her services would no longer be needed. She'd end up on the street—like an escaped sheep.

She knew Wiley Fingerbanana had chained and padlocked all downstairs exits to the building. He hadn't come upstairs until he became apprenticed to Gerald Foon-Package, and he'd arrived by way of the stairway on the opposite side of the building. The second-floor delivery entrance had escaped his notice and padlocks.

Fearful that the revelation of the deep, dark secret would probably result in her dismissal from the company, she was nevertheless aware that the second-floor delivery entrance was the surest way to escape the peril they now faced. Something had to be done to save the group; Felicia needed to come through for them.

She swallowed hard and took a deep breath. "There's no need to take any chances that might get somebody hurt. I know a way out of here that'll be quick and safe. Follow me!"

She clambered through the piles of rubble and office furniture, giving the ragged hole in the ceiling a wide berth, leapfrogging and bunny-hopping over fallen obstacles, and finally arrived at the aisle near the conference-room door. She urged everyone to join her without delay.

The walls and ceiling creaked, cracked, and groaned threateningly. "I strongly recommend we do as Miss Greenthing insists," said Old Man Spuggett, "for I believe our poor building is becoming rather insistent itself."

Bimbo and Cheezy stooped to help Gerald and Sauce to their feet, receiving goopy handfuls of the potatoes au gratin that covered both scientists.

"*YUCK*! You guys are *gross*!" exclaimed Bimbo.

"This is Gerald's cure for excess hair growth," Cheezy explained to Sauce. "You're supposed to *eat* the stuff, not wear it!"

Felicia stopped at the doorway to her office and motioned for the refugees to follow her into the room. Once they'd congregated, she headed to the second-floor delivery entrance vestibule, the refugees shuffling after her.

Barley, supported by Alpha Rae and Dr. Pudbid, reached the door to Felicia's office and stopped, asking the two to pause for a moment and step to one side so others could pass ahead of them. He took one last look into the ruined main office. He'd chased Fandango Slamson around and around and around this big room when his tour group had first arrived. It seemed so long ago, and so much had happened since then—on *two* floors!

He looked across to the far, western wall. Barely visible in the dim distance and the flickering light were the two signs that hung there: the big banner and the hand-lettered sign. Barley focused on the smaller of the two.

From Stupidity Springs Lucidity

He smiled.

His life had been filled with stupidity until he came to this place. He'd been stupid in his business dealings, stupid with his idea of what success should be, stupid with his attitude toward people and the rest of the world. He'd been stupid not to realize the value of true friendship when he had it, and he'd been stupid to let it go.

But he was leaving this place with a newfound clarity and feeling of purpose. Now he had roots and a history to fill in the blank spaces of his existence, teaching him valuable lessons and doing no less than changing his whole life.

All in one day.

The veil of stupidity had been lifted, and the view ahead was clear. The hand-lettered sign made perfect sense. He gave the smashed office one final, wistful perusal and turned back to Alpha Rae and Dr. Pudbid.

"Okay, let's go. I just wanted to take one more look for old times' sake . . . before the *new* times begin."

The three joined the others.

Felicia led the ragtag band of refugees into the anteroom separating her office from the rear stairway. On the right side of the small vestibule was the hand-lettered sign that read,

---

This is definitely **NOT** a delivery entrance!

It is only a **FAKE** door, not a real one! Ha-ha.

The joke's on you.

If you try to use it, you will plunge to your

death and be killed!

The sign hung on the second-floor delivery entrance door, undiscovered, unused, unopened, and unlocked in anticipation of the arrival of the filthy-rag deliveryman with his daily delivery of filthy rags for Faisal—an arrival that hadn't taken place today. Felicia walked up to the sign and deftly tore it off.

Bagmo came into the small room in time to witness her doing so. "Felicia, what are you doing? We can't go out through there; that's a fake door! We'll plunge to our death and be *killed*!"

"Lies! All lies! I put this sign here to fool everybody. I thought I'd lose my job if you knew I'd actually found what I was supposed to find. I've betrayed you all! I feel so . . . so *evil*!"

She broke down and began sobbing hysterically.

Old Man Spuggett entered the room in time to witness Felicia's confession.

"There, there, Miss Greenthing. Please, don't cry! Everyone's known of this door all along!"

"They . . . they have? Then why didn't anybody *say* anything?"

"Because it was *your* job to find the delivery entrance." The old man placed his wrinkled hand on her head and gently stroked her hair. "There's no one here, myself included, who'd presume to tell you how to do your job. Until the time came when you informed us that you'd located the door, we simply found it prudent not to acknowledge its existence.

"Congratulations on a job well done, my dear! You've not only accomplished your assignment successfully and with great aplomb, but you've done so at a most opportune moment. We shall now use the successful results of your labor to make our way en masse to safety."

Felicia stopped her anguished crying. Had she heard right? Instead of receiving rebukes and reprimands from the old man, she'd been applauded and thanked. The fear and anxiety she'd harbored through years of keeping her deep, dark secret a deep, dark secret had been entirely unfounded.

"Thanks, Felicia," said Bagmo. "You saved our life!"

"Not at all, Bagmo! Just doing my job! Just doing my job."

With a horrible grating, ripping sound of disintegrating plaster, an agonized screech of twisting metal, and loud cracking and splitting of wood framing in the main room, the wounded ceiling and weakened roof gave up the ghost and caved in, crashing thunderously to the floor. Every functioning light in the building flickered wildly and went black, plunging everything and everyone into inky darkness.

The refugees huddling in the small vestibule and Felicia's office edged closer to each other, staring at the invisible ceiling. So far, these rooms seemed to be holding together. So far . . .

Felicia focused on her mission, fighting to keep her wits about her in all the bedlam. "Did everybody make it out of there? Is everybody here?"

Each individual answered. Everyone was present.

"Let's *vacate*!" she cried triumphantly, hurling her hand-lettered sign to the vestibule floor and flinging open the door to the second-floor delivery entrance—or as it had now become, the second-floor delivery exit. "There's a stairway outside the door that leads to the alley. Watch your step in the darkness. We don't want anyone tripping or falling!"

"Yeah, *buddy*!" cried Frog.

Despite the seriousness of the situation and perhaps as a nervous response to it, Faisal burst forth with another surge of belly laughter. Knowing they were seconds from safety and freedom, the rest of the group tittered, snickered, giggled, chuckled, and finally guffawed at his display of comedic histrionics, their sense of relief manifesting in an ever-growing chorus of mirthful release.

Soon, everyone was convulsed with laughter. The entire group of refugees traipsed through the door of the second-floor delivery exit, high-fiving Felicia as they walked past her while she held the door open for them. They emerged into the cool, crisp air of the springtime evening and shuffled down the stairway, laughing all the way, step-by-step to the alley below.

45

As the laughing band of refugees reached the bottom of the stairs, their attention was drawn to the fiery, reddish-orange glare coming from Clown Balls Avenue. At the far end of the narrow service drive, the space between the Bumps & Spuggett building and the structure across the way was aglow with a hellish luminosity that lit the night sky. The reddish-orange cast shimmered on the polished surface of the Bathwater Boys 'n Girls Gang's black sedan.

They neared the street. A low, ominous hum became audible—an insistent, growling rumble—the perception of which replaced the vestiges of their carefree laughter with uneasy silence. What would they find when they rounded the corner?

They continued down the alley toward the fiery light. The dark shape of a person appeared ahead at the corner of the building, silhouetted in the glow, peering up the darkened alley in their direction, pointing an indistinct object at them.

"*Halt!*" called a voice from the shadowy shape. "Identify yourselves! Did you come from this building?"

"Indeed we did!" answered the company founder. "My name is Spuggett, and I'm the owner of this building and this business. My employees and a number of our friends have just escaped from inside!"

The shadowy figure stepped from behind the corner of the building into the center of the alley. He switched on a flashlight. They saw the object he pointed at them.

A gun.

"If you please, sir, could you kindly refrain from directing that weapon at us? We've already had a fair share of firearms poked in our faces by Mr. Jelly today!"

"*Billy Jelly*? Where?" shrieked the man, dropping to the ground, scanning the refugees with his weapon. "Is he with you?"

"Heavens *no*, sir! Mr. Jelly lies immobilized and incapacitated in a room on the first floor of this building. He is no threat to anyone. Who might *you* be?"

The man scrambled to his feet, lowering his weapon. "Officer Ninepoodles, Special Weapons and Tactics, North Corners Police Force!" He focused the flashlight beam on the old man. "We've come to rescue you, but it looks like you've already rescued yourselves. Is everyone in your group okay?"

"We're relatively and thankfully unharmed, Officer, although there are several individuals among us with non-life-threatening injuries being attended to by our physician, Dr. Humaylius Pudbid."

Officer Ninepoodles's eyes brightened. "Dr. Pudbid? He helped deliver me after I was born! How's your horse, Doc? Got any lollipops?"

"Frank Winslow's fine, Officer, and thanks for asking—but I'm afraid I'm temporarily out of lollipops. If you'd like to stop by my office tomorrow, I'll give you a whole handful."

"Roger that! Now, back to business. Um, where *were* we anyway?"

"I was informing you, sir, that Mr. Jelly remains inside the building on the first floor, the northwest side, in an empty office. The door is padlocked."

"You said he'd been immobilized and incapacitated; is he okay?"

"I believe that would depend on what you meant by 'okay,'" said the old man, recalling Margaret's treatment of Smelly Billy. "He was unconscious when we left him, not seriously injured, and definitely incapacitated."

"That means his head *hasn't* fallen off!" added Bagmo.

"Right! We'll get on that!" Officer Ninepoodles snatched a walkie-talkie handset from a holster on his chest. "Ninepoodles here: have made contact with a large group of individuals heading down east-side alleyway from within subject building. All ambulant, several with non-life-threatening injuries, kindly Dr. Pudbid in attendance as physician—no lollipops . . ."

The officer paused in his transmission and scanned the ragtag group. "Are there any weapons we should know about? We were informed that you were being held hostage and threatened with a gun; you just confirmed that. Does that remaining person on the first floor—Billy Jelly—have a weapon? Do any of you have weapons?"

"There were two handguns," replied Barley, "but both are unloaded and upstairs inside the building. All the downstairs entrances have been padlocked from the inside, so you'll probably have to break down the doors to get in, and the building is without power. I wouldn't recommend using the exit we just emerged from; as of a few minutes ago, that portion of the building no longer exists!"

Officer Ninepoodles nodded and resumed his radio transmission: "Unconscious male individual in padlocked office on building's first floor, northwest side, believed to be suspect, Smelly Billy Jelly. No threat of firearms. Repeat: no weapons. All exterior doors on lower level barricaded from inside, building's interior is dark—will require forced entry. Over."

The radio squawked with static, and a crackling voice came back in reply:

"*Copying, unconscious male, unarmed, in secured office on building's first floor, northwest side. Confirm kindly Dr. Pudbid as attending physician to injured parties. Did you say 'No lollipops'? Over.*"

"Affirmative. No lollipops. Over."

"*Roger that. Will respond. Out.*" There was obvious disappointment in the voice on the other end.

"Now, let's get you out of this alley and away from the building," said Officer Ninepoodles.

"Lead the way, Officer! We shall be pleased to follow obediently." The company founder addressed the group. "I believe we're out of trouble at last, good friends! Let us follow brave Officer Ninepoodles to safety!"

"*Amen!*" cried Reverend Snortworthy. The beleaguered band let loose with a rousing cheer of joy and relief. Faisal exploded with a new burst of laughter, and most of the group joined him.

Wiley Fingerbanana was one person *not* overjoyed at the prospect of being in the protective custody of the North Corners police. His prior involvement with Smelly Billy and his complicity in the darker side of the day's activities left him concerned for his future, a future that seemed so much brighter since joining forces with Gerald Foon-Package. As they trudged down the alley, Sauce whispered furtively to his new partner: "Gerald, am I gonna get busted? I don't wanna go to jail! I wanna work with *you!*"

"Relax, Wiley! We'll explain the situation to Mr. Spuggett, and I'm sure he'll understand. You didn't hurt anyone, and before we fell through the ceiling, your contribution to our experiment resulted in a major breakthrough. I'll tell Mr. Spuggett that I need you in order to complete the work."

The Bumps & Spuggett scientist-in-residence and his aspiring assistant accelerated their pace toward the front of the procession until they caught up with the old man.

"Excuse me, sir," whispered Gerald, "but I wanted to put in a word for Mr. Fingerbanana here. I don't feel he should be looked upon as a criminal in today's escapade. I *do* feel that if given the chance, he'll prove to be a valuable assistant to me and our company as well!"

"Please, Mr. Spuggett, sir, please don't bust me!" begged Sauce. "I never meant to hurt anyone or cause trouble—or break any of your rules!"

The old man looked at Sauce in surprise. "*Bust* you?! Judging by the multitude of new friends and opportunities that have arisen from today's events, Mr. Fingerbandage, I believe you've done us a great service! You padlocked us into the building, which enabled us to get to know each other better, which in turn enabled us to become faster friends. And it sounds to me like you've made yourself indispensable to our Mr. Foon-Package here!"

"Does that mean I don't have to go to jail?"

"How could the world benefit from your scientific talents if they were sequestered behind bars, Mr. Finglebazamma? Gerald needs you, we need you—the *world* needs you, sir. Consider yourself a part of the Bumps & Spuggett family!"

Sauce sighed with relief, his heart filled with happiness and a new sense of self-worth. Gerald beamed proudly, and the two Bumps & Spuggett scientists in residence walked toward the front of the building with their heads held high, albeit dripping with Gerald's cure for excess hair growth.

"Wiley, I feel confident that our future as scientific associates is going to be a bright one," whispered Gerald as they walked. "In the short time we collaborated before my laboratory fell through the floor, you made a significant contribution to my cure for excess hair growth that augmented the quality as it's never been before! You have a natural gift for creating an embellishing accompaniment to improve a product without changing the product itself—to *enhance* rather than obscure it. As a tribute to your talent, I'm giving you a new nickname!"

"A new nickname?" gasped Wiley, humbled by Gerald's compliment and faith in his abilities. "I'll do anything to get rid of the nickname I have now! What's the new one?"

"From now on you'll be known as . . . 'Sauce' Fingerbanana!"

Sauce looked at Gerald in puzzlement. "But that's already my nickname!"

"But now the nickname 'Sauce' has a new connotation! A *respectable* connotation! A *prestigious* connotation! Now it's Sauce as in 'Saucier'—a creator of embellishing accompaniments—and I believe you'll be a great one!"

"Sauce Fingerbanana," mused Wiley. "Hey, I *like* that. Thanks, Gerald!"

"And I thank you—Sauce!"

They shook hands proudly.

As Officer Ninepoodles and the mirthfully possessed Bumps & Spuggett employees and guests rounded the corner onto Clown Balls Avenue, the mysteries of the fiery reddish-orange glow, the ominous growling sound, and the huge explosion were solved. The sinister glare radiated from many red-and-yellow emergency flashers and revolving lights atop a semicircle of black-and-white police vehicles, a huge fire engine, and a hook-and-ladder truck filling the street in front of the building.

Parked behind the official vehicles was a delivery truck, and next to it sat a police paddy wagon. Positioned between the police cars and along the front of the building were numerous SWAT officers, all gazing curiously at the disheveled band of refugees, particularly the old man and his younger twin in their rumpled bathrobes, the goggle-eyed woman wobbling with a stack of paper tied to the top of her head, and the once-well-dressed-but-now-tattered blue-headed lady with poofed-out hair.

The source of the deep growling hum turned out to be the onboard water pump of the gleaming red fire engine, chugging and idling next to Roland Chumbuckets's parked tour bus. Standing at curbside by the front entrance was a man with the bearing, appearance, and apparel of a captain of the fire brigade, although he seemed to be missing his pants. The fire captain directed a gaggle of firemen manning lengths of the truck's unspooled fire hose, one end of which was attached to a fire hydrant at the corner of the intersection. The fire captain looked familiar to the Doodlebody tour group.

Roland recognized him immediately: Captain Moolly Chubbychuffle!

Upon closer scrutiny, the group realized that chief of police Binky Bohoguss was perched on the wide brim of the fire captain's helmet, chirping orders to his deployed officers in his cute little voice through a teensy-weensy megaphone. His men acknowledged their chief with crisp salutes and big, indulgent smiles.

The source of the huge explosion sent collective gasps of astonishment through the group. Propped at a precarious angle against the curb in front of the Bumps & Spuggett building was a Sherman tank! Its rear end sat in the street, its front end straddling the curb so that it stuck up into the air with its cannon elevated, the big gun's barrel smoking from the round it had discharged into the building. The same tank whose errant cannon blast had blown out the windows of Roland's bus and sent the inaugural tour on its way had just blown up the building and ended it!

Spiffany Tonguehoister sat atop the monstrous metal beast, her crown-bedecked head sticking out through the hatch in the tank's turret. She was weeping and shrieking, vehemently protesting that it was an accident, she didn't mean to do it, she was so very, very sorry, and would take complete responsibility for repairing the damage. A contingent of North Corners SWAT policemen ringed the custom-modified hulk of war matériel with guns drawn, insisting that the self-styled monarch get out of the stilled behemoth and come down to the street with her hands up.

Officer Ninepoodles shepherded the refugees past the hulking tank and politely excused himself to resume his duties. Kindly Dr. Pudbid ran to Roland's tour bus to retrieve his battered black medical bag.

"Chief Bohoguss!" cried Barley, spotting the tiny law enforcement officer. "You're safe! How did you get out here?"

Binky squealed with delight and waved, nearly tumbling from Captain Chubbychuffle's helmet brim. He shouted to Barley in the cutest voice imaginable, telling him that as soon as he was finished directing the operation in progress, he'd rejoin the group. In the meantime, Barley would need to get the details of what happened from Mux Muggsley. Chief Bohoguss resumed his chiefly duties, squeaking orders, pointing here and there, aware that he was being lovingly observed and admired by all of the newly liberated refugees.

Barley was puzzled. *Get the details from Mux Muggsley? Chief Bohoguss knows I don't speak cocker spaniel!*

Mux stood with the fire captain and Chief Bohoguss, watching with interest as they performed their official duties. Old Man Spuggett cried out to his heretofore-missing employee: "*Mux*! *Here*, Mux! Here, boy! C'mon over here, Mux! *Good* boy!"

Mux heard the familiar voice and his eyes brightened. Instead of bolting wildly toward the group on all fours to receive their welcoming hugs, head pats, and "*Good* boys," he walked upright and briskly on two legs to his fellow employees and tourist friends, who gawked at his decidedly un-canine approach.

"Mux, my boy, we're so happy to see you unharmed!" exulted the company founder as the cocker-spaniel man walked up to him and extended his hand in greeting.

"You could've been shot, Mux! You could've gotten lost!" scolded Yump. "*Bad boy*!"

"Indeed, Yump, it was foolhardy, but I believe everything has ultimately worked for the best. I also believe there's a good possibility, had I *not* run off, that you might not be standing here with me right now!"

The refugees gaped at him. Mux was not only speaking but doing so quite articulately. Yet one more miracle in a day crammed with miracles! Only little Margaret seemed disappointed at Mux's transformation.

"What happened, Mux?!" asked Alpha Rae. "Both you and Fandango were running around like a couple of loonies, and that gangster was taking potshots at you! You're lucky you didn't get your little doggie butt blown off, young man!"

"You ran down the front stairs and disappeared!" added Yump. "That's the last we saw of you. What happened after that?"

"Yeah, what happened after that?" chorused the entire group.

Mux let out a long sigh and closed his eyes. "My friends, so much happened. Let me begin where it all began . . ."

Realizing that Mux was about to launch into a revealing narrative, Rapunzel grabbed Biff Spoozma, pulled a sheet of paper from the stack on top of her head, spread the paper across Biff's wide back, and scribbled furiously.

"You'll recall that both Fandango and I were in a panic, running madly around the room, foolishly trying to dodge and outrun the bullets the gangster was firing at us," Mux began.

"But you *did* outrun 'em!" interrupted Bimbo. "He missed you by a mile!"

"For my part, it was purely luck, Bimbo. All I did was confuse the guy. The only fireball I know who can outrun a bullet is Fandango."

Fandango grinned sheepishly.

"In the midst of my aimless travels around the room's perimeter, the futility of it dawned on me. Seeing the doorway to Lollie's reception room just ahead, I ducked in there, continued down the front stairway to the lobby, and was pleased to find the front door unlocked."

"You got out before it was padlocked," said Barley.

"Indeed! There was still daylight outside; I turned the corner, sprinting up Guggbutt Boulevard toward Gob Street and the rear of the building. When I reached the corner of Guggbutt and Gob, I heard the sound of insistent screeching and squealing! I stopped to listen; the high-pitched noises were coming from somewhere just above me on the side of the building. I looked up to the source of the commotion and saw little Chief Bohoguss straining to extract himself from an air-conditioning vent on the wall, crying out to attract my attention."

Barley smiled. The resourceful little chief had utilized his expertise at squeezing through plumbing, heating, and air-conditioning ducts to get out of the building, as he'd done in his former life as "Hoboken BoBo," the seven-inch-tall bank robber.

"*Aha*!" cried Old Man Spuggett. "That explains a great deal! You see, at the moment when Mr. Smellyball first interrupted the wingding festivities, Puddles and I were in my office with the little chief; Mr. Doodyfoodle had entrusted him to me for safekeeping, lest he be inadvertently trampled in the midst of the freewheeling celebrations.

"Witnessing the gravity of the situation through my office door and realizing that our presence there was as yet undetected, Puddles and I removed the little law enforcer through the secret passage, downstairs to the relative security of the library. I woke the little fellow from his trance, related our dire situation to him, and placed him atop a bookshelf, explaining that it was for his own safety.

"Later, when Mrs. Kookerly, Simpleton, Bagmo, and I descended to the library and found the trussed-up Mr. Slamson, I was chagrined to see that the little chief was nowhere to be found! However, I noticed that the grating to an air-conditioning vent had been removed in the wall above the bookshelves. Our little hero pursued his own course of action and used the vent to make his escape from the building—and now we'll learn what happened once he did!"

Mux continued: "I assisted Chief Bohoguss out of the vent and realized we were the only two who'd escaped. He climbed onto my shoulder, and I ran on all fours to the rear Gob Street entrance. It was locked. We were about to head up Guggbutt Boulevard again when a delivery truck careened around the corner. I thought this might be the delivery truck that brought filthy rags each day, so I darted into Gob Street and chased the truck, barking my head off! The driver saw us and pulled over, undoubtedly shocked to see a full-grown human being chasing his truck like a tire-biting mutt."

"*Yes!*" cried Faisal. "Driver is Jobby Gimpthwinkle! Jobby is every day to me bringing the filthy rags for delivery. Now I am knowing why he is not bringing to me today. He is helping Mux and little police person!"

"And he's with us right now, Faisal! I believe Felicia knows Jobby; he passes through her office every day, making his deliveries. Allow me to introduce Mr. Gimpthwinkle to *all* of you."

Mux beckoned him to join the group, and the deliveryman shuffled over. "Ladies and gentlemen, meet Jobby Gimpthwinkle, whose involvement in our plight today has helped to make our happy reunion possible."

"Howdy," said Jobby shyly. "Glad to help out."

The refugees burst into cheers and applause. After Jobby had shaken hands all around, Mux continued his story: "Mr. Gimpthwinkle noticed Chief Bohoguss clinging to my shoulder and burst into laughter! The chief was trying to explain that we were in trouble and needed help, but the more the little guy screamed, the funnier Jobby thought the whole thing was! He doubled over with laughter, rolling around on the floor of his truck."

Jobby's face flushed with embarrassment. "Sorry, but the little guy just sounded really funny when he talked. I thought the whole thing was a put-on!"

"Chief Binky's efforts were getting us nowhere," Mux continued. "It was time to reclaim my humanity—to be a person again. The fate of our friends—all of *you*—depended on it!

"I picked Chief Binky off my shoulder, stood upright, and re-explained our grim circumstances in my most articulate American English. Jobby was taken aback by the abrupt change in my doggie behavior. He stopped laughing and listened to me—at least, as long as Chief Bohoguss didn't say anything—eventually grasping the seriousness of the predicament and, I would suppose, realizing that our timely interception of him had helped him to avoid walking into the middle of the debacle himself."

"You got *that* right!" laughed Jobby.

"I told Mr. Gimpthwinkle to drive to the nearest police station. We sped off in the delivery truck, wending our way through the city until we spied the military monstrosity you see on the sidewalk before you: the Sherman tank belonging to Queen Spiffany Tonguehoister, who was performing her daily vigilance patrol of North Corners. Chief Bohoguss was aware that Her Majesty's tank is equipped with a police-and-fire radio and scanner, which she utilizes to monitor the transmissions of the two agencies. Mr. Gimpthwinkle stopped his truck so we could flag down the tank and commandeer her radio.

"We jumped into the street in front of the approaching tank, waving and screaming, 'Emergency! Emergency!' The tank lurched to a halt, and she poked her head with that silly crown out through the top of the turret and peevishly asked, 'Whaddaya think you're doing, interrupting my vigilance patrol with some stupid emergency?'

"We explained the situation and revealed that the North Corners chief of police himself was a member of our party. Queen Spiffany became polite and amenable to assisting us, especially when she saw how adorable little Binky was. She allowed us to climb aboard the tank so the chief could use the police-and-fire radio in the cockpit.

"But a new frustration presented itself to us: when Ms. Tonguehoister contacted the police on her tank's radio, she was met with derisive laughter and a stinging rebuke—I guess her well-known eccentricities are looked upon either as a source of amusement or as a nuisance. She was told to get off the frequency and keep her nose out of police business.

"We fared no better when Chief Bohoguss tried to communicate with them. They laughed at the sound of his tiny voice, wouldn't believe that he was addressing them, and couldn't take anyone seriously who was associated with Ms. Tonguehoister. We were being frustrated at every turn, and time was ticking away!

"Finally, it was Queen Spiffany herself who suggested we travel to a fire station she knew to be close by. Maybe we could convince them to contact the police for us. We took off in the tank, and Mr. Gimpthwinkle followed in his truck.

"The sun was sinking on the horizon, but at long last Ms. Tonguehoister pulled the tank into the driveway of the fire station. We scrambled into the building, waking the slumbering fire captain and his men—and extracting the poor gentleman's head from a large boot it became wedged in after he leaped from his bed through a hole in the floor. Captain Chubbychuffle was exceedingly gracious and sought to give us all the help he could—although he seemed unaccustomed to solving *problems*."

"That's good ol' Cap'n Chubbychuffle all right!" laughed Roland. "Pants or no pants, he's a real character!"

"That he is, Roland!" Mux smiled, cast an admiring look in the fire captain's direction, and continued, "He and Chief Binky remembered seeing each other earlier in the day, and after we related our predicament to him and were regaled with several odd aphorisms, purportedly from his aged father"—Roland smirked—"the good captain agreed to assist us in contacting the police.

"Evidently his credentials carried more weight than ours; he succeeded in mobilizing not only his own crew of firefighters but the North Corners Police Special Weapons and Tactics team as well! However, when he asked us where we were going, Chief Binky and I realized with a great deal of embarrassment that we hadn't a clue. Fortunately, Mr. Gimpthwinkle did."

"I oughta! I drive here every day!"

"He pinpointed the location of the Clown Balls and Guggbutt thoroughfares for us, and Captain Chubbychuffle informed the SWAT team of our destination. Chief Bohoguss and I jumped into the captain's car, and we set off, accompanied by the fire engines but with their sirens silenced so as not to alert the criminals inside the building. Mr. Gimpthwinkle followed in his truck, Ms. Tonguehoister in her tank.

"We arrived on the scene simultaneously with the police. Once the officers saw that it truly *was* Chief Bohoguss who'd contacted them, they immediately complied with the little guy's orders and deployed into the positions you see now. While Chief Binky and Captain Chubbychuffle were organizing their respective crews, Ms. Tonguehoister showed up—but in attempting to maneuver her Sherman tank around the assembled fire and police vehicles and into a spot at curbside, she inadvertently steered the tank up onto the curb itself.

"The jarring jolt knocked Ms. Tonguehoister off balance, and she bumped the cannon's firing mechanism. A round accidentally discharged, and the secrecy of our deployment fell by the wayside, along with a large portion of the building—which brings us to now. You're all safe, and my joy at seeing you thus is boundless. It's been quite an adventure."

"Wow, that's an amazing story, Mux!" marveled Bagmo with a low whistle. "If I didn't believe it was true, I wouldn't believe it was true!"

"Nonetheless, we're happy that you're safe as well, Mr. Muggsley," said Old Man Spuggett. "I must say, your rediscovered vocabulary suits you far better than a canine bark. And Mr. Gimpthwinkle, we thank you again for your timely involvement."

"Shucks, 'twarn't nothin'," replied Jobby.

"Oh, yes it '*twar*!" countered Bagmo.

A commotion at the front entrance. The North Corners SWAT team, under the absolutely adorable direction of Chief Bohoguss, was preparing to enter the building. Several of the officers hoisted a small battering ram while the rest of the contingent stood by with weapons drawn, waiting for the front door to be broken down.

"It looks like there's more action brewing," said Barley, "but this time we don't have to be a part of it. I suggest we sit back and watch the show."

"Yeah, *buddy!*" seconded Frog.

As the employees, tourists and guests watched from the curbside, the SWAT team bashed in the door and entered the first-floor reception room and lobby. They located the padlocked door to Old Man Bumps's former office. There was more door-bashing, followed by horrified exclamations, loud protestations, and noises of extreme revulsion as they beheld the gangster, lathered to a frenzied froth by Margaret Wubbleduster.

The refugees listened with amusement and Margaret smirked with satisfaction as cries of "*You* pick 'im up! I ain't *touchin'* 'im!" and "I think I'm gonna be sick!" and "That's the grossest thing I've ever seen!" issued from within the office complex. The officers reached an accord. They emerged through the front door, grimacing in disgust but dragging the reviving Billy Jelly by the hands and feet to the sidewalk and propping him into a seated position against the building wall. Other incredulous officers formed a semicircle around the groggy, soggy hoodlum with drawn weapons, witnessing Margaret's handiwork with morbid fascination. The rescuers hurried off to wash the slime from their hands and arms.

Among the policemen was Officer Ninepoodles, who whined, "*Now* what're we gonna do with him?"—but it was Roland who conceived the solution. He walked over to pantsless Captain Chubbychuffle, who'd again been summoned into action before being able to don his complete firefighting wardrobe.

Chief Binky saw Roland and squeaked a cute little greeting. Roland returned it with a happy "Hiya, Chief! Glad to see you're safe, sound, and in charge."

Then, to Moolly Chubbychuffle, "Hi, Cap'n! It's me, Roland Chumbuckets! Remember?"

"O' course I remember you, Roland! I thought this bus here looked familiar, blown-out windows and all. This is the third time I've seen you today—in the third separate location. You certainly do seem to get around, son!"

Roland laughed. "I'm a bus driver, Cap'n! Getting around is what I *do*!"

"*Ha-haaa*, so it is!"

"But, sir, we have a problem here at the moment—"

"A *problem*? Well, we're not used to solving problems normally, but we are here to help. We're always here to help! We're firemen!"

"Yes, sir, but this is a problem you've already solved today."

"Then why is it a problem?"

"I'll explain. It's actually a *new* problem but one you have the experience to solve because you already solved the *old* problem."

Roland reiterated the problem and its solution to the captain, who agreed to implement the old solution to the new problem posthaste. He barked a few instructions to members of his crew manning the length of fire hose. The firemen dragged the hose to where Billy sat and stood a few feet from him while one of the men pointed the hose's brass nozzle at the soiled gangster.

Captain Chubbychuffle called to the fireman standing at the hydrant on the street corner. "Stand by to release the water, Floyd! Everybody else, *stand back*!"

The policemen obliged, moving away from the wall where Billy sat groggily wagging his head from side to side. The befuddled gangster had been regaining consciousness since the SWAT team dragged him from Old Man Bumps's office. He opened his eyes; the residual gooey film from Margaret's HIVED-ing blurred his vision and prevented him from focusing. He tilted his head back and forth, blinking. All he could discern was the hazy, glaring glow of the flashing red-and-orange lights, and the presence of many individual-but-indistinct shapes in front of him.

"Where am I?"

Sitting on the curb with the refugees, Mayor Wubbleduster heard Billy's bewildered query. "But soft! Yon wicked knave from slumber doth awake!"

Billy heard the mayor and strained to see where the voice—a disquietingly familiar voice—was coming from.

"Unauthorized *obrigado* recalls amalgamation with atypical extension!"

Billy's head snapped around to the sound of Ebenezer's voice—*another* disquietingly familiar voice. Where had he heard these voices before? He shook his head in an attempt to clear the cobwebs.

"Sha-lah-lah *boom*! Sha-lah-lah *boom*! Lamma-lamma-lamamba!"

Billy couldn't see his hecklers, but their babbling struck a responsive chord in his reeling brain. The answer came to him: Gloxnarians! The aliens who wanted to take him to their planet and perform hideous experiments on him! They'd covered him with a creamy cocoon of crud to paralyze him and take him back to Gloxnar in their yellow-and-orange-flashing spaceship. He'd outfought them before; he'd do it again. Steeling himself to quell the pounding in his head, Billy staggered to his feet, his back to the brick wall.

"Verily, the brigand hath arisen!"

"Reregistered retaliation! Alas! Amuck!"

"Mapala bumba! Mapala bumba!"

"'Mapala bumba' *yourself*, you alien bastards!" Billy shook his fist defiantly, still unable to see his adversaries clearly. "Bring it on!"

Roland turned to Captain Chubbychuffle. "Cap'n, I think it's about time to solve the problem we discussed, don't you?"

Captain Chubbychuffle smiled. "Like my old daddy used to say, 'If a juggler won't stop juggling, you've just gotta grab his balls.'"

"Yeah, *buddy*!" chuckled Roland.

Captain Chubbychuffle dropped his raised arm and cried, "*Let 'er rip!*"

Floyd the fireman gave the big wrench a sharp yank, and water roared forth from the hose's nozzle, barreling into Smelly Billy with the force of a Spiffany Tonguehoister tank cannon round.

"*Thar she blows!*"

The thug was pounded and pummeled like a wafer in a waterfall, sprayed and splattered, bounced and beaten, hammered and hurled against the brick wall by the powerful stream of water. He skidded and scooted, rolled and writhed across the sidewalk in front of the refugees and police and fire personnel, who gawked at the tremendous hydro-force being unleashed against him. Frog, Biff, Mimsy, Reverend Snortworthy, and Dr. Pudbid winced in remembrance of their similar beating outside Pockets Full o' Pucky.

The captain realized he had once again forgotten to change the hose nozzle's setting from "Riot Suppression"—*Oops!*—and signaled for Floyd to cut off the water. The violent stream eased to a trickle, and Billy ceased flopping like a fish on a boat deck. He lay unconscious on the sidewalk, a sodden, disheveled shell of his former nasty self.

Gerald Foon-Package and Sauce Fingerbanana, covered with the gooey cure for excess hair growth, were certain they were headed for the same fate as the luckless hoodlum. Their fears were assuaged when Officer Ninepoodles reappeared to escort them to the police paddy wagon. After profusely reassuring Sauce that he wasn't being taken to prison, the officer handed them a stack of wet towels to wipe off with and two dry police jumpsuits to put on, motioning for the two scientists to step inside the van and change clothes. When they were dry and dressed, they vacated the paddy wagon, and the SWAT team placed Billy Jelly inside.

Billy's traveling companion would be Spiffany Tonguehoister. Spiffany had performed many unrequested, unanticipated, and unappreciated structural demolitions in the past, and had avoided prosecution by rebuilding the structures herself and at her own expense. However, those buildings had been *unoccupied* at the time; the Bumps & Spuggett building was full of innocent, unwary people, and the police were fed up with Spiffany's incompetence and unsolicited interference. This time, they were going to put her away.

The van's rear door was locked, and the vehicle sped away, red lights flashing and siren blaring, to deposit Spiffany Tonguehoister in the town poky and Billy Jelly behind the walls of the North Corners High-Security Prison for Overly Aggressive Individuals.

46

Sauce Fingerbanana watched the paddy wagon disappear into the distance.

"So long, Billy! I'd like to say it's been nice knowin' ya, but that would be a lie. My days of lyin' are over."

"As scientists, we must always deal with the truth, Wiley," said Gerald as he stood by his new assistant's side and watched the receding police van, "even if the truth is hard to find and we have to search for it *forever!*"

"If that's the case, you guys are lookin' at great job security," said Bagmo.

"But what about the rest of us?" asked Yump. "Now that the Bumps & Spuggett building is ruined, the rest of us are out of a job. What're we gonna do?"

"What we're going to do is regroup, rebuild, and return," replied Old Man Spuggett. "Let no one be dismayed by our present circumstances. Do you really think the only reason any of you had a job was because we had a *building?* It was only the building we lost today. What we gained was infinitely more valuable and important: entire lives were changed for the better, new friendships were created, and important lessons were learned by all of us.

"Remember this: a building is constructed of brick, concrete, steel, glass, and mortar—materials of physical strength, to be sure, but no building could be built as solidly and strongly or mean as much as the bonds of friendship forged between us today. That strength transcends the physical."

"*Amen*, brother!" seconded Reverend Snortworthy.

"Verily, 'tis a sentiment well spoken, laden with truth indisputable!" agreed the mayor.

"As far as reconstructing the building is concerned, I have a solution for that," Barley said. In his mind he envisioned the work being done by none other than Spiffany Tonguehoister, as penance for her transgressions in lieu of a jail sentence. "Just leave it to me; you'll be back in business before you know it!"

"Before you know it? Wow! That's *fast!*" marveled Bagmo.

"For the time being, Mr. Doodlebody, all *you're* going to do is rest and recuperate," insisted Dr. Pudbid.

"You'd better do as the man says, Barley," agreed Alpha Rae.

Dr. Pudbid was amazed. Earlier, Alpha Rae would have bitten his head off for attempting to preempt her own efforts. Now, she supported him. He reasoned that once the executive secretary finally rediscovered who and what she was to Barley and Frog, she could accept the good doctor for who and what *he* was.

But the doctor had a momentous pronouncement to make. He collected himself and announced to the group, "Excuse me, everyone—I found my lollipops!"

The kindly doctor opened his black medical bag to reveal a cache of the revered confection. "I forgot I had these. I always carry a bunch in my bag when I make house calls. With all the chaos of today's activities and the fact that I left my bag on the bus, they completely slipped my mind. I think everyone deserves a little treat after what we've been through!"

"The doctor found his lollipops!" cried Cheezy. He shouted to everyone at the front of the building: "Dr. Pudbid's got free lollipops for all of us! Come and get 'em!"

Cheezy's invitation was enthusiastically accepted. People scurried to the curb where Dr. Pudbid distributed the candy on a stick to anyone who asked, then sat themselves down or leaned against a parked vehicle to enjoy a few peaceful moments with their respective lollipops, chatting quietly with each other about the day's events.

Narducci and Ebenezer sat apart from the rest, engrossed in deep discussion—such as *that* must have been.

Old Man Spuggett, Mrs. Kookerly, and Brufyss sat side by side on the curb, the old man engaging Brufyss's pretty female partner in a quiet dialogue:

"Mrs. Kookerly, you and Mr. Bathwater seem to be something of an item. Please forgive my prying, but are you married? If so, whose name is the married name? I haven't heard you referred to as Mrs. Bathwater, nor is he referred to as Mr. Kookerly. I'm a bit confused!"

Mrs. Kookerly smiled. "Don't be, Mr. Spuggett. I'll explain it to you: Brufyss and I are definitely an 'item,' as you call it, and have been so for forty years or so, but no, we're not married. My parents actually *named* me Mrs. Kookerly! My full name is Mrs. Kookerly Kookerly."

"My, what an unusual name."

"Yes, when I was a young girl it was a source of confusion to many people, and of embarrassment to me, but I got used to it. I even enjoy the confusion it creates."

"My dear Mrs. Kookerly, I can understand what you've had to deal with. I've had to cope with much the same situation myself!"

"What do you mean?"

"Well, I suppose at one time or another you've probably heard me called Old Man Spuggett, correct?"

"Er—yes, I have. I must admit, I've called you that myself! I'm sorry, sir; I meant no disrespect by it."

"Not to worry, my dear. Fact is, my parents actually *named* me Old Man Spuggett on the day I was born, 103 years ago! I have no idea why— perhaps they were just looking hopefully toward a future of longevity for me. Nonetheless, that's the name recorded on my birth certificate, though I normally just use the initials *O. M.* Even when I was a young man, I was Old Man Spuggett. It used to drive Puddles crazy!" He chuckled at the recollection. "But like you, I learned to cope with it. It just took me many long years to grow *into* it!"

Brufyss addressed the old man: "Sir, I've been thinking about something that Bagmo told me —something I still don't quite understand. Perhaps you could elaborate on his explanation for me."

"Certainly, Mr. Brewmeister. What's your question?"

"It's regarding the banner that hangs on the wall in the main office— the one that says, 'It's not *what* you do, but what you do *with* it . . .' Can you explain what it's referring to specifically?"

"The banner! Why, yes, I can explain it to you. The banner is referring specifically to the seventh sense. 'It's not *what* you do' means it doesn't matter what kind of activity you're engaged in. When one utilizes the seventh sense, that doesn't really matter.

"'. . . but what you do *with* it ' is talking about how the seventh sense is *applied* to the activity—how one perceives the activity. When one utilizes the seventh sense, one's level of perception ventures into the realm of *non-*sensibility; what made sense before must no longer make sense. That's the starting point. From there, a whole new way of looking at things begins. A new sensibility is created that provides an answer or a solution where none existed before, no matter how unorthodox or unfathomable it might be.

"It's not *what* you do with the seventh sense—breed thoroughbred race horses that tap-dance to the finish line, build nuclear submarines out of used toothpicks, campaign for Congress, or even manufacture radically stupid suggestions. That's not what matters. What you do *with* the seventh sense—feel productive, make someone laugh, offer a fresh and innovative contribution or perspective, change your way of looking at life and the world—*that's* what matters. As long as it's positive, it's all that matters!"

"But that seems to be on the verge of nonsense to me," said Brufyss.

"It's not on the verge, sir. It's smack-dab in the middle of it! Nonsense is what the seventh sense is all about. It was the perception of nonsense that enabled us to overcome a very serious predicament today. You see, Billy Jelly chose to pursue violence as his course of action. Violence occupies the lowest level of human perception. The best way to perceive violence is from a higher level, and in doing so, one easily sees the absurdity of it. Once the absurdity has been ascertained, it can be dealt with as such.

"My employees perceive the world in a way that permits them to assign whatever degree of importance or unimportance to events or circumstances they choose. By utilizing the seventh sense, they chose to confront the menace of Mr. Jelly as something of a game rather than the earth-shattering, life-threatening, fear-inspiring entity it would be perceived as from a lower level.

"A case in point would be Bagmo's confrontation with Sauce Fingerbandana. Instead of recoiling at the sight of Mr. Bingerfanna's gun and the dire predicament he'd just walked into, Bagmo chose to engage Sauce in his favorite activity—a quiz! The resulting confusion eventually caused Mr. Finglebinger to relinquish his control over the situation, and Bagmo set you free. Mr. Jelly never stood a chance against our group when it came right down to it. The seventh sense—nonsense—was the sense that made sense when dealing with him. Violence cannot prevail when the seventh sense pervades!"

"Okay, I see it now," said Brufyss thoughtfully. "Nonsense makes the most sense when dealing with senselessness."

"You got it! The best way to combat absurdity is to strike back with nonsense!"

Captain Chubbychuffle approached Old Man Spuggett and his

group, carrying little chief Bohoguss on his shoulder.

"Good evening, sir. Captain Moolly Chubbychuffle, North Corners Fire Department, at your service and pleased to meetcha! I understand you're the proprietor of this business."

"That I am," replied the old man as he shook hands with the fire captain, "or at least, that I *was*. It appears that both the building and the business have become casualties of the day's events! Nevertheless, I want to offer my sincere thanks for all your help."

"We're *always* here to help! We're firemen—although today we've hosed down more people than we have fires! Still, I'm sorry about your building. Wish there was a fire we could've put out for you. It's just been one of those days, I guess."

"Indeed it has, Captain. One of those days. One of those *wonderful* days!"

"Wonderful? How so?"

"I was privileged to meet a host of new, interesting, honest, and dedicated people whom I now call friends. I had the extreme pleasure of running into an old college chum of mine I hadn't seen in years. I witnessed the amazing transformation of a person who'd formerly been a heartless, calculating exploiter into a brave, caring, resourceful, and loyal individual who put the welfare of others before himself. I observed a war between two longtime enemies come to a happy end, resulting in the rebirth of a fast friendship.

"I watched a huge number of people who'd never met one another prior to this day band together to overcome a threatening adversity. I saw a mother regain her two lost sons, and a family reunited. I witnessed an employee of mine who'd once retreated and hidden inside the personality of a dog become a *man* again, performing deeds of heroism that helped free us from our tribulation. I observed the redemption of a former criminal who's become a rehabilitated and valued member of our company and society.

"I've seen the blossoming of more than one romance. I've seen the unlikeliest of heroes born out of fear, chaos, and confusion, and witnessed their triumphs . . . and, by George, I even had the chance to put my heretofore unproductive hobby of creating explosive devices into practical application! Yes, Captain Chubbychuffle, it's been 'one of those days'; one of those incredible days that a person may only have the opportunity to experience once in a lifetime, if at all!"

"*Wow*! You sure did a lot of stuff today, Mr. Spuggett," marveled Bimbo.

The old man laughed heartily at his employee's simple assessment. "Mr. Spazzgate, *we all* did a lot of stuff today! We laughed, we cried, we failed, we succeeded, we felt fear, we realized courage, we were overwhelmed, and we overcame. Isn't that what life's all about?"

"Yeah, buddy!" cried Frog—as if he actually *knew* what life was all about.

"The only thing we haven't done today is *eat*!" stated Bagmo. "Anybody here got a big ol' cheeseburger?"

"The big ol' cheeseburgers will be on me tonight," Barley said.

"Hold it right there, Mr. Doodlebody." It was Dr. Pudbid. "We've got to get you to a hospital tonight!"

"You've done enough today, Barley," said Brufyss. "You need the kind of medical attention a hospital can provide. We'll all come to visit you while you're in there, and we'll all be waiting for you when you get out."

The group voiced their concurrence, but Barley held up his hand. "I appreciate your concern for my health, and I'm humbled and gratified by your support and friendship. Until today I was 'a heartless, calculating exploiter of others'—and then I met *you* people! I've never felt so unconditionally accepted, so welcome, so useful—so needed—as you made me feel today. I owe you a debt I can never repay. You helped me find myself amid the ruins of my past life!

"Now I finally know who I am and who my friends are; there's no way I'm going to the hospital tonight by myself! I'd like Roland to take me there in the bus with all of you, but not until we've stopped off at Molly Glumglutton's 24-Hour Cheeseburger Chompeteria and gorged ourselves silly on big ol' cheeseburgers. I've come this far with you, and I'll hold together long enough to finish the day. Besides—I'm *hungry*!"

Everybody laughed and burst into a rousing cheer, whooping and hollering, clapping their hands and shouting, "Attaboy, Mr. D.," and "We're with ya, Barley!" and "We couldn't have done it without ya!"

Bagmo was jubilant. "I could chomp cheeseburgers 'til I nuggmuck!"

Mrs. Kookerly laughed and sighed wistfully as she thought of Flagella "Bubbles" Nuggmuck, her exploded high school cheerleading buddy who was the word's namesake.

Brufyss smiled at Barley. "A lot went down between us today, Barley, but I'm glad it did. You proved to Mrs. Kookerly and me, and I think to Daphne too, that you were sincere about mending our friendship, and I'm ready to begin again if you are."

He extended his hand to Barley. Barley grasped it with his own, and the two shook hands warmly.

"Thanks, Brufyss. I'm glad you believe me, and I'm glad we have the chance to start over. It felt good to be in a partnership with you again—for a *good* cause this time. It also reminded me that we make a great team! If you feel the same way, then as far as I'm concerned the Doodlebody-Bathwater Boys are back in business." He turned to Rapunzel and quickly added, "But this time, Ms. Trashtrumpet, there'll be no *monkey* business—and you can put that on the record!"

"Okay, everybody on the bus!" called Roland. "Cap'n Chubbychuffle! Chief Bohoguss! Follow us to Molly Glumglutton's! And Mr. Gimpthwinkle, you come too—just follow my bus!"

"We'll be along shortly, once we secure the building, Roland!" shouted Captain Chubbychuffle. "My old daddy used to say, 'What's past is past—it's the *future* that counts, although the future will someday become the past, so everything eventually becomes the past, which doesn't really give us much to look forward to . . .'" The captain paused mid-maxim and thought for a moment. "That's gotta be the dumbest thing my old daddy ever said."

Everyone laughed heartily—Faisal in particular—and the Bumps & Spuggett refugees made their way to Roland's windowless tour bus, piling into every seat until the vehicle was filled to capacity.

The fire crew, SWAT team, and North Corners Police Force secured the battered building and the slumbering Sherman tank, and cleaned up the mess left from Billy Jelly's epic hose down. Once finished, they jumped into their respective vehicles to form a convoy with the tour bus that would wind through the streets of town to Molly Glumglutton's 24-Hour Cheeseburger Chompeteria, one of the few North Corners eateries Barley didn't own—which probably accounted for its great popularity.

The refugees waited on the bus, babbling contentedly with one another. Ebenezer and Narducci boarded, stood at the head of the aisle, and clamored for everyone's attention. Narducci addressed them:

"Ladies and gentlemen, tourists, guests, employees, Mr. Spuggett, Mr. Doodlebody, Mr. Bathwater—oh, yadda-yadda-yadda! You know who you are."

"Yadda-yadda-yadda!" mimicked Lollie.

"Now that our day's adventure has come to an end, my new songwriting partner and I have composed a song commemorating the event which we've entitled 'The Ballad of Bumps & Spuggett.' We'd like to perform it for you now; please feel free to join in and sing along at any time."

The tourists, guests, employees, and yadda-yadda-yadda all gave their full attention to Narducci and Ebenezer, and Rapunzel Trashtrumpet scribbled on her sheets of paper as Narducci began to sing:

> *"The day is done and some may say we could have done without it,*
> *But, nonetheless, it's over now, and we can laugh about it!*
> *The start was innocent enough: two groups of strangers meeting,*
> *And in a wink becoming friends with each successive greeting!*
>
> *We danced the danzenfreekenboingadoinga 'til we dropped,*
> *Then Brufyss and his gang showed up; the celebrating stopped!*
> *A confrontation thus ensued—Brufyss encountered Barley.*
> *Old animosities returned, a most distressing parlay*
>
> *'Til Mr. Spuggett intervened. A truce was then affected*
> *Between the two old enemies—the wingding resurrected!*
> *But in the midst of all the fun, an evil guy named Billy*
> *Showed up and threatened with his gun to blow us willy-nilly!*
>
> *He wanted Mr. Spuggett's cash, this crass, conniving clown,*
> *But Brufyss stood defiantly and faced the gangster down!*
> *Bill's finger on the trigger paused and Brufyss cried, 'Don't pull it!'*
> *The villian fired anyway—but Barley took the bullet!"*

Narducci paused. Ebenezer stepped forward and belted out his contributed chorus:

> *". . . Ho-tucka-hey! Ho-tucka-haw! Resiliency resplendent!*
> *A morgus mupple hitherto! A fogus independent!*
> *High knucklemuggets unperturbed, low-budget buckaroola—*
> *We rondelay 'til Saturday, a-booma-locka-loola!"*

Narducci picked up the song's next verses:

"A scuffle then erupted, followed by a frenzied chase
That led down to the dark first floor, a cold, forbidding place.
Bad Billy trapped the big guys there—the tide turned in his favor!
He locked them up in Sauce's care, a victory to savor,

'Til Yump and Roland ventured forth and found the big guys' prison!
When taunted, evil Bill pursued, just like on television,
And Roland lured the gangster on through offices, down hallways—
Around the labyrinthine floor through many large and small ways,

Then lo! The hoodlum's luck ran out with Roland's inspiration:
A well-placed javelin—no need for further confrontation!
Brave Roland knocked ol' Billy cold! The threat was now diminished,
But never sell a gangster short! This crook was not yet finished . . ."

Ebenezer jumped in once more with the song's chorus:

"Ho-tucka-hey! Ho-tucka-haw! Resiliency resplendent!
A morgus mupple hitherto! A fogus independent!
High knucklemuggets unperturbed, low-budget buckaroola—
We rondelay 'til Saturday, a-booma-locka-loola!"

Narducci resumed:

"Meanwhile, Bagmo and Sauce engaged in thrust-and-parried questions;
Bagmo confused the big guys' guard with answers and suggestions
Until poor Sauce was so perplexed he fled upstairs in terror,
And Bagmo freed the captives, thanks to Billy's judgment error,

For Billy never had a clue that Sauce would soon desert him,
Surrendering to Gerald's care—but now Bill couldn't hurt him,
And Sauce became a scientist, a step toward his redemption!
As far as going to jail went, reformed Sauce earned an exemption!

But back to Billy Jelly: he was currently detained
Downstairs in our headquarters room—if only he'd remained!
Instead the hoodlum gave the slip to Marshall, Biff, and Lollie,
The mayor, Ebenezer, and Fandango too, by golly!

The crafty thug ran through the halls, evading apprehension,
'Til little Marg'ret brought him down in ways too gross to mention!
Thus ended Billy Jelly's threat—the crook at last was muzzled,
But meantime, up in Lollie's room, our Alpha Rae was puzzled.

Strange memories and feelings long forgotten now returned
To taunt her mind and haunt her mind—lost lessons left unlearned.
When Barley and his brother, Frog, lay injured and defenseless,
Our secretary sang to them, and though the two were senseless,

Unconsciously they heard her song, responding with a chorus!
Two brothers found their mother in that room right there before us!
So many miracles this day! So many near disasters!
So many of us found ourselves and turned from slaves to masters!

We gained a life experience most valuable for seeing
What we can all accomplish, what we're capable of being!
So many times adversity sought vainly to disarm us;
We put our faith in one another—nothing then could harm us!"

Ebenezer rang out another chorus, and sent it back to Narducci:

"The heroes who emerged this day require some attention,
And if you will allow me to, I'll make honorable mention
Of one or two—or quite a few!—whose deeds when faced with peril
Placed our welfare over theirs, and Bill's over the barrel:

Our stalwart Barley, Brufyss too, and Mr. Spuggett, surely;
They took the reins and led us through the seamy and the surly,
And Roland, braving shot and shell, lured Billy like a spider,
While Lollie faced a great unknown with Marshall there beside her!

When Bagmo forced Sauce to retreat, our quizmaster remained
With Cheezy to release our guys; their freedom was regained!
And noble Noodles, Dork as well: those Nordic two were fearless;
Their brav'ry was exceptional, their dancing simply peerless!

And let us not forget ol' Mux, the former cocker spaniel!
When it came time to improvise, he threw away the manual
And joined with little Binky B.—the two of them proceeded
To bring assistance to our cause and aid where it was needed!

And when we mention 'aid,' good Dr. Pudbid we acknowledge:
The kindly old physician, Mr. Spuggett's pal in college!
With many years of practice, he's experienced and wise;
If lollipops could cure all ills, he'd win the Nobel Prize!"

After another chorus from Ebenezer, Narducci continued:

"Frog Puppleman revealed the grit that no one knew he had;
He's everybody's 'buddy' but a bull when he gets mad."

"Yeah, *buddy!*" exclaimed Frog happily.
Narducci picked it up without missing a beat:

"Bimbo and Cheezy, Faisal too: three gents awash in whimsy,
Contributed their own fair share along with Yump and Mimsy,

And Alpha Rae: she took control when things became chaotic;
Her connection to her long-lost sons seems now so symbiotic,
But at that moment, unaware, she just did what she had to
And in the process gave us hope. Give kudos? We'd be glad to!

The mayor and Biff Spoozma, our two friends from city hall:
Big Biff was our protector, and translated for us all
The mayor's staunch pronouncements, full of wisdom, wealth, and worth,
In language seldom heard since Shakespeare walked upon the earth!

Rapunzel of The Daily Poop, the conscience of our town:
We're happy she was present; everything that she wrote down
Will one day jog our memories of all we saw and heard—
A chronicle we'll cherish, and the truth in ev'ry word!

Faisal kept us in stitches when the tears threatened to fall,
Fandango set speed records as he sped from hall to hall,
And hail, Mafumbus Snortworthy! When called, the man defended
The principles of love and truth that Billy had upended!

And how could we ignore brave Mrs. Kookerly and Daphne?
Their strength and courage never flagged and . . ."

Narducci paused again.

"Frab-jahola glaff-schnee!"

"Right, Ebenezer! There isn't anything that rhymes with 'Daphne' *but* 'frab-jahola glaff-schnee'!"

"And how could we ignore brave Mrs. Kookerly and Daphne?
Their strength and courage never flagged and frab-jahola glaff-schnee!
We've no shortage of heroes—they appear when most we need 'em,
Like when the ceiling fell: Felicia led us all to freedom!

A positive conclusion, that's the way our story ends!
The conflicts that we faced are gone, yet we remain as friends,
And what do we take with us? What's the moral, anyway?
That friendship, love, and loyalty will always rule the day.

That honesty and bravery, compassion, faith, and trust
will conquer all adversity and grind it into dust!
When circumstances went awry we each came out a winner,
So, Roland, fire up this bus! We're overdue for dinner!"

The whole bus joined in and sang Ebenezer's final chorus:

"Ho-tucka-hey! Ho-tucka-haw! Resiliency resplendent!
A morgus mupple hitherto! A fogus independent!
High knucklemuggets unperturbed, low-budget buckaroola—
We rondelay 'til Saturday, a-booma-locka-loola!"

"The Ballad of Bumps & Spuggett" came to its rousing conclusion, followed by sweeping bows from Narducci and Ebenezer. The bus exploded with cheers and applause.

"*Bravo!*" cried Cheezy. "That's gotta be the greatest song you guys have ever written together!" It was the only song those guys had ever written together.

"Heck, t'ain't nothin'," declared Narducci modestly.

"Oh, yes it *t'ain!*" countered Bagmo.

"It's a great song, Narducci," agreed Mux, "portending a prolific musical partnership between Ebenezer and yourself, the likes of which we shan't soon see again."

"Oh, yes we *shan!*" countered Bagmo.

"And it's based on a true story, I might add," added Narducci.

"But, Narducci! You left Ebenezer and yourself out of the song!" It was Old Man Spuggett. "You're discounting the importance of your own contributions in the course of the day's events."

"Sir, Ebenezer and I didn't think it would be appropriate to extol our own virtues in the song, since the two of us wrote it! That would be kinda like bragging!"

"Then let me do the 'extolling' for you!"

The old man addressed the rest of the group: "Ladies and gentlemen, I'm sure you wouldn't begrudge Narducci and Ebenezer a place of honor in their song! It's about *all* of us, wouldn't you agree?"

The crowd concurred with enthusiastic cries of support for the two modest songsters.

"Very well, then! Here's a minor addendum to 'The Ballad of Bumps & Spuggett,' with my apologies to its creators for my obvious lack of lyrical skill!"

The company founder began to sing his own words to Narducci's melody:

"When Ebenezer Snugnards, normally a fearful soul,
Was faced with dire circumstances out of his control,
Instead of fleeing in despair, as he'd been wont to do,
Brave Ebenezer took control and saw the problem through!

He faced his fears and with his gift of garrulous descriptions,
Confounded Billy Jelly—sent the crook into conniptions!
Though harried, Ebenezer never once gave up the ghost!
He seems incomprehensible, but makes more sense than most!

Narducci Palpatooti is our self-appointed bard;
He kept our spirits buoyed with song through times when times were hard!
Contributing whene'er he could in any way requested,
Our boy's artistic skills prevailed, albeit sorely tested!

Our gallant in-house troubadour—his main desire? Our pleasure!
A song for ev'ry up and down—his music is our treasure!
A ditty here, a ballad there, he does his tuneful duty;
A debt of gratitude we owe to our best Palpatooti!"

After one more rousing chorus by everyone on the bus, Narducci and Ebenezer's "Ballad of Bumps & Spuggett"—with the "addendum" provided by the old man—concluded with another hearty cheer. The song had summed up the day's events in a most musical and satisfying way.

Now the day was done.

The Doodlebody tourists received much more than their money's worth from this inaugural—and final—Bumps & Spuggett tour (Barley would happily refund every penny). The Bumps & Spuggett employees would leave with the knowledge that they'd keep their jobs and their ravaged building would be rebuilt; Barley and Brufyss would leave knowing their friendship was stronger than it had ever been; Alpha Rae Sapoopa-LaBoobis would leave with the knowledge that her two lost sons had been found, and the three of them would be a family from now on.

Most importantly, everyone knew their lives were changed for the better because they met, discovered wonderful things about each other and themselves, and together played a hand that life dealt them.

And what had it all led to?

"Cheeseburgers!" cried Bagmo as Roland's bus pulled away from the curb. "Big ol' cheeseburgers for *everybody!*"

"Shiggydaygobah!" added Ebenezer.

"*Shiggydaygobah!*" chorused the busload of celebrants.

No translation was necessary.

Shiggydaygobah, indeed.

AFTERWORD

Dear Reader, let me leave you with one final revelation: I, Rapunzel Trashtrumpet, have been your humble scribe in the telling of this tale.

I penned the tome you've just completed, having written the story from "off the top of my head"—quite literally. The ridiculous-looking paper-stack bonnet I strapped to my noggin and brought out of the ruined building, that so offended Mimsy Borogove's fashion sensibilities, is what you've read as you turned each page, and I swear to you on a stack of gumballs, every word is true.

You can't make this stuff up!

With that, I take my leave.

If you're ever passing through the little town of North Corners, Ohio, don't hesitate to drop into the Bumps & Spuggett offices to say hello. Be sure to have some business to give them, of course, unless you can wangle a freely invited guest pass from Old Man Spuggett—and you probably can.

Be prepared to have your current level of perception altered, elevated, and enhanced. One cannot perceive life through use of the seventh sense without seeing things in a newer, brighter, more illuminating light. One will consequently see everything much clearer in the process—and it's a heck of a lot more fun.

Just make sure you don't forget the rules:

Only one question at a time . . .

ACKNOWLEDGMENTS

This is the portion of the book I've agonized over perhaps more than any. How do I suitably acknowledge and thank the many people who have given me invaluable support, help, guidance, encouragement, and inspiration in the creation of this tale, without those thanks seeming (at least to me) pathetically inadequate? Despite my apprehensions, it is absolutely necessary that I do so despite my own perceived inadequacies, and I'll do my best.

Greg Fields is an award-winning author—to me the quintessential "writer's writer"—who's garnered well-deserved recognition and praise for his literary works. Greg writes with a powerful style that flows as effortlessly as liquid, supporting thought-provoking and deeply emotional insights. He was the first person to read, and later to assiduously advocate for, *A Seventh Sense*, for which I am deeply grateful; without Greg's unflagging support, this novel may never have seen the light of day. I have affectionately dubbed him "The Godfather of North Corners" (much to his chagrin), and I'm very pleased and blessed to have such a gifted wordsmith as an advisor, advocate, and friend.

Caroline Jam Miller is my sister and a tireless, enthusiastic right-hand aide-de-camp (her left-handedness notwithstanding). Caroline has been my sounding board, crying towel, cheerleader, and creative accomplice through the process of bringing this book to life. Her sisterly love, her belief in this project, her confidence in her big brother, and her willingness to contribute and help in countless ways has kept me on my toes and inspired. Thank you, Sis!

The first editor to tackle *A Seventh Sense* is himself a noted contributor in the literary world and a friend to me for many years; Robert Yehling took on the mammoth task of guiding me through the initial process of trimming an enormous, wordy manuscript down to a manageable, intelligible, and presentable size, aided by his many years of experience as a noted editor, journalist, poet, author, collaborator, and ghostwriter. As a novice in the world of literature myself, I learned much from his tutelage, and my gratitude is profound.

Y. J. Nicole Im's experience as an architect was instrumental and invaluable in taking the rudimentary Bumps & Spuggett building floor plans I had drawn when writing the story, and transforming them into clean, clear, professional-looking visual representations. Her drawings are an integral part of the story, her participation and expertise greatly appreciated. Michelle Fry added additional assistance and expertise as well; her skill with the designing software helped to polish a few wrinkles and make the drawings shine.

Hannah Woodlan, senior editor for Koehler Books, was the next editor to tackle the behemoth that was *A Seventh Sense*'s manuscript, and her efforts are what you as the readers are reading. Thank you, Hannah, for handling my book with gentle loving care and revealing its true essence— not an easy task with all the gobbledygook I threw in there!

Lauren Sheldon is the Koehler Books graphic designer who's been instrumental in creating the look and design of both the book's interior and the cover. I believe her efforts have successfully brought my vision of North Corners and its environs into glorious reality. Thank you for your wonderful imagination, Lauren!

A special thanks goes to John Koehler, my esteemed Koehler Books publisher (and a whiz-bang artist with a boomerang, among other things), for his fortitude in guiding, informing, educating, encouraging, and instilling confidence in this author. Like a wizened shepherd, he does it with skill, aplomb, and sensitivity, adeptly applying the salve of reassurance to the apprehensions of newbies like me—and he's a great writer, artist, and "guy just to talk to" as well! Thank you for your confidence, patience, and support, John!

Alan Gibby is not only a trusted and respected friend, but also a gifted, forward-thinking individual with whom I've had the pleasure of working for a long time now. Alan has always been a loyal advocate of my writing, giving me employment, encouragement, trust, direction, and aid with getting *A Seventh Sense* out into the world. As an entrepreneur who's been ahead of his time with many innovations in the world of media, I look upon Alan's support and advice with gratitude.

Thank you as well to my lifelong friends Steve Reed, Joe Brunansky, and Mike McMillan, who graciously and patiently read the early drafts of the book as I wrote it, contributing valuable (and to my mind, unbiased) criticism and feedback. Having witnessed my development as a writer since our early youth, these guys gave me the initial impetus to continue writing the story, convincing me it was one worth telling (and as only dear friends can, unabashedly letting me know how goofy I am).

Though they are no longer here to receive my thanks personally, my parents, Edward and Elaine Jam, were always supportive and appreciative of my creative endeavors as I grew up, and I owe them a debt of gratitude for putting me on Earth and giving me the means—and the genes—to be able to write this book. I miss you, Mom and Dad, but this novel is very much a tribute and gift of love to both of you from me. I hope you like it!

I look upon each one of these wonderful people with great love, respect, and admiration; in thanking them, I accentuate my deep gratitude for their invaluable friendship.

Shiggydaygobah!

—Steve Jam

CPSIA information can be obtained
at www.ICGtesting.com
Printed in the USA
LVHW112257030522
717861LV00003B/71

9 781646 636693